Zoë Fairbairns was born in 1948. In addition to *Stand We At Last*, her books include *Benefits*, a futuristic novel of sexual politics also published by Virago; *Here Today* (Mandarin), winner of the 1985 Fawcett Book Prize; *Closing* (Mandarin); and *Daddy's Girls* (Mandarin). Her short stories have appeared in anthologies including *The Seven Deadly Sins*, *The Seven Cardinal Virtues*, *Serious Hysterics* (all published by Serpent's Tail) and *The Man Who Loved Presents* (Women's Press.) She writes regularly for *Everywoman* magazine, and runs writing workshops at venues including the Hen House, the Arvon Foundation, colleges and schools. Zoë Fairbairns lives in South London.

Zoë Fairbairns

STAND WE
AT LAST

Published by VIRAGO PRESS Limited 1983
20–23 Mandela Street, Camden Town, London NW1 0HQ

Reprinted 1983 (twice), 1988, 1992

*A CIP catalogue record for this book is available
from the British Library.*

Printed and bound in Great Britain
by Cox & Wyman Ltd, Reading, Berks

Contents

The March of the Women

Shout, shout, up with your song!
Cry with the wind, for the dawn is breaking.
March, march, swing you along,
Wide blows our banner and hope is waking.
Song with its story, dreams with their glory,
Lo! they call and glad is their word.
Forward! hark how it swells,
Thunder of freedom, the voice of the Lord.

Long, long, we in the past,
Cowered in dread from the light of Heaven.
Strong, strong, stand we at last,
Fearless in faith and with sight new given.
Strength with its beauty, life with its duty,
(Hear the voice, oh, hear and obey),
These, these, beckon us on,
Open your eyes to the blaze of day!

Comrades, ye who have dared,
First in the battle to strive and sorrow.
Scorned, spurned, naught have you cared,
Raising your eyes to a wider morrow.
Ways that are weary, days that are dreary,
Toil and pain by faith ye have borne.
Hail, hail, victors we stand.
Wearing the wreath that the brave have worn!

Life, strife, these two are one!
Naught can ye win but by faith and daring.
On, on, that ye have done,
But for the work of today preparing.
Firm in reliance, launch a defiance,
(Laugh in hope, for sure is the end).
March, march, many as one,
Shoulder to shoulder and friend to friend.

Cicely Hamilton

Printed by kind permission of J. Curwen & Sons Ltd, London

Preface

One cold evening late in 1978, I happened to be in Virago's office in Wardour Street, London. Carmen Callil had obviously been having a difficult day and had had enough. "I'm giving up publishing," she announced, "I'm going to write a novel and it's going to be a family saga about women."

This was serious. The last thing a novelist needs is for her publisher to become a novelist. Besides, I too had been thinking about writing a family saga with a feminist background. We discussed the matter and soon came up with a division of labour whereby I would write the novel and Virago would publish it. Carmen, and Ursula Owen, suggested many ideas, read and re-read the countless drafts, and offered important and vital insights into the development of the story, particularly at the early stages.

Stand We At Last is, it must be stressed, a work of fiction. It is not the story of my family or of any other family I know. Any resemblance between characters and events in the novel (except where these are obviously historical) and real characters and events, is solely in the eye of the beholder.

But many people have given their time and expertise to help me research the background of the story. These include historians, particularly those feminist historians who have done so much to rediscover women's hidden past; librarians; relatives who have shared their memories with me, and friends with whom I have discussed the book, or who have perhaps unwittingly given me ideas for it while ostensibly discussing something completely different.

Particular thanks, then, to Mrs Alma Devitt, Anna Davin, Ann Dippie, Ben Okri, Frances Widdowson, Isabel Fairbairns, John Clifford, Judy Walkowitz, Leonore Davidoff, Mrs Lorraine Callil, Mandy Greenway, Myna Trustram, Susie Innes and Valerie Miner. Also to all the women at Virago; to the members of history groups and writing groups with whom I have worked, at the City Literary Institute, Holloway Prison and Goldsmith's College, all in London; and above all to John Petherbridge, whose loyal and generous help came into all the categories I've mentioned, and more.

That seems like a lot of people to dedicate a book to, but then it's a long book.

Zoë Fairbairns, London 1982

Helena
1855 . . .

The bare hills encircling the Sussex village of Littledean grew
greener each minute as the sun rose. To seventeen-year-old Helena
Weeks they seemed to tower like waves that would crest and
break and flood the village. She shivered; then smiled to think
what her sister would say if she could read her mind. Twenty-
one-year-old Sarah was pacing energetically a few feet ahead of
her; from time to time she stopped to wait for Helena, as if
remembering that this farewell stroll around the village was being
undertaken in fulfilment of a promise. But Sarah did not much
like going for strolls; when Sarah walked she liked to have a
destination.

Sarah looked at her with the odd, twisted smile that Helena
had thought she affected in order to hide the gap in her teeth
where a cow kicked her once; but by now Helena had realised
that Sarah was as likely to twist her smile to the left, which
exposed the gap, as to the right, which concealed it. The look
was louder than words. *Little, 'fraid-cat*, it said; *you'd see menace
in a bowl of milk, even today, your wedding day!*

But there was affection in the scornful look, and Helena was
satisfied; perhaps she wanted to be teased by Sarah. It might be
the last time it would happen.

Everyone who knew the Misses Weeks agreed that one of them
was beautiful and one was not; however, this unanimity disappeared if they went on to identify which they thought the more
favoured. One observer might be captivated by Helena's pallor
and pinkness, the intriguing colours that sunlight or candlelight
could pick out in her chestnut hair, or her generally shyer, more
agreeable manner; another might prefer Sarah's evenness of colouring, the easy grace of her movements, or perhaps the look in
her eye, the flexible brows and the mobile mouth which seemed
always about to laugh at a joke, a joke which might or might not
be the one that the observer thought he had made. Helena was of
medium height, Sarah was half a head taller; only people who

remembered their mother thought the sisters alike, since each, in different aspects, resembled her.

This morning there was no resemblance. And there would be none henceforward, Helena realised, staring in dismay at her sister's straight back as she strode on ahead. Both of them had dressed hurriedly for this early walk; they did not expect to be seen. Sarah had even fastened her buttons on the wrong hooks. And they had pinned their hair with little care because it would be done properly later for the ceremony. But while Helena felt in her own tangled hair a sense of awkwardness, and of reassurance too because it would soon be put to rights, Sarah's thick locks looked resigned or even happy with their state, as if they liked being blown about. And there was truth in this, and it was the truth about the difference between them and the reason why they were soon to be separated forever; and Helena was seized by a desire to pull out both their heads of hair, tug it up by the roots and fling it to the wind that seemed to want it so much, for why in a whole village of memories should it be the hair on their heads that would remind her of the thing she was trying to forget and make her sad on her wedding day?

If you marry him, I shall emigrate to Australia. Sarah had said it the morning the sisters guessed (correctly) that Jonathan Croft, a former business associate of their father's, was about to propose to Helena. It was not a threat; Sarah did not begrudge Helena her love; it was a statement of fact. Now Sarah's room was full of books from an emigration society in London and her passage was booked. If only it had been a threat! If only Helena could believe that Sarah was merely feeling piqued that her younger sister had found a husband before she had, then she might be open to persuasion! Sarah could be reminded that at twenty-one she was by no means too old to hope for offers, she could be induced to accept Jonathan's gallant offer that, although the Littledean house must be sold to meet their father's business debts, Sarah could come and live with him and Helena at Wenbury Hill in Kent. Helena sighed. How lovely that would be: to live with her sister and her husband under one roof! And in time Sarah would meet and marry one of Jonathan's friends.

Walk round the village with me, and say goodbye to the houses!
Such babyish nonsense!
But you promised, Sarah!

They walked in silence. The road met the stream in the centre of the village, cutting it into almost perfect quarters. There were a few brown leaves floating beneath the surface of the water, heralding summer's end, and shiny blackberries grew on the bramble bushes. Sarah picked a few and absent-mindedly put them into her mouth, forgetting to offer her sister any and leaving a tiny dot of black on her lip. Busy, awakening sounds came from the row of low, thatched cottages; and smells of oatmeal and bacon. A few faces appeared in windows and doorways, figures shaking mats or throwing out food for hens; they smiled with friendly understanding at the girls. Helena's peace of mind was all gone. What had happened to it, the happiness and excitement of waiting for today? She felt fear and sadness as a solid presence within her, like – she tried to stop the nasty thought, but it was too quick for her – like the worm that had killed one of their dogs by living in its stomach and devouring its food.

Impatiently, she forced a smile, it wouldn't do for the villagers to say that she had scowled. But she had not come to see them, she would see them later at the wedding, she had to come to see the village. And she was disappointed in it, angry with it; it was ordinary, unmoved; it ought to glow for her, find some way of fixing itself for ever in her memory.

I may be homesick for a while, Jonathan.

I shan't allow it!

It was easy to smile again, remembering his words, the mixture of firmness and kindness that had always been Jonathan. It was difficult to remember the exact moment at which she had stopped thinking of him as a family friend and started to see him as a lover. He was nearly forty. He was old enough to be her father. And he wouldn't allow her to be homesick. It was a foolish thing to say of course, one could not forbid a person their feelings, but it showed how he meant to take care of her.

The houses of the village stood aloof ready. *You be goin' away then, Miss Sarah, Miss Helena?* they seemed to say, *we be stayin' put.*

The sisters reached the end of the road for the second time, where the hills reared up. Sarah said, "I'll race you up the Beacon!"

"No, I cannot!"

"Cannot, cannot, cannot!" Sarah taunted as if they were both children. "Why can't you?"

Helena thought quickly. "It's unlucky." Sarah was more tolerant of superstition than of cowardice.

"Unlucky? Who says it is?"

"Mrs Simmons told me – it's a saying – unlucky the bride, who walks on the Beacon at morningtide." Sarah frowned. If she guessed that the proverb was less than a minute old, she said nothing about it. She just grinned to the left, displaying her gap (which wasn't a gap at all, and it was unkind of Helena to think of it as one . . . it was just a little space in the corner of her mouth that the neighbouring teeth hadn't grown quite close enough to occupy) and said mischievously. "All right, Two-erum" (the old nickname, their parents used to call them One-erum and Two-erum, like shepherds counting sheep), "I suppose you need luck on your wedding day," and she burst out laughing, and Helena laughed too, because if Sarah had really thought she was doing a wrong or stupid thing in marrying Jonathan she would never have said that, not as a joke, not today. Sarah liked Jonathan really, and Jonathan liked Sarah, Helena was sure. If they argued it was only about little things in the newspapers Jonathan brought on his visits, or who was going to win the cricket-matches that the three of them liked to watch on the village green. Sometimes when they were together, Helena had to pinch herself to remember that it was she and not Sarah who was to marry Jonathan: Sarah and Jonathan had the easy, irritable familiarity together of some married couples, and were kind to her like parents. Once she had found the courage to ask Jonathan why he had chosen her in preference to Sarah. And he had said, "Because you are so kind and gentle." And she had said, "So is Sarah!" And he had said, "Of course! She is your sister." And Helena had said, "She is courageous too," and he had said, "Indeed, and courage is a fine thing in a woman. But where should I be, my dear, if you had the courage to sail to Australia?"

Helena had reported this conversation to Sarah in the belief that the best way to induce one person to like another was to persuade the former that the latter already liked *her* very much; but Sarah had just chuckled. "I'm not courageous enough to marry Jonathan Croft! And he is not courageous enough to marry me!"

Having refused to climb Little Beacon with Sarah, Helena turned her back on it without regret. What made some people courageous and some not? Why did the same thing, the same person, frighten some and only please and amuse others? She had thought it was a matter of age. When she was four she had thought it was just a matter of being eight and then she would be as brave as Sarah. But she did not know then what was going to happen when she was five.

They still had the farm then, and Mother was alive: busy and jolly and pink-cheeked and impatient at the slowness her strange new shape imposed on her: she was all swollen up like a cow in calf. Helena had seen her like that once before, but never so big; it was only a small bulge when it ended in illness and tears and whispers and a quiet, guilty satisfaction in Helena that she could go on being the youngest for a little while longer. But then came the day when Mother went quite cheerfully to her bed and Sarah was told to take Helena off walking on Little Beacon and not come back till evening. They took bread and a couple of the intricate rabbit-shaped cheeses with which Mother had won prizes at the county fair. It was a windy, wintry day: if they opened their mouths they could taste salt in the air. The bushes and the stark, lonely trees bent before the wind, resigned, not even bothering to resume their normal positions when it paused in its blowing. Up and up they climbed; Sarah was remorseless.

"Wait – for me . . ." Helena's words were lost in the grey, turbulent air: there was a button off her coat, there was no use in complaining, she should have sewn it on when she was told; but it meant she had to hold the coat closed and have only one hand free to save herself if her short legs stumbled, or let the wind whistle down her neck. "Sarah – *wait* – we're not allowed . . ."

Sarah flopped down in the grass and waited, having a good rest, then mocked Helena for being out of breath: "You sound like the bellows! Not allowed *what*?"

They were not allowed to climb further up the Beacon. It dropped away suddenly at a terrifying height that was always a shock, for even the steepest slope seemed low and gentle compared with the deep drop down to the sea. The cliff crumbled; sometimes sheep went over. The children were not allowed near the edge: breathlessly Helena reminded her sister.

Sarah pouted. "They *told* us to come up here. I want to see the Seven Sisters. You're not to tell." And she strode on. The Seven Sisters was a curved formation of white cliff far along the coast, so distant and misty it could not always be seen. Helena stood still and cried, watching Sarah climb higher and higher. She wanted to see the Seven Sisters but she was frightened. She wanted to go home but they had turned her out. Suddenly Sarah screamed.

"Helena, Helena, come quickly!"

"What's the matter – ?" she screamed back; Sarah was standing still at the top of the cliff; the wind detached Helena's words from each other and scattered them. She started to crawl. It took longer but she felt steadier that way.

"There – are – only – six – "

Only six Sisters! But Mother said there had been seven since the world began! Helena crept slowly upwards. Her face was close to the earth, watching for cracks that might warn her if the piece of land she was on was breaking under her weight. And then she was there, at the top of the cliff, and she wasn't afraid any more. Even when she looked down the dizzying sheer white drop of the cliff to the flat sea, striped with foam, she wasn't afraid. Even if she fell she could fly and call like the gulls.

She raised her eyes to the Seven – six – Sisters.

"One's behind the mist," she said, "that's all, Sarah." She felt rather superior. But Sarah looked more superior still; she had known all along.

"Why did you make me come up here?" Helena raged.

"So you won't be frightened again."

"When I'm nine I won't be!"

But when they went back in the evening, expecting to see the new baby, there was no baby; and no Mother either; she was ill, they weren't allowed to see her. And three days later she died; and three days after that she was buried in St Mary's churchyard. From then on, Helena was always afraid of Little Beacon.

Their father Thomas Weeks had never had much of a head for farming, or even a heart; he was more interested in gunpowder. The farm had come from his wife's family and she was a competent manager, so he had been content to live off its produce while he pursued the erratic profits to be made from supplying Sussex regiments with gunpowder from the small factory he owned. His wife's death sent him slightly mad; his attempts to manage the farm, or to employ others to do so, proved disastrous. Just the sight of the dairy full of cheeses that she had made, or figures in the accounts that she had added up, would reduce him to helpless weeping. And he worried about his daughters' prospects, feeling quite inadequate to the task of raising them. He sold the farm, bought a house in the village and hired a succession of governesses to make ladies of them. Helena was too young to mind the change; Sarah pined for farm life and never quite forgave him.

He survived his wife by seven years; then he was killed with six of his employees in an explosion which destroyed his factory. When his affairs were investigated, he was found to owe substantial amounts to Croft & Co., the London military suppliers, with whom he had entered agreements not very favourable to himself. Crofts agreed not to pursue the matter until the younger of the two orphaned daughters came of age; then they would require the Littledean house to be put on the market. But before this could come about, Jonathan Croft, son and heir of the owner of the firm, found himself in love with Helena Weeks, and she with him. Since the elder sister had other plans, their marriage presented a solution satisfactory to all concerned.

2

"Of course, it was you, Helena," said Sarah Weeks, "who first inspired me to seek my fortune in Australia." Her tone was teasingly flat and emphatic against the flapping of tarpaulins, sails and ropes, the whistle of the wind, and the tramp of a thousand feet on the dockside.

"I?" said Helena Croft. She had meant to imitate her sister's firm tone, but the word came out as an anguished croak, drawing back her husband's attention from the soldiers he had been watching as they embarked on a distant troop-ship for the Crimea. He said, "Indeed?"

His cheerful, questioning tone might mean anything. It might mean that he saw a final chance for some banter with Sarah and sought readmission to the conversation; or it might mean that he had heard the tears in Helena's voice and wanted to stop her being unhappy.

"Indeed, indeed," said Sarah, "Helena does not remember the occasion, I can tell. She was not quite four years old at the time, and so may be forgiven. We were supposed to be planting seed potatoes. But Helena was never very interested in tasks of that kind, and on this occasion preferred to dig a hole. Like a veritable rabbit you were, Helena, for hole digging. And our mother came by and said, 'What's this, Helena? Are you going to Australia?' Naturally I was curious to know what she meant."

"Naturally, with your enquiring mind," said Jonathan.

"When she said Australia was a place at the other end of the earth that could best be reached by digging, I encouraged Helena in her labours while I concentrated on the seed potatoes. You *surely* remember, Helena? I have never seen your face so muddy."

"No," said Helena quietly, "I do not remember." Sarah was laughing at her, and so was Jonathan. Why was Sarah talking so much, telling over and over again her often-told stories?

"In time I discovered that it was the place to which convicts were sent and I lost interest; but I happened to see an advertisement in a newspaper, at the time when Father was selling our farm, much against my wishes, and the advertisement offered financial assistance to lady migrants. This seemed an excellent weapon in my fight, and I roundly declared that I should have my own farm in any case, even if I must go to Australia for it. Excellent weapon or not, he sold; but when I discovered that Jonathan intended, in marrying you, Helena, to turn me out on to the streets – "

Helena clasped Sarah's arm. "Oh, he never, we never . . . " Sarah patted her hand and Jonathan patted her shoulder. Once again she was being laughed at. Jonathan gallantly pretended to have taken Sarah at her word. "My offer of a home with us still stands."

Helena said, "It's not too late."

"It most certainly is," said Sarah.

Of course it was. There was nothing in the bustle and noise of the wet, thronging harbour to suggest that here was a place where minds might be changed.

Jonathan's eyes wandered again to the crates of equipment being loaded on to the Crimea-bound troop-ship. Helena's eyes followed her husband's and noted (or was the mist over the water playing tricks?) that the troop-ship seemed far sturdier than the migrants' tiny vessel.

Of course Sarah could not change her mind. She was proud. Whatever her fear and regret now that the moment had almost come – and Helena felt Sarah's fear and regret as her own, for why otherwise was Sarah being so jolly and voluble? – Sarah was going to embark on the *Crescent Moon* today, in her new, thick coat of big blue and purple checks, with her green hat clamped closely to her head by her green scarf, tied in a thick knot. At that place where she had been staying (she would not come to Wenbury Hill in the time between the wedding, and her departure, for, as she briskly and sensibly said, "We don't want any old ghosts of me lurking in your new home"), that Ladies Progress place where temporary shelter was given to distressed gentlefolk awaiting emigration, instruction was given too: on religion, on the hardships of seaboard life, on withstanding difficult climates; could not just one of the ladies there have been kind enough to take Sarah aside and tell her that her chosen colours warred rather violently with one another?

As if she read her sister's mind, Sarah began to speak of the place.

"They gave us little handbooks," she was telling Jonathan. "They are quite useful. Mine tells me, for example, that I must not expect agricultural conditions in the Antipodes to be quite the same as those of Sussex. I very much appreciate being told that, for of course it would never have occurred to me. It also says that the character of single lady migrants must not only be beyond reproach, but above suspicion. It is to this end that we are kept under one roof and close observation in the week prior to departure, though what guarantee that provides concerning what we may or may not have been doing beforehand, I do not know. I have been attached to a family of failed snuff merchants called the Morleys, though whether as a jewel is attached to a crown or a horse to a cart remains to be seen. Mr Morley is supposed to protect me on the voyage – from what, I am not certain – and Mrs Morley and I are to be friends, which is to say I am to act as governess to her children and audience to her woes."

Suddenly over the noises of the port, the shouts of sailors and the creaking of ropes, and the sad sounds of goodbyes, rough voices were singing.

My true love she was beautiful,
My true love she was young,
Her eyes were like the diamonds bright
And –

Helena turned. It was coming from the soldiers. They had caught sight of a party of ladies walking with brave, determined tread and heavy bags towards the little boat that would ferry them out to the *Crescent Moon*. They were shepherded by a plump matron in a blue cloak. They were of Sarah's party. Soon Sarah must go.

She's taken a trip on a government ship
Ten thousand miles away –

Their singing was an insult! It was all a great joke to them! They sang with an ironic lack of tune.

She'd a government band around each hand
And another one round her leg.
And another one round her –

They sang of *convicts*! They sang as if Sarah and the others were being sent away! They sang with no respect for their choice or admiration for their courage! They sang, and now they shouted: dreadful words and suggestions from the soldiers on the troop-ship to the women in the small, bobbing boat! Sarah's back was resolutely turned to the boat as she talked on, her words gaining speed, her voice rising in pitch.

"Mrs Morley, Jonathan, to whom I have been attached, lost her home in the failure of her husband's business, and I have heard the account of the loss several times. But whenever I have tried to offer my own comparable experience, she makes it perfectly clear that returning my troubles for hers is no part of my duties. But there. You do not have to listen to people like Mrs Morley. All that is required is a sympathetic set of face, a regular nod or two, and a small repartee of sad sounds. As long as these are provided, you may think what you will – "

I wish I were a bosun bold
Or even a bombardier,
I'd build a boat and away I'd float
And straight for my true love steer –

The soldiers' singing rasped on Helena's nerves. She turned on her sister.

"I think you have no pity – and no gratitude – "

Up went Sarah's expressive eyebrows and she gave a little smile of exasperated surprise (twisted to the left, showing the gap in her teeth, the last time Helena would see it), as if she had forgotten Helena was there at all, and did not in any case mind whether she was or not. She said, "What do you mean?"

"Poor Mrs Morley – she only wants to help you – and she has been through so much trouble – you just laugh at other people's sadness, Sarah! Really, you do!"

Helena had meant to imply that Sarah should have more regard for her own sister's sadness; Helena did not care what happened to this Mrs Morley, she felt only jealousy that Mrs Morley would be with Sarah when she herself would not; but this rebuke was as near as she dared venture to expressing these feelings. And even this seemed to have gone too far, for the colour drained from Sarah's face and her eyebrows descended and the outlines of the edges of her teeth became visible through her lips, biting them together to keep them still. And Jonathan, looking from one sister to the other, said, "That's enough, Helena."

Helena felt her cheeks go pink. He had no business rebuking her like that, in front of Sarah, on Sarah's behalf. How could he expect her to be a proper wife if he treated her as a child? His expression changed and she knew that she could have an apology later if she wanted one.

He looked like a dog, she decided, a sturdy, gentle, slightly mournful dog. His jowls were heavy; there were veins in his eyes. In contrast with his large head, his figure was lean and trim and he was proud of this. He was more concerned about his appearance than she had ever supposed men to be, but then she had never known a man this well. There was a pink circle in the flesh of his neck where it bulged over his stiff collar, for he would not believe that a collar which had fitted him last year fitted him no longer. It must be uncomfortable; the sight of that distended fold of flesh made her uneasy. His dark blue coat was good and thick and entirely necessary on the breezy dockside; but he wore it unbuttoned, and every few minutes, as if casually, he moved his weight forward onto his left leg and thrust his clenched fist onto his hip, pushing the lapels of his coat apart to reveal his new check waistcoat with the gold thread. And now as he did this, he glanced shyly at her and she looked away, because he seemed to be asking for some sort of appreciation, some acknowledgement that she forgave his hasty words because he was such a fine fellow; and it made her uneasy, she didn't like to think why.

She started to apologise to Sarah, but one look at Sarah's face told her this was unnecessary, would not even be heard. Sarah was looking at the little boat that had unloaded its consignment of emigrants onto the *Crescent Moon* and was coming back for more. A blue-cloaked matron detached herself from another group of women huddling at the dockside and bustled towards Sarah, waving in an agitated fashion.

"Mrs Packham. Mrs Packham, please!"

"She cannot mean you?" said Helena. "She has mistaken your name."

Sarah laughed shortly. "So she has!" She made to pick up her bags. The matron bustled nearer. Sarah called rather sharply that the matron need not trouble herself any further; she was coming.

Jonathan stopped posturing and put his hand gently around Helena's back, as if he thought she would faint. Helena looked out again at the tiny ship in the middle of the river: in the short time they had stood there, it seemed to have gathered a mist about itself, and now looked frail as a skeleton, ominous as a gibbet. But she must not say that. She must be brave for Sarah. Why weren't there any words for a parting like this? And why, oh, why, did Jonathan have to be there?

"I think Sarah has to go now, Helena."

"Yes, I know." She grasped her sister's hand and peeled off the soft woollen glove, then peeled off her own kid one; and felt Sarah's vigorous flesh. Suddenly Sarah hugged her, hugged the breath out of her. Sarah's lips found her ear.

"Don't say anything."

"I cannot – "

"To the boat, please, Mrs Packham."

"That woman – your name – "

"Take no notice. She has no memory for names."

"I think the boat is waiting," said Jonathan, sympathetic but sure of his duty.

"I think so too," said Sarah. She replaced her glove, shook his hand, and was gone along the quay without another glance at Helena from her beautiful, humorous, rigidly-held features.

It was like a dream watching Sarah stepping capably into the little boat (while all the other women had to be helped) and sitting aloof from them in the bow, amid a fortress of luggage, her face turned remorselessly from the shore. Why did she neither look nor wave . . . because she was afraid of breaking down . . . and if Sarah broke down she had no kindly husband to press her to him until the storm passed; only the bustling matron whose authority (Helena could tell) Sarah already resented, and the other single lady migrants who were probably not far from breaking down themselves. And Mrs Morley . . . No, Sarah would not look back, she would not wave.

It must be a dream that Sarah was going away for ever. It must be a dream because everywhere was so silent. Helena's mind knew that there was a cacophony of sounds, soldiers singing, oars splashing, wails of children, laughter, even a Roman Catholic priest standing in a crowd of emigrants' relatives, raising a cross and booming out the words of a blessing to carry across the water; her mind knew it all but her ears heard none of it.

Taking a trip on a government ship
Ten thousand miles away –

The little boat was making good speed to the ship, chopping up the waves. Ten thousand miles. Ten thousand miles. It was fifty miles from Wenbury Hill to Littledean . . . fifty into ten thousand goes . . . two hundred! Two hundred times the distance between her old home and her new . . . if she walked from Jonathan's house to the Sussex village and back again one hundred times, that would be the distance. She started to pace the quay, five steps to the left, five steps to the right, going faster in her anguish. The little boat reached the ship and Sarah climbed the ladder – thank heaven for her bright clothing; now Helena could watch her till the very last. A sailor helped her aboard. *Oh sailor, hold her tightly even if she does brush away your arm; I could give you gold to keep her safe; or send her back, refuse on some pretext to carry her, send her back: you could sail round the coast and land her on one of the beaches below Little Beacon and I would run over the stones to meet her!*

In the silence a voice was speaking, a flat, monotonous, gruff voice saying flat, monotonous, gruff words, full of numbers. The numbers were of persons who had made the voyage from England to Australia in recent years and the tiny proportion who had met with any mishap, even though many had travelled in vessels far less seaworthy than the *Crescent Moon*. The voice praised the effectiveness of government regulations on safety and conditions in migrant ships; and it pointed out, with a certain sheepishness, that for it to praise government regulations on *any* subject they would have to be very good regulations indeed.

"I wish you would not stand so close to me, Jonathan!" Helena cried. The very fibres of her coat felt him, like hairs. She saw surprise and hurt spread gently in his big, fleshy features; and she repented. "It's . . . just that I feel you're going to push me over the quay."

"Accidentally, my dear?" he joked, "or deliberately?"

"Oh Jonathan – " She let him embrace her, and laughed a little, and cried a little.

Soon he put her gently to one side and pulled out his watch. It was a very good watch. Then he took out a leather notebook which contained some calculations he had made with Sarah concerning the tides and winds.

"Sailing time is in fifteen minutes or so," he said, "but she won't be out of the river for an hour."

"It's not so long to wait . . . for one's sister."

"But I have to take the ferry," he reminded her. He was to dine at the garrison at Colchester this evening, and was sending her home alone in the carriage.

"Then leave me here," she said.

"Certainly not! What? With all these fellows?" He eyed the soldiers, the sailors, the dockers.

"You don't have a very high opinion of your customers, Jonathan," she said, and smiled nervously because it sounded rude.

"I should think not, as far as my wife's concerned! My dear wife, who sees good in everyone! Come along now." He took her arm with deceptive gentleness. He was actually forcing her along. "Helena. Don't cry. Hm? Hm? Don't, now. Just wish her luck and, er, say a prayer. Shall we? Come along now."

"All right, Jonathan."

"I daresay that old matron's met her match! I'm not sure your sister will be very appreciative of the kind of shipboard supervision she has in mind! What did she keep calling her?"

"Mrs something. Mrs Packham. Jonathan?"

"Yes, my dear?"

"You don't suppose Sarah has been secretly married and is keeping it hidden from us?"

Jonathan laughed. "*Sarah*! Well! Nothing would surprise me." He looked at Helena's face. "No, of course she hasn't. Why should she? Neither of us would stand in the way of any choice she made; and any choice she would make would be an excellent one in any case."

"You liked her, didn't you?"

"I still do, Helena!" He gazed almost wistfully over the water at the *Crescent Moon*. He patted Helena's hand and smiled broadly. "I still do. Very, very much."

Helena fretted about the name Packham as the carriage took her home. Jonathan was right, of course; Sarah would not have married without telling them. That matron must deal with hundreds of unknown women every year; it was natural that she should make an occasional mistake. But Helena wished she could work out why the name Packham seemed familiar. She fretted and worried like a dog at a bone, but could find no answer. It was good, though, to have a specific thing to puzzle over; better than letting the loss of Sarah descend on her like a breaking wave that would carry her away in its cold wet depths.

3

Wenbury Hill was growing fast in popularity as a place for men with thriving businesses in London to live with their families; the roads were wide and quiet, the hillside air fresh, and the journey north by railway to London Bridge took only thirty-seven minutes. Jonathan Croft's house (which he often told Helena was hers too, an idea to which she supposed she would become accustomed, along with everything else) was tall and white and new, half-hidden from the road by young plane trees and young sycamore trees. This would be Helena's first night alone there.

It was dark by the time the fly brought her home. After the brisk autumnal day, the evening had settled in earnest into winter. Here on the hill the air was sharp and clear, but Helena could see fog beginning sullenly to curl about the chimneys in the lower valleys of land that led to London. The stars were very bright, like sparks or slivers of steel shot skywards from the railway as the heavy wheels plunged forwards, shattering the night air. Helena sighed. Sometimes when there was little to be heard on Wenbury Hill, Jonathan spoke of silence; but he knew nothing of the real deep silences of the countryside.

But she consoled herself as she approached the house. It was her house. None of the cottages in Littledean had been fully proof against the wind. And Sarah was out tossing on the cold sea. The white of the walls was not the soft, natural whiteness of snow or chalk or milk, but the hard dazzle of new glossy paint. Even in darkness it gleamed coldly. There were steep white steps up to the black front door, with a black rail to hold on to, to protect oneself from tripping. The day Helena first came to the house, the black paint had still been wet, and her hand in its new glove had stuck to the rail. Jonathan could not have been more apologetic if the hand had been severed at the wrist. She had not minded. They were not her favourite gloves. But now she always hesitated before touching the rail.

The number of the house, number 17, was nailed to the door in bright white-gold brass, which corresponded with the door-knob and the letter-box. Maisie, the housemaid, was supposed to polish the brass and whiten the step every morning, and it was a great relief to Helena that she did in fact do so: for Maisie was a surly girl, very different from the cheerful village women who used to come in to help at home, to be dealt with, in any case, by Sarah. Maisie was strong and competent, and Helena feared that the slightest rebuke might lead to her giving in notice, and then she, Helena, would have to arrange to hire a replacement; she could not do it, she knew she could not. She did not know what to do or say; she simply had not reached the age at which such things came naturally.

Besides, Helena would like to be friendly with the servants. Maisie was nearly her age; and Helena was not so grand.

She took out her latch-key and very quietly let herself into the house. She could hang up her own coat. No one need know she was back, for there was nothing she wanted; the only thing she wanted to do was something rather silly; it was to look in the wire basket under the inside of the letter-box and see if there was a letter from Sarah.

Of course there could not be one. It was silly even to think of it. But, were she Sarah, just the sort of thing she might do would be to post a letter on her way to the docks, to have it waiting for when Helena arrived home. It would not be much of a letter; Helena understood, there was no time for that; but it might say something like: *My Dear Sister, the emotions I feel are so strong that I fear I shall not be able adequately to express them when we meet. If I should appear abrupt, if I seem to make light of the poignancy of the moment, if I even give the impression that I prefer to make frivolous conversation with your husband when I could be exchanging fond words with you, I nevertheless want you to know* . . .

There was no letter.

She went into the drawing-room. It was a long room, gleaming with new furniture. There seemed to Helena to be plenty of furniture in the house but he wanted her to order more. He enjoyed buying things, though he pretended not to. "This is really your department, my dear," he said. He thought she knew about

24

furnishing a house, whereas he feared his preferences fell short of what was generally regarded as good taste.

When he returned from Colchester tomorrow, he would want her to have selected some new easy chairs from a catalogue. "And make sure you choose a comfortable one for yourself, Helena," he had said. "I'm not one of these husbands who wants a throne for himself and expects his wife to make do with a milking-stool!" It seemed very important to him that she did not think him a tyrant.

And he was not a tyrant, he was not! She could not have hoped for a kinder husband. He could be rather thoughtless, but in that matter he seemed not to be able to help himself. And she supposed all men were the same.

The drawing-room wall-paper was very rich. It was of oriental design, in orange and crimson and blue and gold with dozens of pictures that fascinated the eye by being not quite identical. In morning sunlight the blue and the crimson predominated; it could be quite cheering, leading one to ponder (as Jonathan said) on the world-wide wonder of man's genius; but in lamplight or firelight it could look rather sinister, with gold glinting from the lanterns of figures crossing bridges, or the eyes of cats.

She heaved the big furniture catalogue on to her lap. She wondered uneasily if she ought to ring for Maisie, just to let the girl know that her mistress had returned. It was strange to feel so alone in the quiet house. But why disturb her? Helena couldn't think of anything she wanted . . . except perhaps company, and you did not ask your servants for that. Ah – a creak on the floorboards outside the drawing-room – Maisie was coming anyway. Helena called, "Come in!" anticipating the knock; but no one came. She went to the door; the hall was empty. It must just be the house creaking. Did new houses creak? She rang the bell and decided to ask for a light supper when Maisie answered. Nobody came.

Jonathan said they needed more servants than just Maisie and the cook; but Helena changed the subject every time he talked of advertising.

Where was Maisie?

Resting, perhaps?

Perhaps she deserved to rest.

Drawings of easy chairs danced before Helena's eyes. How on earth was one supposed to choose? When every manufacturer called his furniture superior, his craftsmen skilled, his prices moderate and his service personal, how could one know? One could not even necessarily believe in the unsolicited testimonials that were quoted at some length, for the advertisers could have written those themselves.

And even if they were genuine . . . well, they would hardly print letters of complaint, would they? Even if they did receive more of them than the other kind?

Those velvet chairs looked comfortable, but a manufacturer would not keep an artist in his employment for very long if he could not achieve that impression . . . would he?

Helena's neighbours and Jonathan's relatives might think her a little bit of a country girl still, and patronise her with their advice, but she was not to be made a fool of by pictures in a catalogue. She would visit the showrooms in person. She would do it tomorrow, and give Jonathan such a surprise when he returned.

She sat and listened to the sounds of the quiet house. She decided to go upstairs and think about furniture for her own bedroom. It now contained her parents' old bed and a few other things from Littledean. Jonathan was too tactful to say directly that she ought to replace them; but she knew he would like her to improve the room a little, make it more like his own.

Their bedrooms were on the second floor. Then there was a steep flight of wooden stairs leading to the attic where the servants slept.

Helena hardly knew what made her start to climb them. She had never seen the servants' rooms. She was supposed to inspect them, to make sure they were clean. But it seemed so insulting, she did not do it. Perhaps she wanted to know whether the tall narrow house was really as empty as it felt. Perhaps she wanted to hear a voice. Perhaps she wanted company . . . company? One did not go to one's servants for company! Did one? Helena did not know . . . but she did want to be a kindly mistress.

The stairs were wooden and bare and narrow and moved under her feet. Climbing higher, she met an odd, sweetish smell. Was it flowers, sugar? Or was it slightly unpleasant, stale sweetmeats or dirt? It was all of those things, but not quite any of them. Why was she tiptoeing? The house was hers.

The stairs creaked. She heard someone moving around. She looked into the open room. It was a very small room – Helena thought the broom cupboard downstairs might be bigger. Maisie sat on a narrow bed holding a candle and a cheap hand-mirror. The upper half of her body was naked except for a chemise of greying wool, and Helena could see the cold gooseflesh on her arms as she moved the mirror and the light to a favourable position to examine her face. Maisie set down the candle, and her freed hand began to pull and prod at her skin while she peered closely into the glass.

Helena smiled. She felt old and protective. Hadn't she looked in mirrors in just such a way when Jonathan was expected? Hunting for blemishes? Was Maisie courting, then? Helena felt like a mother to her, or an older sister: she wanted to rush forward and reassure her that when a man is in love, he does not notice imperfections so small that they must be searched for with a candle and a looking-glass.

Helena stood still, watching. Maisie put down her mirror. She reached under her bed and from a wooden box took out a smudged glass bottle. She turned it on to her fingertip and dabbed her fingertip under her arms. She looked up and saw Helena. She made a little sound like an exasperated snarl. She pulled a blanket off the bed and covered herself.

Helena said, "It's all right, Maisie, there's nothing wrong."

Maisie said, "Ain't this my place?"

Helena was frightened; servants did not speak to one like that.

The girl repeated, "Beggin' your pardon, mum. But ain't this my place?" The polite formula took nothing away from her hostility.

Helena said, "I rang. You didn't come."

"I thought you and Mr Croft was stayin' away."

Helena fled. *Ain't this my place?* The cheek of it! The house belonged to Jonathan. As his wife, she could go where she pleased.

Half way to sleep, she realised the maid had been lying; if she had not expected her mistress or master home, why had she lit the fire? But Helena decided to say nothing. If the servants didn't respect her, it was probably her own fault.

Helena slept badly in her old bed. It was a low, creaky, wooden bed with one of its knobs lost on the road from Littledean; but soft and comforting in the tall narrow room. When Jonathan wanted to be with her, she preferred to go to his room; she didn't want him disapproving of her old furniture; and she would be ashamed to be with him in the bed where her mother had been with her father.

She needed to get up several times in the night. In between, she dreamed three dreams. In the first she was a child, running up Little Beacon with a huge pail of milk that wasn't even heavy. In the second, she was being pursued down a long flight of stairs by a mahogany wardrobe with claws and Jonathan's face. Even in the dream she saw the absurdity of this and laughed at it . . . but it was real enough, with the stairs becoming narrower and the air more stifling until she emerged into the third dream where she was all alone on a wide, hot plain, and kept saying, "Ain't this my place? Ain't this my place?" Those were Maisie's words; but she felt sure, when she finally awoke into a cold morning streaming with rain, that she had been Sarah in that dream.

There were peacocks on the tiles on the walls of the water-closet. They amused Helena. It was a thoroughly elegant room, considering its function, and she had never seen anything like it. The peacocks had supercilious expressions on their faces, and she wondered why Jonathan had chosen them.

She smiled wanly to herself about this as she sat alone at break-fast, sipping weak tea; she seemed to have spent rather a long time contemplating the peacocks last night, when she wasn't having extraordinary dreams. She felt her brow: it was rather hot. The more she thought about it, the more she realised that she was not well.

Should she send for the doctor? But it was hard to identify what was wrong – impossible to put it into words. And she had a feeling she would not like to answer the questions he would put to her, knowing she was a newly married lady.

Probably it would put itself to rights . . . if there was anything that needed putting to rights. Perhaps her symptoms, far from indicating something wrong, showed that things were happening very much as they should.

She shivered at the thought and listened to the beat of the rain.

Was it possible, so soon? They had only been married a month. And the thing that they did as husband and wife (it must have a name, she supposed, a name different from the farmyard terms she could recall) . . . that thing had occurred with such difficulty and awkwardness that she could not believe it had had its naturally destined effect.

It was too soon, she was too young. She was not yet eighteen. She knew village girls who had had babies at sixteen or less, but they had their mothers with them, they had their sisters. She had known what marriage would mean; she had secretly looked forward to sleeping all night cuddled close to Jonathan's strong arms. She had not been ready for the shock of the different ways he treated her: how she seemed to him to be different people, child bride or fine lady in the daytime, for whom nothing was too much trouble; but at night, hardly a person at all, only a fierce, dark duty from which he turned in sadness when he had done what he could not help.

They had never slept all night, cuddled together. He escorted her courteously back to her parents' bed, his head turned away.

Perhaps it was her fault.

She ought to be more sensitive to his feelings. Wasn't he always telling her how beautiful she was? He was a vain man, and older than she; perhaps he thought her reluctance meant she did not think him good looking, and if he thought that he would be very mortified. And he would be wrong; it was the other way round; it was the very sense of reluctance and compulsion warring in *him* that scared her.

She visited the kitchen to hear Mrs Lyons tell her what they would eat that evening; she asked Maisie if she would be so kind as to clean the bedrooms. Maisie bobbed pertly; Helena understood that there was an agreement that if there was no mention of last night's rudeness, there would be no repetition of it.

She remembered she had intended to visit the furniture showrooms today, and choose chairs; but perhaps it would be wiser to wait and choose with Jonathan. It was raining, the streets would be unspeakable; and she was not well.

Upstairs, Maisie was thumping about busily; maybe Helena could spend the morning writing an advertisement for another maid. She wished she had asked the girl to do her room before Jonathan's; she might want to rest this afternoon.

She decided to clean some brass. Helena liked cleaning brass; she liked the way it rewarded her with a silver-red gleam when it was done. And Jonathan did not like her to do it, so here was the perfect opportunity. Not the front-door fittings; they were Maisie's job; but she spread a covering on the floor in the drawing-room and went quietly about the house collecting everything made of brass.

Soon, tired from the work and with a dragging pain low in her back, she went upstairs. Maisie had finished Jonathan's room and was brushing down the mattress in Helena's. She supposed it would do no harm if she lay on Jonathan's bed for a while?

Why was she so tired? Jonathan had said, "You won't have to do anything, anything at all. Just amuse yourself." Sarah had curled her lip at this. One of the reasons why Sarah had hated giving up the farm was that there was "nothing to do; just things around the house." Helena had meant to do things around Jonathan's house regardless; it was her house too; but Maisie was so competent and everything was so bright and new . . . there were probably jobs she ought to do to prevent them deteriorating, but she didn't know what they might be and she didn't like to ask.

Jonathan's room was very blue: blue walls, blue curtains, blue ceiling. She imagined being under water. She remembered stories Mother had told, of mortal women who married mermen and went to live in the sea. Mother told *such* stories, beside the big crackling fire in the farmhouse kitchen. Sometimes there was fibre and dust in the air from the spinning wheels, and the fire spat.

The huge curtained bed could be a wreck, and she a great female fish. To his own mother's amusement, Jonathan kept a frayed brown shawl from his childhood. It looked like a piece of seaweed.

No wonder Jonathan treated her as a child!

Rain lashed the window panes. Even the neat street outside seemed to be under water. Through the beat of the rain she could hear the soft clopping of tradesmen's horses, or callers at other houses in the street.

How easy it would be to pop next door, where the kindly Mrs Lindsay had vowed always to be glad to receive her; and whisper delicately that she feared something was wrong, something hard to mention . . . and have Mrs Lindsay smile and know what it was (since it was so normal) and find a way of speaking of it that acknowledged its discomfort but made light of it without being unkind: "Trouble in the water pipes, eh?" – yes, that was how she would put it in that jolly Scotch way of hers, and then they might even have a secret laugh together about the cruder words they might once have used, for Mrs Lindsay had been a country-woman too, thirty years ago.

She would go . . . in half an hour, perhaps. Meanwhile she lay still.

She heard Maisie finish in the room next door and stamp down-stairs to her lunch. Still Helena did not move.

She stared at Jonathan's bare fireplace. She was cold but would not get under the covers. The fireplace was made of marble, with pictures from the story of Achilles. Mother used to like Greek myths, and read from a big heavy book. Achilles' mother feared he would grow up to be killed in a war, so she disguised him as a girl and hid him in a palace. Jonathan's pictures showed him revealing himself by choosing a sword in preference to jewels when merchants came to call. He was taken away for a soldier and in due course his mother's gloomy prediction was fulfilled. Helena supposed that it was Jonathan's being a military supplier that made him like the story so much.

The fireplace was only one of the room's glories. The royal blue carpet caressed and swallowed up the feet, and on two of the walls there were guns and swords and pictures of wars and cricket matches.

The wall by the bed was different. It had been cunningly made to allow a variety of little alcoves, shelves, niches and nooks; it was rather cosy after the guns and swords, because these were the places where he kept his souvenirs. Was there ever such a man for collecting souvenirs? Ornaments, buttons, postcards, pictures, snuff boxes, even toys; and feathers, stones and shells. There were some oyster shells that smelled rather strongly if you went close to them; but he would not have them washed. "It's good to smell the sea," he said; but Helena had never smelt the sea like that.

It was strange that Jonathan should sometimes be so fatherly; for seeing all these toys and collections she felt like nothing so much as a mother to him, a mother with a son whose trouser-pockets were full of dead insects and birds' eggs.

She yawned. He would not be home till the evening. She could stay here. But there was no point in ignoring that irritating sensation. Down she must go to the peacocks again! What a funny thing this was! How Sarah would laugh! How Jonathan would laugh if she couldn't sit still through dinner!

At last the sensation eased; and she slept.

She must have slept. She awoke in darkness on the cold blue counterpane. She reached out and she could touch the darkness; she rolled over to the other side of the bed where a lamp was burning.

Jonathan was padding round the bed like a bear in his shirt-sleeves and his trousers and his stockinged feet, pulling the golden tassels at the bed's corners till the unbound curtains fell loose like unpinned hair. She sat up.

"Jonathan, what are you doing?"

"There's a fine welcome!" His broad face smiled with pleasure at seeing her; but he looked a little disappointed too, thwarted in surprising her. She moved to the edge of the bed. "No, stay there," he said, "you look like the sleeping beauty, and besides . . ." The fourth curtain closed and she felt trapped in a box. She heard a rustling sound; was he changing his clothes? Her heart beat so fast she felt sick.

Light returned and the curtain opened.

"There!" he said.

In the middle of the room, draped across a chair, was a fine gown, black, trimmed with scarlet lace.

She stared. "Thank you, Jonathan. I shall . . . wear it next time we have company."

He threw back his head and laughed. He shook with laughter. He stopped when he saw her face and squeezed her hands. "You dear thing! It is a *nightgown!*"

"Oh," she said, "is it? I did not know."

"No," he said, "you did not know."

"Thank you, Jonathan. I was not expecting any presents."

"No, no! Of course not!" He embraced her and she was glad of the reassurance of his return but she wished he would put his jacket back on. It was a rather wasteful nightgown and would not suit her colouring, but it was kind of him. *It's the kind thought, not the gift,* Mother used to say. He was still laughing at her. "Of course not! And if I hadn't given it to you, not for one moment would you have pestered me with 'What have you brought me from Colchester, Jonathan?' It would never have crossed your mind, would it, to think, 'here's a fine husband I've found myself! Leaves me all alone and doesn't even think to bring a – ' " he was mimicking her voice. And he pinched her cheek with two fingers, quite hard. She felt the place burn.

"I hope I am not ungrateful," she said.

"Now, now! Don't pout! Silly girl! You bring out the playfulness in me and until I discover your real faults – so far you appear to have none – I shall have to tease you for imaginary ones. Now. Tell me what you have been doing."

She said stiffly, "Am I to account for myself?"

Again he laughed. "Certainly not! You will have an easier time of it hunting out my faults than I have with yours, but tyranny will never be among them . . . even if your formidable protectrix has abandoned you to my mercy." His tone changed. "No, no, Helena." He sounded hurt. She had not meant to hurt him. "You need never account to me for anything." Anxious lines creased his face. "But Helena, this is the way married people talk to each other! They are separated for some reason and when they come together again they say, 'What have you been doing?' The husband says it and the wife tells him – excluding anything if she wishes, it is no matter, it is just conversation – and then she asks him the same question." He took a deep breath and rubbed his hands together. "Would you like to put it on now, Helena? For me to see?"

"Jonathan! We have not had dinner!"

"No," he agreed. "We have not had dinner." She hurried downstairs, and soon he followed.

After dinner he asked again if she would put it on. She opened her mouth to protest that she was not well, but she realised she would have to wear it sooner or later if she was not to seem ungrateful. She put it on in her own room, then went to him.

"With you in it," he said, "the nightgown is even more beautiful than before."

"You mean the other way round?" she said shyly.

"What, Helena?"

"I mean, isn't it a more usual compliment to say a dress makes a woman more beautiful, rather than – " she stopped, confused. He was laughing at her again.

"Why should I pay you compliments that are *usual*? And Helena, you seem to know more than I do about the *usual* forms of address to a lady in a nightgown!"

She pushed him away. "Don't say that."

"It was only a joke."

"I don't like your jokes."

"Or me. You don't like me very much yet, do you, Helena?"

"I do."

"Come along, then. Come and show me."

What could she say? He had trapped her nicely. She had thought she was growing accustomed to this, but this time was worse than before. The bed rocked with the force of him and the nightgown scratched her skin. She felt outraged. He seemed to be simply spiteful. If he could not be gentle, where at least was his dignity, Jonathan Croft of Croft & Co., who dined with the colonels at Colchester barracks? Had he gone mad? Had some rapid illness struck him while he was away? Or had he always wanted to be like this, waiting for the first month of marriage to pass before revealing himself, bringing her a beautiful nightgown to console her for what he would make her endure while she wore it? He was big and heavy and wet, his movements were out of control, she could almost have pitied him, how dreadful to suffer such a need . . . She found a way to move that lessened his weight, felt better. Felt much better. Or worse: strange, terrifying edges of sensation like licking flames. Like nothing. No, not like nothing, like something she would not think about, like dreams, like childish games, silly childish habits, games with Sarah that the governess caught them playing and said she would beat them like hearth rugs if she ever, if they ever . . .

"Helena." Jonathan was still. "Forgive me. I forgot myself."

"You forget me," she sobbed.

"Helena, sometimes a man . . . don't go."

"I am not well."

As she opened the door, he said, "Don't wear that thing again. Just wear your own things."

"You gave it to me!"

"I know. I should have known . . ." he started to get out of bed and come towards her.

"I *am not well!*" She fled from him to her own bed. He did not follow, but she felt his remorse through the wall.

Forgive him? She might as well. No doubt it would be repeated. No doubt she would get used to it, though she could not imagine that now.

She wanted to sleep but she could not; her nerves were writhing like caterpillars and the rain pouring down the dark outsides of the windows seemed to call to all the fluids of her body to follow in floods, draining her like chalk. She wondered if she was really ill or only nervous.

Time after time she must get out of bed and pad along to the water-closet, half crying with exasperation and pain, half laughing at the absurdity . . .

She wished she knew what this strange ailment was. She wished it would go away.

4

Two weeks later, Helena Croft received an unexpected letter.

She was glad not to have troubled a doctor with the little difficulty that had by now almost vanished. She would hate to speak of it. Her fear and hope that she might be expecting a child had proved unfounded. Jonathan and she had a silent agreement not to refer in the daytime to what passed between them at night; and even that was becoming less frequent and, through familiarity, more acceptable. The red and black nightgown was neither worn again nor mentioned. Helena put it in a box at the back of her wardrobe, wrapped up in tissue paper. Perhaps it would be more suitable when she was older.

As if exacting a debt, her body slept late in the mornings.

She was dimly aware of Janet, the lady's maid Jonathan had employed for her as a surprise, bringing in a jug of water; but she signalled to the girl (who reminded her a little of Sarah, being tall and jovial) to set it down and be gone. She slept on until ten, then rose and dressed herself. She did not ring. As if she needed someone to dress her! She put on a plain green morning dress, then decided it looked rather vulgar with her pallor. She changed to the yellow, which she had once thought sickly but now suited her.

The dining-room was deserted. Jonathan had gone to his shop. Her own plate and cup awaited her, and a rack of cold toast. There was a sugary smear on the tablecloth where somebody had spilt marmalade and scraped it off with a knife. The marmalade jars were arranged neatly in their silver holders as Jonathan liked them to be. And there was a letter by her plate. She recognised the handwriting at once and turned the letter over and over in her hands.

"Should I bring fresh tea, Mrs Croft, or coffee?"

"Oh – tea." She felt the pot. "I don't need any more."

Maisie fussed around. Helena kept her letter and her hands in her lap. She sipped the tea; it was tepid. She spread a little butter on a bit of toast.

"There's fresh toast makin', Mrs Croft."

"Oh goodness – this is perfectly all right. That will be all, Maisie." *That will be all*. That was what you said. It was politer than *leave me in peace*. But she decided to postpone reading the letter until after breakfast. She would find a little place for herself before attending to the morning's tasks.

Back came Maisie, opening the dining-room door with a thump and looking like thunder, all a-bristle with brushes and brooms and pots of polish.

"Good gracious, Maisie, wait until I have finished my breakfast, *please!*" Helena cried.

Slowly and deliberately, Maisie set down her cleaning tools. "Beggin' your pardon, Mrs Croft, mum. But Mr Croft said I was to give the dinin' room a thorough clean out and later on I've got to . . . " She recited a long list of tasks that Jonathan had apparently assigned to her, accompanied by an explanation of why they had to be done in a particular order, all leading up to the moral that there was no alternative to her doing the dining-room now. Maisie's shrewd eyes were eloquent: Mrs Croft was causing her considerable inconvenience by eating breakfast so late. Helena bit slowly on her toast and resented Jonathan; how like him, if he was dissatisfied with the way the household was managed, to go over her head to the servants, as if he and the servants were the only adults in the place!

She stood up. "You had better do as Mr Croft said."

"Thank you, mum. And Mrs Croft – "

"Yes?"

"Beggin' your *pardon*, but Mrs Lyons says can she come and talk to you or can you go and talk to her, whichever is convenient, about tonight."

"Tonight?"

Maisie turned her back and swept plates, vases and ornaments to the end of the sideboard and began to polish. "I understood Mr Croft to say you 'ad company coming."

"Oh yes," she said. "Yes, of course. He – er – mentioned it last week."

"Only told Mrs Lyons this morning. She's in a proper state."

"All right, Maisie. That will be all." *That will be all.* That was what you said.

"You mean I'm not to clean?"

"Clean, of course. I shall go to the kitchen."

Half way down the stairs she thought she had left her letter behind. But she felt it in her pocket, flat and hard against her leg.

Mrs Lyons wasn't in a state at all.

36

"I'm terribly sorry for all the rush, Mrs Lyons."

"Bless you, Mrs Croft, it's no bother. Just the one gentleman coming, is it? But I like to have things specially nice when there's company."

"It's always nice, Mrs Lyons. Will that be all?"

"If you'll just run your eyes over this . . . "

Helena read the bill of fare in Mrs Lyons' neat round handwriting: vermicelli soup, rump steak, roast mutton, pastries and custards. Jonathan's guest was obviously expected to have a good appetite. Really it was too bad of Jonathan: to invite people without consulting her. Perhaps news of the man's coming had only arrived in today's post, but still, didn't he know that she wanted to be a good wife and arrange these things herself?

Suddenly the house seemed to spring to grotesque, decaying life: the furniture and fittings that had gleamed with such newness revealed dust and smears and threatened her with disgrace. Jonathan was right; the whole house must be scrubbed from top to bottom, all the rooms, for what if Jonathan wanted to show off his residence? She must swallow her pride and work alongside Maisie; she must summon Janet and put her to cleaning too. And what would she wear? Was black silk correct for a small dinner? Janet would know. Was that why Jonathan had employed Janet – because he feared his wife needed advice on dressing? Still – time enough to worry about that. It was nearly eleven o'clock. "Don't worry, I'll do the brass, Maisie!" she sang out. And while she supposed Maisie ought still to be feeling grateful for this relief she started lifting up the edges of carpets to check that there were no piles of dust . . .

Perhaps before doing this she ought to have decided what response to make if her suspicions were fulfilled; for there were the flattened dunes of dust. She left them.

Once or twice she sat back on her heels from the cleaning and reached in her pocket for her letter. But she was always disturbed.

The guest was a man from the War Office who wanted to talk about some business with Jonathan. Jonathan was not at his ease: he seemed to want to show his appreciation of Helena for having arranged a good dinner and for looking so elegant in her black silk, but the man would have none of it. "Hm, yes, very nice, Mrs Croft," he said gruffly a few times, then returned to talk of uniforms and equipment.

"My wife is very concerned that the soldiers should be warm enough," Jonathan said once, referring to a conversation they had had and trying to bring her into the party, but only succeeding in making her feel silly and old-maidish "and it does not do to ignore the opinions of the ladies."

"Indeed not! Indeed not!" said the man from the War Office gallantly, his mouth full. " 'Wrap up warmly!' my mother used to say." And then, as if that was enough frivolity, he moved on to mention his concern that British soldiers in red and blue were proving to be rather easy targets in the Crimea. Jonathan nearly choked in his eagerness to offer Croft & Co.'s services in providing uniforms in the brownish colours that so frustrated the army in India trying to aim at the Afghans in the sandy landscapes; the man from the War Office was not sure. Were the soldiers of the Queen to imitate blackies, to scuttle about and hide under rocks like locusts in the desert?

Helena was so near to sleeping at the table that Jonathan had to clear his throat three times before she realised he was indicating that she should withdraw.

Dearest Helena,

How surprised you will be to have word from me so soon! And if I know anything of your darling imagination, you will have devised any number of ingenious disasters to have befallen me and made this communication possible! You will have postponed unsealing the envelope for a day or more in order to enjoy fretting to the full; but you will at last have realised that I cannot be drowned, nor cast away in an open boat, nor even marooned on a desert island, unless it be one with a convenient postal service to Wenbury Hill, Kent!

Sarah's mocking voice echoed softly in the long drawing-room where Helena sat alone, firelight flickering on the gold lanterns in the wallpaper. *Where are you, Sarah? Oh, where are you?*

. . . somewhere off the coast of Portugal and tossing like a cork; it has been a tempestuous night and I and most of my fellow passengers have been wretchedly indisposed. But now, like a reward for suffering bravely borne, calmer weather is promised; and a ship has been sighted, homeward bound . . .

You plan to transfer yourself to that ship! You have already done so – you are in England, now as I read this!

. . . she will be alongside us in an hour; and if the wind has dropped it may be possible to exchange letters, etc.; so I write feverishly to tell you I am alive and as well as might be expected, and recount my adventures hitherto; and trust you will forgive any shortcomings in my letter, having regard to the circumstances.

Helena, I beg you to be honest with me always! Otherwise, how will we remain alive to each other as sisters in all the years we are to be separated? I mean to tell you everything, however it may reflect on me, and I begin by confessing that my first reaction on hearing that we were to have contact with the approaching vessel was to rush to my berth and pack my box, for I thought that if messages could be exchanged, people might too; I was homesick, you see, and never so aware that I was taking *voluntarily* a step that has been thought suitable punishment for the basest of rogues, second only in severity to the gibbet itself! Uprooting myself from all that I knew and loved, including the best sister a girl ever bullied, casting myself on the mercy of the oceans for maybe three months, and then, that survived, facing a life of – what? Drudgery and hardship – for what else will it be, the early years of scratching a living from a difficult soil, rich and comfortable though I mean to be in my waning years (and doubtless a little tyrannical too, I am afraid to say).

There! Confession is good for the soul! It has calmed me and strengthened my resolve: I stay with my ship!

Helena sighed and petulantly bit her lip. A door opened out in the hall; she heard a gruff chop of laughter from the man from the War Office. Were they coming in? She crumpled the letter, made to throw it on the fire, waited tensely . . . the door closed. She smoothed out the paper. Why had she done that? Jonathan would hardly object, indeed he would be pleased to hear that Sarah was safely on her way; but he might wonder why she had not mentioned the letter.

Now – where was she?

Ah – the passage she had longed for.

I fear our parting was rather abrupt. A thousand times I have regretted it – wished I had embraced you and talked to you and consoled you – but now I console myself with the knowledge that you will have understood and known how unbearable tears would have been; and they were very near for me, I do not speak for you.

We single ladies are stowed in the stern like chests of tea. They call us the Poop Governesses. We are not in the poop and we are not all governesses . . . but this is a remarkable thing I have noticed about the presiding dragons of Ladies Progress: a steadfast reluctance to acknowledge my frequently-stated intention to work in no woman's house but my own (nor any man's either), but to be a farmer.

I confess I do not know how long you waited on the quay; I hope you did not chill yourself. I went below at once. It was all I could do; I had to be alone to compose myself.

I was neither surprised nor disappointed by my quarters. The Ladies Progress ladies had warned us about them, adding the encouraging rider that a certain discomfort now would be to our credit in the hereafter, not to mention preparing us for life in Australia.

The doorway is slightly shorter than I am, which fact is permanently recorded in a purple bump on my forehead which I have given no time to heal before renewing it at frequent intervals. I reeled from the first blow and tumbled clumsily to the floor (how easily *you* would have accommodated the inconvenience, Helena, in your dainty stride!), tearing the hem of my dress.

"Oh joy!" I remember thinking. "We have not left port, and already I have something to sew!" You will not have forgotten the delight I take in the needle.

It is very dim below, even when the hatch is open. It is frankly foul now, though it was clean enough, even soapy, on my first arrival. The "beds" are patches of hard floor with wooden ridges to keep us from rolling into one another when the ship pitches. Three feet above are shelves, which I at first assumed were for passengers' belongings but in fact are more beds. What possessions we cannot fit into our bedspace are stowed in boxes in the hold, with access only allowed at certain times. Eighty berths I counted, eighty single ladies. Our great nation is indeed clearing out its cupboards!

I could laugh to think of myself, so bitter and so forlorn. But if I were speaking these words, my voice would crack.

The ship lurched and creaked; I grabbed a shelf, fought panic and scolded myself. "We are still in the river, Sarah; how on earth will you handle the Bay of Biscay?" Never one to allow a rebuke to go unanswered (as you know) I retorted that *that* would depend on how the Bay of Biscay handled me, and silenced my critic. Faint sounds reached me from the deck above and the flat receding shore that I refused to look at, keenly though I felt your hurt. I heard cheers, cries, prayers, the sounds of love. Will you ever forgive me for abandoning you to wave at nothing? It seemed wise to exclude you from my thoughts for the time being, and prepare myself for the company of the eighty strangers with whom I must live in far closer physical, though not, I feared, emotional, intimacy than I have enjoyed with you.

A much-read paragraph from one of our interminable Handbooks rehearsed itself in my mind: "On board ship you must expect to meet and mingle with persons who would not, perhaps, under normal circumstances, be part of your circle. Be tolerant, for God smiles on a harmonious ship – think of it as preparation for your new life in Australia where a man is valued not for what he *has been* but for what he *can do* – " All very good sense, I do not doubt it; indeed I am counting on it, hoping that *having been* the dreariest of young ladies will not prevent me from *becoming* the most enterprising of farmers – but there and then with my feet on the unsteady floor of the sleeping quarters, I had severe doubts. Eighty women in this space, being "tolerant" towards one another? Governesses, housemaids, farm-girls and some whose occupation would not, I suspect, bear investigation, scrupulous though the Ladies Progress enquiries may have been. I sent up a prayer for cleanliness and freedom from infectious diseases, this seeming to me a reasonable minimum requirement; I have always felt it best to make only minimal demands of the Almighty, for there is then less risk of disappointment. It seems I was wise; for apart from seasickness and its accompanying inconvenience, which, for all its being a horrible nuisance, at least has the advantage of being entirely foreseeable, my prayers have been answered; and I have also made a friend.

She came crashing through the doorway in those early moments, exactly as I had done. Rubbing her head and her eyes in the darkness, she uttered a profanity with such sweetness that it could have been a prayer; looked at me in a way both friendly and accusing; and declared that she knew who I was.

"Then you have the advantage of me, Miss – er – " said I, and she replied that she was Miss Jean Flanagan and I was Mrs Packham.

Ah, Helena! I wrote those words exactly as I recalled the conversation; and immediately my fingers itched to delete it. But having vowed always to tell the truth, and having commanded you to do the same, I suppose I must confess it. I have changed my name.

Helena gasped at this: she had been right, Sarah *was* married! Her puzzlement faded into pleasure, until she read on, and puzzlement returned.

. . . not in the conventional way that women do such a thing! There is no Mr Packham, that I know of! It was not done deliberately, or out of any intention to deceive; but since everybody aboard now knows me as Mrs Packham, and I am not disposed to offer them the explanation which I now owe you, I shall have to wait until I am alone again before reverting to the name to which I am more accustomed.

Before I explain (how near the ship comes! Half-a-dozen more tacks and she will be upon us! I must make haste!) – before I explain, and lest you misunderstand, let me remind you of my opinions on the institution of marriage.

I have no opinions. One might as well marvel or express disappointment at a sealed gift box before discovering what it contains. Marriage to a kind, beloved person is, I am sure, a blessing and a happiness, as our parents knew and as I pray you and Jonathan are discovering. Marriage to a brute or a fool would be sheer torture. It is obviously absurd, therefore, to ask the question "What are your opinions on the institution of marriage?" without posing a supplementary question: "Marriage to whom?"

And yet just such a question was being asked, just such a conversation being conducted at the quayside, mainly among the complacent wives, all of them praising the married state, as if the identity and character of one's spouse were of the smallest consequence, and expressing ill-disguised pity for the single ladies on the voyage, all of whom, it was assumed, were going to Australia for the sole purpose of finding a husband and out of desperation of finding one at home.

Make no mistake: I shall happily marry the right man, English, Australian or Hottentot if he comes along, and if he asks me – I see him as rather taller than I, cleverer in some regards and stupider in others to make up; sufficiently good-looking to gladden my eye, yet with enough peculiarities to deter the frequently heard observation that the best-looking men always marry the plainest women. Until, as I say, he happens along; or if he does not; I shall happily remain Miss Weeks.

And yet I was about to explain why it is that on board ship I am known as Mrs Packham! It began as a joke – well, perhaps not entirely so. I was quite beside myself with anger at such unkindness, for it may be that some women are desperate to marry, and how cruel of people who have succeeded in doing a thing to mock those desperate to do it too! And so I said very loudly, "I am not looking for a husband."

And Mrs Morley, who is supposed to be my friend and whose husband is supposed to be my protector, said, "That is just as well, Miss Weeks! For *they* like to be the ones to do the looking."

Her words so goaded me that I could have pulled off her bonnet; or smacked her face; or even pushed her into the water – anything to make her feel as foolish and hurt as *her* words would have made *me* feel, had I been in the slightest degree troubled by my single state. Instead I decided to discomfort her. And I said, "I am not Miss Weeks; I am Mrs – er – Packham; I had reverted to my former name in the hope that I might forget. Yet your talk of the happiness of the married state only reminds me of what I have lost. Oh, poor Packham – and all to save a drowning puppy!"

The confusion of Mrs Morley, on finding herself thus silently accused of taunting a widow was well worth any inconvenience or difficulty that may come to me through thus travelling under an assumed name! For needless to say, I cannot now admit the pretence without risking utter ridicule. But I wonder if you can guess – or remember – why the name of Packham came to me? Sarah Packham: I must say, it sounds rather well.

"Little Sarah is growing to look like Constancia Packham." Our grand-mother used to say that; but I do not suppose you remember our visits to her with Mother; Grandmother died when you were three. Naturally I wanted to know who it was that I resembled, and Grandmother one day showed me her portrait. It was not a very interesting portrait. It was old and the colours had faded.

"She looks very cross," I think I said, and Grandmother chuckled. "Determined, not cross. She was my ancestor, and so she is yours; she owned all the land in these parts – " And she told me some exciting stories about barons and dukes scheming to take it from her and she always outwitting them. I had not realised how firm a root Constancia Packham had taken in my memory until I found the name Packham on my tongue just when I needed one! It is better than having the name of a stranger!

Helena sat perplexed. The long drawing-room was chilly; the fire was dying; she wondered whether to ring for more coal. Were Jonathan and the man from the War Office going to stay talking all night? Would it be impolite if she went to bed? Sarah thought herself so superior, being those few years older! She thought Helena remembered nothing! But Helena remembered the portrait of Constancia Packham perfectly well – better, in fact, than Sarah did, for it was not old and faded at all, it was rather glorious and golden like a figure in a stained-glass window when the sun shone; and Constancia looked neither determined nor cross, she looked kind.

Helena turned back to the letter. The handwriting was racing now. Helena could sense the approach of the ship that would bring the letter home. Sea wind cleared the smell of the dying fire from the room; she heard the flap of ropes and sails.

Enough explanations! You will think me quite crazy, but there is nothing new in that! Miss Flanagan had pleased me by using my new name, but apart from that – as is often the way with new acquaintances who are soon to become firm friends – she pleased me not at all at first. She told me I must come on deck immediately, and I coolly asked on whose authority the command came. She is about my age, her clothes very shabby and covered with darning. Her pink cheeks I now see as pretty, but her eyes and manner were a good deal too knowing for my taste. She informed me that Matron was convinced I had missed the boat, and if I did not come at once and prove her wrong I would find myself without food or duties for the journey.

Naturally I should not wish to be without food, so I followed her up to the deck, grudgingly stopping her from falling when the ship dipped unexpectedly. I lowered my eyes in keeping with my decision not to look on England again, but then realised this looked apologetic, so I examined our deck. The single ladies appeared to be fenced off from the rest of the ship like cattle in a paddock: men in the bow were attempting to catch our attention with shouts and whistles but they were sternly ignored. The married couples and families in the middle deck were making each other's acquaintance and even playing music to keep their spirits up at this poignant time, but no such levity is permitted single ladies, or even fraudulent widows! (Really I must find a way to drop this nonsense!) We must listen to Matron!

Again, you must not misunderstand me. I regard the notion of appointing a woman of *very* mature years to watch over any young and flighty girls on the ship as an excellent one, but I did not and do not propose to submit myself to petty tyranny, otherwise why should I be making this journey? She wore a large badge: MATRON. It has always been my opinion that those with rightful and natural authority do not need to wear symbols of it.

She was reading from a sheet of paper, and it was exciting news indeed. Each of us was to be permitted, per week, 3 lb ship's biscuit, ½ lb beef, 1 gill lime juice – really, Helena, no woman on earth is keener on her food than I am, but to hear it thus reduced to a list of ingredients quite destroyed my appetite.

All around me, bonnets nodded and giggled. Matron finished the bill of fare with a flourish – ½ oz pepper – at which I caught Jean Flanagan's eye and we licked our lips in ironic unison, earning a hurt glance from Matron before she proceeded to the two pillars of shipboard life for single ladies: rules and duties.

But goodness me! You will not want to hear about such matters, for I do not imagine that your life lacks rules or duties! Hopes and plans are more to the point! Jean Flanagan and I have discovered kindred souls in one another, and are determined to stay together once we reach Australia: to evade quickly the kindly-meant services of the Ladies Progress to find us respectable positions in religiously-minded households, and set off into the bush together, as soon as possible. What we lack in money and experience we shall fully make up for in courage and friendship and determination – on which inspiring note I must leave you, Helena, for the other ship is close by. Next time you recognise my handwriting on an envelope, it must mean my journey is over and I am safe on the terra firma of Sydney – many weeks, many dangers perhaps, lie ahead, but I am in good heart now that I have found a friend.

And the letter ended with an abrupt, untidy signature. Helena put it aside angrily.

Had Sarah forgotten her manners so soon on that uncivilised-sounding ship? Was there really no time for the sort of fond salutation that would be suitable at the end of such a letter? A letter between sisters who had loved each other and now were parted, perhaps for ever?

Must Sarah ridicule everyone who tried to help her – good, unfortunate Matron with her half ounce of pepper – must she make jokes about everything?

Did she think that by mocking and joking she made things less real? Did she suppose that by changing her name and then contriving that foolish explanation, she hid her disappointment in not being married, the desperation of her flight to the other end of the earth?

Did she imagine that by writing in that bluff, lip-curling style, as if they were girls together by the fire telling stories, she lessened the distance between them?

But what did Sarah care for the distance between them? Sarah had never loved Helena in any case; just tolerated her, patronised her as a sister. It was Jean Flanagan this, Jean Flanagan that.

What a distance it was!

"Jonathan, where do you think Sarah is now?"

"Not far from the equator, I suppose."

The line that cuts the world in two, where the sun comes closest to the earth, Helena remembered from her lessons.

"Where now?"

"Near Capricorn, I daresay."

The tropics, where the water lies still and glassy and sluggish and ships frizzle up like bacon and the people aboard parch to death, driven mad by the water all around them, and sea serpents coil and huge man-eating sharks thrust up their heads . . .

"Where now?"

"I calculate she docks at Sydney any day now."

It was no relief. How safe that ship seemed, that tall, toppling ship butted by storms, that little vessel charred by the sun, how cosy and secure compared with the great empty country into which Sarah was setting off even now with nothing but her courage and good humour and a few memories of farming in Sussex to keep her alive, and no-one for company but Miss Jean Flanagan.

5

The years after the war were good years for Croft & Co. Jonathan explained to Helena that England had won but it had been a close-run thing: strategies, skills, and, above all, equipment which had always been good enough for campaigns against primitive peoples in Africa and the East, had not prevailed so easily against the Russians. He was confident that the resulting army reforms would bring more business his way: "Many's the officer walking about," he said, "who owes his life to a Croft's Crimean Outfit or Winter Greatcoat; all he's got to do is say so in the right ear. I'm sorry to have to be away so often, my dear, but we shall soon be rich."

"Are we not rich already, Jonathan?" She was weary of his boasting. It was strange how time changed a person's endearing characteristics into annoyances.

"Of course! But you shall have everything you want!"

He met her eye and turned away. Everything she wanted . . . except the one thing they both wanted, and could not be bought.

One afternoon when he thought she was sleeping, she had caught him supervising two men tiptoeing up the stairs with a heavy carved crib, taking it to one of the spare rooms which he had had painted with ducks on the wall. She waited for the men to leave, then started to weep noisily. He came and sat by her. He laid his hand cautiously on her back.

"It was a good bargain! You know I can't resist a good bargain!"

"And I suppose if you hear of a nurse who is cheap you will bring her in too and put her in the room to wait!"

"Helena! We can only be patient! It is only a matter of time!"

He knew, she supposed! Really, he was so thoughtless! He acted as if a child was something you ordered from a catalogue and had delivered; he talked as if mystified by the late arrival of the post!

He talked . . . but he didn't, they didn't talk about it. There were sentences half-begun, there were wistful moments, there were incidents like the one with the crib. But Helena usually changed the subject. Jonathan had his work; he could not be thinking about babies all the time as she was; it was best to keep his mind off the subject, for what if Jonathan began to blame her, even to regret marrying her? One heard such terrible stories of what husbands did if they were disappointed at home. And their physical unions in the dark bed were more tolerable if they were not alluded to in the daytime; it was easier to long for a warm baby to hold if she was not constantly reminded of the only means by which it could be brought about.

People said what a happy couple they were, how well suited. Helena knew people said this because Jonathan's mother reported the conversations to her. She was a kind woman, but Helena felt her eyes probing for signs whenever she came to visit. Jonathan's mother never waited to be invited, nor felt the slightest compunction about prowling round the house. Usually this was to the accompaniment of admiring sounds when she discovered some new improvement; and it was certainly very satisfying, the way she always noticed things. The day Helena caught her coming out of the nursery, their eyes met. Jonathan's mother's eyes were full of excitement and hopeful questioning. Helena's faced showed her she was wrong. Jonathan's mother's expression turned to understanding and pity.

She made a rapid excuse to leave. At the door she said to Jonathan in one of her indiscreet whispers, "Maybe you shouldn't leave Helena on her own so often."

And to Helena she said, "Are you satisfied with your doctor? I can introduce you to *such* a good man."

The good man's questions were alarmingly explicit. He wished to know how frequently Mr and Mrs Croft partook of the marital connection. He made it sound like dinner. Helena wished she could laugh; or at least discuss the matter calmly, as she supposed some women were able to do or he would not speak to her in this way . . . but what if the answer she gave was thought by the doctor to be too frequent? Or not frequent enough?

Was she to carry that message back to Jonathan? Or would the doctor send a note?

She muttered that it varied.

"Is there anything else?"

"What . . . for instance?"

If he would say it, she need only nod.

"Anything you perhaps have difficulty in mentioning?"

"No," she whispered. "No."

"Are you sure, Mrs Croft? You should not allow your modesty to inhibit you."

"My back aches."

They were both relieved. He discussed her back-ache with her for a while. He told her she should rest every afternoon, flat on her back with no pillow and the curtains drawn.

Mrs Lindsay, Helena's neighbour, was rather scornful of this advice. She had had all her children when she was working seventeen hours a day. She described farm labour to Helena as if Helena had never heard of it.

"My mother was like you," Helena said sharply, "and she lost more children than ever lived."

Mrs Lindsay's kindness was only available on the understanding that she was never contradicted. "You," she pointed out, "are not even carrying."

Helena turned away.

Mrs Lindsay said softly, "But maybe you do seem a little tired."

Mary, the pious lady's maid who had replaced Janet, told Helena about her cousin. Five full years had passed between the cousin's marriage and the birth of her first child. The family had been very worried. But the child, a healthy boy, had been followed by beautiful sisters at two-yearly intervals, each one of them surviving to this day, thank God; and if Mary might presume to interpret the motives of God as expressed in the workings of nature, it had always seemed to her that this was His way of preparing her cousin and preserving her strength for each child; and Mary was sure that God in His wisdom blessed a woman with children as soon as He saw that she was ready for them, and not before; and it did not do, therefore, for a woman who had not yet been blessed to question . . .

Helena said, "Why are you telling me this?"

"I was just . . . making conversation. Excuse me, Mrs Croft. Oh! Your hair is the colour of chestnuts today. So beautiful!"

"I shall thank you to mind your own business."

It was intolerable to be pitied by an unmarried servant.

And it was no less tolerable that the one person whose pity she might accept, who might have useful advice to give on even such a matter as this, had become a servant herself. Not that Helena had committed her worries to paper on this matter. Sarah might assume, since Helena's letters contained no mention of any happy event, that there had been none; but the gulf between them made the oceans seem narrow and it was all Helena could do in her letters to list visits and outings and touch on periods of illness, she could not bring herself to write what was in her heart. It was partly the months one waited for a reply, the time that elapsed between saying something and knowing that it was heard; partly an indefinable fear of turning thoughts to words. Helena had not actually disobeyed her sister's injunction to tell the truth, she had not actually lied; but letters were an empty form of communication, they were no communication at all.

Sarah might cover all the pages she pleased with loud, unasked-for protests that a domestic help in Sydney was not the same as a domestic help in London, and that it was quite normal in Australia for a governess to cook and clean floors; but the fact remained that Sarah had gone bragging round the world to better herself, or at least to have adventures, and had finished up no better than this girl who combed Helena's hair and whom Helena had just advised to mind her own business!

Jonathan meant to be kind, but she wished he wouldn't introduce Sarah into the conversation quite so often when they had guests. It was as if he thought Sarah was the only topic on which she could speak, that would be interesting to his friends and their wives. Being a man, he didn't hear the tone in which the wives expressed their interest.

"And where in Australia is your sister, Mrs Croft? I have a cousin at – "

"She is in . . . ah . . . Sydney."

"So her husband is in business there?"

"My sister is unmarried."

"Indeed? Then she has a position?"

"She is a . . . er . . . she helps a family who are in snuff. That is – "

"Sarah is a governess," Jonathan helped

"A governess, eh?"

"Snuff, eh?"

The conversation might pass then, to snuff. There was nothing very interesting about an unmarried sister who was a governess, even if she had gone all the way to Australia to be one.

What had Sarah written in that first letter from the ship? *They call us the Poop Governesses . . . we are not all governesses . . .*

reluctance to acknowledge my frequently-stated intention to work in no
woman's house but my own . . . Yet there she was, in the house of
that dreadful Morley family who were supposed to be protecting
her but whom she so disliked on the ship. Since her plans for
farming had failed, why did she not simply come home?

Why don't you come home, Sarah, to your family who miss you?
Family? I am your only family . . . I wonder if you still think of me
as your family or whether all your allegiance is to the Morleys; you
are so free with your loyalty, Sarah, perhaps it is a shame to call
that a fault, but one might have supposed Miss Flanagan's shameful
behaviour would have warned you . . . *Perhaps when I have a child*
you will realise where you belong and come home and we will raise
him together . . .

I cannot write that . . .

"Dearest Sarah, Last week we had the Huntingdons to dinner,
they have a cousin who is sheep farming in Victoria, I wonder
whether by chance you may have . . ." Helena paused in irritation;
she did not even know the Huntingdons' cousin's name; she
crossed out the stupid sentence and threw the paper away. Why
could she not write a cheerful letter, like Sarah? For all her
disappointment, for all her still having no farm, Sarah always
managed to find the bright side of things to report. Even when
she told of Jean Flanagan meeting a man on the ship and marrying
him on the deck against the rocky backdrop of Botany Bay while
the passengers buzzed with excitement at the nearness of their
journey's end and Sarah only despaired that she was alone once
more . . . even then her cheerful tone belied her disappointment
. . .

I begged that she would explain the rash (not to say treacherous) step she
had taken, but she had nothing to say; she merely looked at me in such
a way as to imply that I was jealous, and summoned her beloved, who
was passing, with these words: "Daniel, please come and make the
acquaintance of my friend Mrs Packham, who fears I have married you
in haste and shall repent at my leisure."

He seemed a good-natured fellow; he shambled over, shook my hand
in his floppy red one, wished me well in my new life and shambled away
again, playfully pinching his wife's nose as he went. I say "playfully", I
am sure he meant no harm; but the pinch was a hard one and brought
tears of pain and anger to her eyes, which wrecked the image of delicate
besottedness that my poor Jean had striven to display.

Poor Jean? *Her* poor Jean? Helena clenched her fingers tightly round the letter. How like Sarah to pity her! Who would pity Sarah? Who would help her? Not the Morleys . . .

I dare say I chose the wrong moment to approach Mr Morley with my request; he was perched like a seal atop the slippery box of his wife's clothes, struggling to close it, and, in between making the most terrifying grunting noises, enquiring of his wife whether she supposed her things had been reproducing themselves during the voyage, or whether she had merely been on a few foraging raids. She retorted that a far more likely explanation for his difficulties was that he was losing strength, at which dangerous point I noticed the heel of a boot sticking out of the end of the box. I removed it quite easily, the lid closed, and Mr Morley fell to the ground. Yes, I must admit it; it was not tactful of me to ask him there and then if he would help me to buy some land when we reached Sydney. Even when I explained that it was not financial help that I sought, only company and male authority to reduce the chances of my being swindled, his look was not friendly. And his wife chimed in with the astounding query as to why I should be wanting to purchase land in any case.

Sydney harbour was coming closer. I could see ships and boats of all sizes scuttling across the wide blue bay in the breeze, and behind them the exquisitely sweet sight of land firm enough to hold white buildings glistening in the sun, trees, churches, windmills . . . exquisite and sweet it was indeed, but awesome too; for I had read enough of my helpful Handbooks to know that the cities are but thin, short ribbons of safety and comfort and the great Bush yawns and lures beyond . . . I knew that if I allowed Mrs Morley's absurd question to unnerve me at this moment, I should never respect myself again. So I replied thus:

"What do I want with *land*, Mrs Morley? What would a person want with land? Have I been talking to myself all these weeks? Why do you suppose I have come to Australia? I am not a pauper who has failed in business or a miserable girl cringing for a husband; I am the descendant of Constancia Packham, a freeborn Englishwoman with farming in her blood who wants to breathe the air of honest toil and bring civilisation to a wilderness – I want to be rich from my own labours! I want to eat the food that I have grown, I want to lie down at night dog-tired under blankets woven from the backs of my own herd!" I proceeded in this manner for some time, I fear, for I was becoming increasingly agitated and Mrs Morley was not moved. Mildly she heard me out, then observed in hurt tones that she had understood I would be remaining with the family; that she had treated me as her own daughter on that account; that the children were devoted to me (which was a great mystery to her, her tone implied) and would be deeply distressed by my going, and that in view of her condition, she must make one last appeal to my better nature. I had not been aware that she was in any condition; but her husband intervened at this point to inform me that the ship's doctor had recently confirmed that another little Morley was on the way . . .

Was it Mrs Morley's entreaty and her plight that unnerved Sarah? Helena could sense the change in the tone of the letter, though the words were as cheerful as ever. And although she still felt angry with Sarah for being where she was, she consoled herself with the bond of their shared disappointment: the sense of having failed to achieve the one thing you really wanted, the thing you had led people to expect of you; the sense of being laughed at, resented; the sense that it was your own fault when you knew that it was not; and the deep, violent hatred of anyone who would dare pity you.

Sarah's letters were vivid. Her experience entered Helena's mind like a memory. Sometimes it was impossible for Helena to distinguish what she had been told from the details she imagined.

The Morleys complained to the matron, and the matron tried again to jolly Sarah out of her nonsense; and then the ship docked and Matron was handing out books donated by philanthropic organisations in England to help the new governesses, and Sarah stood aloof with her hands behind her back (stamping her foot, Helena imagined, and saying "Shan't!") and said that what she needed was tools. An old hoe was found, and a garden fork and even a Sussex trug, and given to her as a joke which she accepted in good part, for who would set out to tame the Bush so equipped? And when she climbed at last on to dry land (wanting to kneel and kiss it), passing louts shouted abuse: "It's Varmer George isself!" and other words which Sarah was too delicate to write but which Helena could imagine, remembering the soldiers on the quayside when Sarah left England.

Sarah sat down on a heap of rope and leaned her back against a barrel. The rope was damp and the barrel splintery, but they felt to Sarah like the most comfortable of sofas. She had thought that the first thing she would do on reaching dry land would be to run and run, but she closed her eyes. It suddenly came to her why men smoked pipes. Tobacco had never appealed to her before. Now she thought how wonderful it would be, in the warm morning air, to have a sweet taste to breathe. The ground lurched under her, Sarah was sure it did; she felt seasick as she had not done since the first weeks of the voyage; she opened her eyes in alarm; was Australia *floating* then? Had they omitted to tell her that it was nothing but a gigantic chunk of driftwood, not anchored to the bed of the ocean at all? But it was just her body remembering the swaying and tossing of the ship; she felt better with her eyes open.

She watched the governesses being shepherded into a big shed with a cross on it, the premises of a sister organisation to Ladies Progress.

As if I needed to travel ten thousand miles to bully children in some stuffy schoolroom! she thought.

Her luggage was in the shed, being looked after; she might collect it when she was ready; and have some food and drink and refresh herself; the matron had been kind in the face of her intransigence; no-one could force Sarah to accept a position she did not want; the services of Ladies Progress were at her disposal nonetheless.

She felt she was being humoured.

"As if I haven't plenty of floors of my own to scrub!"

And then Sarah remembered she had none; her home had been taken from her and so had her farm; she had no home.

"Oh, but you have," Helena breathed when she read this. "Jonathan meant it when he said you could live with us; and if he did not mean it, I can make him mean it."

It was still quite early in the morning (Sarah tried to imagine a wintry evening at Littledean, with wet mist rolling down from Little Beacon) but she supposed she had better not sit here all day! She had come to Australia to start a new life, and there was no time like the present for beginning! She supposed she had to find the office where they sold land to migrants. And having obtained your land, how did you reach it? She supposed she should see about getting a horse. If she only had a notebook she would make a list. *One. Get land. Two. Get a horse.* Still she sat and gazed across the wide blue bay as boats of every size scudded back and forth with their intriguing cargoes having no regard for the collisions which seemed constantly imminent but were somehow always averted. Behind her was the tramp of feet, and voices, strange, rough male voices with coarse accents. Were they speaking of her, to her? She did not listen, she just stared and stared. There was a sweet smell in the air (perhaps it was this that had put her in mind of pipe-smoking) . . . it came from the sun on some dark logs being unloaded onto the quay by little slant-eyed sailors gabbling instructions to each other; and far out where the harbour seemed to meet the open sea, a whaler was tacking in laboriously with a huge blood-soaked whale . . .

I can't sit here for ever, Sarah thought.

The stuffy office hummed with flies. They crawled like some grotesque, living hat on the bald head of the clerk with round spectacles who was trying to hide his fear of the threatening manner of two other men arguing with him over prices, under a mask of official boredom. As Sarah hesitated in the doorway he reached with a paper to swat his head, though not with any conviction that his threat to the insects would be heeded. The flies gave a buzz of joy on spotting Sarah and swooped at her in a dark cloud.

The eyes of the men followed the insects.

Sarah waited. The thick air was full of buzzing and silence and the smell of alcohol on breath. Sarah tensed herself to counteract the failing of her heart. Her voice came out in a whisper. "I wish to buy some land."

The office rocked. It pitched and dipped like the sea, and Sarah had thought she could escape this disconcerting after effect of the voyage by simply keeping her eyes open . . . were they open? It was the laughter of the men that was rocking the place great guffaws as they slapped their sides, startling the flies. The clerk wiped his face and took down a great map from the wall and spread it before her.

He diverted a giggle down his nose and a green bubble appeared.

"Make ya selection. *Ma'am.*"

And suddenly Sarah knew she could not; knew that if she was a fool to be here in this hostile office thinking she could buy land like a pound of potatoes and expect not to be swindled, she was twice the fool for spurning the offer of the matron and the Morleys of at least a roof over her head for the night, at least a chance to catch her breath, and, oh, three times the fool for coming to Australia at all and thinking that she could thereby escape her own folly; thinking that it was enough to be daughter of her mother and descendant of the great Constancia, enough to have been once a capable farm girl who could coax good milk from cows fed on short downland grass . . . she would be dead in five days in the great empty lands, the buzzing voracious flies seemed to think her dead already.

Helena shivered as she read Sarah's painfully honest account of this sudden descent into despair. And she wondered (guiltily, for who was she to compare herself with Sarah?) whether Sarah might have remembered Helena's own sudden outbursts of inexplicable panic as a child, when they climbed Little Beacon for instance, and repented of being so scornful.

Mrs Morley was a Christian woman, and familiar with the parable of the prodigal son; and so she welcomed Sarah back to her with, if not a fatted calf, at least a willingness that she should be as a hired servant. Mr Morley doubted genially whether Sarah had spent the hours of their brief separation wasting her substance in riotous living, and whispered in her ear that once he had found his feet, he would be happy to help her find hers. And so Sarah went with the Morleys, meaning to be with them only three weeks, or three months at most; yet now, after as many years, a succession of circumstances had kept her firmly where she was, sharing three cramped and dusty rooms with the Morleys above Mr Morley's failing snuff-shop in a wide, noisy Sydney street overlooking a treeless park across which dust-laden winds blew; educating and caring for the Morley children, nursing their mother who spent the first year as an invalid awaiting and then recovering from the birth of twins, the second demanding to be taken back to London on the next ship and the third suffering resigned, blinding headaches; and overseeing Mr Morley's book-keeping which, if it could be taken as an indication of how he had run his business in England before becoming bankrupt and fleeing his creditors, provided ample explanation of how that step had become necessary.

Her letters were full of bewilderment and self-blame; she would hear no nonsense from Helena about it being her kind heart that kept her with the family that had become so strangely dependent on her; it was cowardice, sheer cowardice, and lazy inertia. She was disgusted with herself, quite disgusted, and would be moving off "up the country" directly, after little Tim's birthday, when

Mrs Morley was on her feet, when the next quarter's accounts had been prepared. Sarah's exasperation with herself was matched only by Helena's shame as she searched each letter feverishly for news that she had bettered herself, or was at least pursuing the adventurous plans with which she had set out for Australia, for Helena feared that her guests despised Sarah (even though they had never met her) and she longed to impress them. It was hard to think of the real Sarah in the role of servant; it was frightening to think that the real Sarah no longer existed, might never have existed at all.

Suddenly the letters stopped. Months passed and no word came. Jonathan was full of plausible, comforting explanations. And when finally news did arrive of the latest development in Sarah's adventure, Helena took no consolation at all; just wished her sister back in Sydney, even with the hopeless, treacherous Morleys.

6

Dearest Helena,

In all the confusion of my departure, I seem to have quite mislaid my Handbooks on Bush Life. And so I cannot remember whether poisonous snakes are more inclined to be afraid of fire, or attracted to it. If you know, I wish you would say; I know that one definitely either *should* or *should not* light a fire when camped on a dark night alone near a waterhole.

I think I will.

The worst snakes are diamond-snakes and death-adders. Diamond-snakes are very beautiful, death-adders masquerade as sticks until you pick them up. A bite is fatal within seven minutes. There is no sense in you curling your nose up or looking over your shoulder at the slightest sound from the darkness behind you, Helena, because this is the kind of information you need if you are to survive in the bush. Forewarned is forearmed.

By far the most sensible thing to do is to make up your mind that you will not be terrorised by sounds or oppressed by silence; tether your horse, build a fire, cook a dinner – I do not wish to *hear* your protests that food would sicken you, Helena, for you must keep up your strength, then collect your thoughts and order them sufficiently to write an intelligible letter explaining how you come to be in this predicament.

That is what you should do.

You should not be unduly alarmed by the absence of an address for a reply; I am not, it is true, precisely sure where I *am*, but I know where I am going; and I shall reach there tomorrow.

Behind me are imposing mountains and Bathurst, the town some hundred and fifty miles north-west of Sydney where I spent last night at an inn so filthy that I think – no, I *know*, I am resolved – that it is better to be out in the open. If God wishes me to die of snake-bite then I shall die of snake-bite; in the meantime, even the loneliness of this whispering darkness is preferable to being eaten alive by fleas. It is hard to describe the country through which I have been travelling to someone who could not run to the top of Little Beacon for fear that it might crash down on the village! A certain humility, even fear, before the wonders of nature, is quite fitting, even on the Sussex Downs; but I honestly think you might die of awe if you saw the astonishing rock-formations that I have seen, with faces and monsters and marks like the half-written messages of a primaeval giant; or of dazzlement at the contrasting riches and sweetness of the spring flowers, or joy at the riotous bird song. All this is to say nothing of the discomfort and hazards of the coach journey through the mountains from Sydney; I think you might not stand up to them as well as I have. But to cosier matters!

My fire is well alight, and its crackling and whistling is as comforting as conversation . . . more comforting than the conversation of some I could refer to. If any of the sticks I collected was a snake planning a little surprise for me, he now has a surprise for himself! It is a fine night and I need no roof, but I have fashioned a tent with a sheet and a rope tied to a tree – the trees are so strange, with folds and creases in the bark that make them look soft, like flesh. My dinner is cooking merrily, salt beef and "damper" bread; this last is a local speciality and favourite of the bushmen; I shall give you the recipe as you may wish to serve it at one of Jonathan's dinners! You simply mix flour and water to a dough and bake it in hot cinders.

Now that you know you have me safe, I shall tell you how I come to be here, and where I am going.

As you know, when I first went to the Morleys, it was out of desperation. They needed help; I needed a home where I could accustom myself to the new country, make sensible plans for the future, and summon up once again the courage that had so unaccountably deserted me. It was an act of mutual assistance. The matter of a salary was not raised.

But in time I became aware that women in positions such as mine were receiving £30 per year and board. There were days at the Morleys when I hardly received board, either because Mrs Morley was ill and I was too busy to cook, or because there was no money. Many's the time I went secretly to a shop to buy myself bread and cheese; only to repent of my selfishness and bring home a substantial meal for the whole family.

With this, and with the need for clothing and other things, I was moving fast through my savings, and no closer to owning a farm than on the day of my arrival. So I put the position plainly to Mr and Mrs Morley, whereupon Mrs Morley made the assertion that I have come to expect on these occasions, namely, that she had always thought of me as a member of her family.

Once out of her hearing, Mr Morley was more understanding; but no readier with a solution to the problem. He said he was willing with all his heart to give me my weight in gold; when I replied that £30 per annum would be quite sufficient, he explained he was in no position to give me anything. And he did not need to convince me, as his book-keeper. He was very straightforward and honourable about it, and told me frankly that he would think none the worse of me if I decided to seek a position elsewhere; but he also managed subtly to remind me how fond the children were of me (and that of course was mutual) and of the likely effect on his wife's health if she had to manage alone. So we reached a compromise whereby he would give me, every quarter, a note promising to pay such-and-such a sum on demand.

Then came the day when I saw notice in the newspapers of a land auction, including some small selections and one in particular that had been managed single-handed by a widow. Full of excitement and hardening my heart, I presented my notes to Mr Morley.

Well! He rubbed his hands and shook his head and took a pinch of his own snuff and sneezed; and then he wiped his forehead and pulled his whiskers and sneezed again; and generally contrived to look so forlorn that I felt that if he would just tell me what I knew already, namely, that he could not pay and did not see how he ever could pay, and beg my mercy, I would tear up the bills before his eyes and resign myself to a life of self-sacrifice.

But it was not to be. Pride glimmered briefly in his eyes, and he declared, briskly and businesslike, that I should have my money a week from the day.

I became alarmed and begged him to do nothing foolish; his look as much as told me that I had demanded my right and it was not now for me to feel conscience-stricken about the means whereby my demand might be met. If I had known what he planned, would I have persisted? You must be the judge of that, Helena. Mr Morley took the shop's tiny profit that he had been saving against the arrival of new consignments, and went to the races, where he began with a small win and ended with a total loss.

When Mrs Morley heard of this, her fury, anger, terror, resentment were all entirely to be expected, and, indeed, utterly justified. But she turned them not against her husband but on me!

She is deranged and hysterical of course; but that did not reduce my astonished pain at being told, firstly, that she had taken me into her household against her better judgement, out of Christian charity, seeing me so forlorn and friendless on the boat; secondly, that if I wanted a large salary I should have said so from the start and ended the matter there and then; thirdly, that I had deliberately alienated her children's affections from her while she languished on her sick bed; fourthly, that I planned to do the same with her husband, starting by posing as a young widow, which, by the way, she had not believed for a moment; in pursuance of which (fifthly) I had dishonestly and incompetently taken charge of the accounts of the shop and influenced Mr Morley to risk the family's possessions in order to raise funds to finance our elopement!

I think of her now and I am sad for the poor, trapped creature. How natural that she should blame me, for then she could believe that if she rid herself of me, matters might improve. When disaster strikes a family, a wife does not blame her husband lightly, unless she has a good capacity for despair! At the time I was less merciful in my thoughts. I rehearsed a brisk list of all I had done for the family, a shorter list of all I had received in return, packed my bags, and departed, late at night though it was. The children cried after me, but I hardened my heart.

The Ladies Progress employment agency was full of girls and women newly arrived off a ship; the matrons looked at me with suspicion, a dusty, agitated creature who had been walking round the streets waiting for the office to open. I explained that I wanted a situation on a property as far away from Sydney as they chose to send me, and this stipulation seemed to work in my favour, for they wanted to reserve opportunities closer by for the nervous new arrivals.

The matron brought forth a letter from a family called Daggett, whose property is at Threeroads, a day's ride from Bathurst, which you will find on any good map of the colony. The Daggetts are three brothers and the wife of one of them; and unless I am lost (which I think I am not, as I have been well looked after; I travelled by coach to Bathurst, where a friend of Ladies Progress lent me my present mount and directed me on the final stage of my journey) I shall meet them tomorrow.

My horse is watching me curiously in the gloom; I realise I have been speaking aloud as I write this! Well, I trust she has enjoyed it, and that you will too. The only place I can see to post it is a gum-tree, so I will keep it until I arrive and find what the postal arrangements are. I dare say I shall add a few words from time to time.

Now I have arrived, and am in a state of some surprise.

It is hard to remember what I expected; but I am surprised, so it cannot have been this.

Threeroads was the first surprise. There had been talk of a town; and

I had planned to stop there after my night in the bush (which passed uneventfully) in order to refresh myself so that I might meet my new employers in as good a state of refreshment and tidiness as circumstances permitted. But to call Threeroads a town owes more to optimism than to truth; the three roads of the name are mere tracks, seeming to meet more by coincidence than design; and the only buildings were a ramshackle inn which I dared not enter, and a few hovels. There were signs of an occasional market; and some stakes linked to each other with worn string marked off pieces of land to which settlers will soon, I suppose, be moving.

Do you remember Miss Dean, the dreariest of governesses, who had us sew samplers to demonstrate our competence at particular stitches? I have started to think of Australia as God's great sampler (He will know I mean no disrespect), whereon He demonstrates that not only can He fashion welcoming, wide blue bays, high, fabulously-shaped mountains and bleak regions of desert, but now displayed to me His skill in creating fertile plain; the last miles of my journey were through green, gentle hills, and I was grateful for it.

I saw my first aborigine at close quarters: a tiny boy, black as coal, not more than four or five years old, his body painted with white lines and circles. He startled me, standing as still as a small tree. I did not notice him until I was upon him. He looked neither hostile nor interested as I rode by. I greeted him and waved. He stared through me as though I were a ghost.

Then I started to meet straggling sheep, and whole herds, and men with them whom I supposed to be other employees of the Daggetts. One grabbed my bridle and talked to me in what I guessed to be English but which I could not understand until I had dismounted (gathering from his blackened smile that he was friendly) and could watch his lips move. He gave me water and a cold roast sheep's rib. He asked, what was the news from Threeroads, from Bathurst, from Sydney? Where was I going? I could not read his expression when I said I was going to work for Mrs Daggett. He offered me some advice; I accepted eagerly, but it had nothing to do with my employers; mine was a fine hat, he said, but out there in the bush with no one to see, might I not consider wearing the veil at the back, where it would provide protection for an area of the neck peculiarly vulnerable to sunstroke? That was what I understood him to say, in his rough, snuffling, difficult way; and it seemed sensible advice. And had I spectacles to protect my eyes? I told him my eyesight was perfect, but that was not what he meant: he showed me a pair whose plain glass lenses had been held in smoke till they were black; the soot would block the worst dazzle of the sun, he said. Would I like a pair? Finally he gave me a pipe, saying there was no call for airs and graces out here, tobacco smoke was God's own protection from mosquitoes. Coughing mightily and half-blinded by the spectacles, I nevertheless went on my way in good spirits: such is the effect of a little human kindness in a wilderness.

As I climbed a little, my ears told me I was near my journey's end: I could hear a great commotion of voices, some men's but mostly the bleats of surprise and indignation that accompany the shearing of sheep. Sure enough, I reached the top of a low mound and looked down into my new kingdom: a cluster of buildings, a sea of sheep, a handful of men, and a river.

Three men, whom I took from their proprietorial air, to be the Daggett brothers, stood together thoughtfully watching the sheep being driven into the shed; I decided to make straight for the house and meet Mrs Daggett. First the house had to be identified, none of the buildings being, at first glance, markedly more domestic or welcoming in appearance than the others. But the sight of a chimney and a half-built verandah on one convinced me that here was where I should try my luck. It also had the beginnings of a fence and an ill-kept garden, in which a few patchy chickens scratched and a cow wandered on a tether. I could count her bones. She kept straining helplessly to reach a water trough; the tether was just too short. She would strain till the rope looked as if it must break; and then she would give up in despair and walk as far from the trough as the rope would allow, as if thirst was enough to bear without humiliation too. My opinion of Mrs Daggett, through whose negligence this animal was being tortured, may be imagined! I reined in my horse, dismounted and went to attend to the animal.

When she had drunk, I turned and found that the men I had seen by the shearing shed were standing looking at me. The shortest of the three made a sound which can best be rendered as, "What ya think ya doin'?" I replied that the animal had appeared thirsty, whereupon the man who had spoken turned to the others, wheezing with laughter, and, imagining (I must suppose) that he was imitating my manner of speech, repeated my words. Then he added, "Thirsty, eh? Better get her a mugga beer then." And another man laughed inordinately.

The third seemed to be searching his mind for some explanation of who in the world I was; rather with the air of a distracted housewife who knows she has set down her duster *somewhere*, it is just a matter of staying calm and hunting systematically. At last light dawned and he asked whether I was "the Progress lady".

I admitted it, introducing myself simply as Sarah Packham, since I am now as much accustomed to this name as if I had been born with it. I offered my hand, which he stared at with interest, and, finally understanding that I meant him to shake it, he displayed his own, filthy with grease and mud and blood, and indicated with a shy gesture that it was goodwill, rather than any lack of it, that restrained him from returning the greeting. He was James Daggett, and he introduced his brothers as Bill and Arthur. Bill's and Arthur's hands being twice as dirty as James', and both of them having witnessed their brother's chivalrous refusal to touch mine, they grinningly insisted on the most expansive of handshakes.

But that is the Daggett boys all over. I think of the two younger ones as boys, though I suppose they are my employers and they are older than I am: I estimate all three are in their thirties. They are very alike in appearance, tall and sinewy and black-toothed, though in James' case this seems to be due to dirt rather than decay – I suppose I must therefore dub him the handsome one of the three. They wear loose trousers tied at the waist with rope, torn shirts, and hobnail boots.

James is very shy, or otherwise has poor command of words; he indicated speechlessly that I should follow him and he would show me round the place. His awkwardness affected me and I did not speak; I just went with him, hoping he would make short work of the out-buildings, then take me to Mrs Daggett, who must, I assumed, be Mrs James Daggett; it was impossible to imagine any woman choosing Bill or Arthur.

There are pools, paddocks, pens, and wool-houses; some rough stables, an overgrown orchard, and a malodorous dairy which shows no signs of having been used recently, but then, I reflected, that unfortunate cow did not look as if she would provide excessive labour for a dairy-maid.

The state of the dairy saddened me. I had not allowed, in my imaginings, for Mrs Daggett to be sluttish or lazy. On the contrary: she was going to be a clean, efficient, slightly tired, slightly lonely woman, and we would be firm friends within minutes of meeting. We would teach each other the skills of our different farming experiences, and together we would make a partnership. I had not expected to have to teach her the importance of cleanliness in a dairy, or water for a cow.

And when I finally entered the house with James Daggett, my worst suspicions about her seemed fulfilled, for there was no sign of house-keeping anywhere. One can hardly call it a home: it is more like a stable or a hutch or any other place where an animal seeks only shelter, rest and food, and cares little for the civilising touches that are supposed to be characteristic of humanity, or at least the female half of it. It is made of logs and bark; there is no division between eating, sleeping or sitting areas: blankets, plates with half-eaten meals, tools, tin cans, boots and bottles lie carelessly where they have been left, like a high-tide mark after a storm. There is no glass in the windows and the door does not fit, so the difference between being inside or outside is small, as far as annoyance by dust and the ever-present insect life is concerned. In front of the unswept fireplace are a few boxes, one of which, being full of bits of meat, I must take to be the larder, and another, containing some cutlery hardly less interesting to the flies than the meat, on account of the wide variety of foods with which it is encrusted, constitutes the sideboard. As I write of this from a kind of bed, an improvised curtain shelters me from the worst of the horrors – it is surprising what comfort a piece of cloth can give – but when I first saw it and took in the realisation that *this was to be my home* and that people who could live this way were to be my sole companions – I was near to tears. I looked and looked. And the more I looked, the more I realised that it was many years since a woman had been mistress of this house.

My realisation blazing in my eyes, I lifted them to James Daggett's face. He looked at the ground. I said nothing. I did not trust myself. What was I to do if I was right? The prospect of remaining alone in this place with these men for even one night was outrageous; the prospect of returning to Sydney, or even Bathurst, made me feel weak with fatigue and frustration. I did not want to know beyond doubt that I had been tricked until I knew what to do about it.

Besides, it might not be a trick. Some tragedy might have overtaken Mrs Daggett; or maybe she worked in the fields, and would come in later with the men, expecting me to have a good dinner ready.

I opened my mouth to question James; but he was gone.

His flight confirmed more strongly than ever that the Daggetts' letter to the Ladies Progress asking for help for Mrs Daggett had not been entirely truthful.

I looked around the place. Even the prospect of clearing somewhere for myself to sleep was beyond me. Heaven knows, I have lost whatever fastidiousness I ever had, but I thought I would as soon sleep on one of those blankets as in a London gutter.

I investigated further. They had not even thought to build cupboards or shelves. No wonder everything was higgledy-piggledy; "everything" could not be "in its place" when there was no place for anything! Nor could the Daggetts claim as excuse that they had not been long in the house, for the piles of dust, dung, and dead insects have built up into veritable sculptures in the corners, and such things are not created in a day!

Disconsolately I caught sight of a parcel with English postmarks; it was open and I was surprised to find it contained magazines and books. The possibility of the Daggett brothers being of a literary turn of mind had not occurred to me. I pulled out a book; how I wish that I had not!

It was literature of the lowest sort. I shall not specify further. Had the illustrations been of dumb animals I should still have felt myself sullied, but these were people! And which was the more horrible to suppose, that the artist had drawn from a diseased imagination, or that he had human models? There was an accuracy of detail to make one despair. I regret even mentioning the matter to you, Helena; but I wish you to know the kind of place I have come to, and to understand my state of mind.

I became aware that I was watched. Arthur Daggett stood in the doorway, blocking the sunlight; trying to put the book down without him seeing that I held it, I smiled and bade him good afternoon. He returned no similar courtesy but simply enquired, if you please, how I had come to lose a tooth! I was sufficiently disconcerted by his grossness to offer an explanation of that childish incident with our cow Butterbell, which you have probably forgotten; but I quickly recovered myself and added, "It would take a nimble animal to get the better of me nowadays." Hoping that he had heard the warning in the words, I enquired sharply as to when I was to meet Mrs Daggett; and was further disconcerted to see him snigger and leave the house.

I set down my things and started to clear a corner with my bare hands. In due course, James Daggett returned, and the conversation which followed led me inescapably to the conclusion that I was not to meet Mrs Daggett in the near future, because there is no such lady.

James Daggett hemmed and hawed and clutched the hat he held in his hand; and I berated him for having brought me here under false pretences, for having told lies to a Christian organisation set up to protect ladies such as myself from fates such as this; I expected him to answer me back; I expected abuse; but what he said quite cut the anger from under me. He told me that he felt responsible for his brothers (he could not have expressed a more tender concern for them had they been three and four years old!) and that they had never had a real home. This at least was manifestly true, and I made to enquire about their parents, but refrained, realising that the answer would either be a lie or else something I did not care to hear. James Daggett himself cut a pathetic figure: he hung his head like a child receiving a rebuke from a governess, yet even in that attitude he was taller than I. Meanwhile a gust of wind caught the door of the house, it went *bang – bang – bang,* chopping at the buzzing of the flies, chopping at my nerves. "It was their idea," James Daggett mumbled, meaning it was his brothers who had decided to tell Ladies Progress that there was already a female in their household; I lost patience at this. "They held your hand while you wrote the letter, I suppose?" I demanded ironically; he replied that he did not know how to write.

The wind died and the door stopped banging. I could hear human voices far away, men's voices and the bleat of sheep. "Better have a drinka tea," said James Daggett, "before ya go."

I drank the tea which he clumsily made for me; but I did not leave. I rested; I listlessly explored; I wrestled with indecision, starting several times to tidy the house and giving up in fury and despair. When evening came James Daggett brought a sheet and a hammer and nails and somehow rigged up the curtain behind which I now shelter, writing to you, trying to sleep. I have eaten a little, with the brothers and the shearers, but the meal was a wretchedly awkward occasion.

The air is thick with the smell of meat and alcohol and men; I long to push away the piece of metal which covers my window and let in some fresh air, but I hear the beat of the insects against the outside, striving to join their fellows in my hot little tent. Most of the time the men are silent, chewing their food, pouring drink into mugs; or one will speak, a whining monotone in which I catch one word in six; or they will laugh together and resume their silence. Occasionally James Daggett's voice will be heard, warning someone not to finish the remark he had started.

It occurs to me that if I am safe tonight, I am probably safe for ever.

There is time enough to make decisions tomorrow. I did not come to Australia to be safe and conventional. I had thought I might live alone, or with just one woman. I think I have at least one protector in James Daggett, who seems to be a good man. And look what became of my sojourn in Sydney with a respectable married couple!

Bill and Arthur Daggett may be good men too; what did I expect, woven waistcoats and drawing-room conversation? Heaven forbid!

I cannot bear to think that you are anxious about me. But I think you did not approve of my being a governess, whereas now you may tell your friends I have joined the landed aristocracy! I think I am safe for now. God grant that I am right.

Your weary sister,
  Sarah

7

"I am going to be very frank with you, Mrs Croft," said the doctor, "and I am going to ask you to tell me the truth in return."

"That's what Sarah says," said Helena, trying not to be frightened of him.

"Sarah? Ah, Sarah! Sweet Sarah the shepherdess! Wasn't there a song . . . ?"

I beg you to be honest with me always – otherwise how will we remain alive to each other as sisters?

The doctor had a silver pen shaped like a hard feather. He never wrote with it. He just moved it about in his hands while he talked. It glinted in the gloomy light from the white window. Helena watched the pen, to keep her eyes off his terrifying hands.

"Affection between sisters is a beautiful thing. But Mrs Croft, perhaps . . . it is important that you are honest with your doctor, too."

She had not told him any lies. She had not told Jonathan any lies. Could he say the same? This doctor was a specialist in ladies' nervous disorders. Jonathan thought she did not know that. The doctor himself thought she did not know. Outside in the street the sky was grey but through the surgery window it looked white, dazzling white, nothing whiter in the world except the rain-drops.

"Your husband tells me you have been upsetting yourself."

"You see, it was the red jackets."

"The jackets?"

"He was telling a man he could make red jackets. For hospital orderlies."

"Yes?"

"But don't you *see*?" How could he not see? "Don't you see why they have to be red?"

The doctor smiled. "War can be a nasty business. You shouldn't think about it."

How could she not? She imagined jackets stiff with blood, looking good as new. She should not think about it. She had promised Jonathan that she would not. And anything she told the doctor would be reported to Jonathan. She had to be careful. Jonathan had said she need not come to the table when he had army people in if the conversation upset her. He might change his mind if he knew she was disobeying him. She was twenty-two but he still treated her as a child.

"I want to have a baby, Doctor."

They all knew that.

"Ah. Yes. And you have been married, ah – "

"Five years, Doctor."

"And you and, ah – "

"Yes, yes!"

"And that is, ah – "

"Distasteful. Yes, yes."

He seemed pleased.·

"Mrs Croft, I am going to be very frank with you. And I am going to ask you to tell me the truth in return."

The silver line of his pen moved through the air.

"Is it a toy?"

"Mrs Croft?"

"Your pen. Can you write with it?"

"Mrs Croft – tell me – if your wish were granted; and by some happy chance you were able to leave here today with the news that you are expecting a baby – would you be a perfectly happy woman?"

She had not considered this. "I sometimes think I should have gone with Sarah." She felt safer if she talked about Sarah.

"Ah, Mrs Croft!" He laughed sadly, kindly. "It is a hard life."

"That's what she says! She writes angrily. She says I am lucky. She doesn't understand, about – "

"About what?"

"About not having any room, Doctor."

"Ah, the wide open spaces!" She wished he would stop saying "ah". She could not tell if he was breathing in or out. "I hear you have a beautiful home, Mrs Croft."

"But he is always bringing things."

"Things? What kind of things?"

"Doorknobs." It was all she could think of. Carpenters had filled the house with the sound of sawing as they fixed doorknobs to match the finger-plates. And a film of sawdust floated on the evening's soup. "And china."

"My dear Mrs Croft, this is a new complaint and I am not sure I shall not write to the journals about it! A wife driven mad by a husband bringing her *too many gifts* . . . That was, of course a manner of speaking. I am not seriously concerned for your sanity, nor indeed your physical health. Your husband tells me of your backaches and your headaches, your fatigue and your frequent tears. You tell me of other difficulties which you cannot discuss with him, and about which I feel you are not entirely frank even with me, your doctor . . . "

White rain beat at the window.

"But Mrs Croft, there is nothing physically wrong with you."

He thought the talk of china was a joke. That was a relief. Jonathan had not told him, then, about the nineteen dinner-plates. She was ashamed of her tantrums. Jonathan would stand there wringing his hands, always managing, in his determination to say the right thing, to make matters worse. Poor Jonathan! When all he required of his wife was that she be happy, wasn't he entitled to that?

"Nineteen dinner-plates! Nineteen, Jonathan! Why – might I ask?"

"It was only meant to be sixteen, Helena. Those fools at the shop."

"You want fourteen children – right away?"

"Helena, you know I like company."

"I know you like certain kinds of company! It is only fitting that your bloodthirsty friends should eat off those things." They were dreadful plates. Blood-red roses twirling on snaky stems. Sixteen, and then another box of three. "I suppose I am not enough company for you."

"You're not the best company these days, Helena. To be frank."

That was when she had started to think there might be another Mrs Croft somewhere. One heard of such things when a man was disappointed at home. A Mrs Croft and a Miss or Master Croft who did not have to have army people to dinner.

The doctor droned on about honesty and frankness, but Helena told him nothing of this. If she was wrong she was mad, if she was right she was at fault, for there were those other arguments.

"Helena, this is a natural thing between husband and wife! And you cannot expect to have children if – "

"Do you think I do not know that? I was raised in a farmyard." He flinched. "I think I do my duty," she added.

"But Helena, to some women it is a joy and not a duty."

"Then go to those women."

There! She had authorised him to do it. She had not authorised him to humiliate her with bits of china!

She would not tell the doctor this.

The silver pen floated back into her vision.

"Tell me about your sister." That genial voice, changing the subject.

"She has a farm, with three men."

"Good gracious!"

The interview was over.

"She says she did not go to Australia to be conventional or safe."

"I can see that. Now, Mrs Croft, I would like to see you again next week. And I am going to be very frank with you then, and I am going to ask you to tell me the truth in return."

*

Sarah had written:

What! You wish that you could be with me? Then I am an inaccurate writer indeed; or you are living in fairyland! But then you always were a little goose in your reminiscences of our farming days; how you annoyed me sometimes with your chatter when we became idle young ladies: your only memories, it seemed, were of running through the buttercups and daisies on a spring morning, never of trudging knee-deep in icy mud at 5 A.M. in February! I remember you chattering to Jonathan about the "restful whirr of the spinning wheel!" – more restful for the hearer than the spinner! Pretty little Helena was never kicked in the teeth by a cow; it would have had to be a nimble cow indeed, for pretty little Helena kept her distance! And you always had a chill or a fever, didn't you, when there was anything more strenuous to be done than a toothless calf to be taught to drink from a pail, or a message to be carried a hundred yards!

Goodness, how I rage at you, and for childish grievances long forgotten! Forgive me. Ever since the letter in which I sternly exhorted you (if I remember correctly) not to be cowardly about snakes, you will have gathered that whenever I am angry with myself, I turn my wrath on you! Whether the years of soft domestic living have weakened me, I do not know; but I know that my hardy memories of our agricultural childhood that led me to suppose I could tame and make fruitful the soils of the Antipodes were every bit as romantic and foolish as your prettier dreams!

My exhaustion and loneliness and anger are constant and inexpressible. I am a drudge, and I am glad you cannot see me.

In their advice to us, the Ladies Progress had much to say of English-women's "civilising mission" in Australia; I assumed this referred to a spiritual mission only; but when I had literally to resort to a pitchfork to "civilise" the Daggetts' home, I began to see what is really involved. The younger brothers are like animals; except that animals treat one another with respect, whereas Bill and Arthur Daggett's attitude to what they are pleased to regard as lower forms of life is one of cruelty and contempt. They even shear lambs! Can you imagine such ignorance? It is a difficult job and yields only a few ounces of wool, but the brothers and the shearers say it will improve next year's fleece. So the lambs rush around like naked orphans, and even in the heat they shiver. The sheep here are a mess of cross-breeding, prey to the most disgusting ailments and absurd mishaps. Bill and Arthur love to discuss these over supper, particularly, I think, as they perceive how their talk disgusts me; and sometimes James joins in too. How such a sheep's feet smelled as the hooves rotted! How such a lamb squealed as it was branded in the face and the iron (hissing) touched its eye! How deeply a man must plunge his arm to assist the labours of a distressed ewe! The cost of it when a ram was flung into the river to wash its wool, and the weight of its horns dragged down its head and drowned it!

"Never throw a ram in a river, Sarah!" they shout, perhaps not ill-naturedly, throwing their chewed mutton-bones on to the dirt floor. If asked, they would deny hotly that they mean me to pick the bones up. They expect the bones to pick themselves up.

"Thank you, I shall remember," I reply stiffly. I still do not feel at home here, though I am sure I am indispensable, and James Daggett occasionally thanks me for my labours. I am suspicious that any kind or humorous remark may be at my expense, after the business of the bunyips. Bunyips are a mythical Australian animal, the staple fare of simple minds wishing to make sport of "new chums"; no-one enjoys a joke more than I, but the way I was introduced to the animal seemed peculiarly cruel. I am trying to revive the orchard which had been sadly neglected, and one morning Bill Daggett rushed to me with the news that a female bunyip was nesting beneath one of my apple trees, and if I did not go immediately her young would follow their normal practice of burrowing upwards through the trunk and devouring the fruits from within. Helena, I spent a whole morning turning hard soil under my trees looking for the wretched beasts and probably damaging the roots into the bargain, before the glowing eyes of Bill and Arthur Daggett coming to watch me revealed the truth . . . I hope I have not entirely lost my sense of humour, but what is the point in telling a simple untruth to a person whose state of ignorance and dependency are such that she *must* believe, and when a person needs every ounce of her strength for *real* work, what kind of person amuses himself by inducing her to waste it?

Anyway, Mother always used to say that a cow is a fine education for rough-mannered farmers, since she will not be bullied, and only patient, knowledgeable care will induce her to give down her best – and so I have persuaded James to buy three cows to replace the poor tortured creature whom I met on my arrival and who lay down and died three days after it. Bill and Arthur were incredulous when I said I wanted a hundred sheep penned in a field to turn and fertilise the soil for pasturage, and it continues to amuse them when I carry sweepings from the house and spread them on the grass, but so far I have had no complaints about the milk and butter that the much-improved grass thus produces. There was also a tremendous row about them tramping into my dairy in their unspeakable boots to inform me that all this nonsense about scalding the churn was a waste of time and where was their dinner? "Who's robbing this coach?" I snarled back, borrowing one of their favourite expressions, which translates freely as "Mind your own business," and I won.

Let them laugh and have their jokes; I am in Australia and I have a farm. In time I mean to put it to James that since I am doing all the work of the dairy, I should keep the profits, in addition to my salary, which of course I am saving, sewn into my mattress, there being little to spend it on. In the meantime my cows and your letters are company enough, though I could wish the latter were more cheerful, Helena, and more mindful of your general good fortune and easy life. You write of *fatigue* – when you have risen as I have at five in the morning (after a night rendered sleepless as often as not by extremes of heat or cold), seen to the cows, built a fire, fed breakfast to three sullen brothers, as well as such assorted tramps and failed gold seekers as have honoured us with a visit, only to move on in search of easier money, just as (James says) they were beginning to be useful, set the house to rights (beating back tides of insects and mud, emptying the tin cans which catch drips from the roof), cleaned the dairy, churned, struggled with unbudgeable rocks and tenacious weeds in the orchard, served endless meals (as my gesture to Ladies Progress and *civilisation* I refuse to adopt the practice common on stations where there is no woman, or only a sluttish one, of keeping a pot of stew permanently on the simmer for anyone who is hungry to eat when he wishes; I insist that we eat meals together, sitting at a *table*; I state my wishes plainly to James, and he conveys them to the brothers), pickled, preserved, and yes, even sewn; when you have done all these things without help or human company worthy of that name, then I will listen to your talk of *fatigue* – "

"I make everybody so impatient!" sighed Helena Croft.

"Now, Mrs Croft," said the doctor, "the time has come for plain speaking. What I have to ask you," he went on, "is a matter of some delicacy. My colleagues and I can find nothing wrong with you, physically speaking."

Summoning all her courage, Helena said, "There might still be something, Doctor."

"I beg your pardon?"

She had rehearsed this; it had seemed so easy to say in her head.

"We can't always . . . see everything."

"Mrs Croft, I don't understand you."

She rocked back and forth in her chair and stared at the doctor's silver pen, immobile in the air between his fingertips. Maybe she should not appear to argue. Wasn't this just what distressed her about Jonathan: that with his plates and his doorknobs and his sudden dinner-parties he trespassed on her sphere, made her feel of no account? Was she not trespassing on the doctor's sphere by saying this?

"Just because . . . you cannot find something," she gasped, "doesn't mean . . . there might not be something." She looked at him imploringly. "Does it, Doctor?"

His eyes narrowed. "It's very unlikely."

"But maybe there is something in my . . . in my womb, which . . . a growth, or something."

He smiled very kindly. He laid down his pen and rose from his chair. He stepped away from the chair and indicated it with a flourish of his hand.

"Perhaps you would like to sit there? Then you can be the doctor, and I shall be the patient."

"I'm sorry – "

"Don't mention it, Mrs Croft." He resumed his seat and his pen. "Mine is a solemn business for the most part, and it is not often that I have a patient with whom I can joke . . . besides, we are beating about the bush." His voice took on a hardness she had never heard before. "We both know what the trouble is, do we not, Mrs Croft?"

"I don't – "

"My fallible colleagues and I – in our ignorance – encounter – I will not say *many* – but *too* many cases such as yours. Infertility without cause; extreme nervousness . . . you cannot deny that, Mrs Croft, you are shaking like a leaf; irritability and tears that cannot be explained by any fair-minded person having regard to your domestic circumstances – "

"But if I had a child – "

"No, Mrs Croft! Do not interrupt me, please! And do not mistake symptoms for causes; you are not in your present state because you cannot have a child, on the contrary, sterility is the *result* of your condition. And it has a known and disgraceful cause."

"No." She shook her head. The movement cut through the tension in the muscles of her neck. She went on shaking it. "No."

"Mrs Croft, nervous exhaustion . . . resulting from over-stimulation . . ."

"Please – "

"You prefer plainer words?" He took a deep, terrible breath, and stopped. He was like a colt they once had at home, who used to take a run at hedges. He never jumped; just stopped at the last

72

minute as if he had never meant to jump, turned away sheepishly and cropped grass. "Mrs Croft, did you ever, as a child – it is rare in girls, but it occurs. Curbing it is part of the civilising process, as vital as the teaching of religion or cleanliness. Cleanliness of body and mind. Ah."

This time he was certainly breathing out. Exhaling all the words he had dreaded to use. Helena saw them floating in the air. He had not needed to utter them. She had confessed. "I see from your face that we understand one another, Mrs Croft. Matters may not be as bad as they appear. The practice of which we speak . . . I do not entirely share the opinion of those of my colleagues who hold that childhood indulgence is necessarily disastrous in its consequences. And you are not so far out of childhood, my dear Mrs Croft. But it must cease. It must cease, Mrs Croft! There are ways of ensuring beyond doubt that it does cease. The preferred remedy is self-control. I wish to see you once a week from now on, and I shall know whether or not you have obeyed me. I shall know by looking at you, you will not need to lie or indeed tell the truth. If you do obey me, then I look forward to an immediate improvement, and later the pleasure of giving you and Mr Croft the news for which you long. Otherwise . . . Mrs Croft, only yesterday I visited my private asylum. I could tell you some terrible tales, I could show you some pitiful cases, and all of them were healthy men and women until they became addicted to the vice of which we speak."

The vice of which we speak.

What – that game, that foolishness, that remedy (ugly, she had thought, but at least private) for her nervous tension and pain after allowing Jonathan to satisfy himself with her. That aid to sleeping when sleeping-draughts failed? *The vice of which we speak.* The doctor had not spoken of it and neither had she. But they both knew.

She had always known it was dangerous and wrong. She had not known the consequences. Now she knew: insanity, sterility.

But Jonathan did not know. Provided she obeyed the doctor, it was their secret. Jonathan never complained about not having children. He seemed to mind more about her difficult moods. What would he do if he knew they were both her own fault? Would he beat her? Some husbands did. Perhaps it was what she deserved, perhaps it was the only possible cure.

The carriage took her home. She looked out of the window at

the hurrying crowds of people. They looked back and she hid her face.

"It is time for my rest," she told Eliza, her maid, who opened the door for her.

She lay on her new white bed. The room was very cold. The old farmhouse bed had been sent away. Jonathan found woodworm in the posts.

Jonathan had never punished her, but he would punish her if he knew about this.

Our Father, lead me not into temptation . . .

Just once more. She would permit herself a last indulgence, a final reminder of how wicked it was.

8

Sarah seemed settled in Australia. She had worked out a way of living with the brothers, and it seemed to have little in common with what Helena knew of relations between domestic servants and their employers. Sometimes Helena read bits of her letters to Jonathan: how Sarah had shamed James Daggett into fixing a proper floor or walls between the rooms, or offered the brothers a brisk choice between washing their hands and not eating.

Jonathan was amused. "Your sister," he said, "is a veritable virago." And he hummed the *v*'s like a bee.

"Those Daggetts are no gentlemen," she retorted.

"They will be. They'll surprise themselves."

She did not read him the frightening parts of the letters: the tale of the time when the river broke its banks and edged to within yards of the house, or the nights when the Daggetts stayed out with the sheep, and wild dogs and wild men, seeming to know a woman was alone, sniffed and scratched at the door till Sarah scared them off by firing a gun. The desolation entered Helena's dreams, animals howled, and the arrival of each new letter brought terror, even though Helena knew that its very coming was proof that the particular dangers it described had been survived.

Worse were the sudden paragraphs of melancholy: so darkly vivid that even though Sarah's moods of depression seemed to have the most trivial matters as their cause, Helena was left wondering whether this was the voice of the real Sarah, and the cheerful day-to-day accounts that so entertained Jonathan were mere bluff;

like Helena's own bright tone when she reddened her cheeks to visit the doctor and tell him she was quite well, much better, quite well, thank you.

There were three trees, of marvellous height and girth, dominating a clump of forest which the Daggetts wanted to clear to extend their grazing. Sarah loved the trees for their still, scornful majesty. She said they reminded her of herself.

But the Daggetts said they must come down. "Very well then," Sarah wrote.

"let the pines be felled at the whim of sheep and their loathsome caretakers, but you would think, would you not, that Arthur and Bill Daggett could go about it in a manner befitting one of God's species showing respect for another? Let them take their axes and chop the trees like men – but no; such a proceeding would be too close in its resemblance to hard labour for my gallant lads, who have found that if they cunningly slice rings of bark from the trunks, the trees will die of their own accord.

And so they do. Last summer, clouds of brave green foliage clustered on the branches, flinching from the sun and the hot winds but steadfast and beautiful; now the trees are sick and dry, dying by inches. At evening the red sun lights them like bloody skeletons and I am filled with distress, as if they, being insentient creatures, have transferred their pain to me, the only being who will care for them – I would rush out and bandage their scars if I thought it would help.

Yet why do I care so much? I am a farmer, not a visitor to a botanical gardens. Ruthless use must be made of living things if these stubborn soils are to yield their gifts; *you* were the one to mourn the death of piglets and swear tearfully not to eat a morsel (until you smelt the sweet pork crackling in the oven) – but it is as if what is happening to the trees is happening to me, I am drying out, withered. When I first came here I feared all kinds of danger from being a woman, alone, with three rough men – yet I have almost forgotten the fact, the Daggetts giving me no reason, good or bad, to remember. They wish me no ill, my bark is whole, it is like armour; but I feel so old and plain, unsexed and . . ."

And here Sarah had crossed out a word that Helena was sure was *barren*. And the crossing-out was more painful than if the word had remained intact.

Then Sarah wrote mourning a cow. Constancia had died of fever. Sarah bled her and held her head in her lap as she died.

"She was my only friend," her letter wailed.

Helena resisted the mild temptation to write back spiritedly, reminding Sarah how scornfully she had condemned Helena's own sentimentality about animals. She knew the saying about last straws and camels' backs. Sarah was about to break, but was too proud to admit it.

Even the brothers, in their clumsy way, had seemed to perceive this. Helena felt her first glimmer of warmth for them as she read on.

I expected only teasing in my distress over Constancia; but was surprised to receive a certain rough sympathy from the brothers, which, however, only served to unnerve me more. I began to weep at table. They did not know what to do about me. As I struggled for composure I cursed the social constraints which, even here, made it impossible for any of the three of them to offer me a shoulder or an arm, or for me to request such comfort. When did I last touch a human being? I could not remember. The brothers bent low over their plates and chewed their food in a ruminative, respectful silence which Arthur Daggett broke by remarking "Gotta go sometime." When I realised this was not some sheepish imperative but a philosophic comment on the inevitability of death for man and beast alike, I was even more deeply touched. How the roughest kindness can ease the mind! I went to my orchard. I felt near to death myself. I sat down under the apple tree where I had been told the bunyips nested.

Time passed; it seemed long, but the sun hardly moved. Flies fed off me and I didn't brush them away. A few figs plopped to the ground. A branch moved: James was holding it back and looking at me. He asked whether I was all right now; I replied that I was; he asked whether he or his brothers might help me in the dairy. The offer was kindly meant, I know, and I am not proud of myself for curtly rebuffing it; but I could not allow those sheep-mannered men to touch my cows, already distressed by the loss of their sister.

He looked foolish holding the branch. He seemed to wish he had not initiated this encounter and was wondering how to end it. How impatient I used to become, Helena, over all our tuition in social graces and saying the right thing; yet only when one attempts social intercourse with someone who has not mastered these skills does one realise their importance. Not that I recall being taught appropriate expressions of condolence for a foolish woman who has lost her cow.

James said, "We buried the cow." Again, this clumsy kindness! They might as easily have left me to dispose of her, or fed her to their dogs. But I was in no mood for it. Something determined me to raise another matter that had been on my mind; something told me that I should get my way. I approached the subject by remarking that it was in my head to give my dairy a name: the Constancia Packham Dairy. He clearly thought me absurd to wish thus to commemorate a cow, and I informed him that this was in fact the name of a great lady, adding, "The dairy is mine, is it not?" Some demon had hold of me; as if years of resentment must pour out at the first sign that they would be heeded. "Your dairy was nothing when I came; now mine is the best stall at Threeroads market. I think I should own a share of the profits; in addition to my salary, of course. Otherwise, what reason have I to increase the profits?"

He saw that this made sense, though it was obviously not what he had had in mind when he came to offer me comfort. And, to tell the truth, I myself wished the words unsaid. He said that he would talk to his brothers, and was gone.

I sank back on the ground, exhausted. What did it matter what we called things, or who owned which money? It was just that I had been feeling myself increasingly a partner rather than a servant and would have liked that status acknowledged. Somewhere in me there was concern, even hope, for the future when I might have my own property; but for now I was content. My fruits were ripe, my leaves green; there was endless work to be done and some of the trees I still could not get near for undergrowth, yet peaches and pears winked at me like little suns, urging me on and reassuring me that they are tough, they will grow as long as I try and am courageous. I started thinking about my poor dead cow, and how the Daggett brothers buried her; how it had dawned in one of their dull brains that here was a kindness they could do me – and they had done it. *All dead things go into the earth one way or another.* I thought; *my cow, my mother, my father, their parents, right back to Constancia and beyond; they fertilise it and new things grow; I will see about a new cow next time I go to market.*

I stayed in the orchard till night, picking figs. I carried several baskets back to the house. The lamps were lit and it was very quiet. I could smell mutton frying. James bent over the pot, prodding with a stick. I brushed him aside and built up the fire which was not hot enough. Idly I asked where the brothers were; he replied that they had heard of some good rams up for sale and had gone to investigate; and bade me draw up a chair and eat. I was not hungry, but could not spurn his kindness yet again. It was as well that I did manage to swallow a little, for I needed my strength for what was to come.

He began with what might, from a man more gifted with words, be termed a short speech on the duties of brothers to one another; it was certainly a brave attempt at one. He told me what he had told me on my first arrival at Threeroads: that he felt a special responsibility towards Bill and Arthur, that they were "pals" as well as brothers. And he added that it was not right for there to be discord within families.

Fearing this signified that my earlier rash suggestion had caused an argument between them, I immediately urged him to forget all about it since it had not been meant. But this was not what he wanted. He filled his mouth with mutton, and uttered the following words:

"We thought if you and me got married."

That was all. It was neither statement nor proposal. We sat in silence, each waiting for the other to speak. I closed my eyes, then opened them fast to escape what I saw behind the dark lids. Pictures of myself, worn, ragged, aged beyond my years. Back at home, being teased by Father for being strong and muddy as a boy. And then, ridiculous in fashionable dresses, wondering why on earth all my efforts never succeeded in making me look one-tenth as appealing as you in the most ordinary clothes; the despair of dressmakers, the constant striving to joke, to show that I didn't care, for I didn't, I didn't. Even at your wedding when everybody had me marked as the spinster elder sister running off to Australia. And pretending to be a widow. And now: myself as I was, as I am: brawny and burnt, gnawing sheep-bones with muddy fingers. We have no mirrors, I never see myself, but I saw myself at that moment: the surplus woman shipped out to the colonies where husbands may be picked off the trees.

"Your proposal is very gallant, Mr Daggett," I said. Five minutes before I would not have dreamed of attacking his clumsy speech with sarcasm. I would as soon have beaten a child or a weak animal. Now, though, he had forfeited any right to my compassion, for where was his for me? They, the brothers, had decided it all between them. I could hear it. "She wants what?" "Ain't we payin' er?" "What are we doin' that for?" "She's here – might as well – who's gonna 'ave 'er?" "You?" "Me?" "James is the eldest." "And us two'll make ourselves scarce and give ya both a chance ta get used ta it." And there would have been other, less seemly, comments.

I raised my voice above the imaginary din and as if imparting an interesting fact that had just come into my mind, remarked. "We have a number of traditions surrounding the subject of engagements in England, Mr Daggett. One is that the lady always says no – the first time." It was lost on him. He simply stared into his greasy plate as if an alternative choice of bride might appear. I continued thus: "Another is called courtship. Wooing. It is customary, you see, for the gentleman to honour the lady he wishes to marry with expressions of fondness. A foolish fancy, some say. They say that fondness develops after marriage if not before. Alternatively, a gentleman might comment on the lady's beauty. He might not always be strictly truthful, but he will find something in her face or figure to admire. And if not, then, he might admire the strength of her arm, her courage in undertaking long journeys, her willingness to adapt to difficult circumstances. It is no part of my upbringing, Mr Daggett, to respond to a proposal that bears a remarkable resemblance to a low bid at a land auction."

His only reply was to ask how many offers I had had. When I answered that there had been none he expressed surprise, and I fled to my room to escape the fabricated compliment that would follow. The simple-minded creature would have understood me to say that if he paid me one tribute I would accept him.

I could not sleep. I tossed from mortification to guilt, from guilt to grief, then down again into dank sadness. I heard James shuffle past my room to bed.

It was late and very dark when the brothers came back, riotously drunk and unaccompanied by the rams they had supposedly gone to buy. I concluded they had been drinking at one of their shepherds' out-stations – they reined in their horses outside my window and sang a song in whose words I caught my name and James'. It pretended to recount the events of the first night of our marriage. I went to the window and called out that some people were trying to sleep. They appeared to find this amusing. I heard them make their unsteady way to the room they shared with James. They exclaimed with shock and ribald disappointment to find him there; it seemed they expected him already to be with me.

So that was it! How foolish and cynical of me to have supposed that they wanted the marriage in order to keep the proceeds of the dairy and save the cost of my salary, when all they really intended was a more equitable distribution of bedrooms.

I am sorry to disappoint them on both counts.

I suppose Sarah will come home now, thought Helena. *It was bad enough that she stayed at that place once she discovered there was no woman . . . now that Mr Daggett had made clear his intentions and she has refused him . . . poor Mr Daggett! I wonder if he loves her very much? He does not sound the sort of man I would choose for my brother-in-law.*

But Sarah did not come home. She grew colder and colder in the dust and the heat.

. . . your latest letter fills me with nothing but impatience Helena! Do you ever do anything but grumble? Do you even read my letters, for instance? Apart from a courteous reference to "having received mine of such-and-such a date" you show neither sympathy nor amusement nor shock nor *anything*! It would be bad enough to wait four, five, six months for a response to my words if that response were worth the reading when it came! You are a little bit self-centred, Helena, a sister can and must say it; and your *troubles*; well! That you have some I allow (who has not?); but you will forgive me if I do not shower you with pity!

You are tired, are you, of Jonathan's mother's interference and his friends' dull wives? Do you realise that I do not meet a member of my sex from one week's end to the next, and that only at market where the opportunities for pleasant chatter are somewhat limited? Would we not give all we have (not much, admittedly) for an hour in an easy chair in a cool clean drawing-room following the rules of "not more than three successive remarks on one subject"? Our talk is of bush-fires, ticks, sheep-dip and blighted fruit! There is other talk, from which I feel excluded, having no children about whose ailments I can fret; they grumble about their husbands too, in a resigned sort of way. I used to join in, for I could surpass with a tale of one or other brother the worst that any of them had to complain of, but I have learned to hold my tongue since I heard one rather sharp-nosed lady enquire of her companion: "That woman got three husbands or what?" The answer (in case you too are wondering) is no; neither three nor one; the subject of marriage has not been mentioned again; I help myself to what I regard as my due from the proceeds of dairy and orchard; and as soon as I hear of a property that a woman can manage alone, I shall be gone. James continues to treat me with a sort of fond, speechless protectiveness which sometimes makes me feel I am a thankless hussy being courted, and sometimes leads me to congratulate myself for having gained many of the advantages of wedlock while remaining my own woman.

The brothers are surly but I take no notice.

And as for your health, about which you write at such length while communicating little or nothing! Pardon me, Helena, but are you not enjoying invalidity in the smallest degree, in the absence of anything better to do? I detect an unappealing note of self-pity in your complaints, for if you really wished to be well and thought my advice could help you, I think you would find the courage to overcome your misplaced delicacy and tell me *exactly what is wrong.* Am I a doctor? And if I were, could I diagnose and treat you from this distance? Goodness me, I wish I had the luxury of refusing a doctor's attentions here! If I should be unlucky enough to fall ill, I should have to make the journey to Threeroads for treatment, and if the journey did not kill me, the type of doctor who would set up practice in a place like this undoubtedly would.

I tell you this, Helena: if you go on complaining, I shall come home on the next ship and bring you back with me, and then you will see what hardship is . . . !

"Sarah is coming home," Helena said, "to fetch me."

Was it a joke or was it a threat? She could not tell from Sarah's handwriting. She could not even tell from her own tone of voice. She would see how Jonathan reacted. Then she would know.

He looked up from his cricket report. He put his finger inside his collar where it chafed at his pink, thickening, wrinkled neck. He was growing old. Was she making him old? Would he be glad or sorry if Sarah took her away?

"My wife is to be stolen from me?"

It was a joke, then.

"I think she means you to come too."

"Well, not this week." He boomed with genial laughter, his sign, Helena was sure, of feeling awkward. "This week I am needed at Colchester."

"One of these days," she said gaily, "I shall come with you to Colchester, and see what you do there." Sarah's words stung. If she could exasperate at such a distance, what must she be like as a companion?

"Of course, my dear, of course. I shall arrange it. But today I was thinking of coming with *you* to the doctor's."

"How did you know – "

"It is your day – is it not?"

She had said she would go with him to Colchester. He had replied by offering to come with her to the doctor. Was going to the doctor her profession, then? "I don't know if the doctor would . . . allow you to come."

"As a matter of fact," he waved a letter that had come in the morning's post, "he has asked me to call. There is something he wishes to discuss. Perhaps there has been a misunderstanding over the account, though I think I have paid him promptly. But I would enjoy your company if you would enjoy mine, and I have been meaning for some time to congratulate him on the progress you have been making." *It is I who deserve the congratulation, Jonathan,* she thought desperately. *I have been acting! Acting for him and acting for you!* Jonathan seemed unconcerned by the doctor's summons, even cheerful; he wondered aloud whether the doctor planned to give the two of them some good news.

One look at the doctor's face as they walked into the surgery was enough to confirm for Helena that there was no good news. A year had passed since the doctor's first accusation. A year in which she had struggled between temptation and disgust and fear; a year in which she had reddened her cheeks and brightened her tone and thanked him weekly for the advice which had done her so much good. She had thought him convinced. Now his anger was terrible and she knew that he was not.

He had on his desk a heavy leather body-belt with buckles and straps and a lock. He held it aloft like a prize.

"It is good of you to call, Mr Croft. I had hoped it would not be necessary to speak of these matters to you. I have advised your wife and warned her; to no avail, it seems."

Jonathan looked in bewilderment from Helena to the doctor to the belt. "What are you saying, Doctor?"

"I am saying that treatment has failed and kindliness has failed, Mr Croft! You may abandon all hope of having a child. Your wife may think she can deceive me, but I am telling you both that *this*" – he indicated the belt – "is all that stands between her and the insane asylum."

Helena started to laugh. She saw the belt standing on its end, barring her way to a turreted institution. She saw the two men watching her. They would beat her with the belt, the two of them, together.

But Jonathan faced the doctor, trembling with sudden rage. His words seemed to seize the doctor by the lapels. "What are you saying, sir? Remember it is of my wife that you speak."

"Perhaps if Mrs Croft were to leave the room – "

"She will do no such thing! If you have anything to accuse her of, you will do so to her face!"

"I have already done so, and she has admitted it. Mr Croft, I know this is upsetting, but please do not shout. Your wife's disgraceful habit has already deprived you of children; if you wish to avoid being the husband of a certified lunatic, you will purchase this belt from me and ensure that she wears it night and day in order to prevent her doing more harm – "

It was like being at a play, Helena thought, as the two men shouted at each other in that still, decorous surgery, and the doctor declared he could no longer treat a patient who did not co-operate with the treatment and Jonathan took the belt from him and turned purple in the face trying to tear it apart and finally gave up and threw it on the floor and put his arm tenderly round Helena's waist and escorted her back to the carriage.

"Why didn't you tell me he was saying such disgraceful things?"

"I was afraid you might believe him, Jonathan."

"If you thought that for one moment, then I have failed you. Failed you utterly. The man is a scoundrel. To speak in such a way – "

"He is a doctor, Jonathan."

" – to my wife."

The carriage neared the house. "Did not your mother die in childbirth?"

"Yes."

"There it is then. There is obviously a defect in your family."

"Jonathan – "

"I mean something physical – unavoidable – nothing to be done about it. We must accept it as, er, God's will." He never spoke of God in his own words. "What I mean to say, Helena, is that if that doctor has been troubling you with this filthy talk, it is no wonder your nerves have been bad! You will not think of blaming yourself. Do you think I want children so badly that I will sacrifice your happiness as a price?"

He still didn't understand. She wanted children *and* happiness. But she smiled at him and kissed him impetuously. His astonishing display of quite unearned loyalty had made her believe for a moment that she could have both.

9

My dear Helena,

How many times I have taken up my pen and laid it down again in cowardice!

Perhaps time plays tricks and my last few letters to you have been less full of unkindness and rebuke than I remember – *judge not, that ye be not judged* – what I have to tell you will demand all your patience and forgiveness; I will not say understanding, for I would not ask you to understand this.

My story begins with the departure of the Daggett brothers, Bill and Arthur. (If I seem to digress before reaching my confession, it is less out of a desire to put the case for my own defence, than to summon up what little pity you can find for me; pity that will override your disgust at what I have done.)

Rumours came of a new gold-find; and our shepherds left at a day's notice. James pleaded with them to reconsider, or at least delay their departure, for the sheep's sake if for no other, but they had their answer ready: Scotsmen, they declared that they would not be in Australia at all had they not been driven from the Highlands by their landlords' wish to graze sheep, so why should they have any concern for the beasts? James even made a clumsy and misguided (as I could have told him) appeal to their chivalry, pointing out that their flight would put a heavy load of work on my shoulders: but of course, as an Englishwoman, I am to them in the same category as landlords or sheep.

Soon afterwards, the brothers announced their intention of following. James raged, almost cried; appealing to me as if they had already gone: "What do they want? Everywhere. Places left. Women left. Men goin' off to the back a' beyond – for what? Gold? It's nothing. Ya can't eat it, can ya? It's the – " he looked down at the wooden floor I had made him build. He stamped and pawed at it as if angry at its failure to supply him with the words he needed. "It's the good things outa the land we need. Food, and milk, and – " He stared at me as if begging me to take his side, but I would not give the brothers the satisfaction of reminding me I was only a servant. "Ya know what it's like up at them diggings? Man set against man – they'll take the shirt off ya back if ya don't bind it on and take turns sleepin'." The grin the brothers exchanged told us they did know, and if there was any robbing to be done, they would be the robbers, not the robbed. James raged on, it was pitiful to hear: he cursed the gold, cursed the country where men wouldn't settle, blamed himself – and the brothers listened to him with little smiles and promised to be back for next year's shearing.

The night they left, I was alone in the house. The air was thick and still, warm syrup without sweetness. Even the mosquitoes seemed to lie stunned by the effort of flying through it. I fought my fears. I had heard of women being abandoned on remote stations when the men went for gold, but James was only out with the sheep. I fought my longing to hear the detestable chink of bottles and rough conversation. The only sounds were uneasy sheep bleats and the occasional bark of a wild dog. James could not stay out every night; I would have to take my turn as guard. I can shoot straight, I thought; I will not be afraid out there alone in the darkness. But what will become of my cows and my orchard if I am to turn shepherd?

He tried without success to find men who would stay with us.

Some nights the sheep must graze unguarded, when our sheer exhaustion meant there would be no point in our staying with them.

There were losses, to dingoes and bushrangers.

There were nights when I heard James weep from his bed: great deep dry groans that made my stomach churn with fury against those who had hurt him.

"This is how they thank him!" I thought to myself; and one night I must have spoken it aloud, loud enough to be heard through the wall, because James called back: "They're still my brothers, Sarah." "More shame to them, then," I retorted. There was a silence; and then I was placed in a dilemma which led me to regret having revealed that I was awake, for he asked if he might come into my room and talk to me. He could not sleep, he said; he was like a little boy.

What was I to do? He was terribly distressed and needed comfort. We were alone in the house; we would be for months, maybe for years. If he ever wished to harm me, I thought, he could do it at any time or place, he need not invent pretexts to invite himself into my bedchamber. Whereas if I rejected his plea for compassion (a plea which possibly cost him dear, strong man that he is), if I clung, far from gossiping tongues, to my maidenly modesty (a notion which, it occurs to me, becomes increasingly ludicrous with the passing of the years) I would be telling him that there was no trust between us, that we could not even be as brother and sister, who think nothing of talking together in their night attire. And thus untrusting we must work alongside each other.

So I let him in. I meant no wrong; and neither, I would swear it, did he. I arranged myself decently in bed, a shawl covering my shoulders and breast; he wore his day-shirt and trousers, hastily pulled on. To cover the awkwardness I humorously rebuked him for sleeping in a dirty shirt.

But there was no laughter left in him.

Do you remember my telling you, after Mr Morley confessed about the money, that I never wanted to see a man cry, least of all a man who stands as my protector? If that weakness is in them, I do not wish to know. I did what all my instincts told me to do, seeing a fellow human being in distress: I took his hand. But his thoughts were still with his brothers. He said, "Don't blame 'am, Sarah." There was no life in his hand. I let it go and spoke briskly. "Then don't you blame yourself, James. They'll come back when it suits their convenience. Why, every day I expect them to appear in the kitchen as penniless as they went away." I tried to imitate their manner of speaking. " 'G'day, Sarah. Any tucker?' " James smiled through his tears. I suggested another possibility: that they might indeed find gold. James turned bitter at this, and unaccustomedly eloquent.

He said, "If they find gold, they'll find whores to take it away. And they'll deserve it. No decent woman would – ah, what's the good a' talkin'? You wouldn't even have me, Sarah. I'd've treated ya right. I always 'ave when I could. Now I'm makin' a drudge out of ya, not like I planned when I saw ya come ridin' outa the trees the day ya came, payin' no attention ta nothin' except that cow that was thirsty as a bone." Can you imagine my emotions at this stream of words? I felt honoured – ashamed – frightened. He continued, as if talking to himself. "The boys laughed. Said ya'd come a long way ta find a 'usband, an' they could see from the look in yer eyes that if I didn't make ya an offer, ya'd make me one. I let 'am laugh. I thought, I'll take my time: let 'er take 'ers. Then that day I saw ya cryin' like a rainstorm fer that no-good heifer." He paused as if lost in a private reminiscence. "Well. Ya refused me, Sarah. Yer a proud woman. I felt like a snake ya'd found in the cookin' pot. But I thought, all right. I'll treat 'er fair and square just the same. She can 'ave 'er dairy and 'er table manners, I won't 'ave 'er wear 'erself out with the sheep, she can stay pretty. And now I'm 'avin' ta make a drudge of ya, Sarah, I'm 'avin' ta work ya like a man." At this point I stopped him. The situation seemed dangerously near to getting out of control and I feared that he would come to regret his outburst when he was once more master of himself. Fatigue, simple fatigue, I was convinced, was at the root of the distress we both felt; and I determined to suggest a practical solution and return him to his bed. I declared firmly that we must make every effort to find an honest, reliable man who would stay with us and help him; whereupon he informed me that the only way we could hope to find such a man would be for me to bear him a son.

Helena, he is so innocent and honest that I could not find in my heart the outrage that I know you will feel on reading this; I think for the first time I looked from his point of view down the years that lay ahead. The brothers would not come back, or, if they did, they would always be unsteady. Perhaps we could hire more hands, but they could never be the same as a family. What were we working for, why (I became myself again) had I come to Australia? Indeed, *not* to trap a husband, but had I not gone a little too far in my admiration for my own spirit of independence? Was it not just a prettier phrase for selfishness? No-one can truly live alone, and James had admitted his need for me. Was it not time for me to examine my own heart? His second proposal had been even cruder than his first; but perhaps, after all, he was simply honest. I know I anger you by writing these things; but you will be angrier yet before I am done. More in response to my own self-questioning than to him, I uttered the word yes.

It was not a promise to marry, still less was it assent to what happened next – yet that is how James interpreted it – it is so painful to write this, yet I must or I will run mad – I will *not* have you believe I was willing, yet equally you must not think James guilty of this worst of crimes. Well – the die is cast, I have told you; you cannot think any worse of me for adding this: you have hinted that you find no pleasure in this matter, yet I found myself profoundly moved, even (it seems strange to say it) honoured that he seemed to love me to such distraction; and the simple joy of touching another human being after so many years – I will not go on.

The moment was past as soon as it had come, and as inexplicably. What pitiful creatures we are. He fled, muttering sounds that were not words, were not even identifiable as to tone, somewhere between pain and a kind of love.

Can you understand? God's judgement is quick and sharp. The incident was not repeated, nor even referred to. In my company, James avoided my eyes; he sought every excuse to be away from me, spending nights out with the sheep. And now that there is no doubt, I will tell you before I tell him: I am with child.

I trust you will allow me still to sign myself.

Your sister,

Sarah

Shaking with disbelief, Helena started to read the letter again. When her anger prevented her from holding the paper, she tore it lengthwise down the middle. She tore each of the long strips in half, and in half again. Then she tore them across into fragments, smaller and smaller. She set the shredded fragments down in heaps, little heaps to count the months since the letter was written: the child was almost born.

Jonathan put his head round the door. He said genially, "Did you have a letter from Sarah?"

She said, "Never mention her again."

"Wh-at?" He laughed, and stopped.

"She has taken everything from me."

"Helena – "

She started to sob. She had not cried for ages; she had been better. A child, Sarah was having a child, had one already! The bastard child of an Australian – Helena supposed that they would marry now – let them, let them – she would never acknowledge the brat as other than it was!

Jonathan said, "Helena, stop screaming." He spoke in that firm, gentle, exasperated tone he used to use when she was ill, before she got better by understanding it was not her fault, there was something wrong in the family that made it impossible for its women to have children . . .

"I am not screaming, Jonathan."

"But you are." It was the air that was screaming, why did he blame her? So that he could slap her face – hard – *crack*, like that – and then, when she protested, he could defend himself:

"I had to stop you screaming."

He had an excuse for everything.

"What was in the letter?"

"You shall never, never know."

She wrote to Sarah, hardly able to hold the pen.

"NEVER WRITE TO ME AGAIN."

"I wish you would tell me what is wrong with you *now*," Jonathan grumbled, "or at least what is wrong with Sarah."

"Sarah? Nothing, I heard from her yesterday," Helena lied.

"But you are still upset; or ill again."

"I am neither."

She was both. She kept to her room but could not sleep. She did not want to be in the same world as Sarah, as Jonathan. Her body came to her aid. Once again, pains shot up and down her spine, her legs, and her bladder tormented her.

"Perhaps the doctor – " Jonathan began heavily.

"He is a scoundrel, you said so yourself."

"He is a specialist."

Now Jonathan was blaming himself for taking her away from the scoundrel-specialist's care. Jonathan thought she was having a relapse. It would be so easy to tell him about Sarah and the baby. It would be easy, it would be impossible.

"I don't think you want to be well, Helena! I'm getting rather tired of this!"

Everyone was tired of her.

Even Sarah seemed to have taken offence at the little note Helena had sent her. Admittedly the note had forbidden Sarah to communicate with her, but Sarah ought to know she had not meant it.

Perhaps Sarah had died in childbirth.

Or perhaps some other disaster had befallen her.

Or perhaps – yes, this was the most likely explanation – perhaps Sarah had written – was writing – dozens and hundreds of letters, and Jonathan and the doctor were conspiring to keep them from Helena in case they made her ill again.

Helena never heard from her sister again.

Sarah
1866 . . .

It was a warm summer morning in 1866, eleven years after the marriage of the Crofts and the departure of Sarah for Australia. The gardens of Wenbury Hill glowed pink and white and yellow with roses; the sun shone on the gleaming white houses and their black doors and railings. A cab containing one passenger laboured up the hill; on the passenger's instructions, the exasperated cabby paused outside number 17, moved on, turned with difficulty, stopped again outside the one she had said could not possibly be number 17, and helped her down with her luggage.

"Good to be 'ome, eh, ma'am? Nothing like England."

"I wonder why the blinds are down," said Sarah.

"I wouldn't like to say, ma'am."

She waited in the sunlight at the top of the white steps for him to bring her luggage before she rang the bell. The brass was dazzling. She had thought she was used to sunlight. She was glad she had never been to Helena's and Jonathan's house before she went away. As soon as she stepped through the door she would be able to escape from the maddening combination of strangeness and familiarity that had been England hitherto. She waited to be let in. The sun cast around a spurious brightness but did not warm her. She looked down at her travelling clothes, blue and purple checks, just as she had gone away, so she had returned, blue and purple checks, green hat, excitement and fear in her heart. The checks were fading, the hat was frayed; she was thirty-two where she had been twenty-one. She felt the excitement of a homecoming, the fear of what she would find; the fear too of the confrontation that would inevitably come with her other reasons for leaving Australia. Had it been the only possible response a loyal sister could give to a garbled appeal from a clearly deranged woman; or had Helena's letter, the first for three years, been a convenient excuse to run away, coming as it had at the height of a disgrace and failure that Sarah would not think about?

She would not think about it. She had come home, she would

be joyous. She had written from Threeroads to tell Helena she was coming, and then found the letter unposted in her pocket when the ship left Sydney. So her arrival would be a surprise.

The house behind the frightened maid who opened the door was dark as a burrow.

"Is this the Crofts' residence?"

The girl nodded speechlessly, then asked what name she should say.

What name? What name indeed? "I am Mrs Croft's sister." She refused to see the girl's eyes as she showed her into the dim drawing-room. She refused to be given the news by her.

She waited. The maid had not seemed surprised by her arrival. She had not said whom she would fetch. Sarah waited numbly. She shivered. Was this house always so cold and damp? No wonder Helena had become delicate. Already Sarah's eyes ached from looking at the busy figures on the wall-paper. She knew about this wall-paper because Helena had written once, "Jonathan is very proud of his Chinese wall-paper."

The door opened and Jonathan Croft came in and there was no more room for wondering or pretence. Helena had died two months ago. Sarah had known as much as soon as she saw the drawn blinds through the window of the cab.

As if from a great distance, Sarah observed her brother-in-law. He was like a puppet, she decided: perfectly attired in full mourning, his every word and gesture, his every patch of pallor and flush testifying to his meticulous fulfilment of his role as distraught widower.

It was a cruel thing to think. It was true that she had never trusted him, but it was equally true that she had never known why. She therefore had no right to doubt the sincerity of his feelings.

She herself felt nothing at all. For of course, none of it was true. She had not left James Daggett, or Australia; she could not possibly be in England, staring at Jonathan Croft's shiny wall-paper; and if she were – well, the door would open and Helena would come in, full of life, full of life.

She looked into Jonathan's stagnant, watchful eyes.

"How can she be dead?"

"I am trying to tell you, Sarah."

"It's difficult . . . to listen."

Helena had always been delicate, said Jonathan. "Yes, yes,"

said Sarah, dismissing this as she had dismissed the vague complaints in Helena's letters, some ordinary female trouble arising from not having enough to do, nothing fatal, surely? Helena had been unhappy about not having a family, Jonathan continued, and blamed herself, suffering increasingly from hysteria and depression. Many treatments (here Sarah noticed that Jonathan avoided her eyes) were tried but failed; surgery was at last proposed. And Helena died in the nursing-home, of blood poisoning. "He was a first-class surgeon," said Jonathan, as if he himself stood accused.

Sarah hardly heard. *Forgive me for judging you harshly. I hope your child is a joy to you. Please come and take me to Australia, as you once promised. Helena.* That was the note that had brought her: Helena's first communication with her after three years' hurt and furious silence following Sarah's confession of her condition. The relief of forgiveness had vied in Sarah's heart with uneasy puzzlement as to what the note could mean. Now she knew. Helena had always been afraid of doctors.

Something white swam into Sarah's vision and she became aware that Jonathan was offering her a fresh handkerchief for her streaming tears. She took the handkerchief and he sat back; again she was reminded of a puppet, controlled by the unseen hand of correct behaviour. And again she rebuked herself. Who knew what he was suffering?

"Sarah, why are you here? It was so sudden. You cannot have received my letter."

She considered possible answers to this. What did Jonathan know of her correspondence with Helena, its ceasing with Sarah's pregnancy, its resumption three years later in that pathetic, childishly-scrawled plea?

"My husband turned me out," she said.

He almost smiled before seeming to remember that he should not. "Why, Sarah! I did not know that you were married."

I do not know myself if I am married.

The gloomy, death-filled drawing-room closed in; the crack of sunlight between the closed blinds at the window yawned open into hot, wide plain, shimmering and dotted with sheep. She shivered and hugged herself, and Australian sunshine blistered her skin. She heard the soporific buzz of insects, the liquid murmur and cackling of birds.

"James, I think I am with child."

He smiled, for the first time in months. "You sure?"

"There are signs."

He helped her to a chair; she thought, *very nice; but in a minute you will have me outside rolling logs.* "Can ya tell if – "

She knew what he was trying to ask. She teased him. "If what, James?"

"Sarah, I won't be sorry if it's a gal, only . . ."

She cried. He wrung his hands. "Hey, Sarah. It's good news. Don't waste the water."

"I'm frightened."

"Nah. It's just like with the ewes."

"I've seen how you treat your ewes."

Abashed, he said, "We'll get a woman to ya. You'll see."

"But she'll know."

"That we're not wed?" He nodded to himself, pleased at having sensed the cause of her misgivings. "We will be. You'll see. Wait there." He was full of surprises. He brought a sticky, dusty *Book of Common Prayer* that she had never seen before. Many of its pages were uncut. "Find it, go on." She turned to the Solemnisation of Matrimony, afraid for the blasphemy; he made her point with her finger as she read the words and he repeated them. Outside the wild dogs howled. Were they man and wife? She did not know then; she did not know now.

A week later she collapsed in the dairy; James was out in the fields; he came in to find her and the dairy covered in blood; and the pathetic dead creature born of her wrapped in a cleaning-cloth.

She buried it in the orchard, whispering christening prayers and funeral prayers.

She considered telling Helena; but she had not yet received her response to the news that she was pregnant. And when the rebuke finally came, she was too bitter to risk another. Helena had decreed the silence between them; let Helena be the one to break it.

Now, sitting in Helena's drawing-room, she wondered what Helena had thought about her as she died; or whether she had thought of her at all.

Somehow tea was brought. Sarah made no move to pour out. Jonathan did it with clumsy hands. There was silence between them now, a sense of everything having been said. Did he expect her to drink her tea and leave?

"She agreed to the operation, I suppose, Jonathan?" She did

not want to offend his delicacy by enquiring as to the operation's exact nature. But she saw that the question hurt him in another way.

"Are you asking if it was done against her will?"

"Forgive me. Was she very much afraid?"

"A little. No more than I would be myself. You see, she thought, we thought, the doctor said that it would make it possible. A child." Long dark lines tugged down the sides of his mouth like ropes. "Sarah, you're smiling."

"I mean no disrespect."

Of course, of course. He had not suggested, he certainly had not thought – her smile was one of reminiscence and understanding, but she did not want to share either with him. She knew how longing for a child could make a woman desperate and brave.

How many times? They merged into each other, became part of the calendar. It always seemed to be a bright day in spring or a golden day in autumn when the changes in her body became unmistakable, and, each time with a little less conviction, she told James they might hope once again. And then came the worst time, always a week of drought or ice when exhaustion or a fall or a fever did its work and the baby was lost.

She might have agreed to an operation on herself, had one been offered.

It was difficult to believe that Helena had died not here, but in the nursing-home. The presence of death was so strong in the house. The bright ornaments, the luxuriant hangings, the smart, polished furniture, mocked in their stillness. How unbelievably extravagant and vulgar it all was; how on earth had a man with such taste chosen a delicate creature like Helena? Why had he not selected some brassy, noisy creature who would fit into his house? Scarlet-patterned dinner plates raised nausea in her throat.

Jonathan was sharp with the servant. "Why these plates?"

Sarah raised her eyebrows.

"Cook said being as you 'ad company – "

"Miss Weeks is not company, she is family."

"It's a while since I was called that," said Sarah when the servant was gone.

"Forgive me. Of course. What is your married name?"

Had she one? It would be too painful to be known as Mrs Daggett. "I am accustomed to . . . Sarah Packham."

He inclined his head. It did not matter. She would not be long in this house.

He asked no questions as to her plans. She might treat the house as her own. There were weeks when she hardly saw him. She remembered Helena complaining that his business often took him away from home. Sometimes she wished he would order her to go; challenge her failure of nerve about returning to Australia. Her limbs felt leaden, her mind would not think; and her nightmares were terrible. It had been a dreadful voyage from Sydney; even the crew were seasick and scared and said they had never seen storms like these. She was not ready to venture forth again. Eleven years of weariness demanded rest.

She said one day, "Would you like me to sort out her things?"

He was grateful. "You must keep whatever you want."

He took away some clothing wrapped in tissue paper, then let her loose on the wardrobe and the chests of drawers. She wept a little and laughed a little over the clothes, fine dresses, savage corsets, good coats, tight boots, the clothes of a stranger. She buried her face in the clean lace underclothes. For three days she could make no decision. Then she started to pile the things into two heaps, those that would be useful for a woman in Australia, and those that would not.

2

Dear Sarah,

Yu shouldnt of run off like that. I miss yu like a dried-up creek. Everyday I look to see yu ridin out of the trees like that first day yu came to us like a blessin of God. I no I said things I shouldnt but yu got a sharp tongue too Sarah. Its what I like yu for, got spirit like a good colt. When are yu comin back? Evrythins good now. My brothers have come back. (Arthur Daggett Esquire at your service mam. Rightin this at my brothers dictation. Gooday Sarah!) They found gold like we never believed. Were runnin a good mob of sheep now. They got fine clothes and good things for the sheds and the house you wouldnt reconise it and wives. Theyre good girls but not too clever. Theres mud in the dairy I can just see yu flyin into a passion over. They brought a girl for me but I said I was married to yu. But they said it aint legal in the eyes of God nor man. Has to be in a church like yu said. First thing when yu come back eh Sarah! If yer comin. If yer not I guess Ill have to marry her. It aint right to hang it on with her. I wait for your reply and I hope yu can

forget about all the other things like I have. Now I got to see the men about wiggin the wethers, they got so much wool theyre near blind but I aint and Ill keep turnin my head to see yu ridin out of the trees.
Yours Truly,
    James Daggett (His Mark)

Sarah thought: *Marry her then, since it is clearly what you wish! Do you suppose you can bribe me with your gold!*

She thought: *Your letter cuts me to my heart; I thought never to hear from you; yet I cannot say I hoped not to; for in all the rush and agitation of my departure, I did not neglect to leave a sheet of paper as if casually bearing my address; and you did not neglect to find it.*

She thought: *So Bill and Arthur are back, to gild with their easy, dirty money the place to which I gave my children's lives; to lounge in greasy complacency in the home I built; to set their women dirtying my dairy; to turn James' head with some sprightly slut from the bitter drudge of a woman who was his right arm and thought she was just beginning to love him.*

In her mind she watched Arthur Daggett's fingers on the pen, moving across the page; she heard him snicker. There were gold rings on his fingers, and black ones on his nails. It was a thing that had sourly amused her when she lived in Sydney with the Morleys: the way the newly rich there loved to flaunt their wealth, it never occurring to them that pink-and-white fingernails were a better indicator of gentility than any weight of jewels.

But she must stop this. She must read the letter again, calmly. She must resist the bleakness of soul that Helena's death had left. She must see that the letter was kind. James wanted her to return: perhaps even more than the words of the letter suggested, for she knew Bill and Arthur detested her, and Arthur would not be above a little editing of a too-strongly-worded plea. Her heart shifted with tenderness – and met her stomach that heaved with fear and disgust.

What! Tolerate once more the smug superiority of the Daggett brothers, whose manners (she would take her oath) would not have improved!

Make that journey again, before her feet were fully settled on dry land after the last one? Feel again the seething terror of the towering waves, and the nausea, in whose midst the only thing greater than fear of imminent death was her longing for it? Cross the craggy Blue Mountains in that malodorous coach, feel the wheels slip, dread snakes and bushrangers and dingoes in the dark bush night? No, no, it had been a woman ten years younger in time and fifty years younger in health and spirits who had done those things. He was watching for her through the trees . . . or so he said . . . or so Arthur wrote . . . but that tender touch could easily be the product of the brothers' sense of humour. She could arrive there and find herself unexpected, she could come upon James in the middle of his wedding-party, she could realise that they had once again resorted to trickery to acquire a cheap servant. And this time there would be no coming back.

"I no I said things I shouldnt but yu got a sharp tongue too Sarah." Was that to be read as an apology? As forgiveness? She hardly knew which she deserved. She had been trying not to think about James Daggett. When memories forced themselves upon her, she alternated between anger and hot, flushing shame.

But neither of them would forget. If ever they came together again, it would lurk beneath the surface of their every exchange; it would embitter every moment of sweetness; it would hang like the smoke of a bush fire over the slightest, most commonplace and harmless spark of domestic anger. *I remember the things you said to me! I remember what you did!*

It was a barren time. The brown grass crackled underfoot; shrivelled, bitter fruits hung like stones in the orchard. The cows were dry, the ewes were dropping more dead lambs than living. Even the riots of bird song were silenced into dry, rasping sounds; bark peeled from the trees; and the flowers turned in on themselves as if ashamed of their colours at a time when the sun blazed so angrily and the earth suffered its punishment.

To lose another child at this time seemed only fitting. It was the least distressing of all Sarah's losses. She lay in her bed as she might at night; participating in the ordinary rhythms of nature: darkness for sleeping and summer for miscarriages. She was too dry and resigned to cry.

James brought her a big plate of steaming meat. Lumps of fat swam in the gravy. She turned away.

"Gotta keep ya strength up, Sarah."

He was kind, for a husband. The women she met at market were cynical about husbands.

But was he her husband? She was increasingly troubled by the memory of the little ceremony they had conducted. There was no sign of an end to the drought. Her bed chafed her but she was too weak to move. Scanning the sky through her little window she saw not the faintest trace of cloud in the searing blue; it was easy to believe that the earth had come under a divine curse; and she with it, in punishment for sin.

Once she would have rebuked herself for such a thought; these were modern times; only in the Old Testament were women cursed with barrenness. The God Sarah believed in was too grand and generous to play such petty tricks. For to Him it would be petty, to single out one woman to punish for a sin that many must commit, especially as He must know that she and James were as truly married as the circumstances (which were, after all, God's doing) would permit.

Yet now, here, in this great, hard, crudely-etched country, with its brilliant colours, its shrieking, whispering, mysterious sounds, its savage extremes of climate, it was easy to believe in the terrible, unsubtle God of man's beginnings. Once she had remarked that the wild varieties of scenery were like workings on a giant sampler: God's sampler, where He practised His handiwork. Perhaps here too was where He vented His anger in clear, uncompromising ways; perhaps the face He turned to this young, ancient country was indeed the face of the Old Testament.

They must marry! Somehow it must be possible, must be made possible. After her convalescence she would demand to be taken to Threeroads and given a wedding. She would make her peace with God; to whichever Testament He belonged, He would surely do no less with her?

She dreamed feverishly of Helena's wedding in a cool church in Sussex, fragrant with flowers; she stood behind Helena while Helena took her vows; Helena turned; Sarah stepped back, waiting to see her, radiant; but Helena's head was a death's head, and maggots crawled in her eyes.

She made her request as soon as she felt well enough for two days' ride; James was angry. What? Was she still nagging about that? Were they not married already? Had he not made a good husband, despite her disappointing him? She wept; he softened. "It hurts a man, Sarah," he mumbled, "when his wife don't trust him."

"Why don't you take me to the fair," she wailed, "and sell me?"

"Wouldn't get much for ya," he said, as if seriously considering it, but adding, as her tears flowed anew, "nappin' ya bib like that." She knew she had won but she let him argue. He told her that word was abroad in the bushranging community that Daggetts' had the welcome mat out for robbers, protected as it was only by one man and a sickly woman: "Since we are so little deterrent to the lawless," she retorted, "it will hardly matter whether we are here or not." He asked who would milk the cows. She reminded him they were dry. He worried about the sheep. She reminded him they were in no mood to roam in the heat. At last they set off. Their horses sensed the differing moods of their riders: James' mount was sullen, Sarah's frisky and triumphant.

"Smells like rain," James said once.

"Excellent," said Sarah. "We shall return to full tanks."

"We oughtta make sure they fill up right."

"The rain has always completed its journey from the skies without our intervention in the past, James."

Shrill bird song filled the air; James was right; there were no clouds to be seen but the sense of rain was unmistakable. A white fluttering crowd of cockatoos rose above them; Sarah wanted to cry at their beauty; let Helena have her white wedding-dress, she thought, her flowers, her wedding party; these were all the guests and celebrations Sarah needed.

And so they went to marry, but they never married. For when they stopped and asked for shelter at a lonely farm, they were treated with suspicion and fear. And only when they had allayed this, satisfying the farmer and his wife that they were an ordinary, decent travelling pair, did they learn the reason for their unease. The previous night there had been a raid: not a swagman or black fellow fancying a leg of mutton, but skilled raiders intent on rounding up the whole herd. Only the chance occurrence that the farmer's brothers were visiting enabled the thieves to be driven off disappointed, and total ruin averted. James said nothing while this story was being told, just chewed his food and stared at Sarah. If she had been one of the thieves herself, she would not expect to see such merciless reproach and fury in the eyes of the man she had thought was soon to be her husband. He asked the farmer which way the raiders had gone; the farmer was not sure.

His meal unfinished before him, James stood up. Very quietly and politely, he loaded his belongings and took his leave. He ignored Sarah. *Come or not, as you like*, his angry back seemed to say. "At least sleep the night," she begged. "There is nothing we can do now." Their hosts politely ignored the quarrel, but Sarah knew they could not fail to know what it was about. Their sympathy was matched only by their incredulity: had they left their property unguarded to go to town on some womanish whim? Sarah was too shy to say what it was, though it was intolerable that this couple should think it something unimportant. When she flatly declared that she would not budge tonight, the wife gently urged her to go with her husband; obviously, thought Sarah bitterly, she did not want a fool under her roof.

So they rode back through the dark, ominous night, arriving as the red dawn opened like a wound between the trees. To say the worst had happened would not approach the measure of Sarah's anguish. They started to meet solitary stragglers from the herd, some covered with blood, trembling under the hedges. They rounded up twenty, perhaps thirty, this way; they found a dead, dismembered cow. White with shock, Sarah struggled to find consolation in the robbers' having omitted to burn any buildings; the house was whole, though the kitchen was stripped of implements and food. There was evidence that they had sat round the table and eaten a meal; and then run riot through the bare, tidy home, casting clothes and shoes and lamps and papers and pans and bottles to the ground. *It's like the day I first arrived,* thought Sarah, *and saw the mess; but that was nothing; that was just the neglect of three men who had not achieved civilisation; this is the work of men who have declared war on it.*

The last of the cheeses had gone from the dairy; and the low branches of the fruit trees had been stripped bare; until, Sarah supposed, the robbers realised the fruits were blighted and parched; and decided to spare themselves the trouble.

She waited like a dog for James' reproaches. But his iciness was almost philosophical, and that was worse. He made her list everything that was gone, dictating prices to write beside each item. Sometimes – too seldom – when he barked the name of some article she was able to say:

"No, James. It is still here. Look."

"Hm."

"So you see, it could be worse."

"How?"

"We can replace – "

He gave an angry shout. He strode to his room. He exclaimed with irony that the robbers had not thought it worthy of their attention. "Perhaps you have been right all along to keep it in such a disgraceful state," said Sarah, meaning to lighten a moment that could hardly be made worse. She heard him grunt; she heard him move the wooden board behind which he kept a locked moneybox and a book of accounts. Often in the evenings he made a great display of secretly counting the money, covertly marking figures in the book. She had watched this procedure with fondness and mounting irritation. He wanted to show her that if he could not write words, he could still add figures. Then he should show her, discuss with her. She was haunted by the memory of her father's failure, and Mr Morley's. She knew she had a way with numbers. Yet he never told her anything. Now she did not want to know; but he laid the books ceremoniously before her and up-ended the box: the books were a tangle of scribbles and scrawls; three coins fell from the box, spun and danced on the table and fell to the dusty floor.

"Not worth the bother," he said. "Replace 'am? What with? Leave 'am," he shouted fiercely as Sarah bent to rescue the coins, "We're finished, Sarah! We're finished!"

She tried to understand. She was suffering on his account as well as her own, but she had to know. "They have taken your money?"

"Nah. Didn't have none."

Her drawn breath whistled through the air. "I have money," she said. She went to her bed and started to unpick the place in the mattress where she kept her savings.

He followed her and stared.

"You – what?"

"Not much," she said, snipping and unpicking.

"How – "

"Some money I brought from England. And what do you suppose I used to spend my salary on? Before we were . . . married, I used to think I would go away some day and set up on my own. Oh, James, don't be angry; of course I wouldn't leave you now that misfortune has come upon us; and I have a little saved from market, so you see we shall set ourselves to rights again in no time." She heard her low, cautious tones become higher and more absurdly optimistic; for she did not see the relief in his face that she had hoped for; she saw disbelief and hate.

"You bin keepin' back money?"

"But you knew, James; you agreed! Don't you remember the

day the cow died; and I was so sad, and you said I could keep what I made from dairying?"

"But Sarah. That was when we were, like, master and maid. I owe money all over. An' you've bin sleepin' on it."

"You never told me!" she flashed. It was true. And in fairness to herself, she knew that if he had told her he was in debt, she would have handed over what she had. But it would not have been without a qualm. In all the years of her so-called marriage, the ambiguity of her position had never been far from her mind. Her modest store of money was her protection; her way out, if she ever needed to go. Why could James not see that; especially now that it seemed her foresight had saved them? Perhaps he did see it; perhaps that was the trouble.

"You let me worry. You let me work like a bullock – "

"I have not been idle myself, James!"

"Near cut myself in half with worry, I have – "

"You never told me! You tell me less than when I was your salaried servant – "

He looked at her with disbelief. "But you're my wife."

"But I am not."

"Damn right you're not! You shoulda gone with Arthur and Bill if it was gold ya wanted – "

"Yes! I should, should I not! Yet I am here with you, in spite of the ruin to which you have brought me! I could weep for myself: the brave, optimistic young girl setting out ten years ago; now look at me! Broken and barren and blamed by the very man whose livelihood I am about to save for being in a position to do so!" He turned away. She had forgotten the resolution she had made years ago never to beat him with words. "James – I know what you are thinking – perhaps you are right – it must appear to you – but if you were right, would I be sitting here, James? If I meant to take what I could from you and be gone, would I be sitting here offering you everything I have – ?" His eye looked scornfully at the unpicked place on the mattress where she had kept the money. She felt dark colour flush up from her neck. She saw the coins on the bed where she had laid them. It was a grand gesture. But she was frightened to see them there and longed to pick them up.

He stepped towards her. "Everythin'?" he enquired. "Everythin'?" – looking at the tear in the material – "You sure, now Sarah? Sure you ain't got somethin' else hidden away – *just in case?*" She felt his hand on her neck; she slapped it down; it was a loud slap but it could not have hurt him; he withdrew his hand, but his voice still lashed her. "None a' my business anyways. You look out for yaself, Sarah: that's the girl! Why don't ya get a pot a' paint, eh? Why don't ya?"

"What for?"

"An' put ya name on what's yours, eh? Mark a line down the middle of the floor – an' the bed too, why don't ya?"

"James, you forget yourself."

"Mebbe," he said, "and mebbe not."

"James," she screamed, "you will tell me what you mean by that!"

"Whore," he whispered, "slut."

"Seducer, thief and liar!"

Soon there was nothing left to be said.

Sarah had not remembered London being so dirty. It had been summer when she was here before, and her heart had been full of hope. Now the streets near the offices of Ladies Progress were narrow and dark; the wheels of the fly skidded on the greasy cobblestones and little patches of fog lurked like pools trapped in rocks after the tide goes down. She looked hungrily out on patches of sooty grass, the suffocating remains of village greens, spared in a moment of forgetfulness by the city's encroachment of stone. She saw ragged children, sick-faced, toothless men – add brawn and sunburn and any one of them could be a Daggett – they peered at her in her fine carriage. Jonathan was generous with the loan of the fly. "Go anywhere, Sarah," he said. He did not add, "And don't come back."

She was moving but everything seemed still and solid. She seemed to realise as if for the first time where she was. She seemed to lose at last the sense that she need only rub her eyes and the dreary vistas of England would roll back and she would see a wild, wide horizon, red and blue and gold. She shivered. Would she ever be warm again?

She had thought the office was a brighter room. She had remembered a brisk, friendly place with helpful staff and eager migrants, poor but clean. And the map on the wall had been broad and tall and new, not torn and faded and shrivelling at its corners.

There was a horrible noise: like an animal in pain. But it came from a human being, a stringy waif of a girl in hopeless confrontation with a bustling woman in the pompous uniform of a Ladies Progress matron. The girl held her hands in front of herself, spreading her sticks of fingers in a pathetic attempt to hide the unmistakable bulge in her belly.

"I wanna go to Orstrilia!" the girl howled.

The howl tore at Sarah's nerves. She wanted to pity the girl but she could not stand her noise, her degradation. The matron, with a rigid arm, was showing her the door. "You certainly cannot travel in that state!"

"I ain't in no state! Whatchoo sayin'? I'll get my lawyers – "

"We are a respectable organisation – "

"I'm, respectable! You'll 'ear from my – "

The woman turned to Sarah with the air of officious relief of one greeting her own kind. "Good morning, madam. Can I help you?" She had raised her voice an octave or two to keep out the drumming, wailing sound of the girl now apparently taken with a fit: she was beating her heels on the ground and making a thwarted, whistling sound through her teeth, a child thwarted, boding no good for the younger child growing within her.

Sarah caught the matron's eye and felt even colder. The look was clear: *Please state your business and we may consign the creature to non-existence. How fortunate that we are not all as she is!* How many times Sarah had imagined just such looks in the eyes of disapproving womankind as she waited in the bush for the birth of the children of James Daggett. And how often she had consoled herself: *There's nobody to know. There's nobody to see.* She gave one last look at the girl hobbling out through the door, despairing; perhaps she had woken this morning in some dreary room and thought, *I know! I'll go to Australia! Then everythin'll be all right!*

"You do still," said Sarah, "send women to Australia?"

"Of course! But not . . ."

"No, no. But poor women – with no means."

"Assisted passages. Certainly, I shall have to write down your particulars." She brought out a large book.

"No, I – " *I'm not ready yet. I'm still tired.* "I know you sometimes need things. Clothes."

"It depends," said the woman.

"I know what is suitable," said Sarah. She went out to the fly and had the boxes brought in.

"There are some good coats for winter. People don't realise how cold it can be. I've been there, you see – on one of your

103

assisted passages." She watched the woman's stubby fingers sort through Helena's clothes as if they were dirty. She was miles away from the anger she felt. She had been like this for so long she could not remember being any other way, she could not remember being one person, she was two: one, like Jonathan, a puppet, who rose in the morning, dressed, ate, passed through the day; another who observed quietly, sardonically, angrily, mocking the creeping of time.

What was going to happen to the rest of her life?

She looked into the woman's eyes for thanks; but the woman clearly thought the interview was at an end.

"Is there anything further – "

"You were saying – Assisted Passages – "

"But you have already had one. Why did you come back?"

"Family business."

"It would be irregular for anyone to have two."

"It doesn't matter." It was a relief. She could not go after all. Not yet. One day she would go as an ordinary passenger. She would have a cabin, not a shared hold with gabbling women and matrons. Jonathan would pay. Jonathan would be glad to get rid of her. Jonathan looked at her these days as if he had killed Helena – and Sarah was the only one who knew. She turned to go. A voice from a deep recess in the building could be heard shouting "Don't forget to ask her to sign the petition, Miss Havers!" A strident, commanding voice; a door crashed open; and a tall girl with a willowy figure and hair in absurd black pigtails strode in. Her hands were too deeply and comfortably entrenched in her pockets for them to have been suddenly replaced there; she must have kicked the door open. "How are we going to get five thousand signatures if you keep forgetting to ask people, Miss Havers?" She seemed to be very short in respect for her elders, this girl, and the matron gave Sarah an exact replica of the look of pained conspiracy with which she had dismissed the howling waif who could still be heard grizzling out in the street.

"Petition?" said Sarah. It would be something to do with improving conditions on migrant ships. The younger generation were soft.

"There is soon to be another extension of the franchise. We want ladies to be included this time."

"Which franchise?"

The pigtails tossed in disbelief. Sarah knew this kind of person.

Such was their obsession that they could not conceive of anyone having not the least idea what they were talking about. "The vote. For Parliament. *Then* we shall see some changes! I am always telling Miss Havers – and she agrees, don't you, Miss Havers, even though you love to argue – and I can see you agree too, Mrs, er – that it's all very well sending women to Australia because there is no livelihood for them here, but sooner or later we must see about making England a country that – " she seemed to consider her case so indubitably proven that she substituted a shrug for an end to her sentence. The vigour of the shrug was such as to draw the long red hands from the pockets; the girl looked at the hands with surprise; then concluded that as they had presented themselves at such a timely moment they might as well be given a task. She fetched a sheet of paper from the bottom of the pile of similar sheets in a far corner of the office (which location caused her to give Miss Havers a glance of affectionate exasperation) and presented it to Sarah to sign, which she did, and turned to leave.

"Oh! Don't you want to read what we're asking for?"

"You have just told me."

"Packham! Fancy that! One of our precedents is a Packham."

"I have no relatives living," said Sarah shortly, but the girl's enthusiasm, which was making her sick at heart, was not to be resisted.

"I have a passion for history and the Suffrage Committee has appointed me to research precedents for freewomen and noble-women possessing the right to vote for Members of Parliament in the Middle Ages! You should see me with my documents! I have a passion for documents, Miss Packham: less than a hundred years ago a case was discovered of women burgesses' names being entered on a list of parliamentary electors; I have made perfect copies; I shall show you; I have them here somewhere . . ."

"Please do not trouble yourself, Miss, er – "

But the girl was determined to show her her list of burgesses. Sarah forced a smile and made to go; but the pigtails were still not satisfied; for there was another document, their owner insisted; she was *sure* it was here somewhere; ah yes; here it was; she had found it in a town hall in Sussex after much searching and many troublesome enquiries from the officials as to what a chit of a girl could want with such a thing! "There!" she said triumphantly, "Fifteen-seventy-two! Look at that, Miss Packham! One small part of the weight of evidence proving our historic right to the' franchise! Is it possible that you are descended? Do you come from Sussex?"

It hardly hurt at all to deny it; she felt a danger of becoming involved; she did not want to be involved; she was tired, so tired; she just wanted to be left alone. She glared at the pigtails, then bent her head to read.

" 'To all Christian people to whom this present writing shall come, I, Dame Constancia Packham, widow, late wife of Sir Robert Packham, Lord and Owner of the Town of Littledean, sendeth greeting . . .' "

In spite of herself, Sarah heard the ringing tone of the words. Then she heard herself laughingly changing her name to Packham: as a joke, it was only a joke. She remembered the portrait; she heard her grandmother: *Little Sarah is growing up to be like Constancia Packham.* Once, perhaps; not now.

" '. . . know ye me to have appointed my trusty and wellbeloved Thomas Smith and John Hastings Esquires to be my burgesses . . .' "

Know ye me! The regal haughtiness of it! It brooked no argument! It was like something from the Bible.

" '. . . and whatsoever the said Thomas and John, burgesses, shall do in the service of the Queen's highness in that present parliament to be holden at Westminster, I do ratify and approve to be my own act . . .' "

"Isn't it interesting?" the girl with the pigtails breathed.

" '. . . as fully and wholly as if I were or might be present myself.' "

"I suppose it is," said Sarah.

"But it *proves*, don't you see, that there is no precedent for disenfranchising us!"

"None whatever," Sarah agreed, "as long as we own towns."

Driving home to Jonathan's, she felt some remorse. She had no quarrel with the girl or her petition. But she had felt a curious, fierce anger at having Constancia Packham's name thrown at her like that, all unexpected; as if she had caught the girl wearing some of her clothes or rummaging among her things. And she had been tormented by the crying of the dirty creature outside the door who had been refused an assisted passage to Australia; if Ladies Progress and its interminable committees could do nothing for her, how had they time to send strong, bright girls

off to dig up documents about other people's relatives? She had
bent to talk to the girl who was weeping bitterly; started to tell
her Australia was not necessarily the answer to all life's problems;
stopped, knowing she had no alternative to offer; and wished she
had saved one coat, one warm skirt, from Helena's boxes. While
she stood there, the girl looked out over Sarah's shoulder at
someone behind; Sarah turned, saw a gross man winking unmis-
takably and beckoning; when she turned back, the girl was hauling
herself to her feet, wiping her nose with her hands.

"Quick, my dear, how much will he give you?"

"I'll ask for a shillin' but I'll go lower."

Sarah gave her a shilling. The girl pocketed it and went after
the man.

Pearl
The 1860s . . .

Pearl was found in an oyster-shell; she was not born in the usual way. She was glad of it: she had seen the St Laur fisherwomen stagger on the mud-flats with bulging bellies, she had peeped with other children through cracks in curtained windows where births were taking place, she had thought it a terrible, awful thing. She had seen the red or grey scraps of life that resulted. Sometimes the scraps filled out miraculously into babies, sometimes they vanished and went to the Good Place. Pearl hoped to go to the Good Place herself, but not yet awhile; she was glad she was born from an oyster shell.

Her mother Lizzie loved to tell the story and Pearl loved to hear it. Lizzie was quite a young girl at the time, she was lonely, doing her dance on the mud. It was a magic dance that only Lizzie knew how to do. It was a chilly summer evening with a storm blowing up in the estuary. The lines where mud and water became sky were dim. Wind shot across the Essex marsh from the edge of the world, and tiny hairs stood erect in lumps on Lizzie's arms. She let the wind carry her till suddenly it dropped. It told her what to do next. The mud oozed between her toes. She reached down as the wind told her and felt something hard. It was an oyster. Lizzie considered. You were not supposed to pick oysters in the summer. They were sick, and if the bailiffs caught you, you might find yourself brought before the Conservancy Court in Colchester and fined. St Laur might even lose its licence to dredge. But the wind had told her; and she had to obey the wind!

"So what did you do, Mother?" Pearl asked, although she knew.

Lizzie grinned, showing her crooked white teeth. "I takes it o'course, gel. No-one there to see."

"And what was inside?"

"What a gel you be for questions! An oyster o'course!"

"And – ?"

"And milk, and brood – "

"*And – ?*"

And, and, and! And a round, hard, white baby! Tiny as a stone! Lizzie took her home, cleaned out the shell and kept her there with a sheet made out of a handkerchief! It was seven days before Pearl opened her mouth to accept food and her limbs softened! If ever she doubted the story, Pearl could check it with a glance at her own flesh. It was white and translucent and did not turn red or brown in the sun. Her hair was pale brown, so pale that it looked as grey as an old woman's in some lights. And she had a fellow feeling for oysters. The oystermen teased her, pointed fingers at Lizzie, declared Pearl to be the first giant pearl to come from a St Laur oyster since the Romans landed, but Pearl reasoned that if it could happen with her it could happen with others, and she would not eat her cousins.

When she was ten she wanted to go out on the smacks. Ever since she could remember she had helped with the sorting and counting, and her courage for hunting crabs, grabbing them out of reach of their claws and filling barrels with them, was legendary in the village; the little ones could be boiled for soup, the big ones sold or eaten, and besides they were a menace to the oysters. Pearl was content to be the scourge of the local crabs but she wanted to go out dredging too. The colder the morning, the cosier her little bed, the more exciting it seemed as she watched through the window: heads down, wet already, laden with nets and rope, the oystermen made for the shore and pushed out their boat.

Old Sam Saxton was kind but firm.

"I don't take no gels in my boat, Pearl."

"Why not?"

" 'Tis unlucky."

"Oh, I wouldn't be unlucky! I wouldn't!"

Sam's son Jake said she should take the test.

"What test?" Pearl demanded.

"You be ten years old now? Do you eat ten oysters then," said Jake solemnly.

"Ten oysters," Pearl repeated.

"Ten's nothing, Pearl," Sam coaxed, "think o' me, I be fifty-seven."

His son was already lining up the horrible feast. He opened the shells with his knife. No pearls, no babies, but still . . . ten plump grey lumps. She ate them, her last oysters; for she never forgot those ten shattering gulps and the icy salt trails the oysters left down her gullet, or the three heaves with which she brought them up again, good as new, one minute later. The Saxtons laughed at her; they said she should try again, but she ran away.

"I won't never catch another crab for you! You see if I does!"

Mother would be cross to hear her talk so, like a village child; and Mr Croft would tease, next time the train brought him. *I do*, he would make her repeat, her hands folded as if doing her lessons, *I do, he does*.

The railway company had built and fortified a long, dry dyke to carry the track to St Laur, for it was almost an island and the marsh still steadily encroached. St Laur had not even been included in early plans for the route, for who would want to go there? But luckily the man through whose land the company had wanted to build had made difficulties; and rather than pay him what he wanted the company passed the track round a long loop, netting St Laur and giving it a Halt. Four times a day the train halted. The villagers pretended not to like the railway; but they nursed a secret pride to know that each of their four trains connected at Colchester with a London train.

They complained about the noise, they complained about the smoke; they fretted about the outsiders the railway brought; they even made a fuss about the mud the train churned up as it eased itself along, parallel to St Laur's main street.

Lizzie had no sympathy. "You'd think mud weren't never seen in St Laur 'fore the railway came."

St Laur was unimaginable without its mud. If the train brought a little extra on its great wheels, it carried some off too. Every day the women swept the street. It was never easy, even when the weather was dry. Then there was a sticky dust to be chased; it coated the bristles of the brooms, needing bare fingers and sharp fingernails to scrape it off. When it was wet the street must be cleared with shovels. Even the houses were never free of it. It came in on feet and clothes and wind; it nestled in the thatch and rained down on to beds and chairs and food and plates. Sometimes the mud even took lives. St Laur was so small that on a dark, misty night a stranger might ride through it all unaware. Just beyond the church the road bent deceptively. It seemed clear enough: obviously the good road was the wide one, while the wet path winding away to the left was more hazardous; but let an unfamiliar foot step carelessly on the safe-looking road, and let it be the wrong time of year, and let there be no-one about with a mind to help, and a man might disappear into the marsh in less time than it took him to repent him of his sins.

Once Lizzie and Pearl built a warning sign; it was gone next morning; and the following Sunday in church the sermon dwelt on the goodness of a God who gave man visible reminders of the truth that *broad is the way that leadeth to destruction*.

Lizzie shared her daughter's pale-skin, but her hair was a thick, yellow tangle much coveted by Pearl. Pearl loved to stroke and brush it but it was often salty and full of knots and Lizzie lost patience with the pain. Lizzie was often in pain. "Oooh-ah! There's no-one knows what I goes through along o' the backache!" And she had funny moods when she drifted off into sad, absorbing dreams behind her eyes and could only be called back at the peril of the caller. One of the many good things about the times when the train brought Mr Croft was that his very presence seemed to cure Lizzie's pains and moods.

The village women assumed sullen expressions when Lizzie and Pearl went by with Mr Croft; they envied them their rich visitor from London and the grand gifts he brought. Everyone knew about the bed that nearly filled their cottage, for it had taken all day to move it through the doorway; it had to be sawn in half and reassembled. When the oystermen came in cold from the boats on winter evenings, Lizzie sometimes invited them in to her house for rum-and-milk; then they sat on the bed, for there was nowhere else. This made their wives very angry, and the publican too, for who would buy his rum-and-milk if Lizzie was giving it away? But Lizzie was unrepentant. The oystermen were her friends, they made her eyes sparkle and her cheeks glow with their tales: "No sense in livin' if we doesn't have *friends*, Pearl." She laughed at the village women and called them a flock of mouldy biddies. She tossed her thick yellow hair at their husbands and laughed to see the women scowl. They said Lizzie was a lazybones who should work for her bread; yet when she bound her hair in ribbons and set off with them on the Colchester train with baskets of oysters they would stand all the way rather than sit by her. Left alone in the village, Pearl could not close her ears to the gossip that flooded like the tide: they said Lizzie sold other things besides oysters, they hinted it might not be too long before another little pearl was found in one of her shells, they said Mr Croft was Pearl's father.

It was not true. He was just a kind friend who knew they had not much money. He said when he gave Lizzie things, "There! Now you won't need to go to Colchester to sell oysters for a while." Pearl guessed he would not like it if he knew how often Lizzie did go, even with his money still jingling in her purse.

He seemed to Pearl to be a magnificent man, and she loved to look at him. He had a round, kind, if slightly sad, face, soft whiskers, a broad chest always encased in one or another of his interesting waistcoats, and legs which seemed not quite to fit him. Pearl could never work out why she had this impression; she never said anything in case she might be thought rude or silly, but it was another thing about him to look at. Once Pearl asked him if he was a hundred, and he said, "About half."

He was smart and rich because he came from London. But he was not happy there; he was only really happy in St Laur. He lived with his wife who was ill and his wife's sister who was horrible. Her name was Sarah and she lived with Mr and Mrs Croft because, Mr Croft said, she was too fierce to marry. She had gone all the way to Australia, married someone, and been sent back. Sometimes, in the evenings, Pearl sat on Lizzie's bed with Mr Croft and listened to his Sarah-stories. If it was winter, Mr Croft and Lizzie shared a bottle of stout and a plate of oysters. Pearl averted her eyes and ate cakes from London. The Sarah-stories (which Mr Croft admitted were not necessarily true, enjoyable though they were) always ended with Sarah getting into some sort of scrape.

When it was time to sleep, Lizzie made up a little nest with blankets and pillows for Pearl by the fire. Then Lizzie and Mr Croft climbed into their own big bed and pulled the curtains round. Sometimes Pearl felt lonely. They were having a lovely cuddle together in the darkness! There were rude words, Pearl knew, for a man and a woman together in the same bed, but they did not apply to her mother and Mr Croft. She pretended her nest by the fire was a smack far out on the estuary and she was hauling up nets full of pearly babies . . . the big bed rocked. She could reach out and touch it. Outside on the marsh, forlorn birds called across the lapping waters. Mr Croft was in her place but she must not be jealous: he brought so many things, he was so kind, the bed was his, it was only fair that he should sleep in it when the train brought him. It rocked again. It had never been quite steady on its legs since they took it apart to get it through the door.

Sometimes they whispered; yet it was lonelier still when they talked in normal voices and Pearl knew she was not expected to join in. She wished her mother would speak properly as Pearl knew Mr Croft liked, even though he never teased Lizzie as he teased Pearl.

"I'll have to think about a bigger place for you," he said, "when business is better."

Lizzie said, "In Colchester?"

"You know I don't want you in Colchester."

"You be shamed o' me and Pearl, Jonathan."

"Oh, Lizzie." The bed rocked. "You know how it is."

"I *know how it is*." Lizzie's voice was fierce.

"Don't you like St Laur? I love its peace."

"I likes Colchester best."

"It's not a good place for a child, Lizzie."

"My friends is there."

"You know I don't like you associating with – "

"I doesn't tell you who to 'sociate with."

The silence made Pearl nervous. Lizzie should not anger him. What if he went away and never came back? More gently, Lizzie said, "It were Colchester where I met you."

"I know," he whispered, "I don't want you meeting anybody else."

Lizzie's voice was very low now. Pearl knew she should not listen but it seemed important.

"Jonathan, maybe I be wicked to ask this, only – "

"Questions can't be wicked, Lizzie, only answers."

"If so be your – if Mrs Croft, Heaven forbid, were took – "

"Lizzie – "

"Would you stay in St Laur, along o' me and Pearl?"

"Lizzie, Lizzie, how can you even ask?"

They thought they were very clever, talking in whispers and half-sentences and secret code; but Pearl understood. If Mrs Croft died, which Heaven forbid, Mr Croft and Lizzie and Pearl would be together for-ever: there would be presents and cakes and stories every day of the week. Pearl clenched her fists. Mrs Croft was very ill and might die. But Pearl must not wish for it. That would be very wicked. What would be, would be.

The morning was as mornings always were, when the train that had brought Mr Croft was about to take him away again. He was brisk and anxious to be gone; Lizzie was irritable; Pearl was in agony for a promise of when he would return.

"Next time I have business in Colchester."

"When, oh when will that be?"

"Don't you be botherin' Mr Croft now, Pearl. Mr Croft be an important man."

He took out a leather diary and named a date some weeks ahead. Pearl jumped up and down; Lizzie pretended not to hear. But Pearl knew she liked to know when he was coming, so that it should not be a day when she went to Colchester.

The three of them walked through the mist and the mud to the train. Mr Croft looked very dark and solemn in his tall hat and long coat. Pearl wore her best dress, one of his gifts: dark blue with white cuffs and a sailor's collar. "Just right for a little girl who lives by the water," he had said. The air was chilly and wet but she did not want to cover the dress with a shawl. She wished Lizzie had put something nice on too. She wore an ordinary grey dress and her yellow hair was tangled like a bird's nest. Pearl knew she was angry with Mr Croft for going away, but looking cross and ugly was not the way to bring him back, was it? Lizzie should be grateful, as she was always telling Pearl to be, for the presents; and if Mr Croft was as important as she said, she ought not to bother him either. He had enough crossness and ugliness at home, with Sarah, his sister-in-law. Lizzie was far, far away. The only thing that brought her back as they walked through the village was the twitch of a curtain in a candlelit window. Lizzie gave a little bow and an unpleasant smile.

"Goodbye, goodbye!"

The train whistled and hissed, and heaved itself off into the grey, marshy dawn.

"Is Mr Croft my father?"

Lizzie seized Pearl's hand and strode off, dragging her.

"Is Mr Croft my father?"

"Mr Croft, Pearl, is our neighbour we must love as ourselves."

"Somebody said – "

"Then Heaven help somebody, whoever somebody be." And then, when Pearl said no more, Lizzie added, "I found you in a shell. I told you."

2

St Laur crouched on the raw, exposed bank of the estuary and took the icy sea-winds like slaps in the face. Hauled out of the water, many of the oysters would shudder and open and die, their shells flopping like the wings of a dead bird.

When spring came, it came in slow, grudging stages. Trees that sprouted early blossoms soon regretted their haste as they were blown bare by the savage easterly gusts. "Blows in from Russia, they does," Pearl heard a train driver tell a village woman. Russia sounded like the opposite of Australia, as far away but in another direction, icy and dark, whipping up winds from nowhere. Nights were heavy, wet and gritty, like black sand; days refused to lengthen. With the thaw, water seeped up through the dyke that carried the railway. For a whole week the trains did not run. A plague of green-bellied crabs set upon the oysters. A few daffodils came out, only to be felled in the night by frost. Pearl had holes in her boots. Lizzie said it was her own fault, running about on the beach. Chilblains burned her feet, but at night in the big bed Lizzie pushed her away: "Keep your nasty cold toes to yourself!" The mood of the weather seeped into Lizzie's soul: her eyes were full of pain and fear and anger and Pearl hated to look at her as she sat wrapped in shawls, staring into the fire until it died. More and more often she let it die. Once she slapped Pearl so hard that her ears rang all day, just for putting more wood on the fire without permission. Meals were scant, and there was no word from Mr Croft.

But he came again with the warm weather. He sent a note that the train would bring him soon, and meantime here was a huge hamper from Lackington's stores. No-one in St Laur ever had anything from Lackington's. Opening the hamper was as good as a second Christmas. The basket itself was alive with glorious possibilities: Pearl could hide in it, play in it, fill it with shells or flowers. She might even sleep in it for a few months, if she did not keep growing so fast. She buried her arms in the straw, finding new treasures at every plunge: a leg of mutton that she could hardly lift, a duck pie, cheeses, sausages, currant-cake; jars of jelly, marmalades and consommé; apples ruddier and shinier than Pearl had ever seen; biscuits, fruit-juices, stout and wine. Saliva poured into her mouth; she asked her mother if she might eat a piece of currant-cake, glad to be told no, she must wait till this evening; Pearl knew what real hunger was; this hunger that knew its fulfilment was only hours away was almost a pleasure.

The house filled up with delicious smells as Lizzie made ready the mutton. "Is he coming yet? Is he coming?"

"That train won't come no quicker for you shoutin' 'bout it."

"It's coming, it's coming, I hear it!" But she realised it was only the afternoon train that she heard.

"I'll tell 'em, I'll tell' em," Lizzie muttered, sweeping furiously, her eyes tight shut against the dust she raised.

"What will you tell 'em?"

"I know, I know! The minute they smells that mutton! They'll come a-sniffin' and nosin' round! 'Good meat, Lizzie,' they'll say. 'Don't often get a smell like that in St Laur! Don't suppose you'll have much left over! Not even for folk as can't remember the taste o' meat like that!' Some people ain't got no pride! 'Good meat, Lizzie!' "

"If they do come, Mother, will you give them any?"

"I'll give to them as doesn't turn up their noses at me! Or whisper scandal in your ears!"

Pearl dressed gloomily in her sailor dress. There would be hard words; the day was spoilt. It was too cold for the sailor dress but she wanted to look her best to meet Mr Croft. With the night, thick mist descended; the spring had gone back into the ground. Pearl heard the train before she saw it and had to run fast to reach the Halt before it did. Her chest ached. To have waited all day and now be late! To have had all day to make herself ready and now to arrive muddy and tousled and out of breath!

The black engine stopped, showing its contempt for St Laur and its mist with a stream of loud, thick steam. Beams of light from the carriage windows cut into the night like blades. Doors opened, time seemed to stop. Mr Croft was always the last to get off; perhaps he did it on purpose.

A lady stepped down from a third-class carriage. Ladies did not usually travel in that part of the train, which was why she caught Pearl's attention. Her clothes looked expensive, if not a very good fit. Her hat was skewed, her collar ruffled, and she seemed to have lost a glove. She looked back into the carriage for it in an impatient way. She seemed very annoyed. She was older than Lizzie but not as old as Mr Croft; her face was dark and weather-beaten, like a fisherman's face. She gave up the search for her glove, and, looking over her shoulder, disappeared briskly into the mist. Pearl turned anxiously again to look for Mr Croft; she did not want to return along that road alone.

Down he stepped from the first-class carriage, broad and nimble and grey-whiskered, putting on the hat that made him even taller as soon as his head was free of the door. She ran to him.

"Well, my little Pearl!"

"Well, Father!"

She had not meant to say that. If she had thought about it, she would have held it back. Lizzie would be furious, and Mr Croft's anger was an unknown thing. But if he heard, he did not respond. He just took her hand in his big glove.

"Mother's cookin' mutton! I mean cooking."

"Why, have you been out catching sheep again?"

"*You* sent it!"

"Did I?"

As they approached the house, Pearl heard Lizzie arguing and bantering with some men around her door. She had brushed her hair about her shoulders and was wearing her best yellow dress with the big graceful sleeves. She laughed and shook a broom at the men. "Do you go home now to your missus!" Pearl glanced up at Mr Croft's face; it was blank and tolerant. It was happy. It made her think of times when she had had something heavy to carry, and the lightness in her bones when she set it down. He strode through the mist and took Lizzie in his arms. The men went away, tipping their caps.

They settled in warmly for the night. Pearl busied herself pushing rags against cracks to keep the mist out and the delicious smell of meat in. She tried not to watch as Lizzie and Mr Croft sat on the bed eating oysters. Lizzie opened them, she said Mr Croft was all thumbs. She wrapped the oyster in a cloth, held it at eye-level and inserted the end of her knife. Then she lowered it, giving the knife a little twist: the shells of the oyster fell apart. Sometimes they fought. Lizzie said that was a good sign. An oyster that opened too easily might not be fresh. Sinewy strings held the oyster tight against the blade. Pearl winced. Lizzie discarded the flat shell into a bucket where it could be saved for building paths. She raised the round shell with the grey fish in it to her lips and tipped. The fish slipped sullenly into her mouth and went down whole. Pearl saw Lizzie's throat move. Lizzie smacked her lips and sipped again, this time at the puddle of seawater and juice that remained, of which she was always telling

Pearl, "Do you drink this, Pearl, and you'll live to be a hundred and one."

Mr Croft tried and failed to open one: it clattered to the floor. "Take care, Pearl, that oyster be comin' for you!" Lizzie cried, chasing her, and they all fell on the bed, rocking and laughing.

"Was that someone at the door?"

"No – it's the bed – creaks to wake the dead some nights Jonathan – you'd best take it back to the shop." But the knocking continued and Pearl went to answer. Lizzie shivered and grumbled as she pulled away the rags from the bottom of the door. "This place only just got warm. Tell em we've et it all."

Pearl opened the door. It was the lady from the train. But she did not look so angry now; she looked cold and inquisitive. Her glance shot past Pearl and took in the scene, the warm room, the big bed, the playful poses and expressions in which the inhabitants were frozen, and her eyes shone with a sudden red mist as if she would cry. Pearl thought it might be embarrassment: the lady had come to the wrong house, she would apologise and be on her way; but the tears dried as fast as they had come. The lady pushed her way into the house, leaving muddy footprints on the floor. She planted herself squarely in front of Mr Croft; Pearl saw his lips in the midst of his whiskers, soft and trembling like a woman's.

"Well, Jonathan! You seem to have a very cosy establishment here!"

"Good evening, Sarah." *Sarah!* Pearl stared.

Lizzie dropped an oyster shell with a loud clack and stood up. "Shut that door, Pearl!" she barked. Mist was swirling into the room. "There's no-one knows what that wind'll blow in next." She glared at the mud the lady's feet had brought. Sarah met her eyes and apologised stiffly for it. She sniffed the fragrant air, then seemed to catch sight of Pearl for the first time. She looked from her face back to Mr Croft's face, several times.

"Won't you sit down, ma'am?" said Pearl politely.

"Why thank you! Where should I sit?" Sarah did not want to sit on the bed. "What is your name?"

"Pearl."

"And mine is Sarah Packham. You may call me Aunt Sarah, for it seems we are related in a kind of way."

"Don't jump to conclusions, Sarah," warned Mr Croft.

Dogs acted like this: mangy dogs that got lost on the marsh and wandered into St Laur to sniff at gutters and rubbish. When they wanted a fight, they did not go straight to it; they sniffed and circled, warned and snapped, getting the measure of one another, trying to make the other give in and go away. A moment would come when the tension would break, when each would realise that the other was not going to give in or go away; then the first to attack, to go for the throat, would have the advantage.

Mr Croft went for the throat. "You followed me. Like a spy."

"I too have business with the women of Colchester, Jonathan. I suppose it is permitted."

"Sarah does *rescue work*," Mr Croft said.

"What do she rescue?" Lizzie sneered. "Ducks?"

Mr Croft was looking round the room, as if for a means of escape. Finding none, he attacked again. The fear and cruelty in his voice made Pearl colder than the draught of wind at her back.

"She is collecting women to rescue, reform and export to Australia. Admirable. But Sarah, I did not know that you had extended your field of operations beyond Leicester Square."

"You dare to mock me, Jonathan Croft! How long – how old is this child?"

"Ten," said Pearl, and cowered before her mother's raised fist.

"Ten! Ten, eh? And it is fifteen years since you married my sister."

"I said don't jump to conclusions, Sarah!"

"I shall not, then! I shall maintain a completely open mind! I shall place no interpretation whatever on what I see! I come to Colchester on business for Ladies Progress – "

"Secretly, you come!"

"No, not secretly! Without your knowledge, perhaps, but I think I am not accountable to you, even if I am at present forced to accept your hospitality, every bit as unwillingly, I assure you, as you give it! I wondered if I might meet you – if we might by some chance have the pleasure of travelling to London together – but when I caught sight of you burdened with parcels at the station in Colchester, I found you were not bound for London after all."

"So you decided to follow me."

"I did. Call it curiosity. I wonder if my sister was ever similarly curious about your visits to Colchester. I hope they did not cause her too much anxiety, her health being so delicate."

Pearl stood very still as Mr Croft tried to pace up and down but kept blundering into things. "How did you – " he began. "I have learned many things I did not know about life." Sarah said, "through my work with Ladies Progress." "Damn your Ladies Progress!" said Mr Croft. "And amen to that, say the gentlemen of England!" Sarah retorted.

Lizzie whispered behind him, "Who be this, Jonathan?"

Mr Croft said, "I have the honour of presenting my sister-in-law – "

"Sarah Packham. The late Mrs Croft was my sister."

Lizzie said softly, "The . . . late . . . Mrs . . . Croft."

Pearl could think of nothing but whether a lady who had been sent home from Australia by her husband should be called Miss Packham or Mrs Packham.

Lizzie repeated, "The late Mrs Croft." And she stared at Miss Packham, who stared back at her. Pearl wanted to grab Mr Croft's hand and run away with him, leaving the two women transfixed by each other's accusation. "What be she sayin', Jonathan? The *late* Mrs Croft."

"You mean he did not tell you she is dead? Well, no. He would not. He has been a widower these four years."

Mr Croft opened his mouth. Pearl knew he was planning to lie. She knew well that feeling of nervousness. She knew the feeling of deciding not to as well. He did not lie, he did not speak. Pearl wept. The smell from the mutton was sour and smoky. She was not hungry any more, but she could not bear the waste. She glared at Miss Packham's hard face and twisted collar, her red hands clenching and unclenching, cold from her lost gloves. Why could she not disappear as she had come? Then Mr Croft and Lizzie could get married and they could all be happy.

Lizzie was ordering Miss Packham from the house.

"I have no wish to stay. But where should I go?"

"Devil take you, spreadin' lies."

"If it were a lie," said Miss Packham, "he would have denied it." And the two of them looked at Mr Croft, sitting on the bed with his face in his hands.

"Is there another train?" No-one answered. Pearl knew there was not but she would not speak to her. "How did people get out of St Laur before there was a railway?"

Lizzie sniffed. "They walked. But they wasn't fine ladies from London."

"I am unafraid of the elements, I assure you," Miss Packham retorted; and she strode out into the cold, wet night.

Savagely Pearl bolted the door. She hurt her fingers cramming rags against the cracks. When the job was done, she did it again, her teeth biting against her lips; she did not want to turn round, she did not want to hear what she heard or know what she knew; she just wanted to wake up. Burning points of cold on her body told her where the wind was still coming through, told her she was not asleep.

"Lizzie, Lizzie – "

"Lizzie, Lizzie! Four years is it since your poor wife was took? And you never breathed a word! Was you 'fraid of keepin' your promise and marryin' me? Don't you worry, Jonathan Croft! Soldiers' woman you may think me, but I be too good for the likes of you!"

Memories of her birth from an oyster-shell slipped from Pearl like a distant dream . . . how could she have believed such a thing . . . yet it was safe in the tight grey darkness with the mud overhead . . .

The mud overhead . . . what if Miss Packham chose the wrong path as she strode out of the village? What if she sank in the marsh?

Let her! Pearl had already wished her dead many times, when she was only a character in Mr Croft's stories! How much more could she wish her dead now!

But to sink in the mud . . .

"Get out, get out, get out!" Lizzie's voice rose till it sounded inhuman, the command was directed at Mr Croft but Pearl took it for herself, she snatched madly at the rags around the door, chose the biggest one for a shawl, and ran out after Miss Packham.

The cold on her burning cheeks calmed her. She heard her muffled footfalls on the street and stopped to listen for others which she never heard. Miss Packham could not have gone far. Perhaps she had found the inn and taken a room for the night. The Halt loomed up, with its three-plank platform. Maybe Miss Packham was sheltering there, waiting for the morning train. She would be cold . . . let her freeze to death, then. Pearl just did not want her sinking into the marsh.

"Miss Packham! Miss Packham!" Her voice sounded strange. Birds cried back from the marsh; and that was all. She would call once more, then her Christian duty was done: Miss Packham had found the inn.

"Miss Pack-ham. Miss Pack – !"

"Help, Oh, help me!"

Suddenly Pearl did not want to help her. The cry was more like an irritated command than a desperate plea for life. The dim shapes of the village seemed far behind; she shouted across the darkness. "I'll fetch ropes, I'll bring the men! You should lie down, Miss Packham, lie down on your back – "

"Are you mad, child? I am quite muddy enough."

"Then you won't sink – "

"I am not sinking. I am just stuck."

At last Pearl found her: not really in danger, only ankle-deep and frightened and cross. Pearl shouted the way to a path built by the men out of upturned shells. Miss Packham gave off a damp, fishy smell.

"Goodness me, Pearl."

"You be safe now. Don't you be frightened, Miss Packham." She had said she might call her Aunt Sarah; but Pearl did not want to.

"Did you think I was frightened? I've been in tighter spots than *that*."

"In Australia?"

"How do you know about that, Pearl?"

"Mr Croft told me." *He told me stories about how horrible you were, and they were all true. I can hear my mother crying, after what you said to her.* Pearl stopped herself. For the first time she realised that the woman everyone was so angry about – the late Mrs Croft – was Miss Packham's sister. If Pearl had a sister and she died, might not the sadness make her angry too? Miss Packham was shivering, brushing off mud and talking about Australia, as if to herself. "Shivering wouldn't be the problem there! At this moment it is a hot, golden day at my farm in New South Wales."

"You should warm yourself before you catch cold."

"I'll freeze to death before I go back to Jonathan's love-nest."

Love-nest sounded nice. "Poor little Pearl, I shouldn't talk this way in front of you, should I?"

"I'm not a baby. I'm ten."

"I know, and you came to rescue me when I'm sure you don't like me much. But there are things in the world that there's plenty of time for you to know."

Pearl took her to the inn. Was it true she didn't like her? She felt sorry for her being so cold and muddy, and because her sister was dead; she pitied the icy hand in hers. But she wanted to let go of it; to let it fall in the mud, melt in the darkness with the rest of Miss Packham. Why had she come? Would bringing misery to St Laur raise her sister from the dead? It would not. Lizzie was shouting furiously from far away.

"Should you like to come and visit me in Australia one day, Pearl?"

"Here's the inn."

"If it's going to be full of gossip," Miss Packham warned, "I shall sleep in the open. I've slept in the open in Australia."

"But shivering wasn't the problem in Australia," said Pearl.

"Mock me, would you?" Miss Packham's voice sounded amused, but she spoke sternly. Then she solemnly shook hands. "I shan't forget that you saved me from the marsh, Pearl!" It sounded like something between a promise and a threat.

3

Mr Croft came once more to the village. The morning train brought him just one week after the cold dark night when Miss Packham had come and revealed the secret that made Lizzie send him away "for ever". He came bent double with parcels and abloom with flowers. Lizzie ignored the presents, stamped on the blooms and told him to get back where he came from. Pearl cried and pleaded. He might have brought her some new boots, so that at least her feet could be dry. Mr Croft said Pearl might keep the parcels even if Lizzie sent him away. Lizzie turned a terrible face on Pearl.

"If you take a farthin' from that fine gennelman, then off you goes to London along o' him, for you're no daughter of mine."

And so Mr Croft went away with his parcels and they never saw him again in St Laur; and Pearl missed him and cried for him, though she was glad enough of his place in Lizzie's bed; and she wondered what had happened to Miss Packham and if she and Mr Croft still lived in the same house, fighting like dogs, or if Miss Packham had gone back to Australia and perhaps drowned on the way. It was a sad, hungry time, as the last of Mr Croft's gifts of food ran out and Lizzie made less and less money from selling oysters and the season came to an end; but Pearl did not regret the choice she had made, when Lizzie said she must either refuse Mr Croft's parcels or go with him, for she never wanted to take the risk of seeing Miss Packham again. She felt uneasy as she had never felt before about town folk and city folk; perhaps the village women were right about there being no good in the railway that brought them to St Laur; and anyway, St Laur was her home.

And so Pearl did not know quite what to think when the summer came and Lizzie announced that they were moving to Colchester to work at an inn, where there would be enough to eat and friends to talk to and they would be far away from gossiping tongues.

"What would Mr Croft say?"

"Who?" Lizzie's voice was dangerous.

Pearl remembered words whispered from the bed: *You know I don't want you in Colchester. I likes Colchester best. It's not a good place for a child.*

He thought she was a child.

"Mr Croft. I was wondering. If he sees us in Colchester."

"Mr Croft don't care for us no more, Pearl. Sometimes gennelmen is like that. They pretends and acts kind but they doesn't mean it."

Another time, Pearl might have hotly denied any slander against Mr Croft. But Lizzie's voice shook and she buried her face in her hands and cried; and Pearl longed for a trace of anger in her sadness, for Lizzie often said things she did not mean when she was angry; but she was not angry, she meant everything. Pearl stroked helplessly at her mother's yellow hair, waiting, when she caught her fingers in the tangles, for the cuff and the shout of rage that never came.

Lizzie sold the bed and all the furniture and bought first-class tickets for the journey from St Laur. They were very expensive, but Lizzie wore her best dress and was determined.

"I be goin' of my own free will," she said.

"So am I," said Pearl.

"I won't have them a-thinkin' I'm runnin' away."

The seats in the first-class carriage were purple velvet with gold braid: if Pearl raked her fingers across the fabric, they left white trails which slowly melted back into purple as the threads rearranged themselves. It reminded Pearl of fields of crops with the wind rushing through them. She fiddled with the adjustable leather arms that divided the seats into four. Lizzie told her to sit still but she could not. This was her first train journey, apart from the short rides to the end of the line that drivers sometimes allowed St Laur children when the train was not full . . . her first time to Colchester, most definitely her first time in First Class! Whistles blew, doors slammed. She pressed her face against the window, peering hard at the glass to escape the feeling of shyness that would accompany her last sight of St Laur. She saw streaks of soot on the window, and streaks of soap, and streaks of salt. When she breathed out a fine mist appeared: she started to write her name. Lizzie clicked her teeth and asked what if somebody saw – they were alone in the first-class compartment, but that made no difference. Each time the train stopped, Pearl hoped and dreaded that someone would get in with them. Some grand person might order them from the compartment – or some kind gentleman might raise his hat and bid them good day.

The wheels of the train screamed on a curve. The low grey roofs of St Laur were lost from view.

"We can come back whenever we want, can't we, Mother? On the train."

Lizzie did not reply.

It was a bright, sunny morning, and the low-roofed farmhouses and the brown-and-white cows looked scrubbed and freshly rinsed; there were patches of brilliant green in the wet, sparkling fields. Pearl could see birds with their beaks open, mouthing songs: the noise of the train stole the music of the songs.

The wheels sang: *Lovely oysters, threepence a dozen, lovely oysters, threepence a dozen.* When they changed speed they shouted: *Oysters from St Laur! Oysters from St Laur!* Pearl did not know she was joining in until Lizzie slapped her.

"Folk will think we be oystergirls."

Pearl was puzzled. But she shrugged her shoulders and changed the subject. "Will we see Colchester soon?"

"Not if we doesn't look."

Pearl looked. The carriage was enveloped in white steam; it might be flying through the air in a cloud. As the steam thinned and cleared, Pearl saw a face watching her. She started. It had been there a long time. It was Miss Packham! No, it wasn't. It was her own reflection, that was all. The moment of thinking it was Miss Packham was a short one, but enough to make her hands go wet with shock. It was Pearl setting off to make her fortune! Perhaps Miss Packham had had the same brave expression when she set off for Australia; did you go by train to Australia? Of course not: you went by ship. Pearl supposed that the branch line from St Laur to Colchester was not in quite the same category of adventurousness as sailing to Australia, but then Miss Packham was a grown woman. How many adventures had Miss Packham had when she was ten, Pearl would like to know! And why did she keep thinking about her anyway, when it was her fault that Mr Croft had gone away, her fault that they were leaving St Laur?

Pearl was so deep in thought that she almost missed seeing what was happening with the railway: a second single track snaked towards them down a slope, to be scooped up by their own track into a thicker one. Pearl waited for another train and hoped it would not hit them.

Lizzie hugged her fiercely. "Pearl. Look!" And there was Colchester: a huge city, bigger than ten St Laurs! Red, white and brown brick buildings gleaming in the sun across the field! Little clouds of smoke above hundreds of chimneys! Factories and churches, big houses, little houses, and then the great cathedral! To have lived in St Laur was like a childish dream: to have played in a single muddy street, to have waited, excited, for four trains a day. Pearl felt herself grow taller as the train pulled into the station; and then she knew no more for several hours.

Lizzie told her later that she had fallen asleep as suddenly as if she had been hit over the head, and had to be carried from the train and taken by cab to the Periwinkle; humiliating though this allegation was, Pearl had to believe it, because in the weeks that followed she kept falling unexpectedly asleep, not only when she was tired, which she often was, but when she was excited or overwhelmed or confused; and she was often all those things too, in her new life.

The Periwinkle was in a narrow, winding thoroughfare between two main streets: it reminded Pearl in a funny way of the marsh outside St Laur, for it looked much wider and more accessible to carriages than it was, and blockages and collisions were common. It was near the barracks and very noisy: day and night, people shouted and fought, chased each other and laughed and cried and sold things; they were like the tide on the river at St Laur, sometimes in ebb, sometimes in flow, sometimes vigorous and thronging, sometimes soft and lapping, but never still.

A wooden sign swung from a metal hook above the door. The hook looked eaten through with rust and the sign very heavy, as

126

if it would fall; but Pearl liked to stand under it, looking at the hole in the plump black periwinkle pictured there with a few bubbles going up through the blue water. Each day she fancied she saw deeper and deeper into the hole, and wondered if the artist had actually painted a creature inside the shell.

Mrs Chicksey said the Periwinkle was three hundred years old and had been falling down from the day it was built. Scars, cracks and patchworks of different stone in the walls seemed to prove this was true. It was a Chicksey family tradition never to turn away a soldier, even if, in the past, it had meant packing them in like feet in tight boots, and building annexes; Mrs Chicksey regarded the recent building of the new barracks and consequent reduction in demand for private billets for soldiers as a personal insult to herself, her inn and her annexes.

The annexes, the repairs, the shoring-up operations and the walls half-erected to conceal these and then forgotten about, all resulted in the exact shape of the Periwinkle being a great mystery to Pearl: she could never be sure how it was that she climbed five flights of stairs to reach the little bedroom with the curtain down the middle that she shared with Lizzie, while from the outside it only seemed to be on the third floor.

Sometimes, just before she fell asleep, she thought she understood; but the explanation disappeared in her dreams.

She had to clear bottles and pots and glasses and tankards from the bar-room to the kitchen. Being small helped: the people who came to drink in the Periwinkle found the most ingenious places to hide their glasses. Sometimes Pearl thought they did it on purpose, as she crawled under tables or placed one chair on another to reach a shelf. Evenings were the busy time: Mrs Chicksey roared furiously if she ran out of glasses. Pearl never dared to say how tired she was; but she took every chance for a cat-nap, sometimes finding a corner to curl up in, sometimes losing consciousness without warning, as suddenly as she had in the train and a good deal more awkwardly.

Lizzie was strange. Finding Pearl asleep, she was as likely to cradle her in her arms and smooth her hair (waking her up, but Pearl didn't mind) as to shove her roughly and shout, "There's work to be done!" When there was no work, she was as likely to say, "Do you go out, now Pearl! I never knowed such a gel for hangin' about!" as she was to rage when she returned: "What have you been at? I never knowed such a gel for mischief!"

Pearl did not get into mischief. She wandered in the little streets near the Periwinkle, went to the barracks, the market. She looked in shop windows, working out how long it would take her to afford the things she saw there if she saved the penny-a-week Mrs Chicksey gave her. There was a woman with bandaged legs at the sink of the Chickseys' kitchen who claimed to have been a governess and offered Pearl tuition by shouting words whenever she saw her and demanding that Pearl spell them. This stopped when the woman asked Lizzie for a small fee, but Pearl went on learning. She looked at notices on walls, combining what they looked as if they ought to say with what she knew of letters, and taught herself to read. Crowds pushed her forward, shoppers and beggars and soldiers, and pressed her back. She felt in her pocket for coins and went to a coffee-house. She was the only child there on her own and the serving girl demanded to see her money before bringing her anything. The curious frowns of ladies behind silk veils were the last things she saw before opening her eyes again – she had slept for hours, the coffee-house was closing. A gentleman stood over her, said she should come with him if she had no home; she skipped away, laughing. Lizzie was angry when she told her.

The Periwinkle never closed its doors. The hardest work was in the evening. The customers had worse manners than in the daytime. They got in Pearl's way, crowding at the bar to talk to the barmaids, especially Lizzie, who was the prettiest. Pearl was proud of her, standing there with flushed cheeks and sparkling eyes, but she wished she would stop putting paint on her face. She was following the example of the women who lived at the inn, the ones who called themselves "Queen's Women" as a joke and weren't proper customers but didn't work behind the bar or in the kitchen. They seemed very rich and had beautiful clothes, but Pearl did not think they were proper ladies. Not that she had met many ladies, but she could not imagine Miss Packham, for instance, sidling up to a soldier, slipping her arm into his, whispering and joking and leading him away, and then asking him his name! But the Queen's Women were jollier than Miss Packham by a long chalk! Then there was Ratty. He looked after the rats that fought with customers' dogs, and collected the money for bets. He looked like a rat. He had red, darting eyes and yellow teeth and ice-cold fingers. Pearl could not understand how he could be so careful and affectionate with his rats, naming them and stroking their necks, and then put them to fight huge bull-mastiffs, sometimes starving them for days beforehand to make them fiercer. He pretended to get his words muddled when he talked to Pearl, calling her "Girl, my little pearl", instead of "Pearl my little girl".

"Come and stroke Prince Albert, girl!"

"It's Pearl," she said.

"Is it? Well bless my soul."

Prince Albert was a long, sleek black rat with ribs that stuck out. "I don't want to stroke that one."

"How 'bout this un, then? I be thinkin' of callin' her Pearl."

"If you do," said Pearl, "I won't talk to you any more."

As the evenings grew late and the great firelit room filled up with people and laughter and songs and smoke, Pearl wished she was tiny, she wished she was ten feet tall. How quickly she could push through the crowd if she was thin and flat like a sheet of paper . . . soldiers' uniforms danced before her eyes in a zigzag of red and gold, and the Queen's Women teased her for taking their bottles away before they were empty, she was crushed and wished she was taller for then at least she would be crushed face-to-face, and not face-to-belly or backside; and then, if she was taller, she would be able to see her mother all the time, not just in glimpses, pink-faced, her hair spread out and golden like a saint's, chattering and laughing while she pulled beer from the pumps and tested gold coins on her teeth . . . She was like a lamp, lit up for the night, Pearl wished she could light up her mother's spirits as the men in the Periwinkle could, as the oystermen in St Laur could when they came to the cottage for their rum-and-milk, as Mr Croft could once.

Pearl wasn't tired. She couldn't remember what it was to feel tired. She felt leaf-light on her feet, the crush of people only irritated her, stopping her moving as fast as she could. Her head spun with energy, she learned to carry ten, twenty, a hundred glasses, she need not even carry them, she could toss them and Lizzie would catch them and smile and she could dart once more into the forest of drinkers, she was growing taller, she was whirling high above everybody's head and plucking bottles out of the air, tipping beer down men's throats to get the bottles and everyone was laughing and someone was cross . . . and she was asleep, she was awake again. It was dark early morning. Everyone had gone; she lay on the floor in the dust. The fire was dead. She had been left without so much as a shawl to cover her. She crept shivering to bed, passing a soldier and a Queen's Woman giggling on the stairs.

Lizzie's bed was empty. Pearl crept stiffly between her own cold sheets. She didn't know how much later it was that she heard her mother tiptoe in behind the curtain.

"Where've you been, Mother?"

"Ssh, go to sleep."

"You left me behind."

"You looked so peaceful, sleepin' there."

Pearl had to be content with that.

"Mother."

"Oh, what now?"

Pearl yawned. "Wouldn't it be nice if you had Mr Croft in there with you?"

"Him! We doesn't need him no more, Pearl. We got lots of friends." Lizzie started to snore. Pearl supposed she had better follow her example. She could hear the sounds of the Periwinkle starting to wake up, and soon another day's work would begin.

4

When anything went wrong at the Periwinkle, Mrs Chicksey blamed the soldiers. If there was a fight, soldiers started it. If windows or plates were broken or lost, soldiers were at fault. If the washerwomen complained about filth on the sheets it was because soldiers went to bed with their boots on.

Pearl thought this ungrateful and unfair, considering soldiers were the Periwinkle's best customers: also, they were in Colchester to defend the Empire for everybody. It was Pearl's private opinion that the trouble with Mrs Chicksey – and Lizzie too, for that matter, for Lizzie was as ready as anyone to slander a uniform – was that they didn't see the soldiers at their best. Let them come with Pearl up to the barracks one morning and watch them parading and training and it would be a different story!

Lizzie had not actually forbidden Pearl to go to the barracks, but then Pearl had not actually told Lizzie that she went. She had a feeling it might be banned. You met all kinds of people round the walls, some of them very rough. You had to pass houses and inns far more tumble down than the Periwinkle, with broken windows where sluttish women glared at you and tipped things down into the street; and children rushed at you, begging and threatening, children so dirty and ragged and thin that Pearl thought herself the most fortunate of girls, and felt guilty about her decision never to take money with her when she went to the barracks.

It was a shame not to have money; there were always good things to buy: oranges, roast chestnuts, ginger-beer, hot green peas and apple pies. There were women who would wash soldiers' shirts better and more cheaply than their neighbours would, and would fight to prove it; and flower-sellers who sidled up to officers with ladies and shamed them into buying a bloom or two. And, come September, Pearl supposed there would be oyster-sellers as well; this must be where Lizzie used to come.

After the stifling chaos of the Periwinkle, Pearl loved the order and regularity of the parade ground. The barracks were like a little town in a big town: rows of wooden huts, all level with each other, and some finer houses for the officers, and flags, and stables, and strange frames and equipment which intrigued Pearl even though they frightened her. Sometimes she saw six straw sacks hung on a frame in soldiers' jackets, and real soldiers practised running at them and stabbing them with bayonets. The soldiers growled and roared and dug into the sacks till Pearl was sure blood and guts would run out. However hard and often they did it, the head soldier shouted that it wasn't good enough, they must do it again. From their ferocity, Pearl supposed they were pretending the sacks were Prussians, or French. Pearl preferred parades.

When the soldiers formed themselves into rows and lines, and great wide rays of sunlight lit up the reds and whites and blues and golds of their uniforms and they started stepping across the parade ground, hundreds of men acting as one, she started to tremble till she nearly fell off the wall where she sat. The banging of their feet thumped into her heart. The commanding officer barked like a dog. When the band played, it was almost too much for her: the beauty of the trumpets and the drums and the pipes and the trombones made her feel sick. And she would have to go away and find a quiet spot for a snooze and sometimes a happy little weep. And she would be drowsy and giggly and irritable for the rest of the day and nobody would know why.

Once when she was watching at the barracks, two of the Queen's

Women from the Periwinkle came by. Everyone called them "the two Di's". Their names were Dinah and Diana and they were inseparable friends. They were alike too, both plump, with round eyes, round noses with round nostrils, and wide mouths which they tried to make appear round by applying bright red paint. They always spoiled this effect by smiling too much. Two minutes after putting on the paint it would have spread all over the lower parts of their faces, like an egg in a frying pan.

People thought they were sisters, but the two Di's scoffed.

"Woman 'ud have more sense than give two girls the same name."

"And what woman ever turned up trumps twice anyway?"

Still, they were remarkably alike. Perhaps it was because they dressed similarly. They drew many admiring glances today, in their white silk blouses and full, rainbow-coloured skirts all a-flutter with petticoats. As they hurried along, Dinah's skirt caught the sun at a different angle from Diana's, emphasising the blue of the rainbow, while Diana's looked more greenish and violet. People shouted, asking where they were going. Pearl wished they weren't wearing those hats, though. There had been talk in the Periwinkle about the Di's having bought new hats and here they were. If you bought hats like that it was only to be expected that you would want to give them an airing on a bright sunny day, but why orange and why bright scarlet? They were like loud sounds drowning out the soft whispers of the rainbow. Still, their friends here outside the barracks seemed to admire the hats. And it was nice to see the Di's. Pearl slithered down the wall and ran to them.

"Hel-*lo*, Pearl! What are you doin' up so early?"

It wasn't early at all, it was nearly midday. But people's getting-up times were an endless source of chaffing in the Periwinkle.

"Grabbin' the best lads, are you?"

"Not much chance for us, eh, Di?"

"Not much, Di."

Pearl grabbed Dinah's hand and skipped along beside her. "Where are you going?" She didn't really care where they were going, it was just something to say while she worked out how she was going to bring the conversation round to the subject of ginger-beer, at which point it might occur to them to buy her some.

"Nowhere," said Dinah quickly.

"Always askin' questions," said Diana at the same time.

And they quickened their pace. Pearl felt frustrated but crafty. So it was somewhere interesting! And she couldn't go!

"Tell me! Oh tell me, please!"

"We be goin' to the hospital and we be late already," said Dinah. Diana glared at her.

"Are you bad?"

The Di's nudged each other and giggled. "Hope not."

"The hospital's the other way!"

"Oh, the hospital's the other way, *is* it?" They teased her for talking in the proper way Mr Croft had taught her. "It's the soldiers' hospital, Pearl. We be goin' to visit a poor friend. Ain't we, Di?"

"That's right. Now do you stop makin' a bother Pearl, or he'll be took by the time we gets there. You want some ginger-beer?"

They left Pearl sulkily eyeing the coin they gave her, the same coin which caught the attention of a tall, dusty boy of about her own age with holes in the knees of his trousers. He approached her.

"Who's that? Your ma and your aunty?"

She remembered, *You may call me Aunt Sarah, for it seems we are related* . . .

"They're Queen's Women," she told him.

He guffawed hugely in his squeaky voice. *"You don't say so!"* He was mocking her speech too. "Goin' up the meat-market, be they?"

"They've gone to the hospital to visit a soldier."

He said again, "You don't say so!" It struck Pearl as an absurd thing to keep repeating, when she quite clearly *did* say.

"I do. And you are a very rude, dirty boy. So please go away." She wanted her ginger-beer but she had no intention of buying it with him waiting for a share.

He spat. "I knows what you doesn't."

"Know what?"

"Where they be goin'."

"To the soldiers' hospital, to – "

"You don't say so!"

Pearl eyed the boy and considered. She should not have anything to do with him, he looked neither honest nor healthy. But he had whetted her curiosity. The two Di's had a secret. If they had told her what it was, or even if they had told her it was private and none of her business, she would have accepted that. But they had lied to her. And liars deserved to be unmasked.

"Do you really know?"

"Everyone knows," he jeered, " 'cept you. Little know-nothing."

"Tell then."

He glanced around in a lordly way, and spotted a man selling hot green peas. "Buy me some o' them and I'll tell you." She hesitated. "I be that hungry," he said.

She bought him some, knowing he planned to gobble them up and still not tell her. Cunningly, she put on a peaceful expression and watched him eat a spoonful. Then she snatched the dish. "Now tell!"

"They looks at their arses," he said.

"Who does?"

"The doctors. They takes down their drawers, and – "

"They do not!"

"All right, *they do not* then!" He made a grab at the peas. "Gimme those, little break-promise!"

"But you haven't told me!"

"I have! They be Queen's Women, they gets pox on their arses and they go with soldiers and then the soldiers is poxed."

"Why?"

"Because the soldiers fucks them."

Pearl threw the dish of peas on the ground and ran. She knew that word. She had heard it at the Periwinkle. She had never asked its meaning. She felt she knew already, not a proper kind of knowing in her head, but a horrible sick feeling. It was only ever said jokingly, or as part of a sly conversation that died away with her approach. It was a hard, horrid word, even spoken silently. The two Di's didn't look ill. But if the pox was *there*, you wouldn't see, would you? Did Lizzie do that thing, might she become poxed and have to go to the hospital to be looked at? Might Pearl herself get a disease? She knew about some diseases: fevers and colds in the nose and skin diseases and diseases of the insides that the women in St Laur sometimes died of when they had babies . . . but diseases *there*? Having to take your clothes off and be looked at *there*?

She would never feel the same about the two Di's.

She crept back to the Periwinkle, past the kitchen where Lizzie was having a good laugh with the kitchen maids (had they got diseases?) and up to her bed where she slept and slept. It was dark when she came sheepishly down to the bar-room and started gathering glasses and mugs. Lizzie took her aside and berated her for her laziness. She told her Mrs Chicksey paid her and kept her to work, not sleep and make a nuisance of herself. In future she was not to wander off alone. Pearl guessed the two Di's had told her mother she was at the barracks, asking questions.

Pearl made her face as repentant and innocent as possible. "Is he better?"

"Who?"

"The poor soldier the two Di's went to visit at the hospital?"

Lizzie's brow cleared. She laughed with surprise and relief. But Pearl noticed the hesitation before she said, "Oh, he be fine, Pearl," and Pearl knew she was lying; which meant that the two Di's had also lied; and the dusty boy had told the truth.

5

The weather grew colder, the leaves began to fall. Oyster-sellers appeared on the streets of the town with the new season's grey pungent crop, and Pearl had her birthday. Mrs Chicksey gave her a silver sixpence and the two Di's gave her a doll. It had a china head with eyes that opened and closed and a soft cloth body. The woman in the kitchen with bandaged legs gave her a special spelling lesson: now that she was eleven, she ought to know how to spell words like elephant, catastrophe, certificate, comb. Lizzie said, " 'Course I didn't *forget*, Pearl. How could your mother forget? I didn't buy you nothin' because I wanted to ask you what you really want."

"I want to go back to St Laur," said Pearl.

"What, that muddy place? And them small-minded folk! I be 'shamed of you, Pearl, when Mrs Chicksey's so kind to us."

"I'm tired," said Pearl.

Her mother laughed. "Then you'd best take yourself off to London, to that there Jonathan Croft, and be a lady of leisure."

Pearl said no more. She still thought about Mr Croft from time to time, and Lizzie's idea was appealing, but only if Lizzie would come too. And Lizzie had not meant that.

"How would you like a holiday, then, Pearl, bein' as it's your birthday? Shall your old mother put it to Mrs Chicksey that you be 'titled to a whole day off to spend that sixpence and please yourself? I thinks you've learned your lesson and won't go disobeyin' me and playin' round no barracks. 'Course there's no holidays for the rest of us, we be that busy, but I can do your work for a day. Eh?" And Lizzie hugged her till she smiled, and gave her another sixpence.

A shilling! A whole shilling! Pearl was planning already. Did she dare? Could she go to St Laur and back for a shilling? Dared she? Could she be sure of getting on the right train?

But before she could have her holiday, something so dreadful happened to Pearl that she thought she would die; if the thing itself did not kill her, the terror of it would.

It was three in the morning and her back and stomach and limbs ached with fatigue. But she could not sleep. Lizzie was snoring behind the curtain. The night was still and thick and she was frightened of the near, white moon. She had never been frightened of the moon in St Laur, where the ripples on the estuary broke it into soft round pieces. Here it was hard and staring, like the two Di's in the morning before they put on their face-paint.

She lit a candle. The flame threw a dark shadow on her white nightgown. She moved the candle but the shadow stayed like a wet stain. She screamed softly: it was a wet stain, it was blood. She stood up. The blood spread, it was coming from her, it was coming from that part of her where the dusty boy said the two Di's had diseases, the part that the soldiers' doctors looked at.

She tore aside the curtain and rushed to her mother, leaving a trail of spots of blood on the floor. "Bloodmotherlook!" But Lizzie slept on, each deep outward breath filling Pearl's frantic lungs with the smells of beer and smoke. "Mother, Mother, I shall die!"

"In the mornin', Pearl."

At last Lizzie sat up. She was very cross and Pearl had to tell her three times what was wrong. Each time she felt more wicked and mortified by the words she must use. Lizzie gave a strange, twisted smile, a bit like the smiles she gave Mrs Chicksey or the Di's when they said something that was not to be repeated in front of Pearl; a grown-up sort of smile. "Is that all?" She rolled out of bed. She pulled off Pearl's bloody nightdress and left her shivering while she put it in a china bowl of cold water. She went to her own cupboard and brought some rags that looked freshly washed but not very clean. She tied them round Pearl to catch the blood, as if she were a little baby who would not keep dry.

"Mother," Pearl whispered, "will I have to go to the hospital?"

"Most certainly, if you lets a man touch you now."

"Have I got a disease?"

"It's your monthlies." Lizzie yawned deeply.

"If a man touches me, will he get it?"

"Look, Pearl. Don't you wake up the whole house. You be growin' fast, you be a young woman now; you can have babies – "

Pearl remembered the women staggering on the mud-flats in St Laur.

" – I means, when you be wed. It'll be gone by next week, Pearl. Then do you tell me when it comes again."

Again? It was going to come again?

"Mother, are you wed?"

Lizzie gave her that smile again and blew out the candle. "Back to bed now, shoo!" Pearl became weaker and more frightened with each little seeping feeling between her legs. Sometimes she thought she could not sleep; sometimes the sky seemed suddenly paler and she realised she had slept a little. Her throat ached; she could see in her mind the china bowl with her bloodstained nightgown floating in it like a dead fish. She was thirsty. She tiptoed down the quiet stairs: there was no-one in the kitchen, and Mrs Chicksey always promised the direst penalties for any of her employees caught stealing food in the night; but Pearl did not care. She took down a huge stone jug of milk and poured herself a cup. The feel of its wetness on her lips increased her thirst and she filled and emptied the cup three times. She sat like a criminal waiting to be caught; and Mrs Chicksey came in and caught her. She was only saved from being fined sixpence by a hasty whispered explanation from Lizzie; after which Mrs Chicksey stroked Pearl's head benevolently and sent her off to amuse herself for the day.

And wouldn't it have to be today that she met Jake Saxton from St Laur, Sam Saxton's son, the one who had forced her to eat ten oysters on her tenth birthday a hundred years ago! Yet she had no sense of anger when she came upon him in the crowded market, scarcely recognisable in the smart uniform of the Essex regiment. Scarcely recognisable as himself, as the loping, ragged boy who lazed about St Laur and shot with a catapult at children younger than himself; but not recognisable either as a soldier, for beneath the smart red of his jacket and his new, bushy, defiant whiskers, Pearl thought he looked rather lost and younger than he was.

Still, wasn't it grand to have a soldier greet you in the sunny market-place with the cold sun bright on the barrows of produce; and lift you up with a cry of delight and surprise, making you almost forget the nasty chafing bloody rags between your legs which had earned you your holiday and at the same time spoiled it!

"Pearly, Pearly, Pearl, and we all thought you'd run away to Lunnon!"

"Put me down, Jake!" she laughed, "*put me down!*"

"Why should I? Tell me that."

"Mother says you shouldn't touch me."

Jake's eyes danced and he gave a huge shout of laughter. He never used to laugh like that, his laugh used to be gentler in sound but cunning and sly, like little pools lapping in the marsh; now it was like a hard rock thrown into the air. The soldiers laughed like that in the Periwinkle. "Lizzie ain't talkin' like that to you yet?" Their eyes met and he set her down rather suddenly as if he knew. "Maybe, maybe. But Pearl, you be like my own sister to me!"

They walked together hand in hand, like other soldiers and their ladies, some of whom raised their eyebrows and winked at Jake. He told her his father had sent him to enlist. Sam Saxton had said in a few years there wouldn't be any living to be had from oysters, they were going away from St Laur; and Jake must make his own way in the world. He spoke sadly. To cheer him up, Pearl said, "You looks *grand*, Jake! I be so proud! Aren't you proud?" She was thinking of how, in St Laur, where everything was grey and misty, people seemed to fade into their surroundings, their flesh took on the colour of their clothes and if there were two colours the line where the one became the other was always uncertain; yet Jake looked so bright and magnificent, and she was wondering in agony whether she might persuade Lizzie to let her go to the barracks just once to watch him march in a parade. Let her see him, that was all! Then she would have to agree! Lizzie might even come too!

"Oh, I be proud enough to serve my Queen, Pearl."

"Are you a Queen's Man, Jake?"

"I should say so!"

"I," she said, "am a Queen's Woman." And he looked at her

138

as if he couldn't decide whether to laugh or be angry. Instead of either, he squeezed her hand; and bought her a glass of ginger-beer from the ginger-beer stall.

She said he should come to the Periwinkle to see Lizzie; she had quite forgotten her plans for a secret trip to St Laur, and anyway wasn't it as if St Laur had come to her? The bar-room was full and noisy; but as Pearl walked in with the magnificent figure of Jake Saxton in tow, conversation seemed to drop. The two Di's gasped and giggled; Lizzie paused in pulling a beer-pump, pushed her hair out of her eyes, and stared.

"Pearl! Do you *come here at once!*"

"Wait there Jake; Mother doesn't recognise you."

"Pearl!" Lizzie's voice trembled. She was angry but that wasn't all. Pearl had noticed the trembling before. Lizzie didn't drink whole bottles of beer like the other bar-maids but she took sips all the time as she worked. She said it helped her to keep on her feet, but Pearl thought it also caused her voice to tremble.

"Pearl, don't you never, never, *never* talk to no soldiers in the street! You hear! And as for bringin' them here – "

"Mother!" said Pearl. "It's Jake."

"I doesn't care if it's the King of France! Don't you – " She raised her hand but Pearl was saved by the brusque summons of a customer: "Lizzie! Liz-zie! Get you over here, gel! My tongue be burnt black wi' waitin' – !"

Lizzie darted along the counter; ashamed, Pearl glanced towards Jake, who, impatient with hiding to give Lizzie a surprise as Pearl had suggested, was pushing towards the bar. He asked Lizzie for a glass of best ale and Lizzie gave it to him without comment, but when she handed back his change her face lit up like the sun coming out.

"Jake! Jake Saxton from St Laur!"

"I *told* you!" Pearl shouted, but Lizzie didn't hear. With a shout of delight she threw Jake's money back at him. She laid her hands flat on the counter and with a wild whoop vaulted over it, showing her petticoats and frilly drawers while everybody cheered. Pearl looked away in horror; when she turned back, Jake had done the only thing a gentleman could do, and caught her. To further cheers, Lizzie kissed him on the mouth.

"Well, my little oyster-catcher! Ain't you the fine man!" And she summoned Mrs Chicksey and the two Di's and even Ratty, whom she didn't usually speak to, and began to introduce him.

It was all "Please make the acquaintance" and "Allow me the honour of presenting"; not Lizzie's way of speaking at all. Everybody smiled and laughed; they paid no attention to Pearl. Lizzie had a hasty consultation with Mrs Chicksey, and then, having been granted permission, left her work and led Jake to a table, her spare hand twirling an imaginary parasol.

Pearl stared at them talking together at the table and sipping their beer; Lizzie kept leaning forward so that he could see her pretty neck. Jake had forgotten all about Pearl's bringing him here! He was *her friend*! Lizzie was laughing and sparkling as she used to be with Mr Croft; yet she could almost be his mother; and she had never had any time for "them Saxtons" when they were in St Laur!

Pearl felt a sickening pain in her stomach and looked down anxiously at the floor to see if any blood had dripped. She needed some more of those horrid rags. How could she ask for them? And what about her holiday? She sighed. She picked up a tray and started collecting glasses. Perhaps Lizzie, or even Mrs Chicksey, would see and say, "There's a good girl!" Unnoticed, she worked methodically towards the table where Jake and Lizzie sat. She overheard them talking. Lizzie was being very tender. Jake was very sad.

"You knows I ain't 'fraid of hard work, Lizzie."

"I knows you ain't 'fraid of *nothin'*, Jake."

"He calls me a lazy – I won't say the word, Lizzie."

"They has to say that, Jake. They has to make a tough man of you. Come next year, you'll be a-sayin' it to the young uns."

"Come next year, I'll be dead as mutton."

"Jake! My Jake ain't a coward!"

"I knows it, I knows it."

Pearl grabbed his arm. "Nobody will dare hurt you, Jake!"

The two heads turned in surprise. "Run along, Pearl," Lizzie said.

Pearl looked pleadingly at Jake, but he turned away.

"Mother, I've got a pain." She tried to put her real meaning into her eyes.

Lizzie said, "You'll find them things you be wantin' in my cupboard."

Pearl ran away with burning cheeks: how could Jake fail to know what she was referring to? Lizzie went on listening to him,

140

her eyes rolling in sympathy, her painted lips savouring each word as she consoled him.

6

Jake Saxton came to the Periwinkle whenever he could. Forlorn and hangdog, he looked for Lizzie. All he ever said to Pearl was "Where's Lizzie?" Lizzie didn't have time to sit at tables with him, so he perched on a stool at the counter and watched her serve the other men. Sometimes, when they were too friendly with her and she was too friendly back, he looked sour and angry. This gave Pearl a guilty pleasure. Soon there would be a fight and Jake Saxton would be banned from the Periwinkle.

It was not that she wanted him banned exactly. It was not that she minded him and Lizzie being friends. It was just the nights. When Lizzie sent her to bed early, so that she should be asleep when Lizzie came up with Jake. She never was. Once in outrage, Pearl sat up in bed and said, "I just hope you don't get diseases, that's all!" and Lizzie said, ominously quietly, "I be pretendin' not to hear that, Pearl."

Pearl grew accustomed to the idea of bleeding every month. It was a horrid nuisance but there was no getting away from it. And at least she knew it wasn't a disease. One morning, amid much teasing (and jokes directed at Lizzie: "You'd best come too!"; at which Lizzie just smiled) the two Di's dressed up again in their rainbow skirts and their best hats and went off to the barracks to "get their certificates". Only Diana came back. Dinah had been found to be ill and had been put in the lock hospital. She couldn't be a Queen's Woman any more.

Pearl grew bigger, and all her dresses had to be lengthened and let out. Old Ratty died and left a prodigious amount of money from his betting, to be used for a grand funeral. On his deathbed he made Mrs Chicksey promise to cut the throats of all his rats personally, and personally lay them in the coffin beside him. She wouldn't do it, though. She said it would be disrespectful. She sold the rats instead.

Jake's regiment was posted overseas and then kept back at the last minute. He was frightened. Pearl hoped he would go soon. She knew there was no chance of Lizzie agreeing to return to St

Laur while Jake was in Colchester. Sometimes he didn't come in for weeks, and then Pearl guessed he had set sail. Then he would appear, and Lizzie was very cool.

"Evenin'."

"I'm sorry, Lizzie."

"Oh, I be just the bar-maid."

"We gets punished if we – "

"Pooh! There's always plenty of soldiers here."

"Maybe they doesn't mind – "

"Maybe they be men."

Lizzie forgave him of course. Pearl was disappointed in him. A soldier shouldn't abase himself like that. He should stride in exactly when it suited him and make excuses to no-one. He ought to be willing to risk punishment to see his lady-love, but because he wanted to, not because she demanded it. He wasn't like a proper soldier; even when he drank beer, it didn't make him boisterous or rowdy, it just made him droop and complain. He didn't seem to be getting on very well at the barracks either. He said he couldn't eat, the meat was full of maggots. Lizzie called him a namby-pamby. He said his commanding officer called him that too. Once, when he was learning to use a bayonet, the commanding officer was so dissatisfied with Jake's yells of hatred as he plunged the blade in the swinging stuffed sack, that he made him stay up all night practising the yells in the darkness. And the louder he yelled, the louder his comrades yelled back from the barrack-room where they were trying to sleep. Pearl laughed. Jake pouted.

"I thought you was my friend, Pearl."

He should just make up his mind, then! If he was her friend, he ought to pay her more attention! If he was Lizzie's friend he ought to be more grand and grown-up. He ought to walk with a proud step, and the three of them ought to go walking on Sundays: Jake in his uniform, Pearl in her sailor dress, Lizzie in yellow with her hair piled high and a nice bright bonnet. In short, he ought to be like Mr Croft.

She sighed. Where was Mr Croft? He always used to say he had business in Colchester. But he never came to the Periwinkle. Surely one of these days Pearl would meet him by chance as she had met Jake? But then hadn't Miss Packham also said, "I have business with the women of Colchester"? Pearl did not want to meet her by chance.

Sometimes, when Lizzie was asleep, Pearl and Jake talked through the curtain.

"Are we your only friends, Jake?"

" 'Part from Ginger."

"Who's Ginger?" It sounded like one of Ratty's rats.

"Don't know his real name. We calls him that 'count of his hair. Red as carrots."

"Oh."

Lizzie groaned and they started to whisper.

"The lads doesn't like Ginger, Pearl. So him and me's friends."

"Why don't they like him?"

"He don't drink beer or curse or nothin'. He be a godly man, Pearl; puts them to shame; and me, I don't deny."

He sounded very troubled. Pearl guessed he wanted to say something else. She said, "I don't always remember my prayers either, Jake."

"They tricked him," Jake said. "They lay in wait and tricked him. His comrades, his brothers-in-arms. They played some foulness on him, then they told him he had to drink a bowl of beer-and-whisky mixed as a forfeit."

"Like you made me eat oysters," said Pearl.

"He ran wild, Ginger did. Fought – he never fights. And the major was a-walkin' with his lady and Ginger goes to them and tells her she be no better than a whore and she ought – and then he pukes on her dress."

"What did they do to him?"

Jake's voice sounded as if he were crying. "They put him in irons."

"I'll put you in irons," Lizzie barked in the darkness. "Hush up or go home."

Pearl saw his shadow get out of the bed and start to dress. She could hear the street beginning to wake up: doors opening, the clop of hooves. What a sight Jake was when he appeared from behind the curtain! His trousers were rumpled where they had lain in a heap on the floor, and all the buttons on his jacket had been put in the wrong holes.

"Shall I come for a walk with you, Jake?"

In the lightening street, a few people were hurrying about. A girl was trying to run with a bread-box wider than the span of her arms. She dropped loaves on the cobbles. A drunken soldier rushed at Jake from an alley, tripped on a loaf and didn't get up.

Jake continued the story of Ginger, his words coming slowly then fast. Ginger's clothes had been taken away and he had been put in a cold, wet cell to sober down. Then they took him out and flogged him.

"In front of everybody?" It was the worst thing Pearl could imagine.

Jake was furious. He yelled at her: "You stupid girl! Not a schoolroom swishin' – they took the flesh off his back! They might as well have took a butcher's knife to him! They tied him to a cross and marched us so close we could see his face, waitin'! He were tied so close to that cross he must have smelt the fear of whoever were there before!"

"I'm sorry, Jake."

"And then they beat him with long cats dipped in brine."

She thought of long, mangy animals being swung on to a man's back by their tails and felt a desperate urge to laugh. She said, "Brine?"

"You knows how it is when you cuts your hand and the salt gets in!"

Pearl flinched to think of it. Jake was talking of how the man's white bones showed. And black flies came and fed off him. Jake said, "I could've put a stop to it. If I were man enough."

"How could you?"

"It ain't allowed no more. Floggin'."

"What do you mean?" She had supposed soldiers of senior rank could do as they pleased.

"I'm tellin' you! It's against – "

"But don't they know?"

" 'Course they knows. They thinks we doesn't."

"Could they go to prison for it?"

"Pearl, I fainted like a girl! They was ploughin' up his back like a field, and I was thinkin', *say somethin', Jake Saxton, do somethin', you knows what's right* – next I knew, they were throwin' water over me, and I says to the sergeant, 'it ain't allowed, sir, it ain't allowed.' And he says to me, 'I'll be watchin' you, son. Put another foot wrong and we'll see what's allowed and what ain't.' " They were near the barracks. He glared at her. "Go home," he said. "Go home to your mama. You're only ten."

She said, "I'm nearly twelve." She stalked off and left him. The Empire would be in a fine state if all soldiers were like him! And yet she was sorry for him. She had been just about to tell him her plan. But he was so nasty to her, she almost decided to keep it to herself. A bugle called across the morning, that meant he had to be somewhere, or he was in more trouble. She turned to see what had become of him; he was crouched in a heap by the wall, his head in his hands. She could not stop herself running to him. She could bend down to him, crouched like that.

"Jake. Let's go home."

"Home?" His eyes were desperate.

"St Laur."

"Desert – "

"We could build a house on the shore. We could eat fish."

She heard her words and knew they were nonsense. They could not go back, any more than next year could become last year. But Jake's eyes told her he wanted to believe it; and so he believed it; and so she did too. They hurried to the station. They were like toys, Pearl thought: a toy soldier and a toy girl in a clockwork railway. They didn't seem to be deciding anything any more, it was simply happening. It was magic! Back they would go to St Laur and somehow live happily ever after. Lizzie, the army, the Periwinkle, didn't matter, all that mattered was the little eager train, the silver railway track winding across the fields, gleaming in the sun . . .

"*Sax-ton!*"

They had been seen. With only minutes to spare before the train carried them to safety, the army had caught them. And Pearl had two one-way tickets in her hand.

"*Sax-ton!*"

Jake shuddered into life. If he was clockwork, the mechanism had broken. He trembled and stiffened. He choked and saluted. Two men were elbowing rudely through the crowds on the platform. Their uniforms were like Jake's, but with more stripes and braid; their moustaches were wide and thick, like black gaping mouths.

"Goin' somewhere, Saxton?"

They paid Pearl no attention. Thinking quickly, she crumpled and discarded one of the tickets to St Laur.

"Just-seein'-my-girl-to-the-station, sir."

"Here's my ticket, see, sir!" cried Pearl, "only one!"

The officers were not interested in the ticket. They wanted to know why Jake wasn't on parade. They wanted to know if he was deserting. Pearl shivered. That was the word Jake himself had used, and she had changed the subject to talk of fish and cottages and made him do it.

"Just a minute! Ain't you the regimental lawyer?"

"No-sir."

"No-sir. No, sir! But I think you are, Saxton! I think you are! I think only yesterday you was givin' the drum major the benefit of your advice as to what he could and could not do." He barked orders then, which did not sound like words but which Jake seemed to understand: he stamped, he jerked, he turned. And he marched away.

Pearl was left with the other man, who examined her one-way ticket to St Laur.

"St Laur, eh? Long way from home. What are you doing in Colchester?"

Pearl felt a rush of spirit. It was on her lips to tell the man to mind his own business. Frightened she might be, but she was not in the army! She checked herself. She must think of Jake, he might be in serious trouble. She must put herself in his place, work out what he would say; then she could back it up.

"Seeing Saxton, sir."

"Bit young for that."

"I'm fourteen," said Pearl.

"Got your certificate?"

The last doors slammed on the train that was to take Pearl and Jake to St Laur.

"Yes."

The whistle blew.

"Let's be seeing it."

The train pulled out of the station and along the silver track, across the gleaming fields. The whistle that was to have been a cry of triumph at having escaped, was like a sad moan.

"Your certificate, girl, look sharp."

"It's – " She could not say the Periwinkle. What certificate? She was frightened. "What have you done with Jake?"

"You'd best come with me," he said, "if you ain't got no certificate."

He grabbed her wrist. She bit him. She felt like Prince Albert the rat going for one of the bulldogs. He howled and she ran. The crowds were thick and curious, but Pearl knew how to get through crowds. She dodged and crawled but the soldier was gaining on her. Jake, where was Jake? The Periwinkle, where was

146

the Periwinkle? If she could just get back to her little bed and pull up the covers . . . if she had only not got up this morning at all! She dived into a mass of people round a vegetable stall and doubled back, fleeing up an alley she recognised. The man did not follow; she paused for breath. Suddenly he appeared again, she turned and ran smack into the arms of another man. She was relieved; he wore an ordinary black coat; he wasn't a soldier; he would let her go home.

But matters grew worse, not better. The nightmare began. Pearl's terror grew as her understanding diminished. The man in the black coat seemed to be some kind of policeman. She screamed, "I ain't done nothin!" which was what you learned in the Periwinkle to say to policemen; but the soldier was talking about her to the policeman, saying he had caught her "soliciting", saying she had no certificate. What was soliciting? Was it worse or not as bad as helping a soldier to desert? Had it anything to do with solicitors? They were to do with the law, Pearl knew that; probably, then, it was not as bad as helping a soldier desert. So she did not deny it.

She was taken to a cold police station. She wondered if Jake would be there. He would tell the truth and save her. But the truth might get him into trouble! Weren't soldiers shot for deserting? Would she be shot? Shot dead, this bright morning? Never to see St Laur again, or Lizzie, or collect glasses in the Periwinkle? Her tears rolled as they sat her on a bench. At least it wasn't a cell with bars on the windows as she had imagined. What was the penalty for soliciting? And what would Lizzie say? They brought her a mug of hot tea but her throat was so tight with shame and fear she could not swallow. They took her before a magistrate. The court was as solemn as death, everywhere were wooden walls, she could not see what was happening, she could not understand, whatever it was, just let it be over as soon as possible. She said "yes", she said "no", she wrote her name, she said she was fourteen because that was what she had told the soldier, and she was led away; they said they were taking her up to the barracks. The policeman was holding her behind her neck as if she were a St Laur crab and he afraid of being nipped.

A new regiment was in town and the crowds had gathered round the barracks. Through her confusion, Pearl thought of maggots on dead fish. Why were they going to the barracks? Was Jake to be shot, was she to watch? She knew why the crowds gathered for new regiments. She had heard talk in the Periwinkle. Booty to be had! Pay-day, and what has a soldier to spend his money on? Soldiers without wives or children; or none that they'll acknowledge! They'll pay, and glad to, for food and tobacco and smiles! They'll hand over shirts for washing to a pretty smile, and the pretty smile may then sell the shirts! They'll complain of maggoty beef and watered ale; easy, then, to sell them pies and sweetmeats, especially with a smile for nothing! (The smells tightened her throat, even tighter than the policeman's hand.) Pearl tripped, the policeman bent her arm back, the women in the crowd sent up a howl, something about her delighted them, disgusted them. What if Lizzie could see her now – her mother, who had forbidden her to go to the barracks! Would she ever see her again? She saw a little girl watching from a wall; she wanted to shout, *Go home, oh, go home*. The women howled like dogs and pointed, they pointed in her direction, but they could not be pointing at her, there was nothing about her that was worth pointing out, something must have happened over her shoulder if she could only turn and look; their urgent, greedy faces – she felt ashamed of the coarseness and cunning of her own sex, as if soldiers' lives were not hard enough without this flock of carrion crows gathering wherever they laid down their bundles and rested their heads!

It was a long, light room. There were notices on the wall, brown bits of paper with royal crests and curling edges. At one end of the room a group of men gathered in uniforms different from Jake's. One of them had whiskers like Mr Croft's. They talked among themselves, consulting lists, checking instruments on a table which filled Pearl with foreboding because they told her she was in a hospital or a place of torture; and sent glances, sometimes mean, sometimes quite humorous, to where Pearl sat on a bench with four women.

The four women didn't seem to think they were going to be tortured. They were glum but not afraid. Maybe they were just brave.

There was a high bed in the middle of the room. There were steps to climb to reach it, and a sort of slope in the middle.

Pearl wanted so much to go to sleep . . .

"There's older arses than yours needs a rest!" She was rudely shoved from the place on the bench where she had lain her head by a new arrival, a dreadful-looking woman with no teeth, her face pitted with scars. Pearl started to cry again at the sight of the woman; the woman offered her a reeking bottle. "Your first time? It ain't as bad as all that."

A thin waif of a woman about Lizzie's age, with jet-black eyes, scoffed, "Speak for yourself, Aggie Teal! We all know you counts the days – "

The woman with the bottle said to Pearl, "I should take no notice. Not a bit of notice, none. You come and sit with me and keep out of trouble."

Pearl was taking no notice. She was watching the doctors. They were starting to allocate instruments amongst themselves, gleaming silver instruments dipped in steaming pans. Pearl remembered Jake's whips soaked in brine.

The black-eyed girl was very angry about something. She kept looking at Pearl and muttering. Pearl looked away. The girl burst out: "You don't know what yer here for, do yer?"

Pearl said nothing.

"Don't s'pose you can even write yer name."

"I can," said Pearl.

"Bein' kept against her will, this one is!" the black-eyed girl shouted, "it's a case of 'abeas corpus!"

This created a bustle and a stir until somebody produced a piece of paper that Pearl was said to have signed. They called it a voluntary submission. She sat very still. She watched as the black-eyed girl took her turn on the examination bed. She wanted to look away but her muscles no longer obeyed her. The doctors made the black-eyed girl take off her lower garments and lie down. Then they put their hands up her skirt. Then they put one of their silver instruments where their hands had been. The black-eyed girl grumbled that the instrument burned her, and they told her not to be a baby, it would burn the germs, and she said she would burn them, given half a chance, and everybody laughed. That was what Pearl could not understand: all that cursing, all that laughing. At last one of the doctors lifted the skirt of the black-eyed girl and peered between her legs.

Then they let her up and called Pearl's name; and Pearl ran for the door.

It was locked. The black-eyed girl, on her way out and proudly brandishing a piece of paper, held Pearl gently. "Go on, love, you signed yer name. It's for yer own good really. Tell you what, I'll wait for you, eh?" Pearl bit her, received a hard wallop and was handed over to the doctors. As she felt their strong hands she stopped struggling. She felt sleepy and far away as they started to do it to her.

Their voices spoke some nonsense.

"Seems a shame when she's never been touched."

"You *sure*?"

"Take a look. Virgin as the Mother of God, if you'll – "

"Yes, well, there's virgins poxed a man before now. They sew themselves up."

The pain was sudden and savage. She was being opened wide like an oyster.

She tried to scream but she could only make little mewing sounds, and the doctors laughed. When they looked at her she kicked and they threatened to tie her up. But it was only a joke because they had finished with her. She stood, her legs wobbled, blood dripped. But this time she had no reason to fear that the blood heralded disease; for they gave her a piece of paper with her name on it, and the royal crest; it said she was a (she spelled it out) registered prostitute of the city of Colchester; and it said she was entirely free of disease.

"You're a Queen's Woman now," said a doctor hesitantly, opening the door to let her go.

She walked towards the barracks gates, holding her certificate. She carried herself carefully, legs slightly apart. She watched the walls come nearer. She wanted a good stout wall to press herself against. People were sitting on the wall, watching something. It was no concern of hers. Black, misshapen lips moved with scorn and wit. Tongues licked mouths, but the eyes were not looking at her.

At the first *swick!* sound she did nothing. She heard it but she did not think what it might be. She was too busy trying to remember and forget what had happened, trying to walk without it hurting. *Swick!* It came again and the crowd hooted and laughed. Then she knew someone was being flogged.

Jake Saxton was being flogged. She knew it was Jake, even from far away. They had been caught trying to desert. She had had her punishment and now he was having his. He was strapped to an X-shaped cross in front of a row of soldiers; and the *swick!* was the sound of the salt-soaked whip cracking across his – but wait a minute?

It *was* Jake. There *was* a man with a whip. He swung it through the air quite terrifyingly. But just as it was about to meet Jake's flesh, the man wielding it gave a little flick and the tails fell harmlessly to the ground, as Jake flinched and the crowd booed and jeered.

It was like when Lizzie raised her hand to her in a terrifying threat; and then thought better of it, let her off. Jake Saxton had been *let off!* And she had not!

As she reached the wall she heard him howl in fear and anguish. And the crowd's voices rose in indignant response.

"What's 'e cryin' for?"

"Never touched 'im!"

"Bloody Parliament, makin' nancies of English soldiers!"

"Spoilin' *your* fun, you mean."

They wanted him flogged, they wanted him flogged properly.

A ragged boy whom Pearl might have met before grabbed her certificate and read it aloud.

"Another for the Queen's service!"

Swick!

"And clean too! Not fer long, eh?"

"Go on, give 'im one! We won't tell!"

Swick!

"Which d'yer like best, Pearl, a doc' or a cock?"

"You shouldn't be dressed so shabby, my dear. You're a nice young girl. I could give you a nice home, nice gentlemen – "

Swick!

"Go on! What's his blood made of?"

"They're not allowed," said Pearl, "to flog him."

"What did you say, dear?"

"Come with me, dear."

"I've stroked that lad's back many a time," a woman chuckled.

Suddenly Pearl started to shout. She hardly recognised her own voice, it was like a boiler being raked. Gone were the soft tones of St Laur and the polite way of speaking Mr Croft had taught her. She sounded like the crudest, the worst person ever to come to the Periwinkle.

"Let 'im 'ave it! The bloody desertin' coward! Rip the skin off 'im, let's see 'is bones! Give them rats their dinner, lay it on now! Take a butcher's knife to 'im!" The crowd was shocked, and stepped aside to let her through.

7

Lizzie ran quite mad. The Periwinkle was used to her alternating tantrums and high good humour; but when Pearl came home that day, white and speechless, clutching her certificate (for *don't you lose it now!* the man had said), Lizzie's anguish rocked the rafters and shattered glass.

No chance now of keeping it secret! Mrs Chicksey clucked and sighed and clumsily set a plate of beef and gravy before Pearl. Di laughed philosophically and promised not to tell, moving from group to group of her friends in the bar-room, making them promise not to tell either.

"Let me look at you Pearl, let me look at you! Dear God!" Lizzie tried to tear off Pearl's clothes. She was mad with strength and even Mrs Chicksey dared not restrain her, but she was reckoning without something new in Pearl: the cold knowledge that nobody would ever touch her again unless they killed her first. It did not feel like defiance as she stepped out of her frantic mother's way, easily dodging her wild lunges. It felt like the fulfilment of some prophecy that nobody could change: nobody would ever touch her again.

"My baby, my little girl!" Lizzie flung herself against the walls till china and cutlery and glass fell in a silvery cascade. Mrs Chicksey brought smelling-salts and sharply ordered Lizzie to stop breaking things and get back to work.

"If you ain't satisfied with my work, Mrs Chicksey, we be goin' right away."

"Lizzie – "

"Pearl! Do you pack your things at once! We be goin' back to St Laur to starve."

"St Laur?" Pearl whispered.

"Do no such thing," said Mrs Chicksey.

Lizzie dug her fingernails into Pearl's shoulder. Pearl brushed them away like flies. "Did he touch you? Did he? Pearl! Did that Jake Saxton – ?"

"Not like he touches you, Mother."

"Oh! Oh?" Energy left Lizzie like air from a balloon, "Knows everythin' now, does you? My daughter be tellin' me what's right and wrong? My daughter, a Queen's Woman, a slut, a bag o'– " Di looked warningly from the doorway. "I knows I shouldn't

152

have brought you here – " Lizzie moaned, adding, as she saw Di,
" – this bawdy house full o' loose women and – "

"Take care, Lizzie," said Di.

"Ain't no man ever paid me! Ain't no certificate on my wall!
If I gives myself, I gives myself for love! That Jake Saxton: I
loved him like my son and my husband and look – "

"Huh," said Di.

Pearl watched the quarrel with cool contempt. She struggled to
lift a big pan of hot water from the stove.

"Take care with that, Pearl," said Mrs Chicksey.

"I want to wash myself."

"We be needin' that hot water."

"Then I'll jump in the river," said Pearl. Mrs Chicksey seemed
to see that she meant it and let her have the water.

Jake Saxton did not return. Perhaps he had been posted abroad
at last. Or perhaps he was ashamed. Coolly, Pearl watched her
mother. Pearl felt nothing about her experience. As long as she
kept the memory of it deep inside and nobody ever touched her
again, it would be as if it had never happened. But Lizzie still
raged, and cried when Pearl would not kiss her good night. Pearl
knew the real reason. It was because Jake had gone away.

Once a soldier who looked like Jake came into the Periwinkle.
Pearl's heart leapt in spite of herself. Lizzie picked up a bottle to
throw.

"Any more of that," Mrs Chicksey said, "and you leave here."

"After what he did to my little girl – "

Pearl smiled loftily. "I'm not a little girl. I'm a Queen's
Woman."

"Don't you dare, Pearl! You be goin' to school soon!"

"I am not," said Pearl.

"All little girls goes to school."

"Queen's Women don't," said Pearl, "do they, Di?"

"They won't know," Lizzie wheedled.

"They will if I tell them," said Pearl.

"Then you ain't goin' out of these doors," Lizzie raged,
"without me."

"I don't want to go out," said Pearl.

She preferred to be inside. She worked and ate and slept; she
ate huge meals till Mrs Chicksey said they might as well keep a

horse in the house. She grew fast and Lizzie complained about the constant need to sew new clothes. Once Di offered to cut down the other Di's rainbow skirt for her, but Lizzie retorted, "Keep your rags!" and strutted off to the draper's. Every month, Pearl bled; and with the bleeding came nightmares about diseases and doctors with silver instruments. Lizzie fussed. She must always be told when it happened, and it was treated as Pearl's fault if it was late. Pearl yearned for privacy. She tore up her own rags and pretended to forget to tell Lizzie, watching her anxiety mount. Once she caught Lizzie spying on her.

Then the stranger came to the Periwinkle. Just a face in the crowd: he wore a heavy cape like a highwayman and carried a bit of paper. Customers stood aside as he strode rudely to the counter and demanded to see Mrs Chicksey without ordering a drink. Hearing his voice, Pearl recognised him: he was the plain-clothes policeman who had caught her that day in the market-place and taken her to court. She eyed him coolly and wondered if he knew he was in danger of being killed.

Mrs Chicksey took him into a back-room. He left after an hour. Mrs Chicksey called Pearl.

"I haven't done anything," said Pearl.

Mrs Chicksey hesitated. " 'Course you haven't." Then she sighed. "I'll talk to your mother."

Pearl heard them.

"She'll have to go for her inspection, Lizzie."

"Over my dead body, Mrs Chicksey!"

"I won't have girls arrested here! That policeman says she's missed her day; he wanted to take her, but I said she'd go tomorrow."

"Mrs Chicksey! She ain't goin' through that again, she's not the same since! She be clean, I swear it! She ain't been out of my sight!"

"I'll take her along," Di offered, "and look after her."

"Either she goes," Mrs Chicksey warned, "or you both do, Lizzie. Out from here. This is a respectable house."

"Respectable!" Pearl heard Lizzie laugh. "What about her?" She meant Di. "And her poxy friend in the lock hospital!"

"Careful what you says, Lizzie!" said Di. "I be a patient woman."

"That's what the men says!"

"It's like keeping fighting cats!" Mrs Chicksey said. "What you girls do is your own affair till you make it my affair by breaking the law and keeping a registered girl without her inspections."

"Then it's a wicked law, a wicked, wicked law!"

Pearl heard no more. It was late and dark and she was meant to be asleep. She lay listening to the beat of her heart. It beat in her chest and then with an answering beat in the place where the doctors had prodded and looked. She would not go. She would kill somebody. She would kill herself.

Lizzie burst in. "Pearl, get up." Pearl dressed. Lizzie was flinging a few things into the bag they had brought from St Laur.

Pearl was spellbound. Was it really happening? Had Lizzie decided at last? Were they really leaving and going back to St Laur, the smells of mud and fish, the lapping grey waters? Away from the smoky crush of drinkers and Di's jokes and soldiers and talk of diseases – their little house? It would be bare, they had sold all their furniture, they would be poor with only oysters to eat, but Pearl would even eat oysters if it meant going back to St Laur. Jake Saxton would not be there. Mr Croft would not come, the gossiping tongues would wag, but what did any of that matter if they were going home? Were they going now? There were no trains. Then perhaps Lizzie meant them to walk through the darkness with the railway line silver in the moonlight to show them the way. Dawn would come up and there would be St Laur, sleeping by the estuary.

"Pearl, listen to me."

"Yes."

"Does you remember that there lady as came after Mr Croft and told us his poor wife were dead?"

Pearl swallowed. "Miss Packham."

"Miss Packham! I were that angry, I didn't take account of her name. And did he say – remind me now, Pearl – did he say she do *rescue work*?"

Unease crept up Pearl's spine. She didn't like this talk of Miss Packham when they were going back to St Laur. Of course she remembered that night perfectly, every word, every gesture, even the smell of burning mutton. But she must be careful. What was Lizzie planning? What was she going to do?

Lizzie bent down and took her by the shoulders. She was half-coaxing, half-terrible, and commanding. "He did say that, didn't he? And now, you remembers: what was the name of the society she do her rescue work for?"

"You said she rescued ducks," said Pearl.

Lizzie slapped her face; her face didn't hurt; the hurt was deep inside. "Ladies . . . Progress," she whispered.

"Ladies Progress! That's it!" And she dragged Pearl out, protesting, into the night.

Lizzie strode across the dark cobbles, up streets, down alleys. Pearl dragged her feet, but Lizzie's grip on her wrist was firm. Lizzie hadn't even troubled to put on a shawl; yet she had dressed Pearl and packed for her as if for a long journey. Every time they came to a corner, Lizzie looked left and right over her shoulder; once two men approached them and they hid in a doorway. At last they reached a dark church with a little house beside it. Pearl's heart nearly failed as she read "Ladies Progress" over the door. Lizzie beat on it like a mad woman; Pearl hid her face from the sight of Miss Packham who would appear, tall and terrible.

The woman who came sleepily to answer was not Miss Packham; but it was Miss Packham Lizzie asked for, dropping a little curtsey.

"Miss Packham?" The woman's voice was puzzled but kind. "She's at our London Headquarters."

"But you knows her?"

"Everyone knows Miss Packham."

"And you rescues girls?"

"Well. Yes."

Lizzie thrust Pearl forward. "Here's one needs rescuin'." Lizzie clutched the woman's shoulder and spoke in her ear, fast, harsh whispers. The woman nodded and looked at Pearl. "Poor little thing."

"Mother!" Pearl shrieked. "What's happening to me?"

Lizzie brushed her eyes with the back of her hand. Then she smiled, a bright, wide smile. "What you was always wantin', Pearl! You be goin' to London to your father! This kind lady'll take you to Miss Packham, and Miss Packham'll take you to Mr Croft and then you'll be safe."

"But you come too! You come too!"

"If so be he sends for me," said Lizzie, "I'll come too."

"But Mother – "

They could hear a carriage approaching in the darkness. Lizzie snatched herself away from Pearl's grasp; there was nothing Pearl could do.

"Come inside, dear," said the woman. Pearl struggled against

156

her soft, fat arm; but Lizzie had turned her back; Lizzie was walking away, hiding her face, walking fast, running; Pearl felt a rush of remorse, all the times she had disobeyed her mother, gone to the barracks, been jealous about Jake – Lizzie hadn't even kissed her! Pearl would call her and she would come back for a kiss at least! Just a kiss, just a minute! "Mother, just a minute!" But already there was nothing to be seen of Lizzie as she disappeared into the darkness, nothing except the soft light from a window gleaming through her wild yellow hair.

Sarah
The 1870s . . .

In the evening of the day of Pearl's surprising arrival at Jonathan Croft's residence at Wenbury Hill, Sarah Packham sat staring into the fire in the ornate fireplace of the guest bedroom. She listened to the rush of water in the pipes in the wall and the roar of the bathroom geyser as Pearl was given a bath. *Dear God, what is to happen now?* she thought.

Six years had passed since Jonathan said, "You must stay as long as you wish, Sarah." He had said it affably enough, but then that was Jonathan Croft all over. Affably enough he approached the events of each day. Sarah had no doubt that he had been every bit as affable a husband as he was now a widower and a brother-in-law, and would be a father. His relationship to the world in which he moved seemed to be one of mutual aid and admiration. Misfortune struck; consolation was round the corner. Wars, for example, even little skirmishes in outposts of the empire, were misfortunes to most people; they sent Jonathan hunting for more orders. A barren wife, he had seemed to think, could easily be remedied by taking his seed elsewhere. A dead wife . . . ah, that was different. She smiled sourly. She did not suppose he took much consolation in her presence.

When he said she could stay, he had probably thought she only planned to remain long enough to recover from the shock of Helena's death. He had thought she would return to Australia. He did not know that she could not rid herself of her terror of the sea; he did not know about James.

At last, she had said, "I have to modify my plans somewhat, Jonathan."

"Yes," he said. She could still hear his cautious tone.

"I am not leaving just yet."

"No."

"What do you mean . . . no?"

"I mean, I see that you are not."

"Do you want me to go?"

"Sarah," he said, "stay as long as you please. My house is large."

"Yes." She sniffed. "Thank you."

"Can I be of any assistance?"

"What do you mean?"

"Financially?"

She remembered thinking, *He will pay me to go away*, but graciously saying, "Thank you. A small loan, perhaps, when the time comes." She ought to explain. "I cannot go back to my farm, you see."

"Has something happened to your husband?"

His eyebrows had lifted slightly in his round face as he said this. He did not believe in this husband . . . her own disbelief had communicated itself, perhaps. He referred to her as Miss Packham, which suited her well enough; she was not inclined to explain. *How fortunate to be a man*, she thought sometimes with exasperation, *and not be called upon to reveal or disguise your personal circumstances every time you give your name!* She replied simply, "Yes."

His reminders that he would pay her passage became so frequent that she once said, "Goodness, Jonathan, how eager you are! Do you plan to replace my sister as soon as my back is turned?" And he said quietly, "Helena can never be replaced." And she almost sensed pain in him, but she still did not trust him.

Why not? Why that mistrust? With the living evidence of how right she had been upstairs in the bath-tub, Sarah traced painfully the development of her conviction that Jonathan Croft had a secret life.

"You see, I shall need hands," she told him once, explaining her continued presence.

He spread his own. "I have only two, but they are at your disposal."

"I mean workers, of course."

"You mean to take men out with you?"

"Women." She had a picture of a manageable little property in New South Wales. "I mean to reclaim poor women and put them to honest labour." A row of robust, pink-cheeked former prostitutes swung scythes in the sun. Sarah was secretary to the Rescue Committee at Ladies Progress. She shrewdly eyed the rescued girls. Somehow they never fitted her dream. Was that her fault? Was she foolish to have faith in a dream that was so picturesque?

Sometimes she even found herself complaining about them to Jonathan. "Really, they are the most provoking creatures."

"Who?"

"Fallen women."

Jonathan guffawed, then stopped himself. She might have laughed too. The conversation had its comic side. She had not yet come to the suspicion that Jonathan knew at least as much about the habits and characteristics of fallen women as she did. "Even when reclaimed?" he said.

"*Particularly* when reclaimed."

"What is the difficulty?"

"Oh, they accept our charity. But they do not wish to journey further."

"They don't want to emigrate?"

"Well, faint hearts are not wanted over there! Did I ever tell you, Jonathan, about the time when I – "

"You may have."

She scowled. He treated her as the worst kind of bore. And perhaps she was. Spinsters with a vision were. Especially when, beneath that vision, their hearts failed them. She would not complain to him again about her girls. It would be disloyal. Without doubt he too had dealings with knaves and fools, in the army, the War Office, the textiles business, but he managed to maintain the complacent bearing of a man in whose world all was right, save for the unfortunate circumstance that he had lost a wife and unaccountably acquired a sister-in-law.

Still she wished the act of being rescued did not render so many of the girls spiritless; some of them had lived through hardship and danger that would surely earn them medals were they soldiers! She had hoped to find them strong-willed, noble creatures under their degradation; fellow-creatures to herself, who had fallen on hard times. Never, never would she condemn them, she had thought, for who if not she could know how moral standards could shatter under the wind of circumstance? There were times when she thought one would not even have to find oneself alone in a wilderness with a strong, passionate man to fall . . . there were times when she lay awake and thought loneliness the greatest temptation to wrong, thought there was nothing she might not do for the touch of another human being in the night. Perhaps this was what frightened the girls and sent them back to their pimps

160

and their customers, clothed and fed at Ladies Progress expense
and laughing about the strange lady who had wanted to take them
to Australia and put them to shearing sheep . . .

"Of course, some of them are simple-minded," said Dr Graves,
the pious, handsome young doctor, who placed one afternoon a
week at the disposal of the often wretchedly-ill girls. He was a
kind man with a pretty wife who helped him with his work; as a
result of her collaboration, he was accustomed to speaking in a
very direct way with ladies. It never seemed to occur to him that
certain subjects ought to be veiled in euphemism, if mentioned at
all.

"They test my belief in a just and merciful God," he said, "to
its limits."

"What do you mean, Dr Graves?"

"The sins of the fathers are visited on the sons – and the sins
of the mothers on the daughters. Then the daughters grow up too
disfigured to marry, too sick and simple for honest employment,
and there is only one road for them to follow. And so it goes on."

"You are referring to syphilis?"

"I am. There is more justice in syphilis' little sister gonorrhoea;
it is not inherited, and death rarely results. Thus only the guilty
suffer. The commonest outcome is sterility; which, you might
think, is only right and just. Those who abuse God's gifts forfeit
the right to them . . . perhaps it is His way of preventing sin from
propagating itself."

"Do you think immorality is inherited, Dr Graves?"

"A predisposition, perhaps . . . but there is no woman beyond
redemption. Remember the words of our Saviour! Go, and sin no
more . . . God speed the Ladies Progress! And you, Miss
Packham." It was always a pleasure to converse with Dr Graves,
even on such distasteful matters. He burned with such zeal for
hard work, for medicine, for virtue, you almost felt you could
warm yourself on his words. "Of course it is not true that
gonorrhoea only afflicts the guilty. I happen to be of the opinion
– though I could not offer it to many ears other than yours, Miss
Packham – that undetected gonorrhoea is one of the main causes
of sterility and ill-health among virtuous married women."

"I do not understand how that can be."

"Virtuous wives do not always have virtuous husbands, Miss
Packham," he said. "Unfortunately." To this day she could not

161

remember whether she exclaimed, or whether her face passed through some eloquent changes, but the doctor coughed, apologised, and wondered aloud when the weather would improve.

What followed was like an illness too, or a tempest in the head, that blew everything she knew, every remembered snippet from Helena's letters, every move Jonathan made, in the same direction.

The bright-eyed doctor lent her books. Reading them was like biting down on a toothache but she could not stop.

"An insidious aspect of this cruel disease is that the patient may show no symptoms at the time when she is at her most infectious . . ."

". . . Thus havoc and tragedy may be wrought through countless lives, while the primary source of infection never suffers . . ."

". . . The need for regular inspection of prostitutes is thus paramount . . ."

Indeed, indeed! And yet weren't such inspections, required under the law, the target of a Ladies Progress campaign at just this moment? Did not her colleagues call them unjust, degrading, tyrannical?

"Tyrannical?" Sarah stormed at her committee. "What of the tyranny of permanent ill-health? What of the injustices of being deprived of children, of death at an early age?"

They said, "Then let the men look to their morals! Or let them too have their private parts assaulted in a lock hospital on the Queen's authority!"

Such remedy had more justice than probability on its side! Sarah held her peace. She would watch Jonathan more closely in his daily life and see whether anything gave rise to suspicion. She avoided arguing with the ladies, but stayed away from meetings where this matter was discussed. She considered "indecent assault" to be a rather strong phrase to use of women who were not, after all, unaccustomed to allowing liberties to be taken with the parts in question.

That was what she thought. That was what she had honestly thought, until the child came.

That child – Pearl – that pale, sturdy creature Sarah had immediately known as Jonathan's the day she saw him in Colchester and followed him to St Laur; the child who had looked at her with such fear and horror even before she spoke, and then said, "Won't you sit down, ma'am?" The child who had sat with tears rolling down her white face while Sarah revealed to her coarse, brassy-haired mother that Jonathan Croft was a liar and a cheat, that his wife was dead, that nothing stood in the way of his marrying her but his own preference for the present arrangement. (What on earth had the child thought? What had she understood?) The child who had listened as a few sharp words between adults shattered all she knew of the world, and had then come running out into the cold marsh to save the life (or so the child must have supposed) of the woman who had brought the terrible news and hurled a bombshell of hate into the cosy cottage . . . *that child* had been taken, branded as a prostitute, and subjected to the hateful inspections; and sent to her father, and to her, Sarah Packham, asked for by name by the mother, for protection! Protection by her, Sarah Packham, who had not been able to see anything in the Contagious Diseases Act beyond the aching suspicion that, had they been properly enforced, her sister might be alive now . . .

The injustice of it! She rocked in agony by the fire in Jonathan's guest bedroom and listened to the rushing of water in the pipes and the roar of the bathroom geyser as Pearl was given a bath. That woman – Lizzie – was she the source of the disease? But *she* had a child. That was the unfairness of it. If Helena had had a child, might it not be Pearl's age? Sarah stared into the fire till her eyes watered. What was she to think? It might still be true that Jonathan's behaviour had been the cause of Helena's illness, but she had no evidence . . . she ought not to make such a serious charge, even in her own mind, without it . . . in fairness . . . ah, but did fairness come into it, really? Was she not simply exchanging an accusation that could not be proved for one that could? Did she not simply want to blame someone for Helena's death, someone other than herself, or God, or an irrational universe? With or without disease, Jonathan's infidelities (for who was to say there were not more little families dotted around the garrison towns of England, waiting for nemesis to descend?) had sent Helena into a nervous decline, necessitating surgery, leading to death. That was enough!

But what of Pearl? Sarah herself had offered to take her to the bath. Pearl's grey eyes had hardened like stones. "Don't touch me," she said. "Don't you touch me." She was like a dog and her body was the bone. Sarah let her go with the servant. Now

Sarah listened to the gurgle of water running from the bath, and the servant's soft, kind voice as she took the monosyllabic child downstairs to her father.

Her father! That was another thing! If he had wanted to be a father to her, he could have defied convention and married that oystergirl! Yet now she heard Jonathan greet Pearl from her bath, his voice booming with kindness and good spirits. And Pearl chatted back, shy, frightened, but not hostile. Sarah pulled a shawl round herself and bent low over the fire. She was thirty-eight, muttering as she warmed herself in someone else's house, neither wife nor servant, neither governess nor aunt. How could Jonathan Croft be so wicked and have so much?

2

Pearl said firmly, "I doesn't want to go to 'stralia, Miss Packham." Sarah corrected. "I *don't* want to go to *Au*stralia." She was sure the child did not have this coarse way of speaking when they met in St Laur. Compared with the mother, she had seemed a refined little thing, with a delicacy of feature beneath her bland fleshiness that had immediately convinced Sarah that her ancestry did not belong entirely in that degenerate little community. "And you may call me Aunt Sarah." "Yes, Miss Packham." Now that it had fallen to Sarah's lot to educate and amuse the child, it seemed that she was ignorant, obstinate and greedy. With Sarah, at least; the return of affection that Sarah hungered for, Pearl bestowed unstintingly on her father; and he, Sarah was sure, wanted only to be rid of her.

Nothing had been further from Sarah's thoughts than taking Pearl to Australia, so why was the child so frightened? Was it Australia she feared, or being alone with Sarah? She puzzled and hunted for a reason; and remembered the night on the St Laur marsh when – more as a tribute to the child's generous courage than out of any real intention – she had said, "Should you like to come to Australia one day, Pearl?" She laughed softly. Children's memories played strange tricks. But it was a relief. Better to think that Pearl was tormented by a fear that time would show to be unfounded than that she knew (Would Jonathan have told her? Could he stoop so low?) that Sarah had actually made speeches in favour of the very laws under which she had been violated.

"Don't worry, Pearl," said Sarah. "I'm not going to Australia yet, and neither are you; we're going to stay here and be the best of friends."

Friends! There were no friends in this house.

"I shall send her to school, Sarah."

She looked at Jonathan with cool hate. "That child has been sent away often enough."

"But she must have an education, Sarah." He seemed puzzled, as if he thought she could not see this.

"I shall educate her myself."

"That is . . . a very generous offer." She noted with satisfaction that it was not, however, the arrangement he had had in mind. "But I thought you were returning to Australia."

"We cannot always please ourselves, Jonathan." Sarah disliked the prim voice in which she said this, just as she had always disliked the kind of person for whom morality consisted solely of doing without what one wanted. Yet she would not stand by while he got what he wanted in this: a peaceful house, the slate wiped clean, the reaffirmation of his right to take easy pleasure where it suited him while others paid for it.

He was ageing before her eyes, a process made strange less by its speed than by its unexpected contrasts: his hair was retreating across the dome of his head only to sally forth with renewed vigour down the sides of his face, his lips and his chin; he might pass as a Biblical hermit with his greying bushes of whiskers, were it not for the smartness of his dress. A respectable businessman, he wore dark suits, stiff white collars, permitting himself bits of colour only in the check waistcoats at which he would glance down from time to time, following this with a glance at Pearl or Sarah, as if seeking admiration. Sarah watched the unchecked advance of grey hair across his face. It reminded her of a curtain at a window, behind which shameful deeds were done. The inclination to pity him the burdens on his conscience was outweighed by the suspicion that he had no conscience, or at least that what conscience he had carried no burdens. His life simply continued. The arrival of a misbegotten daughter, demanding those things which a daughter has the right to demand of a father, had required modifications in his life, but not disruption of it.

He rose early to breakfast alone, but hurried home in the evenings and kept his travels to a minimum. He gave over his weekends to outings and general entertainment for Pearl, in which

Sarah might take part too, if she wished. He kept a close watch on her education, taking and giving pleasure by testing her on spelling or tables that he knew she knew well.

He filled the house with toys and fashionable dresses, which were of no use to Pearl, who was at an age that despised the former without aspiring to the latter, but Jonathan was not to be discouraged.

He even changed his friends. He did it quite openly. Old friends came less and less frequently to the house; they were replaced by recent acquaintances, to whom Jonathan could introduce "my daughter" and refer to "my late wife" without their questioning that the one was the product of the other.

He did it all with such an air of innocence and purpose; as if he had read a book of etiquette for just this social dilemma. Sarah watched him closely, watched, when he was with Pearl, for a sign that he knew he had amends to make and was making them. When she saw such signs, she wished she had not looked. Their mutual affection shone like twin beacons. He played with Pearl, admired her, treated her. He left Sarah to teach her, to mould her, to discipline her. It was all so neatly arranged, Sarah felt she could scream.

Instead she asked sharply one day, "What do you propose to do about the child's mother, Jonathan?"

"Do?" He might have forgotten the woman Lizzie existed. On the other hand, he might be visiting her once a week. After all, he would doubtless think, why not?

"Pearl said she promised to come if you sent for her."

Jonathan coughed. There was a book in his lap, some official publication from the War Office. He read such things as if they were the most absorbing of novels. "I think Lizzie gave up Pearl to my protection because she felt unable to provide such protection herself. And she long ago gave *me* my marching orders. Does Pearl miss her? Does she mention her?"

Sarah swallowed her incredulous, unspeakable rage. "It is *because* she does not mention her that I *know* she misses her."

He nodded earnestly, as at a new idea. "All right, Sarah. There's a lot in what you say. I shall make some enquiries. What was the name of that public house? May I ask you to find out, as discreetly as possible?"

"Ask her yourself!" The man's behaviour defied belief. The idea of Lizzie being summoned to become mistress of the house was as unappealing to her as it was unlikely; but she knew too many tales of women being seduced and abandoned by their social betters not to be outraged. When she went to work at Ladies Progress (rarely now, with Pearl to attend to) she saw in the flesh what Jonathan's behaviour meant; how could she condone it when she came home, better though that might have been for this counterfeit family's daily happiness had she been able to do so!

He had a hundred reasons for going away; he had regular appointments at Colchester barracks for fittings and consultations. But Sarah knew without being told when he went to look for Lizzie.

Pearl seemed to know as well; she was listless and irritable and asked over and over again where he was.

When he came back, Sarah could not read his face. Perhaps it was because she did not know what she wanted the news to be.

"You had better," he said, "prepare Pearl for some sad news."

"I have always believed in telling what has to be told directly, even to a child. The preparation of which you speak is more for the teller's comfort than the hearer's."

"Quite so." Jonathan swallowed. "You had better prepare her never to see her mother again."

"And why? Is she dead?"

"You had better tell her so."

"You had better tell me the truth, Jonathan."

"She asked me to . . . to lead Pearl to suppose that she is dead. She thinks it is for the best. Perhaps it is . . . but I have no choice in any case, having given my word."

Pompous self-justification . . .! And he wanted her to be the one to tell Pearl this lie. She declared hotly that she would tell Pearl nothing; but when, an hour later, Pearl asked for news about her mother, the words, "She is dead, Pearl," were out of Sarah's mouth before she considered. And yet she had considered. A woman would send a message like that to her child for only two possible reasons: either because she could not hope to see her again; or because she would not. Was Lizzie in prison, then, or rotting to death in the lock hospital? It would not be surprising. Or had she found a new partner for her life, a man who did not care to have another man's child in his household? Sarah had heard of such things. Let Lizzie be dead, then. If Lizzie thought the news of her death would be a lighter burden to bear than any alternative explanation of her abandonment, she was probably right. It was probably the wisest, most motherly thing that woman had ever done.

Pearl cried in the night, soft, private sobs. Sarah lay and listened, burning with rage. At last she rose and went to her. Her consolations might not be welcome; but she would tell her the truth, whatever it cost. Not that Sarah knew the full truth; she would not stoop to insist that Jonathan tell her Lizzie's true fate, though she was sure she could force him; but she knew that Lizzie had abandoned the child. To know that would hurt Pearl, of course it would; but how much worse to hear her weeping over what was not true than to give her the slightest of slight hopes, even though Sarah knew the other side of hope was pain.

Pearl lay on her side clutching the doll that an unsavoury-sounding person called Di had given her at the public house. Her crying was like waves on the sea building up to the great seventh wave: six little mewing sobs and a great wail that she buried in the doll's soft cloth body.

"Pearl," said Sarah helplessly, "tell me what is the matter."

The pale face shuddered, as if the worst thing that had ever happened in Pearl's life was to be found hugging a doll and crying by Sarah Packham. "I be hungry," she said.

"Now, if you'll just say that again correctly," said Sarah, "I shall fetch you a piece of pie."

She heard herself with the child's ears and stopped wondering why Pearl hated her. What would she, Sarah, have thought of a maidenly governess who posed as an aunt and came to her on the night of her mother's death to ask what the matter was and correct her grammar? But she did not mean to be unkind. She meant only to be normal, her normal self; a little gruff, perhaps, but kind and practical. She meant only to convey by her manner that life goes on, even in tragedy, and that the love of one lost person is often replaced by the love of another.

But Pearl said coldly, "I *am* hungry," holding herself stiffly, as if her tears were gold coins and Sarah had come to steal them. Sarah tiptoed down the stairs to the dark kitchen, cut a slice of apple pie, Pearl's favourite, wrote a note for the cook so she would not blame the servant girls, and took the pie to Pearl. She would not remind her to say thank you. Pearl remembered.

Sarah watched her as she ate the pie in three great gulps.

"Better now?"

Pearl lay down and shut her eyes.

"Good night, then."

Outside the door she met Jonathan in his red and black dressing-gown, sheepishly carrying a tin of biscuits. For one painfully absurd moment, she was reminded of James Daggett in his nightshirt.

"I've given her some pie," said Sarah.

"But I promised to leave these in her room, and I forgot."

Sarah said, "It's not good for her, to eat between meals."

"But she tells me she wakes up feeling hungry, and I promised."

"Well, she doesn't need them now," said Sarah, taking the biscuits from him and blocking his path.

"Oh," said Jonathan, nonplussed. And they gave each other a curt goodnight and went to their beds.

Jonathan
1880–1882

After the shock of Pearl's arrival, seeking sanctuary in his house, seven years were to pass before she was to give Jonathan anything but pleasure.

She brought delight to the closing years of his fifth decade, the opening of his sixth; a delight quite undeserved, he solemnly reminded himself. He had to keep reminding himself because he could not really believe it; sin was sin all right, and he was a sinner, or had been; but if sin produced Pearl, and Pearl produced delight, what was the meaning of sin after all?

He watched her grow up, watched girlhood and womanhood warring in her body. He was amused by the majestic clumsiness of her in delicate clothes, the way her light brown hair sat shining and flat and straight on her head, oblivious of all attempts to make it curl. He was charmed by her sweet nature and relieved that it gave way less and less frequently, as she grew up, to her moods of dark melancholy, in which she clutched her old doll and lapsed into the Essex speech that he had rarely heard her use in Essex. He worried a little about the prodigious quantities of food she ate, especially pies and cakes, for she was rather plump. But he consoled himself with the knowledge that not all men shared his preference for slenderness. He would find her a husband, when the time came, one who would make her happy. Meanwhile, he rather fancied he was in love with her himself, though only, of course, as a father might be.

He often wondered sadly why wisdom must wait for old age before it came to a man. The whole trouble with Helena, poor girl, was that he had wanted her to be a child and wife all at once. You could not protect and cosset and delight in a woman's frailty, and then expect her to love you as a woman. If it wasn't for the needs of procreation, those aspects of marriage should perhaps be kept solemnly apart. Perhaps savages in Africa had the right idea: three wives apiece, he had heard! And yet, had he not, in a rather untidy way, managed just that? Helena for love, Lizzie for his child, and now Sarah for . . . for what? To educate his child? To be a worthy sparring partner for him? He could never consider her as a wife now, of course, but if he had his time over again he might have made a different choice between the daughters of his father's old business partner down in Sussex.

Jonathan ordered his life according to a strict routine. He vowed to himself that the day he failed to rise at 6.30 A.M., sit down to breakfast at 7.15, and catch the 8.03 from Wenbury Hill to London Bridge, would be the day he would hand over everything to his indispensable assistant, Reeves, and go into retirement.

The force of this warning kept him in order. He had no wish to retire. He thought of himself as an old soldier who would die in the saddle. His bones ached from time to time and his doctor muttered vague warnings about his heart; but Jonathan knew his health was good for a man of sixty-five. The prospect of retiring seemed not only less appealing than the prospect of dying; it was also less believable.

There would be no undignified fading away into dribbling senility for him, on that he was determined. He had seen it even in acquaintances not many years his senior. In his case, a train would crash with him in it, or his heart would fail him as he struggled with a column of figures; one minute he would be there, diligent, in full possession of himself; then he would be gone, pouff! like the flame of a candle, snuffed out for ever. As part of his devotion to order, he took nineteen-year-old Pearl to church every Sunday and listened there with equanimity to talk of judgement, heaven and hell. There were always plenty of Lessons to show that God understood about a man's weakness. Understood it! Had He not created it? Or was He not after all the creator of all things? There was much that puzzled Jonathan about God (such as why it had been necessary for Jesus Christ to come to earth and die on the cross after all; if God wanted to forgive mankind its sins, why could He not have simply done so?) but one thing was sure: a grown man did not go about in 1880 believing in eternal hell fire as punishment for sins committed so long ago that he could hardly remember what carnal desire felt like! Nevertheless, he sometimes secretly envied Sarah her brisk, almost comradely relationship with her God; she was as likely as not to miss church, declaring, "I worship by works, Jonathan; and I have a positive mountain of correspondence to attend to." But he wondered how deep it went, beneath her bravado; there were secrets in her past too, that man in Australia whom she once claimed to have married but about whom she never spoke, referring to herself always as *Miss* Packham; was it possible that she never worried about what lay beyond the grave?

But that was enough of this! Had not Christ Himself said, "Well done, good and faithful servant!" to the man who invested his talents and traded successfully? Jonathan had intended to have those words engraved on a scroll and hung on the wall of the office of Croft & Co.; he had somehow never done it. But the words were reassuring. Routines, order, kept the days in check, kept a man's mind on his work and away from disturbing thoughts of what might have been and what was yet to be; a man could go mad contemplating the ineffable emptiness of Time. Better then to bridle time, to cut it into portions that could be managed, yearly seasons, daily duties. And it all began with a good breakfast.

Before him lay the white expanse of the table-cloth: a neat blue place-setting for himself, and two others for Sarah and Pearl who, if he was lucky and faithful to his routine, would not come down until he was finished. It was not that he minded Pearl's peaceful round face at the breakfast table, but Pearl had mastered a lesson which had always been incomprehensible to Sarah: that breakfast was a time for silence and respect, for reading the day's newspaper and the day's post, anticipating one another's wants and not discussing them. Sarah was at her most voluble over a plate of sausage and egg or kedgeree. He had learned to be tolerant of the way she always received the lion's share of the post, using his home to receive mail for her rescued prostitutes or whoever it was; but it was the way she dealt with it: she wore spectacles to read, thin-rimmed glasses that were thrust into place with such vigour that they seemed, over the years, to have etched a tiny groove in the bridge of her nose, slightly too high to do her not-unappealing features credit, for they seemed to push back her eyeballs and push up her brows, giving her an appearance of permanent surprise. To read a letter without comment was foreign to Sarah's practice; she liked to gasp or chuckle or exasperatedly command him to "Fancy that!" But if ever he ventured to obey, or even enquire what it was that he was supposed to fancy, she would look at him with reproach as if to enquire whether, having sacrificed the best years of her life to educate his daughter, she was not even entitled to privacy with her correspondence.

He noted that the marmalade dishes and the honey-pots were not arranged as he liked them, symmetrically by size, and proceeded to remedy this, placing the flat pot of gentlemen's relish in the middle of the row. Sarah said it was bad for one's digestion to eat gentlemen's relish at breakfast and that it should be reserved for tea; but as Jonathan was only in to tea on Saturdays and Sundays, this would constitute an unwarrantable deprivation. Besides, what he really liked might bring on a fit in Sarah at whatever time of day it was served: toast, and gentlemen's relish, and marmalade.

It was remarkable, he mused, how Sarah had mellowed, even to the extent of concerning herself, as a wife might, with his digestion! She still had her vinegary moments, and Pearl was rather a trial to her, showing not the slightest interest in her campaign for women's rights to do this or do that. But at least she no longer looked at him as if he were a murderer! At least she no longer followed him about! He could smile now to remember the horror with which he had faced Sarah's announcement that she was going to stay and bring Pearl up.

He had begun by then to think of Sarah as a wearisome dinner-guest, with her interminable offers to depart, never fulfilled. The kind of guest who announces as midnight strikes that he really must be on his way; and announces this again at one o'clock from the depths of an easy chair while the host yawns behind his empty glass and the servants' manners move through sullenness towards insurrection. At last the visitor calls for his coat, the finding and donning of which takes another fifteen minutes, then he lingers in the hall until the front door might be opened for him without it appearing too bald a hint, and finally, with the brisk night wind blowing through the weary house, setting the lamps a-flicker and dislodging ornaments from shelves, some final matter of importance suggests itself, discussion of which, while not requiring further adjournment to the drawing-room, nevertheless will not wait until another meeting. And so it is discussed, half-way inside the house and half-way out, in whispers, so as not to disturb the street . . . At last, at long last, the guest is down the steps and crossing the front path, edged on his way by his smiling host, and then some forgotten item is remembered, a parcel, an umbrella, the man returns, conversation is resumed, the front door is closed, a bottle brought out . . . and the host, despairing of ever seeing his bed again, suggests the man might as well stay for the night.

So it had been with Sarah. She had come, she had stayed; and if she had not exactly conquered his heart, she could be an amusing companion, when she was not objecting to his choice of breakfast food, or blaming him for some more general wrong to her sex about which she had just heard from her committee friends and for which she held him, Jonathan Croft, as the male person nearest her at the time, personally responsible. And if she had not exactly overwhelmed Pearl's affections either with her plans for training the girl for a profession, or entering her name for a public examination or at least teaching her to bowl straight in the garden cricket matches – which Sarah had seemed to think were essential for the young Pearl's healthy physical development – Pearl owed her a lot and expressed her knowledge of this debt in a polite affection and a self-control which ensured that only when she and Jonathan were alone together did she give voice to her opinion that "Aunt Sarah can be most ridiculous at times!"

Jonathan passed with pleasure from his thoughts to his breakfast, and thence to his post: the flat package was the new edition of the Army Dress Regulations, and he would be one of the first civilians in England to have received a copy. He supposed he was foolish to feel proud of this fact, but proud he was. He liked its attention to detail. It was essential to have clear instructions to give to his tailors and seamstresses; he could respect an army that set out clearly what it wanted, and the army in return respected him for providing it. "Unless otherwise specified, loops, frogs and buttons on the front of the tunics etc, will be at equal distance." Excellent! Obvious, perhaps, but the obvious often bore repeating in a slapdash age. "Buttons generally will be an inch in diameter and 'small' buttons three-quarters of an inch. When loops of lace or cord are worn across the breast, the top loops will reach to the sleeve seams and those at the waist will be four inches long." Jonathan Croft wiped his plate with his bread, and, hearing the sounds of womanly awakening from the rooms above him, hurried for his train.

Croft & Co was in Anthony Lane between Oxford Street and Piccadilly, conveniently placed for officers to drop in after a good lunch at one of the military clubs. Jonathan liked the negotiating and supervisory aspects of the business well enough, but best of all he liked the shop. Obtaining military approval for a paper pattern of a coat or a greatcoat and an order for five hundred of them to be dispatched to Colchester or Aldershot by the seventeenth of next month was the work that kept his bread buttered, but the shop was more like the business of . . . well, business. Soldiers were well equipped these days, but a regulation kit was not enough for any man, private or general. It was human nature to want to own more than one was given, how else were the wheels of enterprise to be kept turning? So Jonathan stocked the shop with clothes, boots and equipment of slightly better quality than the minimum laid down, and with little extras which he referred to in his own mind as "toys" but which he trained Reeves to promote as necessities. This practice carried advantages both immediate and in the long term.

Once convince a soldier of an article's indispensability, and it was on its way to being incorporated as standard kit. For instance, Jonathan had high hopes of his new Frontier lightweight combat jackets with the reinforced front panel. He took the opportunity whenever he could of talking to the lower ranks when he visited barracks (despite the disapproval of their superiors) and wrote himself copious memoranda: he knew, for example, that the Afghan tribesmen had a particularly savage way of murdering English soldiers, striking terror into the comrades who found their bodies. The Afghans carried butchers' knives and slit a man in half from his neck to his thigh, undeterred by such trivial obstructions as the rib cage; the cuts were so clean, deep and swift, the soldiers told Jonathan, laughing wildly, that a victim's last sight on earth was of the fluttering of his own heart and the writhing of his own gut. Jonathan gave this a lot of thought. In reality there was little he could do. No cloth on earth could protect flesh from this cowardly brutality, but he might do something about the fear in soldiers' hearts about such an end. A panel of stiff milled fabric stitched inside the front of the jacket might at least make a man *feel* safer. He watched them try on the jackets and was sure that he was right: they did not always know why, but the jackets made them brave. There was no deliberate deception, he was scrupulous about that: Reeves must at no time state that the jackets offered better protection from Afghan knives than standard military issue. But if the men concluded from the feel of the jackets that they did, it was their business. And in an odd way, it might be true. A soldier who feels safe is a brave soldier. A frightened soldier is often an incompetent one, and more likely to be dead at the end of the day.

Jonathan paid off his cab in Oxford Street and approached his establishment on foot. Anthony Lane was narrow and so choked with traffic that it was quicker to walk; also he liked sometimes to arrive unobtrusively. He trusted Reeves absolutely, but now and again he liked to keep an eye on him; and to wander incognito round the shop, watching the customers, glowing inwardly with more than financial satisfaction when a sale was made, taking careful note of criticism. Sometimes he even considered wearing a disguise, but that would be to risk making himself ridiculous.

He entered the shop. He noted the squeal of the door hinges and a slight delay in the coming of the *ping!* from the bell above the door that should warn of a customer's arrival. Reeves would have to make himself busy with an oil can. And where was the man? With a customer, Jonathan hoped, for his own sake, for no other prior occupation would excuse him bounding forward, all agog to serve.

The shop was empty; there were no customers. But it was early. Jonathan's heart shifted with pleasure. The air was dim, and light-beams danced in the little clouds of dust that always hung in the air above the piles and rails of goods: short coats, long coats, greatcoats, light jackets, blankets for men, blankets for horses, trousers, shirts, leggings, drawers. He moved to the back of the shop where the "toys" were kept. These were what he loved best, and not only because he was their owner. It must almost be worth being a soldier to benefit from such miracles of design: it seemed there was no necessity or luxury known to man that could not be made in a folding or portable form, to be carried with ease north or south, east or west, to wherever the British Empire was expanding or resisting threats. Baths, beds, armchairs; tents, writing cases, canteens, even soda-water factories complete with bottles and flavouring. These were somewhat beyond the means of the private soldier on twelve shillings a week, but for him there were smaller "toys": knife, fork and spoon sets in stout leather wallets, "huzzifs" with needle and cotton for mending tears in uniform, but equally useful, Jonathan knew, for sewing up wounds in an emergency. There were button-holders, boot-polishing kits, razors, combs with good bone handles, neckerchiefs . . . inexpensive these may be, "toys" in the eyes of some, but each item had been personally selected for its quality by Jonathan from many dozens offered to him by manufacturers who would be only too glad to number Croft & Co. among their customers, but who, competition being what it was, were mainly doomed to disappointment. The whole atmosphere of the shop was one of trust. Croft & Co., its suppliers and its customers, trusted one another to recognise quality when they saw it. Reeves had strict instructions not to make customers feel they were under any obligation to buy. If they wished simply to examine the stock, Reeves was to bow and say, "Your right and our privilege, sir." If they did not buy today, they would return and buy tomorrow; indeed, if they did not feel compelled, by the quality they had seen and the service they had been offered, to return and take advantage of them, then Croft & Co. had failed in its aims and there was no purpose in Reeves' existence, or, indeed, Jonathan's.

At last Reeves emerged from the back of the shop, tall, clean and eager, a trifle too eager perhaps, for was not a certain insincerity betrayed by the way he said, "Ah good morning, sir, welcome to Croft & Co., what can we do for you – " all in one breath and before he had looked at the customer with sufficient attention to establish that he was not a visitor but his employer? Jonathan would speak to him about it. He assumed an expression of formal reproach for the man's tardiness, but in reality his respect and liking for Reeves was limitless; he would never be late for anything without good reason. He came of a very good family who had lost heavily in shipping; but Reeves the boy had done exactly the right thing in the circumstances, found himself a position as office-boy and factotum in a promising firm with an employer willing, nay eager, to reward effort and ability; worked hard, observed, listened, learned, done as he was told; and now Reeves the man had his reward, manager of the shop at thirty-two, with every prospect of rising higher, indeed, to the highest point imaginable if things continued the way Jonathan liked to think they were going.

"Just as well I'm not a customer, eh, Reeves? Could have walked round the corner to Haviston's in the time you took to serve me!" A long, apologetic explanation followed, too complex and commonplace to be of interest; it was a combination of Reeves having been absorbed in a difficult order, a salesman being ill, and Reeves himself "not being entirely myself today, sir", a failing for which Reeves accepted full responsibility; but would clearly not be displeased if Jonathan enquired into the reasons for it.

Jonathan decided that he would do so, but in good time; his fatherly interest in Reeves was suddenly tinged with unease, he did not know why.

"You'll have to learn to hold your drink, Reeves; we can't let our indulgences impede our alertness, can we?"

"Not a drop has passed my lips, sir," said Reeves, his honest, square face colouring slightly, "since – " he made an effort to remember " – one month ago." Here was an admirable man! Seemingly so free of vices that he did not even make a vice of virtue! The occasions on which he drank alcohol were sufficiently rare as to be memorable; yet he did not make others uncomfortable by joining the tee-total brigades! Jonathan decided to reward him here and now for being such a thoroughly decent fellow by enquiring into the nature of the news that made him "not quite himself" and responding to it with only one aim in view: the aim of giving the response Reeves wanted; even if, as Jonathan was beginning to fear, the news was that Reeves had been made a tempting offer by another employer.

"What then? I can't make up my mind, Reeves, whether you look as if you're on your way to the gallows or on your way to dinner."

"Neither, Mr Croft. I'm thinking of getting married."

Jonathan set down his hat and hung up his coat, went into his office and sat at his desk. Reeves followed uncertainly. Remembering his resolution, Jonathan put a cautious smile on his face, struggling to master his true feelings.

"Indeed, Reeves! Indeed! Well, good heavens! Tying the knot, eh?" It sounded frivolous. Reeves looked hurt. "I can tell you this, Reeves. I've never been a happier man than I was when poor Mrs Croft was alive." Jonathan wondered if that sounded right. "You say *you* are thinking of marrying. Has the lady in question any views on the subject?" He could be wrong. He might be about to be given a delightful surprise: Pearl might pop out from behind a row of greatcoats, place her white hand in Reeves', and Jonathan would then know that his last ambition had been fulfilled.

"She has accepted me, sir," said Reeves. "Miss Okeley – Julia – has done me that honour. Now it is simply a matter of ascertaining your views on the subject – "

"Well, good gracious, Reeves, you're somewhat over twenty-one, aren't you?" Jonathan heard his voice bluster and shake.

He must control himself. If anything could be worse than this disappointment, it would be the humiliation of having his feelings known. Thank God he had not told Sarah of his hopes for Pearl and Reeves! Thank God for that at least! He would be spared her crowing! Now – what was Reeves asking him? Reeves surely did not think him the kind of employer to stand in the way of his manager's marrying, even if . . . ah, no. This was it! Jonathan saw behind the words that tumbled over one another along Reeves' tongue and out of his lips. It was not that Reeves was ungrateful – nothing could be further from his thoughts than ingratitude when Reeves contemplated the accommodation with which Mr Croft had been kind enough to supply him, the single room above the shop, between the storerooms; nor was the future Mrs Reeves in any way fussy or particular as to where she lived, as long as (she had been kind enough to say) she could be with Reeves; it was just that it had crossed Reeves' mind to wonder – it was just that he so wanted to start Mrs Reeves off in a nice home, consisting of two rooms at least –

Jonathan was finding it difficult to speak. Was this encounter with young love making him sentimental? He had been to, or heard of, dozens of weddings over the years, friends' weddings, friends' children's weddings, customers' weddings, and they had not given him pain, but Reeves' talk of *two rooms* had put him in mind of Helena's endearing bewilderment in the big, beautiful house he had given her . . .

"I dare say we could empty one of the storerooms for the time being," he said gruffly. "Is Miss Okeley the kind of woman who'll want to be measuring for curtains and so forth?"

"Very much that kind of woman, sir." Reeves glowed.

It was a slow day; the morning's good spirits leaked from it like oil from a faulty lamp; in the evening a fine rain fell, and the shadows of empty jackets lengthened on the floor of the shop. Jonathan told Reeves to shut the shop and come with him to a restaurant. They must celebrate! They had large plates of roast beef.

"You know, Reeves, you have to be careful with women," Jonathan said, in one of the many pauses in the conversation. "Don't give them too much."

"I beg your pardon, sir?"

That was not what Jonathan meant, that was not it at all! He was sounding like one of Sarah's tyrants, he did not *mean* that!

179

He meant . . . but it didn't matter that he could not put it into words. An excess of material possessions was unlikely to bewilder Miss Okeley in the immediate future. There were other things Jonathan wanted to say to Reeves, hardly less awkward.

He began cautiously, "My daughter will be surprised to hear your news, Reeves."

Reeves' ears turned pink at their tips, and he said, "I don't think she'll mind, sir."

"Oh?" Nothing more was offered, so Jonathan ventured a little further. "There was a time when I thought you and Pearl might, er, be coming to care for one another." Reeves was silent. "My mistake, eh, Reeves? An old man wanting to tie up a few loose ends. Don't mind me, Reeves. I wouldn't have been sorry to have you as a son; but I shall think of your Julia as another daughter." Nevertheless, Jonathan resolved to let Pearl know in no uncertain terms that one of her best chances was gone. His daughter could afford to be particular, but not too particular. And the crimson spots that had appeared on Reeves' ears at the mention of her, coupled with a few incidents Jonathan could remember, told him that he would be failing in his duty as a father if he did not take Pearl aside and warn her that suitors do not like to be mocked or humiliated. Was it the time Reeves came to Sunday tea and Pearl fell asleep over a book while he was there? Was it the time Reeves took her walking and Pearl left him standing alone while she conversed with her favourite pie-man at his barrow on the corner of the street? Was it the time when the four of them, Pearl, Reeves, Sarah and Jonathan went to watch the visiting team from Australia play cricket at Kennington, and Sarah, not content with creating a disturbance because she and Pearl were not admitted to the pavilion, suddenly became an Australian patriot and an expert on cricket and drew considerable unwanted attention down upon their little party with her loud and largely accurate comments on the day's play? Jonathan was fond of Pearl, accustomed to Sarah; but it occurred to him that with the former's inexplicable moods of shyness and obstinacy, and the latter's determination to prove that a woman was the equal of a man in any circumstances where this might be in dispute, keeping a suitor happy long enough for Pearl's affections to become engaged was not going to be as easy as he had once hoped.

"I'd like a word with Pearl," said Jonathan; and then, since he had decided that Sarah was equally to blame, if not more so, added, "and with you."

He noted grimly her astonishment at this brusque summons. She even forgot to be offended. She straightened her skirt and parted her hair, and, in an ironic but passable imitation of the demeanour of a maid appearing before a mistress for a rebuke, enquired, "Is anything wrong, Jonathan?"

"Something most certainly is!" His temper had risen in the train on the journey home, and now he felt dangerously near to making a fool of himself. After all, what had he to say? What had happened? "Reeves is engaged to be married." It was enough. A look of perfect and scornful understanding passed over Sarah's face and she said, "My goodness, Jonathan. You are anxious to be rid of her."

"Of course I am not! I simply feel that if she – and you, Sarah! – had been rather less discouraging than you were to Reeves – well, she could do a lot worse, Sarah! I had hoped to leave him the business!"

"Leave it to Pearl," said Sarah.

"Now you are trying to provoke me."

"Perhaps Pearl does not want to marry."

"If that is the idea in her head, Sarah, I cannot imagine who put it there."

"In the circumstances, Jonathan, would it surprise you to know that Pearl has a deep fear and disgust of anything to do with men or marriage?"

"I suppose that is the sort of thing she confides in you, Sarah," he said. "You are another woman."

"You say that as if it were an accusation! I must plead guilty to the second half, at least. But Pearl does not confide in me – I wish she did, for she is sometimes very unhappy and I would like to be able to help her. I can only speculate . . . and I have wondered, that is all, whether what I have said might be the explanation for her apparent lack of interest in the suitors you so assiduously provide."

"So you have noticed that."

"Naturally."

"And you encourage it."

"I do not, I may have mentioned that there are worse things in the world than never having married . . . "

Jonathan rose to the challenge.

"Weren't you married yourself once, Sarah?"

She glared at him. "That was in Australia," she said. He raised his eyebrows. Her tone implied that only an imbecile would imagine that anything that occurred in Australia was real or serious or even interesting. He must remember that next time she was comparing the bowling styles of the English and Australian cricket teams. It was strange, and sad somehow, the way her passionate interest in Australia and determination to return there with a select group of rescued fallen women had dwindled into this faintly ludicrous patriotism. But that was what years did to you; there was no escaping them. Sarah was forty-six. He knew because he had given her a pair of gloves on her birthday.

"Well, Pearl!" cried Jonathan genially, "here is some good news!" Pearl and Sarah were down to breakfast early before setting off on some excursion, and Pearl was tucking into a pair of good Scotch kippers. She raised her eyebrows politely to indicate that she was paying attention but must not speak with her mouth full, and Jonathan informed her of the invitation that had come from Colonel and Mrs Sanderson who were holding a ball at Bristol and would be happy to welcome Pearl for a week's stay.

"They have three sons," said Jonathan, "and a daughter."

"And a daughter," said Sarah. "Fancy."

Pearl lowered her white face and operated carefully on her kipper.

Sarah said quickly, "What a shame it is out of the question, Jonathan! Pearl and I have already arranged to attend Dr Birkett-Hamilton's lecture on 'Why the Liberal Party Must Enfranchise Women' on the Wednesday of that week."

Glancing at his daughter, Jonathan reflected that anyone unfamiliar with the expression "Out of the frying pan, into the fire" had only to look at Pearl's face for full clarification.

"Which must I do, Father?"

Jonathan and Sarah rushed to outdo each other in expressions of regret that Pearl should feel she "must do" either: visits to Bristol, lectures on politics, both had been arranged entirely for her amusement and as such were completely optional. She might even do neither, if she preferred.

Pearl looked from Jonathan to Sarah and back again, then down at the bones of her kipper, and sighed.

"We will let you choose," said Jonathan.

"And we will abide by your decison," said Sarah, "won't we, Jonathan?" The triumph in her voice as she said this turned out to be a little premature, for Pearl elected to go to Bristol; and Jonathan was very tempted, as he watched Sarah button her coat and tighten her lips to go to the lecture alone, to suggest that this was what came of allowing women to elect anything.

Pearl came back from Bristol pink and talkative; which was to say, rather less pink and talkative than Jonathan would have hoped a girl in love might appear, but still pinker and more talkative than was usual with Pearl. His spirits soared as she spoke endlessly and fondly of somebody called Alexander; and fell again when Alexander was revealed as a horse she had ridden. Hope rose when a letter arrived for Pearl with a Bristol postmark; slipped a little when Jonathan asked teasingly if he might read it and Pearl passed it over without a word; recovered itself as he noted that the letter, while not being a love-letter exactly, contained some very respectful compliments; and was finally dashed to death when he said, "Well! You seem to have won the heart of young Archie Sanderson!" and Pearl said, "Archie? I thought it was from Roger. I couldn't tell them apart." Sarah's expression showed that she considered herself fully avenged for Pearl's missing her lecture.

And then there was young Madsen Briggs who was down from Cambridge and came to call with his mother. Pearl excused herself with an upset stomach.

"Do you really think the child is afraid of marriage?" Jonathan asked Sarah.

"She is afraid of young Briggs, and who can blame her? That absurd laugh! It would be like setting up house with a donkey. And the way he shambles about."

"I think you should have a talk with her, Sarah."

"I?"

"About her . . . experience. You may be right. She may not have forgotten."

"Forgotten! Of course she has not forgotten! I have not forgotten – why should she?"

"But Sarah, it must not be allowed to – "

"I am hardly an advertisement for the institution of marriage,

Jonathan," she said, and added so softly that he was not sure if he heard correctly, "and neither are you."

"Please, Sarah," he said weakly, "talk to her."

He never knew whether she did or not. It was three months later when Sarah burst in on his peaceful breakfast, looked about her and said, "Oh."

"Not a very communicative remark, Sarah."

"Pearl isn't here?"

"As you can see. Unless she has been transmogrified into these excellent sausages." Sarah did not usually object to a little joke in the mornings, so when she responded to this one with a glare and a door-slamming departure, he knew something was wrong. He found her looking down at Pearl's empty bed; it had not been slept in. Nobody had seen Pearl since last night.

"Perhaps she's – " he bade this sentence to supply itself with a reassuring end.

"Run away?" said Sarah.

"Don't be absurd, Sarah. What would she run away from?"

"I cannot imagine."

Ah, no. In all the anxiety of the moment, he would not allow her to get away with this. Sarah was jealous of Pearl's affection for him, she always had been, that was clear; but he would not let her suggest that Pearl had thought him tyrannical. And yet the only alternative was that the child had been abducted.

"Sarah, if you know where she is, you have a duty to say so."

"Don't tell me my duty. I do not know where she is."

His alarm grew (and Sarah's did too, he was sure, except that hers was tinged with triumph) as they searched through Pearl's belongings and found a number of her good clothes missing. Did abductors allow their victims to pack? It was possible, he supposed.

At last Sarah said, as if casually, "Perhaps she has gone to look for her mother."

"Her mother is dead!" He did not know that. "At least – Pearl thinks so."

"We told her so, you mean. It does not mean she necessarily believes it. Who knows? It might have crossed her mind that her father and her – her aunt are capable of lying. You never even told me the truth, Jonathan. What happened to Lizzie?"

He drew breath. What he felt was like real pain. Why bring this up now? He liked to pretend he had forgotten; but he would never forget the sound of Lizzie, his mistress, his former mistress, the mother of his child, announcing her own death. *Tell Pearl I be gone to the Good Place, Jonathan.* Sent to look for her at Sarah's bidding, he had found her after a long search, not at the Periwinkle, not even in St Laur, but in the chilly household of a non-conformist minister. Her yellow hair was cut and hidden from view under a tight handkerchief; her eyes were dim, she swished a mop, she was a housemaid, she had turned her back on her wicked life, she said, after listening to the kind ladies of Ladies Progress and Mr Cupar, who had led her to see that the dreadful thing that was done to Pearl was God's way of making Lizzie know how deeply she had failed in her duty as a mother; and what was best for Pearl now was to forget that she ever had such a mother as Lizzie; and so Jonathan was to say that Lizzie was dead. He remembered thinking that he ought to have been glad, glad that such a reformation had been achieved, glad that Lizzie was safely employed and provided for, and forgave him and made no claim on him; but the sight of her moved him more than anything he could remember since Helena's death. It was as if all the life had been cut from Lizzie with her hair. It was as if she had always been this mousy, humble creature, mouthing half-understood phrases from the New Testament, it was as if she had never screamed with laughter or rage or taken the top from a bottle of stout with her teeth or swallowed oysters . . . or rolled in a bed with a passionate man, making him feel that passionate was all that a man need be . . . he dated the waning of his own passions to that encounter. Like a man held up by robbers, he gave the essence of this story to Sarah.

Sarah said, "And that was that, was it? You are at peace with your conscience over it?"

"Sarah! It was her wish! I did as she wished! You would surely not have wanted me to act on the assumption that a woman does not know her own mind?"

"Shall we call the police?" she interrupted. He might suppose that she had wanted him taken away. He anticipated their questions. *Has she any suspicious acquaintances?* He would have to tell them everything, and they would trawl the alleys and gutters of Colchester for her. And what would they find? That Pearl had found her mother and hated him? Or that Pearl was not there. But in the course of their enquiries they would reveal to Lizzie that Pearl was lost. And Lizzie (if she was still alive) would turn

185

white and toss her yellow hair and declare, *You ain't been no father to her, Jonathan Croft! I could have kept her myself to lose her!*

He glared at Sarah, who had somehow imposed this dilemma upon him. Why on earth had she been allowed to remain in this house, accusing him?

"You blame me for Helena's death too, don't you, Sarah?"

She seemed startled. She said quietly, "That was a long time ago, Jonathan."

"Even so!" He started to shout. He had no control over his words. "Well, let me tell you this! Since you are so fond of attaching blame and speaking plainly! It was the opinion of one of her doctors that the condition from which she suffered, and which required the operation, was entirely her own fault! Her own bad habits had caused her mental weakness and inability to bear children! There! What do you think of that?"

Sarah stared at him as if she had not understood. Then she turned and walked out of the room. He sat down heavily and rested his head on the arm of the chair. Damn Pearl, oh damn her! Breaking down this frail comradeship, forcing him to say disgraceful things . . . but it was true, wasn't it? Had not the accused man the right to speak?

Pearl . . . he almost expected her to walk into the room. He had forgotten that she was missing. How dare she inflict this anxiety on the people who had raised her? When she returned, he would punish her, old though she was. No, he would not. If she came back safe, he would forgive her any mistake she had made, any wrong she had done. Just let her be safe.

His resolution was tested to its limit when she returned with colour in her cheeks, defiance in her eyes, a ring on her finger, and a brand new name. She was Mrs Hamish Barrington. She had married the man who had made pies and sold them from a barrow on the corner of the High Street.

3

"Be kind to them now, Jonathan. I have asked Pearl to bring him at four. The thing is done."

He glared at Sarah. What pleasure she was taking in this! She knew he was not accustomed to being told that "things were done" so he might as well "be kind".

"She's our . . . your daughter still, Jonathan."

"Hah! Say 'our' daughter if you want to, Sarah! Or leave me out of your calculations altogether, you seem to have had more influence over her than – "

"Jonathan, you surely don't think *I* – but he's not a bad boy. He has prospects."

"Prospects! A pie-barrow!" He flinched from the vision of Pearl selling wares in the street.

"He has saved enough to rent a shop."

"And is Pearl to sleep under the counter? The thing is outrageous!"

"There is a flat. I think it's rather sweet."

Jonathan watched them arrive from an upstairs window. He had seen young Barrington on the corner of the street, of course, but, not realising they were destined to become related, had not paid him much attention. Now he noted that he was not much older than Pearl, wore an out-at-elbow brown suit of good but very old tweed, and generally had the chubby, cheery look of a pie-man in a book of nursery-rhymes. Jonathan heard him and Pearl being nervously greeted by Sarah, and there were remarks which he did not quite catch about somebody being "upstairs taking umbrage", somebody who would "soon see sense".

Sense, eh? Barrington was a seducer and a thief and had Sarah on his side; somehow, Sarah, Pearl, and Barrington had put him in the wrong without a word being spoken; yet he was damned if he would tremble on his own staircase before entering his own drawing-room to tell the fellow exactly what he thought of him!

He paused in the doorway as three heads turned towards him. Barrington stood up with a vigour that suggested army training, and swayed slightly on his legs like a wary bull. Young though he was, he had the beginnings of a paunch; what a gross character he would be when he reached Jonathan's age. Pearl's cheeks were very pink and her eyes were the eyes of a stranger: he had never seen them pleading like that, or warning. The blood drained from his head.

"Here, sir – sit down."

Jonathan sat and recovered himself; he waited for what seemed like an hour to be ready to speak. His heart beat a tattoo in his throat. He looked at his sleeve where Barrington had touched him; he wanted to see floury fingerprints there and brush them away.

"What I can't understand," he said, addressing himself to Barrington in a quavering, hateful voice, "is why it had to be so secret? Eh? All this hole-and-corner business? Perhaps I wouldn't have chosen you. But I would have liked the chance to show . . . my daughter that her happiness is the most important, the only important . . ." He had exhausted his stock of words. Must stop this, stop it, at once. No point in discussing it. As Sarah said, the thing was done. Nothing Barrington or Pearl could say would alter what now stood revealed: that Pearl saw him as a brute and a tyrant to be run away from at the first opportunity. Nothing more to be said. Shake hands and let the girl go.

Pearl looked very pretty in her pink and white frock. She had worn it to go to Kew Gardens with Jonathan once, and he had told her she looked like a rose.

She said, "I knew he wouldn't like you, Hamish."

"Like! How do you know if I like him when I've never – Pearl! I've spent all these years trying to show you that I love you, to make up to you for – " Pearl's furious warning look told him there were some things she had not told her husband. "Do you think I wouldn't have given you a wedding? Do you think I wouldn't have walked up the aisle with you?"

Pearl began, "I didn't want – "

Sarah said, "Perhaps as you've been saved the expense of a wedding, Jonathan, you might put some capital Hamish's way for the shop."

It occurred to Jonathan's outraged mind that young Barrington appeared to be something of an actor, for he seemed as stunned as Jonathan was by this piece of cheek; and Sarah herself might one day look to the stage for a career, so convincing was her appearance of regret at having spoken, almost as if she had sought only to interrupt Pearl in a remark that might be even more painful for Jonathan to hear than this cool demand for a dowry . . . but Jonathan was not deceived. They had planned it all, together. He eyed Barrington's bulky frame from head to toe.

"You're a shrewd investor, young man!" he said. "But you'll get nothing more from me."

When they had gone and he was sitting alone with Sarah in the quiet drawing-room, he ostentatiously wrote a letter to his solicitor.

"What are you doing, Jonathan?"

"Writing a letter," he said, "to my solicitor."

"Cutting them off without a shilling?"

"Most certainly." He glared triumphantly. The infuriating creature did not even look surprised behind her absurd spectacles. "Don't you know that sort of pompous behaviour died with Mr Dickens, Jonathan?" He sealed the letter and called the housemaid to take it to the post, late though the hour was. If Sarah and Pearl really thought him a tyrant, let them see what tyranny was! Let them tremble at the thought of the destitution that awaited them on his death! And let Sarah know, above all, that it was she, mocking his justified rage behind her spectacles, the most exasperating of wives with none of a wife's compensating benefits, let her know that it was she who had goaded him into this most dreadful of gestures!

"We know nothing about him!" he shouted.

"Perhaps that is our fault," said Sarah.

"Oh? Oh?"

"We never asked her."

"You mean we never said, 'Pearl, are you by some chance planning to elope with the pie-man?' "

"Perhaps we were both so busy with our plans for her that we forgot *her* entirely," said Sarah. "Perhaps that was why the idea of running away seemed so exciting, instead of waiting for your agreement, which as you have said, you would have given eventually. Perhaps she wanted this choice to be *hers*."

"And perhaps the advantage of having a woman about the house to bring up a daughter is that I might benefit from insights such as that! I hardly think my efforts to make a suitable marriage for the child are to be compared with yours to turn her into a – "

"A shrieking harpie, an unsexed creature, a lady, so-called, with knowledge of that of which she were better ignorant? Have I supplied you with the phrase you were hunting for, Jonathan? I have heard them all – and I assure you I might as well be deaf, for all the pain they give me."

"Might you, Sarah?"

"Of course! For our final victory is in sight. We have the solemn word of a number of Liberal Members of Parliament that the eighteen-eighties will not pass without some extension of the franchise, and this time it will include women. And then our work with poor women will wither into disuse, for the *fair* sex, the just sex, will control its own destiny."

The notion of besting her in agreement seemed suddenly irresistible.

"Do you propose that women shall become Members of Parliament too?" Logically, she must. Yet even Sarah could not, surely . . . "Prime Minister too, perhaps?"

"Naturally."

"Oh. And what legislation will you seek?"

"Well, I – "

"Come along now, Sarah, come along. I hereby elect you as my Member of Parliament. What changes will you bring about?"

She had no answer. It was enchanting – better than he could have dreamed. *She wants the vote but she doesn't know what for!* She said, "Too many to put into words, Jonathan," a lame answer if ever there was one, and walked quickly from the room with her head held high. He rubbed his hands triumphantly and felt somewhat restored. But his mind was made up as far as the will was concerned. He kept his appointment with his solicitor, who showed no surprise over the document he was required to draw up.

The gloom that settled round Jonathan was almost tangible. It was as if his own personal rain cloud had descended from the heavens to stifle and dampen his spirit. He might have thought he had brain-fever if he did not know so well what was wrong. He had never thought cutting people out of one's will would be so complicated. He realised he had forfeited the right to send a peace message to Pearl and Barrington, Sarah's presence became nearly intolerable as he thought of her tramping off to the workhouse after his death. And there was no refuge in the shop, because going there meant seeing Reeves with the wicked weariness in his eyes of a newly married man, and thinking of that aspect of things.

"Are you not going to work today, Jonathan?" said Sarah. He made a sound that could mean anything. It was a wet, cold August; a fire had been lit for breakfast in the dining-room; damp logs crackled reluctantly, begruding their smoky heat.

"Might I take the newspaper, Sarah?"

"I was reading it," she said, and he shrugged his shoulders and walked out of the house and round the corner and bought another from the boy who shouted there. (Matters might have been worse, Pearl might have married him!) He took it into a coffee-house.

The coffee was bitter and he put in spoonful after spoonful of sugar. He read his paper and discovered what had absorbed Sarah so. The Australians were playing England at Kennington, normally he would have gone, this year he had not even noticed! He felt deep empathy with the home side; they were slightly ahead on the first innings, but struggling. Rain washed the windows of the deserted coffee-house.

When he calculated that Sarah must have gone out, he went home. His mind was made up. He would have a quiet day alone with his thoughts, and tomorrow he would decide that young Barrington was just the son-in-law he would have chosen for himself. After all . . . was not love blind? Did it not laugh at locksmiths? Could it not, then, only be expected to flick its fingers in the faces of fathers? He felt deprived of the chance to oversee Pearl's marriage, for was that not both a duty and a privilege of fatherhood? But he still had the chance to show himself a kind and reasonable father. Whatever his faults, however he had been misunderstood, he had always tried to be kind and reasonable to those close to him . . . hadn't he? In fairness to himself, he could not think of an occasion when he had not.

He was at his writing desk when Sarah came upon him.

"I thought you were going out."

"I thought you were."

"We can't just mooch around all day, Jonathan. Life goes on, you know."

It certainly does, he thought. *And what do you propose to do with yours?* "What do you propose?"

"I propose that we ask Cook to put together a bit of lunch for us and that we go to Kennington."

"Ah! So you have noticed."

"Of course I have noticed that my countrymen are about to give yours a trouncing they will never forget."

As affection and irritation warred in him, he felt his spirits rise a little. "Come along now, Sarah. The colonists have never beaten a full English side in England. And they never will, not in my lifetime." She replied by jeering at W. G. Grace, yorked for four. "They won't play today," he said. "Look at the rain."

"It will stop."

"We'll go tomorrow."

"It will all be over by tomorrow."

Why did Sarah have to *know* everything? Were the words "I think" or "I suppose" or "It's possible that" quite foreign to her vocabulary?

She folded up the newspaper with three sharp crackles, in the way she had of rendering it unreadable. Once when he had protested about finding page 8 unaccountably upside down opposite page 2, she had retorted that the publishers of newspapers deliberately made their products too large for ease of management by the average female arm, the more susceptible to render women to such male complaints. "I am going to Kennington," she said. "You may please yourself."

"Thank you," he said. "I shall stay here."

4

By the time they reached Kennington the rain had stopped. The air was still cold and wet, but the crowds of people round the gates and the sense of occasion improved his humour. He almost thanked Sarah for making him come, but he was reserving the right to leave her on her own in the public seats and watch from the pavilion if she did not behave herself.

The stand was draughty and the seats were wet; but the magic seized Jonathan as soon as he sat down. The grey sky was lightening hopefully and the six great gasometers brooded at their separate heights, reminders that while Englishmen played at their timeless, tireless game, the heart of the Empire throbbed with energy. Occasionally a watery sun peeped through, and a cloud's shadow darted across the green turf. He listened to talk of the sticky wicket, the soapy ball, the wisdom of this selection and that exclusion from the teams.

Beneath and all around the stand went the tramp of feet, new arrivals searching for a good position, like unusually good-humoured lost souls.

He sat and glowed while England dismissed the Australians for 122. He did not give Pearl a thought. Even Sarah's behaviour caused him only flickers of irritation. When Lucas dropped Massie at thirty-eight she chortled; when Massie hit his fifty she jumped up and down; but when Grace took advantage of the inexperience of the young Australian Jones to run him out, Jonathan fancied that had Sarah been offered the choice between immediate enfranchisement for herself and lingering death for W.G., she would have chosen the latter.

"If that's the kind of play you want to resort to," she sniffed.

He pointed back over his shoulder. "Over there, I think, Sarah."

"What?"

"A little booth, selling copies of the laws of cricket." He gave her an avuncular smile. "I'll give you a penny and you can buy yourself one. Then we needn't argue."

A smile circulated in the tight-packed neighbouring seats. Sarah's comments were creating quite a stir. She did not care. "The laws of the game are quite familiar to me, Jonathan," she said. "There is more to fair play than laws." He smiled: that was an important admission from Sarah, one that might be quoted in other contexts.

People started to drift away from the stand to find a bit of lunch; Jonathan stood up to rest his stiff bones. He waited for Sarah to open the picnic-basket but she sat and brooded, her chin on her fists. She looked so miserable with her defeat imminent, not only in front of him but in front of all the other people who had been audience for her unsought commentary, that he almost felt like being kind to her, even admitting that Grace's behaviour had not been quite within the spirit of the game. But then . . . how much mercy would she have on him if the situation were reversed and his side were losing?

"I think you may have been right after all," he said thoughtfully, intending, when she enquired what he meant, merely to agree that the game would be over by this evening. She said nothing. He repeated the remark. She said, "Ssh. Listen."

He listened. There was nothing unusual. He heard heavy feet, excited conversation from thousands of throats, rowdy shouts from the inexpensive end of the ground, an extraordinary turnout, twenty thousand he estimated, at the very least. "Listen!" she insisted.

He heard a lone, loud Australian voice regaling the crowd with musical vulgarisms concerning a ruffian who stole sheep and what he did with them when he had done so. Jonathan could not decide, from Sarah's expression of wistful, painful concentration, whether she was about to cry or join in.

"The Daggett boys used to sing that," she said, "when they were drunk."

He said softly, "Were you in love with one of the Daggett boys, Sarah?"

She turned on him. He expected one of her exquisite rebuffs. It would be no more than he deserved. She said, "I think he was with me. For a while."

"And you?" He was very close to her. The lines round her eyes were surprisingly deep.

She gave a desperate little laugh. "I didn't really know how to do it."

He had never thought of loving as something you had to know how to do. He wondered when she was going to be angry with him and wished the players would come back.

"I wonder why I told you that," she said. "I've never told anyone else. Even when I wrote to Helena . . . I just ridiculed him. I was kind to him though," she added, in sharp, sudden defence.

"Do you still think about him? I still think about Helena sometimes."

"It's a strange feeling, isn't it?" she said. "When someone's in love with you? It's rather nice."

"Sarah, if his name was Daggett, who was Packham?"

"Packham?"

"You took his name."

She looked puzzled. Then she laughed. "Ah, Packham, Packham was another one."

"Another husband?"

"Another dream. I never had a husband."

He had intruded too far. He was in unknown land. He ought to retreat. He wanted to stay. He was not sure how to.

"It is 'rather nice' to be loved," he said. "I can remember." He took a deep breath and went for something safer. "But Sarah, it's a thing I've often wondered about. Worried about. With all your talk of equal this and equal that – I mean, what about love?"

"What about it?"

"Look, Sarah. I know you'll think I'm an ass, but you've thought worse of me than that. You said, 'There's more to fair play than laws.' "

"Yes?" The single syllable might have been a challenge, it might have been agreement.

"But aren't you implying that the law *is* all there is to it?"

"What else is there?" Sarah enquired.

"There's *love*!" Her face seemed to withdraw into itself, its lines deepening, the eyes sinking only to glow back with a fixed brightness. The warning was clear, but he had wanted to express this for as long as Sarah had been interested in Women's Rights and had never found the words until now. "You may win your so-called rights, but have you ever thought you might lose something too? We men *love* you for your appearance of frailty – which is not frailty at all, of course – and where we love, we protect – "

She said, "Where you love, you *what*? That is the sort of nonsense we hear every day of the year from those who would *protect* us from membership of the human race. You have protected me from a kind of destitution, even, yes, I will admit, loneliness, by allowing me to live in your house all these years, and I thank you for it even though perhaps I should have gone away, but I think it is safe to say that *you* do not love *me* – "

The bowling had started again. "Ssh!" said the crowd. "Stop this, Sarah!" Jonathan begged. She lowered her voice, her only concession. She was counting on her fingers the instances that proved him wrong. She was hissing in his ear.

"James Daggett, on the other hand, most certainly loved me, and yet protected me from nothing. You say you love Pearl; but you have disinherited her! And as for Helena, so far from protecting her from danger, did you not bring it to her door and beyond?"

They could not talk about this here! He watched the bowling of a few overs and wondered uneasily what she meant. The crowds were coming back, he had to move closer to Sarah to make room, their elbows touched, the feel of her sleeves was like bone on bone. *What did she mean*? She was applauding the Australian bowling with cold, furious, regular claps. "I told you what the doctor said!" he whispered. And then, regretting those words, added, "I will be seeing my solicitor again. Pearl and Barrington and you too, Sarah, will be provided for."

"What a pity all wrongs cannot be undone by seeing one's solicitor! How dare you make reference again to that doctor. Did he not prescribe the treatment that killed her? For myself, I have a much simpler explanation. I have often wondered – though not very much recently, until you raised the subject – to what extent your own morals and habits were instrumental in rendering my sister an invalid."

People were starting to stare at the pale-faced, furiously whispering couple, and she said no more. She watched the game with a tight, rigid face. She might have been commenting on the fall of the first five English wickets of the second innings for sixty-six runs. She might even be regretting saying what she had said.

How on earth had she reached such a conclusion? And what was he to say in reply? Admit that, yes, he had had a touch of gonorrhoea a month before he married Helena, but an army doctor had cured him? Tell her (since no subject seemed forbidden between them) about the treatment, a modern one from France involving ingeniously-designed instruments with sharp points and a ruthless disregard for a man's sensibilities? Tell her how much he paid the doctor, who had grinned and said, *You're a lucky man, Mr Croft! With any other treatment, you'd have had to cancel your wedding, and then you'd have had some explaining to do!* Silence and unease descended on the Oval cricket ground. The situation was serious. England might be defeated.

"Ah, well. All's not lost," said a man nearby.

"Certainly not. Five wickets down means five wickets standing."

"A half-empty bottle's half full."

"Only want nineteen to win, what!"

"Whistle and keep up your spirits," said Sarah in a clear, dead voice.

Sarah believed that he had infected his wife, her sister, with that most loathsome thing: a venereal disease. Helena: his dear little wife, to whom he had only wanted to be kind! Was it possible? Might his army doctor have lied to get his fee, sent him to marry before it was safe because he knew that was what Jonathan wanted? What else did Sarah know – or think she knew? Did she know how difficult it was for a man who must wait until middle age to marry? Did she guess how varied his tastes and adventures had been? And how difficult it had been to wean himself off them once he realised that his wife was going to provide no substitute for them in the physical aspect of marriage? He had blamed himself for even expecting her to. He felt a blush begin at his neck as he remembered the time he bought Helena a French night-gown in the hope that she would turn into the sort of woman who wore such things. He had been in moral and physical turmoil in the first few years of his marriage, but he was sure he had never let Helena see it. He thought he had reached such a just and satisfactory solution, with Lizzie and Pearl in St Laur and Helena

196

at home. If only Helena had not become ill. But then if Sarah was right, she would not have become ill if . . . and it didn't matter whether she was right or not. It was possible and that was enough. He was guilty.

England added four more runs. Fifteen were needed. And another wicket fell. The sky seemed to darken, the gasometers crouched.

"Appeal against the light," a man suggested at the top of his voice. "That's the thing! Well, don't look at me like that, madam, even if you are an Australian. It's only a game."

Another wicket fell without score. Jonathan heard thumping in his ears, felt pains stabbing all over the top of his body. Didn't these diseases lie dormant for years, then kill you? He realised he was forgetting to breathe. He opened his mouth, the air of the packed stand tasted foul, scraped at his throat.

"What *about* that fellow Spofforth, then?"

"Damn silly name. Like a man sneezing."

"That's how he does it," Sarah remarked to the air. "Sneezes and blows your bails off." She turned her head a fraction of an inch towards Jonathan; she might be slyly seeking approval for her wit; but it seemed to give her intense pain to move. "Jonathan, I – "

Two more English batsmen came and were dismissed. And now Peate and Studd must make eight: the issue hung on eight runs.

"A six and a two will do it."

"No, *no*. Better to go for singles. No point in taking risks: we can bat all day tomorrow if we want to."

"This will be the ball," Sarah announced, "that will finish the match." She was right, of course. Boyle hit Peate's wicket, hit it, just like that, with the ball. The stumps parted in disbelief, the bails fell to the ground, the match was over: the Australians had beaten England, *in England*, by seven runs. Even the grass seemed to gasp.

The applause sounded to Jonathan like rifle-fire, the polite, glum, incredulous applause. Sarah Packham placed herself where she could glare at anyone who did not clap. But they clapped, of course they clapped; it might hurt, but England had been beaten, fair and square! Jonathan clapped till his hands ached, he would clap till midnight if need be, only one team could win, the best one . . . but if the sound of the clapping would only quieten, if it would only remain in the thundery air and desist from

penetrating his heart and stamping in the soft matter of his brain
. . .

He heard an explosion louder than any hand-clap, right inside his head: the sound of the clapping had done some horrible damage, a blood-vessel had burst, he knew it, an artery in his brain had given way before the pounding of his blood and in a minute the pain would come, the pain that would never end because blood would pour in darkness before his eyes, the darkness of death, and he would be standing before God who perhaps did send men to hell for all eternity. And he would not even have the excuse that he had been a kind husband and a reasonable father. He had foully bullied his wife; and his daughter had run away. What was left?

Sarah was looking at him with concern, though not the alarm she would surely have shown if he had been weeping blood. He put his hands to his eyes; the fingertips were not red. He tasted them. The fluid was not blood. It was salt water. It was tears. It was only tears.

Only tears. *Only* tears. Jonathan Croft of Croft & Co. was weeping before a crowd of twenty thousand at the Surrey County Cricket Ground!

"Jonathan," said Sarah, "it's only a game."

"And what you said to me, was that only a game?"

"No," she admitted after a long pause, "it was a suspicion and it cannot be unsaid. I had long ago resolved not to mention it since we can never know the truth and no good could come of it if we did. You made me very angry, Jonathan . . ."

Was this an apology? How would he recognise what he had never encountered before: an admission from Sarah that she might have been wrong?

His groan came out like a wave, deafening and shaking him. Another broke, and another. Crowds of people flattened themselves against each other to avoid him, unsure whether to disapprove or sympathise.

Sarah stood by him like a lighthouse in a swelling sea.

A man said, "I know how you feel, sir. But we'll live to fight another day, eh? The Cornstalks beat us fair and square."

A lady said, "Is he ill?"

Sarah said, "I am taking care of him."

The tears dripped on to his shirt. He shivered. He could hear nothing but the tramp of boots and talk of defeat. Defeat! By seven runs! At home! He heard the whine of telegraph wires, the chatter of presses. In the wilds of tropical jungles, on barren, hot mountainsides, in deserts and plains where Englishmen wearing Croft & Co. uniforms received bundles of newspapers every six months, and where for morale's sake they read them only one day at a time, dressed in their best for dinner in a tent, savouring the suspense of waiting for the next day's score for a match whose stumps were drawn half a year ago . . . stunned, they would read of how the home side had let them down. Needing nineteen runs with five wickets standing, they had lost.

A bottle of brandy appeared from somewhere: he drank it to its dregs.

Sarah took his hand. Hers was surprisingly soft. "Do you feel better now?"

"I think so."

"Can we forget what I said, Jonathan?"

"Can you?"

She smiled sadly. "No."

He said, "Neither can I."

"But we can forgive, perhaps; forgive each other, and ourselves. If it makes it easier, Jonathan, there are things in my past too; I may have regrets, but I do not torture myself with guilt. Perhaps if I had been as . . . unlucky in the outcome as you were, I should. Yet the outcome depends on chance; the impulse, the act may be the same."

"Will you be entering the Church before or after you enter Parliament, Sarah?"

"Excellent! You are fully restored to your fighting self, Jonathan, and I am not to be deprived, as I had feared, of the opportunity of reminding you of today's glorious victory at least once a day until you dare to challenge us again."

"Go home now, Sarah."

"I can't leave you like this."

"As you have observed, I am fully restored to my fighting self, and since I am wise enough not to give you orders, I *ask* you to go away and leave me alone."

She went. She waved to him once before descending the steps to the ground.

The early dusk of the wet August day was gathering. The huge gasometers seemed to sink before his eyes. Soon he was hurrying along Kennington Road towards the darkening heart of the city.

The pain had returned to his chest and his eyes and the faster he walked the more it hurt . . . but he would not stop. He would walk right through the city and right through the pain and come out at the other side to peace and tranquillity.

He stopped in the middle of Westminster Bridge and looked down thirstily at the dark waters. The brandy and the crying had dried his mouth. A flower-seller approached him with only some blown roses, the last of her day. He bought them, bought them all, for two pounds. He gave them back to her.

"Thank *you*, sir."

His gaze swept the London skyline as if he had never seen it before, back and forth, until when he closed his eyes he still saw it, black against blue-grey. He turned and looked south into the suburbs and the slums. Somewhere in that jungle of chimneys and roofs and cranes and factories were Pearl and her pie-man.

He really must have a talk with his son-in-law about giving up pies and going into Croft & Co.

He really must do something about this great, sharp weight over his heart; if he did not know that it was caused by England losing to Australia *in England*, it might be rather worrying.

He thought he might as well go and have a look at the river. He walked down the bank. Face-to-face the water looked black and icy and foul.

He really must step back. He was rather unsteady on his legs, his poor old legs that had carried the burden of him for sixty-six years.

He had once been very frightened of dying because however he hid from it, he knew in his heart he was a sinner, and that all the worst stories were true about what lay beyond the grave. But now he was able to realise that you might as well be afraid of water which (in spite of its icy, foul blackness) opened a warm space for you and lapped over you with words as it thrust its way between the banks, washing up slippery mud for an old man's feet, you might as well be afraid of that as afraid of death, for there was this to hold on to: the God who sent people to hell had also been human Himself; He would hardly blame Jonathan Croft for having been in the same deplorable condition.

Pearl
The 1880s . . .

Hamish Barrington's pie-shop was in Crossing Lane, Stalcross; the lane, little more than an alley, ran between the High Street and the railway station, an excellent position for business, Hamish said. Stalcross was very different from Wenbury Hill: it had several large factories, the employees of which, Hamish further explained, were much too tired and busy to cook their own pies; and high over Crossing Lane, a great agglomeration of eaten-away walls, leaning chimneys, and sad, sooty windows brooded. That was where the factory people lived.

It was difficult for Pearl to believe that her new world was on the same railway line as Wenbury Hill, with its wide, quiet streets and its fresh air. Stalcross was nearer to London, of course; just a mile and a half south of the Thames. Every fifteen minutes, a train thundered over the nearby level-crossing, shaking the pie-shop from the cellar to the little flat above, screaming and belching soot into air already thick with odours of oil and machinery, of burnt sugar and overripe fruit from Maddison's Jams, and foul leather from the tannery. Pearl Barrington thought she would never grow accustomed to the smells.

"I can't smell anything," said her husband.

"Or the noise!" shouted Pearl as a train went by.

"What did you say? I can't hear you!"

The shop was to be called Barrington's Pies. Hamish painted the letters himself while Pearl held the ladder and dirty-faced children gathered to watch. Pearl smiled in what she hoped was a friendly way, and the children stared back. Hamish seemed to have quite a talent with the paint brush. "How do you make the letters stand out like that?" she called. Somehow, with black lines round the twirly gold strokes, he had made the letters look solid.

"Prospective," he explained.

"Per-spective," she corrected. "Prospective means future." She giggled. "Mr Reeves was supposed to be my prospective husband."

"If you're so clever," he said, "come up and do it yourself."

"All right, I will." She let go of the ladder and set her foot on the bottom rung. The ladder swayed with the weight of the two of them, tipping her off, leaving him dangling. The children cheered, dogs barked all along the lane.

"Just you wait," Hamish warned cheerfully, when Pearl had restored him but not his dignity.

Some of the adults were as bad as the children, if not worse. The first day they opened for business, a vulgar man came in for a 3-pound ham pie. Pearl supposed it must be for his family, but he took a moon-sized bite out of it, right there in the shop.

"Whass this supposed to be then?" he asked rudely.

"Ham," said Pearl. "The best." It was her first sale.

"Hm! Well, ham-ish!" The man went away, chewing and chuckling. "I think that man was drunk," said Pearl. Hamish took her hand in his red, floury one and told her she had many things to learn, one of which was that the customer is always right, even when he is wrong. They would change the name of the shop to Hamish & Pearl, which sounded friendlier; and the ham pies would be known as Hamish Pies.

"Will there be Pearl pies?"

He considered: "We might do oyster patties."

She shuddered. But he was only teasing. He teased her all the time, for giving herself airs and graces, for marrying the pie-man, for having to be taught by her husband to roll pastry, for being frightened of him at night.

He made her feel so foolish she sometimes wondered if it would be easier for her if he were angry or cruel.

"It's only me, you know," he said sometimes as they lay side by side and heard the trains rattle by. She wished she could stop feeling so cold and stiff. He must think she hated him.

Laughter might help. She tried to joke.

"Is it? I thought it was Mr Reeves."

"Reeves, eh? It shall be pistols at dawn." He tickled her, they wrestled in the dusty little room that the bed almost filled – if this could only be all – he was very close, he held her tightly, she wished she were little. If she were a man she would want a wife she could lift and carry.

"I'm like a lump of pastry," she said.

"Of course, that's why I love you, I shall roll you out and make you sweet."

202

"I thought you said I was sweet already."

"Even sweeter, you shall be."

"No, Hamish, don't – "

He had spoiled it! Why couldn't he just be kind and say things? How could he want to do such a thing when he had just said she was sweet? How could he think she was sweet, how had she deceived him so successfully? What would he say when he found out, what would he do? She rolled away from him, got out of bed, stood at the window and cried.

It was a relief to cry and she indulged herself. She looked at the tightly packed smoky chimneys and wished they lived nearer the river, or a field, or even had a garden: something to stop her feeling so trapped. Her sobbing seemed to free her a little; then she looked at her husband. Poor Hamish! What must he be thinking? His eyes were streaming too; the shock dammed her own tears.

He said, "I thought I'd keep you company." His voice was steady and normal.

"You're not really crying!"

"What's this, then?" He proffered a teardrop on a fingertip.

"It looks like a pearl."

"Perhaps it is."

"Don't poke fun at me, Hamish!"

She stayed at the window.

"It's not that I mind sharing the sight of you," he said.

"What do you mean?"

"When the trains go by you're all lit up like a peep-show."

She stepped angrily away from the window and examined the bare walls minutely. She felt cold in her nightgown. It would be nice to paint the walls a good, warm red. She suggested this.

He yawned. "You can start housekeeping now if you want to, Pearl. I'm going to sleep." She watched him turn over and become still.

"Hamish."

"Hm."

"Are you really going to sleep?"

"I was, till you woke me up again, Diamond."

"Don't call me Diamond."

"All right, Ruby."

"It's *Pearl*."

"Pearl?" He sat up in his striped red nightshirt and rubbed his eyes. "So it is! Miss Pearl Croft! Bless my soul, you've followed me a long way for one of my pies, Miss Croft; what's it to be, apple?"

"Hamish, I'm your *wife!*"

He looked puzzled. "What are you doing over there, wife?"

"Just . . . looking."

A church clock rang out two.

"This is a funny time for a wife to be out pacing the floor."

"You won't touch me?"

He got out of bed, smoothing down his night-shirt with his big baker's hands. She pressed herself against the wall but he did not come near her. He went behind the little screen where he changed his clothes and came out with the plaited cord of his old dressing-gown.

"Hamish – no!"

But he put it into her hands, then turned his back and pressed his wrists together behind him. "Go on," he said, "tie 'em." His huge shoulder-blades challenged her and she could see the hairs on his back making a pattern on the underside of the striped fabric of his night-shirt, like a badly stuffed cushion. "Tie me up," he insisted.

Wants to be tied up, they does, and then you flogs 'em like schoolboys. The Queen's Women in the Periwinkle. Would they never leave her alone? She had thought that running away and getting married would make her into a new person. Perhaps it had . . . she meant to be nicer with Hamish than ever she had been with her father or Aunt Sarah; but the new person had not forgotten the old person, the child.

"What for?"

"Then I can't touch you."

"Oh Hamish – "

"No, no. You've as much right to sleep easy in your bed as anybody else."

"You wouldn't sleep very easy with your hands tied up."

"That's true." He abandoned the cord. He said, "I know." He took the bolster on which they laid their heads and put it down the middle of the bed. When he had rearranged the sheet, it looked as if they were to have a third companion for the night.

"Where will we put our heads?"

He frowned and rubbed his face. "If you put your head on my shoulder, it would be *you* touching *me* and then it wouldn't count."

They slept at last without bolster or bonds, side by side.

He was a slave-driver, there was no other word for it. When he rose early to light the ovens, he wanted her making his breakfast; he expected her to learn his recipes quickly and be ready to replace him when he set off for market. He was merciless in the face of her confession that she had expected only to stand behind the counter in a nice dress and sell pies. He called her "Ma'am", and threatened to return her to her father and ask for his money back if it turned out she had only one pair of hands and could only be in one place at a time. Pearl laughed at this. Poor Father! What would he say?

The shop had been a butcher's before Hamish took it, and although Pearl scrubbed every day till her hands were raw, the smell of old meat was always with them, mingling with the other unsavoury odours of Stalcross and grossly slandering Hamish's shopkeeping and Pearl's housekeeping habits: only the freshest produce was good enough for Hamish & Pearl, but their predecessors had allowed rank, slimy accumulations of gristle and bone and offal to lurk in hidden corners and between floorboards and in the end there was nothing for it but for Pearl to get down on her hands and knees and pull them out with her fingers.

"This is the nastiest job I can think of," she said. "Why don't you do it?"

"Very well, Pearl, my darling, and you can fit the new oven – "

There was no point in complaining. There was no point in thinking of how she used to spend her time: the sewing sessions, the outings with Aunt Sarah, the long, sleepy hours in the drawing-room doing nothing very much. "Aren't you bored, Pearl? I'm sure we could find something for you to do at Ladies Progress." "I'm tired." Aunt Sarah and her Ladies Progress were enough to make anyone tired! "I'll teach you the meaning of work," Hamish had said, "if you marry me." So Pearl could not say she had not been warned. And she was managing quite well, she thought. It was almost as if hard work was less tiring than doing nothing.

She started to tell Hamish about how full of energy she had been as a child when she collected glasses till far beyond midnight in the bar of the Periwinkle . . . and stopped before the cold amazement of his stare.

He knew nothing of this. He thought she had always lived in Wenbury Hill. He thought her mother was her father's dead wife, Aunt Sarah's sister. She had never told him anything different. And once they were in love, it had seemed that the only way of preventing him finding out was to persuade him that running away was the only solution, her father would never consent to their marriage. She had arranged all that, so that Hamish should not know; and now she was simply telling him!

"Little Miss Croft was a *barmaid*?"

Her lip trembled. "And a Queen's Woman."

"Wha-at?"

He might as well know everything now. At least he would understand, when he sent her away, that it was not any lack of love that made her shrink from being fully his wife. It was easier to begin talking about St Laur and her mother and the man she knew as Mr Croft; then she told him about Colchester, the Periwinkle, Ratty, Mrs Chicksey; and then the two Di's edged in, the barracks, the soldiers . . . his hands stopped working in the bricks behind the oven, his great strong hands that could make the lightest pastry and had wanted until this moment always to be touching her; she watched them to escape his eyes as she told him about the day she was taken to the military doctors at the barracks. When she dared to look at him at last, all she could see were tears and anger: her own tears and his, sharp, venomous jets.

"And I swore that if anyone touched me again I would kill them." It did not need to be said; he would not want to touch her now.

He wiped his eyes with the back of his hand. He turned and continued with his work.

Say something, Hamish.

"I didn't know I'd married a . . ."

Say it.

". . . spider."

Spider? Was that another word – ? "What do you mean?"

"Spider couples with his missus and that's the end of him. She bites his head off."

"Oh, Hamish! I wouldn't bite your head off."

"I'm not saying it wouldn't be worth it."

"Hamish – "

"Be quiet now, Pearl, I've got to think." He hammered furiously at the bricks, breaking them. "Was that *true*, what you just told me?"

"Yes."

"God bless my soul. God bless my damned rotten soul!"

"Hamish!"

"It's the most – " He beat his fists against the solid black stove, grazing his knuckles, beating again, – "it's the most – the tsar of Russia doesn't treat twelve-year-old girls like that!"

"No."

"What happened to your mother?"

"She died."

He stood up, wiping his hands. He came to where she was scraping dirt from between the floorboards. He reached for her but pulled back his hands and looked at them with disgust as if they belonged to a hangman.

"Hamish, it isn't your fault."

He stood there helplessly till she rose to her feet and put her arms around him.

The bell rang over the door to the shop.

"Customer," said Hamish.

"I'll go. Look at you!"

But it was not a customer; it was Aunt Sarah, bringing the news that Pearl's father had not come home after a cricket match; after a few days' waiting, during which Aunt Sarah had not wanted to worry Pearl, he had been found drowned, floating in the Thames.

2

Aunt Sarah said she had taken him to Kennington, sure that the inevitable English victory would cheer him up; but when Australia won he had taken umbrage, drunk a lot of brandy and gone for a walk on his own. She had wanted to go with him, he looked ill, but he had sent her home . . . the doctor who examined his body guessed he had fainted and fallen into the water.

"Your hat is crooked!" Pearl shouted in fear and anger; she had been wanting for years to tell Aunt Sarah how absurd she looked in her clothes; now she could! Her father was dead, she was a married woman, she could say anything she wanted! Aunt Sarah had gaps in her teeth too.

"Pearl!" Hamish rebuked her. Aunt Sarah said, "Never mind. It's the shock."

Shock? Was it? There had been times when Pearl had hated her father. The way he did nothing when she first came to him as a child and told him her mother would come too if he would only send word; his ill-concealed relief when he heard that her mother had died. The way he thought the past could be erased by the simple expedient of never speaking of it, the way he never found her when she was crying, abandoning her to Aunt Sarah's clumsy consolations, the way he thought it was enough to give her things, new dresses, tins of biscuits, dull young men to marry. She had exulted to think she could end all that and have her revenge by running away with Hamish, going back to the sort of life where she belonged, a simple life of hard work and perhaps even poverty, in a strange way she had thought she owed that to her mother's memory . . . but now that she would never see her father again, she realised it had always been at the back of her mind that she could rely on him, even go back to him. She knew that once you were married it could not be put asunder, but still there was that feeling that if things went wrong they could be put right again, by him.

"It must have been a shock for you too, Miss Packham," said Hamish politely.

"Well . . . yes. But Hamish, I should take it as an honour if you would call me Aunt Sarah. You and Pearl are the only family I have now, you see."

Now? What did she mean, *now*? The black, battered hat dipped over Aunt Sarah's left eye. Was she going to pretend that Father had been *family* to her, that she was *sad* that he was dead? They had detested each other, Pearl should know, for wasn't she the one over whose future they had played out their rivalry? Aunt Sarah wanting her to train for a profession. Father wanting her to marry Mr Reeves? Hadn't she dished the two of them! The occasional times of laughter and politeness between them had not deceived her, and neither had their carefully staged arguments over cricket scores!

Hamish who, as Pearl's husband, ought surely to be consoling *her*, seemed very concerned about Aunt Sarah. Aunt Sarah said she had other things to talk about but this was not the time, she would go home and come back tomorrow.

"You can't stay all alone in that big house," said Hamish.

Aunt Sarah gave a short laugh. "Where else?" she said. "Besides, I shall not be there long."

"What do you mean?"

"Pearl . . . Hamish. I have something very difficult to tell you. I know it will seem as nothing compared with the loss of your poor father, but you see . . . he has left you nothing."

Hamish said sharply, "We know that. It was just about the only thing he said to me: 'You're a shrewd investor, Barrington, but you'll get nothing more from me.' "

"Now, Hamish, he didn't mean that."

"But it seems he did."

"Well, yes. At the time. He was very, very distressed; and I cannot blame him. What you did was . . . unkind, you must both admit that. He changed his will, cutting you out, Pearl, leaving everything to Mr Reeves and his wife. But I nagged him and teased him into changing his mind again, and he was going to see his solicitor. There's a letter making the appointment."

There was a long silence. Pearl was thinking of her mother and the wretchedness of St Laur. Had she realised that her life with Hamish, with its early mornings, its late nights, its endless work, was to go on for ever? She felt she was realising it for the first time now. And yet she would not have wanted Hamish to give up pies for Croft & Co. She didn't want those hands of his, that could connect the back of a baker's oven to the flue and make good the masonry, then wash themselves and roll the lightest of pastry, reduced to measuring colonels and calculating into how small a space a tent could be folded. Aunt Sarah went away. As Pearl watched her stiff figure weave its way down Crossing Lane to the station, avoiding the knots of children, the scrawny hens, the ragged washing hung out to dry, she wished she could have found a kind word for her. How would she manage on her own? You grew accustomed to someone if you lived in the same house with them for years and years . . . even if you didn't like them very much.

Hamish said, "Does your aunt have money?"

"Oh . . . yes. She works at that Ladies thing."

"But is that a living?"

"I don't know. I suppose so."

"Pearl! You've said yourself, she was like a mother to you!"

"But what can we do? She can't live here. Anyway, I expect she'll go back to Australia; she was always talking about it."

She avoided his eyes, they were making her uneasy. They worked together in silence. She felt his pity, but there was something else. She blurted out, "Oh, Hamish, what if he killed himself because of us?"

"I shall be very angry," he said, "if you ever say that again."

"Yes, Hamish."

"Or think it."

"You won't know."

"Of course I shall know. A husband always knows what his wife is thinking, by Act of Parliament. Listen, Pearl. We should be glad to know he made that appointment and never kept it. Because it proves he forgave us . . . you, at least . . . and proves he didn't know he was going to die."

That made her cry. He closed the shop and sent her up to bed. Five minutes later, he arrived. He climbed in beside her and took her in his arms. "There's a few more things I forbid you to think about, while I'm giving orders."

"What?"

"Doctors, soldiers, hospitals, and being hurt." Not think about it? Sometimes months went by without her thinking about it. Sometimes, though, there seemed nothing else . . . "Why don't you give them to me to think about for a while? Have a rest from them," said Hamish.

"But if you think about them, you won't love me."

"Is that what you think? Let me show you you're wrong, Pearl. Let me be your husband."

She didn't answer; thank goodness, he didn't ask again; she didn't want to have to give an answer; it would not be no, but if it were yes, she could not change her mind . . . he went on gently arranging her, like flowers . . . "Oh, Hamish, you're right inside me!"

"I know, is it so terrible?"

"It's rather funny."

"Laugh then, you're not in church."

"We'd better not do this in church."

She laughed a little with him, it was like a strange itching and not wanting to scratch, it was as if she were floating over the smoky housetops or down a river (*no, don't think of rivers, Hamish*

has forbidden . . .) and then there was a feeling of hardness that
might have come near to the edge of pain if it weren't so sweet,
he was probing and hunting for the very centre of her, like that
doctor with his . . . (*no, no need to think of it. Hamish is taking
care of everything. Hamish is taking care of me*) . . . and then,
nothing. After all the fuss she had made, she didn't like to ask
him to continue.

He seemed very tired.

3

Hamish really liked Aunt Sarah. There were times when Pearl
felt herself seriously relieved that Aunt Sarah was spinsterish and
nearly fifty and need not be seen as a rival. She liked to come
over and help them, and she and Hamish had long talks about
politics, from which Pearl felt excluded. He even agreed to sell
pies at a reduced price to one of her Ladies Progress homes,
without consulting Pearl. She was quite glad one day when they
looked as if they were about to quarrel; but although Hamish's
face reddened as he heard Aunt Sarah's words, he remained
respectful and polite.

"I went to see Mr Reeves," she said.

"Oh yes," said Hamish.

"I took with me the letter which proves that Jonathan had
intended to change his will. I explained that although no-one
doubted Mr Reeves' legal title to all the property, there is more
to fair play than laws, and since you and Pearl are so hard up – "

"That wasn't necessary, Aunt Sarah."

"You may say not, Hamish. But I am nearly destitute."

"I beg your pardon, Aunt Sarah. But Pearl and I don't need
anyone to go begging for us."

There he went again! *Begging* was hardly the word; but even if
it had been, Pearl would have said, if consulted, that she would
not have minded swallowing a little pride if it meant she could
afford to employ a girl, for instance, to see to the flat while she
worked in the shop.

"Mr Reeves is an honourable man, and I feel sure he would
have been willing to accept his clear moral obligation, but his wife
is a different matter entirely. She cannot believe her luck and does
not intend to let any of it slip through her fingers; she delivered

herself of a fine lecture on the obligation of the living to respect the wishes of the dead. I think she fears Jonathan might come back and haunt her if she hands over so much as a shilling. One concession, though, she will allow – "

"What is that?"

"She will allow me to remain in the house. As housekeeper."

Pearl struggled to hide the relief she felt. So Aunt Sarah was to be provided for! The alternative was . . . well, she had seen it sometimes in those wealthy homes where she was sent by her father to capture the affections of suitable young men: anxious, charming, ageing maiden ladies, their hands adorned with modest rings on every finger except the one that counted. Somebody's sister, somebody's aunt, not quite family, not quite a nuisance, not quite welcome; always slightly too eager, jumping up to ring for the servant before everyone had finished eating, laughing at jokes before the important line was reached, finishing other people's sentences to show that they understood and agreed, oh so utterly, with what they were saying, yet finishing them with the wrong words . . . poor, spare creatures, every step an apology, every breath a plea for pardon for having nowhere else to go. It was not just for her own peace of mind that Pearl did not want to see Aunt Sarah like that.

Pearl was sleeping badly. She was so tired, she was terrified. How long could she go on like this? Up before dawn to scrub and cook, send Hamish to market and smile at the pinched faces of customers wanting a small pork pie to break and share among three on their way to the dark factories that belched their sickly smells into every corner of Stalcross, the shop, Pearl's clothes, her body . . . and smiling all day as she rushed between oven and counter? Stealing moments to go upstairs and set the flat to rights, working, smiling, moving all day and half the night, and then too tired to sleep as the trains thundered by, flinging patches of light into her eyes and shaking the shop? Even when they stopped there was no rest, for she lay shuddering for the next one, listening for the innocent sneering of the church-bells that told her she was foolish not to take this opportunity to sleep, for soon . . .

She woke in a panic. The ceiling was coming down, the walls were getting nearer. The room was too small, how could she live here? There were still packing cases in the corner. Hamish said, "The shop first," whenever she tried to plan to make the home nice . . . but now there was to be a baby! Where would it go? She didn't want it to grow up as she had, lying lonely on the floor while its parents cuddled together in the bed. She staggered out to the store-room, which was slightly smaller than the clothes-cupboards in her father's bedroom, in that big rich house where she dreamt she had once lived; there was no light, she heard mice scratch and squeak, she wrenched the door open, put in her hand and felt cold flesh.

She screamed . . . maybe the scream was only in her head, for Hamish would have come if he had heard her scream yet she still heard him snore. Flesh – there was a cold man in the store-room, a dead man, a passing train flung light, it was a hand of pork on a sack of flour next to two boxes marked BEST APPLES. She heaved at the sack and the boxes and brought Hamish running.

"What are you *doing*, Rube?"

He had a series of nicknames for her: Ruby, Diamond, Emerald.

"Don't call me that! Can't you see – ?"

"Breaking up the happy home?"

"Oh, you and your happy home! Do you think I'm going to keep my baby in the larder?"

"Your what?"

She pointed at her belly. "There's a baby in there!"

"I didn't know!"

"You never know anything!"

"Are you sure?"

"I just know!"

He groaned at the sound of the church clock reminding them they must get up in two hours, then he laughed like a fool. "I don't know what to say to you, Pearl."

Why didn't he just say he was pleased? Perhaps he wasn't pleased. She thought of the village women staggering across the St Laur mud-flats with their heavy bellies, she thought of the poor women who came into the shop with their beloved, skinny bundles, begging for the broken bits of pie that Hamish couldn't sell.

"Where are we going to put it?"

"Seems safe enough where it is."

"But we've got to have a nursery and a cradle and linen and a nurse and all those things!"

"What, now?"

213

He coaxed her back to bed and brought her a cup of milk. He petted and teased her and told her it had better be a boy. She said it was definitely a girl. He said he had nothing against a girl except that he might love her as much as he loved her mother and that would wear him out. Then he turned serious. "As soon as we can, we'll get a bigger place to live, why do you think I'm working you so hard? And if we need a nursery before that, we'll make that store-room into one, only not in the middle of the night. So you don't have to worry about that. Now listen, Pearl. I told you when I asked you to marry me what I'd got and what I hadn't, and you said your father might help, and I said, well, if he does, he does, but we can still manage if he doesn't. Marry me, Miss Pearl, I said, and I'll give you nothing but a room above a shop, a stove to stoke, pastry to roll out and a lot of larks. Do you remember me saying that?"

Pearl nodded.

"So there's no call for you to start saying it's not good enough for you now."

"But the baby."

"Do you think you're the only one who cares about that? Do you think I'll let my child want? But it won't want, Pearl, it'll be a good bonny baby, a little bit of me and a little bit of you, and it'll prosper through the hard work of its mother and father and it'll be beholden to nobody."

With that she had to be content. Hamish seized the few remaining moments of sleep, holding her. She hadn't meant to hurt his pride. But she couldn't stop thinking of the big, comfortable house where she had once lived, and where Aunt Sarah still lived, even if only as a housekeeper.

The noise from the street seemed louder than usual, and Pearl went to the door, wiping her hands on her apron. Her hands didn't need wiping, but she liked the feel of her stomach through her clothes.

When she saw the cause of the commotion, she thought, *Oh no*! And again, aloud, she said, "Oh no!" Bouncing across the cobbles, encircled by screaming children, was Aunt Sarah on a bicycle, seemingly in no more control of it than if it were an unbroken stallion.

Even for Aunt Sarah there ought to be limits! She was nearly fifty! She stuck out a brown-stockinged leg to halt the thing; there was a hole just above the ankle. Pearl shut her eyes and sent up a silent prayer for the glass in the shop window.

When the children's cheering had died away and Aunt Sarah's voice was saying, "What do you think of my new way of getting about?" she supposed it was safe to look. Aunt Sarah's black skirt appeared to have been cut in the middle and sewn up like a pair of wide trousers.

"Where did you get it?" Pearl asked faintly.

"It is not mine, unfortunately. How would I afford such a magnificent thing? Mr Reeves bought it for his wife, but it offends her dignity . . . having none, I am allowed to borrow it whenever I wish, so I thought I would pop over and tell you I am *delighted* about the baby."

"How did you know?"

"Why, Hamish wrote to me of course . . . ah, Hamish!" He appeared beaming in the doorway with white floury arms. "Pearl seems concerned that I am bringing down ridicule upon your shop."

"Not at all, Aunt Sarah," said Hamish solemnly, examining the machine.

"I suppose you have to wear those clothes," said Pearl.

"I suppose I do! And I suppose you are now going to tell me that I am too old for such things! Well, I am hardened to it! I have just been told that I am too old to go to Australia, so – " She stopped talking and laughed and turned away to lean her bicycle against the wall of the shop. Pearl felt a twist of shame and anger at the person who had said such a thing.

The story soon came out. Aunt Sarah was bored and weary already with being the Reeves' housekeeper, and Mrs Reeves, for her part, had expressed her dissatisfaction with the arrangement by employing another woman with superior skills for the same job. Aunt Sarah was told that she might "help", but her position as a recipient of charity was clear. Aunt Sarah was also exasperated by a tendency she discerned among members of the Ladies Progress Suffrage Committee to abandon the apparently hopeless struggle for the vote and devote themselves instead to ensuring the return of Liberal Members of Parliament. Not sharing her colleagues' faith in Liberal Members of Parliament, Aunt Sarah had accosted the new secretary of the Emigration Committee.

Aunt Sarah stood at the counter of the shop as she told the tale, pausing to attend to customers; working behind her with Hamish, Pearl could not see her face.

Aunt Sarah said, "She is certainly an absurd creature, no less so than her own name, which is Miss Flagstaff, if you please. She is not much older than you, Pearl, yet reserves the right to speak to me so."

"How did she speak to you?"

"She is one of these women who clearly considers herself born to sit behind desks and be officious. It would not surprise me to know that she has hinges at hip and knee."

"Fun for her husband," said Hamish.

"Hamish!" said Pearl.

"Oh, there is no husband, but there will be, I do not doubt Miss Flagstaff's determination. She will fly any colours that are offered to her; but we cannot blame her for that, poor soul. Would anyone go voluntarily through life with a name like Flagstaff? She invites humour of the most obvious kind: very tall and straight, yet corsetted to look as though she had been planted in an egg-cup. 'To Australia, Miss Packham?' she said. '*You?*' 'I have been before,' I replied, and she said, 'Yes, I *had* heard,' the implication of her tone being that I am the worst of bores on the subject. 'In the eighteen-fifties, was it not?' 'Yes,' I said, 'before *you* were even thought about.' "

Hamish murmured, "Well said, Aunt Sarah."

"She said, 'You surely don't imagine that you will be going under our auspices?' 'I most certainly do, Miss Flagstaff. I have worked for this organisation, poorly paid and hardly thanked, for more years than I care to remember, and if it cannot now afford – ' 'Oh it is not the *cost* Miss Packham! It is just that you are not the *kind* of emigrant we like to send nowadays.' "

"What did she mean by that, then?" Hamish demanded.

"She meant that Ladies Progress has *progressed* from being an organisation whereby single women without means may find a useful life for themselves in a country which, unlike their own, has a place and a welcome for them, into a . . . wife-finding agency for Australian farmers. And women who are resigned, or even content, with their single state are no longer eligible . . . of course, she did not express it in those terms. But she showed me a sheaf of letters from Australian men offering tempting-sounding positions – 'Five thousand acres, the labour is light, the climate

216

fair, the roof nearly built', that kind of thing – and when I pointed out that none of these letters mentioned a salary, her face displayed the coyest and sweetest of dimples – a feat I should have considered impossible, such is the dearth of flesh – and I understood that the man was not looking for a salaried employee at all. 'Having been there, you will know that Australians are only human,' she said, 'and they will be looking for sweetness of face and youthfulness of figure.' 'Then it is fortunate that cattle make no such stipulation,' I retorted, 'I shall beg on the streets to raise the fare, and go alone.' But it was bravado; her words had done their work; sweetness of face and youthfulness of figure are of no concern; but I am simply too old to go alone. It is nearly twenty years since I so much as milked a cow; I have been pampered, I do not even have the bodily strength I first went out with, far less the courage, and even then I was not equal to . . .''

The shop was very quiet. Aunt Sarah's back was stiff and straight. She sniffed. "Goodness, is someone cutting onions?" "Sorry, we don't notice it," said Hamish, but there were no onions; Hamish was cutting rounds of pastry and laying them in greased dishes, Pearl was taking the stones from overripe plums and dropping them into the dustbin. She had never considered feeling ashamed on Aunt Sarah's account for running away and marrying Hamish, her thoughts had always been for her father; but suddenly, she realised, Aunt Sarah would have gone away years ago if it had not been for her arrival, Aunt Sarah had sacrificed her hopes to bring Pearl up, all the while hoping that Pearl would have a career and fight for things. What must it be like to be Aunt Sarah now, now this minute, as she struggled for composure, while behind her Pearl made pies with her husband and grew a baby inside herself?

Hamish said cautiously, "What made you go to Australia, Aunt Sarah? It must have taken courage."

Still Aunt Sarah would not turn round. "You ask that!" She sighed. "But how should you know? Hamish, if you had to choose between safety in a prison cell – a very comfortable prison cell, but a prison cell – or the dangers of freedom in the wilderness, how much courage would it take from you to choose the wilderness? I see your shop, I have my answer; this very day, Hamish, you could be filling orders for Croft & Co., and Pearl could be sitting idly in her father's old drawing-room. But you have chosen honest work and struggle and love instead, and the knowledge that everything you have comes from your own efforts. That was why I went, Hamish. My mother was a farmer, I was a muddy farm boy of a child, I loved the rewards of *growing things*, of being at the centre of where life begins and what life is, but it was all taken away, Australia seemed to be the only way of claiming it back! I was happy enough to see my sister marry your father, Pearl, but it was not the life I wanted for myself, pushed to the periphery of things. Australia! A vast continent of land waiting to be tamed; I should have stayed, oh I wish I had stayed, somehow we would have made it right."

"Aunt Sarah," said Hamish firmly, "that Miss Flagpole of yours was quite right to say that an ordinary woman of your age cannot emigrate to Australia and start from nothing. But you are not ordinary!"

"You are quite wrong, Hamish. I am utterly ordinary. I thought I was special and clever and would make something of my life, but I was quite wrong. I thank you for your kind words. I only wish you had been at hand to say them twenty years ago. I shall not stay at the Reeves'. I must find myself some employment – though what I am good for heaven alone knows, and heaven has not told me – and some lodgings. Take care of Pearl, Hamish, and if you need any help – or if your child requires a great-aunt – I shall let you know where to find me."

Word spread rapidly along Crossing Lane that the funny lady was about to re-mount her bicycle and be off; children rushed at her, mothers appeared in doorways. "Roll up, roll up!" Aunt Sarah muttered, "Look to your money-boxes, fat ladies, trapeze artistes, headless men; there's no finer spectacle than Sarah Packham falling off her bicycle!"

"Was she always like that?" said Hamish, as they watched her go.

"What do you mean?"

"Smile on her face and a breaking heart. Were she and your father . . . fond of each other?"

Pearl laughed to cover her discomfort. "They were like cat and dog. Her heart isn't breaking."

"Do you know what I'm going to do?" said Hamish. "I'm going to give her a job."

"What job?"

"I was just thinking, I need a delivery boy."

"Hamish! Aunt Sarah can't be your *delivery boy*!"

"Why not? She needs a job, she wants to be with us, only she's too proud to ask. We'll tell her she's doing us a favour. We'll get her lodgings at Mrs Chivers', and all the time I shall chaff her and joke with her and make her believe she's *not* too old to go anywhere in the world she wants."

This last part of Hamish's plan gave Pearl a guilty sense of relief; if the idea was to cheer Aunt Sarah up enough to send her on her travels, Pearl supposed she could tolerate having her live nearby for a while. But she was a little bit angry with Hamish: she had not realised they were rich enough to employ anyone yet, and she would need things for the baby.

4

Aunt Sarah came to live in lodgings nearby. She did the pie-shop's accounts and delivered pies on the rusty bicycle that was bought for her. At first she was regarded as a joke. People ordered pies from Hamish & Pearl out of curiosity to have them delivered by a straight-backed lady bicyclist in a divided skirt; but soon they grew used to her. They started giving her things for Pearl and the baby: clothes, shawls, a wooden crib which she towed home noisily across the cobbles.

Pearl watched her with mingled gratitude and unease. Had she not married Hamish to escape Aunt Sarah? And yet she was glad of the help. She was so heavy and frightened.

The winter seemed never-ending: the days were like small, grudging patches of white in the endless blue-black of cold darkness. Factory folk trooped in in the mornings, their faces a-glitter with threads of ice; the women lingered to take their revenge on those who could work in their own warm kitchens, those whose bellies bloomed proud.

"When your time comes, dearie, you cry all you want. Don't mind us, your neighbours. Don't you keep it in."

"Such a time I had – "

"Don't look till they show you; that's my advice. There might be things as a mother's better not seeing – "

"Keep away from the Cross, dear. You'll never come out of there."

The Cross was the Stalcross Lying-In Hospital. Stalcross women seemed to know more of its horrors than the horrors of hell.

Aunt Sarah found her a midwife, a grey spider of a woman with thin hairy arms who lived amid a tangle of rooms, steps and dark corridors in a dim building. Pearl always dreamed, after visiting her, of the Periwinkle, of rats, of pregnant women without heads staggering over beaches.

Then she lay awake, unable to find comfort. One morning it came to her that she could run away. She had an hour before Hamish would wake. Shivering, she got out of bed and pulled on his coat. Her own no longer fitted her. She cried as she packed a few things, thinking how hurt Hamish would be, but he must understand that she was not as strong or brave as she had thought and she could not continue living like this. When she died, he could marry someone else, he might even marry Aunt Sarah.

But would they change the name of the shop?

Passing a dark row of shops, she saw herself in the light from a passing train. She was shocked by her own huge shape; it was like waking up in a condemned cell, the baby was *still there*, still in front of her, its struggle to get out was still in front of her, the impossible struggle that could only end in her being torn apart and killed.

Hamish was looking anxiously up and down the street when she returned; he started to shout at her, but stopped when she made no reply.

"You can grease those tins," he said gruffly, "and then weigh me out three pounds of flour, three times."

"I can't," she said.

"Come on, Pearl, you can sit while you do it!"

"Leave me alone! Oh, leave me alone!" She dragged herself as quickly and loudly as she could up the stairs to the bedroom, lay down carefully and cried into the pillow. She kept listening for Hamish's comforting tread on the stair, a careful tread that would tell her he was carrying something, something on a tray perhaps, but he did not come.

If only he would appear in the doorway with a bundle and say, "Look, Pearl! The baby's here."

She drowsed. Downstairs, Hamish and Aunt Sarah seemed to be conducting brisk business. The door of the shop tinkled and banged, delicious fragrances floated up. They might think to ask if she wanted anything, they might even light a fire for her . . . evening seemed to come very suddenly. She might think she had slept, except that she knew she had not. She could hear Hamish and Aunt Sarah chattering away; she could not identify actual words, but the rhythm of their conversation was brisk, friendly and controversial.

Had they forgotten her? She would not call for them. Nothing would make her shout.

She watched the day slope from iron-grey into darkness over the roof-tops; she started counting chimney pots but her eyes misted over. She wanted to run and run; she lacked the strength to turn over.

A fat worm of agony twisted inside her. She gasped but could not scream; and when it had passed, she dared not make a sound in case it came back at her, like a burglar disturbed in his work.

The midwife had said the early pains were nothing. What, then, was to come?

If she just kept still and quiet, it would stop – shouting would hurt, she dared not –

Now! That must be as bad as it would get. That must be the end of it. Slowly she raised the sheet and peered at herself. Still her stomach towered. Everything that had been inside her when she got into bed was still there, except for a dark smear on the sheet between her legs.

When Hamish and Aunt Sarah finally came to her, she raged and sobbed that she had been in agony for hours and nobody had cared; Hamish said, "Nonsense!" (kindly, but he did say "Nonsense!"), he had looked at her every fifteen minutes all day, and she had been snoring with her mouth open most of the time. She gritted her teeth and vowed revenge on the two of them: she had no time to do more, the pain was getting ready to tear her again and she must get ready to bear it, certain though she was that she could not.

Stephen Hamish Jonathan Barrington took twenty-one hours to come into the world; Pearl alternately howled, sobbed and rebelled, she cursed the midwife and pleaded with her, she clung to her soft grey hand and recoiled from the complacency of her touch: "You're doing fine, darling, you're doing lovely." Hadn't she once promised to kill anyone who touched her . . .?

At last the midwife offered her the white-wrapped bundle; Pearl refused it, its mouth opened and closed, it was asking for things already, had it not had enough? The midwife shrugged her shoulders and hummed as she scuttled round the room gathering together the bloody cloths and dreadful instruments with one hand, holding the baby with the other.

Pearl groaned with pain and fatigue and fear for the future. She remembered another time when she had cried in this bed. She had run to the window and Hamish had come after her and suggested that if she did not feel safe with him, she should tie him up.

"I should've done it!"

"Come along now, darling, take your baby. I'm going to call your poor husband, who's in a fine state, and your auntie, who's pretending not to be but doesn't fool *me*."

"I don't want him."

"Take him away, then, shall I?"

"Yes, oh yes!"

The midwife chuckled. "Your boy or your husband?"

"Both of them."

But laughter leaked weakly from Pearl at the sight of Hamish, all rumpled and ashamed, like a child caught with his spoon in the jam pot. "How's . . ." his eyes darted from his wife to his son, his tongue unsure as to which he should enquire for first.

"Very well indeed, sir," said the midwife. "They always make a fuss with the first." And she passed him the baby. The first! Pearl closed her eyes, then opened them again: "I haven't held him yet." Hamish carried the baby in a desperate, terrified clutch, as if unsure whether the little mite was going to smash to smithereens on the floor or punch him on the nose.

"How's business?" Pearl asked.

"Oh, we couldn't open, not with – "

"Not with the noise, I suppose! Oh, I'm sorry! I never meant to upset the customers! I'll try and be quieter next time!" Pearl shouted. Better to wait and choose the right moment to tell him there would never be a "next time".

"That'll be a day's profit lost," said the midwife sympathetically to Hamish.

Pearl held her son. There were parallel wrinkles on his knuckles, fine as hairs. "May I come in?" said Aunt Sarah; Pearl could not read her expression. "Boy or girl?"

"Boy," said Pearl, "as a matter of fact."

Did Aunt Sarah's nose twitch? Well, of course; having failed with Pearl, she would be waiting for a daughter.

"There are some women downstairs," said Aunt Sarah, "enquiring for you."

Yes, they would be there. Cunning, black-toothed factory women, their faces white and nauseated from the foul air of the places where they lived and worked, ragged busybodies, breathing warnings laced with the smell of alcohol, whispering advice; she had thought all that would stop with the birth but she knew now that it would not: once they knew that Stephen was safely born, that he had two arms, two legs, two eyes, they would cover their envy in smiles, but they would watch like hawks, watch for sickness, watch for pallor, watch for marks, listen for omens in his cries. *Mine was just the same, dear,* they would say; *the healthiest baby you ever saw, then suddenly* . . . And if they saw nothing, if Stephen throve and she recovered, they would cast spells. They would call down curses. They would come one dark night and exchange Stephen for one of their own flat-nosed stunted scraps . . . oh, why was she here? She did not belong with these people; it was like a wicked game in which she mocked the poor by pretending to be one of them, and they hated her in return. In one of her history lessons, Aunt Sarah had told her once about Queen Marie Antoinette of France who liked to dress as a pretty shepherdess while the real shepherdesses were starving . . . and the real shepherdesses turned on her and cut off her head.

"That's kind," said Pearl. "Tell them we're well."

5

Pearl kept to her bed for a month after the birth, her body a jumble of pains and weariness and fever. Aunt Sarah started coming early in the morning and staying till all was quiet at night, doing whatever was required with the baby, in the flat or in the shop. "What would we do without her?" Hamish asked repeatedly, to remind Pearl of her initial reluctance to have her nearby.

When at last Pearl was well enough to get up, she was utterly changed: even Hamish noticed, he started to call her Mother. Her month in bed had been like fifty years in those terrifying legends she had heard, when the young hero wanders into an enchanted cave, plays chess with a witch, and goes home an old man. She had thought all the extra flesh would disappear with the birth but

223

it hung on her like the sacks of mud they used to put against the walls of houses in St Laur when the river was in flood. Her breasts drooped heavily, aching with milk; Stephen's appetite was voracious but she always had too much for him. She was happy to be a mother, she liked the slowness that had come upon her, it made her feel dignified, regal; but if she was a queen, Hamish was no courtier. He seemed to think that now the birth was over, she could work as before. Waking in the night to feed Stephen did not excuse her from waking early in the morning to feed Hamish and then the factory-workers of Stalcross; the new burdens she must carry were in addition to the old burdens of sacks of flour and trays of pies, not instead of them.

"I can't serve at the counter now. I have to bath Stephen."

"Aunt Sarah can do that. She loves to bath him."

Of course she did! Who would not? Pearl loved to bath him too, and she was his mother. She defied Hamish, to hold his slippery pink son in a bowl of water, watching his lips widen into a grin that was all gum. Hamish said Aunt Sarah had to go out on her bicycle to do a delivery, he was cooking and could not keep rushing forward to serve; the customers liked to be served by Pearl, to enquire after the baby while they made their purchases. "I'm bathing my son," said Pearl obstinately. "Good for you, Stephen!" Hamish breezily retorted, "Your parents may go bankrupt but you'll never be dirty!"

She could not make up her mind how she felt about the one thing he did excuse her: he still kissed and cuddled her often, but as a child might, or a relative. For now, she did not want him in any other way; her mind would not even accommodate the thought of another child; she wanted only to sleep and sleep . . . but she wanted him to want her, and for a long time she was not sure that he did.

When finally he set her mind to rest on that score she was unprepared for the indifference and pain she felt. Panicking, she feigned the old pleasure.

Soon, cold with resignation, she found that she was pregnant again. Leonard's birth was slightly less of an ordeal than his brother's, but it did not feel that way at the time; the midwife declared that she had permitted a lot of crying and fuss with the first birth (which was not true) but now it was time for Pearl to start behaving more like a grown woman and less like a market-girl.

The bare walls of the cramped flat, the stuffy shop, the noise of the railway, the odours of Stalcross, closed in on Pearl as she staggered to attend first to one child, then the other, then Hamish, then the shop; there seemed never to be a time when all four of them could simply sleep; there seemed never to have been a time when bed was a place of rest. Leonard would wake and squeal, she would offer him her breast, relieved that her body possessed such a simple remedy, moving as softly as she could in order not to waken Hamish, who slept at the other side of the great mound of flesh that seemed no longer to be her own. She loved the way the sight of her feeding their babies awed him and made him affectionate, but she wished it could stop there . . . she knew that if she refused Hamish he would not insist, but she dared not refuse too often, for what if he turned elsewhere, as men did, to young girls whose flesh was firm and who were full of energy and laughter and health?

Hamish called her Mother; Aunt Sarah treated her as a child: a child among children. When she was heavy with the third baby, Aunt Sarah and Hamish arranged everything together before informing her that they were to move house. A larger shop was vacant in the High Street, with four rooms; with some economies and harder work, the rent could be afforded. One of the economies would be Aunt Sarah's salary; she would no longer be paid; instead, she must live with them.

"It was meant to be a surprise!" Hamish roared, hurt by Pearl's anger. "You always say you're tired – I thought you wouldn't want to be bothered with this. There's no pleasing you!"

"She organises my life!" Pearl sobbed.

"Good God! What would you do without her?"

The day they moved, she felt very sick. She was sent up the road with Stephen and Leonard to wait in their bare new home for the arrival of the furniture. It was a hot day; the old factory smells were only an echo in the air, instead there were the smells of horses and the hot crush of people as the High Street moved like a steaming, swollen river in some tropical place. There was not even a chair to sit on in the bleak rooms. Leonard slept in her arms on the mound of her stomach as she sat on the floor and rested her back against the wall; Stephen irritably chased beetles. He was nearly four and deeply resented not being allowed to help Hamish and Aunt Sarah load the cart with their belongings.

Sometimes he turned and stared at Pearl with wondering,

disturbed eyes: he had not seemed much aware of the birth of Leonard, but now his silent questions were loud. She thought of telling him there was a baby in her strange new belly, that he need not worry, it could never happen to him; but she did not know what words to use. Perhaps when the baby came, she would say she had found it baked in a pie.

She stood up to ease her spine; she opened the window and looked out at the stalls, the pedestrians, the vehicles, the horses, moving in the gleaming heat: the room filled up with dust. Stephen put up his arms to be lifted, started to whine, Leonard shifted in his sleep. Pearl lifted Stephen to the window with her free arm.

"Where they going, Mama?"

"Where do *you* think they're going, Stephen?"

" 'Stralia."

She sighed and closed the window. That was what he had said the day he ran away from home. Hamish had smacked him for putting out his tongue to a customer, and Stephen had stamped off down Crossing Lane. Hamish had darted along a short cut and met him at the end of the road: "Hel-*lo*, young man! Where have you been?" " 'Stralia." "Well, come home now and tell your Aunt Sarah all about it."

"Open window, Mama!"

"No! Be quiet; if Leonard wakes up, I'll – "

"Dog, dog!"

A mongrel bitch, sniffing the gutters, had caught his attention. Her belly hung low, seeming to scrape the skin to paper-thinness over the points of her spine.

"Come on then, we'll go out." Stephen was not excited by his new home, and why should he be? As for Pearl, she refused to be sitting in the rooms like a piece of furniture when Hamish and Aunt Sarah arrived, with their belongings.

She pushed her way along the street, heavy with her sons. Her dress stuck to her; her eyes and nose twitched with the dust. Stephen kept darting away to look for the dog.

They found the dog at last by the side of the road, a mound of shifting, steaming meat where the wheel of some vehicle had ploughed uncaring through her. Pearl covered Stephen's eyes and dragged the children home. Aunt Sarah was there with the first cart-load piled high, flushed and pleased with herself. Leonard started to scream; Pearl put him down, blind to his fury, blind to everything: "What are you *doing* with my husband?"

Aunt Sarah wiped sweat from her face. "I beg your pardon?"

"You – you – he likes you better than me!"

"Pearl, let's get this chair inside and then you can sit down."

"Don't tell me it's my condition! I've thought it long before I was in any condition!"

Aunt Sarah rubbed her back. "I don't think anything will surprise me any more."

"What do you mean?"

"That I should be thought to be doing wrong with that *boy*– "

"My husband is not a boy!"

"To me he is: a dear, darling boy, and I am devoted to him. As a son. And he likes me. I cannot now recall a man who has simply liked me. Perhaps if I had met a man like Hamish . . ." Aunt Sarah turned away. She said stiffly, "But of course if I am disturbing your happiness, Pearl, when I only wanted to help you . . ." and she walked off in the direction of her old lodgings.

Pearl took deep breaths to stop herself shaking. Now what would happen? She could not unload the cart by herself; soon Hamish would come with the second cart and the heavier furniture. He had men to help him, but what would he *say*? When would she ever find time to lie down and give birth? How would they set up shop and serve these huge impatient crowds of people, how would they raise the money for the new rent, how would they feed the children?

Hamish demanded, "Now what have you said to Aunt Sarah?"

"That's right, Hamish. Blame me."

"Very well, then, what did she say to you?"

He talked as if it did not matter! He had no loyalty. He might be Pearl herself, intervening in quarrels (as she imagined she would do) between two children whom she loved without preference: *I don't care who started it, just stop it!*

"Nothing."

"Pearl, what's the matter? I'm trying to do my best for you, but you've got to help!"

Tearfully, she told him the story of the run-over dog. It had upset Stephen, she said.

"Never mind Stephen, I think it upset you," he said.

He thought that was all it was.

She listened for the sound of the bicycle wheels above the hot hubbub as she arranged things in their new home. The furniture and possessions that had seemed to trap her in the two rooms in Crossing Lane, reaching out to bruise her and concealing anything she was looking for, seemed meagre and lonely in the wide, bare space. She thought of winter and shivered.

Hamish made no mention of Aunt Sarah. Aunt Sarah herself was doubtless waiting with her nose in the air to be sought out and have her pardon begged. Pearl would not do it! As the days went by it was more and more difficult to remember why; a feeling of doom oppressed her, no good would come to this third baby if it was born without Aunt Sarah's friendship; but Pearl could not remember anything sensible that the quarrel had been about, all she could think of was Hamish's version, which was that Aunt Sarah had been willing to help them in return for being a member of their family and Pearl felt . . . what? If she could not find the words for why she had been angry, how could she find the words to apologise? How could she have begrudged a little space in their warm home to the woman who had brought her up? How could she be jealous that her husband offered friendship to a woman old enough to be his mother, especially when, as Aunt Sarah said, he was the first man to like her? How could she explain her unease, ask for reassurance and pardon?

It was Aunt Sarah who found the words. Pearl did not know if Hamish had sent for her, but she arrived with her belongings and moved into the smallest bedroom as if nothing had happened. At last she said, with stiff fluency as if she had been practising, "Pearl, if you can find it in your heart to forgive me for not being your mother, I shall endeavour to overlook your failure to be my daughter."

6

The new baby girl was kinder to her mother than her brothers had been, coming smoothly and quietly into the world, sorry for making even the minimum of commotion. The midwife frowned anxiously over her and promised to visit twice a day; but the child evidently considered herself unworthy of so much attention when everyone was so busy, and on the third day sighed regretfully and died. They named her Ruby Sarah and buried her in Stalcross Cemetery.

Uninjured by the birth but sick at heart, Pearl wept. How had she failed the child? Had she not loved her enough because the birth was easy? She had heard of that. Or was it because she was a girl? But Pearl had only wanted boys because girls faced such a hard life.

"You're glad, aren't you!" she shouted at Hamish. "We couldn't afford to feed her, you didn't want her!"

"I'll show you how much I didn't want her," he retorted, "when the next one comes!"

She closed her eyes; it was she, then, who had not wanted Ruby.

The shop prospered. It was called Barrington's Pies because Hamish said that was more dignified for a High Street shop; and anyway, the whole family helped, not just Hamish and Pearl. Stephen could cut pastry into perfect rounds; Leonard picked bad fruit out of the big boxes Hamish brought home from the market, reminding Pearl of herself as a child chasing crabs. There were plenty of passing customers from the High Street, and Barrington's Pies became quite famous: big hotels in the West End of London sent orders, and Aunt Sarah delivered them on her bicycle. She wasn't as nimble as she had once been, and often complained of stiff bones, but even when Hamish hired a boy, he left the deliveries to Aunt Sarah. She was as good as a trademark, Hamish said.

After a long struggle, Hamish was at last able to buy the shop from the landlord and stopped paying rent. Three more sons were born: Sam, Anthony, and Charles. They grew robust and cheerful with enormous appetites that alternately filled Hamish with pride, and terrified him. His cheeks, florid from the ovens, sprouted thick ticklish whiskers, and Aunt Sarah's lined face and ageing figure took on a dignity that even the bicycle did not dispel. But Pearl was beginning to feel that she herself was turning to stone.

Her flesh was a burden; there were days when every step seemed to awaken pains in different, inaccessible parts of her body. Wearily, she listened to her growing boys' demands and teasing and wondered what more they wanted of her and for how much longer she would be able to give it.

Since the quarrel the day they moved into the new shop in the High Street, Aunt Sarah had seemed to make a special effort to help without interfering, and she rarely sat with Hamish and Pearl in their occasional moments of leisure. She would say she was tired, and go to her room. Pearl appreciated the thoughtfulness behind this; her old irritation with Aunt Sarah had faded, along with all the other emotions, into a lethargy that sometimes threatened to paralyse her. For all Aunt Sarah's curt little acknowledgement that she was not Pearl's mother and Pearl was certainly no daughter of hers, she was the only one who seemed to understand how she felt, the only one who ever bade her rest or ordered the boys to keep quiet, for couldn't they see that their mother was *tired*? Yet she had one act of outrageous interference up her sleeve, and that Pearl would not tolerate.

She brought home a book which she handed to Pearl with a steady hand and a look of nervous defiance. "Call me any names you please, Pearl, but read it." Pearl obeyed, her incredulous disgust increasing as she turned the pages. This was low literature indeed! It gave explicit directions as to how a husband and wife might enjoy the marital connection without conceiving children. There were even diagrams.

"Where did you get this, Aunt Sarah?"

"I bought it for you. Oh, Pearl, don't look so shocked."

"It's the worst thing I've ever seen!"

"Then you have been very fortunate in your life, Pearl! I have seen far worse things! Poor women worn out by repeated childbearing – "

"I'm not *worn out*!" Pearl threw down the book. "I just need to get a bit of rest. I won't have that thing in the house! What if the children found it?"

" – as I was saying, poor women worn out, children neglected and underfed, good husbands led into temptation – "

"My children are *not* neglected or underfed!"

"Why do you suppose I was speaking of you, then? All these poor women need to do is take a small sponge and a little vinegar – "

"You want me to drink vinegar?"

No, Aunt Sarah did not want her to drink vinegar. She was brief and direct as she explained what she did want Pearl to do with the sponge and the vinegar. Pearl was revolted. When she reported the conversation to Hamish, her indignation was such that she was able to quote Aunt Sarah's words verbatim. But Hamish seemed so unsurprised that Pearl was forced to the conclusion that he already knew about it, Aunt Sarah and he had planned it. She could hear them, scheming: *I'll talk to her, Aunt Sarah. No, Hamish, I will; then she can vent her anger on me and you can calm her down and persuade her.* Were all her feelings to be planned in advance?

Ten months later, Ruby Sarah Elizabeth Pearl was energetically born. With a polite glint in her eye, Pearl invited Aunt Sarah to be godmother, which role the old lady had politely but steadfastly refused for all the other children, waiting, as she had been, for just this eventuality.

Despite the failure of the vinegar plot, Aunt Sarah exulted in Ruby. The child was as round and scarlet as her name, and made it clear from the beginning that it mattered not one whit to her whether she was baby sister to the five sons of a pie-man, or the future Queen of England. As an infant she claimed it as her absolute prerogative to decide when she would feed, sleep or play and when she would not; she was as intolerant of inattention as of the wrong kind of attention; and once she was able to walk, her father gave it as his gloomy opinion that she would need her own personal policeman.

"Oh, the boys will look after her," Pearl said, watching her offspring troop down the High Street on some dubious expedition, neatly arranged by size, the pattern broken only by the tiny, dark-haired girl who refused the degradation of being shepherded at the back by her youngest brother: she would hold Stephen's big hand, or she would hold nobody's.

"I don't doubt it," said Hamish, "but who will look after them?"

"Is it the twenti-eth cent-ury yet?" demanded four-year-old Ruby from Aunt Sarah's lap, on the last night of 1899. Pearl smiled in the quiet kitchen. They were celebrating at home, just the family. Stephen, who was sixteen, was out pursuing some wholly unsuitable girl. But Hamish would have none of Pearl's anxiety: "You were pretty unsuitable yourself at one time," he reminded her, "but you've grown up quite respectable, all things considered." The other children had conducted a seven-day campaign to be allowed to sit up and watch the clock pass the point of midnight. Years of anti-climax on birthdays, when they had been sure that being able to say, "I'm five now!" or "I'm ten, double numbers!" would yield some remarkable transformation, and it had not, counted as nothing against their conviction that the world must surely turn upside-down when 18 vanished for ever from the calendar. They would not miss it! But Charles and Anthony had started yawning at eleven o'clock, and Sam and Leonard glared with such fixity at the clock's minute hand that they could not keep their eyes open beyond quarter-past. Soon only Ruby remained with Pearl and Hamish and Aunt Sarah, screwing up her face like a dishcloth and responding with equal rage when Aunt Sarah let her nod or tickled her into wakefulness.

Pearl considered the turn of the century with awe and satisfaction. Some of her nearly-forty years had been difficult, but she bore their scars with quiet pride: her husband loved her, six of the seven children she had borne were alive and healthy, and she had not yielded to the temptation to cast Aunt Sarah out. They were not exactly rich, but none of the family wore rags or went to bed hungry; and with the extra rooms that had been built on to the back of the shop, they had a comfortable home.

"You tell me what the time is, Ruby," Aunt Sarah coaxed. "What does the clock say?"

"The little hand is on twelve and the big hand is on ten."

"And what does it have to be for the twentieth century to start? Try and remember."

"They both have to be on twelve."

"I should go to bed if I were you, Rube," Hamish teased.

"I don't have to, do I, Aunt Sarah?"

"Of course you do, if your father says so." And Aunt Sarah hid the top half of Ruby under her shawl. "What a relief, Ruby's gone to bed. Now we can talk about what a naughty girl she is." Pearl watched Ruby's legs twitch with suppressed indignation. At last the clock struck twelve, and there were cheers and kisses and glasses of sherry for Pearl and Aunt Sarah and brandy for Hamish. Ruby had some milk and then went straight to bed, unbidden, uncomplaining and struggling to hide her disappointment that the new century felt remarkably like the old one.

When Pearl came back from kissing her goodnight, Aunt Sarah and Hamish were talking about politics; Aunt Sarah was walking round the room, fast, but in the slightly bent posture that she had when she had been sitting still for a while. Pearl suspected that her sixty-five-year-old bones troubled her more than she let them know; she had hung up her bicycling skirt for good. Pearl pushed a little stool near to Hamish and sat on it, nuzzling his hand; he pinched her cheek in affectionate answer but his words did not falter. He and Aunt Sarah were outdoing each other in expressions of indignation that the South African War was being fought at all: they were pro-Boer. Pearl did not know about that. All she knew was that her father would be proud to know that the British soldiers out there were wearing khaki, for had not Croft & Co. always maintained that that was the colour for desert warfare? She felt sympathy for the mothers who had sons in South Africa, and hoped Mr Reeves had maintained her father's old, high standards, for if men had to go to war it was the least the grateful nation could do to send them properly equipped.

Aunt Sarah's grey head nodded up and down with the vigour of argument that was not really an argument, for she and Hamish thought the same things. But Aunt Sarah loved to argue. She would go to her grave arguing! Or would she? If the years had brought contentment to Pearl, how much more must they have given Aunt Sarah, who, after all, must have abandoned hope of a home and family of her own and expected to wither away alone in some spinster lodgings. Aunt Sarah had looked after Pearl as a child, and again as a young mother, and again and again and again and now she helped look after the children: "You must stay with us forever, Aunt Sarah!" Pearl blurted out, and Aunt Sarah turned from Hamish and the South African War and blinked and said, "Why, thank you, Pearl!" as if she had taken *that* for granted, but was glad to hear it re-affirmed nonetheless.

Sarah
1905–1911

Sarah was used to head-colds: they, and her intermittently excruci-
ating rheumatism, were her body's way of leering its reminder
that it had allowed her her allotted three score years and ten, and
guaranteed nothing further. At least the colds ran a predictable
course, warning her with a day of wet, snuffling misery, then
laying her out for no more than a week.

But this feeling of dryness and distance from the world, of
fullness when she had not eaten and cruel irritability with the
children, seemed to be a warning of something more ominous,
however often she impatiently told herself and everyone, "It's
only one of my colds."

She was reminded of pebbles sucked hissing along a beach by
the undertow of waves; and how they lay gleaming and shuddering
for the return of the pounding surf. She was reminded of that
terrifying journey from Sydney all those years ago, except that
then she had been so miserable with sea-sickness and thoughts of
James Daggett that she had thought she would not mind if the
next wave killed her.

I'm not ready to die, she thought now. *There's something I still
have to do, even if I don't know what it is.*

"You'd better go to bed," said Pearl, and Sarah obeyed, not
for herself, but for Pearl, whose gruff exasperation seemed to say
that she had quite enough to do without nursing an old woman
whose most serious disease was her obstinacy.

It would be convenient for Pearl if Sarah died, for if she lived
she might exact some of the debt she was owed, of loving care.
But Hamish would miss her, dear Hamish! And the children too,
even though they saw her precisely as she herself would have seen
an equivalent old lady living on the edges of her childhood. "Good
old Aunt Sarah!" "Eat your crusts and you'll live to be as old as
Aunt Sarah!" "You're not my mummy, Aunt Sarah" (this from
Ruby) "so I don't have to do what you say." "Aunt Sarah, how
do you spell baboon?"

Still the wave of whatever this illness was reared up and did not break. She feared influenza: it had raged through Stalcross's factories and back streets last winter, claiming victims old and young. She shivered and pulled up her blankets. Was this the wave breaking . . . no, it was a surge of wet heat, she was boiling and wet, she thrust off the covers and looked at herself in disgust and despair in her darned, yellowing underclothes. Her knees were knobs, her fingers talons, her skin creased and faded. Did any animal or plant or tree age as absurdly and pathetically as the human female?

The doctor said, "Hepatitis," and left a bottle of black medicine. Sarah would not drink it.

"You obstinate old woman!" Pearl raged, trying to force her lips; Sarah gritted her teeth and flailed about with one skinny arm. At last she was defeated, down went the bitter black stuff. Sarah slept, and woke vomiting all over the sheets.

Pearl's thoughts were transparent as she cleaned up the mess: Now Ruby is too old to dirty sheets, I have this!

Hepatitis, what was that? Something to do with the liver. Extraordinary! Internal organs paraded through Sarah's mind in grisly single file: flat, deflated lungs, quivering heart, womb dried out like a water-hole in a drought, no longer bothering with its insolent monthly reminders of its presence . . . but liver? What did the liver do? And what were the consequences if it did not? The doctor had not looked worried, but perhaps he was being polite or perhaps she was not seeing straight. Did the liver affect the eyes? Their lids were like blades scraping across their dry surface when she blinked. Her mouth was like a dusty gutter. All the fluids of her body were pouring from her in an icy sweat – was that what the failure of the liver meant? All the fluids in the wrong places? She had never given her liver a thought; was this its revenge for her neglect? It pressed against her ribs in a sickening, aching lump. She could taste it, the taste of decaying liver, her own.

Why couldn't people age like trees? Why couldn't they be at their strongest and most beautiful at the time when they were wisest?

Wise? Was she? What had it all been for if she had not reached a wise old age? She sometimes thought that the wisest thing she had ever done was to set sail for Australia aged twenty-one, her break for freedom, her statement that she would *not* dwindle and fade just because she had no farm and no money and was a woman and counted for nothing. But if that had been so wise, why had she come back? If she believed those things about women's rights, why had she changed her mind so often? If she had been right to think that marriage was not an adequate career for a woman, why was she so miserable and Pearl so happy?

"If you had begged me to stay, I would have," she told James Daggett, who appeared by her bed in his ragged trousers and no shirt: he was still young.

"It was ya pride, Sarah."

"I have no pride, I have nothing to be proud of."

James turned into Hamish, who said, "You're the proudest old woman in the world, Aunt Sarah, which is why you're not going to give in to a chill on the liver."

Not give in? She had always given in! She had thought herself so strong, so clever, so different from ordinary women; but she had given in to Helena's plea to come home and rescue her, given in to Pearl, now there was Pearl's son Stephen grown up, walking out regularly, was there no end to it, to this cycle of people growing up, needing her, marrying, needing her, while she remained always the same age, too old, too young, her turn never coming?

Her turn *for what?*

Best not to know now, now that she could never attain it.

She was floating up a dark shaft. Sometimes she floated, sometimes she must climb. It was a chimney, a sewer, a mine; she must keep climbing, for at the bottom she was dead. A light was burning high overhead and somebody was waiting for her.

I am not sure that I like dying, thought Sarah, *I think I prefer to be either ill or well, not this mixture of nausea and lightness; and this sense that everything is over is quite intolerable, I know I had things to do . . . and I fear I am not ready to meet my God.*

The light burst on her – *We have left undone those things which we ought to have done.* Did God expect you to say words from the Book of Common Prayer, like a sort of school-inspector?

But it wasn't God, it was a lady, a lady in very old historical costume, faded, like a tapestry with fraying stitches or a portrait with the paint flaking off . . . a portrait, yes, it was that portrait she had seen at her grandmother's with Helena, for at the lady's feet was a little plaque: Lady Constancia Packham.

Then it wasn't God that you met at death, but your ancestors!

Wait till she told them that back home! But maybe she was only being allowed to know that because she was dead and could never go home.

It would never do to let people know that there was no God after all! Think of the immortality that would result!

Immorality, she meant.

The thing to do was to feel her wrist, feel if a pulse beat there. Her brain sent a message to her right hand to feel for her left.

But she had no hands. Her body was quite gone.

Dead, then –

"I don't want Aunt Sarah to die!"

Ruby's voice, howling from far away. She was not allowed in the room for fear of infection.

I don't want to make Ruby cry, but there's something I have to tell Lady Constancia –

As she fought for words in her dried-out throat, Sarah started to fall. Back down the dark shaft, down and down and back to bed.

"Whew! You gave us a bit of a scare, Aunt Sarah!" said Hamish.

"But I wanted to – "

"Don't try to talk," said Pearl.

"But I wanted to tell Constancia – "

Someone asked someone, "Who is Constancia?" No-one knew, no-one asked her.

Her liver had resumed its duties. The fluids had come back to her body. They poured in rivulets down her cheeks, cutting great canyons in her flesh.

In the long reluctant months of her convalescence, Sarah was haunted by what she had seen. She told no-one. They would not understand: they would say it was a dream, and of course it was, a sick and sentimental old woman's hallucination . . . but knowing that did not console her for not having told Constancia the things she wanted to tell her. She wished she had told her. There would be a sense, then, of having left something important in safe hands, to be collected later, not very much later, she thought, she feared, she hoped.

She had only wanted to tell her that she admired her and wanted to be like her. Flying up that dark shaft towards that strange liquid light, it had felt true. Yet now she knew it was so much nonsense. Her tongue stuck to the gritty roof of her mouth. Just two feet away at the edge of the bed was a glass of water, but would the pleasure of drinking be worth the effort of reaching for it?

At last the doctor said she could get up; she overheard Pearl and Hamish working out how they might send her to the seaside for a while. Sarah declared that she had no intention of being wheeled along some esplanade in a bath chair; if she was going to be alive, she might as well be useful. She would sit outside the shop in the May sunshine, she would smile at well-wishers and peel apples.

But the sight of the living, thronging High Street brought her no comfort. She felt as if it was beginning all over again: she had come back, a coward, from a great adventure, and all that remained was dreariness and grief. The people who came into the shop were the lucky ones; what about the others, in their dozens and their millions: the gaunt-faced, the dirty, the begging children to whom she could not deny her carefully peeled apples?

What had Constancia to do with them? (*I changed my name to yours, my lady. Did you, my dear? Why was that, pray? To hide my shame at being unmarried.*) She remembered that girl at Ladies Progress (*Ladies Progress! I trust they progress apace, sending wives to Australia and Liberals to Parliament!*), that girl who had been so excited by the discovery that Constancia had once appointed two gentlemen to represent her at Westminster. And Sarah, who had brought her dead sister's clothes, had turned on her in fury: that was not Constancia, a haughty lady who owned a town! Sarah did not wish to own a town, only her own life.

And soon she would not own even that. The street cleared and was momentarily still for a modest funeral group: one plumed horse, a sorrowing family, a tiny coffin. The dazzling sunshine taunted her; she closed her aching eyes. The funeral passed, the street resumed its rattle and its buzz, but over it all the words of the burial service tolled in her ears: *We brought nothing into this world, and it is certain we can carry nothing out.*

2

Sarah's head nodded. The apples on her lap weighed down her skirt and tumbled across the road. She woke with a start to the commotion: rumbling wheels, shouts, music, tin-whistles, shrill singing. *Now I am really dead*, she thought, for the sight was quite impossible: an omnibus lumbering up the street towards her, a private omnibus hired for some party, it seemed, for it was festooned with streamers, brilliant with colour, and the women aboard kept calling to passers-by to join them and stopping to let them get on; and they were wearing spring hats; and there was a sign on the omnibus that said, "Votes for Women", next to the one that said "Pear's Soap".

"Pearl. Pearl!" Sarah limped into the shop with a speed and agility that surprised her. "I think I may be seriously ill!"

Pearl wiped her hands, sat Sarah down, and bustled out to investigate. She returned with a twisted smile on her face, the kind that usually marked the discovery by Ruby of a new game. She said she had talked to the women on the omnibus, they were going to the Houses of Parliament to support a Bill that was to be debated to give votes to women.

"Then bring me my coat, Pearl!" Sarah commanded, "and fetch your own! And where is Ruby?"

"Aunt Sarah, you can't – "

But she was already there, her foot on the step of the omnibus, begging the young women to let her board; she went on begging long after they had smiled and stood aside and beckoned her to a seat, she could not believe they would let her come. She felt Pearl's soft, fat hands on her bony shoulders, wrapping her in a coat, she heard Pearl beg the young women not to take her, but soon she was sitting in the bus and they were decking her with flowers . . . and the vehicle was moving off and Pearl stood in the road with her hands on her hips and a tolerant expression, managing a little wave as they turned the corner.

The omnibus that brought Sarah home that evening, sleeping with her head on someone's shoulder and a smile on her lips, was rather subdued; but it was not only defeat that made it so, or even concern for the quiet streets. Yes, their Bill had been lost today; or rather, not lost, there would have been some honour in that, to have had it honestly debated and honestly defeated, but it had been talked out by a trickster, a mover of a trivial little bill about roadway lighting. The women showed their contempt by jeering softly at every street-lamp they passed; and in between, they were making plans. They woke Sarah up to elect her honorary secretary of the Stalcross branch of the WSPU.

239

"The what?" said Pearl, pressing food on her and urging her to bed.

"The Women's Social and Political Union . . . don't you know what that is?"

Pearl said she had a feeling she was about to be told . . . Sarah smiled. Pearl would change when she told her; if only Pearl had come! How could even Pearl have failed to be moved and excited by that great throng of women, the variety of them, rich and poor, factory girls and university women, young and old (though few as old as Sarah) overflowing the lobby . . . that beautiful creature from Manchester with her daughters, one of whom had seized Sarah's hand (Would she ever forget? Would she ever wash that touch away?) when Sarah told her she had historical proof that an ancestor of hers was a woman who had voted, told her she herself had collected signatures on petitions for the vote in the 1880s . . . "Thank you for your early struggles, Miss Packham," the girl had said with fire in her eyes, "We mean to win this time."

"The WSPU, Pearl! This is no Liberal Party auxiliary! It is beyond party, above party! They have one aim: to win the franchise for women, and win it we will, whatever it costs! And then we will not see such outrages perpetrated in the mother of parliaments as a matter of basic democracy being *talked out* in favour of a Roadway Lighting Bill!"

Roadway lighting! Roadway lighting, indeed! Sarah tossed in her bed. What was she to do with all this energy that her body was giving back to her after her months of illness? The soft glow of the gas-lamp winked from the streets through her window. Roadway lighting. She pulled on a coat and shoes, went out and selected some stones.

With the lamp shattered and nobody disturbed she returned to her bed and lay satisfied. It occurred to her that she had just committed a crime and could be sent to prison. But what did "crime" mean, when a matter of basic democracy could be talked out of the mother of parliaments . . .

In the morning Hamish and Pearl looked at the broken street-lamp, stoutly denying to a suspicious policeman that any of their boys would have done such a thing. And Ruby could not throw so high. It would have been awkward if any of them had been blamed. But Sarah gazed back blithely into Pearl's knowing eyes: "No, Pearl, I heard nothing . . ."

As the years passed and Sarah's stout heart forced her body to forget its age and do its duty as secretary of Stalcross WSPU, and Hamish allowed his premises to be used as headquarters only on the condition that no lawlessness was planned there (though a good deal of lawlessness was planned and executed elsewhere as the men in Parliament showed that the Roadway Lighting Bill was only one of the weapons in their well-stocked arsenal for keeping women from their birthright), Sarah never admitted what she had done. If glorious Christabel Pankhurst and dear Annie Kenney (what an inspiration they were, these young girls!) wished it to be thought that theirs was the first act of militancy, who was Sarah Packham to deny it?

It became increasingly difficult to keep her promise to Hamish. As more and more women were abused on their campaigns, maltreated by the police, arrested and imprisoned; as stories came out of Holloway of their courageous hunger-strikes and the grotesque response of the authorities with their gags and their forcible-feeding tubes, Sarah knew that a comfortable office over a law-biding pie-shop was no place even for a woman of seventy-six. She made no plans on the premises, she owed Hamish that much; but out in the street she could plan what she wished. Having decided what to do, all her excitement evaporated into fear; it was one thing to glow with pride at what one's comrades were suffering at the hands of male politicians and cruel ward-resses, quite another to suffer oneself. But there was no going back now. Not a street-lamp would burn in the street she selected (far from Stalcross, to keep suspicion away from the family) once her stones had done their work. Her age was no excuse; it was the reverse, for what had she, really, to risk? She had nearly died once already.

It was like a dream; her aim was straight, glass fell like rain, the whiff of gas hung on the air. She was quite alone when she did it, her young comrades had discouraged her, there was talk of a truce, they said, and besides, Holloway would kill her. *Kill me!* she thought, *kill me!* She wandered chuckling among the broken glass, the policeman scratched his head. "Er, excuse me, madam . . ." "I did it, yes, it was I!" "Then I shall have to ask you . . ." *Prisons, where are your locks and keys? Counterfeit courts, where is your authority?* "Yes, I did it, yes, it was I! Votes for women!" "Twenty-eight days." "You and your twenty-eight days,

I have lived seventy-six years!" *We are moving now, rumbling through the streets to martyrdom, I and this poor girl convicted of abortion and this surly pickpocket who thinks she is old. Courage, my sisters, with your years to serve, you think me fortunate, perhaps you think me mad with my singing and my smile, but together we will break down all walls! A great gate is opening, stop peering through the cracks of our dear Black Maria if it distresses you, sing and shout with me and do not hear the gate clang shut behind! Poor things, you have done no wrong and neither have I, you think your years are eternity but I am going to my death and my place in history!*

The back of the van opened; they were in a dim, turreted courtyard. The air was full of shouted orders, the clang of keys, what an inspiration those keys and turrets and orders were, *there is no escape, what it is to be free of fear!* And Sarah was marched up stairs and along corridors by a blue-uniformed heavy-shouldered wardress with a face, above her square, strong body and uncomfortable-looking white collar that looked surprisingly young and frightened.

Frightened! Well! If they were frightened, Sarah Packham might give them something to be frightened of! Not this one, though; she was a singularly ill-favoured girl, with her great square features, but she might have a kind heart. Sarah rebuked herself a little for having imagined wardresses to be one with politicians and policemen; she would set this big awkward girl at ease.

"You remind me of the matron on the ship when I went – "

"Silence! In there!"

The wardress pointed at one of a row of cupboards. Sarah understood that she was to go inside and wait. It was a WC: how unpleasant! Was she to spend twenty-eight days looking at a WC?

She listened to the unfamiliar sounds of women ordering one another about. She heard the rush of water and the regular crash of doors. It was like being inside a machine.

The water must be for baths. She had heard they made you bath. It would not be necessary in her case; she knew about the dirty bath-water and had washed herself carefully in preparation. Perhaps they had been able to tell by looking at her that she would not need a bath and that was why they were leaving her here in this cubicle while they bathed the others. Perhaps they had forgotten her; she would not be able to hunger-strike, for they would not bring her food. The smell in this place was most unpleasant, most insanitary; she would not be surprised if she caught a disease. She started to call: "Wardress! Ahem! Wardress!" "Silence!" was all she heard. The smell was making her feel sick. At last heavy footsteps approached her cubicle.

The Wardress
1911 . . .

Packham, Sarah. Single. Age Seventy-six. Church of England. Twenty-eight days for damage, obstruction and refusal to pay fine. The young wardress wrote the details carefully in her large, round handwriting.

She had only recently completed her training course and did not want to make any mistakes.

Know your prisoner, they said. She put down the pen, folded her arms and eyed the white-haired old lady from top to toe.

The young wardress knew that this was a posture that added to her girth and so to her authority; despite her smart dark uniform and the clank of her keys as she walked, she did not feel very authoritative yet. She could not make up her mind which was uppermost in Packham's face: nervousness, unease and impatience at having been kept waiting; or clear determination to be a nuisance.

Whichever it was, the wardress must make it clear to Packham, old though she was, more than three times as old as the wardress, that she was in prison now.

Suffragettes did not always appear to know this. They would go through Admissions with the air of Lady Visitors who couldn't wait to get home to their tea-tables and tell about their day out.

The prison had not been expecting any suffragettes. They had heard that the leaders had called a truce, following some promises from government. Perhaps Packham was not a real suffragette. It was the wardress's private opinon that the suffragettes' behaviour provided an excuse for all kinds of madwomen to draw attention to themselves. There was sense in what they said, the real ones, but they were campaigning in the wrong way. If they were ladies, they should behave like ladies. They should be patient. It took time for people to get used to new ideas. Meanwhile, why should Holloway staff have all the bother? These were the terms in which the young wardress had considered the matter. But it was not her place to form an opinion on any prisoner's crime; she had just to "wait on them hand and bloody foot while they're here," as the older wardresses sometimes joked in the mess.

Address and next of kin were the next questions.

"I am quite alone in the world, my dear," Packham said.

The wardress bit her lip. It was usual for suffragettes to tell this lie. They didn't want their unfortunate relatives rushing in to pay their fines. It was difficult. Pretend to believe her and she would think she had tricked you. Challenge her, and you might lose.

"Occupation?"

"Er . . . farmer."

The wardress felt as if all sympathy had been cut from her with a knife. "In Stalcross? Nice down there for a spot of farming, I've always thought. What do you keep, rats? I think we'll be able to arrange for you to exercise your profession here."

"Have I said something to upset you, my dear?"

"You call me miss," the wardress barked. "And if you *do* ever say anything wrong, you'll soon know." Even in her anger, it was hard to speak so roughly to such an old lady; and yet it was the easiest thing in the world in that place. "You've got to have a bath now."

Packham started to protest; she was quite clean, she said; the wardress ordered her to the only vacant cubicle. It was not the one she would have chosen for her, angry though she felt – the last occupant had been very dirty; but she had to be free of Packham for one moment, to calm herself after her outburst and the remark about farming. There had been farm-women here before, there would be again. Holloway took all sorts and the wardress knew her duty . . . but this Packham was no farm-woman. Those hands had worked, but not with soil and animals. Perhaps she had a few flowers in pots; or perhaps she was a witch who had read the wardress's mind and knew how to taunt her. Either way; the wardress was in no mood for her nonsense.

Deliberately she delayed, picking out clothes, hearing the listless swishing sounds from the various baths. It was like a sort of gloomy baptism, the wardress had thought, this business of the baths: water, a number instead of a name, new clothes, a new life. New life! The wardress felt like spitting with rage. Twenty-eight days! What about those who were in for years, for life? Packham would enjoy her bit of martyrdom, then she would go out to pester her highly-connected friends about "the conditions" inside, bringing about "reforms" and "improvements" which were anything but reforms and improvements for the poor devils who worked there, adding nothing to their lives but trouble.

When she guessed Packham had finished her bath she took her a bundle of clothes. But Packham was still fully dressed, looking at the warm, grey water. "I can't get into that, my dear. It doesn't look very clean."

Without a word, the wardress bent down, pulled out the plug and drew a fresh bath of clean, cold water.

"Now," she said, "clothes off, and in."

Packham glared at her; the wardress looked back steadily. It wasn't easy to look into that wrinkled face and see it realise for the first time where it was, but she knew she must not be the first to drop her eyes. At last Packham started to unbutton the front of her dress. The wardress hid her relief. It would do her no credit if she had to summon help and bathe Packham by force, and she could not guess how much resistance she would offer. Laying hands on her might break her like dry sticks; or it might not.

A button tumbled off its thread under Packham's clumsy fingers and went spinning under the door. "Leave it," said the wardress.

Soon Packham was quite naked. The wardress had known that she was seventy-six but had not taken in what that meant. Packham must have been a strong woman once, it might even be true about her being a farmer after all. There was a lot of flesh to her, but it hung in folds in the wrong places, making her look both plump and wasted. The wardress thought of her own large body; for a second it was as if she were the naked one. She was only twenty-two but already she thought she had detected the beginnings of a looseness, a slackness that had not been there when she was sixteen. She remembered her uniform. Packham's eyes enquired whether she must really get into that cold bath. The wardress's eyes indicated that she must. Packham might think she was in trouble for not bathing when she was first told, but what about the trouble the wardress would be in if she was behind with her admissions?

Packham gripped the edge of the bath and dipped her toe. The water rippled as she climbed painfully in and started to sit down. Her legs bent slowly. At last they could not stand her weight and she sat down fast. She let out a long, hissing breath. A wave of

246

shuddering began at her feet, climbed up her body and was quelled. She looked up in triumph.

She had spoken the truth. She was clean. The wardress did not insist on a thorough wash. "Let's get you warm and dry," she said gruffly.

Packham managed to look smarter and neater in the brown dress, white apron and white cap of the prison than she had in her own clothes.

The wardress said, "Do you know why that bath was cold?"

"I imagine you had something to do with it, my dear."

"Do you know *why*? Call me miss."

"I expect I said or did something you didn't like. Miss. I have been saying and doing things that people don't like for at least three times as many years as you have been alive, miss, and when you get to my age you will find that the odd act of cruelty or disrespect is neither here nor there."

The wardress heard a voice calling her to attend to another prisoner and look sharp about it. "Look," she said, "I can make things good or bad for you."

"Good?"

"Less bad. But you've got to remember where you are."

"How can I forget?" hissed Packham as she hobbled ahead of the wardress down a long, echoing gallery, past locked doors. "I am where I belong."

2

"It was her own fault," the wardress wrote, "she asked for it, Davey! I hope you know I'm not the kind to look for ways of making it harder on them than — "

Her pen paused. *I hope you know.* That seemed a funny way of putting it, as if she didn't know herself what kind of wardress she was. As if it was no longer enough for her conscience to tell her the difference between right and wrong. She shuddered. Through the window of her tiny bedroom, the wintry night seemed dead and full of ghosts. Gusts of wind brought the sounds of the prison to her. The prison was never quiet, the wardresses were never free of it. Shouts were borne on the wind, secret words were tapped on the pipes, a slammed door seemed to set the world a-shudder. *I hope you know I'm not the kind* – The wardress supposed she had been as kind-hearted as anyone when she first came in. But it wasn't the same, it couldn't be the same when you were dealing with criminals. Perhaps, though, she would not tell Davey about forcing that old lady to sit down in a cold bath.

She stared at his photograph, nailed to the whitewashed brick. Around it were other pictures, advertisements cut from magazines to brighten the room up, but Davey had pride of place. He stared back at her. What did he think of her, how did he remember her, out there in Virginia growing tobacco? It was only a year since he'd gone; he wrote every month, cheerful letters about acres and prices and rainstorms and droughts, the feel of the sun on his back, and the house he would build for the two of them and their children when he could; he wanted everything to be nice, she understood that, it was because he loved her, it was why she loved him, but how could she tell him that if he didn't send for her soon she was going to change, it wouldn't be her fault, it was the prisoners, it was the place, but she was going to change into the sort of person who . . . who . . . locked people up for a living and goaded and tortured old ladies. How could she tell him that without turning him against her? She abandoned her letter and lay down to sleep.

Her blue serge uniform hung from a hook. It swayed slightly in the draught from the window. It looked so huge to her sleepy eyes, she couldn't believe it was hers.

You had to be firm with them. You had to. She was beginning to remember something. It was important. She pulled herself back to wakefulness to remember it properly. Then she could sleep more easily.

She had been very new and green at the time: just a week out of training school. Another very old lady had come in, not like Packham, pretty as a child with clear blue eyes and soft white hair. The wardress had only seen her from a distance, didn't know what she was in for, but felt sure it could not be anything serious with her looking so sweet and frail.

The old lady had stayed on her mind. She had wished she was on her wing so that she could look after her. Privately, to herself, she had called her Granny.

Then one day she was sent to the wing where Granny was, to fetch something. And her attention was drawn by a loud beating sound from one of the cells. She peered in through the spy hole. And there was Granny chasing a wasp. She was chasing it like a demon, going *wham, wham, wham!* with a shoe in one hand and a Bible in the other. The sweet blue eyes blazed and blood ran down the old lady's chin from where she had bitten her tongue. The wasp was dead and crushed to bits but still she went on beating, *wham, wham, wham,* with her ferocious sticks of arms. Then she saw the wardress watching her, and stopped, and her peaceful expression returned, and she licked the blood from her chin.

The horrified wardress had asked casually what she was in for. It turned out that what she had done to the wasp, she had done to her baby granddaughter one night when she cried.

Lying in her bed, the wardress remembered this as an important moment. It proved that you shouldn't make pets of prisoners. It proved that you couldn't be too careful with old ladies. Soon she slept.

Sometimes the wardresses said to each other that the only difference between themselves and the prisoners was that the prisoners had homes to go to. Certainly it was a lonely life. You didn't get much time off, you were tired when you did, and you couldn't have visitors, for who would want to visit you in a prison? Sometimes a wardress coming off duty would hail a wardress going on duty with the traditional greeting of an old lag to a newcomer: "*Whatchoo* in for?" And back would come the answer: "Life." The wardress did her best to avoid close friendships. After all, she wouldn't be here long.

Elizabeth Sammington was one exception. Sammy, everyone called her. She was one of the oldest wardresses, kind and wise. Maybe that was why they put her on deathwatch duty whenever there was someone condemned to death. The young wardress thought she would die herself rather than accept the task of sitting with some wretch as she counted the days and the hours . . . even if a reprieve did usually come through.

It was all in a day's work as far as Sammy was concerned.

"How's yours, then?" the young wardress asked when they met in the mess.

"Oh, still hanging on." The young wardress shuddered admiringly. "Clever little chess-player she is, too. Seems a waste. Want a bun?" Sammy passed a bag. The wardress guessed the buns were not hers to offer, but she took one to be polite. "What've you got that's new?" Sammy asked.

"Suffragette," said the wardress, which was difficult with a mouthful of dry bun.

Sammy groaned. "Is all that starting again?"

"I suppose there's right and wrong on both sides," said the wardress.

"You suppose. Why do we have to deal with it? What's yours like?"

"Oh . . . old as the hills, mad as a hatter."

"Does she eat?"

"Eat?"

Sammy sighed. "They're right, you know. Votes for women and out with the government. You wouldn't catch me voting for politicians who'd pay the likes of you and me to force-feed fine ladies who never knew a day's hunger in their lives till they found this new game – "

This was an aspect of Packham that the wardress had not yet considered. Would she eat, or would she be the prisoner on whom the wardress was destined to learn the techniques of forcible feeding? It involved gagging them and holding them down and forcing tubes up their noses or down their throats. The wardress had heard talk. She didn't like to think about it. It was just like the Middle Ages. She remembered Packham forcing her quaking old bones down into the icy bath-water. She arranged her features into an expression of toughness, folded her arms, and stared at Sammy. "Packham," she declared, "will eat."

Sammy winked. "One way or another, I do believe she will."

"Sammy."

"Yes."

"Have you ever seen it done?"

Sammy shook her head. "It's done before they know it. It's the waiting that's the real punishment." She sat down with her cup of tea. "They have this trick, see, they put the mask on the prisoner and she thinks she's still got a few more seconds till the rope comes. What she doesn't know is that the rope's attached to the mask, and while she's waiting, phht!" Sammy flicked her fingers and rolled her head loosely on her neck. Suddenly she stopped, flushed up, and buried her face in her tea.

"I meant force-feeding," said the young wardress.

"Oh. Yes. I've done it." She started to talk about how they brought it on themselves, but the young wardress was thinking of hangings now.

250

"It's not right, is it, Sammy? Not for women."

"Ah well, there it is, you see. If you want the vote, you can't expect not to be hung."

She forced a smile. "I'll tell that to Packham."

"You do that. You had a letter from your boy today."

"How do you know?"

Sammy smiled kindly. "Your face, love."

The young wardress wondered whether Davey's letters signalled their arrival to the whole prison on her face; and whether it was happiness that people thought they saw, or its opposite.

She almost laughed to see Packham, sitting by her cell-door, sewing a shirt. She was having trouble with it. But she looked very demure in her white cap. The wardress noticed that her slop-pail contained uneaten gruel and there were two small prison-issue loaves under her bed.

"Eaten your shoes, have you, dear?" she enquired.

"I beg your pardon?" said Packham.

"Never mind begging my pardon, it's granted, only I was just wondering whether you've put your shoes in your belly, being as you've put your food under your bed."

Spoken loudly and scornfully, this drew a titter from the cell next door. Packham said, "No."

"No what?"

"No, miss, I have not eaten my shoes. My shoes are on my feet, as you see. They don't fit, by the way; but then the clothes have not been made that will fit me properly, Pearl says."

"Pearl? I thought you hadn't any family."

"We are not related," said Packham quickly.

The wardress picked up the loaves, which were dirty. "I shouldn't do this," she said, "but I'll fetch you some clean bread and you'll eat it. I'll take these home to my mother; she'll be glad of them."

Packham's smile was respectful and sympathetic. But she said, "I shall not eat again until I eat as a free woman."

"You'll be a dead woman. You look a bit feverish."

"I wonder how that came about," said Packham, and the wardress knew she was thinking about the cold bath. She put her fists on her navy-blue hips and moved her foot to make her keys jingle. "No-one hunger-strikes on this wing."

"I shouldn't worry about the Home Secretary, my dear."

"I don't worry about the Home Secretary, I worry about you."

"Why? Because you are repenting of your efforts to give me pneumonia? No charge of murder will be laid at your door if I or any other woman dies here; women don't exist as far as this government is concerned, and that applies as much to you as it does to me, whether you choose to think about it or not. And when you reach my age, you will find that avoiding death is not very high on your list of priorities."

There were new admissions to see to; there was laundry to sort. The wardress was tired of being shouted at by her superiors for wasting time. But it would be to her credit if she could persuade Packham to eat.

"What is, then? Votes, I suppose."

"That, and girls like you, pretending to be cruel and harsh when you are not a bit like that inside. Why are you here, bullying an old lady? I am equal to you, but you are not to know that. You ought to be out in the sun, doing something glorious; instead, you are a prisoner yourself." Packham spoke with a kind of disgust; the wardress went away, quickly.

The doctor said a day or two without food would do her no harm provided she drank water and rested. After that he would move her to the prison hospital and forcibly feed her.

The wardress persuaded the principal of the wing to let her try tempting Packham with some special food. She took her chicken in a fragrant gravy, and a little orange jelly. Packham's nose twitched, her thin tongue ran once over her lips. "It smells so good," she said at last, "that I don't need to eat it."

"We don't get food like this," said the wardress.

"Eat it, then," said Packham. "A girl who works as hard as you do should be well-fed . . . I expect you're still growing."

"Hope not," said the wardress with a grin, then reassembled her frown at once. She felt oddly hurt. She had always been tall and broad and had never liked it. When she started to shoot up and fill out as a child she had imagined there was a spell on her and she would one day break free of it as a delicate, pretty creature. This was silly. It was good to be strong and Davey liked her as she was. That grin she had given Packham was the grin she always gave when people talked about her size, to hide the hurt. She was forgetting herself, she ought to tell her to stop being impertinent. "I hope you're well-paid, at least," Packham was saying. The wardress considered. Perhaps Packham too was forgetting where she was. She had permission to stay with her to try and make her eat. A little cunning was the thing to use now.

"I manage to save a little," said the wardress. "There's nothing to spend on, here."

"What are you saving for?"

The wardress dipped the bowl of the spoon into the chicken-gravy and put the handle gently between Packham's fingers, where it stayed. "To emigrate."

One bony hand tightened its grip on the spoon; the other reached up and rested on the wardress's shoulder. A faint wisp of staleness reached the wardress's nostrils from the close, old body. "Good gracious!" said Packham. "Why didn't you say so before?"

"Why should I?"

"But you are just the type who will make a success of Australia!"

"America," said the wardress.

"I suppose it is the same," said Packham.

The wardress heard her name being called. She went to the door of the cell and whispered there with the officer who wanted her. She was told that she might try a little longer. Packham was still holding the spoon. Breezily, the wardress said, "I'll be out of here and over the sea as soon as my boy sends word."

"But why don't you go now? Of course. You are saving for your fare. Oh, my dear, I wish I had money! I would gladly give it to you."

The wardress slipped her hand under Packham's hand and together they lifted the spoon. "I wouldn't be allowed to accept it. Anyway, Davey doesn't want me to go until everything's ready."

"Everything's *ready*? But what is the point of emigrating if everything is *ready*? You would miss all the fun!"

The spoon with the gravy had nearly reached her lips.

"Perhaps," said the wardress, "perhaps I'll go sooner, then." Just half an inch to go, and Packham would be eating. Slowly, now . . .

"You wicked girl!"

The push Packham gave was angry but light; she was not strong, but the wardress was off her guard. She staggered back, chicken, gravy and orange jelly spilled down her apron onto the stone floor.

"You call me miss!"

"Telling me lies so that I will forget myself and eat!"

Choking with anger, the wardress wiped herself with the edge of Packham's apron and left her. She met some questioning glances in the corridor: "I think she's weakening," she said.

3

Packham was in the third day of her hunger-strike when a new group of suffragettes came in. The papers said their truce was over. They came by the van-load, guilty of riot, obstruction and damage, singing, shouting, embracing each other as their Black Maria opened and they jumped out, then subdued a little by the sight of the towering walls, the grim procedures of admission and the realisation that they couldn't go home. Packham knew nothing of this and they knew nothing of Packham. The principal wardress of Packham's wing told the wardress she wanted this ignorance to continue.

Packham's forcible feeding could not be long delayed, and the wardress was told to go and fetch the trolley with all the equipment. She wanted to argue. Packham looked dreadful. Her skin looked yellow and dry as old paper and she lay on her bed all day without moving. Everyone said it was because she was not taking food. Only the wardress knew the shameful secret of the cold bath.

She said, "If we feed her now, the new ones might hear."

"It'll be done tomorrow, in the hospital wing. Just bring the trolley and let her see it."

The new admissions were having their baths. They were obeying every rule (but only out of consideration for the wardresses, they said, who were women like themselves) except the one that required silence. The wardress shivered as their singing echoed in their bath-water and washed along the corridors, seeped under locked doors. What if all the prisoners just once stood together and rebelled? What chance would the staff have?

"Rise up, women – " If Packham heard, the song would give her courage. The wardress didn't want Packham to have courage, " – our battle song – " It would make her steadfast. It was even filling the wardress with emotions she didn't care to think about and couldn't afford to feel. It would be wicked of these newcomers to encourage Packham to persist. They were young women, healthy and strengthened by food and good fellowship. It could not be their wish, it could not further their cause to have a lonely old lady suffer torture, even death. But the wardress could not speak of that to them, she could not plead for their cooperation, ask them to ask Packham to eat, could she? It would be to forget her position entirely.

The feeding-trolley was ready. One of the wheels was loose; it trundled along with an uneven grating sound. The wardress looked at the things that it carried.

A jug and a mug for the food. The food would be liquid, milk or thin gruel, for ease of pouring and digestion. A sharp metal gag to hold open the prisoner's mouth if she would not co-operate. A long rubber tube. The wardress was shocked by its length. Was it really that distance from a person's face to her stomach? Perhaps the tube had to lie coiled in the stomach like a snake. Sometimes it must go up the nose and down again, instead of going into the mouth; that must require extra length. She found a little white dried crust of something on the side of the tube, and scratched absent-mindedly at it with her finger-nail. She stopped as she realised it might be stomach-fluid, this very tube might have been inside a woman's stomach.

Noisily, she wheeled the trolley to Packham's cell. She jangled her keys, searching for the right one, and flung back the door till it hit the wall. Packham lay still and undisturbed in the half-light from the barred window. The half-light made shadows on her, like stripes. The wardress listened for her breathing, was she breathing? She was breathing, was there difficulty in the breathing, a hiss, a rattle, anything to betoken pneumonia brought on by the cold water? The wardress would not listen. She shouted, "Packham, do you know what they're going to do to you?"

Packham opened her eyes. She had not been asleep, she knew exactly where she was. She said quietly, "I imagine that pie-barrow will have something to do with it, my dear."

"You think you're so brave now, but you'll fight when it comes to it! You will! When the tube gets in your throat, it'll feel like suffocation and you'll bite and kick at me and the doctor and all the other people who don't want, who don't want – " The wardress stopped shouting, she was near tears and there wasn't any point. Packham said, "Have you done it to anyone?"

"No, but we all hate it and we all have to take our turn."

"I would not wish to distress you, my dear," she whispered.

What was this? A plea? An offer? The effort was almost physical as the wardress tried to place herself in Packham's mind, imagine what she felt, discover what on earth would make her eat. Fear of the feeding was not enough; fear of death was even less; it was understandable that you dared not fear death at seventy-six. The wardress wished she knew more of her history, of why she was here; was there not somebody she loved who might intervene? Packham would not say.

"You're very brave," said the wardress.

"And *you* are brave enough to join us."

"What, the suffragettes? Aren't I in here already?" She had not meant to say that.

"Then you are brave enough to emigrate."

"I am too. Davey's got me all wrong if he thinks I can't put up with a bit of hardship." She wanted to stop, she wanted to go on. She would not be able to bear it if Packham thought this was another trick. "I should go while I'm young. I shouldn't wait."

"You shouldn't. If you wait, one day they'll tell you you're too old. And the worst of it is, they'll wait until it's true to say it."

"I could just go," said the wardress, half to herself. The bars on the windows were nothing to her. "I could go tomorrow. I've got enough saved. I wouldn't have to feed you then. You could please yourself."

She had been hoping to read Packham's mind; but Packham had read hers. She said, "And what will your Davey say?"

The wardress laughed. "Can't send me back, can he?" She seemed to have been standing looking down at Packham's still form for hours. She shifted her weight to her other foot and heard her keys jingle softly. "Anyway," she said briskly. "I'm not leaving you in this state."

"Are you proposing some sort of bargain, my dear?"

The moment of silence was shattered by clangs and wails and shouts for help from the gallery below; someone was fighting, an emergency, a member of staff in danger perhaps, the wardress tensed, one day that might be her: "We don't make bargains with prisoners," she said gruffly, and hurried off to help her colleagues calm the young pickpocket who had gone mad, smashing and tearing the things in her cell, ramming her head against the stone walls. Blood poured down her face, two wardresses were injured too. Other staff converged on the cell like bluebottles to a bone on a hot day. Soon all was quiet again; as quiet as it ever was, the wardress thought bitterly, in a place where such events were part of the day's routine.

As the day wore on, the wardress returned, as she put it, to her senses. *Are you proposing some sort of bargain, my dear?* That, of course, was out of the question, even if Packham had meant it. And simply going to America was out of the question too; but she might write Davey a letter, in as firm a tone as she dared, saying she was tired of waiting. She sighed. Meanwhile, Packham must be transferred to the hospital wing to be forcibly fed. And to get there, she must pass along the corridor where the new suffragette prisoners were being held. And whatever work had been done by the wardress's words, and the sight of the trolley, and the fact of the transfer, would be undone by their songs and their steadfastness. Packham would accept the torture, exulting. She would be like a Christian martyr.

In the meantime, the wardress had a plan. She consulted quickly with the wardress in charge of the suffragettes, and received her permission. Then shortly before Packham was due to be brought along, she went from door to door of their cells, unlocking them and making a little speech.

"Now, ladies, if you'll just be quiet, please," she said respectfully. "We all know why you're here, different people have different opinions and we're all entitled to them, I'm sure. You act on your opinions and we act on our orders and so it goes, but what I'm going to say now isn't an order, it's a request, a request that those of you who are so eager for the rights of women will agree to I'm sure, when I tell you it's a request to show a little kindness to a woman in her last distress."

The wardress was shivering a little inside, at her own fluency and her daring untruths. "In a few moments we've got to bring a woman along here who's under sentence of death."

One of the suffragette prisoners said, "Shame!"

"Shame it is, shame it may be, it's not our doing and it's not yours. But if you think it's a shame, then the kindest thing you can do for her is to stand back from your doors and keep a respectful silence as she goes by . . . I think she thinks she's already dead, poor soul, and if that's so, it would be a shame to bring her back to life, wouldn't it, by your shouting and carrying on, with all she's got to go through."

A girl said, "You wouldn't be playing a trick on us, would you?"

"You're in prison," the wardress barked. "I don't need to play tricks."

It worked beautifully. The suffragettes kept as quiet as mice while Packham was half-helped, half-carried by. Maybe they were even a little afraid, thinking death was so near. Packham offered no resistance. When they reached the hospital wing, she was settled in a cell with a dish of fresh broth by her bed to tempt her. "Tomorrow – " she was warned. And once again the feeding trolley was wheeled past the open door of her cell for her to see. Then the door was slammed shut.

The wardress could not sleep that night. The perpetual tip-tapping on the pipes seemed to rise in a sinister crescendo. How were the prisoners able to communicate this way when they met so seldom and were mostly strangers to one another? Did they learn a code outside in the underworld? Were they planning an uprising, were they planning a murder? Davey wrote sometimes of the great majestic silence of the nights in Virginia; would she ever grow used to that after this, would she ever hear it, would there ever be an "after this"? She put on the light and wrote wheedlingly, "It might seem a mean thing to do, Davey, but I only want her to eat and not to die, she's an old lady, she'll starve to death or she'll die of the feeding . . ." Once again she decided not to tell him and crossed out her words. He would say the suffragettes were a lot of nonsense, but she did not want him to think her cunning and sly, not when she was writing to beg him to let her come – now, soon.

In the morning she dressed slowly, thinking. It was early, she had time to go to the governor. She would ask to be put on another wing, transferred to another prison perhaps, where they didn't have suffragettes. High above the walls the wintry sun lit up the cold courtyard. The sky was blue and free, the same sky that covered the world outside, the same sky that Davey looked anxiously at in Virginia, wondering if the weather would be right for his tobacco crop. This way the governor, that way the wing; this way her quarters, that way the gates. How had she been led to believe that she was a prisoner? She returned to her room and exchanged her prison clothes for her own. She told the guards at the gate that it was her day off, and they didn't bother to check. Soon she was out walking through busy London streets. Whatever happened to Packham, she would not be there to see it.

4

It felt like a grand gesture to walk free like that. It unleashed great energy. She felt she could walk for miles, all the way home to Camberwell, and not feel tired. That would be wise, for she must watch her money now. She strode vigorously with the flow of the traffic, chilly in her unfamiliar light clothes. She stopped in a café for tea and a bun. Far away over the rooftops she could see the dominating column of the prison's tall ventilation shaft, and her mind could see the walls, hear the crash of doors. Never again! She felt no different, she decided, from all the other women who had come out one morning through those great gates, determined to start a new life and wondering how.

A man who seemed to know the café's proprietor sat down beside her and asked if she had anywhere to go. Coolly, she enquired what he thought she was. Doubt stilled his features, he begged her pardon, he went away.

She walked south, through the busy city and over the river. It was late afternoon when she reached Camberwell, and wintry dusk was gathering over the tight-packed houses, the smoky streets. As a tangle of brothers and sisters rushed out to greet her, she thought, as she always thought when she came home, how the house seemed to be getting smaller and smaller. The youngsters were getting so big.

"My tooth's loose, look!"

"Bet got the cane yesterday."

"Test me on my six-times!"

She pushed her way through them, smiling, looking for her mother. Her mother seemed very tired. She had some bad news that she had been keeping till the wardress came home. The eldest of the wardress's young sisters was in trouble and would have to marry her boy soon. There was nowhere for them to go, they would have to live here.

The wardress's high spirits fell away from her like a warm coat on a cold day. She realised for the first time what she had done, giving up a good job and expecting to be taken back at home with nothing but a welcome. Her father was working, but that never lasted.

Her mother forced a smile. "Don't look like that, love, it's not the end of the world. Are you staying the night?"

When the wardress told her she had left the prison for good and could offer no explanation, her mother started to cry. She tried to console her with promises to look for another job the next day, but she just wept and wept. The wardress could understand. Weren't a woman's oldest girls supposed to be a help and comfort to her as they grew? The children sat down to bowls of porridge, the wardress said she wasn't hungry and her mother said she wasn't either, so they just drank tea.

She slept the night in with the youngsters. She had hardly nodded off before they started pestering her.

"Tell us about the murderers."

"Ooh . . . I haven't had any murderers for a while?"

"Pickpockets?"

"Ssh, go to sleep." But they wouldn't, without their stories. "We've had some suffragettes."

Suffragettes were not as interesting. "What do they do?"

"Sometimes they break shop-windows with a hammer."

"And nick things?"

"No. Not usually. And when they come to prison, they don't eat the food."

Every stomach in the bed seemed to rumble with awe. "No food?"

"Not a crumb."

"Not the potatoes?"

"No."

"Nor the bread?"

"Nope."

"Do they eat the suet slices?"

"They do not."

The wardress started to wish she had invented something about murderers. The children were enjoying the story. "Some of those ladies get as thin as sticks."

"Are they ladies?"

"Some of them," she said, "are ladies."

"I know what you do. You put a tube up their nose, and – "

"We tempt them," she interrupted, "with roast chicken and jelly. And now we're going to sleep." In the morning she would do two things. The first would be to write a letter to Davey and say she was coming anyway, whether he agreed or not, if he didn't want her she would set up on her own. The second would be to

260

look for a job. She could not be another mouth for her parents to feed. And she had to give Davey a chance to reply.

In her letters of application, she said she had left Holloway in protest against the forcible feeding of suffragettes. It was all she could think of, to explain why she had no testimonial. No-one would want a girl who had left her previous position without giving notice, unless she had a very good excuse. They might think (rightly, as it happened) that she planned to do the same to them. She would just have to hope that one of her letters would fall into the lap of a suffragette sympathiser.

At last she was summoned to the Kensington house of a Mrs Janetta de Witt. It was a small, neat house, well-furnished, and easy (the wardress guessed) to care for. Mrs de Witt had two children and a husband in textiles; far from being suspicious of the wardress's past, she listened with great politeness, her chin in her hand, to her list of domestic skills, and then asked, "How long were you at Holloway?"

"Just a year, after my training, ma'am."

"And did you wear a uniform?"

"Oh yes, ma'am, navy blue skirts and blouses and capes. And bonnets." She tried to change the subject; she did not want to talk about Holloway. "I'm a handy cook," she said, "plain food mainly, but fancy if required, and if you're prepared to take a chance on the results, begging your pardon, ma'am."

"And what do the convicts eat? Bread and water, I suppose."

"Er, no, ma'am, only as a punishment, that is."

"I see. And what other punishments do they have? Do they whip the women? Have you ever whipped a woman?"

"No, ma'am . . ." It went on. Nothing about the suffragettes, just the prison. How big were the cells? How many lived in one cell? Were there bars at the windows, rags on the beds? Were the women lousy or diseased, had the wardress ever examined a woman for lice or disease? What sound did the doors make as they closed? Would the wardress be kind enough to close this door just the way she would if it were a prison cell . . . was it that kind of sound, or louder?

"Mrs de Witt, ma'am, I seem to be taking a great deal of your time when I feel sure you have other candidates to see."

Mrs de Witt sighed. Her bright eyes dimmed. She was like a

child at the end of a treat. "Yes, I suppose so, and I must choose one of them. I have so enjoyed our little chat, prisons are my passion."

"Begging your pardon, ma'am, but might I have reason to hope?"

"Hope?"

"That I might, er, have the honour of entering your employment."

Mrs de Witt's frown was answer enough. But the wardress wanted to hear her say, "You see, it's the children."

"Begging your pardon, ma'am, but I am experienced with children. There are seven of us at home."

"Yes, yes, but you see – " Mrs de Witt paused, "it would have to be a kindly person. For them."

The wardress started to protest that she was a kindly person, but the words stuck in her throat. Mrs de Witt had never had any intention of employing her. Prisons were her passion, her passion for talking. She probably had a little group of ladies who sat and talked about prisons. How could she pass up the opportunity of talking to a real wardress? The wardress felt sick, sick at the thought of all these law-biding souls who were so glad to know about prisons, slept safe at night because of prisons, had collections for the ex-inmates of prisons . . . who did they think worked in prisons? Monsters? Machines? Next time she applied for a job, she resolved bitterly, she would say she was a reformed pickpocket.

But it did not come to that. By great good fortune she found a family in Richmond who wanted a maid-of-all-work for five months, till April. The wardress was relieved that she would not have to lie about staying permanently. April it was, then, whatever Davey said.

For a long time he said nothing, and as the weeks crept by and the snowdrops and crocuses began to peep through cracks in the winter, her nerve failed her. Then at last his answer came. "What a girl you are! I believe you aren't joking as I had thought! Well, come with the spring, then, but I will hear no complaints that the accommodation isn't good enough! I shall meet you off the boat at New York, with a bunch of flowers in my hand."

"We'll all come on the train with you! To Southampton."

"Oh, Mum. You can't afford it."

"We'll manage, love."

The wardress knew what her mother's "managing" meant, and insisted on going alone. She said she preferred the last goodbyes to be said in private. By the time she reached Southampton Docks she hardly knew what she would have preferred. Would she want her family with her if she didn't know it meant them skimping on food to pay the fare? It would be good for them to be out in the fresh sea air. And she would like her unaccountably knowledgeable brothers here, filling her ears with technical information about the ship she stared at and must soon board. At the same time, it was better to be alone with her terror.

She hated the ship. She hated it. It was enormous, bigger than the biggest imaginable wave. That ought to reassure her. It was just that she had never thought it would be so big. She urged herself out of her foolishness. How did she think she wanted to travel if not in a modern liner? A wooden sailing ship, perhaps? That must be how that old lady in Holloway had gone to Australia . . . if her story was even true. The wardress was glad to have left Holloway when she did. The old lady's death – if she was dead – was not her doing.

It was in the past. The wide sea was the future and its breeze blew on her face. The dockside was packed with people, excited and tearful. Bands played and streamers flew. Porters and dockers wove in and out with their burdens, cranes whisked heavy crates high into the air.

But the ship was like a solid black wall. The wardress's eyes inched up the rows of portholes to the white upper decks. The funnels towered higher than the ventilation shaft over Holloway.

Why was she thinking of Holloway when she was about to cross the sea, the sea that she had never set eyes on before, except from the train as it sped along the coast to Southampton? It covered the earth and stretched to Davey. It was hard to believe it could carry this ship when it looked so blue and pretty. But it was not blue or pretty here in the dock; between her and the ship, it boiled black, full of sticks and weeds and rubbish, far, far. "All aboard," came the cries. "*All* aboard." And back from the high decks came the answering cry to the ship's visitors, "All ashore that's going ashore, all ashore that's going ashore." Bells rang and she joined the queue at the steerage gangway.

Her ticket was checked, her eyelids were turned back and looked at by a surgeon, her medical certificate was in order. She was given a number and led away down steep stairs by a silent woman in a uniform.

She tried to count the stairs. Soon she was sure she must be below the water-line. Did they have cabins below the water-line? She should have asked her brothers. She hoped the sides of the ship were strong.

The cabin was tiny, the four berths were like shelves. She wished she were smaller. "It's a bit like . . . where I used to work," she said.

"Don't know you're born," the stewardess retorted, "you steerage."

The ship vibrated into life. She couldn't believe she was on her way. Even when she went on deck and saw the land slipping away, she couldn't believe it.

The ship called at Queenstown to collect more passengers, and three Irish girls came to share her cabin. There were always a lot of Irishwomen in Holloway, some of the staff said they had crime in their blood; the wardress had always turned away from that kind of ignorance, there was good and bad in all races, but now she felt uneasy and wished she could afford a cabin on her own. She wanted to think about Davey; he was not real to her, she had to make him real. She was going to marry him, how could he not be real? She loved him but she could not imagine him. She had five days to sort this out. The nights were the worst. In the daytime she could sit in the lounge or pace the deck, feeling the air getting colder and colder, staring into the flat blue whiteness of sea and sky. At night, the girls chattered and prayed. Sometimes she wished she knew the words of their strange, Roman Catholic prayers, and could join in. Then they would pause and look at her and say, "Will you listen to us! We're disturbing *her*!" They said *her* with great reverence and proceeded in whispers. The wardress took to walking on the deck in the darkness. "You'll catch your death! Stay here and we'll be quiet," the Irish girls promised. The wardress just smiled. "It's nice up there."

A white dot winked far out at sea. It drew near enough to identify itself as a ship, far smaller than the great liner. For a moment the two ships were level, blazing with light; there were figures standing at the ship's rail. The wardress found herself waving, like a child waving at a train. No-one waved back. Where were they going, who was aboard? Soon the passing ship was a white dot again, enfolded into the blackness. The wardress listened to the low throb of her own ship's engines, the swish of water as it cut through the flat, icy sea. Some people were up late. From the celestial first class, high above her head, the orchestra played its stately tunes. Nearer at hand, in the third-class saloon, the piano thumped, and dancing figures flung shadows against the windows.

The wardress looked up again at the first class. Had somebody called her? She wasn't sure, but her attention had certainly been caught. The most puzzling thing about the incident, when she thought about it later, was how normal it had seemed.

It was as if she had been expecting to see the prisoner Packham standing there in the purple, green and white of the militant suffragettes, smiling triumphantly and beckoning her up to those opulent regions.

"Packham!"

She felt no surprise when the voice came back clear and strong despite the distance between them and the other noises.

"*Miss* Packham now, don't you think, my dear? Why don't you come up and tell me all about it?"

She answered back quite normally. "We're not allowed in first class."

"Nonsense! Go through that little door there, turn left, up the stairs, then keep walking to the barrier and I shall meet you."

She didn't even consider disobeying or disbelieving. The journey up to the forbidden regions was a good deal more complicated than Packham's directions had suggested, and she got lost several times in the web of corridors and stairs, but she was not stopped until she reached a sign: FIRST CLASS PASSENGERS ONLY BEYOND THIS POINT.

A steward politely sent her back. She asked if she might wait for her friend, but of course nobody came.

Back in her own cabin, the Irish girls said she looked terrible and asked if she was sea-sick.

"I think I just saw a ghost."

"Mother of mercy!" Out came the rosary beads.

The wardress wished she hadn't said such a thing. Even if it were true (and sometimes she believed in ghosts, and sometimes she didn't) they would be praying all night now. She had only assumed that Packham was dead, she did not know for sure. But what would she be doing on the first-class deck of this ship, in suffragette colours? The girls pestered her for details but she lay silent; she preferred them to pray; it was a rather soothing sound.

She woke very suddenly, she felt she had slept for hours but it was still dark. Her companions were awake too, staring at her as if for some explanation. She had none. She asked them, "What was it?"

"What?"

"A sort of . . . bang."

The wardress had heard no bang. What she heard was worse, for being hard to identify: more of a tension than a sound, and restlessness in the adjoining cabins, like morning, with people waking up and asking questions. The ship did not seem to be moving. That was it, the sound was silence, the ship had stopped.

"I wonder why we've stopped."

One of the Irish girls went to find a stewardess. She came back with a big smile of relief on her face.

"It's nothing," she said, "We're to go back to sleep."

"But what is wrong?" said the wardress.

"Nothing," said the Irish girl, lying down, her eyes wide open.

The wardress pulled her coat on over her nightgown and went on deck. A few of the third-class men were there, looking at its strange new covering of broken glass. The slivers and chunks twinkled, green, black, and blue, like jewels. Up on the high decks there were women wearing real jewels in their hair, and fur coats. The silence was broken by a roaring sound that felt to the wardress like her ear-drums and spine shattering: steam was shooting from a funnel. That was all. Just steam shooting from a funnel and some bits of broken glass and the great ship stopped dead in the middle of the sea. There was nothing to worry about. She smiled and scanned the upper decks nervously. She looked back at the faces on her own deck and found they were smiling too. It was exactly the same smile on every face, a smile that said their hearts were afraid though their minds had not yet been told the reason. It was like being in the middle of a family gathering where there was a strong family likeness. She picked up a piece of the broken glass, shaped like a cake. It melted into a cold puddle as she watched.

She stood for a long time watching the activity on the upper decks, not seeing what she saw, not thinking what she thought. And when she returned to her cabin, the Irish girls had gone, gone somehwere in great haste, for their bedding and many of their things were on the floor, darkening as they soaked up the black, seeping water.

"Just wait here, please. There's no cause for alarm." The stewardess was trying helplessly to make herself heard, make her voice prevail over the worried gabbling of the third-class passengers, each one of whom, the wardress noticed, as if for the first time, seemed to speak a different language.

The wardress knew the look in the stewardess's face. She knew the stewardess had her orders.

"Then why is there flooding in the cabins?"

"Er . . . a water tank has burst. You will all be moved."

"Then why is there ice on deck?" a man's voice demanded.

"A small iceberg, a small collision, it's nothing." A steward had come to his colleague's aid.

"Then why are the lifeboats going down?"

"Please put on your life-jackets. It's boat-drill only. Please put on . . ."

Numbly, the wardress strapped on the bulky thing she was handed. The crowd calmed down with the relief of something to do. Then they stared at each other in the tight-packed corridor. Somewhere a child screamed. The noise rose again. The wardress stared with disbelief at the picture unfolding in her mind: she had paced every inch of the third-class deck. There were no boats there.

"This way!" she shouted, "We must go up . . ." A crowd followed her, but they met locked doors. Her brain churned. There was another way up to the first class. She had been there this evening. That . . . person had directed her and she had found it. She felt sick. Shouting for anyone to follow her who would, she darted back on to the tilting deck and in through the doorway that she knew led up to the first class. She knew because Packham had told her.

There it was again: FIRST CLASS PASSENGERS ONLY BEYOND THIS POINT! And this time no steward on guard: only a barred gate. She looked to see who had followed her: a handful of people only,

267

she thrust her strong shoulder at the gate, she urged them to do the same, they howled with pain and panic and at last the gate gave way.

They raced through lounges and corridors and a splendid dining-room.

Heaven and hell . . .

Then what was the boat-deck? Purgatory? Pressing faces, some tortured, some deathly calm. Screams, arguments, orders, information: there were plenty of boats, the boats had all gone, the boats were here, the boats were there . . . she followed the press of people and gunshot cracked the air.

A sailor stood by a boat that was half full. He waved his pistol at the crowd: "Anyone tries to rush this boat, here's what you get! It's women and children only, women and children – "

Only a few male heads separated the wardress from the boat now, thank God, oh thank . . . .

"Back you – it's women and children," the sailor told her roughly.

"But I'm . . ."

He heard her voice, looked again, said she could come, the boat was filling up, precious time was lost.

"Go on, my dear," said a voice in her ear.

She spun round. The old lady's face was staring at her and then the crowd closed and it was gone.

"Miss Packham, oh, Miss Packham, give me your hand . . ."

The hand was like ice.

The wardress pulled at the hand, pulling it through the crowd. She would not look back, just pulled at the hand that felt real enough. She lost her footing as she neared the lifeboat, grabbed at a woman's bonnet in front of her, pulled it down off the woman's face, the crowd howled to see it wasn't a woman at all but a boy, white with fear, about to take his seat in the boat.

The sailor pointed a gun.

"All right, *girlie*. It's women and children. Out of this."

The boy whimpered, the sailor pushed him aside, reached for the wardress, his arm like a snake in writhing undergrowth. "You going or not?"

"But my friend, help my friend, the old lady." She could no longer feel the icy hand.

"I can't see no old lady."

"*Help her* – "

"No, my dear, help yourself." In the confusion, the boy had resumed his bonnet and was back in the boat. Only one seat remained. Packham's eyes were blazing in their sockets. She still wore purple, white and green. "You must see that I cannot possibly take a seat on that boat. Let that young man have it."

The wardress never remembered entering the lifeboat. Suddenly she was there, that was all; she might have been lifted above the fighting crowd. Then the boat was inching, creaking, tipping, down the streaming sides of the crippled ship, hitting the black water with a splash.

Someone put an oar into the wardress's hand and she felt her strong limbs respond, as if quite separate from her. Someone shouted to her to pull like hell or they would go down with the ship. No one knew where they were going, just get away, get away from the screams of the stranded, get away from the glorious floating palace of dreams that now reared up hideously for the plunge, get away from the ghosts of the dead and those about to be dead . . .

She pulled and pulled with her eyes shut tight. The other women took turns on the oars, but whenever anyone offered to relieve her she told them to leave her alone. She knew it was not only the cold that would kill her if she allowed herself to be still.

The boy with the bonnet took it off and put it on again, took it off and put it on again, in wretched gestures of fear, defiance, apology.

"She gave up her seat!" the wardress shouted when she could find no words.

"Who did?"

"That old lady!"

"What old lady?"

Nobody had seen the old lady who wouldn't get into a lifeboat ahead of a frightened boy because she believed in equal rights. All the other people in the lifeboat were first class, but they didn't know anyone called Packham.

The ship sank. The wardress saw it all, through closed lids. She saw the stern high in the air like a finger. She saw the funnel fall off in a spray of fire. The lights went out, the water groaned and screamed. And then the ship slipped down out of sight and the water was full of people drowning and freezing to death.

She realised then that shock was playing tricks with her mind, that this awful scene was reminding her of forcing that old prisoner into a cold bath, and none of the things she thought she remembered, from the vision on the upper deck to the cold hand in hers as she fought for a place in the boat, none of them could have been real.

She heard prayers for rescue, for light. She did not join in as she heaved on the oars. Rescue she did not care about, she felt she could row to America and all round the world and home again. And she did not want light. She dreaded it. She was right to dread it. The sickly blue morning, when it came, revealed mountains of ice all around them and dreadful things in the water: desperate, empty little rafts made of chairs strapped together, trunks and wreckage and bodies, even a tiny bloated baby dwarfed in a lifebelt with its limbs hanging down like seaweed. The boy in the bonnet nearly upset them by reaching out to rescue it, but someone else told him to unfasten its lifebelt and let the baby sink, better, they said, than to have it float for ever on the face of the ocean. The wardress closed her eyes again and pulled on her oar.

Hours passed. People groaned with the cold. Thin cheers made her look: another liner had appeared. She felt no trust in it, she could not move except to row . . . hoisted aloft on a rope ladder, warmed and consoled with drinks and blankets in a lounge hushed with horror, she heard herself being praised for her strength and courage, heard that she had rowed all night and helped others up before she left the lifeboat, heard she was ill. They wanted her name, for London and New York must know who had survived. One corner of her icy heart warmed to think of her family's relief back in Camberwell; but New York? Who in New York would care? Davey . . . he was waiting for her with a bunch of flowers . . . Davey, who had not wanted her to come. How would she face him?

New York was a nightmare of glaring lights and towering buildings and driving rain. Little boats besieged the laden liner, beat at her sides, certain to ram a hole in her or themselves. Men on them had microphones. They were newspaper men. "What happened?" they shouted. "What happened?" And their cameras flashed like guns. As the ship docked, she knew she could never get off. Rain poured down in sheets. The crowds broke forward, wave upon wave, and mounted policemen beat them back. How could she step into that? What else could she do? Once she had thought that when she and Davey were rich they would go home and visit their families; now she knew she could never go to sea again. She was here. She had got what she wanted. She could never go back.

Davey carried no flowers. She recognised the arms round her; she would never have known his face. He was coarser than she remembered, and thickly bearded. Over and over again he said her name in his strange new voice, till she forgot that it was hers.

"Oh Davey, you said I shouldn't come."

"Yes, but I'm glad you did."

"Are you? Are you really?"

"Of course. Aren't you?" What could she say but yes?

They stayed for a day with friends of his in New York for her to recover. The friends were kind; the woman gave her clothes. Davey wanted to be back with his crops. They took the train to Virginia, a great-wheeled snorting thing, whistling its contempt for her awe at the wide green countryside. It set them down at last in the middle of a dark wilderness: a man with a mule-cart helped her down. "Ladies first," he said. "We're proud to have you with us, ma'am." He was Davey's neighbour.

The morning revealed that Davey had told the truth when he said the living was rough; the hut was bare, each meal the same, the neighbours stolid farmers and their suspicious, imperious wives. But she did not mind; rest, luxury and conversation were the last things she wanted. She wanted to work, break her back with it, die of it.

"I guess the first thing we do," said Davey, "is get ourselves married."

"Yes, Davey."

"You say that as if you don't want to."

"Of course I want to."

It was strange to be Mrs David Blatch, the tobacco grower's wife. Still: better than locking people up for a living! Spring became summer, the fields were green, the sun was warm, she learned the work, made friends. Davey had grown rough mannered living alone, but she could usually humour him. He worked hard. There was no sign of any grand house for her and she wondered how long she would have waited.

"Now, now, don't look like a wardress," he said sometimes when they quarrelled.

"I'd be a wardress to this day, if I'd waited for you," she retorted.

Sometimes he laughed, sometimes he scowled and said he only wanted the best for her.

It was true, he was a hard-working man and she was content. When she found she was expecting a child she hardly knew whether to hope for a boy to please Davey, or a girl so that she could call her Sarah, which she remembered writing in the register at Holloway as Packham's first name. For a long time she had blotted Miss Packham from her mind. Either explanation – that she had drowned in that icy black sea, that she was a ghost – was intolerable and set her shivering. But the nightmare was fading as her new life became real. A stream flowed near the wooden hut that was her home, and it was good, in time, to grow used to the sound of water that was sweet and alive. Sometimes she stood by it in the evenings and watched the sun go down, her bones aching after a day's work, her body seeming to grow before her eyes. *You showed me the way to the boat deck, in any case. What is it now, votes for mermaids? Rest in peace, old lady at the bottom of the sea, or wherever you are. I won't forget.*

Ruby
1913–1937

"Bother Aunt Sarah!" Pearl Barrington sat heavily at the table in the little kitchen above Barrington's: Manufacturers of Superior Pies. Her face was in her hands. Her voice was faint with tiredness and exasperation.

From the other side of the table, her daughter Ruby watched her uneasily, wondering why she had to cry so much. There they had been, having a perfectly reasonable discussion about Ruby's future, and now her mother had to spoil it by bursting into tears. "I never mentioned Aunt Sarah!" said Ruby righteously. She meant to win the argument but not with unfair tactics, not at this stage. Her mother was still grieving. Of course she knew as well as Ruby did that the old woman would have been an ally for Ruby in her determination to follow her brothers and take a job and earn her living. It was not necessary to remind her.

"All my life, Aunt Sarah has told me how to manage my affairs! Heaven forgive me, but the one consolation I might have found in her dying was that I might be mistress in my own home, at last! And now you start, Ruby! It's wicked of you to bring her into this, wicked! I simply don't see why it is that you can't wait to be out of the house. When I was – "

"I have to do something, Mum."

"There's plenty to do in the shop!"

Ruby yawned. "There's more to life than pies, Mum."

Her mother's face, writhed with a sarcasm which, Ruby thought, was a new development in her character, only used on her daughter. "Is there, Ruby? Do be sure and tell me what it is when you find it, you impudent girl! And in the meantime, no, for the tenth time, I am not coming with you to the Misses Parley Typewriting Agency for an interview; it would be a waste of our time and theirs, because even if they accept you, you are not going to work there and *that's final*."

Her brother Charles came in at this point: the last of the brothers left at home, he was very cocky. He whistled as he walked. "Going to be a typewriter, Rube?" She sniffed. "Go back to your drains, I was talking to my mother." Charles was learning to be a plumber.

At sixteen, Ruby Barrington was a steadfast arguer. Her father said she had been born arguing, with little clenched fists, but she knew quite well the origins of any slight obstreperousness that might be in her character. Her eldest brother, Stephen had never bothered with her much, and Leonard was kind; but with Sam, Anthony and Charles, it had been a simple matter of self-defence. If she had not learned how to stand up for herself, she would have been flattened like a cat beneath an omnibus. The present controversy was a precise example of what she meant. When Stephen and Leonard had left school, it was taken for granted that they would go into Barrington's and open new shops. Sam went into the army. Anthony was a clerk, and Charles had chosen drains. No-one had minded, everyone was delighted, but now that she, Ruby, with help from no-one, had applied for a job and been invited for an interview (bringing her mother with her) everyone was getting upset: would it be safe for her to travel every day into London on a train and type in an office? Wouldn't her mother be lonely?

Ruby sighed. It was not "everyone" who was saying these things. Her father was quite encouraging, and her brothers only teased. It was her mother who opposed her; and it was so unfair, because Ruby was sure there was an element in her opposition of getting revenge on Aunt Sarah. Ruby might have understood this better if she herself showed any signs of going the same way as Aunt Sarah, bringing disgrace on the family and having to be rescued from Holloway prison, but Aunt Sarah's activities had been as mortifying and inexplicable to Ruby as they had been to everyone else. Ruby believed in the Vote, everyone did who was modern, and she always bought the suffrage newspapers if she happened to pass by a girl selling them (she had found her job advertised in one of these, though she had not told her mother that); but the militants were going about it in the wrong way. You only had to pick up an ordinary newspaper to discover that someone else had completely lost patience with the cause.

Ruby knew that she would never have the courage to go to prison, even if she thought it the right thing to do; but that was not all. The scorn and anger of her brothers, when some new suffragette outrage was reported, frightened her. She was used to argument, used to teasing, but this was something different. It was like the way they talked about Aunt Sarah, in death as in life: as a good sort who could take a joke, and make one, and would help you out, but not really a person to love, not a person to take seriously.

Charles had said the worst thing of all, when the news came that the *Titanic* had gone down after hitting an iceberg. He had said, "I expect Aunt Sarah was steering at the time."

There had been a few days of sincere, respectful grieving as the enormity of the disaster became known; but the jokes soon started again, as if Charles, who had shed a tear or two at the memorial service, had frightened and angered himself by doing so and wanted to restore his normal personality as soon as possible. Ship or no ship, he pointed out, time was running out for any seventy-seven-year-old who insisted on acting the fool the way Aunt Sarah did. Their parents told him sharply to be quiet. He made no more of his remarks in front of them, but he often said to Ruby, with an expression she could not read. "You'd think they'd have let an old lady into one of the lifeboats, wouldn't you, Rube?"

She was a short, plump girl with black hair that needed no attention from her to form itself into tight curls. She had a new blue suit and her neat hat matched. Her mother had crept into her room this morning with a surprise gift, a white blouse with blue embroidery and a peter-pan collar. Waiting now on the draughty station at Stalcross for the morning train to London Bridge, Ruby felt the slightly tight new collar cut into her neck. But the discomfort was nothing compared with her sense of victory. Ruby Barrington was going to work.

In the end, her mother had given in. She always did.

The platform was crowded with smartly dressed strangers. Ruby tried to look relaxed, as if she did this every day. She followed their example and glanced anxiously up the track for some sign of the train. Seeing none, she looked up at the station clock and frowned. She could not be late on her first morning!

That was a fear . . . but oh, the luxury of having it as a fear! Some of her old school-friends had jobs, and some had to stay at home and help their mothers. Few of the jobs were as exciting as Ruby's was going to be, but she had no doubt which group was going to have the better life.

She looked fondly at the level-crossing. She knew her parents had had their first shop here, when they were young and poor: look carefully at the name of what was now a haberdasher's and you could just make out a layer of faint lettering: Hamish & Pearl. And there was the gap in the fence where Charles, Anthony and Sam used to challenge local boys to play Last Across. Ruby shuddered to think of the risks they took; the game was strictly forbidden, of course, and Ruby used to collect a percentage of the winnings as the price of her silence. Once a boy from school, Alan Morris, fell before a train and it ran over his hand. He was lucky. He only lost the tip of his little finger. He came to enjoy it. He chased new girls at school with the stump: "That was the finger I used to take wax out of me ear. Who'll take the wax out of me ear now?"

Alan Morris! What had happened to him? She recited the names of all the people she could remember from school: Mary Stibbings, Lucy Tadpole, Michael Gold. School was only months away, but these once-familiar names had lost their faces; they sounded like a mysterious incantation. How quickly time passed! If it were not so exciting, it might scare her.

The train came. She found a seat. It was very cold in the carriage. As the train rattled into London she found she was not the only person discomforted by this. The men were battling with their newspapers and the few women held on to their hats, but there seemed to be a private agreement to leave the window open, so of course Ruby, as a newcomer, could not take it on herself to close it.

Her mother had said, "Don't talk to strange men on trains." It was a relief, then, to reach London Bridge without being accosted. The next thing she must do was catch the bus to the Misses Parley Agency, and here another warning must be borne in mind. "Never take a window-seat in a bus, Ruby. A man could sit next to you and trap you." On the other hand, it would be nice to watch the city speeding by at close quarters, the city she had visited before on childish treats but where she now felt she had a place. So she took a window-seat and sure enough, a man sat down and trapped her.

Perhaps "trapped" wasn't quite the right word, but he contrived to sit in such a way that he took two-thirds of the available space. She gave way at first before the pressure of his hip-bones and crushed herself against the side of the bus; one glance at his face, however, was enough to tell her that he had no sinister aim, it was a very clean, young face, pink and honest, with a neat, sandy moustache and a slightly turned-up nose. He was just selfish in the way of young men, she thought, she could imagine any one of her brothers overwhelming a bus-seat in just such a way. Spotting that similarity gave her the courage to shift herself hard against him, asserting her right to half the seat, not one inch less or more. And he gave way.

She sat and blushed with triumph. He was looking at her. He said, "New job?"

She bristled. Did it show? But then he was quite bright and spruce-looking himself, and not much older than she was. For all his talk, it might be his first day as well. So he had nothing to be so high-and-mighty about!

"All right, don't answer," he said. "I don't need to be answered to go on talking. The only way you'll get me to stop is if you say I'm being a frightful bore. That would crush me. What is it now, let me see . . . a telephone girl?"

This was too much. "I type," she said coldly. The conductor came for their fares. She paid her own without saying where she was going, another of her mother's suggested precautions.

"Do you? I say, how clever. I'm by way of being a poet and my poems always look much better when I can bully Miss Collins into typing them for me. Miss Collins works at the bank. She types very fast, faster than you, do you suppose? She does shorthand as well, do you? If she was here, by the time I got to the end of what I was saying, she'd have it all typed out with a carbon copy. And I do talk rather quickly."

"And rather a lot," said Ruby.

He grinned and started to get up. A sunbeam danced in his fair hair. "I have to get off, the bank's there. But I don't know anything about you, your name or anything."

"You don't know anything about lots of things," said Ruby, "manners for instance."

She was rather pleased with that. Her mother should not worry. All the practice she had at home made her more than a match for bus-travelling scoundrels who would trap her in her seat. The young man need not suppose that she was flattered by his attentions. She had hardly spoken ten words to him.

"I'm *so* pleased you are not late, Miss Barrington. It is scarcely credible that a girl would be late on her first morning, but I have heard of it. I would have had to rebuke you quite severely, for your own good."

Ruby took in this greeting from Miss Ada Parley, wondering whether she was expected to thank her employer for her willingness to have regard for her welfare, or to apologise, on account, as it were, for those future mornings when she might be late. But Miss Millicent Parley appeared behind her sister and welcomed Ruby with such charm that she could only stare at the two beautiful, gracious creatures with admiration and envy.

She had been given strict instructions as to how she was to address her employers. If only one of them was in the room, or if it was otherwise clear to whom she was speaking, "Miss Parley" would suffice. Otherwise she must call them "Miss Ada" or "Miss Millicent", and she must always distinguish accurately between the two.

This was not difficult. They were both handsome women, approaching thirty, but there was no danger of confusing them. They complemented each other, almost as husband and wife were supposed to. Miss Ada's hair was bobbed, revealing an elegant neck, and she wore a dress of lime green, Miss Millicent's clothes were sterner: she wore a necktie over a tailored blouse, which was gathered in at the waist, along with a black skirt, under the sharp command of a wide black belt. But her figure and features were so much softer, fuller and fleshier than those of her sister that the result was winsome rather than severe.

The office was small and smelled of oil, both from the watchmaker's shop downstairs and from the heaters. There were four typewriters, one new and covered and apparently not in use, two slightly less new with paper already in place, and a fourth old battleship of a machine which Ruby guessed was to be hers. She looked at it and shivered.

"Are you cold, Miss Barrington?"

Ruby tried to collect herself, to remember where she was, to focus her eyes through the tears that had leapt there

"No, Miss Millicent."

"But you are trembling, and it cannot be that you are afraid of *us*. Ada, our little trainee is perished with cold; are the stoves functioning?" There followed a great confusion of concern, with both the Misses Parley going down on their hands and knees to tap and sniff at the oil-stoves . . . but Ruby was looking at the typewriters, at the one that was to be hers.

Votes are not enough. Teach that child to type. She could hear Aunt Sarah's voice as if it were she, and not the Misses Parley, who reigned over this office. Aunt Sarah had had a typewriter just like that one in her Votes for Women headquarters. And Ruby, aged ten, had leaned on the door-handle, squinting at it, curious about Aunt Sarah, curious about the typist who sat there, her fingers moving like lightning over the machine, turning handwriting or words in the air into firm, unarguable print. *Teach that child to type.* Each day, Ruby had stood for fifteen minutes beside the typist and learned where all the letters were. Aunt Sarah had known Ruby would want to earn her own living. And now it was too late to thank her for making it possible.

"Miss Barrington, my *dear* – your first day at work should not be a time for tears."

"I know – ." But she could not rid herself of the spectacle of Aunt Sarah being brought home, a sulky ghost, from Holloway. She had been furious. It was as if she had wanted to be forcibly fed. But the authorities had lost their nerve and let her go, made her go. *Hah!* she had cackled, *where am I to go when even prisons will not have me?* " – I was thinking of my aunt."

"Ah well. We have had a few aunts in our time, haven't we, Millicent?"

"But none the very thought of whom reduces us to tears."

"Miss Barrington's aunt must be a particularly intimidating example of the species."

"She was on the *Titanic*," said Ruby.

The two sisters looked at each other with an amazed horror that was almost delight. Dully, Ruby wondered why she had told them: the shipwreck was nearly a year old, but it still had this effect on people. They wanted to know everything: had Aunt Sarah drowned or merely frozen to death? Why was she on the ship in the first place? Ruby explained listlessly about the American suffragettes who had wanted a visiting speaker from England; not a famous leader this time, they had said, one of the troops; a rich American lady would pay her passage, first class, in the best ship available; it could be a rest-cure, perhaps, for someone, newly released from prison. Ruby did not mention anything about the prison. She did not know what the Misses Parley would think. But she would never forget the malicious glee with which Aunt Sarah had sought and seized the opportunity to go to America, positively glowing with contempt at all Ruby's mother's objections. "At least somebody appreciates my importance! Free me from prison against my will they may, Pearl, but they cannot prevent this!" And the whole family had gone to see her off at Southampton, and she so pink and talkative about when she was a girl on a migrant ship; and the stewards having to help her up the gangway into the luxurious first class . . .

The Misses Parley were eyeing her closely. "And are you going to follow in your aunt's footsteps, Miss Barrington?"

All kinds of people advertised in the suffrage papers. She did not know the Misses Parley's views. She had better play safe. "I want the vote of course," she said, "but I'm not a militant."

She could not understand the expression that passed between the sisters; but soon they wanted her to get to work.

She took a deep breath as they set her before her typewriter. Would she remember where the letters were? She eyed the keyboard in a panic: where was *k*? She could not find *k*! Was it possible that they would give her something to type that contained no *k*'s? *Kay of the Door*, that was the name of the play script she must type, a heap of tea-stained pages. *Kay* of the door? Should that not be *Key* of the door? But no: there appeared to be a character called *Kay*. It seemed to be a joke. It kept appearing in the text with stage directions: "laughter". She typed the title without mishap, and realised that while her brain had been worrying where the *k* was, her fingers had found it. She felt much better now that she was working.

The Misses Parley had told Ruby that their Agency handled a variety of important documents, working with which would give her an unrivalled knowledge of the world in all its diversity. One day she might type a manuscript for a professor at London University; the next day, a lease for lawyers. Mr Walter Orange's play seemed more exacting than either. It was very modern and not always clear. His handwriting was difficult, but even when Ruby had deciphered it more problems were revealed. Mr Orange's characters were not above answering questions they had not been asked, or making reference to people not previously mentioned. Characters would "Exit" and then participate in the conversation again before they had "Re-entered". Ruby leafed through the pages to check that the mistake was not hers. Her ceasing to type cut the volume of clattering noise in the office by one-third, and the Parleys noticed.

"Is something the matter, Miss Barrington?"

Ruby explained the difficulty she was having.

Miss Millicent's teeth flashed with her sister's. "Fancy this, Ada! On her first day, Miss Barrington is turned author."

"Type it as it is written," said Miss Ada sharply.

"But – I beg your pardon, Miss Ada – you did say I was to correct errors."

"Of course! Errors of spelling, punctuation, grammar and known fact." Miss Ada counted on four fingers. "For example, if the celebrated Mr Orange had definitively stated that Rome was the capital of France . . ."

"Paris is," said Ruby.

"Quite. That sort of thing comes within our terms of service. But our customers are at liberty to scribble whatever nonsense they please, Miss Barrington."

It was the first hint that the Misses Parley might despise their customers, or indeed think unkind thoughts about anybody. Ruby became uneasy. When clients came in, the Misses Parley were all smiles. "Well, of course, we shall be delighted! But I wonder you have need of our services, Mr So-and-so, when you have such a neat and legible hand!" "It is such a pleasure to work for you, sir, you might almost charge *us* a fee!" But as soon as the door of the cramped little office closed, if Ruby looked up, she would see the sisters exchanging glances of superiority and contempt; and this worried her particularly when she was sent out for her lunch, for what might they be saying about her?

"I shall go to Lyons' for my lunch," she had airily announced before setting off this morning. Her father had signalled to her mother to say nothing, then he himself had suggested that she take some cold pie in a bag, just in case Lyons' was full. It was not full but the prices made her heart flutter: the Parleys were only paying her fifteen shillings. She found a bench and ate her pie and watched the world go past.

The afternoon was very long. She struggled with Mr Orange's script. An early darkness gathered; the Parleys closed the windows to keep out the draught, and the office filled up with fumes from the heater. The *s* on her typewriter kept sticking. Her finger hurt from hitting it. Miss Millicent remarked on her slowness; she explained about the *s*. She was sent to make tea, and when she came back, Miss Ada was tinkering with the machine with a brush and a screwdriver.

"Perhaps I could use that one, Miss Ada," she said, glancing longingly at the brand-new machine sitting unused in the corner of the office.

"You most certainly could *not*."

"That is a new machine," Miss Millicent explained. "It comes from the United States of America."

"Oh," said Ruby, "Sorry, Miss Parley."

"I think we might let her go," said Miss Ada, "don't you, Millicent?"

"I think we might," Ruby was alarmed. "She has been such a good girl on her first day, hasn't she?" Ruby smiled. Of course they were not sacking her! They were letting her go home early as a reward. She had finished her first day at work, she had done nothing wrong, and her employers were pleased with her. On the bus to London Bridge, she looked round for the poet, but he was not there. This was just as well for him, for she would have ignored his nonsense. He was there next morning, though, chattering away about how bored he was at his bank and what he really wanted was to see the world and write poetry. Ruby allowed him to sit next to her, and smiled occasionally out of politeness.

2

Ruby was often sent home early from work. Or she was given an hour or two in the day to amuse herself. She would be sent out on some trivial errand with clear instructions that she was not expected back until a certain time. The time allowed was always excessive to the errand, and she came to know a lot of coffee-houses and back-streets with interesting little shops.

When she did go back to the office, the Misses Parley were always very brisk and high-voiced, as if they had been doing something secret. Ruby could not guess what it was, except that the new American typewriter had always been moved from its place. It was never used in Ruby's presence.

She still got bored occasionally, and made mistakes. The Parleys bought her her own eraser, but there were strict instructions concerning its use. "Three mistakes on a page," said Miss Ada, "and you do it again." It was a fair rule, customers, did not like smudgy pages, but it led to considerable tension after the second error. Was it worth trying for perfection, when the very effort increased her clumsiness? Discarded paper rose around her like the tide; still the Misses Parley said she was a "good little worker" and gave her another shilling a week.

On Sundays, all the brothers came to tea with their families. (All except Sam, who was overseas with the army.) It was a happy occasion, with the table covered with pies and potted meat and salads, fruit and tea and cakes. Their father sat, proud and plump, at the head of the table in a clean white shirt, discussing business with Leonard and Stephen, making their mother impatient as she bustled about making the daughters-in-law feel at home and helping them attend to the youngsters.

Ruby felt sorry for the daughters-in-law, particularly Charles' new wife whom he had acquired in rather a hurry and not apparently to the great happiness of either of them; they lived at her parents' house and came rather glumly to the Barrington family teas. Everyone was kind, but the Barrington brothers were a formidable team, and their wives seemed rather left out when the back-chat flew. Sometimes Ruby enjoyed playing hostess and aunt; sometimes she felt so tired after helping her mother prepare the spread that she sulked and wished she too had a partner to bring. All around the table everyone was in pairs, even the children, Stephen's Johnnie next to Leonard's Annie, Anthony's baby Timothy next to Charles' new wife with her rounded stomach. But Ruby was all alone, free to pass plates, fill the tea-pot and crawl on the floor to pick up whatever the children had thrown there. She noticed that her brothers treated her a little like Aunt Sarah; and she wondered in a panic whether that was how her nieces and nephews would grow to see her.

Charles boomed, "And how's the typewriter?"

"Fine, thank you. It needs oiling sometimes, when the s sticks."

"Pass the oil, Leonard" Charles picked up the milk-jug and pretended to pour in his sister's ear. "Rube needs oiling."

"How you expect these children to learn table-manners," said Mother, "I do not know."

"You're a stupid fool, Charles!" Ruby flashed.

"Now, Ruby, don't be rude."

"Ooh, Mum! He can say whatever he wants, but when I stand up for myself I'm being rude."

"Quite right," said Charles. "Respect your elders. Fat little typewriters should be seen and not heard." Ruby put down the jam tart she was eating and left the room in silence. She remained within hearing, however. It was satisfying to hear the sounds of the party fading into awkward silence.

"That's just how it's been," she heard her mother complain, "ever since she started working at that place."

"Probably in love," said Charles with a full mouth.

"Good gracious, she doesn't meet anyone!" said Mother. Ruby smiled. That was all they knew! "If I thought – "

Leonard's voice interrupted. "I know we've always had our fun with Ruby. But why can't we show her a bit of respect as well, Charles? Her Misses Thingummajig seem to think well of her, raising her salary and letting her home early."

"There's something funny about that if you ask me," said Mother. "They're up to something they don't want her to know about."

Oh yes, thought Ruby, still listening, *white slavery*. Her mother thought white slavery lay behind any offer of employment to young girls.

"White slavery I expect," said Charles. "All right, all right, Ruby, I know you're listening and you can come back now. Big brother begs your pardon." Ruby would not budge till he came out for her, and a look of perfect, malicious understanding passed between them. He uttered words of apology which they both knew he didn't mean; she must accept them with a good grace, because it was a low thing in the Barrington family to spurn someone who said sorry. Back at the tea-table she was politely besieged with questions.

"Which train do you catch?" Leonard asked.

"The seven-twenty."

"And what do you do all day, exactly?"

"Well, I type. I'm a typist, you see." She started to explain the separate difficulties and techniques of typing legal documents, verse, playscripts and business letters. Her mother interrupted:

"You see? That's all we hear."

"You *are* in love, aren't you, Rube?" said Charles, and he shared a sickly, mocking smile with his pale wife. Ruby's eyes ran round the table: man, woman, man, woman, child.

'As a matter of fact," she said, "I am."

Cheers and applause broke and Charles was patted on the back for his perspicacity. Mother did not cheer. "It's the first I've heard," she said.

"His name's Robin Fellowes and he's a poet. I met him on the bus."

Charles said, "But you're not allowed to *talk* to men on buses, Ruby. You're not even allowed to get *on* a bus that has a man on it, is she, Mum? To think, a sister of mine!" He stood up and recited: " 'A fallen man again may soar; a woman falls to rise no more.' "

"I did tell you about talking to strangers," Mother said.

"I don't care! I can leave home if I want to, and take rooms! Lots of girls do!"

"And there's a name for girls who do."

"You can call me it, then! I don't care!"

Later, when the family had gone, her parents talked with her quietly. They were kind, and she felt rather foolish. What on earth had led her to say she was in love with Robin? She didn't see him every day, and even when she did, he did not always talk to her.

True, he made her feel very important, sometimes writing her words down in the notebook where he collected "interesting phrases," and begging her to type some of his poems when Miss Collins, who usually did it for him at the bank, was too busy. They were lovely poems, often quite passionate, and addressed to a girl without a name who did not know how beautiful she was or how much he loved her . . . her parents were a little bit worried about her getting into a friendship with a poet on a bus. She let fall that he was also starting at the bottom in a bank and they softened a little and admitted that he might be a suitable friend.

"After all, your mother and I met over a pie-barrow, and her father didn't think much of me."

"All right Hamish, that's enough, that's got nothing to do with it. Ruby, would you like to invite Mr Fellowes to tea next Sunday?"

Ruby was aghast. What would he think? She could not imagine Robin with the family. But he would probably love it, sitting there with his notebook, collecting interesting phrases. She would ask him. There was no harm in asking.

He seemed startled, but he accepted. She felt doubly glad that she had a definite appointment to see him at the weekend when she was typing invoices later that morning, with a stern note for defaulters: "The Misses Parley will be Obliged for Prompt Settlement, as we wish to Close Our Books."

Miss Ada, glorious in purple with a white ribbon in her hair, said, "Miss Barrington, dear, you won't mind, will you, just jogging your friend's memory about those few shillings he owes us?"

"Which friend, Miss Parley?"

"Well, dear, you did type his poems in the Agency's time."

"And on the Agency's typewriter," said Miss Millicent.

"And paper."

"And I daresay you made use of our eraser."

Miss Ada beamed. "Ah, I think perhaps not, Millicent, I rather think that when Miss Barrington types her friend's poems, she gets them right the first time."

They smiled at each other and resumed their typing. What a dreadful misunderstanding! She had typed the poems at a time when she was not busy and with the Misses Parley's permission; she had never thought that Robin would have to pay! *The Agency's time!* It was as if they thought they owned her for that time. They did, in a way. Promptly and generously, they paid her every Friday. And now she was going to have to pay them, because the more she thought about it the more she realised that you could not ask a young man to tea and then present him with an account for fifteen folios at 2d each!

She did not see him again that week; but the arrangement for Sunday was definite.

"I met Mr Fellowes for lunch, Miss Parley," she said, on payday, "and he asked me to give you this." She passed over two-and-sixpence.

The glance that passed between the two sisters might have been scorn, it might have been disbelief.

"Lunching with a young man, Miss Barrington? Do your parents know?"

Ruby sighed. "He's coming to tea on Sunday."

"Is he, my goodness? I hope we are not about to lose you, Miss Barrington," Miss Millicent teased her as she put the money away in the cash-box.

3

The Barringtons had one young maid, but of course this had to be the Sunday when she stayed in bed with a chill. So Ruby had to work even harder than usual to prepare the family tea. Her mother had never been convinced by the argument that since Ruby was at work all week and contributed to the family budget she should be allowed to rest on Sundays, and this time, with Ruby's own guest expected, it was not even worth trying. By the time Charles arrived, bounding into the kitchen through the back door with his wife in tow and dipping his finger into the hot jam of a tart, Ruby was scarlet from baking. She hastily applied powder to her face from a compact she had bought.

"Had your head in the flour-bag, Rube?" Charles hooted. "Is Romeo here yet?"

"His name is Robin, and he's just a friend."

"Of *course!* What else?"

She scowled. She had plenty of time for revenge. She was sure Charles did not much enjoy being married; she knew he did not relish his impending fatherhood, or having to live with his wife's parents. He could be reminded at any time of these facts. But for now she just wanted a little peace and harmony.

"Don't worry, Rube, I'll behave myself. Heavens, we don't want to scare your last chance."

"That's all you know," she said.

"Oho! Whole busloads, are there?"

"Perhaps."

"Anyway – where is he?"

"I'm meeting him off the train."

"Oho!" Charles shouted again as people started to arrive.

"Don't take your coats off, we're all going to the station."

"If you follow me, brother dear," said Ruby "it will be the last journey you ever make."

The air was crisp and biting after the hot kitchen: there was a hint of early dusk. The streets seemed clean and peaceful; the few passers-by were dressed in their best. Even the boys playing Last across on the railway line looked scrubbed and pressed, as did the little girl watching with her fists clutched tight. Angrily, their parents called them to the platform as the train pulled in. Four doors opened and four people got out.

"Well!" said Ruby, not realising till she saw the station-master looking at her that she was speaking aloud. "He must have missed it! I'll just have to wait for the next one. He can't have gone straight to the house because I didn't give him the address. I particularly wanted to meet him at the station so that I could warn him what they're like."

"Waiting for someone, miss?" the station-master enquired.

"Er, yes, my friend did say she might – " her voice was high and casual. Why had she said that, pretended she was waiting for a girl? What would the station-master think, when Robin arrived on the next train and she walked off with him, when he thought she was waiting for a girl? "My friend might not come," she continued quickly. " 'If I'm not on the four o'clock,' my friend said, 'expect me on the four-thirty, but if I'm not on the four-thirty, you'll have to assume I didn't get back in time from, er, my aunt's.' So you see, my friend might not come at all!" She tried to stop herself chattering. After what she had said, she could not wait beyond four-thirty without the station-master guessing the truth, and if Robin came on the five o'clock he would be quite lost! She watched the clock. Had it stopped? She had better not ask. Of course he would be on the four-thirty, had he not said he would come? Anyone could miss a train. She could hear the far rumble of the train coming. She could shrug her shoulders and say, half to herself, half to the station-master, "Oh well. I suppose I'll wait for one more train." But that would not be necessary, Robin would be on this one. The air was getting cold. At home they would be boiling water, waiting for her and laughing. The train stopped, let off its passengers, went away. "Oh well," she said, "I suppose I'll wait for one more train."

By five-thirty it was quite dark, and she left the station. And the first thing she saw was a familiar figure coming down the road towards her. Her heart leapt: it was Leonard. One chance, then! She might have given Robin her address and forgotten about it, he might be at home waiting for her, or he might have sent a telegram. One look at Leonard's quizzical eyes told her these things had not occurred.

He told her a lot of lies, kind lies, but lies: nobody was laughing at her, he said, and there might be a dozen acceptable explanations for her guest not turning up. "I expect you're ready for your tea, Ruby."

"I'm not going home" – this was rash – "while Charles is there."

"Then I'll take you out to tea." This was obviously planned: he would have sent his wife home. They went to the Daisy Chain, which specialised in sugar cakes. The tables were tiny and close together.

"I'm not hungry," she said.

"Of course you're not," said Leonard, ordering scones and sugar cakes and Cherry Ripe iced biscuits. "I'm just getting these for us to look at. What d'you suppose happened to your friend?" He tagged the question so innocently to his nonsense about biscuits that she found herself answering.

"Nothing much. I'll find out tomorrow."

"Do you see him every day, Ruby?"

"Mostly." He did not talk to her every day, of course, but that was not what Leonard had asked. She could not remember when she had last been alone with Leonard. She could see the strange line on his cheek where his hair became whiskers. She could see threads of broken veins worming there, as if Leonard were old already. He was: ten years older than Ruby, he had been ten when she was born. And if another baby had been born when she was ten, how would she regard it? Even now? As a child, of course. Everyone thought she was a child.

"I should hope it was something pretty serious," Leonard was saying stoutly, "for Mr Fellowes to let you down. Are you sure he said he would come?"

"Oh yes, and why would he say that, if he didn't mean to?"

"Well," said Leonard.

She bit into a scone. It was fresh and warm with plenty of fruit and butter. "I mean, he didn't have to say he would come. He didn't have to be polite." She had been most careful. She had actually offered Robin the words: If you're not doing anything else, of course, she had said. And even when he accepted, she had offered him another way out: Or perhaps some other Sunday. If he hadn't wanted to come, he could have said, Yes, Ruby. Some other time. No-one's feelings would have been hurt, and the matter would have been closed. But he had said yes, he would come.

"Did you ever wish any of us were sisters?" said Leonard, as if changing the subject.

"Oh yes," Ruby changed her face, "all the time."

"I wish so too."

"Did you want to be a girl, then?"

"Not likely! Not with all those brothers!"

"You weren't very nice to me, all of you. I got my revenge sometimes, though."

"You certainly did," he said with feeling. She poured tea. He looked gloomy, as if he were the one with troubles, "But you see, Ruby – just having us – well, we've never really treated you as a boy should treat a girl. You wouldn't expect it. But it's all been a bit – free and easy. And now you've got to learn about, well, men, and we don't want you hurt. You may not believe this, but we'd all kill dragons for our little sister, even Charles."

She thought about this. Any friends the brothers brought home had certainly taken their cue from them and treated her as if she were their sister too. And as far as her own friends were concerned . . . having all those brothers had given her a certain popularity among girls who wanted introductions, but boys avoided her, as if they were scared.

"What do you mean, learn about men?"

"Look. Don't be hurt, it's not your fault. I blame Mum and Dad a bit, for encouraging you to invite him. But if I met a typist on a bus and she invited me – well, anywhere, I'd think one of two things. Either I'd think, I know what kind this is – no, let me say this, Ruby, nobody with two eyes could seriously think that about you – or else, I'd think, she's on the look-out."

"What for?"

"A husband."

"You'd think that."

"I might. If I didn't think the other thing."

She broke a biscuit into tiny pieces. "It's a good thing not everybody's like you." She stood up.

"Sit down, Ruby."

"I won't! It's disgusting! Tell me something else! If you thought those things and you didn't want to go, would you tell the girl you were going and then not go?"

"I know," he said ruefully. "We're a rotten lot."

She sat down again to look more closely at her brother's face. It was unbelievable. *We're a rotten lot!* Who did he mean: Barringtons? Men generally? Some group that he belonged to. One thing was sure: whatever the group was, he didn't think they were rotten at all, his words were smug and complacent. He felt fine about the whole thing; and taking the blame like that made him feel better still!

"You'd actually do that! You'd agree to meet a girl on a station and then leave her in the cold with everybody laughing at her? Because they are laughing, aren't they, Leonard? And they sent you out to say this to me! You'd do that – when you could've said no in the first place? Even when the girl had typed your poems – and paid for them!"

"You've given this chap money?"

She felt so broken under her anger that she told him about the poems. He pushed half-a-crown across the table at her. "Just don't go after him, Ruby. Catch a different bus."

She looked down at him with scorn. Catch a different bus! From now on, she would not be catching any bus, because she would not be travelling to work from Stalcross, because she would not be living in Stalcross. There was a boarding-house near the Parleys, she had noticed it particularly. If her family thought she was staying at home for ever, to be laughed at and pitied and lectured on how to behave, just because some men hadn't the manners to say *No, thank you* when they didn't want to do something, they could think again! The half-crown would be plenty for tonight; tomorrow she would plan properly.

4

It took Ruby a long time to find the boarding-house. She remembered it as a rather cosy, inviting building, but in the dark of the chilly Sunday evening it looked dangerous, just waiting to fall down.

A man in a big, dirty apron met her and asked for how long she wanted the room. She said, "For ever," though she knew she could only pay for one night and supposed she would have to go home sometime, to fetch her things. It was lucky that she was wearing her Sunday clothes, they were good enough for work tomorrow.

Well – she had done it! She had threatened, and now she had done it! It was a tiny attic room with a sooty skylight: the night outside was black and there were no stars. She could sit on the bed and touch the wall opposite. There was a key on the outside of the door: when she moved it to the inside, it would not turn.

She could not hear the strange, starved, ugly-looking people she had seen on the street, so different from people in the daytime. She was quite alone. There was a chest of drawers with three legs, and a railway timetable for the fourth. There was no wardrobe. Where would she hang her office clothes if she came to live here, to keep them nice? She was hungry, but dared not go out. She thought of her little room at home, with the sounds of her mother bustling about and smells from the bakery waking her in the mornings. The sheets were dirty, she would not get between them or take off the clothes that she had only put on to walk to the station . . . she wrapped her skirt round her legs and pulled down the sleeves of her coat to protect herself from cold and dirt, and the mice that she heard but never saw.

She thought she had not slept, but suddenly the skylight was smudged with grey so she supposed it must be morning.

No-one brought her any water, and she dared not ask. She made herself ready as best she could: the first thing she would have to do would be to ask the Misses Parley for a week's pay in advance. They would agree, they trusted her; but trust or not, they would not take very kindly to her walking in looking as the room's broken mirror told her she looked. Her face was red and streaked with old powder, and sand stung in her bloodshot eyes. Then she spread her fingers into the shape of a comb and tried to repair her hair. Her dress was terribly creased, her best dress, her Sunday dress, put on to meet Robin Fellowes at the station . . . she felt sick. She had run away (as far as she remembered) because she could not bear her family to think her a fool; but she was a fool; a fool to have spoken to Robin on the bus in the first place, twice a fool to have asked him to tea, three hundred times a fool to have minded when he did not come. Like a neighbour looking over a fence, she saw herself as she had been only this time yesterday: bright and excited, with a home, and a job and a young man. Now she had nothing but aching limbs.

"A little late this morning, Miss Barrington." It was true. It was past nine. Her mother always woke her at home, and gave her breakfast. "And I don't suppose you've had any breakfast." Why should Miss Millicent suppose such a thing? They never discussed breakfast. But a cup of tea was placed before her (an unheard-of courtesy: Ruby might have supposed the Parleys did not know how to make tea) and two shiny apples in a paper bag. Ruby ate one but she was not lulled by their kindness: they knew the truth, and it was only a matter of time before they spoke of it. Her mind felt strangely bright and dazzled: she felt she could do a day's typing without a single mistake, if ónly it were not such a noisy business. The typewriters were covered and silent, but her brain flinched from their imagined clatter every time she looked at them. The Misses Parley wandered round the office, pretending to do this and pretending to do that, until at last Ruby could stand the tension no longer and said, "How do you know, Miss Parley?"

The direct question changed the mood of the office with a snap. Ruby's tea cup was snatched away, and the place on the table wiped where she had laid down her apple. Paper was brought from the stationery cupboard. "Your mother was here, Miss Barrington," said Miss Ada, in terrible tones, "with a policeman."

"A policeman?"

"What did you expect, good gracious? They were all for setting the entire Metropolitan Force after you, but we dissuaded them from that, thank goodness. We knew that you would be in to work as usual; 'If there is breath in her body, Mrs Barrington,' we said, 'your dear Ruby will not have abandoned us, whatever she may do at home.' Ruby imagined this encounter with some awe, while the Parleys informed her that her mother had gone home and was awaiting a telegram: if it had not arrived by 11 A.M., the police forces of the capital would be placed on alert. "And we are not going to have that, are we, Miss Barrington?"

She stared down the table while something white floated into her vision: a telegram form. A pencil was pressed into her hand.

"Write, Dearest Mother . . ."

Her hand was immobile.

"Am safe at work . . ."

Am safe at work –

"Home tonight sorry for trouble caused – "

She wrote, *Love Ruby.*

Miss Ada plucked the paper away from her and waved it in the air with triumphant scorn.

"Look at this. 'Am safe at work love Ruby.' No doubt your poor mother will be suitably thankful for the 'love'. Was there ever such an ungrateful girl, Millicent? We are perhaps well free of the trials of motherhood."

"Perhaps she is trying to save herself money," suggested Miss Millicent, "by keeping the telegram short."

"She will save us money when we are no longer paying her a salary."

"Oh Miss Millicent, Miss Ada, please don't, please don't dismiss me! I'll work just as hard, it won't make any difference I'm a good worker, you said so! It's got nothing to do with – "

"Nothing to do with it, indeed!" Miss Ada echoed. "That's not how your poor mother sees it, or all those moaning Jemimas out there who declare that the minute a young girl sets foot on a train to an office she is straight on the path to rebellion and ruin!"

Miss Millicent said kindly, "Give me the telegram, Miss Barrington. I shall take it to the post office for you." When she returned, she said, "I took the liberty of adding the words 'home tonight'. Don't worry about the cost, we'll deduct it from your salary at the end of the week."

Without thinking, Ruby flashed. "It's none of your business whether I go home or not."

"It most certainly is, you impudent miss!" Miss Ada retorted. "It most certainly is our business if the police come crawling round here like woodlice, poking their noses in and asking questions."

Ruby knew everything was lost. There was no point in controlling her tongue now: on the contrary, she might as well fire her last shot.

"I know why you don't want the police here!"

"What does the child mean?"

"There's something funny going on, with that typewriter." She eyed the new American model, which again had the look of having been recently used. She felt like a detective in a story. "You never use it when I'm here, only when you send me out of the office! I know what it is, it's white slavery, that's what my mothers says." Her employers' stunned faces frightened her. Why had she said that? It was the thought of her mother here, talking with them about her, planning how they would together make her return home. "At least, she doesn't say it about you, but she says that's what a lot of jobs you see advertised for young girls are really."

"Good gracious me," said Miss Millicent.

"Good gracious," said Miss Ada. And after a pause, she turned to her sister. "Obviously Miss Barrington hasn't been benefiting as we had hoped from her little holidays from the office. We always supposed she was using her time gainfully, didn't we, filling her lungs with fresh air and taking exercise to avoid curvature of the spine. Instead, she has been indulging in libellous fantasies – "

"Oh, I haven't, I haven't!" She started to cry. All the tears that she had not dared to shed in the cold night came out. "It's just that everyone treats me as a child, and you send me out of the office to have your secrets, and my mothers puts the police on to me if I'm out of the house for five minutes and Robin doesn't come and Leonard huffs and puffs and says, 'Well, Ruby, all men are rotters,' as if he's proud of it and my feelings don't matter *at all*, and I don't think you're white slavers, Miss Parley, Miss Parley, only please don't take away my job because if you do they'll never let me have another one."

She reached the end and sobbed some more and felt she could stop; but what would happen when she did stop? The sisters were hearing her out, but what would they say when it was their turn?

At last she ran out of breath and sat silent and aching. Her handkerchief could do no more for her: Miss Millicent offered her some blotting paper, and when Ruby looked up into her face to see if this was a joke, she said, "Do you feel better now?"

Ruby nodded foolishly.

"There's nothing like a good cry. Your mother told us that your young man let you down. But my goodness, dear! If that's the worst thing that ever happens to you, you will be a fortunate young woman!"

Miss Ada interrupted. "I think Miss Barrington is much more interested in the white slavery side of the business, Millicent."

"Of course she didn't mean that. Did you, dear? She just has a vivid imagination, and why not? We are a little mysterious about our lovely American typewriter. Perhaps Miss Barrington would like to sit at it, and take dictation."

"She can type an invoice for two dozen white slaves."

Offered this chance, Ruby wanted only to sit at her old stiff machine and struggle with the *s*; she was flushed and hot and tired and confused. Probably she would break the new one. But the Parleys removed its cover, inserted paper and set Ruby down before its gleaming keys. As she put her fingers in position, and Miss Millicent opened her mouth to dictate, Miss Ada's cold hand closed on Ruby's wrist, immobilising her.

"This is only on condition that you go straight home this evening."

"Yes, Miss Ada."

"And since you have our word that we are not in the white slavery business, what are you about to type is between you, us and the machine.

"Yes, Miss Ada."

Miss Millicent dictated slowly, to allow Ruby to accustom herself to the keys, some of which were in the wrong place. And there were some strange symbols that she had not seen before. Apart from that it seemed quite normal, apart from its spotless newness, the darkness of its black parts, the gleam of its metal. Her fingers moved easily, she thought she must be asleep. The keys obeyed the lightest touch of her fingers: she skimmed over them, hardly seeming to make contact. It was as if Miss Millicent's words were passing through her body with no action on her part: only the strangeness of what she had been asked to type stayed with her as an uneasy comic memory after she finished the task and returned to her own machine to try to make sense of *A Board in the Hand* by Mr Walter Orange.

She went home that evening, on the bus and the train, as she had promised. Her father was angrier with her than she could remember seeing him. His round face reddened; his big fists thumped the table.

"That was a terrible thing to do, Ruby! Don't you care how much suffering you cause?"

She felt punished and cleansed by it. "I'm sorry, Father."

"The thing I don't understand," her mother said, "is why you didn't confide in me. I am your mother."

Ruby looked at her, heavy and pale in her chair, fingers knitting restlessly, fingers never still, knitting something for her next expected grandchild. What did she mean? That Ruby was supposed to lay her head and weep on that soft, spreading breast because Robin didn't come to tea? What? As if she were a child, and the hurt no more than a grazed knee? The thought of it set her teeth on edge. She remembered once her mother had sent some rude boys out of the shop and they shouted at her and called her an old bag, and the brothers (they were children then, and all still at home) had pursued them in a troop to avenge the insult; but if you took away the revulsion of it, that was what her mother really looked like, a worn-out kit-bag, frayed and bruised by its years of burdens, a bag that would be kept, out of sentiment and affection, but would carry no more.

"I just didn't feel like it," Ruby said. "I wanted to be by myself."

"Respect your mother's feelings another time," Father barked, "and not just *I want*."

"I've said I'm sorry," said Ruby.

Her mother leaned towards her with a look in her eye that made Ruby flinch. "I do know how it feels to be in love," she said.

"Well, I don't!" Ruby shouted.

5

When Ruby saw Robin Fellowes watching her expectantly through the window of the bus, she bit down hard on her lip and strutted straight past him to a vacant seat next to another man, a butcher in a blood-stained apron.

"I say! Ruby!" Robin called along the packed bus.

She turned and hissed, "Ssh!" But her heart sank. She wished she had not looked at him. He looked so nice and friendly and innocent with his smart white collar and his fresh morning face. How dared he look so innocent? If he thought he could just carry on as if nothing had happened . . .

The butcher left the bus and she looked up desperately for a standing passenger to whom she could offer the vacant seat. But Robin was in there with the agility of an acrobat.

"Anyone would think you were avoiding me, Ruby."

She sniffed, to indicate that to do even that would involve more thought than she cared to give him. "I daresay you have paid your fare. You may sit where you please." The good dark cloth of his trousers brushed against her navy-blue skirt. She was surprised by the racing of her heart: she must be angrier than she knew.

"The most ripping thing has happened!"

What would happen if she summoned the conductor and said, *This man is bothering me*, as Mother always said she should?

"Father's bought a Renault!"

"A Renault. How pleasant."

" 'How pleasant.' Wait till I've written that in my notebook Rube, and I'll give you a good shaking."

Rube! A good shaking! If he thought he could talk like her brothers, she would soon show him how she treated them.

"If you lay a finger on me, it'll be the last thing you ever do, *Mister* Fellowes."

"I say, Ruby. Have I done something to offend you?"

"An ant crawling along the ground isn't big enough to offend me, and neither are you."

"Ruby." He was sincerely admiring. "Have you ever considered writing poetry?"

"I'm much too busy typing it, actually," she said, adding, "for people who don't pay their bills." Fortunately this was lost on him, for it was a little unfair. She hadn't even asked him to pay. He chattered on happily, about how they had got the car at the weekend, how they had spent the whole of Saturday tinkering with it and polishing it and learning how to make it go, and then on Sunday the whole family had piled in and –

"Oh Ruby! How will you ever forgive me?"

In rigid control of herself, she enquired, "Forgive you? Why? What have you done?"

"You invited me – oh, Ruby. What a bounder I am. An utter bounder!"

"Aren't you supposed to get off the bus here?"

"Not till you say you forgive me. And give me your address so that I can send your mother a large bunch of flowers."

"Well," said Ruby, "my mother loves flowers, and if you want to send her some, that's no business of mine. But do let me into the secret of what you've done wrong."

With glee she watched him wonder if he was mistaken; no, he was quite sure. He had been invited to the Barringtons' for Sunday tea and he had accepted; and then he had allowed the excitement of the new car to drive the engagement from his mind. She took a deep breath. She laughed. It was a good laugh. She might even get a part in one of Mr Orange's plays if she could laugh like that.

"It's open house for tea at the Barringtons' on Sundays," she said. "I thought everybody knew that. We hardly notice who is there and who isn't. And now, you may not be going to work today, but I am. Excuse me, please." And she left the bus.

She tripped briskly up the stairs to the office. Her heart sang a vindictive little tune: *He said he was sorry, he missed his stop!* Perhaps she should have yielded enough to give him the address for sending the flowers. "Is everything all right at home?" Miss Millicent enquired. "Yes, thank you, Miss Parley." She longed to tell of her triumph, but there was a large pile of legal documents waiting for her, and the clock indicated that she was nearly one minute late. She sat down. She hated the way lawyers wrote. Their vain, picturesque handwriting was hard to read, and there was nothing of interest in their words even when they could be deciphered. They had such petty minds, always working out ways in which people might evade the terms of their stupid leases and wills and contracts, and forbidding them. Miss Ada saw her struggling to understand what she was typing and bade her not to waste time.

"If lawyers used words that people could understand, people wouldn't pay them, would they? And then they wouldn't pay us and we couldn't pay you, could we, Miss Barrington? So get on with it, dear, and get it right." Lawyers were very particular about getting things right. The slightest error, and they would refuse to pay.

There were no more holidays from the office or early evenings for Ruby. She heartily regretted her thoughtless accusations of white slavery which had had this result. She could almost feel the curvature beginning to stiffen her spine as she sat over her typewriter from morning till night with only a short pause for lunch. And since they had been at pains to tell her what the real secret of the new American typewriter was, she was not sure that she wanted to know.

When she took her turn on the new machine, one sister dictating, the other watching, she was not sure whether what they were doing was a crime or a joke. If it was a joke, it was not very funny: some of the letters they wanted her to send were rather cruel, rather frightening, and addressed to important men. Yet it was silly too, childish; they enjoined her to secrecy – who on earth did they think she would tell? But their very concern that no-one should know suggested that they at least thought it was a crime. That was why they used a foreign typewriter, that was why it was used for nothing else, so that nobody should identify the type. She was polite and obedient when she took her turn, and they interpreted this as agreement with their aims and objects: when they had advertised her job in *The Vote* it was not only because that was a sure way of getting a bright, intelligent girl; they told her that her poor dear Aunt Sarah would doubtless approve. Ruby was not sure. The real suffragettes (she could not think of the Misses Parley as real suffragettes, and they denied that they were: "Just two women, doing our bit!") were still marching, selling newspapers, going to prison and being let out with broken health. Sometimes they did desperate, dangerous things, like setting fire to buildings and letterboxes . . . and what was a threatening letter to a Member of Parliament compared with that? A letter did no damage; the MP probably laughed it off. But it seemed sneaky, cowardly almost, unworthy, like the way the Misses Parley fawned over people like Mr Orange when he brought in another manuscript, and sneered behind his back about his style and his creased trousers. If Ruby were the sort of girl to become involved in politics, she would rather be marching, even setting light to things, than sitting safe in an office using a typewriter and His Majesty's Mails to intrude into a strange man's home like a burglar, even if the man did not want to give votes to women! Still, there was nothing she could do: her parents would be suspicious if she left her job, and she did quite like it, anonymous letters apart. It wasn't her responsibility; she just did as she was told.

It seemed that Leonard had told no more than the truth when he said men liked to be the ones to pursue friendship. It was an exasperating yet secretly delightful thing about Robin that the ruder she was to him on the bus, the more interested he became. Nothing brought him to her side quicker than the flick of her head in the opposite direction. She sometimes allowed him to woo her into having some fairly interesting chats. One day near Christmas he opened his briefcase and two wrapped parcels tumbled out into Ruby's lap. One was for her and one was for her mother. She thanked him shortly and glanced around the bus in a very obvious way to see who else had received a gift. Unwrapped, they were boxes of Suchard's chocolates with cards. Ruby's said, "To Miss Ruby Barrington, a poet's inspiration". Inspiration she may have been but her mother got a rhyme: rather an awkward one that seemed to be laughing at itself but meant what it said, full of good cheer for every day of the year, and hoping this sweet would be good to eat. Finally, in prose, he hoped that he might soon have the opportunity of apologising in person for his recent lamentable want of manners.

"Well!" said Mother. "Well! He'd better come to tea."

"Oh, I'm sure he'll be much too busy with his motor-car."

"He has a motor-car! Do you suppose he'll come in it?"

"He's rather a bore about it, actually."

This was true, but only sometimes. Ruby supposed everybody

was a bore sometimes, when they had something they were passionately interested in; but she also wondered uneasily whether he might not find her a little dull because she was not passionately interested in anything. But that was another good thing about him. He had so many interests and ideas, and was so insistent that she must have some too, that she found herself making ideas up and arguing fiercely with him over things she had not thought about much before. For he did not want her to have the same ideas as he had; he seemed to like to argue.

"Ruby, what do you *really* believe?" he said once.

"What about?"

"Anything. Beliefs. God, for example."

God, for *example*? "Are you an atheist?" she whispered.

"Good, you know the word. Now, what do you believe?"

"Well. That God loves us, and – "

"*No*, Ruby. That's what you've been *taught*. What's your *opinion*?"

"Oh, shh!" The bus was full and people would hear. She wasn't quite sure why she minded them hearing, it was only a question, and God could hear you anywhere. But there was no stopping Robin.

"If He loves us, why does He let bad things happen?"

"To punish sin."

"Look, Ruby. You're not almighty, are you? Or all good, though I expect you are, nearly."

"No-one is."

"Exactly! But can you think of anything that anyone could do to you – think of the worst way someone could hurt you – that you'd punish half as badly as some of the things God does to people? I mean, even if you could give a cancer to the person you hated most in the world, would you do it?" Ruby stared. Could Robin tell from her face that she had been forced to type precisely such a threat to a doctor in Harley Street who had said the suffragettes ought to be confined to asylums? She had thought it was all right, because, being a doctor, he would know to take no notice . . . "My grandfather died of it. He had a head of hair like mine when he got it. When he died, he was quite bald. Do you know why? He plucked out every single hair, one by one, to take his mind off the pain." Ruby stared with horror at Robin's nice, glossy hair. She tried to bring her mind back to the conversation. She tried to find a kind way of saying that the man might have committed a terrible sin, and the cancer was the punishment. But she knew that Robin would reply that his grandfather was a good man, and anyway, young children also died, innocent babies. She said, "I think we understand when we die. I think that's what dying and going to heaven means. You sort of change, and understand everything. It's like . . . well, when I was a child I didn't think I'd ever be brave enough to go on buses and trains by myself. And now . . . here I am."

"Yes, Ruby." He was full of admiration. "Here we are."

They didn't talk much about God after that. But they talked about many other things, some of them surprising. Beside the memory of Robin's conversation, the jabber of the brothers at the Sunday tea-table soon lost its power to amuse or even irritate her. Sometimes they told jokes that caused Father to say, "Not in front of your mother, please"; beside this, Robin's racy theories of free love seemed almost religious. He said the old moral ideas were out of date, and when women had the vote and jobs and could be independent, men and women could belong to each other and delight in each other . . . his poems were full of this idea, they were like prayers. She said she could not type them any more, but he still showed them to her. She didn't think the ideas applied to him and her. He had never done more than squeeze her hand in greeting or farewell. The ideas did not seem to apply to any mortal person. They might be rather frightening if they did.

"What's wrong with being free?" he demanded.

"Nothing."

"What's wrong with love, especially when God is love, or so you say."

"Nothing."

"So what's wrong with free love?"

Nothing, she supposed, if he put it like that; but she said, "Human beings shouldn't behave like . . . rabbits."

"Oho! What have rabbits to do with it?"

She turned pink. "Nothing." She was thinking of one of Charles' jokes.

"Speaking of rabbits . . ."

"Never mind rabbits."

"My godfather lives in the country, and he's got a rabbit that's forty-five years old. It's as big as *this*, and they have to keep it chained up or it attacks people. I promise you it's true. Would you like to see it?"

"Well, I don't know when I'll be free."

6

She had to invite him to tea before she was allowed to go; this went off not too badly. Then there was a cold spell and the Renault wasn't very reliable for country trips. At last they set off for Surrey one afternoon in May, with blossom bright on the trees. They went along at a fine speed, with Robin looking very dashing in his cap and goggles and big motoring gloves. Ruby didn't think he needed gloves, her own hands in light net ones were quite warm, and she wanted to watch his fingers, the fingers she had only ever seen lying still in his lap or fumbling for change or gesturing while he talked, only imagined covered with dust in his dusty office. She wanted to see them clutched powerfully round the big steering wheel, so powerful that they could move the three of them, Robin, Ruby and the shiny black motor-car, along the country roads to the village of Baxburn.

Ruby had assumed that there would be a Mrs Dotts living with Mr Harold Dotts, Robin's godfather, but there was only another man and an old servant. Mr Dotts was tall and old and military-looking; Mr Winters, his friend, was smaller, younger and rather fidgety. The four of them sat in deck-chairs in the garden while Ruby looked round nervously for the rabbit. Tea was brought: floury scones and cake and some early strawberries from Mr Winters' greenhouse. Mr Dotts said, "Shall we ask Miss Barrington to pour out?" and Mr Winters said, "No, I will."

"And what do you do with yourself all day, Miss Barrington?" Mr Dotts asked, and Robin said, "She's a first-rate typist."

"I used to work in an office," said Mr Winters.

"Oh, why don't you still?"

"They acquired a telephone," Mr Winters said sadly.

There was a long pause, and Ruby said, "Can we see the rabbit?"

Robin said quickly, "I told her about Goliath," and winked at his godfather, who winked back.

"I stammer, you see," said Mr Winters.

303

"You don't!" said Ruby. "I beg your pardon."

"I did when I tried to use one of those dreadful things."

Mr Dotts chuckled. "Rather than use it, he used to get on his bicycle and go and see people. After a while, they used to wonder where he was."

After tea they strolled round the garden, and Robin and Mr Dotts outdid each other with stories of the rabbit. "He might sneak up on us unawares," said Mr Dotts, "so keep your eyes open, Miss Barrington." Ruby knew by now that the rabbit was a joke, but she didn't mind, she was having such a nice time. Mr Winters kept bending down to pull fretfully at a weed, and when Ruby stopped to help him he told her the Latin names of all his plants. Mr Dotts put a stick in her hand and made her prod deep into the earth near the garden wall to feel how deep its foundations were. He shook his head sadly. "Still manages to burrow out, does Goliath."

"Doesn't he leap over the wall any more?" asked Robin.

"Bit old for that, Robin. Rheumatism."

"I still think you should chain him up. It's your public duty."

"I would, my dear boy, if I could find a chain strong enough."

Later when Robin was talking to Mr Winters, Ruby extracted a confession from Mr Dotts that Goliath had been dead fifteen years; but he had been a rather large rabbit, of unpredictable manners, and Mr Dotts and the young Robin had enjoyed making up stories about him. Ruby smiled to herself. So she had been brought here on false pretences after all!

The sun was streaming through the briar-rose as they motored back towards London along bumpy lanes, and Ruby watched herself from beside the road and said to somebody standing with her: *There goes Ruby Barrington and her young man, in his motor car. What a nice couple they make!*

Robin was very quiet. They might have been driving down this red, shadowy lane for ever. The office tomorrow, the clattering typewriters, and the strange behaviour of the Misses Parley might be years away.

"So much for the rabbit!" she teased.

Instead of answering he put on the brakes, slowed the Renault down and stopped it under a tree that was loud with birds.

"What do you mean by that?" He might almost be angry. She might almost be afraid. Only it was not real fear, it was a delicious, make-believe fear, the kind she had felt as a child when Aunt Sarah told her stories of princesses in towers and Ruby always knew they would be rescued.

"How dare you tease me about my rabbit? Don't you believe in rabbits with bad habits?" He put his boyish, mannish face very close to hers and twitched his top lip till two teeth showed, and growled, and took off his motoring gloves and his goggles and put his fingers round her neck. There was a second of panic, but he smiled; he said he had always admired the soft skin of her neck and wanted to touch it; and he stopped twitching his lips and kissed hers.

It was a nice kiss; his moustache was less bristly than her father's; but she was not quite sure what was expected of her, so she kissed him back with a loud smack, just as she did with her father.

"Forgive me about the rabbit," he said, "but I did want to kiss you for the first time in the country, so that I could write a poem about it." And he kissed her again with his nice dry lips that tasted of strawberries.

The secret was to keep her eyes closed. If she could not see what was happening, maybe it wasn't happening.

It seemed a shame not to look, though. If she peeped for a few brief seconds (not long enough to think) it seemed all the more perfect: the green chestnut leaves and the heavy pink flowers miles above them, carefully arranged to let the sun gleam through. The sun was looking but it didn't matter: the sun didn't mind. And Robin was sitting beside her with his white shirt open at the neck and his face so transformed he was like a stranger, a dear, familiar stranger. His eyes were open and he smiled each time she peeped: his smile was like another glimpse of sun, warm and golden and still.

The night he brought her home to Stalcross after that first visit to his godfather, she had looked through her wardrobe and realised how dowdy and childish her clothes were, for a girl who had just been driven out into the country to be kissed. Next day, she spent a terrifying amount of money on a pale blue summer dress at Lines', with a lace collar and buttons that looked like diamonds all the way down the front. Her mother did not like the dress, she said it made her look common: diamonds, common! But now, Robin seemed to like the buttons well enough, so Mother could be left out of this. Ruby sighed. It was too late. The sun and the blossom and the chestnut leaves had shifted in the breeze and rearranged themselves into Mother's face, warning her. She should have kept her eyes closed.

Mother was never very far away. For example, when Robin said, "Come on, Ruby, you're a modern girl," her mother's voice snapped back, forbidding her to go and work for the Parleys: *I suppose you want to be one of these modern girls!* It was a funny word, *modern*.

"What are you thinking Ruby?" His voice rustled with the leaves.

She couldn't tell him that her mother was watching. They both knew where Mother really was: presiding over the tea-table at home, the children, the daughters-in-law, the brothers. Charles hummed *Here Comes The Bride*! whenever he saw Ruby these days, and the brothers clapped Robin on the back as if he were one of themselves. What an insult! Little did they know of Ruby's conversion to free love. The idea of it, at least.

Robin's parents were almost as bad. They had a circular drawing-room with polished tables that reflected back and forth in the round mirrors on the wall; they tinkled with laughter when she said her parents made pies. Their conversation was full of veiled warnings about couples who married young, before the man was established, and lived to regret it. Ruby took no notice. She knew she was quite good enough for Robin if they chose to marry, but they did not choose. Not marrying did not necessarily mean turning into Aunt Sarah or the Misses Parley. Not marrying could be very romantic, while marriage could mean an end to everything, excitement and adventures and even beauty, for babies came and work made you grey . . . she was beautiful now, at last. Even if Robin did not keep saying so, she knew: she was as beautiful as a painting, lying in the grass like a nymph, while her handsome poet caressed her. In fact it would be just perfect if only he would stay this peaceful, if only he would not get his sudden moods of hunger and frenzy.

"Nothing. What are you thinking Robin?"

"I'm just admiring these buttons."

Under the pretence of admiring them he was undoing them! He was actually undoing her buttons! She froze, then relaxed. She would not show that she had noticed yet. She would keep her eyes closed. Suddenly she felt his hand right inside the top of her dress. Only her vest was between it and her flesh! Now she must say something! And yet it felt so – nobody had ever touched her breast like that, not her mother, not a doctor, not even she herself. Now she felt as if this was all that part of her was for, to be touched like this by Robin's firm, gentle, curious hand.

She pushed him away. She sat up sharply and buttoned herself. Robin was not angry. He sighed, smiled, leaned back against a tree, and wrote in his notebook while she composed herself.

"What's wrong, Ruby?"

"Nothing."

"Did you feel something?"

Was he mad?

"Didn't you like what you felt?"

"Oh, it's not that." She didn't want to offend him.

"I won't do it again," he said. "I'm sorry."

"It's not that," she said again, in alarm.

He laughed. "What you felt. Do you know what that was, Rube? You don't mind if I call you Rube?"

"I do," she said, "actually."

"Ruby, then. I'll do everything you want, and nothing you don't. What you felt was passion."

"Passion," she repeated. She thought she could still feel his hand inside her dress but when she looked it was buttoned up tight.

"My mother never felt passion," he said.

"How do you know?" She was shocked, but she could believe it.

"I can tell, by looking at her. Women didn't, in the past. Your mother didn't. Or your grandmother."

Ruby did not know much about her grandmothers: both had died when her parents were young. She felt oddly irritable, like a dog deprived of its bone.

Robin went on. "They *didn't*, Ruby. It was all – a beastly business. Now you can. You're free. You must let yourself, otherwise it gets all damned up inside." He grinned. "I know why you bought that dress, even if you won't admit it."

"Let's go home," she said, and he nodded.

When they got home these Sunday evenings, the brothers and their families had usually gone; Robin would come in for a quick cup of tea and Ruby marvelled to see him being so proper, her parents so reassured. Mother thought him very charming. But then she didn't sit as Ruby did through the long light evenings after his departure, yearning, frightened and indecisive, feeling as if she could jump out of her skin. The clock ticked. Mother's needles could easily have kept time with the tick if only she bothered. Father read out passages from his newspaper. As soon as she could, Ruby went to bed.

She never slept deeply on Sunday nights, and she was tired for the Misses Parley.

Miss Ada, Miss Millicent! Under Robin's tuition, Ruby had taken to looking at women and guessing whether or not they had known passion. He couldn't tell her exactly how he knew, but she got the idea from a game they played on the bus in the mornings: they used a code. It was rabbits. If Ruby thought a woman had known passion, she would say, "That lady over there keeps rabbits." Sometimes he would say that he didn't think so, but increasingly he came to agree with her.

She couldn't make up her mind about the Misses Parley. They were certainly beautiful enough to have known passion, but they could be very cruel and cunning and Ruby never felt quite with them, even when they were being nice. She tried to talk about this puzzle to Robin, without actually telling him about the poison-pen letters . . . sometimes weeks would pass with none being sent, then they would read something in the newspapers that would start a flood; her fingers still ached to remember the savage threats sent to newspaper editors who scorned the noble suicide of Miss Davidson at the Derby: *Take extra care as YOU cross the street, Mr So-and-so* . . . had the Parleys known passion or did they hate all men? Robin said he would pop up one day and take a look and guide her in her assessment.

"Oh, you can't do that. They're very strict."

"Strictness in women is often a sign of not having known passion. Or having known it and lost it. 'Hell hath no fury like a woman scorned.' "

" 'Better to have loved and lost than never to have loved at all,' " she replied. She didn't know where that quotation came from, or why she said it. She had heard it somewhere, and liked it better than his words. He quoted hers back at her on one of their drives into the country. He was driving unusually fast; he turned so sharply into a narrow green lane that Ruby bumped her nose on the windscreen, and he did not apologise. The lane was very bumpy, not built for motor cars; it grew narrower and narrower, then opened into a wide sunlit field.

" 'Better to have loved and lost than never to have loved.' Which is it going to be for us, Ruby?"

She was saved from answering, or even understanding, by the whizz of the arrival of a ferociously pedalling flock of cyclists who had been coming along behind them, unnoticed. They leapt off their gleaming machines, flung them in a heap and took out sandwiches and flasks.

Robin whispered, "Oh, damn it!" and reversed back down the lane. He said nothing as he hunted for another field. At last one suited him. He spread a blanket on the ground and smiled at her.

"Now," he said, "now, Ruby, it's today, isn't it?"

"Robin, stop it."

"Don't push me – come on, Ruby – you're not still frightened?"

"I can't breathe," she said.

"Oh. All right." He seemed a bit grudging about it, considering all she wanted was to breathe. "Now you can. All right? Nice air – smell the buttercups and daisies and cows. Breathed all you want? Now come here. Oh, Ruby, don't make me – I don't want to bully you, I'm not going to force you. But how long are you going to make me wait?"

"Robin, that's *enough*!"

"It isn't, nothing is, nothing's enough for a poet. I want to experience everything. I have to, I'll be too old soon, I'm nearly twenty! Twenty! Oh, I wish you were a poet too, then we shouldn't have this trouble."

"I'm a trouble now, am I?"

"You know I don't mean that. What is it, do you think I'll just cast you off afterwards? Well, I'm not going to marry you, you know that, we'll both be as free as air, but you'll always be special. If you were a poetess, you wouldn't fight nature like this; you wouldn't chop things up into little bits; you wouldn't say, oh yes, I love the flowers and the birds and the sun and the moon and kisses and then stop short at – you'd understand that that would make as much sense as if God hadn't made the world properly round, as if He'd chopped out a segment so it didn't join up – "

"I thought you didn't believe in God," Ruby shouted.

"It's just a manner of speaking."

"That I'd understand if I was a poet."

"Or a poet's mistress."

She pushed him roughly away with all her force, and there was a moment when she thought he was going to use all his force against her in return . . . but he relented. He let her roll up the blanket and strut back to the car while he sat on the grass with his head in his hands. She waited in the passenger seat. She wished she knew how to drive. If she did, wouldn't she just show him! He had said he would teach her, but he never did. He never wanted to do anything these days except this one thing. They never went anywhere except to the fields. What had he in mind for the winter, she would like to know! At last he came forlornly towards her and they headed for home.

"Just because your family's rich and I'm only a typist, you think you can do what you want with me."

"Don't be such a baby."

Baby! That made her think of something else, something she had put from her mind because it seemed that if they could be happy and peaceful just doing the things they did, there was no risk in it. But even this fear he had an answer for. She couldn't remember . . . had he mentioned it, had she? Somehow he had let her know that even this could be taken care of.

"It's wrong, it's sinful."

"Sinful." His face was closed. A hen ran across the road; she was sure he aimed at it. He missed, but Ruby felt the impact in her own shoulder, she felt herself killed.

"Don't drive so fast."

"You haven't heard a word I've said. I don't believe you've ever listened, you let me ramble on like those stupid editors who are always sending back my poems because they haven't got enough *experience* behind them, what expereince do I ever get in a rat-hole under a bank? And you're laughing at me up your sleeve." They were back at Ruby's home. "Go on, get out."

The family tea-party was in full swing.

"Prince Charming not coming in for a scone?" said Charles.

7

Better to have loved and lost than never — this was what he had meant by quoting it back to her. "Which is it to be for us?" he had said. *Love me or lose me*, he had meant. But she did love him. Why was she crying into this wet pillow if she did not love him?

But what made him so sure that if she lost him she would never love? He wasn't the only currant in the bun!

She knew lots of young men who, she was sure, would like to take her out. Some of them nodded to her on the train in the mornings. Then there was Mr Orange, the playwright, who blushed when he said, "Thank you for your *trojan* efforts, Miss Barrington, in deciphering my prose!"

She sighed. She must sleep. Her body felt like a great burden. If only she could discard it, she could turn over and drift away. It was wakeful and hungry.

She had been right to say no to Robin. She hated him. And yet she did not want to be like the Misses Parley, hating all men. And she did not want to be like Aunt Sarah, sitting at a thousand tea-tables as her nieces and nephews grew up and brought their husbands and wives along for approval, and their babies to be cuddled by their spinster aunt.

She was asleep. She knew she was asleep so she supposed she could not be, not quite. It was half-dream, half-memory. She was sitting on a chair that was hard and knobbly. It wasn't a chair, it was Aunt Sarah's lap. Ruby was a tiny child. Aunt Sarah was talking in long words to Father. It was New Year's Eve, long, long ago. Every now and again, Aunt Sarah stopped talking to Father, leaned forward and whispered into little Ruby's ear; *I have known rabbits.*

But you're strict and an old maid, said Ruby, *and not very pretty. I have known rabbits, nevertheless.*

But Robin says . . .

I have known rabbits.

The dream faded.

Robin was at London Bridge next morning, looking very hangdog. He wasn't even on the bus: he was waiting by it, quite prepared to miss it rather than miss her. Seeing him ready to apologise, she tilted her nose into the air; but she let him say, "Ruby, I'm sorry."

"It's quite all right."

"In future I won't even touch you."

"Oh, you can! Only not . . ."

"We'll see. I'll have to sort out my silly ideas." He whispered, "It does terrible things for a fellow's temper, getting all worked up like that."

I'll have to sort out my silly ideas. What did that mean? That he didn't believe in free love any more? That he might want to marry her?

Time will tell, thought Ruby.

Late July brought special excitement to the Barrington household, for Sam's regiment might be ordered home from South Africa as there was talk of a war in Europe. Sam would have a few days' leave in London. They were still waiting for news when Robin's godfather invited Robin and Ruby to visit. It was the Sunday before the bank holiday. They went by train. The Renault had broken down. Robin's father was quite angry about it. He blamed it on the habit of certain people of driving over unsuitable terrain. Ruby laughed as Robin told her. They hadn't driven into the fields for ages. Robin was a reformed character. He never spoke of free love, in general or in particular. He held her hand, he kissed her goodbye; he didn't actually mention marriage but he asked a lot of strange questions, such as where in England she would most like to live if she had the choice and whether she was bright and cheerful when she first woke up in the mornings. She answered briefly and truthfully and wondered. Also, they found many more interesting things to do together, now that it wasn't just a matter of motoring into the countryside to find a field. They went dancing, or to the seaside. Robin had even given her a lesson in driving the car. (She sighed: maybe this had done the damage.) It was all so strange. At the time of the quarrel, Robin had seemed to want what he wanted more than anything in the world. Now he seemed to be treating her especially nicely because she had not let him have it.

The train to Baxburn was full of people wearing flowers and union jacks. Complete strangers kept telling each other that the British Expeditionary Force should be put in without more ado. Robin had nothing to say on the subject. Ruby smiled faintly. At a station a girl leaned over and kissed Robin's mouth before getting off.

"Who was that?" Ruby demanded.

"I don't know." Robin wiped his lips furiously with a handkerchief, and everyone in the carriage said, "Shame!" He kept his mouth covered to whisper to Ruby, "Stupid idiots. War. Bank holidays. It's all the same to them."

The people in the carriage burst into:

Oh soldier, soldier, won't you marry me

With your musket, fife and –

"Come on, Ruby, we're getting out."

"But we're not there yet."

"We can walk from here."

She had to run to keep up with him.

"They didn't mean any harm. I suppose they thought you were a soldier."

He pushed up his sleeve.. "Does that look like a soldiers' arm to you? I'm a bank-clerk, Ruby."

They were silent for a while, striding along the hot road. She said, "Does that mean if there's a war, you won't go?"

"Go?" He laughed bitterly. "Heaven help them if they send for me! Anyway, all those fools on the train are raring to go: let them go first! Then when all that's left is me and some German office boy on the other side – we'll meet in the middle and settle it over a glass of schnapps." He said "schnapps" very fiercely, like a dirty old man spitting in the street.

They came into Baxburn by a new route. It was beautiful. There was a triangular village green, with a pond and rushes and ducks. There was a church with a high spire reflected in the pond. Ruby felt suddenly safe again, far from the noisy people on the train. They would have tea with Mr Dotts and Mr Winters and Robin would forget his anger as they all forgot the war.

But Mr Dotts and Mr Winters had spread a map of Europe across their dining-table and were moving pens and teacups about: "If we attack them here, they can break through *there*, but if we –" Mr Dotts told Robin he could get him a commission in his old regiment because the colonel-in-chief was a friend of his. He reminisced. Mr Winters fumed over the infamous behaviour of the Germans. Belgium might be his personal possession, the way he carried on! Robin sat sullenly with his teacup on his knee and Ruby sat beside him, wishing they had not come.

Mr Dotts nagged away. Mr Winters regretted that the strawberries were finished for the year. Ruby felt a rush of gratitude for this attempt to change the subject. Mr Dotts said, "It's up to you, of course, my boy. But don't blame me when all your chums've got a row of medals and all you've got's a row of figures, even if they *are* added up right."

"A fine soldier I'd make."

"Nonsense, nonsense. I've seen a month's training make mastiffs out of skinnier whippets than you, what! Anyway – " he leaned forward, "if that's what's worrying you, Robin, get in first, eh, and have your choice of the jobs. *Someone's* got to tot up the men's pay."

The gentle Mr Winters was looking at Ruby. "Of course there might not be a war," he said.

"Of course, of course, and let's pray God there's none," said Mr Dotts fervently.

And Ruby burst out, "Yes, let's! Let's all go to the church this minute and pray there isn't a war!"

There was a long silence which Robin broke by saying he wondered what was wrong with the Renault, his father was a bit worried about it.

Mr Winters wanted to play chess with Robin, and when Robin won, Mr Dotts said, "Must play the winner." Ruby didn't understand chess but she knew this was a tense contest between wary equals. Robin was black and Mr Dotts was white and each kept picking up the other's pieces and laying them dead on the table. Mr Winters walked round them, stopping and squinting to get new views of the game. Nobody spoke to Ruby for a long time. She felt shy, then angry, but sat very still. She didn't want to disturb Robin's concentration. His dark pieces seemed to glide about the board with more authority, to cluster with more menace than Mr Dott's white. Outside, the summer sky grew pink, then purple. She stood up. "I'm going to look for the rabbit." Not a head moved. The garden was very still, the air heavy with the smell of roses. The daisies on the lawn were sleeping, curled in on themselves, and huge shadows crouched beneath the trees. If the giant rabbit appeared, she would simply believe it: believe it, and welcome it.

"Come back little rabbit, big rabbit, when he was a little boy."

The words made no sense but she liked the sound of her voice in the thick, fragrant silence of the summer night.

Back in the house, Robin laid the tallest of his pieces on its side, and Mr Winters offered supper. Robin took out his watch.

"My heavens, there's no time for that, I'd forgotten we're at the mercy of the trains." He looked at Ruby as if he had suddenly remembered her. "Are you ready to go?"

The little station was all in darkness. A long train thundered through on the down-track, not stopping. There was a notice: OWING TO THE INTERNATIONAL SITUATION THERE WILL BE NO MORE TRAINS TO LONDON TONIGHT.

"They're taking the troops to the coast," said Robin.

"Why are they?" Ruby hid her panic in anger. "Why are they? What do they mean? I want to go home. Why should they spoil things?" She sounded petulant as a child. They walked back to Mr Dotts' house slowly, in dark silence. She thought, *I must keep him safe, I mustn't let him go. I must keep him.*

How to say it? She couldn't find any words. The words he had used would not be right for her. Somehow she must let him know that whatever he wanted was his for the asking tonight. How did women let men know that? There must be a way, a way to let him know he had nothing he needed to prove to her, he was a man, he need pay no heed to the military blandishments of his godfather. Mr Winters showed her up to the spare bedroom. It was small and very clean. He apologised for all the things in it, they rarely had guests, it served as a storeroom. There were trunks and books and oriental ornaments; there was a bronze boy with slanting eyes, entwined round a three-foot candlestick. Robin was to sleep on the couch in the drawing-room.

When the house was dark and still, she tiptoed down to him. He had not gone to bed. He stood in his shirt-sleeves, staring out at the moonlight garden. He did not turn as she came in. He said, "What's the matter, Ruby?"

"I can't sleep."

"Thinking about the war, eh?"

"No, I wasn't thinking about the war." Cautiously she put her arms round him from behind, pressing her face against his back. Still he did not turn round.

"I've got to think about what I'm going to do, Ruby."

Was he sending her away? The horror of that possibility knocked the breath out of her body. She clung to him. "Robin, Robin, I've come to you." She tried to explain. It felt like an hour before he understood.

Mr Dotts and Mr Winters slept heavily behind their closed doors while Ruby and Robin knew passion together on the drawing-room floor, with the map of Europe open on the table and all the rabbits in the world free to look in at the window if they wanted to. They knew passion as if they had known it all along . . . Ruby felt a little shock at passion's violence, but the peace of its aftermath quite made up for that, the peace spreading from his body to hers. She kissed his neck, his hands, his toes, drinking at the peace of him. At last he said she should go back up-stairs.

"No, Robin. Please!"

"Silly girl, what if they find us? You can't stay here."

She didn't want to be alone in that little room, with that slanting-eyed slave gleaming and winking at her in the night, reminding her of what she had done, whispering, *What if something happens? What would Mother say? What if he goes away?*

"Oh God. Don't make me go, Robin!" She never said God, except in prayer or serious discussion. Was this either? He kept his arm round her, but tensely, as if about to help her to her feet. She cried, she could not help it.

"Don't cry, Ruby, don't regret it, don't wish – how can I stand it if you wish?"

"I don't wish anything."

He let her stay and they looked into each other's eyes as if these were the first eyes they had ever seen. They looked and looked and realised with surprise that they could suddenly see everything and it was nearly morning. She felt dazzled and still and quiet. She wasn't afraid any more because he had let her stay with him all night. She had won, she had got her way, she had prevailed over him. She could prevail again.

8

The hard face of the white cliff was breaking up before Ruby's eyes. She knew it was chalk but she saw it as granite. Sharp slivers of it showered down and cut her skin, pretending to be rain drops. From now on, everything could be hard and sharp. Rock as soft as chalk, gentle rain, had ceased to exist.

It was the spring of 1918, the war's fourth year. The Barrington family had been cut to bits. The latest disaster was Charles, blown up by a land-mine in France. He was in a base hospital, too ill to be moved. Ruby's visits home from the Sussex farm where she lived in a cottage and worked on the land, home to be with her parents at a time of bad news, were becoming something of a ritual.

Leonard was the first: her favourite brother, he had volunteered at once. A German sniper got him in his second week. Sam was torpedoed in a troop-ship in 1915 and while the family was still reeling from that, news came of Anthony dying a "hero's death" in France . . . they later learned his lungs had been burned out with mustard gas. Stephen, the eldest, survived still, somewhere in the Middle East.

Ruby had thought she had learned not to care. She thought she had built steel casing round her heart so that nothing could hurt her. And now, standing on the platform at Littledean Junction where the London train had left her, looking up at the peak in the Downs that they called Little Beacon, a great white wound cut in its side where they had built the railway fifty years ago, she thought, *If he was dead, I would not mind so much*.

The thought stabbed at her conscience like a knife. But she only looked at it with interest. Charles was her brother, but to be honest (and why not be honest, at a time like this? What was more damned honest than the thump of the guns across the channel?) she had not liked him much. Another dead brother, another of her mother's fits of weeping . . . this uncertainty was different. If Charles lived, he would be crippled. Who was to say that was better than death? Who was to say that the agony of bereavement was worse than the guilty torture of hope, especially when you hardly knew what you hoped for?

She could wish Charles dead and at peace. She could not hope to see him maimed or in pain. Was that so wicked, in a sister? What did it matter, what was wicked and what not? Who decided? Her thoughts were her own. That man, for instance: would he not be better dead? A soldier with only one leg was swinging vigorously along the platform towards her on his crutches. She could see his face each time his sturdy single leg took its double load. There was no-one on the station but Ruby and the one-legged man. Ruby's body had hardened with physical labour; her short hair was like wire. She wore breeches and boots and cracked steel casing round her heart. They might be the last people left on earth, she and the soldier. Adam and Eve in reverse . . . only the railway line, gleaming sullenly in the chilly evening, testified to there being other places, and, she must suppose, other people. He lurched closer. He wore a blue uniform and a red tie. She knew about blue uniforms. Leonard had worn blue when he first enlisted. Mother had frowned over her pride. "My father always used to say that khaki was best." But there wasn't enough khaki then, so the new recruits wore blue. Now there was plenty of khaki, and blue was for the wounded, particularly for those whose

injuries were not so clearly visible as this man's to save them from
the patriots and recruiters, to save them from the Misses Parley
brigade. Ruby fought the memory, her eyes fixed on the man's
empty, sewn-up trouser leg, but it was too late. The first day of
the war she had gone into the office with her very veins singing.
(She wouldn't remember why, she wouldn't think beyond that.)

"Oh! Good morning, Miss Millicent!"

"Good morning, Miss Barrington. What are you staring at?"

"I'm sorry, Miss Millicent. But you look different."

"I was hoping you would congratulate me on looking patriotic."
For Miss Millicent had abandoned her customary austerity of
dress: she had draped herself in the Union Jack, or so it appeared:
she still wore a white blouse, but her skirt was rich blue and a
red ribbon flamed in her hair. Miss Ada was the same, and it was
indicated to Ruby that she would be permitted to dress likewise,
they would even advance her two weeks's salary to make this
possible. She obeyed. One day they sent her out to the butcher's
to buy an unplucked white duck. They made her pull out the
feathers and put them in a bag. The little downy ones got up her
nose in the stuffy office. They started to enclose the feathers with
completed orders and invoices for selected customers. They sent
them off anonymously in envelopes. They presented one coldly
to Mr Orange when he came in with the script of *Queen Victory!*
and he departed, scarlet. This was when Ruby's brothers began
to die; she left the Parleys. They had now placed their entire
business at the disposal of the War Office, or so she heard.

If the one-legged soldier had any memoirs, they would probably
type them for him, for nothing.

I wonder what that feels like? she thought. Once, sawing wood,
she had run a blade deep into her thumb. It tingled still but it
had healed. Dark skin grew back, thick and defensive against it
happening again. Legs did not grow back.

The soldier smiled at her. He was not friendly. He was grinning
with amusement at her breeches and her boots. How dare he?
Did he think he was such a pretty sight? How dare he stare,
horrible, common little man? She looked again and saw that if he
did not grin he might have no face at all, he was so pinched and
grey and rat-like. He could be eighteen, he could be eighty.

"Haven't seen a leg lyin' around, have you miss?" She said
nothing. She ought to admire his chirpy courage but she only felt

disgust. No-one should be wounded like that. They should die, or live. They should make up their minds. "Have to keep movin' " he said, and swung past her on his crutches. He could move! He could catch trains! Why should he think he deserved her sympathy?

The train came. It was short and dimly lit. Nobody got out. She watched the soldier to see how he would manage.

"Can I help you?" She said hoarsely.

He opened the door, reached inside the carriage with his crutches, put them on a seat and hoisted himself up. He was agile and capable. His arms were strong. She stepped in behind him and closed the door. She could remember being told by her mother never to let herself be alone in a railway carriage with a man.

"Thanks," he said, "but I got to do it for myself."

"Yes," she said, and thought of Charles. There were no details, just that he was seriously wounded and would be returned home as soon as possible. The stump of the man's leg lay on the seat opposite, pointing at her. A bit of thigh, and then nothing.

He took out a packet of cigarettes and gave her one.

She said, "Where were you?"

"Boys du Palle. We used to call it Pally Woods, because the mademoiselles used to . . . beg pardon, miss. It's them breeches. I forget meself."

The train moved off. Ruby drew deeply on the cigarette. It was good, strong tobacco but she wished she had not accepted it. People expected you to talk to them if you took their cigarettes, and that always led to trouble.

"Which regiment?"

He told her.

"Did you ever . . .? Have you ever heard of the Duke of Baxburn's Regiment?"

"Can't say I have."

She hated herself for asking. She accepted the answer as the punishment she deserved. Her face must be showing something, for she saw pity in his eyes. Pity and guesses. She didn't want his guesses. She had no pity for him. "Probably one of them funny old regiments . . . a lot of 'em are making right idiots of themselves. That's what we call the really brave ones. Mad Harrys. You got someone?"

No point in feeling angry with him; it was her fault. "I don't know," she said. The train stopped. Ruby peered out. All the stations looked the same; hers wasn't yet. *I don't know. Have I got someone or have I lost someone? I don't know.*

"Missing?"

She nodded.

"He's probably all right. Hasn't had a chance to write you. You gets days when you don't know your left foot from your right."

"He never wrote," said Ruby, "never once!"

"Your husband?"

"We weren't married."

"His family heard anything?"

"I went to see them. They said they'd let me know if . . . anything. But they never liked me. I won't ask them again." *If Robin's alive, he knows how to find me, if he wants to find me. But I'm the last person to know what he really wants. I thought I knew. I thought he wanted me very badly, but when I think about it now, when I can't help it, all I can remember is his sending me away. I thought he wanted to be the last man in England to go away and fight, but once the bands were playing and the posters were calling him, he couldn't be stopped.*

The soldier shifted his stump painfully. "War Office?"

"Missing, they just say missing, it's the only word they know."

"We-ell. War Office! Field of turnips!" He had offered the War Office as hope. Now that he knew there was no hope in it, he disparaged it. "They couldn't find a haystack in a bag of needles. War Office find somebody? Ever heard of the time they lost a tank between Woolwich and Dover?"

And now you're going to say, "No news is good news."

"Know what they say? No news is good news."

Ruby said, "If you had a girl; and you . . . came to despise her for some reason, or you met another girl you liked better, wouldn't you tell the first girl . . . knowing she'd worry?"

His eyes narrowed in his pain-filled face. Not meaning to, she had told him everything. He said, "Let me ask you something. If your boy comes back, and he's . . . like me, will you still have him?"

She said, "Southeden Halt. This is my station."

He said. "They got any pubs in Southeden?"

She said, "There the King's Head." It was a dim, dusty little place in the village, peopled with miserable old farmers who glared resentfully at outsiders who tried to sit on the benches, drink from the glasses or farm the land that belonged to their missing boys. Ruby had gone there once with Beatrice and Jane, the two girls who shared her cottage, but they were scared away by the unfriendly atmosphere. When Ruby tried to order a whisky-and-soda alone, the landlord's wife refused to serve her. It would please her to go in with a one-legged soldier; no-one would dare to turn them away. "How will you get home?" she said.

He said, "I'm me own man now, what's left of me. I don't have to be anywhere."

What did he mean? He might mean he did not necessarily intend to go home, he might think he could stay with her, she had heard of such things. He climbed down from the train, spurning her help. His crutches thumped on the stony road. What a thing to think! That part of life was over for him, surely; and for her too, most probably, with the steel round her heart. And what did it matter? It was stupid nonsense, it was nothing. It wore you out, like Mother. It made men like Robin love you till you gave in, then they went away.

The door of the King's Head was open but the bar was empty. Dim light shone grudgingly on the dusty tables; scant warmth came from the dying fire. The owner's wife came bustling in with a hospitable expression which turned to a scowl when she saw Ruby. She was about to send her out, Ruby was sure, but the soldier asked for two whiskies and the woman was too abashed to refuse.

They sat shivering by the fire. Ruby sipped her drink: icy to her lips, it warmed her inside. They spoke of their families, their school days. The soldier sang a few of the songs of the men at the front. He had a voice that seemed to lend good cheer to the miserable place. With three whiskies inside her, Ruby felt a surge of indignation about the fire; she walked unsteadily to the counter and beat on it. "Could we have some more coal?"

The woman said, "It's not worth it."

"What do you mean?"

"Someone's got to pay for that coal. And there's no customers here."

"*I* am here, and so is my friend!"

The woman folded her arms. She looked at Ruby with disgust. "Like I said. There's *nobody* here."

Ruby felt like hitting her. She felt like pulling the last remaining coal from the fire and ramming it into the woman's eye. She stood there safe because soldiers were losing their legs; daily she ate food grown by the land-girls.

"Let's go," she said to the soldier.

"Where to?"

"Anywhere's better than here."

"Here . . ." He handed her some money and she stared. "Get us a bottle."

She bought a small bottle of whisky and held it now to the soldier's lips, now to her own, as they made their unsteady way back to the train.

Suddenly he said, "Where' we goin', then?"

"The station."

"I thought you said you lived round here."

"I do, but – "

"Well then?"

"Not by myself. I live with my aunt and my sister."

"Bloody hell!"

"Where are you going?"

He could move at a good speed when he tried. Or perhaps it was the whisky. He made for the side of the road, for a tree. He leaned against it and dropped his crutches. As she stepped forward to help him he grabbed her. It was as if all the strength of his missing limb had been added to the strength of his arms. She could not move. When the shock had subsided, she dared not try, he might fall, he might hurt himself.

And why struggle, what did it matter? This thing that everyone made such a fuss about was nothing, nothing at all. No harm had come to her. Robin had only gone away, and she would want this man to go away, so why not be nice to him, here, leaning on this evening-wet black tree with the dark silence of the countryside all around and the taste of whisky on his lips and hers?

She would not have thought it was possible, standing like that, like a fumbling, gasping human tripod.

9

The cottage had belonged to Farmer Simmons' shepherd, Smythe, and his wife and two babies. When Smythe was called by his regiment, and Farmer Simmons was sent three girls with a month's training apiece to replace him, along with orders that his

322

flock be slaughtered for meat and replaced with dairy cows, Mrs Smythe had moved into the big farmhouse for the duration. She was supposed to come to the cottage to cook and clean for the girls; but they rarely saw her. Sometimes she stood wistfully on the path, looking up at the cottage, with a child clutching each hand; but she ran away if anyone tried to speak to her.

Ruby's indignation over this was only one of the things that set her apart from her two companions. Beatrice Parker was a vicar's daughter with big bones and apologetic eyes: she made a point of seeing good in everybody, and understood why poor Mrs Smythe would not want to wait on strangers in her own home. Jane Phipps had been a kitchenmaid and would not say boo to a goose; she still had not quite forgotten her habit of calling Ruby and Beatrice "Miss". Beatrice was kind to Jane; Ruby was as polite with the two of them as she must be, living so close, but she raged inside at the domesticity they tried to impose on the cottage, as if it were permanent, as if it were home. Who ever heard of a home consisting of three girls? To make a home there was like goading the war to last longer. It was not as if Beatrice and Jane had not suffered at the war's hands; Ruby could have hated them thoroughly and without guilt then; Jane had lost her father, and Beatrice prayed nightly for her sister, killed with the VADs, and her brothers in the navy. But they could turn away from their sorrows and their fears, as Ruby found she could not; and Ruby thought them heartless for it.

Most of the time, their work was with the cows. They were also supposed to take turns joining a felling team in Long Forest, a sparse wood growing sparser; but Jane was frightened of saws, so Ruby went for her. Hacking trees suited her mood. Cows were too personal. They had names, faces. Beatrice said things like, "Bluebell got out of bed the wrong side this morning," when it kicked her, but even without such nonsense it was possible to imagine they had personalities. And the feel of their pink, wet teats . . . of course cows were milked by machines now. That pleased Ruby. She liked to see the stupid creatures standing two-by-two while a chugging pump and India rubber pads did to them what human hands had once done: how dare they look so hurt and indignant? They were at war too.

Beatrice Parker had not wanted to be a land-girl; she had joined the VADs with her now-dead sister, and then, in her first week on the wards in a military hospital, had fainted at some dreadful sight and left in shame and terror. This much Ruby knew from overhearing a conversation between Beatrice and Jane; no hint had been given as to what horror it was that had shattered Beatrice's nerve, but Ruby supposed her sense of failure was what accounted for the big girl's air of apologetic kindness as she fussed over her companions like a mother, cooking stews at the end of the weary day and urging them to take off wet boots. It mortified Ruby, made her angry. Did Beatrice expect herself, expect everyone, to be strong and perfect all the time? But who else was there for Ruby to turn to as the weeks crept into summer and the gaudy flowers and sickly birdsong goaded her with the terror that the one-legged soldier had left behind?

She came in one evening after seeing the cows were all right for the night and saw the usual sight of four feet steaming on the fender as Beatrice and Jane sat close together on the fraying, over-stuffed sofa. Really, she wouldn't be surprised if there was something funny about those two . . . but that was how it was going to be now, she supposed, now that all the men were dead.

"Come and get warm, Ruby. I've made some soup."

"Not now. Will you come for a walk with me? Just you, Beatrice?"

Jane bounded to her feet: she was terrified of Ruby. "Have I done something wrong, miss?"

"No, but I've got to talk to Beatrice alone." She heard her voice crack, dawdling back to the cottage, she had wondered whether she would have the courage to go through with her planned confession, but now she knew she had lived alone with her panic too long. Jane pulled on her boots. "*I* quite fancy a walk."

She would not apologise. She would not beat about the bush. If Beatrice could not understand, if she condemned her, Ruby would follow Jane and never be seen again. "I think I might be in trouble. I might be going to have a baby."

"Oh, Ruby!" Her shock might even be admiration. "How is that possible?"

"There's only one way."

"Oh, *Ruby!*"

Ruby took out a cigarette. Her hand shook so much she could not light it. Beatrice brought a taper from the fire and helped her, although she did not approve of girls, smoking.

"If that's all you can say," said Ruby, after thanking her, "there wasn't much point in me telling you."

"But what do you want – ? Oh, Ruby!"

"You're the one with medical experience. I thought – ?"

What had she thought? She had thought nothing. She did not really expect Beatrice to help her medically, even if she knew how; neither of them would have the courage. If she was right, there was nothing to be done; she would just have to go home, that was all; show her parents their sons weren't the only people who could bring the war into their cosy pie-shop! She felt sick with bitterness. If the baby ever came to birth it would be a savage creature after nine months inside her.

"I can't do that, Ruby. Even if I knew how, it would be wrong."

"Wrong! Wrong! Is it right for me to bring a one-legged baby into the world?"

"One – "

"He only had one leg! He only had one leg! I felt sorry for him – "

"Oh, Ruby!"

She might as well have confided her fears to Bluebell the cow.

She awoke next morning to the sound of the forestry van driving away. She should be aboard the forestry van. Beatrice's and Jane's beds were empty. She felt sick at the memory of her confidences with Beatrice. Beatrice was in the kitchen, pink-cheeked from early work, mournful with worry.

Ruby accepted a cup of tea without a word. "What time is it? Why didn't you wake me? What about the cows?"

"They're done, and Jane has gone to the woods for you."

"Ha! She'll cut herself in half."

There was a look of shy determination in Beatrice's eye; missionary zeal, almost. That was it! Ruby wondered why she had not had the sense to keep her mouth shut. Having failed as a nurse, Beatrice was going to repay her debt to the world by saving Ruby's soul. "I wanted to talk to you, Ruby. I've been thinking." Out it all came. Beatrice knew the addresses of organisations that could help Ruby, if her fears were founded; she even had a little money and would give her all she could. But (and here it came) she was very disturbed: had she correctly understood Ruby to say that she did not even know the man?

Ruby laughed. "I knew him all right."

Beatrice flushed. "You know what I mean. Were you . . . attacked?"

"No. No twice. No I wasn't attacked, and no I didn't know him. It was just . . . an impulse."

"I see." Ruby watched Beatrice hunt for words. When they came they were a surprise, and the rush of contempt Ruby had expected to feel for her did not materialise. "Isn't there enough destruction without us destroying ourselves?"

"Oh, it's nothing, Beatrice," she said uneasily. "It doesn't mean anything. It didn't mean anything to Robin." She couldn't remember if she had told her or Jane anything about Robin. Probably not. Now she took a savage pleasure in it, talking of the wicked, sensual joys of love, knowing Beatrice had no such memories and probably never would have; and if Beatrice chose to conclude that Ruby had given herself to the soldier out of grief that was better than that she should know about the helpless, hopeless burning hate that she felt for the whole world and herself most of all.

"You haven't heard anything?"

"No. He must be dead."

"If he was dead, you would probably have heard. Oh, Ruby, I'm sorry, but do you think . . . it is possible he might have found somebody else?"

"I hadn't thought of that," she said.

"You don't want to go to his parents, but is there anyone else who would know?"

"He'd take her to Baxburn." Savagely she told Beatrice about Baxburn, Mr Dotts and Mr Winters, the stupid rabbit.

"Then write to them, why don't you?"

"They sent him away! They made him go to the war."

There was a long silence as they finished sweeping the dairy and turned to scalding the churns. Ruby liked the clang of metal against concrete, the sharp burn of hot water on her hands. Let the baby be there inside her, or not, as it chose. She would give it to Beatrice. Beatrice was obviously made to be a mother and this would be her only chance.

"You see, Ruby, the worst of truths can't hurt as much as the least of our imagined fears."

"Where did you hear that, in one of your father's sermons?"

Quietly, Beatrice repeated what she was willing to do to help Ruby: addresses, money, and, of course, prayers. She added that she ought to visit the village doctor. Ashamed at last, Ruby said that she would, though she knew she would not; the doctor had bandaged her hand after the accident with the saw, and had been kind and amused; she had had all the kindness she deserved.

Beatrice was still speaking above the hiss and slurp of boiling water in churns. If at any time Ruby decided to take courage and go to Baxburn and find out the truth, and if she wanted company, Beatrice would go with her. Because, quite apart from her present predicament, there were considerable dangers in her behaviour. Beatrice would not speak of morals . . . but Ruby surely knew that there were diseases? And laws under which a girl consorting with soldiers could be locked up? "Didn't your mother warn you about these things?"

"You don't know my mother," Ruby retorted.

Mother wrote that Charles was back in Stalcross. He would never walk again. His wife was too upset to nurse him, so he was staying with the parents for the time being. Ruby was shocked, yet it was not a surprise. She gritted her teeth and wrote him a letter of sympathy and welcome. Then she walked out into the middle of a field and vomited burning yellow bile over and over again into the grass. At first it was a relief but it went on and on, spasms racking her till she could no longer stand. Bent double she squirmed on the ground, howling with pain and disgust. She rolled in her own filth and still the sense of being torn apart did not leave her. The vomiting stopped but her insides were pouring themselves out in a frenzy that was almost ecstasy. It was not enough to see blood there, she wanted to see her womb and her heart, steaming and throbbing on the grass, every part of her that had ever felt anything. The war wanted death, did it? She, Ruby Barrington, had made her contribution.

Quietly she informed Beatrice that she had been mistaken; everything was all right after all; she thanked Beatrice for her willingness to help, but she would thank her even more if she never alluded to the matter again.

10

She was glad nobody had seen her disgusting display in the field. Even the cows were being milked at the time.

In the ensuing weeks her body was besieged by racking pain and other debilitating symptoms. One half of her suffered and pitied itself; the other laughed bitterly, told her it was no more than she deserved, reminded her that there was a war on and she had a job to do.

One chilly morning in the autumn, Mrs Smythe appeared at the door with the farmer and her children. Her eyes shone.

"My Tony be coming home." And she looked greedily over the girls' shoulders into the room. Ruby was washing dishes at the sink and stared back at her from a long distance.

"Is it over?" Beatrice breathed. And Jane started to cry.

"We're very grateful to you girls," Farmer Simmons said.

Ruby wiped her hands and walked towards the little group in the doorway. They seemed to be saying that something had ended. Beatrice seemed to be offering to pack her things this instance and leave the cottage to the Smythes as if nothing had happened. Jane seemed to have her arms round Mrs Smythe and to be apologising for not looking after the place better. The farmer seemed to be saying that they should not go just yet, and here were a plucked fowl and some bottles of beer to celebrate . . . celebrate what? They talked as if the war had ended! They talked as if they thought they could just do that: end the war as suddenly as they had begun it and expect everything to be just the same! What kind of people were they? . . . She tried to protest, she opened her mouth, she saw Beatrice's square, stupid worried face staring at her, and then the floor, with its darned, threadbare carpet, reared up and hit her mightily between the eyes.

Beatrice Parker was loyal and honourable, that had to be said for her. She alone knew the likely explanation of Ruby's collapse, but she went along with the fretting and fussing, agreed that Ruby had worked terribly hard, suggested that the shock of the Armistice had been the last straw. Ruby was moved to the farmhouse and feted with flowers and eggs; no-one would hear of her making the journey to Stalcross until she was fully recovered: even Mother wrote that they could manage quite well without her for now, which was kindly meant, but sounded ominous. For the first few weeks she felt drained of energy and utterly peaceful: she would not have known that time was passing but for the periodic reports she received: Tony Smythe had come back, his wife could not stop weeping, he was seeing about selling the cows, for he was a shepherd and this was a sheep farm, and the Simmonses had no heart to argue. Jane had gone home to her parents. Beatrice stayed to help look after Ruby, but news came that her brother would be home from the navy for Christmas and Ruby dismissed her. There was an insane moment of forgetfulness when she thought that she herself would like to go home for Christmas . . . but then she pictured the empty spaces round the family table and started to sweat and vomit.

"She can stay as long as she likes, bless her," said Mrs Simmons. Beatrice looked anxious. Ruby marvelled bitterly at Beatrice's sense of duty: she seemed to think it an imposition on the Simmonses, to care for a few more weeks for the girl who had nearly killed herself saving their farm. At last Beatrice went away with a promise to return with the family car and drive Ruby to Stalcross as soon as she received word that she was ready. Ruby knew what lay behind the promise; Beatrice was going to go away and look at Baxburn on the map; and, by the strangest of coincidences, that would be the way they would go. And since they were in Baxburn, Beatrice would say, pathetic in her attempt at deceit, might they not call at the house of those two men who would know by now what had become of Robin? She smiled weakly in the white bed. She was quite well. It was only standing up that made her faint. She would agree, she would agree to anything. It was too far in the future to worry about.

Pale winter-red sun hung over the frosty January downland as they set off. Ruby's stockings were thick, but her legs felt cold without her breeches. Her skirt hung awkwardly; her shape had changed since the time she wore the skirt to take the train to town and type in an office. Her waist was thin from illness, her thighs had thickened with work. Beatrice also looked strange, feminine, pretty almost . . . Ruby had not noticed the tan on her face when she saw it every day, but now she was pale and pink, and she wore a lovely pink scarf on her head, matching the sky, and a thick green coat.

They spoke very little. Ruby felt well in her body but sick in her mind. Beatrice was nervous about driving and had to concentrate. It was an uncomfortable ride. Ruby watched the sparkling countryside with dread, waiting for the moment when it would turn grey.

Beatrice said, "Good gracious!"

Dully Ruby asked what the matter was.

"Did you see that signpost? Baxburn, three miles. Isn't Baxburn that place where you had friends?"

Ruby sighed. "Yes."

Beatrice stopped the car: obviously she wanted to be able to talk firmly and thoughtfully. Why did she bother? Ruby was too tired to argue, it was much easier to agree that, yes, it would be as well to be able to set her mind at rest about Robin, one way or another.

". . . otherwise, you're just going to torture yourself with wondering, for the rest of your life, Ruby."

"You're driving," said Ruby.

Beatrice sighed and drove them into Baxburn.

They came into the village from the south; Ruby was used to approaching it from the direction of London. It looked all wrong. The village green was the wrong shape, a ragged triangle. Dead weeds were caught in the thick ice on the pond; the church spire made no reflection. Beatrice leaned over and opened the door of the car; Ruby got out, shivering. It was strange to feel grass under her good shoes and have no work to do. The sun had disappeared, leaving only a white mark on a cloud to show where it had been. The streets were grey, the little cottages with their unkempt thatches were shut tight against the damp air. The trees were black and bare; no-one was about, except for a man kneeling at a short stone column half-covered with a cloth outside the little church. He was chipping away with a chisel and as Beatrice turned her engine off the clink-clink sound of metal on stone was all that broke the silence.

"Come on, be brave. Tell me where they live."

"It was summer when we came here," said Ruby desperately, "and it didn't look like this." She started to walk towards the church and the man chipping at the column. Under the cloth it had the shape of a cross. A *cross*! A thought to damn her invaded her mind, and she would not let it go: a cross was not enough! One man had suffered on a cross for three hours! What was that, against a million men and four years? And who was this man, chipping out names in the stone? Why wasn't he killed in the war, had they kept him safe so that he could go like this, from village to village? She went closer. She pulled away the cloth.

"Here, it's not unveiled yet!"

He had in his hand a scrap of paper with a brown circle on it where he had rested his cup of tea. He was copying names from it. Ruby snatched it and read it while the man marshalled his indignation. There was no name that she recognised and she handed it back. Robin's name wouldn't be on it anyway; he had been lured into the local regiment, but this wasn't his home. She thought fast and made a final decision. She would not go to Mr Dott's house and see the cosy gathering of him, Mr Winters, their chess-set, their map of Europe, their oriental ornaments, Robin, and his new wife. What did it matter if he was dead or not? He didn't want her.

"Come on, Ruby, what's the address? Is it this way?"

"There's no need," she said, "His name's on the memorial."

"Oh *Ruby*."

"Take me home, please," Ruby said briskly. She felt intensely relieved: in saying it aloud, she had made the lie true. Robin was dead to her, and that was all that mattered. Now all she wanted was never to hear Beatrice Parker say *Oh Ruby!* again.

She started to feel quite kindly disposed towards Beatrice as they neared Stalcross: the poor girl was frowning agonisingly, and clearly very worried that she had done the wrong thing. Ruby hastened to reassure her. "We just have to begin again, I suppose!" she said.

"Oh, Ruby! I'm glad you can see it like that . . . it's best, isn't it?"

Ruby smiled wearily, wishing she could be like Beatrice, who really was intensely kind and seemed to like her. Beatrice had tried to play mother to her, but now Ruby felt fifty years her senior. But she did not snub her. "Won't you come in, Beatrice?" said Ruby formally, as the car stopped outside the pie-shop, "and have tea?"

"No, no you want to be with your family."

"Yes, I suppose I do." With weak arms, she hauled her suitcases from the back of the vehicle and went slowly inside. She looked back once and saw Beatrice's pretty pink scarf fluttering as she drove down the road.

There was a welcome-home tea party for her, and throughout it she observed and marvelled at her own behaviour. She embraced her parents with fierce, real affection, apologising to her mother for not coming before and teasing her father for his loss of weight and receding hair. Then she made the rounds of the rest of the family like a visiting duchess, saying all the right things without a shred of feeling. She congratulated Stephen and his wife Susan on his survival; she murmured words to the widows of Leonard and Anthony, pressing their hands and hoping they were as well as could be expected. She felt no horror as she bent down towards Charles' bitter, pale, pain-filled face, and kissed him; not for one second did her breathing falter as her nose detected the unwashed, decaying smell that came from him. She even managed to greet his wife, who still would not have him home; she had only come today, Mother had fiercely told Ruby, because the children wanted to see their father; she had been heard to say that Charles would be better dead. Freed of feeling, Ruby was able to understand her point of view; it had been clear from the earliest weeks of their marriage that they were not well-suited and had only wed because they had to; but she still did not like the girl. She cuddled her nieces and nephews, with extra-tight hugs for the ones who had lost their fathers. As they all sat down to tea (a meat pie, jam sandwiches, and a sugar-cake large enough for each child to have a slice) she noticed that Sam had left no great sense of loss behind him. But then he had never been at home. He had always been a soldier. And a soldier was always absent, whether living or dead.

Father and Mother were worn out: they were both nearly sixty, but their plans for retirement were out of the question now, with so many mouths to feed. Stephen and Susan would take over the running of the business and the main shop; the parents would try to salvage the near-bankrupt branch that Leonard had started. They were a family; somehow they would manage; they must look after each other. All eyes were on Charles' wife: "It's the stairs," she said. "I don't see how I can manage him with the stairs." "It's all right," said Ruby, still feeling nothing but knowing what was expected. "There aren't so many at Leonard's, and I'm strong." Charles' wife would come round to realising her duty in time . . . and if she did not, what did it matter?

They ate their tea. At one point Charles caused a wave of tut-tuts by bringing out a small bottle and swigging at it. Ruby caught his eye and moved her lips in the smallest of smiles. Perhaps they had something in common after all. She summoned up her courage and lit a cigarette. In the ensuing silence, Charles made as if to lunge at her from his wheelchair, lolled dangerously and restored himself. "Isn't that writer fellow going to make an honest woman of you, Rube?" he asked quietly, "Oh – sorry. Did he cop it?"

Ruby blew smoke into the air. Mother coughed. "Thank you for noticing," said Ruby.

All round the table, repentant sympathy glowed.

"We didn't know."

"You didn't ask."

Everyone was very sorry.

She seized Stephen's arm as he was getting ready to go.

"Will you buy me a typewriter, please?"

"Oh! Have you asked Dad?"

"I'm asking you. You're getting the business."

"Well – I dare say. I'll need a bit of help with that kind of thing."

"You'll have to pay," she said.

He smiled. "You're a tough girl, Ruby. Good luck to you." And off he went, with his wife and children.

11

"Put your arms round my neck, Charles." Ruby leaned over the bed where her brother slouched, resentful at having been woken to begin another day. But he obeyed and she returned a grotesque embrace of her own. Her hands met in the small of his back and she hooked her fingers into each other till they hurt. Together they heaved him up into a sitting position, then swung his legs over the side of the bed. At last, with her knees braced against his lifeless ones, she was able to swivel and manhandle him into his wheelchair. He was heavy and awkward, some days more so than others, though whether his mood or his physical state was responsible she did not care to think. Sometimes her own back hurt so much that she made jokes about ordering a second wheelchair for herself, but nobody laughed.

Breathing heavily from the effort, she brought him a bowl of water to wash himself, dressed him and tucked a blanket about his knees.

"In a hurry this morning, Rube?" he said suspiciously.

"Yes. We're going out. Or rather, you are."

"Where?"

"I'm taking you to visit your dear wife."

"I'm not going."

"No? This wheelchair is, together with whoever happens to be in it at the time."

"You're a hard woman, Rube."

She folded her arms and stared at him. "Oh yes, Charlie boy," she said softly. "Very. But you see, I've got a visitor coming this morning, and somehow I've got to convince him that besides being a small branch of Barrington's Pies, this place is also the Miss Ruby Barrington Typewriting Agency . . . and he's going to find that hard enough to believe without thinking it's a nursing home as well."

"Visitor, eh?" Charles leered.

"Customer."

"Cigarette?"

"Thank you."

She wheeled him out to the street through the shop kitchen, fragrant with pastry and breakfast. She paused to let her parents stop their work and greet their son. Despite the misery of Charles, which sometimes manifested itself in savage, sarcastic moods of depression and sometimes in a pathetic desire to please, which, being so unlike him, was almost worse, it was the sight of her parents working away in this small bakery that should have been Leonard's that made Ruby saddest. They ought to be able to rest now. But they rose before dawn and slowly carried on with the work they had done all their lives. War and hardship had seemed to shear flesh from the two of them; a quick glance might suggest that Father was as round and rosy as ever. Mother as stolid and calm; but living with them, Ruby knew how Father's clothes hung from him, held in place only by braces and belts; she knew about her mother's fits of weeping. But pity was dangerous.

"Here's Charles, I've brought him to see you!" she shouted at his astonished wife, "I'll help you carry him upstairs."

"Oh . . . we were going out."

"Then I'll leave him here and you can take him with you." She ran off down the street, smiling a little at the discomfiture of her sister-in-law, whose determination she must secretly respect, burden her though it did. At least she could catch the bus home. She would have less than an hour to prepare for the most unexpected of visitors: Mr Walter Orange, whose handwritten plays had been such a mainstay of the income of the Misses Parley Agency, and such a torment to her own working day.

The letter had come a few months after she acquired her typewriter and started advertising in newspapers. Its author had seen the advertisements and took the liberty of enquiring whether she was the *same* Miss Barrington – if by happy chance she was, then a long search was at an end, for he knew he could believe her assurances of accurate, conscientious work at reasonable prices; such assurances were, he regretted, more frequently given than honoured in these changed times.

Her parents allowed her to put a sign in the window for Mr Orange, lest he should arrive at the pie-shop and think he was mistaken: THE MISS RUBY BARRINGTON TYPEWRITING AGENCY: THROUGH SHOP. She had expected to conduct all her business by post; she had not bargained for personal callers. She busied herself converting the room into a convincing replica of the Misses Parley's office. She covered Charles' bed, put away his medicine bottles and arranged piles of paper in a businesslike manner around her typewriter. Then she attended to herself: she looked rather dowdy in her loose grey cardigan, so she took it off and wore a fresh white blouse. Caring for Charles could be a rather messy business, and she did not usually bother much about her clothes. She sighed. She did not resemble the Misses Parley either in her appearance, or, she feared, her skills.

It was difficult to picture Mr Orange, now that she tried. Unlike his plays, he had not left a lasting impression. He used to come crashing into the office with his manuscripts and go crashing out again, like a streak of rather clumsy lightning: the Misses Parley used to speculate that he was probably the illegitimate son of an aristocrat, adding, "The House of Lords' loss is our gain!" But of course, Ruby recognised him at once. If she'd seen him in the street she would have recognised him: his surprising height, his shaggy, straw-coloured hair, his long stride and good, ill-fitting suit. She was touched by his apparent pleasure at seeing her, a pleasure that seemed to go beyond the relief of having at last found a typist equal to his work; but her heart shifted with anger too at his obvious good health and high spirits: *You've survived. Why have you survived and others not?*

But perhaps he was not entirely unscathed. She noticed he stammered: it was an unusual stammer, it occurred at the end of words rather than their beginning. It sounded as if he had swallowed the word by mistake and was spitting it out again. She was sure it was new. If it had existed before, the Misses Parley would have made sport of it and she would remember. She wondered why, since he must be aware of the impediment, he had to talk so *much?* Why didn't he just get down to business and go? Time without Charles was very precious to her; but of course she could not tell him that.

He was telling her about his war. His manner of speaking was really most annoying. Sometimes he waved his arms and rolled his eyes in a way that was almost girlish. Sometimes he used gruff monosyllables like a military man. It was touching though, that he did not make himself out to have been any kind of hero. "Damned lucky," he said. "I was in Stores most of the time; think they forgot I was there-ere. Didn't see much action till the end, when they got a rather plucky girl to replace me."

Love behind the Lines. That was what the play would be called. Or *Lanes?* Mr Orange was fond of puns in his titles.

"*Damned* lucky," he repeated. "All those bangs! *Quite* terrified me!" He looked up to the ceiling and shuddered. "Commanding officer worked for Duckbill & Middlesex. Found me a job; Indian Exports, that's what I am now. Need some help with correspondence, busy time, you know-ow. They talked about getting a girl in, but I said, 'Oh, no, it's much cheaper to put it out to an agency at the busy times.'" Ruby looked through the sheaf of papers he gave her and was relieved to be able to learn from them that Duckbill & Middlesex was some kind of department store, for it would not have been good to admit that she had never heard of the firm.

"I thought it would be a play," she said.

"Oh, goodness, sorry to disappoint my one admirer! No time for that now; got to work for a living! That dreadful war! Investments shot to hell, if-if I may put it like that. Now these letters, Miss Barrington – don't mind if I talk to you like a commanding officer for a bit, do you? – these are orders we *can't* fill, and I've scribbled the reasons on the corner, and I'd like you to put it into good English and send them off. For instance, the wine this chap wants simply *doesn't* travel well-ell, and we won't risk our reputation by trying. This one doesn't pay his bills – you can find a polite way of saying that – and that lady hasn't written her address, silly, er, lady."

"So how can I write to her?"

"Ah! Good point! Well done, Miss Barrington! Now, send me the carbon copies with your account, and I shall *personally* ensure prompt settlement."

He was as good as his word; and Duckbill & Middlesex sent a steady stream of work Ruby's way. She advanced from the typing of disappointing letters to the senders of impracticable orders to more demanding tasks: D & M, as Mr Orange called his employers, once he was sure that such intimacy would mean no lowering of Ruby's respect for them, were bringing their mail-order catalogue up to date. This involved Ruby going page by page through the old edition and incorporating scribbled amendments in the margins into a text that would be readable by printers. She enjoyed the work. It was good to feel in touch with a world where the sun shone so fiercely that people needed topis and spine protectors.

It never seemed to occur to Mr Orange that he need not call personally to collect and deliver orders, and it was not always possible to have Charles out of the way when he came. But Mr Orange's reaction to the sight of her brother was such as to make her deeply ashamed: ashamed of having been ashamed of Charles, ashamed of fearing that Mr Orange would not think hers a serious agency if he knew that she was also a nurse. On the contrary: he shook Charles' hand, talked with him in a manly, cheerful way as if they were old friends and Mr Orange had not even noticed the wheelchair, and later whispered, "Don't wear yourself out, Miss Barrington, will you?"

That was all. But it was enough to be very touching. Who else cared? Charles drifted in and out of his moods, and everything must be permitted a man with useless legs and a heartless wife. He never thanked Ruby for anything. It was understandable that he preferred to forget how he relied on her for his performance of the most natural functions; but could he only achieve that forgetfulness by seeing her as one of those functions?

"Would it be difficult to think of me as a customer, Miss Barrington, if you were to call me Walter?"

"I don't think so."

"And might I call you Ruby?"

"Of course. It's my name."

Pink and emboldened, he said, "Would you come to a matinee with me?"

"Why, thank you, Walter. Is it one of your plays?"

"It's by George Bernard Shaw, actually. But it's very-ery good."

It was. She laughed till she thought she would cry; it was rather terrifying, like being tickled till it hurt or beaten repeatedly on her funny-bone. The words the actors spoke were so wickedly, tragically true at the same time as being funny. She quite forgot Walter at her side, with his white fingertips pressed together, his brow furrowed, until the interval when she clutched his arm and said, "Oh, *Walter*! If you could write plays like that, I'd type them for nothing, just for the fun of it!" She saw him flinch and began to repent; but why should she? Why should she watch her every word and hold it back if it seemed it might hurt someone? Who ever took such care of her? She sighed. Walter did. The very fact that he brought her to the theatre, when he could not possibly like her or think her pretty with her tired face and wiry hair and dull grey skirt, showed that he was kind. Who was she to imply that he would never be as good a playwright as Shaw? What did she know?

They went afterwards to a tearoom lush with greenery, quite different from the cramped little place where she had once drunk tea with poor Leonard before running away from home . . . she smiled at the memory of her pink, indignant little self. Why should she be thinking of running away? She was twenty-one and could earn her living. She could go where she pleased.

Music played: two daring girls were dancing together. As the violins built to a screeching climax, the taller of the two whirled the other off her feet in an embrace that was almost passionate; they grinned mockingly at each other, shrugged, went on dancing. Ruby turned away. The waitress brought tea. "It's India-a tea, I take it?" said Walter.

The waitress giggled. "Yes, sir."

"Whereabouts in India does it come from?" He sipped. "Darjeeling?" The waitress did not know, but she would ask; she returned with cucumber sandwiches and a selection of cakes. "Yes, sir, Darjooling."

Pouring tea, Ruby felt very formal. "You seem to be very knowledgeable about teas, Mr Orange. Walter."

"I'm trying to mug up on all things Indian. I may be going out there, you see, in a year or two."

"How lovely!"

"Well. It'll be hard work. D & M are thinking of opening a branch in Calcutta. Seems silly-illy to be forever sending off brown paper parcels when we could have a shop!"

"I suppose so." The casual ease of it! *I may be going out there! A year or two! Seems silly!* "Walter, I hope you didn't think I was being rude when I said that about Mr Shaw's play and, er, yours."

He smiled sadly. His skin was very smooth. Sometime recently he had let fall that he was thirty, which had surprised her. She had begun to detect wrinkles in her own face; he had none. "You were quite right, Ruby. And you see, the thing is – well, you're a clever girl, but you don't go to the theatre *often*, do you? And yet you could *tell*-ell. Shaw's the master. I should stick to what I'm good at."

"And what's that?"

"You're laughing at me, Ruby."

"I'm not!"

"Those two old harpies you used to work for did."

"Oh, them. They laughed at everybody."

He was talking about India now. About how the order books of the last twenty years at D & M had enabled him to build up a picture of the lives of English people there, just as if he were writing a play . . . so all his imaginative work before the war had not been wasted after all. "All the world's a stage, Ruby," he said, and he went on to quote some lines from Shakespeare. She could see what he meant, but he still made her sad, sorry for him. Why should she be sorry for him? Didn't she too know what it was to want something very much, and then find she was not good enough for it? Besides, something else that he had said had found a resting-place in her mind and was gathering other stray thoughts round itself like a magnet: *You don't go to the theatre often, and yet you could tell.* Certainly she could tell. Words were words, all made of the same twenty-six letters, yet one arrangement could make her sick with boredom while another could make her laugh till she wept. And Robin used to collect her interesting phrases and put them in his poems, then seek her opinion on the poems and value it. And for as long as she had been a typist, people had asked her to "put things into good English" and she had done it, never realising until this moment that the very request meant that she had a skill which others lacked. Maybe she could be a writer too! Not plays, perhaps, or poems; but stories! Lots of women wrote stories! And she could do it at home! She did not know yet what her first story would be about, but she was suddenly desperate to get home and start. She waited for Walter to finish his tea, hardly listening to him; it was only after he had shaken her hand on her doorstep and walked away that she realised that, without actually proposing, he had given her to understand that she could go to India with him as his wife if she wanted to.

12

"It's quite impossible," said her father; and his eyebrows hovered like white birds above an expression on his face that Ruby could not quite read.

Mother shushed the squirming grandchild on her knee, covered her own mouth with her napkin, and said solemnly, "You can't do it, Ruby." Even her dead brothers seemed to rise up beside their wives to protest at the announcement that she was engaged to Walter. But she wanted to marry Walter, he was a nice man, very fond of her under his shyness. If her relatives could only see themselves! They were like a row of typewriters with their messages of alarm clicking up in their eyes: *The parents aren't getting any younger, Ruby! And what about Charles? We're not accustomed to worrying our heads about Charles! We're not accustomed to worrying our heads about anything!* Her family claimed her. Well – let them say it. Let them just dare!

Stephen leaned forward. He was trying not to smile. Ruby looked down her nose at him. He exploded into laughter, and the whole table with him. "Oh, Ruby, don't be cross! We guessed, we knew it was only a matter of time and we were just chuckling to think of your name being Ruby Orange!"

Stony-faced, she let them laugh. They moved to congratulating her, to telling her they had discussed everything, and everything would be all right. They laughed and laughed, no-one daring to be the first to stop with her looking so sour. At last Stephen and Susan's little girl ran from the room and came back with a globe on a stand and solemnly told Ruby where India was, pointing out that it was pink and therefore English; and Ruby smiled.

Ruby went with her mother to Duckbill & Middlesex to get all the things she would need. Walter had given her a book that listed

340

all the correct clothes, along with many other useful hints for people going East for the first time, and she had authority to place everything on his account. She bought linen suits, pith hats, dresses for the evening, sports-wear, lots of light cotton underwear and two good trunks. It was like a child's dream of being let loose in a toy-shop: she had never owned so many new things, and neither had her mother. Ruby was sure Walter would not mind if a few bits and pieces for Mother were added to the list, but Mother was anxious not to be seen as a greedy mother-in-law. At last, exhausted, they went to the D & M tearoom and ordered tea.

"Will you be all right, Mother?" Ruby blurted, not meaning to, for the question was superfluous. She felt sad about going, but she was going. In her mind she had already gone.

"Well, Ruby, I was thinking I ought to ask you the same."

Horrified, Ruby said quickly, "It's all right, I know."

"Know what?"

"The, er, things you think you should tell me."

Her mother sniffed to conceal her relief and said, "I won't ask how, dear."

"There are books," Ruby explained, "nowadays."

"Are there indeed? Dr Stopes, I suppose."

Ruby hardly dared breathe for fear of what she might confess. If Mother wanted to blame Dr Stopes – whoever he was – that might be best.

"There are things that Dr Stopes chooses to publish that I never knew about – and never needed to know about, even though I have been happily married for forty years, which is more than she has, and borne seven children and lost . . . five of them."

Five? Leonard, Sam, Anthony, and the baby that died . . . was she thinking of Charles as the fifth lost one? Or of Ruby herself, because she was going away, because she was going to be Ruby Orange?

The waitress brought a tray and spent an inordinately long time arranging its contents on the table. The light, changing-the-subject tone in which Mother resumed speaking showed that she was determined to say her piece, blush red though she might. "Are you and Walter hoping to have a large family?"

"No cake for me, thank you," said Ruby.

"It's just that the climate out there . . ."

"Just bread and butter."

"For your health's sake, you might want to wait until you're more accustomed . . ."

"Moth-er!" Ruby watched her mother's pale jowls moving up and down on the unaccustomed treat of chocolate cake in a tearoom. She loved her so much at that moment but the thought of her flesh made her cringe. Why was it so much easier to share the intimacy of your body with a strange man than to allude to doing so with your own mother?

"You can shout as loud as you want, Ruby, but I'm going to say this. As your mother, I have to. Things are different now. When I got married we didn't even think about such things, never mind talk about them; and I don't regret having *any* of my children. But young people today can consider their own health and convenience more . . . anyway, I won't distress you further, Ruby, but I've made an appointment for you with a lady doctor and she'll be able to say these things better than I can."

Ruby was speechless. Her mother chuckled. "You remind me of myself with Aunt Sarah."

Aunt Sarah! Thank heaven! They would talk about Aunt Sarah! "Where does she come into it?"

"Oh, Aunt Sarah told me once that five boys were quite enough; she meant well; but I produced you to show I wasn't taking that kind of advice from anybody! Then I took it. And a very messy business it was too, sponges and vinegar . . . it's much easier now, I hear."

Ruby could only give way before the cheerful obliviousness with which her mother spoke of sponges and vinegar while all round them tea was sipped and cakes were nibbled. "I suppose Aunt Sarah felt she had to tell you," she said, "if her sister was dead." Her mother looked puzzled. "She was your mother's sister, wasn't she? She wasn't Dad's aunt?"

Her mother hesitated. Then she shrugged her soft shoulders as if it no longer mattered.

"No, she was my father's wife's sister."

"His first wife, you mean?"

"He only had one wife."

"And she wasn't your mother?"

"My mother wasn't married."

"Oh!"

"They called her Lizzie, Lizzie Croft. She used my father's

342

name, though she had no right to it. She used to say she found me in an oyster-shell and that was how I came to be called Pearl." The faintest of country burrs, never far from the shadows of her mother's voice, was suddenly very pronounced. "She used to sell oysters outside the barracks in Colchester, that was how she met him. Then she used to come home to me in a muddy little village. I used to catch crabs, to stop 'em getting at the oysters."

Ruby could see it: a wild little girl running on a beach.

"And did your mother die? Was that why you went to your father?"

"They told me so. I believed so. I sometimes wonder now. But that wasn't why . . . my mother was alive and well when she sent me away. I've thanked her for it, I've hated her for it. It was for my own protection."

"Protection from what?"

Mother pushed away the tea-tray and gathered together their parcels. "You have your revenge Ruby. I've pried into your life, and you've pried into mine. There are some things that there's no call for even mother and daughter to tell each other."

"I was only asking. I didn't mean to upset you."

"I know you didn't, Ruby love. But I am upset, as you can see . . . very silly of me, I daresay. I was only twelve years old at the time. Some things you can't forget, can't talk about. Shall we go now?"

Ruby went home with her mother. She had enjoyed their day out and been intrigued by their talk, even if it had ended in that difficult way. Poor Mother, fancy being so ashamed of having been illegitimate! And fancy Ruby having had an oyster-seller for a grandmother, a Victorian gentleman's mistress! It was very romantic. And she could distinctly remember Robin Fellowes informing her that her grandmother had never known passion!

Would she know passion with Walter? She supposed so; she supposed she must pretend to be completely ignorant, but she was glad that she was not. There were to be quite enough new things to get used to, without that!

The Barringtons had always known themselves to be the cleverest, toughest, wittiest, and most handsome family in the neighbourhood, but Ruby was excited to feel that they were romantic and interesting as well: they were a family of tragic lovers and long journeys, first Aunt Sarah and now Ruby. She was going to be the wife of the manager of a department store on the other side of the world. She would never type another word. And she had remembered Robin Fellowes as a painless little joke.

She felt she had become a whole new person.

13

"They love us to bits," said Mrs Charterhouse. "They're *tremendously* loyal."

Ruby yawned behind her hand. Duckbill & Middlesex had paid for her and Walter to travel out first class. It was a long, glorious rest. Out on the gleaming deck, Walter was playing deck-tennis in white shorts. Mrs Charterhouse had invited Ruby to sit with her in the lounge and help her finish her jigsaw.

"A little firmness at first, Mrs Orange, will pay *tremendous* dividends," Mrs Charterhouse was the wife of an army major, and Walter said it was a great honour that she should befriend the wife of a shopkeeper. "Particularly as you're so young, and not, ah – " Mrs Charterhouse wore a brown crepe dress and a fur; she seemed not to feel the heat. She was fat and spoke in a slightly bored, squeaky tone, never varying its pitch. She was like a queen bee. "Let me see, have you got a blue bit there, with some hair on it?" She was also very stupid at jigsaws. Ruby longed to tell her that if you had to force a piece into place it was probably the wrong piece.

Ruby offered her a cigarette, which she accepted. Everyone seemed to smoke, which was a relief.

"Ill-considered kindness is no kindness at all, Mrs Orange. I gave my sweeper a hen. A gift – you know? I *told* him she would lay. And what did he do? He cooked her and ate her that very evening. I can't imagine *what* he found to eat. There was hardly any flesh on her."

Ruby reported the story to Walter that evening in the cabin when they were changing for dinner. "It doesn't sound as if it was a very generous gift," she giggled.

"I hope you didn't say-ay that to her, Ruby!"

"Of course not. But I wish she'd stop telling me what to do."

Walter raised his chin for her to tie his tie, then she turned her back for him to button her into the pink chiffon dress the maid had ironed for this evening. It was loose and cool and light and gay, and camouflaged her plumpness. She was glad to be the

344

youngest wife on the boat. It allowed some people to think her
the prettiest. She was glad to be the only newly-wed, too; no-one
minded if she used the wrong cutlery or said the wrong thing.
They put it down to her being madly in love, and nudged each
other and smiled.

"You shouldn't be too proud to take advice, Ruby," said Walter
mildly, opening the door for her. He minded. He minded dreadfully that she might not live up to her position. Or down to it.
He fretted if she laughed at a joke that hadn't been meant for her
ears. He turned crimson if she opened a conversation with a wife
of senior rank. "Mrs Charterhouse has experience of Indians, you
haven't."

She beamed at him. "Neither have you," she said as she swept
into the cocktail bar.

Docking at Bombay was all steamy heat and confusion. She
allowed herself to be pushed here and there through the crowds.
She was faint from lack of air; Walter had practically to lift her
on to the train, and she loved him for his tender concern. The
journey across the subcontinent was a parching, bone-shaking
nightmare. The train raced through aching, dun-coloured desert,
the heat flinging itself into her eyes like sand; paused as if to allow
the dense clouds of insects to make a tour of inspection; and
rattled over ravines in the darkness till it seemed it must be flying
and must crash to earth. It stopped at desolate halts and teeming
stations. Faces thinner than she could believe peered into the
carriage, wheedling voices offered curry, newspapers, ice. She
called for gin-and-lime, and lit one cigarette from another to keep
the insects at bay. Snippets of advice danced in the rhythms of the
wheels: *Remember you're British, remember your mission. Adequate
exercise, clean cotton underwear. Kindness but firmness.* Or was it
firmness but kindness?

She laughed.

Stretched out on the seat opposite, with rivulets of sweat
running through his fair hair and on to his linen suit, Walter
watched her. "Something funny, Ruby?"

"No . . ."

"Bit too much gin, perhaps?"

"I hope I haven't saddled myself with a tyrant for a husband,
Walter," she said nastily; and unjustifiably, as it happened,
because he wilted and murmured, "I only wanted to stop you

345

getting a headache." But next time the attendant came, she demanded another gin; and she heard a harshness in her voice and felt sorry and frightened because the attendant looked as though he was used to it and expected no different; and she didn't want to turn into someone like Mrs Charterhouse. The Barrington family had always firmly believed that all men were equal; and when Mother had girls to help with the heavy work she expected Ruby and her brothers to be polite to them. "You're nothing special yourselves," she used to say, if she caught any of them doing what she called "putting on airs".

She was happy for Walter again to take charge of her when they reached Calcutta. He saw to the luggage, got them a taxi, never let go of her hand. Her fingernails ground into his. If she lost him she knew she would be lost for ever in the throng of dark-skinned people who swarmed out of alleyways or the heaps of rotten driftwood that seemed to be their homes, blocked the path of the cab with their children and animals, seemed ready to wind themselves round its very wheels in the desperation for alms.

Fists poked through the windows like guns. She reached automatically into her purse. Walter stopped her. "They only spend it on drink," he said.

"But they're starving! And that man hasn't got any fingers!"

"They cut them off themselves," Walter whispered urgently. "Is that what you want to encourage? I was told that-at by an Indian." He was unnerved too; she could tell by his stammer. But he didn't tell lies. If that was what an Indian had said then it must be true. Some Indians were highly educated. And some were very rich. She buried her face in Walter's damp lapel, and wouldn't look at India again until he said they had reached the European quarter.

A yellow road wound between fertile fields, their irrigation channels gleaming in the sun. There were women planting and hoeing, they looked like butterflies. A boy driving a white ox-cart waved at the cab and got out of its way. An ayah with an armful of bangles pushed a white baby in a pram and two sturdy English-women strode through a gate towards a tennis-court. The bungalow that Walter had rented was cool and spacious; there was a rockery and a waterfall in the garden.

"So much space, Walter," Ruby breathed, wandering from room to room. "What will we do with it all?"

"*You* will do nothing, my dear. The servants will see to all that."

Nothing? It wasn't quite nothing, she discovered. You had to hire your servants, and then you had to supervise them. A dark, supercilious man in a turban arrived at the bungalow shortly after Ruby and Walter did, flourishing testimonials and offering himself as Walter's bearer: Walter was highly delighted, said the man showed initiative and appointed him on the spot, sending him to unpack his trunks. It made Ruby so uncomfortable to have the man in the home that wasn't quite theirs yet, trooping back and forth with armfuls of Walter's suits and books and underwear that she resolved to do without servants at all, for herself; she could care for her own clothes, she could cook for two. But when Mrs Fairfax and Mrs Hobbs, their neighbours, called, bringing flowers and welcomes and offers of introductions to the local club, they were horrified by this idea, which Ruby weakly confided to them. Of course she must have a cook and a sweeper, though she might manage without an ayah until the children came along. The natives relied on the Europeans to provide them with this employment and Ruby would be busy with social engagements. They knew just the man to be her cook. She wasn't to worry about a thing. They would show her the ropes.

The cook was a plump old man who reminded Ruby of her father. Each morning she went to the kitchen to inspect his pots. He set them all out for her on the table and waited like a child eager for praise, she thought, while she sniffed them and ran her fingers round their rims. He beamed dazzlingly when she muttered, "Yes, that's fine, thank you," avoiding his eyes; so she supposed he didn't mind very much. He was a sensible, reliable man, he didn't steal food, not even the nominal amounts that Mrs Fairfax told her that it was the convention to ignore; she felt relieved that she would not be called upon ever to punish him. Administering syrup of figs as a remedy for lying might seem cruel, but it worked wonders, the memsahibs at the club assured her.

"Will you be coming to the hills with us when the hot weather comes, Mrs Orange?" they inquired, kindly waiting until she was acclimatised before revealing that this was *not* the hot weather. Ruby shook her head. The club was a place to have fun with tennis and bridge, but it was also a place of gossip. Ruby knew by now the names of women who had gone to the hills without their husbands, the circumstances in which they had lost their heads (and more) to some wandering bachelor, and she was determined to give no rein to opportunities or desires that might carry her in that direction. Walter and she lived well enough together, even if he was a bitter disappointment to her in ways that she could only wish she did not know. He had little passion and less delicacy. On their wedding night she had been so careful not to let him know that she knew anything that she only just realised in time that he had only the most rudimentary knowledge of what to do. She blushed to think of it. Now he gave a pompous, trembling performance once a week, the very essence, she thought gloomily, of what she had thought of him when she first met him again after the war; half military man, half fop.

She stayed with him. She would forget what she had no right to know, she decided, and crush her restlessness with the same strength of character with which she endured the hot weather. The first time was beyond all imagining. The sun ceased to be a glowing, benevolent god who sometimes overreached himself; he became a leering yellow tyrant flinging down invisible coals, a gloating thief who stole the air. Ruby hid in the bungalow, sponging herself, sucking ice, playing Patience and wondering why she was there. But when the rains came and the memsahibs trooped back from their refuge, she felt a quiet pride. She even found herself comforting bewildered girls newly out from England: "You'll get used to it, my dear! Just tell yourself you won't be beaten!" She felt entitled to call them "my dear", even when they were older than she was. She felt established.

Three years passed. It seemed the right time to have a child. She abandoned her precautions and, rather to her surprise, discovered that all the relevant parts of her body, and Walter's, were in working order. She gave up tennis and let out her clothes. She sat on the club verandah in the armchair reserved for the old, the honoured, and the pregnant. She listened to the memsahibs' tales of the hardships of childbirth in the old days, none of which, they assured her, she would have to go through. She supposed she would endure it all right. She looked forward to having a child. She would make up stories for it. She remembered a plan she had once had to write stories. The picture pleased her: the enthralled child in pyjamas, looking up from a clean white bed. "*Then* what happened, Mummy?" "I don't know, darling. Wait till tomorrow, and I'll make up some more."

Once a week, the memsahibs brought out the letters they had received from their children in English boarding schools and read out the important or clever bits. Ruby smiled politely, but the letters made her uneasy. She remembered her own childhood as one long battle but she would have been desolate if her parents had sent her away. It was a Barrington rule that everyone must kiss everyone else goodnight, and a previous day's quarrel must never be unearthed in the morning. She even used to go to bed feeling warm about Charles.

She stopped herself. There were hardly any English children over the age of six or seven in India, and those that were there became spoilt, sickly, and wild. It simply wasn't fair to keep them; you had to make the sacrifice. And besides . . . her baby was only a bulging lump, pinning her into the back of the chair like a hot insect, and she was letting people worry her about sending it away to school! There was plenty of time to get used to the idea, or else to decide to rebel.

14

Walter liked the life in India. He seemed to grow in physique as he grew in confidence and courage. The man who had trembled at the memory of "the bangs" in the war took to shooting tigers and cutting off their heads to mount on wooden shields and stick on the walls of the bungalow.

He especially enjoyed having his own shop and being answerable to no-one closer at hand than London. He took great pride in fulfilling his customers' most eccentric wants. But he was hurt when an old school-chum, now very high up in the civil service, appointed him his wine-merchant but would not invite him to his house to enjoy the wine.

Ruby didn't care. She knew by now that managers of shops were not very highly regarded by the white upper classes, but she also knew that she and Walter were as good as any of them. She just wished that Walter wouldn't try so hard to compensate for his inferiority complex by showing off and being correct all the time. He wanted their house to be a kind of permanent exhibition of the best of D & M stock. She was always having to make room for new furniture, add to her wardrobe and give dinner-parties. Of course it was lovely to have new things all the time and be a successful hostess. She just wished it didn't always have to be *ordered*.

Walter all but ordered her to produce a son. She wanted a son too; but when she did produce one, there was a tinge of irritation in her pleasure. God ought not to have given in to bullying. He ought to have taken the opportunity to show Walter that certain things could not be ordered, even in India.

Randolph John Orange had a big head and his mother's thick, dark, curly hair. His eyes were perhaps a little too close together, but they sparkled winningly and gained him friends. The ayah Ruby hired (passed on by a friend at the club, whose daughter had gone to England) was devoted to him and very experienced with children. Ruby hardly had a thing to do. When he was two, he acquired a sister, who, unlike him, had none of the chubbiness of the Barringtons: she was pale and blonde, with little curly eyelashes and deep blue eyes. Ruby marvelled at her beauty and hid from a deeper, unspeakable feeling of jealousy.

"I'd like to call her Sarah," she said.

Walter sharply reminded her that Randolph had been her choice. He wanted to call the Baby Emma, after his own mother.

"All right, then Emma Sarah," she said in a faint voice from the bed. If Walter thought it fair to quarrel after what she had just been through, then let him win and let him have joy in it. He muttered that he supposed Sarah Emma would do just as well, but Emma Sarah went on the birth certificate.

Ruby wrote home with the news. Too soon to be a reply, a letter came from her brother Stephen. Her father Hamish Barrington had died in the night from a heart attack. He had been well enough the day before, chasing the grandchildren round Stalcross Common; but he went to sleep and never woke. Mother had lain beside the body for two whole hours before callers at the closed-up shop began to wonder what was wrong, but no-one blamed her for it. She was distraught, of course; it would be hard to be alone after nearly fifty years. Ruby started at Walter in terror and disbelief: fifty years! Would they be together for fifty years? And if not, what? Her father and mother had belonged together, it was unthinkable that either of them could have married anyone else . . . would Randolph and Emma grow to think that of their parents?

350

Mother sent a photograph of Ruby as a young girl with her father. Ruby could not remember it being taken, but Mother said he kept it with him always. Ruby shed a few tears over it, then put it by the mirror and made a critical comparison.

Randolph and Emma had added layers to her, like a tree. But she knew how to make the best of herself. She had a mature, dignified build, she decided, but a young face. She did not look her thirty years.

The dispute over Emma's name was soon resolved by the ayah, who simply called her *missy baba*. Randolph was *chota sahib*. Ruby and Walter fell into using these names too, first as a joke and then as the usual thing, at least when there was no company.

Ayah was older than Ruby, fat and lame. When she walked, she rolled like a ship in a storm. At first she made Ruby uneasy, the way she came in the early morning to get the children up, ran after them all day and squatted heavily down outside their rooms at night until they fell asleep. But she never seemed to tire, and she, after all, had been doing the job far longer than Ruby had. Ruby passed on old clothes to her and she seemed very pleased, though Ruby never saw her wearing them.

The children ate bananas in the cool, silky mornings and then were taken for a ride. Missy looked so adorable, wobbling along on the pony's back, or begging to be lifted up to rub its velvety nose, that Ruby could hardly bear to look. She wished she could spend more time with the children, but Ayah was so good and she was so busy. And Walter was rather worn out and demanding after a couple of nasty attacks of malaria. When the children had their second breakfast with them in the mornings, he did nothing but criticise Randolph's table manners. Ayah would not or could not impose discipline, and Walter wanted his son to eat with the manly delicacy of a *pukka sahib*, young though he was. Sometimes Chota took a pride in doing exactly this, but when the heat made him irritable he would spill things, hold his spoon wrongly, and argue when corrected. Walter bought a cane and hung it on the wall with a flourish. "What on earth is that for?" Ruby demanded. "Randolph knows," Walter replied quietly. It was rarely used, and never with any severity: Walter and his son developed a quiet language of the eyes, warnings and apologies. Ruby seethed inside, as much at her own exclusion as at the cruelty of it, or turned sharp attention on Missy, whose own misdemeanours seemed motivated more by a cunning determination to please herself than by frank naughtiness, and, as such, should perhaps be given a mother's close attention.

An English girl came from the mission-school from time to time to teach them reading and sums; Ayah took them for walks. The bazaar was out of bounds because of diseases, but Ayah took them anyway, wooed into compliance by Chota's glinting eyes. Ruby always knew when they had been, from their excitement and the sugary marks round their mouths from the milky, syrupy and likewise forbidden sweetmeats that they had been given. She did not tell Walter; just hoped they would not fall ill. In the evenings, Missy wanted to be consulted as to which dress Ruby would wear to go to the club; and when Ruby was ready and went to say goodnight, the little girl was generous but honest. "*Bootiful*, Mummy," she sighed when the choice was the lime-green voile which Ruby always thought of as her Miss Ada dress; "Qui' nice, Mummy," was the response to the black lace, even when worn with pearls. "Good night, Missy," Ruby would say, bending carefully to brush her with a kiss; and then, because it was so oddly difficult, she would add, "And you're going to have lovely dresses too, and be beautiful, and go to parties, one day."

"One day" wasn't good enough. Missy pestered and pestered until Ruby and Walter planned a real dinner party for them. They sent them an invitation, and Chota had to write a polite reply, and Missy had to add her name. Ayah dressed them in their best, and Walter's bearer was teased into forgetting his dignity and pulling them up the garden path in a rickshaw. They were helped down from the rickshaw by Ayah, who pretended to be solemn but kept giggling; and Ruby held out her hand. "Ah, good evening, Miss Orange, Master Orange, so glad you could come! Would you care to see my latest dresses, which my husband has imported from England?" They sat round the dining table on the verandah with lamplight glowing on the scarlet hibiscus blossoms. The low moon shone on Missy's delicate, full-lipped face as she strove to eat her roast snipe politely. Ruby's heart ached, she didn't know why: *This is a moment you ought to remember all your life, Emma Sarah, it ought to freeze in your mind like a photograph in colour*. Losing patience with her bony bird and thinking no-one was watching, Missy picked up a gamechip in her fingers and ate it with gusto. "If you can't behave like a grown-up, Emma Sarah," said Walter, "I shall take you to your room."

There was book called *Donald and Clara Go To School* which was immensely popular among memsahibs with young children. It was passed from hand to hand at the club – for some reason there was only one copy – and told of two English children, twins, whose parents lived in India. When Donald and Clara were told that it was time for them to be sent to school, they did not immediately take to the idea. This gave their parents the opportunity of explaining why school was important, and why England, and not India, was "home" really. On the inside back cover Donald and Clara were pictured in blazers and school hats, smiling at the distant towers of their respective boarding schools, and looking forward (the text assured the reader) to their parents' visit, next year.

Randolph said, "Did Donald and Clara go to the same school?"

Walter said, "Of course not, old chap. There are separate schools for boys and girls."

"But their schools were very near to each other," said Ruby. "They would probably see each other from the windows."

Emma pored over the picture. Then she slammed the book shut. "Don't read it again, Mummy," she commanded.

15

Walter's old school friend – the one in the civil service – accepted an invitation to dine at the bungalow. Walter stammered with nerves and issued instructions right and left. Ruby laughed at him.

"Anyone would think he was the viceroy!"

"It's all very well, Ruby – but he's doing us an honour."

"I think we're doing him one."

"Just make-ake sure everything's all right! That's all!" He had the grace to blush as he said it, but Ruby wouldn't wait for his apology. "Have I ever let you down?" she demanded, folding her arms. He kissed her. "No, Ruby. You're a wonderful wife. The best. And I love you very much."

"I love you as well, Walter."

"Don't take any notice of me."

"I never do." She smiled.

They had a long discussion over whom they could invite to meet the civil servant and his wife, who could be relied on. They settled for the Manns, who were in textiles, because Mr Mann had been at Oxford University (even if the club rumour was that he had been sent down). Of course they couldn't explain to the Manns how carefully they had been selected; and when Mrs Mann popped round on the day of the party to say that a cousin of hers had turned up unexpectedly to stay for a few days, Ruby could only say, "We do hope you'll bring him tonight."

The civil servant was pale and quiet-voiced and charming; his wife was one of those women whom Ruby envied because she could make the simplest clothing look stunning. She wore a simple silver-grey velvet dress, a ribbon at her throat, and that was all. Her only jewellery was her wedding ring. Yet she talked and moved with such relaxed grace that she made Ruby feel vulgar and clumsy. Neither she nor her husband was in the least bit condescending, which made Ruby wonder whether Walter hadn't imagined the earlier snub, and wish they had invited them before.

But the Manns' cousin was dreadful. He wore a loud check waistcoat with buttons missing and had dirty fingernails. His face was dark red and he seemed to be drunk. He kept starting to tell stories and then pausing: "Not in front of the ladies, I think!" In the middle of dinner there came a loud crash from the kitchen, and he roared, "You bloody fool, what have you dropped now? Whoops. Pardon my French. Forgot where I was."

Ruby hurried to the kitchen to investigate, and found the best dinner plates in pieces on the floor and the cook raging at the boy they had hired for the evening to wait at table. Normally, Ruby would have been angry too, but she felt deathly calm. She told the cook to tell the boy it didn't matter, put fresh plates to warm in the oven and hurried back to the table where the Manns' cousin was in the middle of a story about his gun-dog.

"Marv'lous little chap. Marv'lous! Just the job. Can't wait for the gun to go off and he's away like lightning. I'll have to train him to wait – I've nearly brought *him* down more than once!" Mrs Mann, Walter, and the civil servant's wife raised anxious eyebrows in Ruby's direction, and she signalled back that everything was all right. "Has the time of his life! You should see his eyes shining! I said to my wife the other day, y'know, I think I'll keep him. I might even pay school fees for him if he'll come out shooting with me when I need him."

Icy silence cut the warmth of the room. He wasn't talking about a dog, then? He was talking about a child? "Who are we talking about?" Ruby asked politely, looking straight at the man, wanting

354

to shame him into not replying, hoping that someone would change the subject, knowing that she ought to. "Jameel," said the man, "my bearer's boy."

Ruby knew she ought to stop herself. But she didn't want to. She said quietly, "I think that's absolutely disgusting."

The man laughed a hard, nasty, slow laugh that sounded like *het-het-het-*.

Ruby waited for the civil servant's wife to say something. She would have been trained to smooth over a situation like this. But she said nothing. She looked at her plate. A slight blush, like a dusting of rouge, settled over her cheekbones. It was her husband who said, "Actually, Mrs Orange, I agree with you."

"I say! Can't anyone take a joke around here?" asked the Mann's cousin, and Mrs Mann glared at him. The civil servant said levelly, "Good manners and mutual respect, it seems to me, are the very least the races owe to each other. Servant or master."

His wife seemed to collect herself. She beamed at Ruby as if she had just arrived. "That's what my husband always says to me," she said, "when my ladies' committee organises purdah parties." Ruby marvelled at the ease with which she had moved the conversation on. How long did it take to learn to do that? Or were you born with it? "He says it's not for us to tell the Indians how they should treat their wives. Which is absurd, of course, because the husbands quite approve."

"They're often too polite to say what they really feel," her husband quietly insisted, "which of course is my point." A glimmer of well-bred mischief shone in his eyes. "But I wonder how you ladies would feel if the Indians started telling *us* to keep *you* locked away."

"I'd like to see them try!" said Walter with feeling; he didn't seem to realise it was funny; there was a pause and then a breeze of laughter that became a gust; and the dinner continued pleasantly enough for everyone except Ruby, who could hardly swallow. Her anger subsided but an obscure fear stared her in the face. Obscure, and yet instantly recognisable; she realised she had brushed with it every day since she came to India but it had been so unbearable that she wouldn't acknowledge it. How did this tiny group of light-skinned people hold sway and privilege over this huge continent, and its dark-skinned millions? Why didn't they rise up and murder them in their beds as some of their daily humiliations might encourage? When the cook heard that man call him a bloody fool – as he must have heard – why didn't he slip poison into his food? Why didn't the slum dwellers simply leave the city and move into the bungalows of the Europeans? Why didn't they? They would hardly need even to fight. They would come in their numbers and do it. The doors were rarely locked. It wasn't necessary. Why wasn't it?

She tried to hint at her unease when she and Walter were undressing for bed. "They respect us too much," he declared. Why did they? Why should they? "We've earned their respect," he insisted, "and that's why it's important that we always do the right thing." He was slightly drunk. He mumbled on about the army, about ceremony and spit and polish being as important as knowing when you had to use a gun or a truncheon. Ruby got into bed. All she could think of was the way at the club they always made the servants draw the blinds and go home if they wanted to play Tag or Murder, in order that Europeans should not appear ridiculous.

Club opinion was unanimous: Emma should be sent to school with her brother. She was a dear, pretty little thing but rather full of herself. And how old-fashioned of Ruby to believe that education was not important for a girl!

"*I* think," she said to Walter, "that the only reason they don't want me to keep Missy here is that it would make them feel guilty about their children."

"What are you talking about? I thought that was all settled."

Settled? It was, she supposed. There were letters from the schools, confirming places for the children. The tickets for the voyage were in Walter's bureau. They might have kept Emma till she was seven or eight; but it was a stroke of luck getting her into a school near Randolph's, and if they waited they might have to send her somewhere else.

"Yes, but – " She gave up. Life for Walter was a list of separate Things to Do. Things to Decide. When each was done, he moved on to the next thing. He had no notion of wrestling with a problem, going back to it.

Then one morning, when Ruby and Walter were drinking tea in bed and the children were out on the pony. Ayah limped in, near to tears, dragging Chota, whose hand was bleeding. Ruby pulled on her dressing-gown and had to sit Ayah down and give her tea before she could find out what had happened.

It was all the fault of the groom. He was supposed to run along beside the pony when Chota was riding. But he had let his attention wander. And a stray dog had come slinking out from the rubbish dump at the end of the street. The dog went for the pony's heels; the pony kicked it in the teeth, sending Chota to the ground; and the dog bit Chota's hand.

Chota was strutting around, staring at the crimson toothmarks, trying not to cry. The wound looked clean. It was nothing very much. But Walter was roaring. His face was red, his pale hair stood on end, he was absurd in his pyjamas. Ayah must get out, get *out*, and not return without the guilty dog! It must be tethered and watched for any sign of illness. A paragraph from a handbook swam into Ruby's stunned, reluctant memory.

"Ayah, the first-aid box."

"Sahib say, catch dog. Memsahib say bring first-aid box – "

"Catch the dog, damn it!" Walter shouted. For the first time. Chota showed fear.

"Will I go mad, Mummy?"

"Silly, of course not! Was it a mad dog? Well, then, I shall have to clean the bite, then we'll take you to the doctor. Are you going to be a brave boy?" Somehow the first-aid box was in her lap. She opened the disinfectant bottle, fingered the blade of the lancet. She wanted to cut off her own hand rather than . . .

She felt the boy's trusting wrist under her fingers; she felt his muscles squirm with outrage as she pressed the blade into the wound and cut and cut, then cut across and squeezed till white bone showed and blood bubbled. Chota shrieked like an animal. She could do no more, there was ringing in her ears, her body felt like a soft wet sponge. She thrust him at his father. "Wash it! Bandage it! Take him to the doctor!" While they were away she drank a large gin.

The doctor was consoling. Ruby had done exactly the right thing. The boy was more shocked than hurt. At the club the memsahibs were kind. One of them could remember having to amputate the foot of a railway official following snake-bite a hundred miles from the nearest medical help.

Packing for Chota and Missy shouldn't have taken long because Ruby planned to equip them with uniforms and warm clothes when they got to England; but it was fraught with woe. Chota was over-excited, Ayah was tearful and Missy was sullen and incredulous. Ayah encouraged her until Ruby wanted to bang their heads together.

"Emma Sarah, you won't be able to have *all* those dolls at school, so there's no point in hiding them in the trunk. I saw!"

"Missy Emma Sarah!" Ayah wailed.

"I'm Missy Baba, call me Missy Baba!"

"You're certainly behaving like the biggest baba in the world!" said Ruby, and she went to find Walter. "When we get to the school," she told him, "if she's really unhappy, I'll bring her back."

But Walter said, "She's bound to play up a little, Ruby. I used to blub my eyes out saying goodbye to my mother, but once she was out of the way, I had a capital time."

Ruby's nerves were raw. "I'm fed up with the lot of you," she declared. "Ayah, please finish the ironing. I'm going up to the club. We'll pack later." A couple of gins and some adult conversation would make her feel better, she decided. Perhaps she would pack tonight while Emma was asleep. There was no point in upsetting the child more than was necessary. And Ruby didn't want her daughter's last memory of India to be arguments and unpleasantness.

An Indian man whom she did not recognise came running towards her across the street. He seemed to be in a tearing hurry. "Memsahib, Memsahib, dog rabbit, dog rabbit!"

What nonsense was this? "Dog rabbit" sounded like something out of the garbled nursery rhymes that Missy had been insisting on Ayah singing to her "just one last time" all day while they packed. But Ruby followed the man. Her body seemed to know what he meant before her mind would accept it.

The dog that had bitten Chota was still tethered to its tree. Walter had been checking its health every day. But today he must have forgotten, because today it was ill. It foamed at the mouth and ran circles round the tree. It yapped at unseen prey, its ribs going into convulsions under its dull, yellow coat. The Indian brought a bucket of water and tipped it on the ground. The dog howled like the devil, and looked as if it would break free of its tether.

"Kill it!" she gasped. "No, don't. Fetch the vet!" The vet confirmed rabies. Ruby struggled to take it in, to think. The dog that had bitten her son had rabies. There could be no delay. Chota

358

must be taken to the Pasteur Institute. It was a thousand miles away. The course of injections would take three weeks.

"Come here, now, Emma Sarah, I want to talk to you. Did I ever tell you where you got that nice name Sarah?"

"No."

"It was after a lady, a *very old* lady, my Mummy's aunty, can you imagine? And years ago, before you were born, before I was born, even before my Mummy was born, she went on a very long journey over the sea, all by herself."

The child's eyes never left Ruby's. "That dog bit me too, Mummy."

"What? Where?"

"Here, on my tummy, you can't see it, it's better now, he took a great big bite and it bled, and I got a knife and – "

"You *wicked* girl!" The slap Ruby gave her left the red imprints of her fingers in the child's cheek. "Darling, I'm sorry – "

Emma did not cry. She gave a howl of shock and fear and stared at her mother dry-eyed. "Are you taking me to England, or not, Mummy?"

"I can't, Emma. I have to take Chota to hospital, and when we get back our boat will be gone and then we'd be late for the start of term – "

"Am I going by myself, then?"

Ruby took a deep breath. "You're certainly grown up enough to go by yourself, but I've found a nice lady at the club to go with you. And then you'll be all settled at your new school when I bring Chota, and you can show us around and introduce me to all your new friends. Won't that be nice?"

Won't that be nice, won't it? The words beat in Ruby's ears with the rhythm of the wheels of the train that carried her and her son up to the hospital in the hills and safety. He was calmly unaware of the danger he was in, or the ordeal that awaited him. The injections would have to go straight in the soft flesh of the stomach. *Won't that be nice, won't that be nice?* Emma had been muttering that to her dolls as Ruby left, slapping their faces: "Wicked girl. Going to England. Won't that be nice?"

16

Ruby stayed with her son for three weeks at the hospital. She insisted on being with him for each of the injections into his soft, bruised belly; she was moved and worn out by his courage. She supervised the preparation of all his food and sat at his side at night until he fell asleep. Ruby herself hardly slept at all: she summoned all her will-power. If she could will herself not to sleep, her will-power was strong. If her will-power was strong she could will the germs in Chota's body to bow before the vaccine and die. Sometimes she would reach for the jug of iced water and pour herself a glass, not because she was thirsty but because she knew that if the rabies virus had taken a hold one of the first signs would be Chota's terror at the sight and sound of water simultaneous with a burning desire to drink.

"Have some of this, Chota."

"I'm not thirsty."

"I didn't say you were. Drink it!"

"If I drink it, can I have my injection in my bottom tomorrow?"

"Be quiet! It has to be in your tummy."

At last the doctors said they could go home. They were sure the infection had been caught in time. But they told her (why on earth did they have to tell her, when there was nothing more that could be done?) that rabies could occur at anytime up to two years after a bite. She watched Chota and watched him. The memory of the dog running in insane circles and throwing itself into agonising spasms burned at her brain. She could not keep Chota for another two years, not with Emma in England. But she could not let him go.

Just another month. Just another month, to make sure he's all right. What if he fell sick on the ship, surrounded by all that sea? What if – ? Ruby fell sick herself. She burned with fever and dreamed of mad dogs. Recovering, she could hardly walk up the road. She found a strict governess for Chota, determined that he should not be spoiled, that when he met his sister again she must not hear of what a fine time he had had without her. Before they could travel, the hot weather came again, and the train journey across the furnace-subcontinent was out of the question. September, then; he would start school in September; just a year late.

Emma wrote: "Please can Chota come to school, because it's not fair." Ruby wrote back with gifts and chiding: was Emma jealous of her brother's sickness? Emma had developed a nice flair for letter-writing, considering she was only seven. "Dearest Mother and Father and Randolph, thank you for your letter. I am sorry for mine. I hope you are well. I shared out the sweets with my Class. It is the rule. Miss Ledder say I am good at sums. We are doing India. I had to stand up in front of the class and answer questions. I got three order marks last week, I deserved it. Please kiss Father and Chota and my dolls and remember me to Ayah. Lots of love from your little girl Emma Sarah. PS Aunty Susan and Uncle Stephen took me for a picnic. PPS when is Chota coming because I want to tell him something? PPPS Granny has died. PPPPS Angela Gramstock says Orange is a silly name but Gramstock is sillier isn't it?"

Ruby did not read this letter aloud in the ladies' lounge of the club. She didn't want the oohs and aahs of the memsahibs increasing the volume of the voice in her head, the voice of the schoolmarm directing her daughter in the correct way to write to one's parents.

Enquire after their health, report on your own; give news of your progress; confess faults, send love . . .

"Isn't it sweet, all these PSs," she said uneasily to Walter, "Something new she's learnt!"

"What do you suppose this is?" he said, pointing to the line about Granny having died.

"A teacher, I suppose, or a pet. They'd hardly have left it to her to tell me if it was Mother!"

But it was true: a letter from the family, delayed in the mail, brought confirmation. Like Father she had died in her sleep; unlike him, she had died alone. Ruby cried like a rainstorm. Walter offered clumsy consolation: "Let's see it as a blessing, Ruby." Yes, a blessing; she had read enough into her mother's restrained letters to know that the days of her widowhood had dragged by; and most ways of dying were so cruel, one must be glad for both's one's parents drifting off in the night after a long life, a happy marriage. Still she felt a horrible temptation to snap back at Walter: *Put her out of her misery, you mean! Like that dog you shot!* Instead she let him hold her and she wept into his starched shirt's neat creases. He was strong and safe. She felt she was making him very happy, letting go like that, but she must recover herself. Mother's death was neither blessing nor tragedy, it was simply part of the way things were. Good things, bad things

. . . you had a lovely wedding when you thought all hope of one was lost, your father gave you away but secretly kept your photograph, your mother cried and kissed you, told you her secrets and made the appointment you would never dare make with a lady doctor . . . and that was the last you saw of them. You sailed away and they died. That was all. The important thing was to behave correctly. Her life had become a succession of occasions on which she must behave correctly. She shivered with a premonition of death – her own or Walter's, she wasn't sure. The very flowers in the vases seemed to wither.

"Penny for your thoughts, Ruby."

She didn't know which scared her more: the thought that she would die, or the thought that Walter would. They must have become one flesh.

"I was . . . thinking about Mother, and widows. And those Indian widows who jumped on the fire."

Walter said stoutly. "We British soon put a stop to that. What's all this, Ruby? You planning to come with me when I snuff it?"

"No . . ." she made herself smile. "I've got my eye on a little place in Cheltenham."

The ship was full of mothers escorting children to boarding schools in England.

At Port Said, where East became West, the desperate little ceremony was performed of lining up the children on the deck to throw their topis into the sea. They did it gleefully, then burst into tears. Randolph did not cry. He asked if he might wear his school cap now.

He was a sturdy boy, big for his ten years, with unruly dark hair and the same flashing, close-together eyes he was born with. *You'll charm the birds out of the trees in a few years, my boy*, Ruby thought proudly. Already he had struck up a slightly bossy friendship with a waif-like blonde girl with a pink-and-white complexion that looked permanently wet. Her mother attached herself to Ruby with dog-like desperation when she discovered that her daughter was going to the same school as Emma. Was it a good school, was Emma happy there, might the two little girls be friends? Ruby was brisk; the child was younger than Emma, and would not be in her class.

The South Coast of England loomed white and ghostly out of the chilly darkness. Ruby dressed Randolph and then herself. She would have to be careful about the cold. She put on the fur coat that Walter had secretly sent for as a going away present. She powdered her face, added lipstick and pulled on her gloves. She remembered vividly her first sight of the vigorous colours of India, the contrast with English grey; she tried to reverse the feeling, to know how Randolph felt. Seagulls flew above the old soot-encrusted buildings; miserable men with their collars turned up scuttled about with ropes and heavy loads.

"Is this where you were a little girl, Mummy?"

"Not exactly! Now look out for your Uncle Stephen!"

Randolph insisted on preceding her down the steep gang-plank. She felt herself tremble in her silk stockings and her good new leather shoes. Her legs were spreading into plumpness, like the rest of her. She had felt so smart in the cabin: now she was a snobbish frump, fat, idle, with a smoker's cough and grand airs to hide her humble origins: she was Ruby Barrington, going to tea with her brothers who would laugh at her. She was their baby sister who had made a clever marriage and become a memsahib, too good to look after her own children. She wished with all her heart that she had not made this elaborate plan to be met by Stephen (in a taxi that she would pay for) and taken to Stalcross before going to Emma's school, whose term had already started. It was cowardice, it was shame; what else would have kept her even one day longer than necessary from her daughter?

But she could not spurn Stephen's welcome. She could not turn from the anxious adult manner with which he pretended to be a grown man, the broad grin with which he behaved as if she had been away for thirteen years. They hugged each other: he was wearing an old tweed coat that used to belong to Father, it rubbed against her fur. He smelled appetisingly of pastry.

"Hel-lo, Randy, young fellow! Have a good trip?"

"Good morning, Uncle."

The three of them were tongue-tied in the taxi-cab. They sat in companionable silence as Ruby stared and stared at the colourless, majestic city. It seemed to go on for ever: she saw landmarks that she had planned to point out to Randolph, she framed questions about the family that she had meant to put to Stephen. She said nothing. She lit a cigarette from her silver cigarette case, and Stephen asked if he could have one. He smoked it greedily in long gulps, like a man who had given up smoking, as people at the club were always doing, to improve their coughs. It occurred to her that he was rather poor; but then she had read that there was a lot of unemployment in England, and that was never good for business.

The old pie-shop, the house where she had grown up, was tantalising in its familiarity and strangeness. Furniture looked different, until, on closer inspection, it proved to be some Barrington heirloom with a new coat of paint. It seemed very cold, rather cluttered and untidy after the neat, sparse, comfortable bungalows of India; but Ruby certainly could not complain about the spread her sister-in-law Susan had laid on for her home-coming tea. She was touched by the presence of so many of her grown-up nieces and nephews, with a confusing array of wives, husbands, fiancés and babies; the wives of her dead brothers came too, but Charles' wife was not there, she having finally run away with a postman, leaving Charles to live with Susan and Stephen. Ruby smiled and smiled, but fretted inside at the passage of time and the untidiness and dirt of what had once been her home. She knew Susan was busy, but Mother had always been busy too and kept everything spotless nevertheless. If there was all this unemployment, the kitchen could do with a good scrub; from the sound of things, Susan had no domestic help. Charles looked gaunt and morose, he had aged more than anyone, except perhaps the children, who mocked the world with their gawky height and serious political conversations, and even, in the case of poor Leonard's daughter Emily, roared with rude but disarming laughter at Ruby's shivering insistence on keeping her fur coat on during tea.

"All right, memsahib," said Charles, "we haven't forgotten where you've come from."

"This is your Uncle Charles," said Ruby very sweetly to the rather overwhelmed Randolph, who had been warned about the wheel-chair and was very carefully not staring. "And if he ever says anything nice about me, write it down in a book and sell it to a museum of rare documents."

"Well done, Ruby!" Charles roared delightedly. "It hasn't been the same without you."

There was one dreadful moment when she so far forgot herself as to shout "Ashtray!", seeing none; and Susan brought it and curtseyed. But the moment dissolved into laughter and Ruby made amends by boiling another kettle to top up the tea, and she went on to enjoy the party thoroughly. Everyone was thrilled by the presents she had brought: silk scarves and bottles of strange, oily, woody perfumes for the women, hand-carved pipes and walking-canes for the men; boxes of sweets to be shared around, and, for curiosity's sake, a single grain of Indian rice per household in a gold case with a magnifying lens. If you looked through the lens you could see the entire text of the Lord's Prayer written on the grain. People wanted to know about India, and Randolph gave a suspense-filled account of his brush with rabies. Christopher Barrington, Stephen and Susan's son who was training to be a teacher but looked as if he was already a professor with his big spectacles, wondered if it was true that the British would leave India soon.

She laughed. "Perhaps! When the ravens leave the Tower of London!"

"But it is true, isn't it?" he persisted, in his bookish, rather disconcerting way, "the Indian people want independence."

"Our people certainly don't!" she said. "Look at the benefits of the Raj! They're a wily people, Christopher, they know what's best for them." He seemed unconvinced. "You must come out and visit us some time," she said kindly, "then you'll know what you're talking about. Not that you don't," she added, for she had not meant to be rude, "but not everything that's worth knowing comes out of books, does it?" He conceded that it did not, and the argument – not that it really was one – was at an end. He was an interesting boy.

It was nearly eight o'clock when everybody left. Ruby took Randolph upstairs to sleep in her old room and introduced him to the phenomenon of the hotwater bottle. When she came back to the kitchen, it was empty except for her nephew Christopher, who was reading a book. Susan was doing something in the shop, Stephen was helping Charles to his bed. Susan called through, "Just sit down, Ruby, you must be exhausted. And Chris, where are your manners? Talk to your aunt, and do try and keep off politics."

Ruby cleared her throat. "What are you hoping to teach, Chris?"

He closed his book. "English literature."

She did not see the warning light that flashed in her head, though she was to remember it later. "And what's that interesting-looking book?"

He passed it to her reluctantly. He obviously thought her

365

unworthy of his attention for not believing in quitting India. *The Modern Age: English Poets Since the Great War.* She looked down the names in the index and said experimentally, casually, "I don't see Fellowes here, Robin Fellowes." She waited for the young man to curl his lip and say, "Who?" But he laughed. "Robin Fellowes? He's in a different class entirely."

It could mean anything. It did not mean Robin was alive or dead. His pre-war poems had been published since the war, that was all it meant. *A different class entirely.* Was that bad or good? Good, apparently, for Christopher was suddenly interested in her for having heard of Robin Fellowes and was bounding up the stairs to fetch a copy he had of one of his books; a thin volume, highly priced. It was called *An Easy Sort of War* and the notes on the cover told Ruby what she would never have understood from the chaotic, difficult verses it contained: that Robin had been imprisoned in Germany between 1915 and 1919 and then spent a long period in a mental hospital, after which he married the novelist Marcia Higgs, with whom he now lived in Leicester with their three children.

"Fancy you knowing Fellowes' work! I've tried writing in his style but I can't get anywhere near it," said Christopher excitedly.

"Personally I prefer poetry that people can understand," said Ruby.

17

The smell of baking woke her early in the dark morning. Randolph was still asleep. She put on her thick winter underclothes and got dressed. Stephen and Susan were busily making pies and serving early customers. Gratefully she heard them turn down her half-hearted offer of help. She pulled on her fur coat and stepped out into the quiet street.

"Going to look for your memories, Ruby?"

"That's right."

Stalcross was dreary and foreign to her. The few people who were up moved softly, spoke in hushed early-morning voices. Even the sparrows were quiet. They sat in huffed-up, flustered rows in gutters. The houses were poky and dark and close together. She found herself at the station. It smelled of soot. The young girls with red fingernails who waited for the train to take them to work took it all for granted: had they had to fight their mothers for permission to go? Not they; it was easy for them now. The shop where her parents had started out together as Hamish & Pearl, now offered permanent waves for 19/6d. It did not seem to be doing much business, or even trying to; through the letterbox, Ruby could see more than a day's unopened mail piling up and the windows were encrusted with grime.

She was rather surprised to remember that she had a child. Two, in fact. And Robin had three, by a lady novelist. Dead to her, he was alive; and all that time while she had yearned for him, he had been languishing in some prisoner-of-war camp or gibbering with shellshock in an asylum. Maybe if she had waited, maybe if she had been brave enough and swallowed her pride and written, or even called at Mr Dotts' house that day when that girl – what was her name, Beatrice? – had driven her to Baxburn instead of killing him in her mind like a sniper . . . when did he meet this Marcia Higgs? Perhaps she was a nurse who had helped with his cure. They lived in Leicester, where was that, exactly? She knew it was in the North. Could you get there and back in a day?

No. She had three weeks in England. And she had promised those weeks to Emma, whom she had abandoned as Robin had abandoned her.

Back at the house, she helped Randolph dress smartly in his white shirt, blue-and-black tie, crested tie-pin, black trousers and blue jacket. She bent to polish his shoes.

"The bearer should do that."

"Chota, honestly, if you say things like that at school – "

There were slices of veal-and-ham pie for breakfast, which Randolph refused so Susan gave him a boiled egg. Ruby felt ashamed but she wanted him well fed for the journey. He shook hands gravely with uncle and aunt and said he looked forward to seeing them in the holidays. Ruby tried tactfully to tell Susan that the money for the children's keep would come well in advance and would be plenty.

Susan smiled and embraced her. "Thank you, Ruby." Her voice was tolerant. "It's all right, just a difficult time. And we're glad to have them."

At Stalcross Station, Ruby bought cigarettes and peppermints and told Randolph about playing Last Across just *here* . . . she stopped, had she saved him from rabies to have him mangled by a train? She told him about the first day she went to the Misses Parley, but she abandoned that too, because that was the day she first met Robin.

They had lunch on the Brighton train: bright red soup, chicken and steamed pudding. Randolph wanted to be the one to pay the waiter. He was relaxed and very lordly. At his school, she bent for a kiss and received a handshake; a hawk-nosed housemaster and a starched, rustling matron flanked him as he trotted away down a polished corridor with chessboard tiles. The headmaster said, "I'd offer you tea, Mrs Barrington, but I've just had mine." Ruby said, "Oh good gracious, Mr Johnson, I have to go to St Hugh's; my daughter is dying to see me."

Emma appeared shy in her purple gymslip, her white blouse and her black stockings. She had grown and filled out but was still painfully dainty and sweet under her bulky overall, tied in the middle with what looked like a piece of string but on closer examination proved to be a white sash fingered and twisted by muddy fingers. She kept Ruby waiting in the parlour for ten minutes; she was busy with her nature table, the mistress said.

"Why, Emma Sarah, you look like the laundry bag!" Ruby took off the overall while Emma stroked her fur coat. "And what's all this about a nature table?"

"I'm in charge of it."

"Just like you used to help the *mali* with the garden in India?"

"I have to pick wild flowers and find out their names. And soon I'll be able to get conkers and sycamore wings."

"I could press some flowers from the garden at home, and send them to you."

"I don't know if we're allowed to have Indian flowers on a nature table. I'll ask Miss Smith."

Ruby booked into a hotel on the sea front half way between the two schools. She visited each child on alternate weekdays and took them out together at weekends. She was shown classrooms and dormitories and playing fields and drank tea with masters and mistresses and heard about her children's progress. She watched Randolph kick a football; she saw Emma's nature table.

They went for walks and bus rides and train rides; they went to restaurants and cinemas. Money was pouring through Ruby's hands like water. Sometimes she just took the children back to her hotel, but they were noisy and there was nothing to do except sit and listen to the wireless. They went to tailors and dressmakers

368

and the children were measured for new clothes with plenty of room to grow. She bought Randolph a cricket bat and a dictionary: she bought Emma a book for identifying English wild flowers. She found a riding stables and hired a pony for the morning. They had the little girl she and Randolph had met on the boat with them that day; she was desolate because her mother had just left for India, but Randolph cheered her up by schooling her as she sat on the horse, loudly criticising what he called her "seat".

Ruby had planned the biggest treat of all, the one her children demanded, for their last Sunday together: they would go on the pier with a bottomless bag of coppers and Randolph and Emma could play endlessly with the slot machines, a recreation forbidden by both their schools. But it rained and the games palled; with no ideas left, Ruby summoned a taxi-cab and said, "We're visitors here, please show us the countryside." On and on they drove in the gathering evening, past wide brown ploughed fields and soft green hills. Ruby told her children that she had once been a farm girl here. Randolph laughed. Emma said, "Where was I?" They passed a cottage nestling in a valley with ivy round the door and a To Let sign. The taxi was going too fast, the cottage came and vanished, but it fixed itself into Ruby's mind like a photograph. As they made their way back towards the schools for the last time, they passed churches with bells ringing for evensong.

Emma said sharply, "I hate that sound."

"It's a lovely sound, Emma!"

"I hate it. When Uncle Stephen and Aunty Susan come the bells always ring when they take me back to school. It makes me melancholy."

"That's a big word for a little girl!"

She told the driver to go to Emma's school first. Lights shone in its towers; it was like an historic castle; darkness rolled in from the sea. The fine rain still fell. "I'll take you in, Emma, but we'll say our goodbyes now because I'll be gone before you're awake tomorrow. Kiss Chota – " she had not meant to use the Indian nickname. Emma twisted up her face.

"What's this?" said Ruby, "making yourself cry?"

"I want to cry! It hurts! But I can't!"

"But Emma darling, if you cry, I'll cry too."

The little girl turned a blank face on her. It declared that she would not cry for a hundred pounds. "Good," she said.

"Emma – "

"I want you to cry. I hate you. But I love Daddy."

"That's a fine thing to say, when I've just decided that Daddy and I will both come and see you next summer." Hope and suspicion warred in Emma's face. "Perhaps you don't want us to? I saw a little cottage to let, and I thought, that's just the kind of place Daddy and I could stay in for a summer holiday with Chota and Missy!"

"Ooh good, Mother," said Randolph.

Somehow Ruby got the children into their schools. She was shaking, but this she knew: once you had made a promise to children, you had to keep it. Walter would see that, angry though he would be that the promise had been made at all. The way they were living was absurd: he would work himself to death if he never took a holiday, and she would be left alone with two children who hated her.

Back at her hotel she bought a bottle of gin and a bottle of lime-juice and tried to fortify herself against the bitterness of her own attack. What an expert she had become in the arts of protecting herself, deceiving herself. If Walter had not exactly made her happy, he had not made her miserable either; he had given her a good life and two children. But having no children at all would be better than having children who hated you! Perhaps it had been necessary, in those years of the war and afterwards, to put up a shield between herself and her feelings, but that was all over now and she should just pull herself together. She no longer knew whether Robin could have been the great love of her life or whether it was all a game, a dream, a foolish flirtation that went too far; but her decision not to look for him had been the right one, the right one for a wife and a mother to take. She smoked till her chest hurt, and clumsily did her packing. She had refused to believe that Emma was unhappy when she thought there was nothing she could do about it. She had read the words of her letters and looked no further. But she had known, oh yes, she had known the violence of the childish horror and outrage Emma must have felt, packed off to England alone with a stranger, Emma, the younger child, the one who had not wanted to go at all, while her brother stayed behind.

Never again would she visit her children like this, like a stranger. She would give them a home, if only for a few weeks, or she would give them nothing! She would not wait on Emma's convenience while she busied herself with her nature table and sought permission from Miss Smith to have Indian flowers on it! Ruby paused in horror; she was thinking of herself again! She was thinking of how she had been: anxious and guilty and resentful and, yes, bored, bored with the children's treats and play! Even now as she remembered that dreadful, heart-rending thing Emma had said about the church bells and about not being able to cry when she needed to, and she cried herself, she could not be sure whether her tears came from relief or pity or gin. Emma hated her. At least they had that in common.

Walter was at the station to meet her, shining in the sun with his white suit and welcoming grin, towering above the tight-packed writhing crowds and striding towards her on his long legs. *That's my husband*, thought Ruby. *That man has been my husband for thirteen years!* and his pleasure glowed and she lowered her eyes shyly like a little Indian wife.

It was a relief to feel so pleased to see him. Throughout the journey from England she had felt so dead inside, so miserable about not having loved her children enough, that she had moved to thinking about Walter and had castigated herself for not loving him enough either, simply because she sometimes thought him a bully and sometimes thought him absurd. But the interval apart had done wonders for her appreciation of him: she found she had at last abandoned her image of him as the talentless youth bounding into the Miss Parleys, to be the butt of their humour. The transformation must have been happening gradually over the years without her noticing it: he seemed suddenly to have become a mature, sun-tanned successful businessman with a dignity not too great to prevent him jumping up and down with delight at the sight of her. So she jumped up and down too, why not? His hair, which she had remembered as the pale straw-colour of the Miss Parley days, was rich gold, streaked with silver; but that was what India did to colours. Even the red veins in the whites of his blue eyes had a magic, an immediacy. She felt as if she had just recovered from an illness during which everything appeared blurred and grey and pale: now she could delight in Walter's hair and eyes and suit and skin, and the blue sky, dazzling fabrics, dark faces, trees, stalls, shops, animals, soldiers, temples, churches, the yellow dusty road up to the bungalow . . . everything was so *bright*. Even the bungalow was transformed, for Walter, knowing she would hate the disruption of decorators, had had the whole interior freshly painted in her absence. She smiled the delight she felt: the colours were pale and clean, creams and pinks and cool blues, marrying well with their rich carpets and tapestries. And there were some new mahogany cabinets that she had wanted, full of her china. She breathed deeply: wood and new paint mingled with the perfume of chrysanthemums and sweetpeas in gaudy vasefuls in every room, nearly every room, she did not go into the children's rooms, she did not want to see them neat and empty, waiting for guests.

"I told the children we'd go home next summer," she murmured, and Walter said nothing, and she let it pass.

The servants seemed pleased to see her, though you never knew what they were really thinking. "My sister-in-law could make use of you!" she told the cook, looking at the welcome-home dinner he was preparing, vegetable curry, her favourite. He bowed: "I would be honoured, memsahib. Perhaps my son-in-law . . ."

They ate on the verandah, watching the sun give way to the pale white moon. There was a special treat for sweet, little baskets made of spun sugar and filled with tinned pears and cream. Natives had such delicate hands.

"Do you remember how Emma used to love these?" she said wistfully. She wondered what the children were doing, now, this minute.

"Tell me all about them," Walter urged.

"Oh Walter! I'm *dry* with talking!" It was true. She had been talking incessantly about England and the family and the weather and the cost of everything.

"More wine for memsahib!" he shouted, and it appeared. The darkness was still and thick with perfumes and the click of insects. Points of light glowed on Walter's cigar, Ruby's cigarette. Rather than discuss the children now, she said casually, "I must tell you this. Did I ever mention someone called Robin Fellowes?"

The words hung in the air like the moon, like the pale pool of Walter's brandy, half-way between the table and his lips, they hung there, still.

"Don't think so, who is he?"

"Oh, nobody. A poet. Used to have his poems typed at the Parleys, never paid his bills."

"Brave man! What about him?"

"Nothing really. Stephen's boy's an expert on modern poetry and he had one of his books."

Walter stared. "You mean he's *published*, and you know him?"

"I used to, before the war." *Before the war*. "Chris said he was 'in a class of his own', or something, I don't know if that's good or bad, I couldn't understand a word, the ones he used to write for me were much simpler, much nicer, for me to type, I mean," she added, seeing Walter's face, hearing her voice echo in the stillness as if she had been talking about Robin non-stop for half an hour. Why on earth had she brought this up? She knew immediately. It had been to test herself, to see if she could talk casually about him to Walter, as she might swallow unnecessarily and repeatedly after a sore throat to check and enjoy the absence of pain. Absence of pain: *her* pain. What about the pain she should have known it would give Walter? She had not bothered about that. And now she feared she had let him know that Robin had been her first love and he, her husband, was only second-best. "Shall we go to bed?" she said. She had never suggested bed to him before. His needs were regular enough to forestall her even knowing whether she had any after all these years; she had certainly not missed him in that way. But he paused just long enough before taking her hand to hurt her deeply. She accepted it as punishment. In their big bed she tried to possess him utterly. She was clumsy and got tangled up in the mosquito net, but she wanted to give him what she realised he had probably never had, the feeling of being helplessly taken. It was a while before he got the idea, and by then she was feeling tired and foolish and slightly cheap. She closed her eyes tightly and rolled away.

"You *have* missed me, Ruby!"

"You didn't mind, did you?"

"I'll show-ow you if I minded. Come here –"

But she didn't want any more of him. She didn't like his jocular mood. He was covering up. She tested this by pretending to go to sleep. She watched him through her eyelashes. He sighed and stared. Snake-like, he eased himself from the bed and went out on the verandah. The slight scent of his cigar sweetened the blue air. She gave him an hour, then went and sat beside him.

"I was thinking about that poet chap."

"It was nothing, Walter – "

He seemed not to hear. "He stuck at it, didn't he?"

"No. Oh, I see. You mean, writing."

"And now," Walter said, blowing out smoke wistfully, "he's in *print*. And I gave up."

She remembered the first time he took her to the theatre, and how humiliated he was by her enthusiasm for Shaw. "No, Walter," she said quickly, "you just decided to do something else. And . . . and your shop does a lot more for people than a few poems nobody can understand!"

"There were a lot of jokes, you know, when you went away," he said. "Usual thing. While the cat's away, and all that. Good old Walter, off the leash now, what are you getting up to, what's her name? D'you know what I did?" What was coming? "I stayed at home every evening and wrote a play."

"Oh Walter! Can I see it?"

"No. I threw it away. It was rubbish. I can't do it any more. It was for the children. There were parts for both of them and I thought we could put it on at the club. For Christmas. Then I remembered. No point. No children, no point." He sounded drunk.

"I miss them, don't you?" said Ruby.

"Well, of course you would."

"Don't you?"

"Sacrifices have to be made," he said stubbornly. "You can't educate children in India."

18

The road to the club was being rebuilt. The ladies set up a roster for looking after the building-women's children while they worked. They sat them at tables in the gardens, fed them, and taught them English nursery-rhymes.

Ruby held a cup of milk to the mouth of a tiny two-year-old. Its eyes were bright but its lips were covered with sores. She watched the women labouring with pickaxes. Their backs bent and straightened like stiff scissors in the swirling fabric of their dresses.

"Little Jack Horner, sat in a corner, eating his Christmas pie."

"A mouthful for Mummy. A mouthful for Daddy . . ."

Ruby had a lot of time on her hands now that the children were gone. She wished she didn't find good works so disturbing.

She finished her turn on the roster and hurried to join the memsahibs in conversation on the verandah. They were discussing somebody's husband who had been perfectly well one day and had gone mad and started smashing up his home the next. The consensus was that he had been partly to blame for his own fate; as had his wife.

"They think they're tough about India – men. They think health and rest are women's nonsense to worry about."

"All the same, we have to keep an eye on them."

"I heard of a man who became *convinced* he was six years old again! Cried for his nanny and sent to England for his teddy-bear!"

Ruby didn't like the way the conversation was going. She was uneasy about the revival of Walter's ambition to be a playwright. But her unease was mixed with guilt about her own motives. She had thought that Walter was upset by the discovery that Robin had been her lover before him. It was sobering to discover that he cared much more that Robin was in print. She detached herself from the group and went to read the paper. She found an advertisement that interested her, put a ring round it and surreptitiously took the paper home to Walter.

"This looks like a nice place," she said, "Leehaven. It's near the schools, I remember seeing the signposts. It's on the coast . . . and here's a firm that 'specialise in short lets for overseas visitors'. Walter, isn't it funny to think of us as overseas visitors?" He said nothing. She ran her tongue over her lips and tasted dust, but mingled with it in her mind was the taste of cool salt spray. "Walter, we *are* going. I promised the children."

"Oh yes . . ." He reached for the paper and laughed as he read. " 'The comforts of the East in the health-giving climate of Sussex.' Gales and blizzards. Ruby, you want to go home, don't you?"

"In July."

"I mean for good."

She dared not think. "What?"

"Wonder if D and M have ever thought about setting up shop in one of these watering-holes. Funny. Chap came in today who's retiring to Eastbourne. Funny old buffer. He said, 'One thing I'll miss, Orange, is this emporium of yours.' Makes you feel good, remark like that."

Ruby clasped her hands together. "Why don't you write to head office and suggest it?"

A shop like Walter's in Leehaven! Stocked with goods imported from India to feed the nostalgia of retired military men and wrapped-up memsahibs there! With Indian staff, perhaps, to give a

touch of authenticity, and the smell of herbs in the air! They·
would live in a little cottage which she would keep nice for the
evenings when the children ran laughing from the school bus!
The advertisement even said there was a repertory theatre in
Leehaven: Walter could write plays for it, in his spare time!

But Duckbill & Middlesex (London) had other ideas. They
would bear Walter's suggestion in mind, but for now they were
thinking more in terms of expanding the Indian end of things.
They were impressed with how many mail-orders he filled from
the interior and the hill-stations and wondered if some of the
stations could support small branches of their own. If they did
decide on an English south coast operation, the managership was
his, but first they wanted him to make a tour up-country and assess
the demand in India..They understood that D & M (Calcutta) was
well set up with Indian staff, and could manage without him for
a few months.

"If that was true-ue, I'd've come home with you, Ruby – "

"I won't allow it! Do they think you're a war horse, to be
worked until you drop?"

"Expansion indeed! When all the talk is of leaving India!"

"And I promised the children – "

"You go, Ruby."

"I won't go home alone, ever again!"

They argued with each other because they knew they could not
argue with Duckbill & Middlesex (London).

"I'll write to the children," said Ruby, "and ask them what
they think. A few weeks in the summer, or home for good in a
year . . . or two." But she didn't consult them. It was a cowardly
idea. How could children of eight and ten make such a choice,
when their parents dared not?

Ruby went on the tour with Walter. She wanted to protect him
from over-tiring himself. She would help him too, for did he
suppose he was going to talk to ladies about all the goods they
needed? And she wanted to say goodbye to India, for now that
their departure was in the foreseeable if distant future, she felt a
sense of emptiness and loss at the years of afternoons she had
wasted in that stuffy, malicious little clubhouse while the real
India lived on without her.

They took trains to the end of the railways, looked out sites
near the stations, then hired horses to visit outlying clusters of

Englishmen's dwellings. In her breeches and boots, Ruby felt like a land-girl again – except that the bearers rode along behind with supplies and good dresses for evenings in towns. Sometimes they camped overnight in the wilderness, and Ruby and Walter helped the bearers put up the tents and cook; and then they all sat round the same fire, playing cards, discussing their families, and identifying the sounds of the night.

Formality broke down in people's homes too; isolated families did not mind that they were merely shopkeepers. They took them in and shared whatever they had; and all the time Walter and Ruby were noting, tactfully and carefully, what they did have and what they did not. Many of them were regular mail-order customers – Walter greeted them like old friends – but of course it was not the same. They were thrilled with the idea of a department store on their doorstep, even if it was a rather large doorstep, say seventy miles across.

"Dearest Emma, you would love what we saw today." Ruby wrote long, separate letters to each of the children, adding to them every night no matter how tired she was. "A nest of tiger-cubs! They looked so sweet, like kittens, but we moved off quickly in case their mother should be about!" "Darling Randolph, I hope you like the stamps. Today we came to a village where the coconuts were so thick on the ground that the horses stumbled and we had to get off and lead them . . ." Meanwhile, Walter wrote lists. Number of Households. Distance from Station. Estimated Income. Needs and Expenditure.

Duckbill & Middlesex (London) were satisfied with his reports. They proposed to select a suitable young man and send him out within the next few months. He would work for a while at Calcutta under Walter's supervision, and then he could be dispatched inland.

"This is torture!" Ruby fumed. She felt very flat after the tour. She wanted a firm date for herself and the children to look forward to. Emma's letters were dutiful and terse; Randolph's were full of requests for more stamps and wooden soldiers, as he had started to sell them to his friends. "We're nothing but his blessed wholesalers!" Ruby exploded.

Walter started to lose patience with his employers. "They're making a fool of me, Ruby. They can't think they can send out some youngster wet behind the ears and expect him to set up a shop in the middle of nowhere! He'll have to nurse it – and they're expecting *me* to nurse him!" At last he wrote a letter, in a tone he had never used to London before. The letter declared that he took seriously his responsibilities as an employee of Duckbill & Middlesex, and he had no cause to complain hitherto about his conditions of employment. But he ventured to suggest that he too had given satisfaction and he would be obliged if they would honour their undertaking to return him to England as soon as possible, since the separation from the children was causing considerable distress to his wife. Otherwise, he would regretfully tender his resignation.

They read the letter together before sealing it up.

"And then what will we do?" sighed Ruby.

"Write plays," Walter mocked.

"We can't send it," said Ruby.

"No," said Walter.

Mr Archibald Middlesex, great-grandson of the firm's founder, arrived with his wife in Calcutta one still and sticky day in May. In vain Walter had urged them to come sooner, to have some chance of acclimatising themselves before the hot weather started. But some personal concern of Mrs Middlesex's had forced them to delay. "And besides," she told Ruby, "we don't propose to be beaten by India. We may as well start as we mean to go on."

Ruby disliked her on sight. She was a large, gauche girl of twenty-five with a huge appetite and a very bossy manner. Somebody had obviously told her on the boat about the need to be firm with Indians, omitting to mention the importance of tempering this with fairness and courtesy. She seemed also not to have been told that you did not order other people's servants about, you did not disrupt their routine. She thought nothing of summoning up between-meal snacks behind Ruby's back; or playing Patience with two packs of cards, expecting the sweeper to set out the second game while she was busy with the first. Ruby had to spend a lot of time with her while the men were at the shop. She tried to be kind, to offer helpful hints; but the girl soon made it clear that she thought she had nothing to learn.

Sometimes Ruby thought she might be shy and terrified, and tried to make allowances; but the worst thing was the way the servants seemed unsurprised by her. Did they see no difference between the Ruby Oranges and the Mrs Middlesexes of the world?

Perhaps there was no difference . . .

Mrs Middlesex patronised the bungalow as "dear" and "little," and wished there was more space for her clothes. A great reader, she knew for a fact that Mahatma Gandhi was in the pay of the Germans, though she did not care to argue the point with those of the club memsahibs (whom she characterised as "priceless" and "wonderful characters," arousing in Ruby a sudden great affection for them) who were convinced that his gold came from Moscow.

"What a *very nasty* day," said Mrs Middlesex, one evening towards the end of their stay.

"I think it's lovey," said Ruby quickly. It was not lovely at all. There was a brooding wetness in the air that made her skin prickle. "It means we've had the worst of the heat."

"My goodness," said Mrs Middlesex, "was that all?"

While Ruby was still reassembling her breath, Mrs Middlesex announced that she was bored and would like to visit the bazaar to pick up a few things before setting off for the back of beyond. For all Ruby cared, she could go, but she supposed she ought to look after her guest. There had been a spate of particularly nasty pocket-pickings lately, involving knives, and crowds who shouted nationalist slogans while they opened and closed ranks to allow the culprits to escape. "We'll wait for the men to get back," she said, "and then we'll all go."

"Perhaps we could have some of your cook's delightful cakes while we're waiting," said Mrs Middlesex.

When the men returned from the shop they wanted only to bathe and rest, but Mrs Middlesex was not to be denied. So the four of them drove back into town, left the car and walked. The streets always seemed narrower than usual, these muggy evenings before the rains. Sweet smells and foul smells curled round each other in the air like lazy great snakes.

Mrs Middlesex wanted some silk; the stallholder was asking a high price, and she wouldn't hear of it. Embarrassment drove Ruby like a motor; of course they expected to be beaten down, but why not pay what they asked, once in a while?

Ruby walked close to Walter, beating off insects, wanting him to turn and take her arm. The dying sun cast a mood of yellow sulkiness. Everything seemed very slow, nothing quite right . . .

like when they had films at the club and the projector ran down. The babble of voices had the right note of shrillness but everything was heavy and menacing. She hoped she was not going to be ill.

They were the only white people in sight.

Ruby searched for space, breathed deeply for any trace of freshness in the air.

Mrs Middlesex strode on determinedly in her green canvas brogues.

To keep herself from fainting, Ruby watched her closely.

It was hard to believe what she thought she saw.

It was necessary to watch closely to be certain. You had to be careful before you made an accusation like that even in private. But she was right. Mrs Middlesex was deliberately varying her path, aiming herself at individual Indians coming towards her so that they must step aside.

"Walter, I'd like to go home soon," said Ruby. He turned. She must have looked ill because his eyes filled with concern and he reached out his white sleeved arm to support her. Mr Middlesex called out to his wife, "My dear – "

Mrs Middlesex did not hear. She strode on, a plough cutting through soil. Walter gave Ruby a smile of tolerant understanding and rolled his eyes.

Then there was an Indian who would not step aside for Mrs Middlesex: a stone in the soil. The sight would almost have been comic, if it were not so shaming. The short, turbaned man held his ground, looked up into Mrs Middlesex's face with an expression at once determined and sweet. Rage glowed from the back of Mrs Middlesex's neck.

Mr Middlesex and Walter exchanged urgent glances and stepped forward, Walter letting go of Ruby.

"Let the memsahib pass," said Walter softly.

The man indicated, with a slight twitch of his bony shoulder that the memsahib was at liberty to step into the gutter.

Mr Middlesex put his hand restrainingly on his wife's arm; the suddenly-hostile crowd cut Ruby off from the three of them. Everything stopped. Life could not proceed until someone gave way. Walter and Mr Middlesex must have suggested that it should be Mrs Middlesex, because her sneer rang out: "Do you two call yourselves Englishmen?"

If this were a film, it could be a comedy. So Ruby never knew why she screamed. Nothing terrible had happened at that point.

The situation could still have resolved itself into a joke, or apologies, or mildly hurt feelings all round. One heard of ghastly incidents, but this did not have to be one of them. Afterwards, when she could think again, she blamed the weather, or – *afterwards*? What good did it do to think about it afterwards? It was her scream that had done the damage, her wholly unnecessary scream that had created reasons for its own existence! Because it alarmed Walter and sent him lunging back towards her and he hit a man, he did not mean to hit him, Ruby would swear it was just his long arms flailing about, but he hit him and the sun shone dully on a knife in a brown hand. Ruby noticed that there was rust on the blade, though how she noticed she did not know because it was only visible for a split second before it disappeared into the flesh of Walter's neck, and then there was only the handle to be seen, an intricately carved ivory handle standing like a lighthouse in a boiling red sea, and Walter was dead by the time help came.

Emma
1939–1942

Now that she was twelve, and in the Senior School, Emma slept in a dormitory with five other girls. In the Babies, she had had to share with nine; but what she really wanted was a single room.

She knew she would never get one. Single rooms were only for people like Fiona MacFarlane, the head girl; and Nancy Smith, who had to sleep with a kettle boiling on a hotplate all night or she would die from her lung-condition.

She wanted a place where she could be alone, to get away from girls and teachers. Most of the teachers were quite kind. But even their way of being kind could make Emma want to scream. And screaming didn't always help. Once she shouted at the algebra teacher: "I don't want to do algebra! It's silly! I can do sums with numbers, why should I do them with letters?" And the algebra teacher, instead of ticking her off, said, "Emma, why don't you go to the gym and have a good scream? It often helps with algebra." And Emma went to the gym and screamed at the wallbars, but it didn't help, and she still couldn't do algebra.

Every morning, just before the bell went, Matron came round with big jugs of water which she poured into the bowls at the end of each bed. Matron was young and vigorous and cheerful and had a fascinating coil of thick yellow hair which Emma longed to touch because it looked like whipped cream. She loved to see Matron come round with the water; hated the bell. It set her teeth on edge. It was bad-mannered. It was like being ordered to do something instead of being asked nicely. Sometimes, if she pretended to sleep through the bell, Matron would come to get her up.

"Come along, Emma. It's Picnic Day, remember?"

May the first was the birthday of Miss Cookmere, the headmistress. The whole school would be going on the Downs in specially hired charabancs. Sometimes you could wander off by yourself.

As soon as Matron was within hearing, Emma said, "Daddy, Daddy," in a sleepy half-sob.

Matron was immediately attentive. She sat down and ruffled Emma's hair. "What is it, Emma? Have you been having another dream about your poor father's death?" Matron was the only person who understood that you wanted people to say "your father," not "your daddy." And she said "dead" and "death", too, not "passed away" or "gone to heaven".

Emma said, "I dreamt he was drowning and I nearly saved him and then I woke up." It wasn't true. Her dream had been of an oasis in a desert. She had been learning about oases in geography. Anything she did or learned in the daytime that had to do with water turned up sooner or later in her dreams, and became, in the morning, the sound of Matron filling the wash-bowls.

Matron comforted her. Emma could see the other girls dressing and wondering jealously what they were talking about. But soon it was over. Matron stood and said, "Cheer up, Emma. Your poor father wouldn't want you to have bad dreams . . . or to miss Picnic Day."

Everyone had to have one set of old clothes, for picnics and gardening and other dirty occupations. Emma's old clothes were a brown corduroy skirt with crossover straps and a scorch-mark from the iron, and a yellow tussore silk blouse. She turned up her nose as she got them out. Everyone always looked so ragged on these picnics, and she hated to look ragged. The blouse smelled. It smelled of dressmakers. Why did dressmakers always smell? Probably because they spent their time in musty little shops, surrounded by bales of fabric, and never went out into the sunlight.

The charabanc smelled too, of sweat and petrol and tobacco smoke.

"Sit with us, Emma!" girls called.

"Over here, Emma Orange!"

She knew they had been told to be nice to her. She remembered once being told to be nice to a girl whose sister had died of diphtheria after having a hole cut in her throat. It was horrible, having to be nice to someone you didn't like, just because someone belonging to them had died. And even if you did like them they frightened you. You dreaded them bursting into tears at any minute, you were shocked when they didn't. You wondered if it could happen to you, and you knew it could. Girls who still had parents in India avoided her as if she had typhoid. She sat by herself.

Half-way to the picnic place, they stopped at a sweet-shop. Emma bought lemonade-powder and asked the man to put it into two bags. She put one bag in her pocket and licked the powder out of the other one as the charabanc went along. Matron didn't like you to eat lemonade-powder in this way, because you never knew where the paper bag had been.

The picnic place was a grassy slope near where a river cut a gap in the cliffs and wound out to sea. You could see for miles, which meant the teachers could too. Emma listened with disgust to the tricks they tried in order to turn the holiday into a lesson.

"Let's gather a birthday bouquet of wild flowers for Miss Cookmere! With no two flowers the same!"

"Let's see if we can find a dew-pond."

Anyone who had been before knew where the dew-pond was. There was always a rusty mudguard in it.

"Don't go out of sight! And if you hear the bell – back here as fast as rabbits!"

She couldn't believe that they had actually brought the school bell with them. There the stupid great iron thing sat on the grass, surrounded by hampers and flasks and rugs, its stupid wooden handle pointing up to the sky.

Some girls said, "Come with us, Emma! We're going to make a camp." They had probably been told to.

She said, "No, thanks, I'm going for a walk."

She asked if she could take her picnic now and eat it on her own, but the teachers laughed and said she would only want more when the others had theirs.

She strolled off and soon she found a dead rabbit. She squatted down to examine it and a few white maggots crawled out onto her shoe. She wished she had a knife. When they had rabbit stew at school she liked to collect up the bits of backbone from people's plates and assemble a whole spine for her nature table.

At the edge of a wood she came upon a group of the Babies with rolled-up sleeves, scrubbing weed and slime out of a stone horse-trough. One of them was Helen Forster, who had been on the boat when Randolph came from India, and who used to go on outings with them, but didn't any more.

"What on earth are you Babies doing?"

Helen pointed to a patch they had cleaned. The bare stone showed through the slime. "We don't want the horses to have to drink dirty water."

"How silly!" said Emma. "It doesn't do them any harm."

They stopped work, drew close together, and stared at her.

"We don't like you," said one.

Emma looked cooly at Helen. "You like my brother."

Helen turned scarlet.

"She likes your brother, but she doesn't like you. You must be very bad." Emma turned and walked into the wood. It wasn't a proper wood when you came to it, just a clump of stunted prickly trees. The Babies went on shouting, encouraging each other.

"You must be – if your mother doesn't want you at home!"

"We're only at boarding school because our parents are in India!"

"But your mother's come home to Leehaven!"

"And she still doesn't want you – "

Emma shrugged and walked into a bramble bush. How silly the Babies were. She started to extricate herself. They couldn't be expected to understand the importance of education. Her skirt was full of thorns. Or to understand that a widow didn't want her children there all the time, reminding her of her dead husband, even if she did love them. She wished it was time for the blackberries to be ripe. She was thirsty, but she didn't want to go back to the teachers. A fenced-off field of cows blocked her way to the river. She inspected them carefully to see if there was a bull. She wasn't sure how to tell, but they looked very docile. Anyway, she knew that a bull in a field of cows wasn't dangerous. She knew why, too. She climbed over the fence.

As she reached the river, she heard the school bell ring. She spat with anger. The cows took no notice, but the entire staff of the school seemed to be galloping towards the cow-field, waving their arms.

It was a wondrous sight.

"Emma Orange! Come here this *moment!*"

"Keep perfectly still, and don't be frightened. Walk very slowly . . ."

She would leave them to make up their minds. She tipped her second bag of lemonade-powder into her cupped hands, lay down on her front in the mud of the river bank, dipped her hands into the water and drank. The lemonade tasted salty and not very nice.

A canoe with a fair-haired man in it appeared round the bend in the river. He seemed to be having a hard job and a lot of fun controlling the canoe. The river rushing out to sea met the breakers rolling in to land and the two kinds of waves slapped each other in the face, whirling and tossing the canoe. It was easy to ignore the shouting teachers with this adventure to watch. The man grinned and flinched from the spray. He brought the canoe close to the bank.

"Hello," he said, wiping his face.

"Hello, yourself."

"Did you know you're covered in mud?"

"I don't care."

"Do you care that there's a bull walking towards you, weighing about a million tons? No, don't look round – "

She couldn't if she wanted to. She froze. She felt the earth shake, she felt fiery breath on her shoulders, she didn't know what was real and what was not. The man paddled the canoe towards her. Very gently he lifted her into the front of the canoe and sat her down. Then he paddled it swiftly out into the middle of the river.

"Look," he said.

Slowly she turned her head. She couldn't understand why she hadn't spotted the bull before, because now there was no mistaking its square head, the ring in its nose, its mean, pink eyes. For a terrible moment it started to walk out towards them. Then it changed its mind and wandered away.

"Young man! Young man!" It was Miss Cookmere's voice. "Bring that child back *this instant!*" She sounded as if she wanted to give him an order mark.

"Who's that, your mother?"

Emma made a face. "My headmistress."

He laughed. "Looks as if you're in trouble anyway. In for a penny, in for a pound eh? D'you want to go on an expedition?"

"Oh, yes!"

It wasn't much of an expedition. All he did was take her up the river, round a few bends and islands, and along to a place where she could be landed safe from the bull but straight into the arms of Miss Cookmere. It was fun going in the canoe, though. It was so low in the water, it was like being a duck. The smallest of ripples appeared like the hugest of waves, but the canoe always bobbed up and rode safely over them. In the front where she sat there was an exercise book full of handwriting and photographs and maps and charts.

"That's my log-book," said the man. "I write down everywhere I go."

"Are you an explorer?"

"Sort of, I want to be, when I leave school."

Emma's heart sank. She had thought he was grown up. He had long, thin, blond, hairy legs and a deep voice. He was much older than Randolph. What a long time you had to stay at school! Miss Cookmere thanked him frostily for the rescue. He didn't seem in the least bit frightened of her. She sent Emma to sit on her own in the charabanc for the rest of the day, without any food. Emma didn't care. She had had a better adventure than anyone else would have that day, and they all knew it.

2

Matron didn't believe in calling the doctor for minor ailments. "Doctors," she said, "can cure a cold in a week. I can get rid of it in seven days." She believed in fresh air and fluids. The windows of the sick-bay were kept wide open. Depending on what was wrong, she gave you salt-water enemas or salt-water nasal douches. At least, she was rumoured to give salt-water enemas, Emma had never met anyone who had had one. The nasal douches were bad enough. You had to sit over a nasty chipped enamel bowl with a mug and sniff the water back into your throat and spit it out. Then there were the drinks. Matron believed in flushing the germs out of your system. Every hour in the sick-bay she brought you a pint mug of icy-cold fruit squash. You could tell when it was coming from her careful tread on the stairs. Then of course you had to keep going to the lavatory. And while you were there, she would make your bed. Matron could make a bed like no-one else. She could straighten the friendly crumples out of warm sheets till they had the consistency of iron slabs. She could tuck them in so tightly that the mattress buckled and you couldn't straighten your toes. She did all this with a cheerful smile and an optimistic manner. She said that was the secret of successful nursing.

When Emma woke up with a sore throat three days before the

end of the summer term, she decided to say nothing. But she didn't eat her breakfast, and was pink and feverish by lunchtime.

Matron summoned her.

"Are you feeling quite well, Emma?"

"Yes!"

"Open your mouth!"

In went the cold, fragile thermometer, stabbing the tender place under her tongue.

"Mm! I think we might as well take you home."

Home!

"It's nearly the holidays, and *I've* had more than enough of you!" Matron smiled. She said she would drive Emma to Leehaven in her car. Emma was going home early! She was going to have three days extra holiday, alone with her mother, without Randolph! The soreness disappeared from her throat. She swallowed anxiously to make it come back.

Her mother had returned to England immediately after her father's death. She had collected Emma and her brother as if it were a perfectly normal visit, taken them to a tea shop, and told them. Neither of them had said very much, and Emma hadn't felt much either. She could hardly remember her father; she had not expected to see him again until she was grown up.

Their mother had explained that they would continue at their schools because that was what their father would have wished; she was going to settle in Leehaven, where there were a lot of old India people, and give the children a lovely time in the holidays. She did, too. However sad she might be feeling inside, she cooked them their favourite meals, took them to the pictures, taught them to play cards for matchsticks and took them up to London to visit the uncles and aunts.

Emma loved the journey to Leehaven. She loved the way the sun made all its roofs appear white. She knew the sea was the same sea as near the school, but it looked bluer, somehow, and sweeter. Sunbeams made rainbows in Matron's hair. Emma felt so happy, she kept forgetting she was supposed to be ill.

"Here we are, then, Emma!" The car stopped outside the antique shop that had the flat above it. The street was very quiet in the warm afternoon. "Can you walk, or shall I carry you?" Emma hesitated. Was Matron teasing? She didn't want to be in

Matron's arms when she met her mother. But if she admitted she was well enough to walk, might she be taken back to school? "Go on, Emma. Run up to your mother. Poor old Matron will bring your luggage."

"Matron – "

"What now?"

"Hold your head just like that – "

"What – ?"

Emma took a deep breath. "I *love* your hair," she said. Then she ran.

At first Emma hadn't liked the idea of living above an antique shop. It was Randolph's fault. He had said the antiques came from dead men's homes. He said that as soon as anyone died, the antique shop went round with a van and took away the furniture. Emma had asked her mother if that was true, and she had said no, of course not, and then Randolph had told her off for mentioning death in front of a widow.

Now she didn't care where their home was as long as she could be in it. She raced up the steps, banged on the door and sniffed. The flat had its own smells. Indian woods, and polish, and baking. Today there was a rather nasty smell, like bad meat.

But the door opened and there was her mother in a grey dress, looking very surprised. Emma hugged her; she had her own smells too: powder and soap and tobacco. Normally, Emma didn't like it when women wore a lot of powder and smoked; but with her own mother, it was just right.

Matron came up the steps with the luggage and explained about Emma being ill. Emma's mother smiled and thanked her but didn't invite her in for tea or anything. Emma was pleased. It might seem rude, but you didn't want school people in your home.

But wasn't her mother going to let *her* in? She stood there with a funny expression on her face, watching Matron drive away. Emma pushed past. The flat was just the same, chock-a-block with furniture sent from India. There was the glass-fronted cabinet where her father used to keep rows of bottles, all different colours. He used to make a great performance of telling the bearer which drinks to give which people. "Now, Mr Sanderson, I think you'll like to try this new malt." Suddenly she knew he was in the flat. There was the big table where they used to have meals on the verandah. She remembered a pretend dinner-party when she was tiny; and nearly being made to go to her room for bad manners. Was that when he had decided she must be sent away?

He wasn't here. Of course he wasn't here. The drinks cupboard was empty except for one small bottle. And on the table there was a typewriter.

"Ooh, Mummy. Are you writing a book?"

Her mother walked quickly over to the typewriter, pulled the paper out of it and covered it with a leather cover. "Of course not, dear. I'm just helping out a friend." She seemed rather guilty. "I used to be a very good typist, you know. That's how I used to earn my living, before I met your father." She lit a cigarette and blew smoke down her nose in beautiful streams. "Now I'd better put you to bed."

"I feel much better now, honestly!"

Emma had seen something else: an envelope marked, "The Miss Amy Anderson Typewriting Agency, Eastbourne."

"Mummy, do you have to earn your living now?"

"Of course not!" Her mother put the envelope away in a drawer. "Let's have tea."

Emma followed her into the kitchen. The nasty smell she had noticed was coming from a pan of bones simmering on the stove.

"Ugh! What's that?"

"Don't be rude, Emma! I'm just making some stock. For soup. I like soup."

"I don't."

"Set the trolley, there's a good girl."

"What kind of cake are we having?"

"Darling, I didn't know you were coming so I haven't made any cakes. Anyway, I thought you were supposed to be ill."

She made such lovely cakes, it had never occurred to Emma that she didn't have them all the time. They had tea out of delicate cups and plain biscuits off a plate with a doily. Emma dunked her biscuit in her tea and her mother pretended to be shocked. "No-one'll ever marry you if you do *that* sort of thing! And you should crook your little finger when you hold your tea-cup – like this!"

Emma giggled and tried it. "I don't want to get married. I'm going to live with you for ever when I grow up."

"That'll be wonderful! Er, Emma – "

"Yes?"

"I think I'll put the typewriter away before Randolph comes. And we won't say anything to him about it.

A secret! With her mother, from Randolph? "Why?"

"Oh well. He'll only want to have a turn, and then he'll break it, you know how clumsy he is." But Randolph wasn't clumsy at all, he was very clever with machines. "You can have a turn, though. Would you like to? Just don't tell him. There's a good girl."

Emma finished her tea and sat before the typewriter and typed out, MISS EMMA SARAH ORANGE. Then her mother showed her how to use carbon-paper. Emma was enthralled by the way it made copies of everything. It was like magic. "Can I have a bit, Mummy, to take back to school after the holidays?" She was thinking she could hire it out to anyone who had to do lines. You could do them in half the time.

"We'll see."

"Mummy, are we poor?"

"That's a strange question to ask your mother," she retorted sharply. "When you go to such a lovely school and have everything you want in the holidays."

It was as if Emma had been hit on the head with a hammer. It started to throb and ache. She hadn't meant to upset her mother. She had thought she had guessed why she had to do typing and live on bones and plain biscuits and didn't want Randolph to know; that was all. And she had thought of something that might help. "If I didn't go to boarding-school, would you still have to be a typist?"

Her mother looked very angry. And then she looked sad, and said softly, "It wouldn't make any difference, I'm afraid." And then she became angry again, furiously angry, but not with Emma. She seemed to have forgotten Emma was there. She seemed to be talking to herself, or a third person whom Emma could not see. "In fact, it would make things worse. Thanks to the *generosity* of Messrs Duckbill and Middlesex, my children go to two of the most expensive boarding-schools in the country but I can't afford to have them at home! They pay your fees, you see, Emma, and for your uniform, and everything." She turned pleading eyes on her. Emma looked away. She didn't want to be pleaded with by her mother. "It all goes directly to the schools. It doesn't pass through *my* hands. Well! We couldn't have that, could we! I might spend it all on high living! You see that!" She pointed at the gin bottle in the glass-fronted cabinet. "That's lasted me a month! And I buy three packets of cigarettes a week, and play bridge once! Do you know what he says, when Mr Middlesex sends me *my* pension? He encloses a little note that says 'so pleased we are able to provide the dear children with the education their father would have wanted.' Hah! As if it was nothing to do with me!"

Suddenly Emma felt very ill. Her head was all stuffed up with her cold. Through her swimming brain she realised why her mother didn't want Randolph to know about all this. And she felt honoured that she knew, but a bit resentful too. Because from now on, whenever her mother gave her anything, she would know where it came from.

And Randolph would be able to enjoy the holidays, thinking they could have outings and treats because they were still rich. But Emma would have to pretend always to prefer things that didn't cost money, like walks.

But there was one consolation. She went to bed. She felt horrible but safe. It wasn't true what they said at school, that her mother wouldn't have her at home because she was bad. Her mother longed to have her at home. It was all Mr Middlesex's fault.

3

Towards the end of the summer holidays, the Prime Minister came on the wireless and said there was going to be a war. Randolph said, "Good show!" Emma looked at her mother. Her face was blank and matt and dead, as if she had known there was going to be a war and had put extra powder on to avoid showing any expression.

Emma wondered what it meant. It was a lovely day. She didn't suppose it meant anything very much. And anyway, they would be all right.

Perhaps her mother had known in advance. When an air-raid warning went off, she knew just what to do. She took them down to the cellar under the antique shop. She even had a key. They sat and sweated among the tall, dark wardrobes and grandfather clocks. They breathed in each other's breath. Emma imagined that when they came out, Leehaven would have disappeared. Grass would have grown over the ruins. It would be like coming up into the middle of the Downs.

The All Clear sounded. It had been a false alarm. Everything was quite normal, and they went for a walk.

The first news back at school was that Matron had left to become an army nurse. Lessons were suspended so that the school could be sealed against bombs and gas. They sewed blinds and curtains, queued at shops for material. No-one must go anywhere without her gas-mask. They practised wearing them. They were smelly and heavy. Emma thought wearing hers was like being in her coffin already.

And every night it was "Have you done the windows?" "Have you done the fireplaces?" The fireplaces must be taped over and sealed in case the Germans sent mustard-gas down the chimney. Emma hated mustard. It burned your mouth. So mustard-gas must burn your lungs. She imagined choking up bloody cinders from her insides. She imagined a German soldier, yellow and gassy like Aladdin's genie, curled in the fireplace, waiting to spring through the flimsy paper screen.

The gas didn't come. But there were air-raids, and the Germans were just across the Channel. Any day they might put their ships into the water and sail to England. The girls sat in their shelters and heard them bombing nearby ports; and listened for the English bombers flying off to fight them, counting them going over and counting them coming back. There were always fewer when they came back, and then girls who had fathers in the RAF cried.

The government wanted to fortify the south-east coast. They wanted to line it with soldiers. They wanted to house the soldiers in Sussex schools. The schools would be evacuated to Cornwall, where they would live in hotels, shared with more schools.

"I won't go," said Emma.

Randolph, whose school was also being evacuated, said, "Some of the chaps are going to miss the train and hide out on the Downs and fight the Germans when they come."

Emma looked at him coolly. "Are you?"

"No fear!"

She was disgusted. It was disgusting. He might have been joking. But it was disgusting, whether he was or he wasn't. She said, "The Germans wouldn't be scared of *you*, in any case."

He just grinned. "I don't blame them! Only sense I can see in

Home Guarding is they'll be the first to know! If I was them and saw the invasion coming, I'd be on my bike and off to the Highlands of Scotland!"

Their mother smiled indulgently. "I hope you'd stop long enough to give the alarm, dear."

"I'd tip you the wink on my way through Leehaven, Mum," he conceded, "and you could ring the bells."

"What bells?" said Emma. Would they have bells at the new school – or hotel – in Cornwall? Probably. And probably they would ring twice as loud and twice as often for twice as many girls.

"If the Germans invade," her mother explained, "the Home Guard will give the order to ring the church bells. Then all over the country, the churches will hear each other and ring *their* bells." She added with pride: "Leehaven's bells may be the ones to start it off."

Emma felt sick. She croaked. "And then what will everybody do?"

"Run for it," said Randolph.

"Now, now, he's only joking. If it comes to it, Randolph will do his duty, won't you dear?"

"It'll all be over by the time I'm old enough!"

"You hope!" said Emma. "I'm not going to stupid old Cornwall. If I see a German soldier I'll throw pepper in his eyes and stick a knife in him."

Her mother made an odd sound. Randolph put his arm round her and turned on Emma. "That's a fine thing to say in front of Mummy! After what happened to Daddy!"

Emma hadn't meant anything. But her mother started to cry. "I'm sorry, Mummy, I'm sorry," Emma implored. But she wouldn't stop for a long time. When she did stop, her mother said, "It wasn't you, Emma. It wasn't your fault. It was just something I thought of. Because I feel the same as you. If they do come, I'll want to kill them. Every one of them. But then I thought . . . that man who killed Daddy. He probably felt the same. That it was his country and we shouldn't be there. And if we do see a German soldier, he'll probably be a married man. With children. And . . ."

Randolph said, "That's different."

Emma looked from her brother who was a coward to her mother who seemed to be supporting the enemy.

Why didn't countries just keep themselves to themselves and leave each other alone? That would be the simplest solution.

It was surprisingly easy not to go to Cornwall. She didn't argue. She packed her things. She had her name ticked off on numerous lists. She took her seat on the train. Then, just as the whistle went, she jumped off and went home to her mother.

Her mother ordered her, urged her, begged her to go. But once Emma had convinced her that she wasn't going, she got quite used to the idea.

"You'll have to go to school," she warned.

Emma shrugged. There weren't any good schools left, and precious few children. A local vicar's wife set up an impromptu school in a church hall. Emma went. But none of the teachers seemed to be proper teachers, and the other children were very backward. Soon Emma was teaching more than she was learning.

Outrage after outrage was visited on Leehaven. The cinema, the church, the toy-shop and numerous houses were bombed into blackened craters. Barbed wire glittered on the mined beaches. Military installations dotted the Downs.

Still, Leehaven knew a few tricks of its own. It wouldn't long tolerate mines in its beaches, not even to keep back the Germans. Its shingle shifted under heavy seas; the mines came glinting to the surface and exploded unpredictably, causing false alarms and deaths. Eventually sappers were sent in to take the mines away. No-one knew if they had found them all. But the immediate danger of invasion seemed to have passed. Leehaven could rely on its barbed wire and its stout heart.

The worst outrage of all came when two officers were billeted in the flat and Emma had to give up her room. She was furious. She wouldn't speak to the officers. This was her home. She had never had a proper home. Even in India, life in the bungalow had been overshadowed for as far back as Emma could remember by talk of going away to school. That dreadful little book! The insufferable Donald and Clara! Emma wanted a home.

Perhaps it was because of what was happening to her body that she wanted it so much. Matron had explained it all one morning when the dormitory prefect woke up with her bed full of blood. "It means that your uterus is spring cleaning itself, ready to be a home for your baby when you get married." For the first time Emma started to think about being married. How lovely it would be, with your own safe hearth and babies. She didn't much like the children at the school, but her own would be different. She loved to watch the rich red blood drip out of her and disperse in the water. She wondered if there was something wrong with her, that she loved it so much. It didn't hurt at all. She just wished it didn't turn so nasty on the sanitary towel.

And the beauty of the blood was nothing compared with what was happening to the rest of her. She could almost see herself changing by the minute as she stared into the mirror. Her hair was light and wavy and soft. Her skin was smooth and pure, her eyes full of expression. She made herself think about death and tragedy and loneliness – they filled with tears. She thought about love and being married – they shone. Her body was slender and round. Soldiers whistled at her in the street. She just wished she had some nice clothes.

It wasn't fair. Her mother still had cupboards full of clothes from India. But Emma had grown out of everything she had had that was nice. The dress-shops in Leehaven were all so dreary. Everything seemed to be designed for fat women of fifty, and there were never enough coupons. Her mother tried to help her to make a dress and a skirt, but neither of them was very clever at it.

"It's too tight," her mother would say, through a mouthful of pins.

"No, it *isn't*. I want it like that!"

But already her mother would be unpicking Emma's laboriously-sewn stitches. Perhaps she was right and Emma wouldn't have been able to walk very easily in the skirt. But how could she explain that she wanted to show herself off?

Her mother wouldn't understand. With all her lovely dresses, she didn't seem to mind whether she made the best of herself or not. She and some other ladies from her club had taken to donning breeches and going to a neighbouring farm to work. Sometimes when she came home in the evenings, she didn't bother to change out of the breeches. Even if Mr Squires and Captain Hamilton were there she didn't bother. She just sat around like a man and smoked and drank and joked with them. No-one took any notice of Emma.

"Why don't Mr Squires and Captain Hamilton talk to me?"

"Because you don't talk to them."

"I don't want them here. I want my room."

One night when Mr Squires was away on manoeuvres, she woke up and found that her mother wasn't in bed. And she heard strange sounds coming from the living-room, where she had left her with Captain Hamilton. She tiptoed out of bed and listened at the door.

"Come on, Ruby! You're a hot-blooded woman! It must be years since you – "

Ruby! No one called her that! In front of Emma, the officers always called her Mrs Orange and were very polite. How dare he call her a hot-blooded woman?

"No, Peter. You don't understand. I have a daughter – "

" – who ought to be away at school!"

Emma grasped the door handle. She would kill that man. She would just kill him.

"Come on, Ruby. You know you want me."

"Yes. Yes, I do, but – "

Shocked, Emma let go of the door and went back to bed. But when her mother came in an hour later, she determined to let her know that she had heard. "Hello, Mummy," she said, in a calm, wide-awake voice. Her mother stared through the darkness as if she had been shot. "Are you going to send me away now?" said Emma.

There was a long pause. Her mother undressed and got into bed. "No, dear," she said softly. It was Captain Hamilton who was sent away. He was replaced by a rigid, taciturn man called Captain Derry. Emma was glad and hoped that Captain Hamilton had been put into a really uncomfortable billet. She just wished his departure hadn't made her mother so unhappy.

They longed for meat, but there was hardly any to be had. Mr Pritchett the butcher made special sausages that could be sold off ration because there was hardly any meat in them. Heaven alone knew what they were made of. They were colourless and floppy. In the frying pan they shrivelled and squeaked, burst, and burnt into cinders, but the officers seemed to like them.

One snowy day when she was fifteen, Emma went to queue for sausages. She was wearing a coat of her mother's and felt shapeless and horrible. She was depressed because she had heard a man on the wireless saying the war could last another ten years. Till she was twenty-five! She would be much too old then to care how she looked.

Instead of Mr Pritchett, there was a sailor in uniform behind the counter. "Yes, madam," he said. She hardly looked at him. She gave him her order. He weighed out the sausages and wrapped them up in a parcel with twine.

He said, "It may never happen, you know."

"What?"

"Whatever you're looking so miserable about."

Emma hated being told she looked miserable. Men were always shouting. "Cheer up, love!" in the street. What did they expect?

He said, "Don't I know you?"

Astonished, she looked into his face. His hair was as blond as hers, and very short. He had a straight nose and gaunt features, but his smile was very wide and cheerful. If he was a sailor, what was he doing serving in a butcher's shop?

She didn't recognise him, but she felt herself turning crimson and nearly ran away.

He said, "I know! I've got it! You *have* grown up!" And soon he was regaling the whole shopful of snow-covered shoppers with the story of how, long ago, he had rescued her from a bull and taken her for a ride in his canoe.

4

His name was Anthony Pritchett. He was twenty. Emma could call him Tony. He was the butcher's son, home on leave from the navy. He had been living in Leehaven all this time and they had never run into each other!

He took her tobogganing on the Downs. He had built the toboggan himself. They walked up the hill through the thick, unblemished snow, dragging the toboggan behind them on a loop of rope. The sky was blue-grey, threatening another fall of snow.

He wanted her to come down on the toboggan with him, lying on top of him. She wouldn't.

"All right then, I'll lie on top of you!"

"No!"

"Then you'll have to go down by yourself!"

"We – ell – "

"Or not go down at all?"

"I'll go down by myself."

He went first, to show her how. He pushed off with his feet

and shot down the hillside in a swish of snow. When it was her turn, she just went round in circles, hit a stone and ended up buried.

"You're supposed to steer!" he laughed, digging her out.

"You didn't tell me."

He put the toboggan sideways so that it wouldn't move and lay her on it. He got hold of her feet and moved them about. "Like that. Only your stupid legs are too short."

He took her to a place where the Downs formed a kind of ridge. He said they would fly off into space. "Game?" he said. "Yes!" She lay on top of him. Faster and faster went the toboggan. And off – and down – and they were rolling in the snow.

"How long are you on leave for?" asked Emma.

"Another week."

She was horrified. "Can I see you *every day*?"

"I say! Hold hard!"

He had been round the whole world. He had seen icebergs as tall as the Downs. He had seen islands where the girls wore grass skirts. Emma was instantly jealous. He had been ninety days on one wave – "

"You have not!"

"Well. Perhaps it was eighty-nine days."

"Oh, tell the truth! Don't treat me like a baby!"

"I'm not. I'm only teasing. Honestly, Emma. I never forgot that day I met you. Did you get into terrible trouble?"

"I don't want to talk about school."

He told her about the awful silence in the middle of the ocean when you turned off your engines to listen for submarines.

"Aren't you scared?"

"Not as scared as when I come home on leave."

"What do you mean?"

"Lying in bed, waiting for the bombs. You women and children are the real heroes. I can tell you."

She looked at him through her eyelashes. "Which am I – women or children?"

"Which do you think?" He kissed her cheek.

Walking back to town they passed a church with a wedding party coming out. The groom wore a soldier's uniform, the bride wore white. Everyone looked terribly cold. There was a page-boy shivering in satin, and an old lady took off her fur coat and put it round him.

"I hate my surname," said Emma. And then she was horrified: what if he thought she was hinting?

"You hang on to it," he laughed, "until someone offers you a better one."

What could he mean? *Emma Pritchett*. It sounded much nicer than Emma Orange.

He went away. She touched his sailor's collar for luck at the station and he promised to write. She dared not believe him. But he did – he sent long letters and begged her to reply because he was lonely and (he admitted it now) frightened. He never said where he was. He wasn't allowed to. It made her angry to think of an officer reading his letters to make sure he hadn't given away any secrets. As if she were a German spy or something. He always ended the letters, "Love from Tony".

She ended her replies, "Lots of love, Emma". She had to post them "c/o the Post Office". The post office would know where he was, and forward them.

He asked her for a photograph of herself. She hadn't got one. But Captain Derry had a camera. She asked him if he would take her picture. In his polite way, he said, "I should be honoured, Miss Orange."

"Who's the photograph for, Emma?" asked her mother with a smile. It angered Emma that she said "who for" rather than "what for". She hadn't told her mother about Tony, and she hoped she hadn't noticed the letters.

"Nobody."

She put on a summer frock that showed her arms. Tony had never seen her arms. Captain Derry took a whole roll, but only three of the pictures came out. In one of them, she was grinning. In another, she had her eyes closed. The third only showed her face, but it had a very serious, grown-up expression. She decided to send that one.

There followed a very worrying time when she didn't hear from him and she hoped the photograph hadn't been a disappointment.

A few days after her sixteenth birthday, she was in the butcher's shop. Mr Pritchett winked at her but wouldn't serve her. Every time anyone else came in, he would serve them and ignore Emma.

At last they were alone.

"Happy birthday," he said, passing her a huge parcel. "Not a word, now, careless talk costs lives." And he made her hide the parcel in her bag.

"How did you know it was my birthday?"

He winked again. "A little bird told me!"

"Tony?"

"No names, no pack drill."

But she knew he had sent a message to his father to give her a birthday present. So he couldn't have been too disappointed with the photograph. He must be coming home soon. She skipped back to the flat and opened the parcel.

It was an enormous leg of pork with lean meat, thick, bristly skin and a plump trotter hanging off the end. Her mouth watered and she turned on the stove and started to cook it. She almost wished she could eat it raw. She looked to see if they had any vegetables to go with it. There were some potatoes, and an onion that was sprouting green leaves. She longed for her mother and the officers to come home and enjoy it. She kept opening the oven door to see that fat dripping and boiling in the pan.

She hardly knew why a certain unease started to mingle with her pleasure. She kept wishing she could share the meat with her mother alone. But it was no good. She and Captain Derry arrived together.

"Something smells good," said her mother.

"I should say so," said Captain Derry.

Then their faces seemed to freeze.

"Where did you get it, dear?"

"The butcher gave it to me! For my birthday!"

"Emma, love, that was very kind of him, but – "

"I won't touch it," Captain Derry declared. "Disgraceful. Just vegetables for me, please."

Emma opened the oven and stared at the beautiful joint. The crackling looked light and crisp.

"You'll have to take it back, dear," said her mother softly. "Tell him you're sorry, but you can't possibly accept it. He'll understand."

"I won't touch it," the captain repeated. Emma flared, "Don't then! It isn't for you!"

"Now listen, young lady. Perhaps it's not my place to say this, but with men risking their lives on the high seas, and your mother working her fingers to the bone to produce food, it's a fine thing when her own daughter's helping the Germans by undermining the ration system."

Emma looked at her mother. Would she stand up for her? She had to. But she didn't. She just looked embarrassed and distressed. How Emma hated these officers! If they weren't here, she and her mother could enjoy this pork in peace! But if her mother wouldn't stand up for her –

"Mummy," she said clearly, "*you* said we *should* help the Germans. Or if we didn't, we would be just the same as that man who killed Daddy."

"No, dear. That's not what I said – "

"You did, you did, you did!"

Captain Derry said, "Excuse me," and went to his room.

Emma wouldn't look at her mother. With trembling hands she spread newspaper on the table, took the hot joint out of the oven, put it down on the paper and wrapped it up. She picked up the fragrant, greasy parcel.

"Where are you going, Emma?"

"I'm taking it back to Mr Pritchett."

"But he'll be closed by now."

"I'm doing what you told me."

Alone in the blacked-out street, she wondered what to do. She could go and knock on Mr Pritchett's door – but how offended he would be! And what would Tony say when he heard? How dare the captain say that wicked thing about men risking their lives on the sea when he himself sat safe in her mother's flat, smugly eating vegetables and sausages?

Heat was seeping through the paper round the joint, burning her hands. She could throw the wretched thing away, but what if somebody found it, what if somebody saw? It probably was black market, and she didn't want to get Mr Pritchett into trouble. She was hungry, but she couldn't eat it all.

She would throw it into the sea. Yes, that would be the right thing to do. When the tide went out it would carry the pork away. Did cooked meat float? Maybe by some wild coincidence it would float out to Tony and he would look over the side of his ship and see it and guess what had happened.

You weren't supposed to go on the beach. The beach belonged to the army, just like everything else. If the Germans did come and take over the town, how would it be different, that was what Emma would like to know.

She came out on to the sea-front. She could hear men's voices above the wash of the sea but they were too far away to see anything.

She wished there was some moonlight to help her through the wire. She would just have to go slowly and carefully. She smiled to remember the day she first met Tony on the downs. What a sight she must have looked, all mud and prickles from the blackberry bush she had just collided with.

The soldiers had removed the steps that used to lead to the beach. She walked along looking for a place where the tide had piled shingle high enough for her to get down. She put the pork on the edge of the sea-front and lowered herself, carefully avoiding the wire. When she stepped on the unexploded mine, the bang was heard all over Leehaven, and bits of her body and bits of pork were found all along the sea-front.

Jackie
1950 . . .

A combination of errors at the War Office and a leg broken in three places on the rugby field kept Randolph Orange out of active service until the last years of the war. "As soon as Hitler heard I'd joined, he surrendered," was how he liked to put it, when it was all over.

He hurried home and married Helen Forster, who had had a crush on him ever since they met as children on the boat from India. Helen's parents lent them the money to buy a large but rather insubstantial house in southwest London, then died and left a thoughtful will which cancelled the debt. Randolph was pleased about this (not having known them well) because the war had upset his schooling and he lacked qualifications for a career. "And I haven't made up my mind what I want to be when I grow up," he liked to amuse his friends and exasperate his wife by saying.

She meanwhile set about filling the house with children: Max, William, Jackie, Julia and Kate.

With two elder brothers and two younger sisters, it soon dawned on Jackie that everyone else in the world had a partner; but she was the clever one, which gave her a special place in her father's heart. And since her father and mother were frequently not on speaking terms she consoled herself with his special attention.

Her brothers and sisters were pale and short like their mother, but she, with her sturdy build and black curls looked just as she fancied her father would have looked if he had been born a girl. She was only sorry that her athletic prowess was not equal to her appearance of strength and agility; she was actually rather clumsy and could not catch a ball.

From her first day at the council primary school which, to his chagrin, was all Randolph Orange could afford for his children, she liked to bring him trophies of her success, books she could read right through without stumbling, spelling tests with ten-out-of-ten at the bottom, and finally, when she was eleven, a free place at the grammar school.

But her father's real love was sport, and in that her elder brothers outdid her. They were always getting selected for school teams and coming home muddy and triumphant, having saved the day.

This sort of thing bored Jackie when it related to her brothers, but she loved to go with her father to his cricket club or his rugby club at weekends. If he was playing, she checked his form; but what she liked best was to be a spectator with him and his kind, deep-voiced friends, to stand on the touch-line or boundary and applaud or groan with them and shout:

"Come on, our side!"

The first time she shouted this at cricket was also the last: it was firmly explained to her that you shouted only at rugby matches, or soccer, if you went to soccer, which you didn't, because it was common. To shout at cricket matches was a sign of poor breeding.

Jackie's father was very keen on breeding. It was the same as not being common, but not necessarily the same as having money. The Orange family did not have money but they were well bred. It was all to do with the war, and India and expensive boarding schools.

Jackie never quite understood, but she got a feel for the idea. Her parents had both gone to good schools, along with poor Aunt Emma who was blown up in the war. Her father spoke of it all with nostalgia, but it struck Jackie as depressing; there were photographs of the three children in dumpy, old-fashioned uniforms, clustered round a miserable pony.

Their street had been badly bombed. Jackie's father called it a suburb, but her mother called it a slum, particularly when they were quarrelling.

He would say, "Where's my rugby shirt for tomorrow?"

And she would say, "On the floor where you left it, I expect."

"What? You haven't washed it?"

"I haven't had time, I've been keeping this slum clean."

Sometimes it would develop further. Jackie knew the words.

"Why didn't you send it to the laundry?" he demanded.

"We can't afford the laundry."

"I'll decide what we can afford and what we can't!"

"Afford a washing machine, then, and a decent Hoover that

doesn't electrocute me every time I try to keep this slum clean."
While she said this, he would grinningly conduct an orchestra
with a fork to show that he too had heard it all before.

Jackie's mother had big red hands from washing for seven in
the deep cracked sink. On washing days her hands and face were
like raw meat. Hanging from her pale, thin, ever-moving body
like growths, the hands would batter nappies, throttle shirts; or
pause, wipe themselves, sharpen themselves into dry fingers and
pick up the wet cigarette that smouldered nearby. She would
drink at the smoke like a baby at a bottle, then a tap of a red
index finger would knock of the ash, and back the red hands
would plunge into the suds.

"How am I expected to keep this slum clean when . . .?" was
the prologue to a hundred guilt-instilling questions. Theirs was
the only old house in the street; Jackie's mother cast wistful
glances at the neat new council houses put up over the bomb
damage at the other end. Her father declared he would drown his
family one by one before he would let them live in a council
house. The tangled patch of waste-ground between them and the
estate he called a *cordon sanitaire*. Yet their house was rather dirty.
Even the Hoover turned up its nose at dust, belching it back in
insolent clouds. "Why can't we live somewhere decent?" her
mother would demand. "My parents never meant us to live here
for ever – just till you could afford something better!" Her father's
riposte was as deadly as the Hoover's: "You wanted five children,
now you've got five children." He managed to say this without
making any of the children feel that he or she was individually
surplus to requirements; it was their mother's fault.

According to Jackie's mother, the bombs had loosened the
bricks. The house, she said, was crumbling as they lived in it.
That was why it was so dusty. And dusting just encouraged the
process. "How am I supposed to keep this slum clean when
nobody ever puts anything away?" Sometimes she dreamed up
schemes: "Homework things *here*, hamster things *there*, and
anything you want washed goes in the *laundry basket* or it won't
be done!" And then she changed the schemes before anyone had
got used to the first one: "I'm going to get a box. A *huge* box.
And *anything* that *anybody* leaves lying about will just be chucked
in. And if it gets broken that's just *too bad*. How am I supposed
to keep this slum clean when I never get any co-operation?"

Her voice rasped all the more painfully on Jackie's nerves for her complaints being utterly justified: everyone had their jobs, written on notices on the wall in intricate rotas, and no-one did them. One of the things that made it easy not to do them was that as soon as their mother had allocated a job to someone, she immediately felt guilty for having done so and did the job herself. "Right! As from today, I'm not making *anyone's* bed; if you lot want to sleep in a heap of rags it's up to you! Four days, a week, of unmade beds would pass, and then, perhaps, it would be time to change the sheets, and since she was changing the sheets, she might as well finish the job . . .

As the eldest girl, Jackie might have become over-burdened, but as soon as she got her eleven-plus her father stepped in to protect her. He would come up behind her as she stood at the sink and say, "Come along now, you shouldn't be doing this, haven't you got any homework? Let your poor old dad who never passed an exam in his life do it." Gratefully she would flee to her room, her conscience clear. For a couple of minutes she would hear her father's hands chinking and fiddling in the sink; she would then pretend not to hear as he went out.

When people asked Jackie what her father's job was, she usually said, "He's a commercial traveller." He certainly travelled a lot. His respect for Jackie's brains did not mean that he held any brief for what he called "ten-a-penny paper qualifications". "But we Oranges can sell anything," he said. "It's in the blood." Once before Jackie could remember, he had sold large secondhand cars that a dealer he knew had bought up during the war when the owners couldn't get petrol; then it was pork pies from a factory belonging to his cousin; and he also did occasional deals with Burgess & Croft Army Surplus, which was why the house, whatever else it lacked, was well equipped with lamps and bits of sheepskin, and the children all had huge winter coats. Sometimes he went door to door with a flashing smile and a briefcase, selling insurance or collecting football pool coupons. Mrs Orange said he ought to get a proper job in a proper office with a proper salary; living on commissions got on her nerves. She laughed at the term *commercial traveller*; she said he was no better than a spiv.

By the time Jackie was wrestling with difficult subjects like Latin and mathematics, the discord at home had become more than a niggling part of normal life, like toothache or colds, and had taken on major dimensions of pain. The house itself seemed to sulk as her mother rattled and bashed round it with her smoky Hoover: *shut up, shut up!* Jackie screamed inside as her parents shouted at each other. She wished she could shrug her shoulders and accept it as normal, as her brothers and sisters did; but she didn't want it to be normal, it frightened her.

She started to go away, as many weekends as she decently could, to the most peaceful place she knew: Leehaven, where Granny Ruby lived. Her father's mother had always been Granny Ruby to the children, initially to distinguish her from grandparents on the other side of the family. Now that there were no other grandparents, the name stuck. It was a nice name: ordinary and special all at once, which was what the visits were.

Her father grinned. "Can't say I blame you, Jackie!" He cocked his thick, dark eyebrows in the direction of wherever his wife was. "I'd come with you if I was allowed."

Her mother's protests at Jackie's frequent going away were usually silent. Once she said, "It's a funny thing, Jackie. When I was at boarding school, I used to swear on oath, that however rich or poor I was I would never, *never* send my children away. Now you can't wait to shake the dust of your home from your feet." Jackie had nothing to say to this, and the remark was never repeated.

2

Granny Ruby never bought a platform ticket. Like the other Leehaven grandmothers she considered it outrageous to be expected to pay to stand on the platform of her own station. So they all waited at the barrier in their tweeds and tailored raincoats, with headscarves and shopping baskets, craning their necks for a glimpse of their particular swan among the other affable but mediocre geese getting off the holiday train.

Jackie thought her grandmother very beautiful; she would be as beautiful as the Queen Mother if she could afford jewels and more new clothes. But Jackie liked her old clothes well enough, they were always in soft, edible colours, coffee and toffee and greengage. It was no duty to hug Granny Ruby and kiss her; she smelled gently of dry-cleaning, soap and fragrant tobacco.

"Well, now! Let me have a look at you! Haven't you grown?" Being told she had grown was part of the price of going to stay with Granny Ruby, a sort of hotel bill. "And hów's my favourite grandchild?"

"How's my favourite granny?"

"That's not much! I'm your only granny."

There was a routine for Jackie's visits. They went to certain shops, and Jackie was asked what she wanted. There was no need to ask. From Heath & Heather a tin of Fru-Grains, a breakfast cereal that looked like bits of driftwood but was sweet and nutty and went down perfectly with sliced bananas and top of the milk. (At home, breakfast was porridge or cornflakes.) Apple turnovers from the baker's. (Jackie's mother said bought cakes were never as good as home-made, but she never had time to make cakes.) A quarter of a pound of Sharp's toffees, and peaches, fresh or tinned. All Jackie had to do was answer a few questions.

"How's your mother?"

"She's spring cleaning."

Granny Ruby coughed delicately. The calendar said September. "You should tell your mother it's just a matter of getting organised." She moved on to ask after Max and Bill and Julia and Kate, but this was a formality; Jackie was the favourite. The shopping basket filled up: chocolate mousse, Tizer, baked beans, a plucked chicken. Jackie knew Granny Ruby only had a small pension, but she took in typing to help with extras. Nobody knew about this but Jackie. Granny Ruby saved the most important question for the end. "How's your father?"

"He got eighty, not out."

"He was always one for sport! Well, he needs to relax now and again. He's got a lot of responsibilities, your poor father."

They shared out the weight of the shopping basket between them. It was like sharing Randolph. In a special way, only they understood him. Jackie wished sometimes that he in turn was nice to his mother. He only visited her as a duty, and talked about her as a joke.

Jackie tried not to breathe through her nose as they climbed the damp stairs to Granny Ruby's flat. Granny Ruby panted slightly and stuck out her bottom in the funny way she had of walking with her rheumaticky hips. Jackie loved the flat. The tiny sitz-bath and the chamber pot you had to use at night if you didn't want to go all the way downstairs to the landlady's lavatory were novelties, not hardships. Everything was so snug and ordered. The carpets were old but looked as if they would last for ever, rippling their Indian reds and golds and purples. The wooden furniture smelled of polish. There were some exquisite glass and gold and ivory ornaments; sometimes there seemed fewer than last time, but Jackie pretended not to notice; if Granny Ruby did not want anyone to know that she sometimes sold things, that was up to her. And there were pictures on the wall, of the family in India: her dead grandfather, her dead Aunt Emma as a pretty little girl on a horse. The pictures were turning brown.

"Now you should tell your mother that if I can keep my home nice when I haven't even got a proper bathroom, there's no excuse for her in that big house."

"Mummy says it's the bomb damage," said Jackie.

Granny Ruby was a bit scornful. "Are they still bombing London? I heard the war had ended."

Jackie did not like to argue with her grandmother. But sometimes her confusion made her mischievous. "Mummy says if Daddy got a proper job, we could move somewhere nicer."

Granny Ruby said firmly, "It's a *lovely* house. Nice and big. I'm quite looking forward to coming to live there in my old age." She said this very cosily, very jokily, very often. "It just needs to be looked after, like all old houses. You should tell your mother she should get some help."

Jackie would not pass on this message. She had heard the reply too many times. "I won't have another woman going down on her hands and knees on my floors! It's all very well for your mother, Randolph; she's never done a hand's turn in her life! She only wants me to get a charwoman so that she can think she's got servants in the family again! Something to boast about with all the other memsahibs!"

Both Jackie's parents referred to Granny Ruby's friends as "the memsahibs": stiff, gruff, amused old ladies who sat in rows in leather chairs at the oddly-named Constitutional Club and talked about "In-jah". Showing off to them was another of Jackie's duties, a difficult one, because the penalties for showing off at home were severe. To counteract Jackie's reluctance as a young child, Granny Ruby had invented a very irritating tactic. It involved standing Jackie in front of the expectant memsahibs and saying something outrageously incorrect, such as, "Jackie, what was that nursery rhyme you said so nicely? Little Red Ridinghood sat in a corner, how does your garden grow?" This would exasperate Jackie into repeating the rhyme correctly, and only the beaming smiles on the lips of the memsahibs told her that this was what Granny Ruby had wanted all along. She was pleased by the attention but felt slightly tricked. That was the kindergarten version; now it was, "Jackie's passed her matriculation, haven't you, Jackie?" And Jackie would blush and say, "Well, it was the eleven-plus actually." The memsahibs were impressed. They all had grandchildren, but none of them, it seemed, had passed anything.

On Sundays they went to church. This was perhaps to show off too, but Jackie didn't mind. They only went at Easter and Christmas at home, and she hoped that these visits to St Stephen's, Leehaven, would count in her favour when it came to the last judgement, about which she had begun to think rather uneasily. After the service she liked to wander round the old church, looking at the brasses and the stained-glass windows. There was a Roll of Honour, a sort of stone book in a glass case, with dead men's names on the pages.

"Why isn't Aunt Emma on the Roll of Honour, Granny Ruby?"

"Well, silly, she wasn't a soldier, was she?"

It was as if it offended Granny Ruby's sense of what was proper: if you lost someone in the war, it was supposed to be a soldier-son, named in the Roll of Honour. Jackie had never met Aunt Emma, but she felt sorry for her and angry with her; she felt Aunt Emma had a lot to do with the tension between her mother and Granny Ruby. As if Mummy had taken into herself the anger and sadness her friend Emma had felt about being sent away from India, and sought revenge on Granny Ruby, since her own mother, who had sent *her* away, was also dead. And perhaps Granny Ruby was angry with Mummy for being alive when her Emma was dead. There had been as much death in Granny Ruby's life as there was hard work and exasperation in Jackie's mother's. Jackie didn't really blame them for being a bit unreasonable at times. But it frightened her.

Jackie wailed inside at her failure to be either athletic or dainty. She was just a lump, she decided. And now her mother wanted to take her up to town for her first bra.

"Why can't we just get one off the counter at Marks and Sparks?"

"They don't fit you properly at Marks."

"Oh, *Mummy*. We can take it back if it doesn't fit."

"It's very important to be fitted."

"*You* never get fitted. You just go to the reduced counter."

It was no good. Jackie's mother had obviously been reading an article in a magazine about the importance of having first bras fitted. She said, "It hardly matters for me." Some days she got so far behind with the housework that she didn't even get dressed; just wore her blue dressing-gown, which made Jackie's father furious. The bra-buying expedition, though, was obviously an occasion. She put on a suit and a hat and a plastic mac in case it rained.

At the shop, a tight-corseted lady with blue hair took Jackie into a cubicle, measured her, and expressed surprise that such a big girl had such a little bust. She sold her a 32, Teenie-Weenie Cup, white. It had to be white, it was a school rule: pink or black would show through white blouses.

"They're certainly very particular at that school of yours," her mother said. Mortified by the saleslady and her tape-measure, Jackie tried to make conversation. "Weren't they at yours?"

"My school! That dump!" Her mother screwed up her face. There was something embarrassing about a grown woman using slang words against her school. "I *hated* it. I'm glad you're not like me and you're going to do well. All your teachers say you're university material." They did indeed. Jackie had not yet clearly established what university was, but it was assumed that she would go to it. People spoke vaguely of all-night coffee parties, delivering post at Christmas and rag weeks. "At that dump, a bell went for everything. A bell to get up, a bell to strip your bed, there was even a bell after breakfast to go to the lavatory to do number two. Shall we have tea?" They never had meals out. Jackie wanted to go swimming. "I sometimes think that's why I can't get organised, as your grandmother says, I'm always waiting for a bell to tell me what to do next."

Tea came. Her mother lit a cigarette. When she took it out of her mouth it was all wet. She never smoked as if she were used to it.

"I used to count the bells at school. They were quite reassuring, funnily enough. If I can just hold on till the next bell – two thousand more bells and my mother will come. One thousand, nine hundred and ninety-nine . . . Emma hated the bells. In the end she simply refused to go to school. But that's the sort of thing that happens, Jackie, to children whose mothers don't look after them properly. It's just as bad if they go out to work. I was reading about it in a magazine." She kept peeping into the bag that contained the Teenie-Weenie bra. She kept wanting to know if Jackie was sure that it had felt comfortable. It was all Jackie could do to stop her getting it out and making her try it on there and then.

3

Jackie found her O-levels easy, even Latin, her worst subject. She came blinking from the exam-room to where her best friend Mary Flannery waited in the sun. Mary had rigid back-combed hair, and, in further breach of school regulations, wore a Flower Power badge on the bulging bust of her gymslip.

Jackie fell laughing into her arms. "Bloody gerunds! Why do I do it? Why not domestic science like you?"

"Ah." Mary gave an inelegant skip. "You're *university material*." She mimed going into a shop. "A yard of university material, please. I want to make some knickers."

"Oh well, no more Latin after today." No more Mary soon, either. Mary was going to secretarial college. School would be a sorry business without her. Three weeks of term remained and the weather was good and hot. Jackie would have liked to rest, go swimming with Mary, make a final attempt to cement their friendship against their imminent parting, to open up enough unanswered questions and unfulfilled plans to ensure they really would see each other and ring up and write; but lessons went on. Mary had a theory about school. "Want it both ways, don't they?" She mimicked the headmistress. " 'Work hard to get through your exams, girls. But just because you've got through your exams, don't think you can stop working hard.' Shall we sneak out and go to Le Disque?"

Jackie shook her head. Le Disque was a coffee-bar frequented by hippies. She had been there a couple of times, sipping gingerly, for the coffee was rumoured to be laced with addictive drugs. It was one on a list of places where the Orange children were not allowed to go because it was common. It was an arbitrary list. Public swimming baths were not on it, but skating rinks were, as were cinemas on Saturday mornings. Cinemas at other times were all right.

They weren't ordinary lessons at this time of year; they were special projects, in which each teacher tried to humanise her subject and pick up extra custom. Some subjects were easier to humanise than others: Mrs Ringer (music) put aside *Linden Lea* and taught numbers by Lennon and McCartney. The biology project was reputed to be about birth control, but only sixth-form leavers could go. Miss Harris advertised Latin for Fun, a title deliberately chosen, in Mary's view, to ensure Miss Harris an empty classroom and a free period. "Come to domestic science," Mary urged Jackie kindly, "then you can lure men to your digs with your fairy cakes."

Domestic science took place in a new, modern wing, well-equipped with the kinds of appliances Jackie's mother was always campaigning to have at home. Mrs Lewis, the teacher, glared suspiciously at Jackie; she disliked the time of year that allowed certain girls to dabble in a subject for which they normally thought themselves too clever. She enquired very kindly what Jackie would like to learn to do: boil eggs, perhaps? And the mounted, framed quotation from Dr Johnson on the wall had been carefully chosen.

"A man is better pleased," it said, "when he has a good dinner upon the table than when his wife talks Greek."

Jackie seethed under this, and her cakes did not rise. Mrs Lewis said the class might as well eat them now, if they wanted to, because she certainly wasn't going to let Jackie take them home. They reflected too badly on the school.

Loyally, Mary ate a fairy cake. But she defended Dr Johnson. "Like it or not, it's true." she said.

Jackie was sure she'd followed the recipe. "I think my mother would be 'better pleased' with a few jobs done around the house than when her husband scores a hundred runs or something."

Mary was determined to be infuriating. "Sounds normal."

Normal? Jackie shuddered.

Things were pretty normal at home these days.

Her father had been in the same job for three years. He was a men's clothes salesman. A man he knew imported them from Hong Kong and he had to drive about in a mauve car persuading shops to take them. He had to wear them too: flowered shirts and pale suits, just the sort of thing he sneered and raged at his sons for wearing. "Dressing up to look the part for work is one thing! Putting them on in all seriousness is another." William was trying

414

to be an accountant and kept failing his exams; Max was unemployed and wanted to start a pop group.

Jackie's mother had mixed feelings about her husband's job. At least it was secure, but she said the money was no more than she needed to keep up with prices. She had her washing-machine at last, when it worked, but she said he had only bought it for his own convenience: he had to have clean clothes every day. "Superspiv!" she jeered. That was quite normal.

She still didn't like the house. Kate, the youngest, was twelve now, and Mrs Orange said she had thought life would get a bit easier; but toys and nappies and hamsters and chemistry sets had given way to clothes, posters, record-players and clapped-out guitars with yards and yards of wire. "How am I supposed to keep this slum clean when – " the plaint was lost in the tell-tale hiss of the washing-machine overflowing and the twangs and howls of Max Orange and the Pips. And the dust was everywhere.

Everyone in the house seemed to be getting bigger and brighter and more exuberant, even Jackie's father in his gaudy, youthful clothes. But her mother seemed to shrivel before her eyes into her blue dressing-gown.

Jackie was seriously worried about the future.

She had had a few disastrous encounters with boys. William and Max had friends, for a start. The bass guitarist of the Pips once suggested to Jackie that she come on tour with them as singer. "But I can't sing," Jackie said, startled. "So what?" he replied, leering, and then Max came in and told the guitarist laughingly to lay off his sister. Or there were the boys in the Colts XV at the rugby club where Jackie still went occasionally. Each time, she thought, *Today I'm going to meet someone!* But they seemed to prefer talking to each other. She knew that if she were even slightly attractive, they would want her as much as she wanted one of them . . . many of her friends had regular boyfriends; some were even engaged.

She liked it when her father drove her to school in his mauve car and his modish gear, because people who didn't look too closely might mistake him for a boyfriend. But she wondered what was wrong with her. There was no point in dieting to get rid of her thick thighs because the weight only went away from the one part of her that was small: her bust. And her curly hair was childish and unfashionable. She tried to wheedle her father into giving an honest opinion . . . immediately he saw what she was asking and leapt to reassure her: "You're just meeting yobbos, not your type at all. Wait till you get to university, then they'll appreciate you. You're a super girl, Jackie; you're not doomed to end your days an Orange."

Was that the purpose of university, then? Nobody had suggested any other, in their insistence that she would go. She wasn't even sure that she wanted to get married, even though she laughed with the other girls at their single teachers and told each other that their bad moods were due to sexual frustration. You just didn't know what was expected. The school pushed you and pushed you to pass exams, go to university, but who got star billing in the school magazine? The ones who got married, that was who. It was rather shocking to see them turn up there with their strange new names. There was Valerie Astor, for instance, last year's head girl, a piece of university material if ever there was one. There she was, in humble parentheses, between her new name, Mrs Michael Root, and news of her baby daughter Veronica. "University material indeed!" Mary had scoffed, "Don't need a degree in maths to work out what happened to her!"

Jackie glanced up at Dr Johnson. "I'm not going to get married," she said, and Mrs Lewis passed by, and Mary and she exchanged knowing glances.

In the afternoon they did history. It was taught by Miss H. Long ago there had been another Miss Harris, which was why the present teacher of Latin and history came to be called Miss H. The nickname took nothing from the authority of her seamed face and pudding-basin of straight grey hair. She liked the nineteenth and twentieth centuries best, and the girls enjoyed speculating as to how much of it was from memory. She dictated from a file of notes, and girls who had had elder sisters, or even mothers, at the school, could confirm that they did not vary from decade to decade. Today, though, was going to be different. Miss H had to please the customers for a change. Her file of notes lay closed on the desk.

"Now, girls, forget the syllabus."

Mary wrote "Forget the syphilis" in her rough book, and showed it to Jackie. "It is important to realise that history is not just a matter of kings and queens and prime ministers, and battles won and lost."

Mary wrote, "Who said it was?"

Three wasps hurled themselves at the classroom window. Jackie looked out at the sun gleaming on the domestic science block.

". . . and so, Mary, perhaps you would tell us a little of *your* history?"

Mary simpered, "Haven't got any, Miss H."

"I think you haven't been paying attention, dear. We *all* have a history; our daily lives are history. What did you do at the weekend, for instance?"

Mary shrugged and stuck out her bust. "Went to see *A Hard Day's Night*. Seventh time."

The class giggled, expecting a rebuke, but to everyone's surprise Miss H took up a stick of chalk and wrote on the board A HARD DAY'S NIGHT in her fiddly script. "Not the clearest or happiest of phrases! But a curiosity for all that! What do you suppose your grandchildren will make of it?"

The class exploded. The reference to grandchildren, and thus procreation, had reminded them about Hilary Buckley, who, according to Mary (who had access to this kind of news where Jackie had not), frequently went all the way with her boyfriend and had recently survived a pregnancy panic. Miss H rapped her desk and explained her idea. She wanted them, she said, to pursue some "living history", that was, she wanted them to seek out the oldest person they knew and ask them for their memoirs. Not just great events, but the little daily details of working and living: what they ate, what they wore, what they did for fun. "When I tell my grandad," said Mary, "that his chuntering on about the past is living history there'll be no stopping the old bore."

Jackie got a whole day off school to go to Leehaven with Max's supposedly portable but very heavy tape-recorder to record Granny Ruby's memoirs. "Clever," Mary acknowledged: she hadn't thought fast enough to invent someone requiring a day's excursion.

Granny Ruby met Jackie at the station in the usual way.

"How's your mother?"

"She's wallpapering."

"Good gracious! Can't they get a man in to do that?"

"Mummy says it's quicker to do it herself."

"Hm! And has your father still got that dreadful car?"

"He's thinking of spraying it orange. You know, to go with the name."

Granny Ruby insisted on their going through the usual shopping ritual, even though Jackie was only down for the day. She wished they could hurry. She thought Granny Ruby would have some good memoirs; she feared there might be a few false starts with the tape-recorder and she did not want to be late back. In the flat, Granny Ruby poured each of them a gin and lime. Jackie's was more lime than gin; she didn't like gin; but she sensed her grandmother's wish to acknowledge her as grown-up, and was grateful. She declined a cigarette.

"I never was very good at history," Granny Ruby said. "English was my best subject. The books I could have written . . .!" She watched nervously as Jackie uncoiled the wires of the tape-recorder.

"Well, it's not really history. It's just memories."

"Is that thing going?"

Jackie pressed a switch, wound back the tape, pressed again, and to the surprise of both of them Granny Ruby's voice from the machine said, "Is that thing going?" Granny Ruby took a long draught at her gin and lime. Jackie sighed. The old lady seemed to have forgotten all her memories in her fascination with the machine. First she swore it wasn't her voice. Then she giggled and was shy and tongue-tied. Then she patted her hair and imitated people she had seen being interviewed on her television set, speaking in a queenly voice. Jackie wished she had contented herself with taking notes. It was hard to explain about Miss H's living history. Granny Ruby thought it was just dates. "I remember when the Queen died in 1901, and there was a general election in 1905, and the First World War broke out in 1914, and – "

"Tell me about the war."

Granny Ruby's face fell. Jackie could have kicked herself. She knew perfectly well that her grandmother had had a terrible time in the First World War, losing three brothers, and having another one crippled. What did she think she was doing, making the poor old thing relive her unhappiness on a tape, to be giggled at by schoolgirls? "I'll turn this off," she said. "Why don't you tell me about India?" Granny Ruby usually loved to talk about India, where she was rich and grand. "Well, they got their independence didn't they?" She sniffed. "Though I don't know whether they think killing your grandfather helped." Jackie couldn't tell whether the sniff was sad or scornful, but once again she felt tactless and suggested going out for fish and chips. Granny Ruby gave her the money. When she got back, Granny Ruby scolded her gently for having started to eat her chips out of the bag and expecting to continue to do so.

"Does your mother let you do that?"

"Of *course*! Tastes better."

"And saves her washing up!"

"P'raps."

Firmly and delicately, Granny Ruby arranged the fillets and chips on plates. "Now, you listen to me, Jackie. Never mind your tape-recorder! You're getting to an age now when you're going to want to bring boyfriends home to tea, and if they see you've got a lazy, slovenly mother, they'll think that's just the kind of wife you'll be."

Jackie felt herself go white. A chip paused on her tongue. She could explode. She said very quietly, "I haven't got a boyfriend and I'm never going to get married."

Granny Ruby laughed in a way that was supposed to be comforting but sounded rather nasty. "That's just what I used to think, before I met your grandfather! What are you going to be, then – a bluestocking?"

Yes. A bluestocking. Miss H. Anything but my mother. "I am going to university."

"You'll meet some nice boys there."

But I won't marry any of them. You'll see! I'll be – I'll be – I don't know what I want to be! It's too far ahead. I can't see that far ahead. I'll do science. If my results are good. I'll be a doctor. There's less competition for science places than arts for girls. I have to get away. A lady doctor came to school once, to do our BCG injections. She was nice. She was married.

Granny Ruby seemed to realise she had gone too far. She said, "If you take my advice, Jackie, you'll do a course in shorthand and typing. It's never wasted. Look at me! I started out as a typist and I'm a typist still."

Jackie looked gloomily at the big black typewriter on the table in the corner of the room. She thought of Mary who was doing shorthand and typing but was staying at home to do it. She let her mind run riot. *If I had all the money in the world and talent for everything, what would I want most of all to be? What's the future I would construct for myself? I don't know. I've got two more years at school. Then I have to decide.* Listlessly, she ate her fish and chips but paid increasing attention to her grandmother, who was talking amusedly about two maiden ladies for whom she had worked as a typist before the First World War. The tape-recorder was off and Jackie didn't want to interrupt her flow by turning it on again, but she managed to make a few notes.

4

The history group reassembled. Mary's grandad had told her about the Depression, at some length. Lucy Long had found an old ration book and brought it in. Alison Town, who could always be relied upon to get hold of the wrong end of the stick, read out *The Charge of the Light Brigade*, by Tennyson.

"And Jacqueline?"

"Here we go," Mary muttered. "The Raj."

Jackie ignored her. "Miss H, my grandmother worked in an office with two ladies who supported Votes for Women. They used to send anonymous letters to politicians who were against it."

The class giggled. Jackie couldn't tell whether Miss H's smile was one of pleasure or ridicule. The Misses Parley certainly sounded rather ridiculous; and evil too, because when the First World War started they handed out white feathers to young men, sending them off to be killed.

"How many of you know who the suffragettes were?" Miss H wrote SUFFRAGETTES on the board, where previously she had written A HARD DAY'S NIGHT.

"Oh, Votes for Women, Miss H."

"Emily Pancake."

"Don't be silly, Mary."

"They threw themselves under horses' hooves."

"And chained themselves to railings."

"Yes, they did all that. And some of them very bravely went to prison. Most of them were law-abiding, though, and lobbied Parliament and collected signatures on petitions and had *peaceful* processions and worked hard as bus-drivers and nurses during the First World War, till eventually it was seen as only fair to give them the vote." Miss H looked younger than Granny Ruby; what did she remember? She spoke without looking once at her notes. Jackie had heard of the suffragettes before, of course, though the

420

class had not "done" them; she had had the impression that it was just a short struggle in the last few years before the First World War; she had not realised it went back more than a hundred years. Again and again, it now seemed, women had tried to get the vote. Again and again, men had argued, refused and laughed. Miss H.'s words were vivid: it was like being at a film. Jackie could hear the laughter: great male guffaws, like when her mother said she wanted to go to evening classes to keep her brain alive, and her father said, "Bit late for that."

It had seemed witty at the time. Jackie had laughed too.

Now Miss H was saying that the men who opposed Votes for Women did so in good faith: they thought it would harm family life because husband and wife would argue about politics.

An outraged voice said, "That's stupid!"

"That's your opinion, Jacqueline, but we must be careful about judging historical events by the standards of our own time."

"We do for other things!" She had never felt so angry in school. She was being rude to a teacher, and she didn't care. "We say the First World War was a tragedy, and – and William Pitt was clever for his age, so why can't we say those men were stupid? Pompous and stupid – like Doctor Johnson!" Harm family life! When did her parents ever argue about politics? Everything else – never politics!

After class, Miss H called her and she waited sheepishly to be told off. "You seem to have a very interesting relation, Jacqueline." Jackie said nothing; she was still angry, an anger at once vicious and undirected and exciting. "Are you continuing with history?"

"No, I'm sick of it, I'm going to be a doctor."

"A wonderful profession for a woman," Miss H. said softly. "Do you know about the terrible time the first women medical students had? The men drove sheep into the lecture hall, to protest about inferior animals being allowed to train."

"How would I know?"

"Don't shout, please, Jacqueline. We have to keep to the syllabus when we're doing exam work. But that's the point of these special projects: to look into the side streets of history, which are often so much more interesting than the main road."

Jackie sulked.

"I could lend you a book," her teacher went on softly, "and

you could do a project for me in the holidays. You wouldn't get any marks, of course."

Jackie didn't know about the project, but she borrowed the book. It was very old: it had a brown circle on its cover from a cup of tea, and in spite of the sterling work of a lot of sticky tape, pages kept floating on to the floor. It told the story Miss H had told in class, and more, and more.

It was fascinating: not just votes and doctors, but education and factory conditions and marriage laws. Husbands used to *own* their wives, own them and their property and their children and everything! She thought uneasily of the essays she had written in her exam, essays about extension of the franchise in which she had not once mentioned women. That would count against her. And had she included Married Women's Property in her list of Gladstone's reforms? She thought not. And there were some fascinating chapters about VD: fancy those prim Victorian ladies who knew nothing about sex, getting up and making speeches on such a subject! She must tell Mary, though perhaps not Granny Ruby. The book ended with the vote won, in 1928. It said, "It is for the future to fulfil these hopes." Had it? All the things the women of a hundred years ago had campaigned for Jackie knew had been won; was everything all right now, and was that why none of this was on the syllabus?

Miss H. had set her an essay question in her inimitable style: "Did Militancy Help or Hinder the Campaign for Women's Suffrage?" Jackie had not meant to write anything, but some devil seemed to seize her, some spirit from the past, perhaps. She cringed under the indignity of being owned by a man, choked in the poisonous air of mine or match-factory, yawned in the drawing-room as her stays bit her flesh. Her brain ached as a deep voice told her it was unseemly for her to have one, it would impair her maternal function; her heart bled as her children were taken from her. And then she broke free. She felt the wind in her hair and a strong voice in her chest: *Votes for Women! Votes for Women!* She felt courage uncurl itself like a waking cat; she mounted a bicycle; she kissed the prison walls and they fell away . . . how fine it must have been! She would get no marks for her essay, it didn't matter what Miss H thought of it; she would write about how she felt.

Her O-level results were mixed. She got grade ones for all her arts subjects, including history, but only passes in science. "A very creditable performance, Jacqueline," her headmistress wrote, "I shall put you down for Miss Harris' A-level history group unless you advise me to the contrary."

Jackie considered this. She was slightly unnerved by her science results, the more so because she had been looking at some A-level science books and they seemed surprisingly difficult. They did not seem to move on logically from what she had learned, more often by rote than with understanding, she now realised. She seemed to have missed something. Would learning by rote be enough for A-level, for university study? She dread d failure, but many very good arts students failed to get into university because it was so much more competitive than science. And those women in that book who had struggled to be doctors . . . she wrote back to her headmistress with some spirit, telling her she would like to do physics, chemistry and biology, half hoping that it would be forbidden.

It was not forbidden exactly; but there were difficulties. The science teacher was inconsiderately leaving at short notice to get married, and Jackie was the only candidate for A-level sciences. The headmistress would see what she could do. Jackie waited, in grim satisfaction and dread. A solution was found. King's Lane Boys' Grammar would be happy to welcome her for physics and chemistry in their new, modern labs.

"Ooh, lucky you!" her friend Mary cooed. "All those lovely hunky sixth-formers!"

Lovely, hunky? They were spotty and uncouth, or lordly and cruel looking. She never forgot the first day. She had Sellotaped her hair to her face to straighten it the night before, and dabbed a little powder on her face on the bus, to hide her nervous flush and the spots that had sprung up. For something to think about, she wondered as to the legality of this: make-up was banned in her school, but they could hardly have such a rule at King's Lane. There was no comfort in the thought. She pictured her friends sitting cosily with Miss H and her file of notes and her map of the Unification of Italy. She was late. She had a new bra on, but her little breasts wobbled as she ran. A curious youth took time off from picking his nose to direct her to the science block. The corridor smelled of chemicals. She knocked on the bubbly glass door: a black figure fluttered up behind it and a master in a gown opened it and bowed.

"Welcome, madame."

She hadn't meant to indicate, by knocking at the door, that she expected it to be opened for her. She was just being polite.

"I'm Jackie Orange."

"I didn't think you were Freddie Trueman."

The eighteen deep-throated laughs were not unkind, *not unkind* she repeated to herself as she scuttled to her seat. Wouldn't girls giggle a bit if a boy came to join one of their classes?

"Have they asked you out yet?" said Mary.

Asked her out? She hadn't even found a tongue to join in their break-time conversations. It was her fault, not theirs. They didn't address remarks to her, but why should they, when she didn't address any to them? She had read somewhere that shyness was actually a kind of arrogance. Her father said she should hold her own: "No daughter of mine need have an inferiority complex with a group of pimply youths." It wouldn't have been so bad if she could get on with the work. But by the end of the first term she knew she had made a terrible mistake in thinking she could do science. She could not even learn by rote something she did not understand *at all*! O-level physics and chemistry seemed positively cosy by comparison with this abstract world to which she seemed to have no access . . . what had any of this to do with being a doctor? Ions, charges, valencies, rays, tables of figures, Greek letters, equations? When she had thought she would be a doctor, she had seen herself as a kind lady in a panelled surgery, being terribly understanding about things like unmarried mothers, and children who didn't want to undress.

Every time the master addressed the class as "boys" she went pink. She didn't mean to draw attention to her femininity. But he noticed and started saying "Boys and girl", "Lady and gentlemen". He was only being polite, he wasn't trying to make her conspicuous; usually he went out of his way not to embarrass her. When they went through the end-of-term papers in class, he mocked the boys for their stupid mistakes, and she agonised over what he would say about her. But he didn't mention her. Afterwards he talked to her privately about her disastrous paper. He was very kind. "Just stick up your hand and stop me if I go too fast, Jackie."

That Christmas was appalling. Her father had met up with an old school friend in York who had six children ("Another spiv," her mother sniffed: Bill Byron was in secondhand cars) and invited

424

them all to stay. The house became like a refugee camp, with piles of borrowed blankets and makeshift beds in every room. The only good thing that came out of it was the fridge. Throughout the weeks of Advent, Jackie's mother enquired, in a steadily rising voice, how she was to cater for eight guests and seven family with all the shops closed and no fridge. She drew up a menu consisting entirely of tinned food to prove the point. The fridge arrived as a surprise on Christmas Eve, half an hour before the shops closed.

The fridge cast its chill on the noisy, discordant festivities. Presents were trodden on, the fathers went for drinks and played stupid jokes with paper masks and stink-bombs, and the mothers hardly left the kitchen. Half the time, Jackie seethed there with them; the other half, she went walking through the empty Christmas streets.

She thought and thought. Those women who had campaigned for women to be doctors couldn't have meant that *all* women should be doctors. They must have realised that some weren't up to it. So maybe it was silly to persevere when the result could only be failure. And it would be her failure: she was being given every opportunity. At this rate, not only would she not be a doctor, she wouldn't even get a university place. And she had to get away, she had to have those three years in which she could postpone making decisions. Already her young sisters were announcing their plans to be a kennel-maid and an air-hostess. Her headmistress seemed disappointed but unsurprised by her decision to change to A-level history, English and Latin, and stop going to King's Lane. "Didn't you like working with the boys, Jacqueline?" she said, with the twisted grimace that was as near as she came to a smile between Speech Days. Jackie sensed suspicion of ingratitude. "Oh, it wasn't that. I'm really grateful for the trouble you went to arrange it, it's just that, I don't think I've got the ability . . ." "Ah well," said the headmistress. "We'll get you a university place, never fear." Mary was shocked. "I bet you were distracted by their bulging crotches, that was why you couldn't study." Miss Harris, who had declared Jackie's holiday essay on the suffragettes "a lively and amusing piece of work", welcomed her back to the history group with an air of muted triumph.

All the talk in the second year of the sixth form was of offers. It might have been a sale-room, or a gathering of hopeful Victorian spinsters. But the offers were from universities, not men. The places offered were always conditional on getting certain grades in one's A-levels. There was neither rhyme nor reason nor justice in the offers, as far as Jackie could see. The universities she really wanted to go to – in Scotland or the north of England, far from home – wanted her to get A grades, or Bs at least. A London college – just as prestigious – was prepared to take her with passes.

"I don't see why you should worry about it," said Miss H., "You're perfectly capable of As. It's all a bit of lottery." And she moved on to something else. She was a great believer in what she called "The Year Between". Many girls didn't get the best out of university, she said (*what? the best of what?*) because they went up too young. She had a little booklet of things you could do in the year between school and university, such as voluntary work or travel; she said the universities were usually enthusiastic about the idea, and quite willing to hold a place over.

Jackie hadn't paid much attention to this. She just wanted to get away from home as quickly as possible. But with the prospect seeming dangerously real of her ending up at London University, she thought again. She knew that lodgings were in short supply, and students from London were encouraged to live at home. This she was not prepared to do. Because something had happened recently that had shaken her to the core, and led her to realise that her parents' marriage, which she had always taken for granted as unlikely, battered, discordant but durable, was heading for the unthinkable. And when it got there, she didn't want to be around.

It had been a phone call. Her father was away, supposedly staying with his friend Bill Byron in York. But it was Bill on the phone.

"Hullo, Jackie. Is your dad there?"

She tried to think. "No, he's not."

"When will he be back?"

"I don't know. Sunday." Her brain ground its gears. "Do you want him to ring you?"

"Nothing special. Haven't seen him for ages. How is the old ruffian?"

She croaked, "All right," and put the phone down. Her mother called to ask who it was, and she said, "Mary, for me." Then she realised what she had done. The first lie. Still, there was a chance she was mistaken. When her father came home, smart and full of himself, she thought a bit and said, "How was Bill?"

"Oh, fine, the old spiv."

That was it, then. It was a lie. Should she say anything? And if so, to whom? Feeling a complete fool, she wrote to a problem page in one of her mother's magazines. She agonised for weeks in case they published the letter and her mother recognised herself. But Jackie got a private reply in her stamped addressed envelope. It was kind. The incident Jackie described certainly did not prove her father was having an affair. She should forget it and mind her own business. Jackie tried to. But many things were slotting ominously into place. Weekend after weekend he went away; night after night he was late, as his dinner spoiled under the grill. And her mother parroted his excuses with averted eyes: "He's in a meeting." "He's on a tour." Her voice was full of fear. So many things fitted. His firm was expanding into the teenage girls' market: Jackie heard more than disgust in her mother's voice as she railed against the mini-skirt.

"Little Madams! Showing all they've got!"

"Oh, Mummy! It's only the fashion!" Fashion or not, Jackie wasn't allowed to wear minis, and neither were Julia or Kate. The thought of her sisters reassured her a little. Nothing could happen while they were still at home.

"I'd be interested in doing something before university, Miss H. Travel."

"You're still worrying about those grades, aren't you, Jacqueline?" They looked together through the booklet of opportunities. She could build a dam in Yugoslavia, she could be an au pair in France or she could play with slum children in Glasgow. "All good experiences!" Or she could go to college in America. "How about this? I do believe it's just the thing for you!"

It was a year's scholarship to somewhere called Deaconsburg College for Women in Virginia. All expenses paid. It couldn't lead to a degree in a year, but there would be a specially designed course of study to give the successful girl a grounding in American literature, history, politics: ideal, it said, for that pre-university year. To apply, you had to send in an essay on any aspect of "Woman's Role".

"What a good thing you've written one already, Jacqueline!" Miss H beamed. "I certainly couldn't recommend you taking time off from the syllabus at this stage."

5

Jackie's A-level papers felt all right, but she knew better than to trust such complacency. She left school; Julia and Kate howled with envy; but it didn't seem real, not when she didn't know whether, when autumn came, she would be catching a train to Manchester or Edinburgh, a plane to Virginia, or a bus to town to go to lectures and a bus out in the evenings to come home again. Things were dangerously quiet at home. William, who had failed his accountancy exams again, had gone to share a flat with friends in Battersea and brought his washing home. Max had joined the army and was stationed in Hampshire. Their father was away a lot, but Jackie never again caught him out in a lie. Her mother was going through a funny phase, alternately awed by her children's growing up and branching out, and depressed.

Granny Ruby's rheumatism was bad, so Jackie's visits were of benefit to both of them. Jackie did the shopping; Granny Ruby kept up her morale through the long weeks of waiting.

"America, eh? We've always been great travellers in our family."

"Well, me jetting off for a year – *if* I go – isn't in quite the same league as your intrepid voyages to the mysterious East."

"Just what I thought when I left for India. I thought, I may not be as brave as Aunt Sarah, but I've still got to be brave. Shall we have a little gin, dear?"

"Not for me, thanks. Who was Aunt Sarah?"

"She wasn't an aunt, exactly; she helped look after us when we were children. Goodness me, she'll come back from the grave and haunt me for not telling you that she emigrated all alone to Australia in 1850 something."

"I thought it was just convicts in those days."

"She couldn't stay in the same place for five minutes, Aunt Sarah. She wanted to go to America too; but the ship sank and that was the end of her. It was that ship – they made a film about it – "

"The *Titanic*?"

"That was it. My brothers were so wicked! They used to say, 'I expect Aunt Sarah was steering when it hit the iceberg.' "

Jackie opened her mouth and closed it again. Granny Ruby didn't seem to think there was anything remarkable about what she had told her, but then lots of people had gone down on the

Titanic and all of them were related to someone, so why not? She decided this Aunt Sarah must have been a very brave and game sort of person, and she would adopt her as her mascot forthwith. She would just have to be careful not to think about mid-Atlantic disasters when she was twenty thousand feet up. If she got the scholarship. If she decided to accept it. No. No ifs about it. If the opportunity arose, she would take it. If a British university offered her a place too, she could always go there afterwards. The longer she put it off, the longer she had to make final decisions about her life. She had to get away.

It was just as well that Jackie had made this decision at least. It helped her to stick to her guns when her mother launched her own bombshell.

It was at breakfast. Jackie had just received the news she was waiting for, but hadn't had a chance to announce it. Her father was chipping irritably at his boiled egg, which was softer than he liked them. He wore a rather raffish cravat and kept glaring at his wife and younger daughters who had come down in their dressing-gowns. Jackie was fully dressed, out of respect for his feelings, which, after all, she wasn't going to have to respect much longer.

Her mother beamed. "I have some news for you all."

Her father waved his teaspoon and said flippantly, "My Gawd. She's pregnant."

"Yes, I am."

"Oh," said Julia peaceably, "that's nice."

Kate said, "Aren't you a bit old?" but she was only curious, not disapproving.

Jackie was watching her parents. She had never seen triumph in her mother's eyes before; or such horror in her father's.

Her mother said, "I'm forty-one. There are lots of things young girls think I'm too old for, but in this case they're wrong." She looked straight at her husband.

"You can get rid of it," he said. "There's a new law."

"I don't think it says I have to, Randolph."

"We can't afford it!" he roared. "Good God!" He got up, tipping over his egg. A tiny worm of soft yolk oozed out. "I'm not going to have a committee meeting about it! I'll talk to you tonight."

Mrs Orange moved her chair to let him go. Then she sat back at the table with a little smile playing on her lips.

429

"Well, Jackie! What was your post? What a pity your father's gone."

Mechanically, Jackie said, "I got Cs. So London will have me if no-one else will. But – "

Her mother said, "That's nice. You'll be able to help me with the baby."

Jackie rushed out of the room. She could not bear her mother's presence. There had been another letter: offering her the year in America. She ought to be over the moon. She ought to be the centre of attention. Why did her mother have to spoil everything? She walked through the house. The brooding dust lay everywhere. The motley collection of domestic appliances, dubiously acquired by her father down the years, had brought no peace. The departure of her brothers as independent adults had added no leisure or rest to her mother's days. Was it true, as she had once told Jackie, that she·was always waiting for a school bell to tell her what to do next? And now there was to be a baby. Jackie clenched her fists. She could see it already: the loft opened to bring down the cobwebby crib, the push-chair; threadbare nappies unearthed from trunks. Wailing at night, the faint smells of disinfectant, milk and baby-shit pervading the house in the day. Biscuits and rusks crunched into the carpet.

"How could you do it?" she yelled.

"I didn't do it all alone, Jackie."

"*He* doesn't want it!"

"Well, he's got it!" So it was on purpose. It had a purpose. "You'll get used to the idea, Jackie. So will he."

"I'm going away."

"But you'll live at home."

"I'm going to America."

"You are going to London University!"

"Yes – next year – 1970! This year I'm going to Deaconsburg College on a scholarship that I told you I was applying for, only you and Daddy were shouting too loudly to listen! My essay was the best and I'm going! I'm going in September, for a *whole year!*" Why had she let herself worry about the rest of her life when a year was for ever, and three more years' study awaited her after that? *Something would happen* . . . Her mother was saying hesitantly, "It seems we should congratulate each other, Jackie." Congratulate her? Jackie felt she could kill her.

★

"Jealous," said Mary, to whom she fled.

"Who?"

"You. Quite obvious."

"You mean I want a baby?"

"Not nec-es-sar-i-ly." Mary drew out the syllables of *necessarily* and pressed her fingertips together like a doctor. "But you don't like living proof of the fact that your parents still have it away from time to time. Ha! Doesn't sound as if your dad's too keen on the living proof, either. Serves him right, dirty beast. But you see, you're madly in love with your dishy dad, and *that's* why you're angry."

Jackie said, "You read too many magazines."

Mary said, "You don't read enough."

She came in late, to miss the gathering storm. But her mother was alone in the kitchen, fiddling with the knobs on the cooker while something burned under the grill. Long cigarette butts piled up. "Smoking two half-cigarettes isn't nearly as bad for you as one whole one, Jackie. All the harmful substances are – "

"Where is he?"

Back it came, pat. "Working late."

"You know he isn't."

"What?"

"Nothing, just don't expect me to believe things you don't believe yourself. It's insulting." Her mother stared. Jackie went on, she could not stop herself. "You know he doesn't always tell you the truth about where he is."

Her mother seized her hand; Jackie withdrew it in disgust. "You mean you know, Jackie?"

"I know two and two make four."

"But you know who it is? You know her name?"

Jackie was aghast. "No, of course not. I was guessing." And hoping her mother would deny it. Mrs Orange seemed to relax. It was very dark outside for a summer night, and the house was unusually quiet. The girls were in bed. "It's just a phase," she said. "All men of his age . . . they're scared of losing their youth. And with all those young girls he has to mix with. Flaunting their legs. It's nothing. It's not the first time. He's so attractive to women. I was lucky to get him at all. I had a crush on him from the age of seven, but I was just his little sister's friend – he'll change when the baby comes. You'll see. Or maybe you won't.

You'll be in America. Go, then. See if I stop you. I wish you could take the girls with you. I do, really. It would be easy then. Just the three of us: me, Randolph and the baby. I'll clean the house from top to bottom before the birth, Jackie. It won't know what's hit it; you get this rush of energy and nesting instinct. Every speck of dust. And when he comes in I'll be rocking the cradle by the fire."

He came in on her words, his cravat creased and stringy, his brow thunderous. Jackie made herself scarce. She put a pillow over her head, not to hear the argument that raged below her bedroom.

Sometimes at Leehaven when the sea was very stormy, a calm patch would appear, maintaining itself for an incongruous length of time between crashing breakers. The next morning seemed like such a patch, so Jackie changed the subject.

"Did you hear I've got a scholarship to America, Dad?"

"Your mother said something. I forbid it, of course. What? To *college in America*? Is that what I brought you up for? Protecting you from Saturday morning pictures and shouting at cricket matches? Hasn't your expensive education taught you anything about life, Jackie? Don't you know there's nothing in the world more common than an American college student? They all chew gum and become cheerleaders and smoke pot and go on demonstrations and get tear-gassed. Do you want to turn into that sort of person? Couldn't you just become something else, like a mass-murderer? Or why don't you just get pregnant – there's a lot of that about. My God, Jackie . . ." She waited. He was joking, wasn't he? He grinned. He ruffled her hair. "*Bloody* well done. Good for you. What an experience. You're going to have a whale of a time." He pretended to lower his voice. "Wish I could come with you, but prior commitments, you know? And did your mother get it right, that it's not going to cost me a penny?"

"It's all paid for," said Jackie proudly, "and if I need any extra I can get a job on campus, that's quite normal out there."

"I'll give you a bit to top it up. But I warn you, Jackie. If you come back in Bermuda shorts saying things like 'on campus' I'll – well, I'll be glad to see you, I suppose." He gave her a congratulatory hug. Over his shoulder, Jackie saw her mother watching them. She was wearing a maternity smock. She didn't need a maternity smock yet. She said, as if Jackie was about to board the plane that minute, "You won't forget to write, will you, Jackie?"

6

Dear Granny Ruby,

I wonder what time it is with you. I can't work it out. It's three-twenty in the morning here. I can see from my roommate Lindi's luminous electric clock-radio. I can't sleep. I dreamed about you. There's just enough light to write to you without disturbing her.

I feel very, very strange, but you will understand. I'm not as far from home as you were, and for me it's only a year.

Maybe it would be easier if I'd come by boat. It's all so quick and sudden, and I've never flown before. Everyone else on the plane was very relaxed, mainly American students who looked as if they'd been hitchhiking. They walked about and chatted to each other as if they were on the Bakerloo line. Me, I sat tight. Even when I had to go to the ladies I thought I might tilt the plane off-balance.

Landing at JFK in New York was ghastly. I thought I was going to be killed. Because shortly after the pilot announced we were going to land, he announced that we weren't after all. And the plane started to climb and fly in circles. I didn't know what was happening, and to make me feel better the man in the next seat told me that pilots have to circle a bit before they make an emergency landing if they can't get the undercarriage down, it uses up the gasoline (petrol to me and you) and reduces the risk of explosion on impact. But it wasn't an emergency, just a midair traffic jam(!), hundreds of planes flying in circles waiting their turn to land. I just prayed that death would be painless and quick.

Lindi met me at the airport, which was just as well, it was so huge and bewildering I'd never have found my way to Deaconsburg. She's very nice and kind and extremely pretty. I'm green with envy. She looks like one of those teenager dolls with golden hair and a wardrobe of fashionable outfits, that you can add items to on birthdays. Mum hates them, she used to say, "How can a child love a doll with *breasts*?" Lindi looked fresh and cool in a flowery summer dress with a full, short skirt. I just had my jeans on for travelling, and as soon as I realised it was her I apologised for being such a scruff. "Scruff!" she said, "That's cute! *You're* cute!" She talks like a film star. And she has a real knack for saying the right things, a sort of model hostess. For instance she said how sensible it was of me to wear comfortable clothes, she'd never *dare* wear blue jeans to fly, and very tactfully reminded me that girls weren't allowed to wear trousers on campus. I was flushed and hot and bothered; she said she'd heard about English rose complexions and now she could see it was true, and how lucky I was not to need make-up. She even had kind words for my ancient suitcase, said it looked as if it had been to lots of interesting places. And then, when I gulped like a frog and nearly disgraced myself by bursting into tears, she said, "I should think you *do* miss your mom and dad!"

Wanting to change the subject, and always the one to say the wrong thing, I launched into an account of what Dad had told me about American students, that they wear jeans all the time, except when they're wearing Bermuda shorts, and she laughed and said he sounded "a real neat guy". Can't wait to tell him. She said it was truer of the big state colleges, especially on the west coast, but Deaconsburg was a private college, very concerned with maintaining standards. I suppose these distinctions will become clear to me in time.

She took me to another terminal to wait for a plane going south. There seemed to be a lot of soldiers about. I asked if there was some sort of parade or something. She seemed surprised that I didn't know about the war in Vietnam (I do, of course, but I hadn't thought of it in real terms, real young men having to do national service, I suppose that's what comes of not having lived through any wars) and even more surprised that boys don't get called up in England. She said her boyfriend Gary has a student deferment, which means he doesn't have to join up till he's through college, by which time everyone hopes Vietnam will be finished. "It's lucky he's clever," she said, "because if he doesn't keep his grade average up – " She seemd surprisingly cheerful about it, it gave me the creeps. It was bad enough having to get high grades to get a university place, imagine having to get them to stay alive. After what she'd told me about the blue jeans I didn't ask her whether Deaconsburg students made any protests about the war; that's probably another thing that only happens in the big state colleges on the West Coast, so Dad can relax.

She practically had to drag me onto the second plane. I'm not used to a country being so big that you get planes from city to city. I told her this. "I've never flown before today," I said, and she said, "Are you kidding me?" which is what she says when she's surprised. "Jackie, I love the way you talk. You're going to be so popular. And don't worry, planes never crash when I'm on board." I could believe it.

I'll tell you about the campus, my room, etc. some other time; I've been too tired to notice my surroundings. I'll tell you about my dream and then I'll try to sleep again. I was walking through the airport and I was very tiny, about three feet tall, surrounded by pilots and soldiers and beauty queens who were giants, moving slowly like a slow motion film, and they kept throwing buckets of water over me. I fought and ran, I had to meet you but I couldn't find you. Then I saw you, in your green summer frock, with your shopping basket and a towel to dry me, like when I used to come out of the sea. I tried to call to you, but you turned and walked away and I couldn't move. You know those awful dreams. When I woke up, I had to tell somebody.

Sorry for this gloomy letter, I'm sure everything's going to be all right.
Love,
Jackie

Dear Mom, Pop, Julia, Kate, Max and Bill if you're around,

Well, hi there, you-all! This is your cute little all-American Jackie calling from the campus hamburger stand dressed in Bermuda shorts and bobby socks, just about to go to my baton-twirling class as soon as I've finished my chewing gum.

OK, I mean all right, you can pick him off the floor now, it isn't really like that at all. Far from descending to his dreaded depths of commonness. I'm actually behaving better, working harder and more smartly dressed than I ever was at home, if you can imagine that.

Let me fill you in on the place. Deaconsburg College is quite small, less than a thousand students. Parts of it are modern, but the original bit is built to resemble an English college, with a grey stone quadrangle and ivy climbing up the pillars. I was suspicious of this ivy from the start, much too green and shiny for its own good, so I approached it and tried to pull off a leaf. Nearly brought the whole plant down. It wasn't a plant at all, it was plastic. Lindi, my roommate, was very embarrassed; she tells me it is usually real ivy, only it got a disease and died, and the plastic version is taking its place until the botany class comes up with a cure.

I don't really talk like the first paragraph. My accent as it is has a considerable novelty value. Lindi wants me to teach it to her, she says it would help her to get a job as a receptionist in the vacation. In class the professors single me out to answer questions, and don't seem to mind what nonsense I talk, which is just as well, because the girls are mostly very clever. I feel a bit confused. Miss H at school always used to tell us that in the sixth form we must develop good study habits because once we went to university no-one would stand over us or make us work. It isn't like that here; it's almost like being in the second or third form again, with registers called at every class and things to learn for tests at the next class. But just when I start feeling superior about this, I'll be reminded of the fantastic range of things the girls here seem to know about, they don't just do a degree in one or two subjects as we do, they do five or six each semester, and then they choose their "major". (As in: "Are you an English major?" "No, I'm just a sergeant.") Registration was like a supermarket; you had to go from desk to desk, picking up little cards for the courses you want to do. Then you get fed into a computer. I'm doing American Literature, American Politics, American History, things like that. Also swimming. You have to do swimming. Marie Curie herself couldn't graduate from Deaconsburg if she couldn't swim. They say there's no point in having academic honours if you drown the first time you fall into the river. Also, it's good for the figure.

Another course I'm doing is Grooming and Popularity. It's a training in not being common. You don't get credits for it, but most of the girls do it, except for a few scruffy and rebellious ones whom Lindi calls upside-down snobs. I like Lindi but she does go a bit far. She has a little chart on the inside of her wardrobe door to remind herself of what she's worn so far this semester; and once she came storming in and said, "That Jane Grey! She's worn that red spotted number *six times*!" Then she went pink with embarrrassment, remembering that I too sometimes repeat my costume. And also that she benefits from my meagre wardrobe because I let her use some of my hanging space. She said, "Well, it's different for you, you've come from England," which was a bit two-edged. I thought. But when in Rome – I've decided to spend some of the money you gave me on getting some more clothes, as although I don't quite belong with the Grooming and Popularity lot, I don't want to be seen as one of the "beats". Lindi's going to come and help me choose.

Also, another of the girls in G & P did a drawing of how I would look if I had my hair straightened. I'll send a photograph when I've had it done. Anyway, I'm enjoying myself and hope you're all well. The enclosed sealed note is for Mum, so mind your own business the rest of you.
Love,
Jackie.

Dear Mummy,
Thank you for writing to tell me about the abortion. Of course I'm not shocked! I'm sure if the doctor said it was the right thing to do, then it was, and I hope you'll feel better soon. Keep taking the tablets!
Love,
Jackie.

7

Dear Mary,
At last after two months I can write to you, remembering your instructions that you didn't want to hear from me till I'd had a date. I've had one and you're bloody well going to hear all about it.

It was a blind date. This is an all-girl campus, and Lindi, the pink-frilled girl I share my pink-filled room with has been worrying as much as you did about my lonely Saturday nights. She has a boyfriend called Gary, and he has this cousin Patrick, and Patrick was staying with Gary and Gary was supposed to be going out with Lindi. So of course the solution was for Patrick to go out with me.

I know you've got this impression that everywhere in the US of A is like Manhattan or else Haight Ashbury, so I'd better tell you right away that Deaconsburg is really hicksville. It's built on two things: tobacco and the college. So there really aren't many places to go, apart from some out-of-bounds bars, the Campus Center that closes at 10, a cinema that shows nothing but hundred-year-old Westerns, and a hamburger joint. This doesn't usually matter as all the girls' boyfriends have cars and can roam further afield, but it helped to make this evening the disaster it was because Gary and Patrick came in Gary's car, and Gary and Lindi wanted to be alone.

You should have seen me getting ready. Proud, you would have been. I looked like one of my dad's models. The girls have taken me firmly in hand, clothes-wise, and taught me how to do eye make-up without blinding myself where you only sneered. I've even been on a diet, gruesome but effective, so that I can wear a miniskirt without frightening people. (You just eat pure protein and drink water for as long as you can stand it. Beware, though; it makes your breath smell. You have to use something for that.)

The high point of the evening as far as I was concerned was the ringing out of those magic words on the intercom: "Jackie Orange! Lindi Pierce! You have two callers in the lobby." (Because of course they're not allowed up in our rooms, even to collect us.) After that, it was all downhill.

Patrick was quite nice looking, tall, dark and etc. in fawn trousers and a polo-necked sweater and a fraternity jacket (I'll tell you what a fraternity is when I understand myself, it's been explained to me three times and I still don't have a clue) but he didn't have much to say. And most of my conversational gambits seemed to fall on stony ground. Honestly, Mary, what's wrong with me? I don't seem to have advanced in my social savoir-faire since my disastrous break-times at that school where I went to do science with the boys. When I'm with you, we never stop talking and arguing and making each other laugh. Why can't I meet a man like you? Why can't you be a man?

For example.

Me (getting into car): Americans seem to learn to drive as soon as they can walk. It's such a good idea, isn't it?

Him: I don't drive.

Me (ordering a dietburger, meaning, no roll, no french fries): Seems to be your national food, hamburgers.

Him: I'm allergic to hamburgers. They give me ulcers. (To waitress):
Miss, could I have an omelette please?

Me (wishing I had ordered french fries): We call them chips at home.
And what you call chips, we call crisps.

Him: Hmmmnnnhhhh.

And so on. Big night out, eh? Lindi and Gary were hardly speaking
either, but they at least had an excuse, Gary's just failed some exams and
he's worried about his grades falling below a certain level and being
drafted. Patrick was making no effort and once I realised this I stopped
feeling guilty for being so boring and just felt bloody angry. So I told
Patrick I was tired and asked if he would walk me back to the dormitory,
at least that way Gary and Lindi would get something out of the evening.

It was raining, I didn't have a proper coat on and he very gallantly lent
me his jacket which I suppose I must count as the most romantic moment
of my life to date. Still not much in the way of conversation, though.

Me: It rains all the time in England. (It's bad enough to talk aout the
weather. Imagine *lying* about the weather.)

Him: Yeah, you're lucky.

Me: We're not, it's horrible.

Then he said, "I'm sorry if you don't like rainy nights, Jackie, because
I guess I'm being about as much fun as one." I was too shocked to agree,
as I should have, and urged him instead to tell me what was on his mind,
which is what a hilarious class I go to tells me you should do if you're out
with a date who is tongue-tied with shyness.

He said he'd had a row with Gary in the car about Vietnam. They were
both expecting to be drafted, and Patrick was saying that if Gary lost his
student deferment he ought to appeal, and Gary said it was their duty to
go wherever their country sent them. Patrick said he didn't know what
he thought, he was just scared, which was quite an admission in the
circumstances. I told him about the debate we once had at school,
remember: "Patriotism is the last refuge of a scoundrel"? And soon we
were having what I thought was quite an interesting conversation, only
by now it was really bucketing down and we'd reached the dormitory
(that's not dormitory as in "The Twins at St Clare's", by the way, it's
just the place where we all live). So I said he should come into the lobby,
where we are allowed to bring men-friends, and I'd get him some coffee.

This was when it got embarrassing. I've never been in the lobby before
on a Saturday night, usually keep to my cloister. You should have seen
it. Talk about the last days of Pompeii. Or do I mean Sodom and
Gomorrah? On the sofas, on the chairs, even on the floor – couples doing
it. Well, not doing *it*, but not far short. I've never seen so many hands in
places where hands shouldn't be. I couldn't look at Patrick, just fled for
the coffee machine in the basement.

When I got back he'd made a space for us on the sofa with couples to the right of him, couples to the left of him, volleying and thundering, you know? I gave him his coffee and we sat and drank it and not all the slurping sounds were coming from us. Then I thought of going to get a towel as we were pretty wet, so I did that, and when we'd dried off he went all strong and silent again so I tried a bit more conversation – the weather again and had he ever been to Europe – and he just grunted, so I thought I'd have another go at what we'd started talking about before and asked him if he was going to run away to Canada, which is what some boys do if they don't want to be drafted. He didn't answer, he just kissed me. Now I don't know whether it was because he didn't think we ought to talk about that sort of thing there, or because with all the other couples going at it hammer and tongs he thought we'd be letting the side down, if we talked about anything, but I do know that he only kissed me to shut me up. And he knew that I knew too, because when he came up for air he said I didn't like him, did I, and I said something polite which was difficult because he was quite right, I didn't by now, and soon he'd downed the rest of his coffee and walked off into the night and that was the end of my date, so I've come up to my room to write to you. Dear Marje, what's wrong with me?
Worried,
  Deaconsburg

PS (much later): What a surprise, I've found a new friend. One of the girls who was in the lobby came up to talk after her man went home. I hadn't noticed her, though I should have; she's one of the ones whom I may have mentioned, always protesting about something or other, in particular the dress regulations that say we always have to wear skirts. The protest takes the form of wearing skirts – scruffy, unhemmed, patched ones made out of what looks like old curtains – that even the college authorities here can't think are more ladylike than a decent pair of trousers. She said she'd heard me ask Patrick about running away to Canada and assumed I must be something to do with the Movement (against the war) and was surprised she hadn't met me because she was too. I explained and she was really interested to hear I'd come from England, though she said she couldn't think why – she's pretty rude about America considering she's American, most of the girls are very patriotic. She cheered me up a lot about the date, she said it was typical of an American middle-class girls' college and that all they want is to get you married off as soon as possible and that the best way to do that was to make sure that boys and girls can never get together in an informal, normal, relaxed sort of way so that most girls never find out what schmucks most boys are. She says they have mixed visiting, even mixed dormitories in some colleges, and everything's more free and easy. She says her women's liberation group want to organise a campaign to have that here and do I want to join in the consciousness-raising? She laughed like a drain when I told her it was an essay on women's rights that got me the scholarship; she said probably no-one else went in for it and she didn't blame them, or perhaps my essay was spotted by the solitary feminist on the history faculty, who's since been dismissed! Her name's Brenda, Bren for short (as in gun) and she's what my father would call good value. At least, he would until he found out that she's a real live Revolting Student. Anyway, I'm going to join her group. Why not?

Love,

  Jackie

Dear Granny Ruby,

  I hope this air-letter reaches you in time to say Happy Christmas, as your present certainly won't. I've been so busy. I'm sending you some books by sea mail. I think you'll be a bit surprised when you see them. Do you remember telling me about those ladies you used to type for, who supported Votes for Women? Well, the cause lives on!

  My roommate invited me home with her for Christmas, but I'm in no mood for turkey and tinsel and all female hands to the kitchen. So a group of us have rented an apartment in Deaconsburg for the holidays. I'm afraid if you could see it, you'd shake your head in that way of yours and say, "Now, Jackie, boyfriends don't like untidiness." To which I now have my reply: "Boyfriends can clear it up, then!" And they do. There are some men staying with us, though I'd rather you didn't tell my parents that, they'd call it living in sin, which it isn't, not as far as I'm concerned anyway, and if Bren and the others want to, that's their business. Sin is a horrible word for it; free love is nicer. I'm relying on you, who after all gave me my first gin and cigarette when I was fourteen, not to be shocked. One of the guys is Black and there are a couple of draft-resisters. It's all part of the same struggle against injustice, can you see that? Racism, sexism, the war . . . oh, look. I'm so used to using these words I forget I'd hardly heard of them before I came away. And I'm bullying you to understand what I don't fully understand myself, though it's becoming clearer every day. At the end of November we tried to get signatures on a petition for mixed visiting in the dormitories. Hardly any of the girls would sign. They said they didn't want boys to see them not properly dressed up. Isn't that typical of women? They paint themselves and twist themselves and spend a fortune on clothes and have sleepless nights in their curlers just to please men. *We* say if men don't like us as we are, that's their bad luck. Next spring we're really going to zap them, there's an appalling college tradition of having a beauty contest judged by the

440

football team of our brother college, and the winners get to be their cheerleaders! We're going to get an entrance form and enter the name of Daisy Boeuf. And Daisy Boeuf will turn out to be a cow and we will lead her in before the judges. Bren knows how we can get a cow. We'll be making our protest against the cattle market. And we're going to have a jean-in and a dorm-in and we're going to get Grooming and Popularity scrapped and have Women's Studies instead. And I'm going to do research on the woman who endowed my scholarship, to find out if she was a feminist. Sorry if I'm rambling on, it's all so exciting I hardly sleep at night, and it's just as well my exam results don't matter.

Lots of love from your liberated granddaughter,

  Jackie

Dear Mum,

  I feel awful that you went to all that trouble to find out Lindi's home telephone number secretly and phoned on Christmas Day, especially as I'm sure you-know-who was chuntering on about the cost. I didn't deliberately deceive you about my Christmas plans, I just changed them at the last minute.

  You didn't say anything about the book I sent you. I wonder if you've read it yet and if it made you as angry as it should. I liked to think of you being so angry and absorbed that you sat down with it on Christmas Day and refused to go anywhere near the pots and pans. Pots and pans on Christmas Day, Mrs Orange, this is your life! But not any more, I hope. I want you really to stand up for yourself now; it's not too late, in spite of the big con trick that's taken most of your life from you, ever since the end of the war when all the men wanted their jobs back and the advertising industry wanted tame housewives at home with nothing to think about but soap powder and washing machines. I can't stand to think about "himself" ordering you about and you never having a minute to fulfil yourself, and now that you're worn out and getting older he turns round and decides he wants some nice young dolly-bird instead, and you thought the only way to keep him was to have another baby. My God, I'm so glad for you that you were able to get that abortion. Do you know England has one of the most enlightened laws in the world on that? You wouldn't be able to here. You'd be signed on for another twenty years instead of free as you are now. Do you really think he'll leave you? I should damn well show him the door. Please pass the book on to Julia and Kate when you've read it.

This is how we sign letters in the movement:

In sisterhood and struggle,

  Jackie

8

Dear Mary,

Picture the scene: the college swimming pool. Fourteen amateur Miss Worlds in push-you-out-pull-you-in swimsuits and floral swimming caps shiver and titter on the edge. Plus me, in regulation college black. Ironic, really. We got the dress regs repealed . . . and half the girls respond by coming to swimming in things they can hardly move in.

One word from the swimming teacher, and we slide into the pool. And as the warm blue water laps at my thighs (I'm doing this course in Pornographic Writing, see?) it sizzles in the heat of my young body. Because I'm HOT. Yeah, you guessed it; it's happened at last; your pure-as-the-driven friend has lost her virginity.

The swimming teacher tells us to lie on our backs. Sounds familiar. And tells us to practise lengths of elementary back stroke. The water's warm compared with the icy February air outside but I almost feel I could breathe it in after the stuffy air of the changing rooms. It cools me where I need cooling, I'm half asleep after my sleepless night. I'm bruised from lust and passion, I wonder if anyone can see. The water cradles me. I feel One with the elements. Just thought I'd let you know.

Love,

Jackie

PS: Oh, you want to know how it happened? You want to know who he is? Oh well, if you're sure I'm not boring you.

I have to go back a bit, to when the draft resisters at our brother college contacted our women's liberation group and asked if we'd come on a picket. Bren wasn't keen. She said if men on the left had shown that kind of solidarity with women in the first place, there wouldn't even need to be a separate women's movement. But someone pointed out that we'd want their support for our beauty contest protest in the spring, and someone else said in a way it was the same thing – boys get drafted to be he-men and killers, and girls get drafted to be sex objects and domestic slaves, so we agreed to go. Bren has a way of showing it when she's not happy. She's little and wiry with a sort of clipped-off way of speaking and slightly buck teeth that she can hardly close her lips over, *except* when she's not happy. When you can't see anything of Bren's teeth, watch out.

Roommate Lindi wasn't happy either, about me going. We came the nearest we've ever come to a row when I told her she should stop weeping about Gary who's off to do his basic training any minute, and *do* something about the war. First she pretended she had to write a paper. Then she almost turned nasty. I say *almost* – you might as well talk about a rose turning nasty, but her cheeks went very pink and her eyes flashed and she said, "Is everything so perfect in England that you have to come over here and tell us what's wrong with our country?" That shook me. But Bren says nationality and patriotism are male ideas, I wouldn't be going as an Englishwoman but as a *human being* who wants to stop the killing.

About twelve of us went on the bus: seven guys who were going for their medicals at the induction center, an organiser and us four women. The organiser (yes, yes! It is he!) had beads in his hair, a T-shirt that said "Fuck the War", and come hither eyes. Of which more anon. He gave us leaflets to hand out. They were horrifying. They were written in this sort of joky, suggestive style, you could laugh until you realised what they *meant*. This sort of tone: We're not saying you *should* become a drug addict, an alcoholic or a homosexual or mad, or deliberately injure yourself, or become grossly over- or underweight, but any of these things *could* make you ineligible for the US Army. Worst of all was the sight of these big, obviously healthy guys hoping that the medical would uncover something wrong with them.

His name is Calvin. That's his first name; says he's forgotten if he ever had a second. Americans really do have names like that. The original would turn in his grave, though as he says, "I'm a bit of a nonconformist myself." Not only does he wear beads in his hair, his hair itself is an amazing colour – deep, glossy black that glows almost blue in certain lights, quite fascinating. At first I was sure it was dyed but now I know better, after all, as he said last night, "You wouldn't expect me to risk carcinogenic hair-dyes *there*, would you, chick?" (Calling me chick is one of his less appealing habits, but I'm working on it.) I hope you're not shocked by this letter. I mean to speak frankly. What else about him? He teases my Englishness and I can't help laughing – jokes about the Queen, our economic plight "Did you hear they robbed the Bank of England last week and took all the money? Twelve dollars, thirty-seven cents", the Empire "Your Queen's going on a tour of the British Empire today, she'll be back by tea-time" and of course he's a revolutionary. For reasons I forget, his birth was never officially registered and he never went to school and he's never had a proper job, so as far as the US government is concerned he doesn't exist. So he's never been drafted and never will be.

Anyway, where was I? Oh yes, the picket. Bren and Calvin got on from the beginning like fire and water. He was trying to brief us on how not to be arrested, things like offering no violence(!), not standing still (obstruction), not dropping anything on the ground (littering), and explaining to the guys going for their medicals that they had a legal right to our leaflets if they wanted them. Bren said to him. "Do you think you're the only person who's ever done picketing before?"

I saw her point – none of the other guys had come to picket and there was Calvin bossing us women about, but there were some pretty mean looking cops watching us and slapping their batons into their hands and I was keen to know what was legal and what wasn't. Bren wanted us all to stand together in front of the building, but Calvin wanted me and him to wait round the corner to catch people coming the other way and to be reinforcements if there were any arrests. But Bren said, "Fucking macho confrontationism, we're not provoking arrests," and told me to stand with her.

I did, and Calvin sulked. Still, all the best love affairs start with a quarrel, don't they?

We gave out the leaflets while CIA men in plain clothes made home-movies of us and policemen paced in circles, sort of snarling and watching for a false move. I felt quite noble and brave, though I guess there wasn't much danger. Some guys took the leaflets and thanked us, others swore and tore them up. At the end of the day, the ones who had come with us came out; they'd been passed 1A, fit to serve. And gloomily we went home.

Calvin practically forced me to sit next to him on the bus which made Bren glare again. Unfair, really because I meant to convert him to feminism on the journey. Conversation went something like this.

CALVIN (looking moodily at Bren) 'She's a women's libber, then?'

ME: 'Yes, and so am I.'

CALVIN 'Me too, chick.'

ME: 'Cluck, cluck. Don't call me that, and don't tell us what to do.'

What we did arrange was for him to support the dorm-in. He actually is quite in favour of feminism when he's not fooling around. He says men are just as oppressed by sexism as women, what he's in favour of is People's Liberation. What he actually said when I asked him if he'd support the dorm-in was (looking at my bust), "I'll support anything that needs supporting, chick." I managed not to laugh. I suppose someone who makes sexist jokes but is there when he's needed is better than someone who's learned all the right words but does damn-all about it.

Scene Two. The Dorm-In. Not quite such a good turnout as we'd hoped; a lot of girls who'd promised to support us and invite their male friends (*not* just boyfriends, that was the whole point) in for the evening, turned out to have sudden, important reasons for being away for the weekend. We discussed calling it off, but Bren wouldn't. It didn't look good, though; a practically empty dorm with about ten of us and five illegal men crammed into Bren's room drinking coffee and coke. Bren was very strict about no alcohol, no drugs, no sex. I felt disappointed for her not having a bigger crowd – she'd practised her speech on me and it was very good. She reminded us that we'd informed the college authorities of what we were doing and they might come and confront us at any time. Calvin was very nasty to her, told her she was taking just the leadership role she'd criticised him for taking on the picket, but she gave as good as she got.

CALVIN: 'Are you in charge, then?'

BREN: 'Right. If they come, I think I'd like for them to find us doing some consciousness-raising, not having an orgy – '

C: 'I only came for the orgy.'

BREN (shouting to drown him): 'We don't often get to do c-r with guys.'

C: 'Prefer to do it with each other.'

At this point I told him to shut up or go home, hoping he'd take the former alternative because it was nice having him there. He was sitting behind me running his hand up and down my spine where no-one could see, sort of lazily and not going anywhere, like someone mowing the grass on a hot day. He said, "Shut up or go home," mimicking my accent, sort of wonderingly, as if he'd never heard anything so beautiful or so funny.

Bren invited anyone, any woman, to say what was on her mind, and I talked about something I'd found out about the woman who endowed my scholarship. Apparently she came out from England early this century and used to be a prison officer. Everyone laughed and said, "That explains plenty," but I must investigate her more. The college administration office said all her money came from tobacco, but I wonder why she decided to put it into women's education. They said there might be some more stuff about her in the library archives.

Calvin wanted to talk about sex. He said why did we have to be hung up about sex, Bren banning it was like the college authorities banning it. She didn't deign to answer and soon he tailed off and it was just us women talking in the usual way of our c-r sessions, only this time with a male audience. It was rather awkward – we were all sick of coffee and coke and tense from listening for footsteps. I began to think they might not come after all. They were just ignoring us. We'd been so tensed up, working out what we'd do if they had the guys arrested for trespassing or tried to throw the girls out of college, we hadn't thought what would happen if they just left us to stew in our own militant juices! And when Calvin started openly rolling a joint, saying it would liven up the discussion and he would swallow it if anyone came, not even Bren argued.

Have you ever smoked pot? It's not true that it's addictive, and it's much nicer than alcohol. Also, as you don't pay tax on it, you're not contributing to the military-industrial complex. It was nice, though it made me a bit talkative and emotional. I think everyone else was the same, but I can only remember my bit, and not even that very clearly. One of the first things that happened was that Bren turned into you, and I said, "You told me I was in love with my father." It wasn't exactly a hallucination – it's LSD that does that and I wouldn't touch it – more a nice mix-up. I mean, if one of my best women friends turns into another of my best women friends, there's a sort of truth in that, isn't there? Anyway – as far as I can remember –

BREN: 'I said that?'

ME: 'No, it was Mary – '

B: 'Do you think it's true?'

ME: 'I think I used to flirt with him.'

B: 'Did he touch you?'

ME: 'Not like that.'

B: 'You'd be surprised how many girls are raped by their fathers.'

Some of the men laughed. She was trying to stop them. My dad's a bastard, but I couldn't think that of him. I still don't know where my next words came from, but, my God. In vino veritas. In pot veritatissimus. (Or something, don't let Miss H see that.)

ME: 'It was safer to love him than my mother. It was safer to take his side, and go to cricket matches.'

B: 'Safer? Why safer?'

ME: 'Because otherwise I'd have to stay at home and clear up the dust.'

CALVIN: 'Dust, what dust?'

I tried to explain about how our house was always dusty and my mother was always fighting it, but he thought I was talking about radioactive dust and started in on that. I was practically crying by now and there seemed to be lots of arms round me. I kept saying my mother shouldn't have married my father and then realising that that involved wishing I didn't exist. At last I said I had to go to my room for a bit. I just wanted some air and to lie down. I remember this.

CALVIN: 'Are you okay, Jackie? I'll see you up there – '

BREN: 'No you won't.'

C: 'What do you take me for, Brenda? If I'm not back in five minutes, call the cops.'

And that's all I do remember until suddenly we were making love, on Linda's empty bed, no less. Calvin assures me I insisted on that.

Mary, I know I started this off very jokily, but I think that was to cover up how I really felt, and feel, which is indescribable. It's as if I became a new person, understanding and liberating myself from the past for the first time. I never got on with men before because I was scared of them, scared of them turning me into someone like my mother – only now I know I can love, have *everything* and not be trapped.

Another thing, strictly between us girls, have you discovered the delights of your clitoris? He was rather shocked that I didn't know about mine. "Whoever heard of a liberated woman who didn't masturbate?" he said – lucky I was still high from the pot and other things, I mean, I've never encountered that word in polite conversation or even rude conversation. But now that I do know how to, er, do that, I'm beginning

446

to wonder how I'll ever find time to do anything else! Ahem. High-minded historical note. Did you know the Victorians used to cut women's clitorises off as a punishment for masturbation? Calvin read it in a book.

So anyway, all that was how come I found myself floating dazedly around the swimming pool on a cold and frosty morning, thighs a-sizzle. I hope they don't censor the post. I'll let you know the other results of the dorm-in.

Lots of love,

Jackie

9

Long strands of cold May rain lashed the double-glazed window of the airliner as it taxied to a halt at Gatwick Airport.

The knowing, exquisite stewardess announced that it was 9 A.M. local time, and urged the passengers to leave nothing behind them.

Jackie got queasily to her feet and shuffled towards the exit. The stewardess thanked her for choosing this airline.

"It was the first flight I could get," she muttered to herself.

In Immigration she found herself standing in the Alien's queue. She changed to British and was waved through. She was home.

What am I doing here? The term hasn't ended. Back at Deaconsburg, they're calling my name on registers. What will people think? What will Lindi make of my empty bed, my bare wardrobe? Am I quite mad? Do I think I'm David Frost or somebody, to go jetting round the world at a minute's notice? The airport floor is soft under my feet. It's busy with people taking early holidays. Nobody is looking at me. I am not David Frost.

The loudspeaker cleared its throat and gave a little ping; the voice was Bren's.

You can get abortions in England, right?

My mother had one.

So get back there. Don't waste time.

Feeling unable to speak, she couldn't buy a railway ticket. She dodged past the ticket collector and dragged her suitcase to the platform. Trains whizzed this way and that. This was for London. That way for the Sussex coast.

The Sussex coast. The first shaft of light since the dark nightmare of the doctor's office. Not the Student Health Center. An

447

impoverished surgery at the far end of town; hers the only white, healthy face.

Do you prescribe birth-control pills for single girls?

I'll have to examine you.

Gentle black hands probing. The black nurse watchful. *Isn't it customary to go to your own kind for this sort of thing? The surgery is full of malnutrition, cancers.* Visions of the Klan, accusing rape of white womanhood.

Are your periods regular?

Well, er, no, actually.

I'm afraid it's a bit late for birth-control pills. Miss Orange.

The first train that comes, I'll get on it. If it's a London train, I'll go home and face things. If it's southbound, I'll take that as a sign that I should go to Granny Ruby, and somehow, somehow, she'll make it all right.

Again Bren's voice came over the loudspeaker. "All stations to Brighton . . ."

Jackie boarded the train with relief. If the London train had come first she would not have got on it. She had to rest before she went home, sleep and eat and vomit and cry.

He said casually, once in the aftermath, I suppose you're on the pill, chick? And I said, yeah, dreamily. Why did I say that? Didn't want to admit the risks I'd already taken, I suppose. They didn't seem real anyway. And I didn't know where to go for help, and couldn't ask Bren who was so angry with me. And when I told Calvin what had happened, he said, can't be mine, chick, you were taking those pills when you were with me.

"Change here for Leehaven . . ."

The rain had stopped for a rest. The air was turning white, bravely pretending it was May; it was sweet, it tasted of salt. The Leehaven train was full of children. Did anyone go to Leehaven but children to visit their grandmothers? There the grandmothers were, clustered at the barrier, not a platform ticket among them. Might Granny Ruby be there? Might she, by some miracle, be passing?

"Can I leave my luggage here?"

"In the left-luggage, miss."

She had never used the left-luggage at Leehaven station before. She had never had reason to. Why was she using it now? In case Granny Ruby would not take her in. In case Granny Ruby could not accept the transformation from earnest grandchild with a bag of homework, maturing sixth-former planning to be a doctor (*when was that?*) into that timeless, pathetic figure, *a girl in trouble*. She felt a wave of fury against Calvin, but even before it spent itself she knew she could not blame him. If he had done nothing to protect her, she had not sought to protect herself until it was too late. *Why not?* She knew how babies were made! Why had she thought it did not apply to her? It was a puzzle to add to all the anxiety . . . when all this was settled, and she was at university (for they wouldn't take her place away, would they, just because she had run away from Deaconsburg?) she must keep her vow to bring the message of feminist consciousness-raising to English women, and discover . . . she might blame Calvin for the casual enthusiasm with which he had endorsed Bren's suggestion that she get back to England as soon as possible, but he had never promised to love her. About that he was quite clear: *Marriage, love everlasting, chick; it's not my scene and you know it, it's why you wanted me, and when it's time to go, it's time to go* . . . All true. Did she miss him? No, not now . . . but she would, she knew she would.

Leehaven had changed. It had not all happened in the months of her absence, of course, but she seemed to see its newness for the first time. Heath & Heather was a Wimpy Bar. The old brown Boots' that used to have a lending library upstairs was blue and self-service. There was a penny arcade on the sea-front. The sky was turning grey, a storm was coming. She must go to Granny Ruby's and shelter.

Unease seized her as she ambled slowly up the street, but she hardly recognised it on top of all her other troubles. The building did not look right. The landlady's downstairs flat was normal, but there were no curtains at Granny Ruby's broken, blackened windows. She climbed the steps, trying not to breathe the smell of old smoke. She knocked on the door, knowing there would be no answer. She peered through the letterbox. The flat was empty. And the walls were charred and blackened from a recent fire.

She took it quite calmly, as if she had known all along. *What do I do now? Enquire at the landlady's, the hospital, the morgue? Visit the fire-station, the Constitutional Club? Or just go home?*

She decided to go home.

She had lost all interest in what time it was, but it seemed like late afternoon. The rain had stopped but her wet hair bore evidence of it. *Damn this English weather, don't they know it's*

May and I've come home? Her cases were heavy. Hadn't she read somewhere that pregnant women should not carry heavy cases? She hitched them up and walked faster.

As she hurried past the council houses, someone shouted "Evening, Jackie!" in casual greeting as if they had not even noticed that she had been away. *I've been away all right, I can prove it.*

The house loomed: grey and dark, with ill-fitting bricks. The council had never got round to building on the tangled bombsite next door. There were a few garish painted posts, the beginnings of an adventure playground. That was new. Thank God something had changed, otherwise she might think she was going mad. As she approached the front door she could hear the sullen roar of the Hoover. At the sound of her knock, it was turned off, she imagined the little puff of smoke shooting out of the motor.

The door seemed to take forever to open, the big, heavy door. She panicked, she hadn't rehearsed what she was going to say. There was her mother with a smear of dust on her face, small and frail in a housecoat with a knobbly cord.

"I thought it was your father." She looked worried. Then she realised that Jackie shouldn't be there. "Jackie! You're so thin!" *Thin!* Jackie managed to think, *dieting! And then not eating!* before tiredness and tears felled her and she sprawled into her mother's tentative, embarrassed embrace, howling, "Oh Mummy, look after me!" Feeling no response from the housecoat, she thought, *God what did I say in those letters?*

Somehow they got to the kitchen and sat down. Jackie's mother's face was all questions. Terrified and unready, Jackie said quickly, "What happened to Granny Ruby?"

"Oh." A little sniff. "*That's* why you're here. Ask her."

"She's here?"

"Naturally her dutiful son offered her a home after the fire." Apparently Granny Ruby had gone to sleep one night in her flat at Leehaven with a cigarette burning and had a lucky escape, saving herself but little else. Jackie remembered Buddhist monks setting fire to themselves in Saigon to protest about the American presence . . . No, no, she was all confused, this was an accident and Granny Ruby was safe in the next room. She got up and left her mother and went to her, expecting a mass of putrid burns. But Granny Ruby sat placidly in an armchair in the family sitting-room that didn't seem to be the family sitting-room any longer, there was a bed in the corner and a tray on the floor with the remains of a boiled-egg lunch. There was a charred photograph on the wall of Granny Ruby in India with her two children and her husband. *Another addition to your family, Granny Ruby . . . might you be pleased?* But Granny Ruby looked at her without recognition, winding and unwinding her bandaged hands, suddenly, desperately older than her seventy-four years. There was a slight smell of urine mixed with disinfectant in the air.

Jackie knelt down beside her. There were dressings on her legs too.

"What have you been *doing* to yourself?"

"I'm all right now. Randolph and Emma will look after me, my son and daughter. It's about time I was looked after, an old woman . . ."

Jackie took her cold hand. The dressings were only light ones. If she were seriously hurt she would be in hospital. Of course she was confused after the horrible shock of waking up in a blazing bed. "Granny Ruby. You remember me? It's Jackie."

"Jackie! Of course!" The old woman's eyes cleared momentarily. Her jaw stuck out in a smile of greeting. Her false teeth slipped, changing the shape of her face, making her unrecognisable.

If Julia and Kate were surprised to see Jackie, they hid it under their pleasure. "Where's the loot, then?" Kate demanded, a family expression for presents, thinking she might prepare them, and herself, with a dropped hint, Jackie said, "I left in rather a hurry, actually." They didn't care; they just wanted to question her about American fashions, records, listen closely and goadingly for any trace of an accent, fill her in on their own news, which was that Julia had been accepted to train as a pupil-nurse and Kate had a boyfriend. Jackie shuddered, averted her new eyes; had they not read her letters, the books she had sent? They were her sisters, her real flesh-and-blood sisters, if she could not stop *them* obediently lowering their heads for a cowlike walk into stereotyped female occupations –

Who was she to talk?

They had tea, all of them together in Granny Ruby's room. Her mother was garrulous and hospitable. What a lovely surprise! How cross Daddy would be with himself for being so late! He was at one of his stupid old business meetings. They were such a good audience, Jackie almost forgot the things she had eventually

451

to tell. Granny Ruby was intermittently confused and alert. Sometimes she reached a sly finger under one of her dressings. Once she did this, Jackie's mother raised a hand as if to smack her, her face half-amused, half-disgusted.

"They'll never heal if you play with them."

"They itch," said Granny Ruby.

"That shows they're healing."

Finally her mother said, "I expect you'd like something to eat, Jackie. I was going to wait for Randolph, but . . ."

He came in when they were sitting at the table, all except Granny Ruby, who stayed in her room. "Well, well, well!" he said, grabbing Jackie. "Well, well, well! Young Lochinvar has come out of the West! Throw you out, did they? I'm not surprised." She escaped him and smiled thinly. He went on, "I thought you'd got shot with the other lot." He showed her the evening paper. Four students had been shot dead in an anti-war demonstration on a campus in Ohio.

"Ohio's not in Virginia," she said mechanically. But she was reading on. Students all over the States were up in arms. Was Bren all right? And Calvin, and the others? What were they doing?

She said, "I've come home because I'm pregnant," just like that, a terrible way to break in, no warning, no preparation, nothing. Well, they should have realised.

10

"Don't cry," Mary said, holding her, "don't cry."

"But – "

"But you're pregnant, okay, you're not the first, you won't be the last."

"He told me to get out of his sight."

"Who, the father?"

"I mean, *my* father. And it's terrible at home, Mary, it's ghastly, I mean, he made her get rid of her baby and my grandmother's ill, and – "

"Jackie. One thing at a time, huh?" At school, Jackie had been the defender, the clever one, sticking up for Mary, getting her out of trouble. Now Mary was relentless. "Weren't you on the pill or anything?"

452

"Look." Jackie clenched and unclenched her fists, she had to say this in the brief moment that it was clear to her. "I'm *sure* it was because of my mother. I mean, my whole life has been built round a determination not to be like her, and that was why I just didn't believe . . . I mean, I just couldn't relate, *personally*, to what I knew was true. Can you – "

Mary waved her arms impatiently. "Do you want the baby?"

"Are you mad?"

"I *knew* this would happen. As soon as I got that letter from you that was like something out of the Kama Sutra. I thought, that girl can't be trusted to look after a puppy, never mind herself. Beads in his hair indeed! You might want the baby. I don't know how deep this lib-lib bug has bitten you."

"If you're going to talk that way, Mary, I'll do without your help." Panic made her angry. They had been friends. How could they be so far apart? "Women's liberation's the most important thing to happen for women since – "

"Sure, but you didn't invent it."

"Isn't anyone going to help me?" Jackie wailed, getting up dramatically, hoping to be stopped, because where else was there to go? "Are you just going to use what's happened to score points?"

"Coming from someone who has just blamed her own mother, who was three thousand miles away at the time, for her unfortunate condition, that is very good."

Deflated and humble, Jackie said, "Please Mary, can you help me get an abortion?"

"Sure, but I think a doctor would be a better bet." She smiled.

"Which doctor?"

"No, not a witch doctor, try your own. He did your mother, didn't he? Oh, look, don't take any notice of me. Your letters were a bit much, Jackie, and after a correspondence course in how every woman but you was living their life all wrong, I wasn't really . . . go and see your doctor. And if he says no, come back to me with a hundred pounds. There are some hygienic crooks in Harley Street who'll be happy to part you from your money and your, ah, little problem if the National Health averts its eyes. Or so I'm told. I wouldn't know, I've never had an abortion." Mary's eyes softened into anxiety and affection, then she was tough again in the same instant. "I've never needed one, Jackie, listen. It is happening here too. I don't know much about it. But I'm sure *this* –", She pointed to her friend's stomach "– isn't what it's supposed to be about."

Once again Jackie lay half naked while a doctor probed and peered between her thighs. Dr Harrad, who had syringed her childish ears and made her cry with his diphtheria injections.

"You're quite right, Jackie, you are pregnant."

"Yes. I know."

"And is there to be a wedding? Any congratulations in order?"

"*No*. I don't want it. I want an abortion." She swallowed, which was difficult, lying there so tense. She had to say, "It's my right."

"I beg your pardon?" He meant, *Who are you to talk of rights?* it made sense. If he wanted her to beg, she had to beg.

But he didn't want her to beg. Not yet. He wanted something else. He wanted to talk, lying there, about Calvin, about her parents, about what she knew of help available to unmarried mothers. She wouldn't. At last he said, "You seem to be in good shape, physically. Are you saying that you fear for your mental health if you continue with the pregnancy?"

"Can I get up," said Jackie, "please?"

"In a minute, I'm not quite finished – " She ground her teeth and looked at the surgery's yellow ceiling. There should be flowers or cartoons or even public health slogans: Give up smoking. An apple a day, the VD clinic is at . . . something to read. At last he let her dress, leaning on his desk and making her talk again before she was ready. He had a waiting-room full of patients, niceties and decencies need hardly be observed between a white-haired medical man and a grown-up child the inside of whose vagina was more familiar to him than it was to her. For the last time she would say it. "I don't want to have a baby. I don't want to be a mother. I've got a university place. *I don't want a baby!*"

"You see, Jackie, none of those things is grounds."

"What do you want from me?" she demanded, finally buttoning her straining jeans. The bulge which had been hardly noticeable when she left America was bounding forward since it knew it was at home and under threat.

"I?" The doctor laughed sadly. "I? Nothing! I thought you wanted something from me! If I am mistaken, this appointment can be terminated forthwith. Sit down, Jackie." She did; he

454

remained standing. "Jackie, my personal feelings for you and your family and my sympathy for all young girls in your predicament are not the point. I am subject to the laws of this country, and so are you. I can recommend you for abortion on certain grounds. Nothing you have told me suggests that those grounds apply to you. I have, you see . . ." he fumbled in his desk and brought out a green sheet of paper, ". . . to sign this. In good faith."

The lines swam. Something about him being of the opinion that her mental or physical health would be damaged by having a baby. She read his sad, lined, not unkind face. *He wants to help me. But he won't take the responsibility. Why should he? He needs me to say I can't take it, that I'll go mad, kill myself. Was that what my mother said? I can't ask her, ever. It doesn't feel true, suddenly, but it would be easy to say. Easy to say, and then he'll sign his name. What doctor would dare disbelieve such a threat from a distraught girl? A few tears would help.*

She said. "This is a waste of time, Doctor. I'll get it done privately."

"The private doctor will still have to sign the form."

Perhaps. But he'll demand cash, not my self-respect.

As she left the surgery, he offered her pink and blue ante-natal leaflets and she took them rather than argue any more.

Mary said, "I can lend you fifty. Just. But you wouldn't believe the rent on this place. What about darling Daddy?"

Her mother stopped sulking long enough to say, "I didn't have to pay for mine."

Jackie said, "No, well, you didn't want yours, did you?"

Her mother roared irrationally, "If you have a baby, I know who'll end up washing nappies!"

"Help me, then! Just fifty pounds!"

"Where would I get fifty pounds? Ask your father."

He was leafing through the proofs of a clothes catalogue. His firm was going into mail order. He was to visit young housewives at home with the catalogues and appoint them as his agents on commission.

She said, "I need fifty pounds."

"Get out of my sight."

"Daddy, I'm not ready to be a mother."

"You were ready enough to be a – " he stopped. Suddenly Jackie saw the pain in his face and was startled by her own rush of compassion. He seemed to have thought of something. He looked like the doctor. He was almost pleading. "Did he force you, Jackie? He did, didn't he? Or did he get you a little bit drunk? Or was it . . . look, you can tell me. I won't pretend I've never smoked pot. I know it can make you a bit uninhibited."

"No, I chose to do it," she said carefully.

"All right." He turned back to his catalogue. He put a big red ring round a misprint he had discovered. "When I think of how I brought you up. What a favourite I made of you. Your expensive education – "

"It was all on scholarships. It didn't cost you a penny!"

"Oh? What did you eat, then? Who bought your clothes?"

She felt as she'd felt in a dream, her first night in America: as if someone had tipped a bucket of cold water over her. He saw her face and seemed to know he had gone too far. He tried a smile. "I didn't mean that, of course."

"Are you going to help me, then?"

"I'll see. Just give me a little time to get used to the idea, will you?"

Now that Granny Ruby lived in the sitting-room. Jackie's old bedroom upstairs was used for the family to sit in. It might have made sense to use the boys' old room as it was bigger, but as her mother said, "Nobody's ever in in the evenings but me, so why dirty a big room?"

From the boys' old room, Jackie could hear her grandmother moving and muttering downstairs in the night.

It was hard to tell how ill she really was. Her burns, miraculously slight, were healing; her rheumatism seemed to come and go with her mind. The doctor said there was no reason why she couldn't go out on her own as long as she took care, but she didn't seem to want to. She was depressed, lethargic and frightened. Jackie guessed she was mourning for her little home, her life, her routine, her Indian things, all burned up in Leehaven; and perhaps she knew there was a crisis in the house, though Jackie had not been able to bring herself to tell her what it was.

Now Jackie listened to her restlessness and decided to go to her. She caught a whiff of cigarette smoke on the stairs and chuckled: her mother had put a strict ban on Granny Ruby smoking. In fairness, she had given it up herself too, though

456

Jackie knew she had a secret one now and again. It seemed that Granny Ruby was up to the same game.

She was sitting up in bed with a shawl about her shoulders. A point of fire in the darkness confirmed Jackie's suspicions. As she entered the room, the point darted like a firefly and disappeared under the bed.

Jackie made her voice gentle. "Don't hide it – not like that." She put on her mother's voice. "We shall all be burned in our beds."

Granny Ruby said huffily, "Anyone can have an accident."

"Well, yes," said Jackie.

"Sit down, dear. Can't you sleep either?"

"No."

"You seem to be having a lot of arguments with your parents."

"Yes."

Granny Ruby pulled her shawl tight and sucked thirstily at her cigarette. "Don't expect *me* to ask any questions, Jackie. When an old woman goes to live with her family, the last thing she should do is interfere in their quarrels." Jackie shuddered at the note of fear in the old voice. Since when had Granny Ruby considered her comments and advice as interference?

"Shall I make tea?"

"Not for me, dear, I'll have a little gin." She brought out a half-bottle and a glass from under her bed and measured a painfully tiny drink for herself. She nodded at Jackie. "I'm having to ration myself till I'm out and about again."

Jackie craved tea and went for some. When she came back with it, Granny Ruby was reaching again with difficulty under the bed.

"I'm trying to get something – "

"Tell me where it is, and I will – "

"I wanted it to be a surprise. Under the bed."

Jackie felt about gingerly. Her hand hit something hard and metallic. "Your typewriter! You saved it!"

"I told the fireman, save it before you save me. What a nice man he was! I knew it would come in handy."

"Does it still work?"

"Of course! British made – in the days when that meant something. It was secondhand when I got it, but I've kept it busy, kept it young. You'll get a good price for it."

"Price?"

"I want you to sell it. Sell it to a museum."

Jackie's eyes burned. She fingered the keys of the old machine. She hit *j*. Granny Ruby slapped her hand. "Don't do that without any paper in. You'll damage the roller."

"Why do you want me to sell it? You'll need it again! You'll need to type! You can't just give up beause of a stupid accident that could have happened to anyone! You'll get better, we'll find you another flat in Leehaven, you'll – "

Granny Ruby's eyes were glazing and clearing, glazing and clearing like some grotesque novelty clock. "I think you need some money, Jackie."

"I – "

"I'm not asking what it's for, Jackie." Jackie said nothing.

She knew nothing about typewriters, but she couldn't believe that old thing was worth fifty pounds. It was pre-war but hardly an antique. Granny Ruby went on. "I always meant to leave it to you in my will. It's safer to give it to you now, then you won't be tempted to bump me off to get your hands on it." She laughed eerily.

"Granny Ruby, I have to tell you what the money's for."

"No, you do not! You haven't seen fit to tell me so far, and it's not the price of my help! You younger generation, you think I'm a stupid old woman who doesn't know anything! You think you've invented everything! Imagine you writing to me to say you believe in free love and you hope I'm not shocked!"

"Granny – "

"Silly old Granny Ruby was a young girl once, you know! And a spot of good luck saved me from a very different life from the one I've had! You deserve the same chance. Now go away, I'm tired." She stubbed out her cigarette with exaggerated thoroughness. Jackie could find no more words, and soon she went back to bed.

It seemed to be a night for creeping about the house. At first she thought she was dreaming when her father came to her in his stripy pyjamas, ruffling his hair.

"Jackie, are you awake?"

"Yes."

"Look – "

She felt very adult and powerful, watching him struggle for words. He liked best to shout or make jokes.

"Look, it's hard for a man to accept it when his daughter . . .

I mean, you're *my doing* in a way, Jackie. Can you imagine what that feels like?"

"Yes."

"You can. Good."

He seemed relieved. He seemed to think he had said it all. How nice it must be to think everything was so simple. How nice. How bloody wonderful.

"Of course I'll give you the money, Jackie. No reason why one mistake should spoil your life."

"It wasn't a mistake and I'm keeping the baby."

"Is this a joke?"

"No. Just thinking. Thanks for the offer of the money. I may take you up on it, but not for an abortion. Will you throw me out?"

He reached out and ruffled her hair. They still resembled each other in their hair. Was thick, black, curly hair growing inside her at this moment? "What do you think I am?"

"A man," she said, "like Calvin." He laughed in the darkness. She didn't laugh. She had not wanted to become the man-hating kind of feminist. But there was something very clean and easy about the bitterness she felt.

"I'd be a fine one to throw you out." She tensed. Some dreadful confession was coming. Perhaps there was a young girl somewhere, pregnant by him? "You see, I'm not going to be here much longer myself." What was this, was he secretly terminally ill? "You know your mother and I – "

"You're leaving her?"

"When Kate leaves school, I shall consider my duty done as far as you lot are concerned. Don't be hard on me, Jackie. Isn't a man entitled to a bit of happiness? Even a man?"

Jackie ignored this. She had thought for ages that this ought to happen, ought to have happened years ago. But what would her mother do?

"What about Granny Ruby?" she demanded. Even he could not expect his wife to take care of his mother while he was whooping it up somewhere as a middle-aged honorary teenager. He couldn't expect that, could he?

"I'm looking round for homes," he said airily.

"They're dreadfully expensive," said Jackie.

He put on the face with which he usually preceded news that he had scored a century or pulled off a deal.

"You mean you can afford it?" Jackie enquired. He nodded. He seemed very pleased with himself: "And I'll see your mother right, of course."

"Oh, you will, will you?" Jackie got out of bed. She couldn't sit still with him on her bed while she said this. She paced round, her voice getting louder in the sleeping house. He watched like someone in a cartoon, his mouth opening and closing. "Oh, you will, will you? You can afford it, can you? You can afford to put your mother in a home, when a year ago you couldn't afford for your own wife to have your baby and a few hours ago you couldn't afford fifty pounds for your own daughter who would have gone on her knees to you for it? But maybe that was the trouble – I didn't go on my knees, did I? Oh, you'll see her right, will you? You can afford that now, can you? So how come you haven't seen her right all these years?"

"But Jackie, I've always given her anything she's wanted; if I could afford it! She wanted the abortion as much as – "

Jackie didn't want to hear this. If she stopped now she would never start again. She knew she was sounding like one of her dreadful, embarrassing, hectoring, know-it-all letters, but this was real and she had to say it. And her father stopped trying to argue. He took it, like a boy being punished at school. "You're leaving, are you? I bet you're not going to another dusty slum like this! You want me to have an abortion now, do you? Well I'm not going to have one so you'll feel better, nor am I going to pass up the opportunity of handing on what *I* know to a new generation, any baby I have will be illegitimate because I sure as hell am not getting married, ever, so it might as well be this one so I won't ever have to *talk* to a man again! And you needn't worry that I'm going to disgrace the family with my *common* behaviour because both I and my baby are going to have an entirely new name . . . "

"When I said that, of course, he immediately jumped to the conclusion that I *was* getting married," Jackie wrote to Bren, "whereas in fact I'm going to change my name to Barrington, my grandmother's maiden name, the one who offered me the typewriter, the only one who tried to help without having a go at me . . ."

Writing this, she wondered if Bren would have a go at her. But there wasn't much chance of the letter reaching Bren in any case. Bren had been thrown out of Deaconsburg for disruptive behaviour. She had sent Jackie a string of addresses where she might be reached. They all sounded pretty unlikely.

Maybe this was wishful thinking . . . but although Jackie carried Bren's letter around all morning before daring to open it, its contents were innocuous. Bren was training to teach self-defence. She was moving to California. Someone Jackie didn't remember had been arrested for a bombing in which she was not involved. Bren sent sisterly greetings to English feminists, and best wishes for Jackie's pregnancy and motherhood.

There was no reason why she should congratulate Jackie on her courage if she didn't feel that way. Or tell her she had made the right decision, or even pretend to understand her decision if she didn't.

It didn't even feel like a decision any more. Her body ballooned out as shop windows filled up with "Back to College" products. All she had had to do to stay pregnant was nothing. Now she started to wonder what was going to be expected of her.

11

The baby was born on November 14, nine months to the day after the dorm-in. That was a relief, at least: no need for Jackie to torture herself with the thought that if she'd only been sensible and gone on the pill straight away . . . after all, nobody was so cold blooded as to go on it in anticipation of losing their virginity, surely?

It was a girl. Jackie called her Dora. Dora Barrington sounded like an MP or a tennis-player. She was slightly underweight and had red hair.

So Calvin's hair really was dyed; there's no red hair in our family! It was the last nail in the coffin of his reality. She thought of him with weary disgust. It was probably all lies: his hair, his romantically disordered background, his support for feminism. It was more likely that he had seen feminism as a sophisticated version of playing hard-to-get, a challenge. Did he ever give her a thought, now? He would assume she had had an abortion. Would he want to know that he was a father? He was probably one already, several times over. He might even be married and living in a suburb. She drove him from her mind. He was nothing compared with the astonishing reality of his daughter. She was so little and clawing and voracious. Jackie stayed in hospital for nine days, elated by Dora and her own returning strength, then they went home.

The house seemed more unfamiliar than when she had got back from America, as if she had been on a much longer journey. Even the gruelling, relentless, unarguable reality of the birth had not, she realised, prepared her for thinking she was a mother, she had a child and both of them were made of flesh.

But it wasn't just that. The house had changed. There wasn't a speck of dust anywhere. Her mother went up into the loft and brought down the cobwebbed crib, she unearthed nappies from trunks. She made a list of jobs and stuck to them. She announced in the mornings what time supper was, and anyone who wasn't there got it cold. And she said, "Maybe you can think about going to university next year, Jackie. And I can look after Dora." Jackie wasn't sure. University didn't seem so important any more; after all, she'd only seen it as an escape, an escape that was now both impossible and irrelevant. She just lived from day to tiring, happy day, blessed her mother's kindly expertise and marvelled at it. They were helping each other as women should, she thought. Jackie remembered her mother's tearful plans for getting organised and making the house nice for her own baby; Jackie hoped Dora was making up a little for the loss. Hadn't Bren always said that the nuclear family oppressed women and children, that an extended family was best? Wasn't this an extended family?

Jackie said, "No wonder it was so difficult for you, with *five*."

Her mother said off-handedly, "I never had five *babies*."

"But I can't do anything except look after her and sleep. And you're helping me."

"Ah," said her mother, "I had your father." And Jackie, not sure if she was joking, said, "I expect he was a great help." And her mother, apparently equally unsure, stared at her. And they scoffed with laughter together and Dora splashed about in her yellow plastic bath.

Dora seemed even to have brought about an armistice between Jackie's parents. Her father started coming home in the evenings and sulked if his grandchild was asleep and he couldn't play with her.

"It's only six o'clock," he protested

"I'm sorry, but she was tired."

"Couldn't you have kept her up? She's got all day to sleep . . . just like the rest of you."

"You've still got a bit of work to do on your father, Jackie," her mother said archly. Her kindness and helpfulness were increasing Jackie's embarrassment about the diatribes she had sent her from America, and she was keeping off the subject of feminism except when her mother raised it, half joking, half goading but always (or did Jackie imagine this?) curious for more. "I knew you'd give up this women's lib business once you had a baby to look after."

"I'm not giving it up. This is part of it!" Jackie shouted very loudly.

"Well, don't tell me! Tell your father!"

Once he said, "Can't you drop this Barrington business now, Jackie? You've made your point."

"I thought you'd be pleased. Saves embarrassment."

"But how can I talk about my daughter Jackie Barrington and my granddaughter Dora Barrington when there isn't a Mr Barrington?"

"Tell them the truth. That I reject my patriarchal name. Or say I'm a tragic widow. I don't care. Anyway, think about it. You can't call her Dora Orange."

"Why not?"

"Say it fast."

"Dora Orange, Dora Orange, Doraorange, Doraorange . . ."

"There! Isn't that common? It's like when carol singers stick an r in 'Gloriarinexcelsis', and you know how you hate that."

He was silent. Jackie liked her new name. The very difficulty of remembering it would remind her of what she was doing, stop her sinking back into complacent motherhood. She felt so proud of Dora, who had brought peace to the house. Her father said no more of his plans to leave. He started bringing things home. Baby clothes, of a quantity and variety to last till Dora went to school. (School! Which school? Jackie's old school? Would she still be here then? Where else? But why worry? She had worried enough for a lifetime, Dora was here and she was here and the sun rose and set and Monday led to Tuesday just as if she had not worried.) He brought an intercom to hear Dora crying all over the house, and a washing machine specially designed for nappies. He even paid special attention to his mother, bringing her occasional bottles of gin, play-acting that this was secret from the rest of the family, taking her patiently to the pub so that she could have a cigarette, and generally treating her with a care that Jackie could not believe was compatible with an intention to dump her in an old people's home at the first opportunity.

Granny Ruby herself was delighted with Dora, and if she could not actually help much with the work of her, created none of her own. She seemed to think it very funny that Dora's and Jackie's name was now Barrington, but understood it no further. Jackie gave up trying to explain. The night-time conversation in which Granny Ruby had offered her typewriter had shown Jackie that there was a depth of understanding between them that words need not reach, perhaps could not.

There were still some disturbing incidents. Cigarettes were found burning on carpets. One day, Granny Ruby disappeared. She didn't say where she was going, just wasn't there when it was time to get up, didn't phone, didn't come home all day. The family didn't know what to do: they would feel foolish calling the police, she wasn't a prisoner and they were always on at her to get out and about when her rheumatism let up . . . she came back in the evening, weary, blank eyed and nearly lame. She said she had been to Leehaven, not for anything in particular, just to look around. Jackie's mother went into a panic: "She's senile at last, Randolph! Now what are we going to do?" But the laugh was not on Granny Ruby. When they searched her handbag, they did indeed find a used day-return to Leehaven. It made Jackie want to cry. She imagined Granny Ruby fingering the wet ashes of her old life. She suggested that she and Dora should go with her next time – what better place than Leehaven for Dora's first big outing?

They waited for a mild day and they went. The train was full of children, all years older than Dora, but children still. Salty wind blew through the strange, unfamiliar town. Jackie's arms ached from heaving the pram in and out of guard's vans, her brain throbbed with the responsibility of a tiny baby and a slow old woman to look after. By silent, common consent they went nowhere near Granny Ruby's old flat, to see it ruined or rebuilt with some new person's curtains in the window. And Granny Ruby was emphatic that she didn't want to go to the club or to visit anybody. They looked at the church and Jackie burrowed desperately in her memory for a trace of early feminist consciousness in the indignation she had felt over Aunt Emma not having her name on the war memorial, but her mind was blank, terrifyingly blank, defending her from pain. "Take your grandmother out to lunch," her father had said, pressing money into her hand; they went to a café that did an Old Age Pensioners' Special and Granny Ruby hid behind the menu in case there was someone she knew. What was it, shame? Or a need not to be reminded of the life she had lost? Jackie tried to pity her but only pitied herself. They ate roast beef with watery gravy; the waitresses cooed over Dora, who blew back bubbles and cried.

They walked along the sea-front where Jackie had run and run as a child, brushing the dust of home from her hair. "How's your leg, Granny Ruby?" she kept asking, harassed by the slow pace. "It's all right, dear. Once I'm moving I can keep going. It's getting started, that's the business!" Quite the opposite was "the business" in Jackie's case. Getting started had been only too easy; how was she to keep going? And where was she going? Dora was a treasure and a delight, but was she all? Jackie was only twenty, and still burdening her mother. Was she herself to be forty before she could make any more choices?

"I'll push the pram if we're slowing you down, dear." Jackie relinquished Dora and started to run. Ahead were the green Downs, breaking suddenly into white cliffs. She could run all the way up and look down at the sea. Her legs ached. It was a long time since she had taken proper exercise, she had striven to despise talk at the clinic of "getting her figure back". She had mouthed what she knew she ought to say, if only to herself: *I've had a baby, why shouldn't I look as if I've had a baby?* She didn't care about how she looked, who was there to see? Dora liked her soft and slow. But now she wanted to be light on her feet, full of energy and real ideas, not just face-saving formulas that seemed to have no meaning.

She ran out of breath long before she reached the beginning of the Downs and the cliff. Slowly she walked back to her grand-mother and her baby.

12

"Baby," asked the employment agency's advertisement in the High Street, "are you hot enough for Manpower?"

"This ad," ventured a sticker, "insults women."

A felt-tip pen had added, "So what?"

"So march on Saturday!" proclaimed a huge spray-painted circle with a cross beneath a fist.

Excitedly, Jackie planned for her family to send a contingent: her mother, her grandmother, herself, her sisters, and Dora. Four generations! But her words fell on stony ground. Julia would be on duty, Kate was going out with Dave, Granny Ruby had a bad leg and her mother was "far too busy".

"Might a mere male show his face?" her father enquired, "I've burned my jock strap."

Jackie walked out of the room and shouted down the phone to Mary, "You've got to, it's your duty. You don't have to join anything, and you know you believe in it really."

"Who are you talking to?" Mary grumbled. "Me or yourself? I'm a working girl, I value my Saturdays. I'm not coming."

But she did, very smartly dressed and made up, loudly blaming Jackie as much for her presence as for the bizarre icy-cold of the spring day that thrust knives up from the pavement through the thickest of soles and socks, numbing feet. Jackie took not the slightest notice. Mary had always liked to play the bullied dupe, but she never went anywhere she did not want to go. She wanted to be here all right, with Jackie and these hundreds of other women with red noses and pale cheeks, walking arm in thickly-coated arm, banging their gloved hands together and dropping money as they bought and sold pamphlets. There were some men with beards too, selling socialist newspapers with photographs of women on the front. They reminded Jackie of Calvin and she gave them a wide berth, but one managed to ram into her hand a closely-typed sheet of duplicating paper which said that women were not oppressed in China.

Despite wearing practically every garment she owned, Dora started to whimper.

"She's cold, poor little sausage," said Mary, reaching for the handles of the push-chair. "I'll take her in there for a hamburger and wait for you."

But a passing woman overheard and sang out, "Don't eat there, there's a boycott, they won't serve unaccompanied women at night."

"Eh?"

"In case we're prostitutes."

Mary sighed. "Oh well, we can't have that, can we, Dora?" And the attention of both was caught by street theatre, women dancing, beautiful, silly, their faces painted, their clothes a delectable parody of the fashions in the glass-eyed shop-windows all around, the fashions Jackie's father sold, they had a wind-up gramophone in a pram, they sang, "Keep young and beautiful if you wanna be loved . . ." and one of them tied a balloon to the push-chair and Dora stopped crying and Mary said "Thanks," gruffly, and Jackie smiled and laughed inside.

A forest of banners, blown all over the road like sails, announced the existence of Women's Liberation Workshops, demanded equal pay and opportunities, abortion on demand and free birth control. Mary kept saying, "You don't have to be a women's libber to believe in *that*. Did I tell you we've got a male typist at the office now, Jackie?"

"No."

"Even if they do call him an executive assistant."

"There you are then! That's exactly the point!"

"They can call him God the Holy Ghost for all I care," said Mary, "if I can stay in bed next Saturday."

"Oh, do stop being a drip," said Jackie.

Film crews closed in and Mary hid her face. She said she would get the sack if the viewing millions saw her carrying on like this. She agreed with Jackie that the police and passers-by were being very nice and smiling a lot, but said it was probably because they thought the march was a joke. And when a woman with a witch's pointed hat on asked them to sign a clipboard so that they could be put in touch with their nearest group, Mary said, "I don't want my name on anything."

Jackie sighed. "But you've got *skills*. They want people with skills. What have I got?"

"Every woman's useful," said the one in the pointed hat.

"What skills?" said Mary. "Oh. Typing."

"Can you cut stencils? We're having terrible problems with our newsletter." The woman showed Mary a copy and Mary said she could see what she meant. "Will you teach us how to cut stencils properly, then? Share skills?"

"Share?" said Mary. "What are you going to teach me?"

"Herstorical research? You can come to our Herstory Workshops. We take it in turns to give papers."

"Great," said Mary, signing her name. "You go to Herstory, Jackie. I'll go to typing. It'll be just like old times."

The Women's Centre was an old shop, with fish and chips to the left and bookmaker's to the right. The window was blanked out with white paint, except for a feminist fist through which you could see in and out. The floor was covered with damp bits of carpet on which the push-chair stuck, and there were bookcases and filing cabinets and boxes of stationery everywhere, and signs which said: CORRESPONDENCE IN. PLEASE KEEP *AND FILE* COPIES OF ALL REPLIES. WHO DO *YOU* THINK SHOULD WASH YOUR COFFEE CUP?

None of the women sitting about seemed inclined either to welcome Jackie, Mary and Dora, or to send them away, so Jackie started to run her eye over CORRESPONDENCE IN.

Dear Sir, Further to the article in the Guardian, *please send a membership form for Women's Lib.*

Dear Madam, I want to be an engineer.

Dear Women's Lib, I have worked and paid contributions for fifteen years, but when I enquired about my pension entitlement . . .

Dear Ladies, Our National Housewives Register Group meets once a month to discuss matters of topical interest . . .

You Cunts, I'd like to Fuck the Lot of You.

"How did you get this place?" Jackie asked.

"Squatted," said a girl.

"Pardon?"

"Squatted. Been empty for years. Belongs to the council, what do they care?"

"You mean you just moved in?"

"That's right."

"Can you just do that?"

"We've just done it."

"Don't mind my friend," said Mary, "she's very law-abiding. Which way to the typing pool?"

"Pardon?"

"I've come to share skills. That is, type stencils."

"It's only the one room. And we've got our Herstory Workshop now."

"Look," said Mary, "I arranged with someone over the phone that I'd come in today and try and lick this newsletter of yours into some kind of shape."

"Oh, that'll be Jo from the newsletter collective. She's gone home."

"Either I do it now," said Mary, "or I don't do it at all. My God. What's that?"

"What?"

"That thing."

"It's our duplicator."

Mary eyed the oily, patched-together contraption sadly. Then she turned her attention to the typewriter which satisfied her more, being newer. She demanded a toothbrush and some methylated spirits and showed some stragglers from the newsletter collective how to scrub the letters for a clear, sharp stencil.

Meanwhile Jackie sat on the floor and tried to keep Dora quiet while she listened to the speaker. Dora kept making little cockcrowing noises, but no-one objected.

"The oppression of women is precisely a function of the capitalist mode of production; prior to the industrial revolution and the division it brought between private life and public life, women's economic position was . . ." Jackie felt her eyes closing. A year ago she had been a student; she could be one now if it were not for Dora, who she wished would sit still. But could she ever be a student if she could not concentrate? She must concentrate. She must not let mental laziness ambush her like this . . . she was in a thatched cottage in the country, a red-cheeked farmer and his white-capped wife who was also a spinner and a brewer and oversaw the dairy, discussed the farm together in easy comradeship, children ran in and out carrying small pails of frothy milk or cupping brown eggs carefully in their hands. A warm fire crackled, meat roasted on a spit, and above it all, behind it all, like the tap of Mary's typewriter, was the restful whirr of the spinning-wheel.

"Learn anything?" said Mary.

It was one of the area's drearier streets. The paving stones tilted at different levels, jolting the push-chair over single lines of defiant, crushed weed. Dora swayed about, restrained by straps. Litter piled up in drifts. The mean little houses had no gardens; the sky was heavy with the scream of an aeroplane.

"I don't want to go home," said Jackie.

"We'll go to the pub then. Oh. We can't. Her."

"Exactly. Her."

Mary waited a while before saying excitedly, "*I've* learned something."

"I'm never going to be free again, Mary. The way we live. In cities."

"I've discovered why they won't call that little youth what he is, which is a typist, and put him in the pool with the rest of us." A bus came and stopped just out of reach. They ran for it; Dora started to yell. It was full. The conductor watched with interest as they began to dismantle the push-chair, then pressed the bell and was gone.

They walked on. Supermarkets proclaimed their special offers, tins and packets of food: *Open here; just add water*. "I see it all now!" cried Mary, hammering one fist into the palm of the other hand. "Clear as day! The rats."

"What, Mary?"

"When you read the newsletter – and you will actually be able to read it this time, because the stencils have been cut by someone who can tell a typewriter from last week's washing, and also because it's going to be run off on the latest model of Gestetner, namely the one in my office, and that only until I've had a word with the girls who work the photocopier about what's going on . . ."

"What is going on, Mary?"

"Read your newsletter. Then you'll see."

It was an article about how employers were dodging the equal pay laws by separating men's and women's work so that women had no men to demand equality with.

Also in the newsletter was an account of a woman's difficulties getting an abortion, and her relief when she did.

A housewife whose husband put a carving knife to her throat and backed her to the top of the stairs till she fell down, said that when she told the police they said they could not interfere and suggested she should apologise. A trade union official urged women to join their trade unions. And a mixed commune in Scotland described how much easier it was to break away from sexist stereotypes when living off the land.

Mary joined her union. She became so busy as membership secretary over the next few months that Jackie hardly saw her.

The commune wrote, "We were really glad to hear from you, Jackie. And it is among our plans for the future to offer a holiday home to refugees from the Smoke. But we're not sure we're into kids yet, living with them, we mean. We have to sort out our own heads first. But when we do, you and Dora are first on the list . . ."

"I hope you wrote back and said, 'Gee, thanks,' " said Mary, when she rang Jackie from her office sit-in.

"I don't see why you have to be like that about it. People are entitled not to have children around if they don't want them . . . I didn't even say I definitely wanted to live there. I was just asking about possibilities. Oh, Mary, will you come round?"

"Sorry, I'm starting the revolution. You come here."

"I can't, I'm worn out and fed up. I'm Granny-sitting and baby-sitting and I've had a row with both of them. I'm telling you, Mary, I'm not sure how much – " Jackie stopped, alarmed. Dora had had her up all night, teething, and Jackie had looked with despair at the white shadows of ivory pushing through the inflamed gums, the savage slowness of it, and wept at Dora's pain and her own, but she thought that was all past; this had started out as a perfectly normal conversation with Mary, nothing had been further from her thoughts than breaking down into tears. Was she really so disappointed about the commune's snub? There had been a rather absurd picture in her mind of Dora crawling free and unsupervised in a field while Jackie herself milked a goat . . . but she didn't care, she really didn't care.

"I didn't know you had rows with your white-haired old grandmother."

"She's got a nasty streak, Mary," said Jackie, glad to change the subject to something specific. "Do you know what she said this morning? I was half-way between some soup burning on the stove and the washing machine overflowing, and Dora found a penny and put it in her mouth. And do you know what my white-haired old grandmother said? She said, 'Now, Jackie, it's just a matter of getting organised.' "

"The honeymoon's over, then?"

It was. Things were grinding back into a normality made all the more terrifying by the way it incorporated such seemingly trivial changes as Jackie growing up, becoming a feminist, having a baby, and Granny Ruby coming to live. Her mother was busy as a hamster in a hamster-wheel. Jackie wanted to scream. The final irony: busy, busy, busy, yet all her work was done. Jackie's mother kept insisting that she could look after Dora while Jackie got a job or went on a course or something, and then failing to live up to some little promise to wash a pile of nappies. Julia was nursing, Kate had her O-levels and her boyfriend, they came home only to visit or sleep. Their father went off on his weekends, hardly bothering to lie; he would claim to be playing cricket and leave his bat behind. Granny Ruby muttered, "Take no notice of me, I don't want to be a nuisance," like a litany, but some unnerving incident always seemed to occur when she was left in the house on her own, some little herald of greater disaster – a cigarette burning on a carpet, some nasty splashes on the bathroom floor.

Summer bloomed briefly and slanted down into autumn and Dora's first birthday. Jackie forced herself to bake a cake, a lemon sponge from a packet. It took her mind off terrifying other thoughts. *One year old. How many more? Why did I keep you, Dora? I didn't have to. Don't grow up so fast and make me wonder. Or, Grow, grow, damn you, and leave me in peace.*

Dora showed no interest in the birthday or the cake. Everyone in the family except Granny Ruby had a prior engagement, and Jackie felt too self-conscious to ask anyone from the women's group to the party. So they sat in silence, the old woman, the young woman and the baby, and Dora ate a raw carrot.

The phone rang. Jackie ran for it with the same unthinking enthusiasm with which she picked up each morning's post, which was rarely for her. Any message might be an escape.

"Jackie? It's Jo. Can you get here?"

"Where?"

"The Centre. We're being evicted, the bailiffs are here."

"It's Dora's first birthday party."

"Jackie, for heaven's sake!"

She flew back to the tea-table. She said, "Granny Ruby, I have to go out." She was surprised at herself. But she felt a mother's fondness for the Women's Centre too. She had helped build it up. She was expecting it to help build her.

"But it's her birthday, dear!"

"*You* can look after her! Just this once!"

"Children know when their mothers don't care, dear!" The deadly remark washed down the street beside her as she ran just ten yards, the crest of the wave of Dora's yell. She went back. "Have I got to take the two of you, then?"

"*I'm* not going anywhere. I'll be all right. I'm having tea."

Jackie hauled Dora upstairs and wrestled her into a clean nappy and a coat. Dora shrieked and turned purple as they fought, and it was only when the purple faded back into pink all over her body except for grip-marks on her wrists and legs and a bruise on her back that Jackie realised she had hit her, she had hurt her, possibly badly, certainly unforgivably.

She did not go to the eviction. She went numbly to the meeting in Mary's bedsitter where women talked of finding another squat, marching on the town-hall. A chill of fear and excitement spread among them with the realisation that their mailing-list had been stolen. A way must be found of informing women that their names and addresses were now in the hands of the Special Branch.

"Or dirty telephone callers."

"Same thing."

Meanwhile, Christmas was coming. Jackie's father's behaviour was outrageous even by his usual standards for the festive season. Jackie was sure that he intended to leave soon, for good, but he still presented his wife with his schedule of proposed parties and guests. After Christmas, then; the new year. Jackie could see his mind working as he encouraged Kate in a casually stated ambition to go to France as an au pair when she left school. *The last bird flown. One returned, but that is her business.* What would he do? Announce his departure, or simply go? Probably he would just set off on one of his weekends and not come back. Then he would communicate with the family through a solicitor, informing them that funds were available for putting Granny Ruby in a home. All his duties done. Jackie shuddered. She would have to set limits to her duties too, or she would break.

The house tensed itself. It was like the departure lounge of an airport. Jackie's mother cut out a list of jobs, called "Countdown to Christmas", from a women's magazine and stuck it up on the kitchen wall. There was no sign of the usual mammoth cleansing and stockpiling operations, but she explained this by reference to the list, which exhorted housewives to order goods well in advance but arrange for their delivery on Christmas Eve; and not to clean so early that it had to be done again.

Three days before Christmas, she pinned her farewell note to the list and disappeared. She wrote:

Randolph! I've beaten you to it!

Don't waste time looking for me, I've been planning this for months, and I've got all the Christmas money too. And don't flatter yourself it's suicide, I'm just starting to live. There may be a few turkeys left in the shops if you hurry. It's only a matter of getting organised.

I've got this to say to you. Get on with it. I'd have stayed and tried to make a success of things with your mother and Jackie and Dora, for better for worse, just like I promised, but not without you. I've spent my whole adult life attending to the details of yours, and your desertion is one thing I won't arrange.

So wash your own shirts, pack your own bags, deal with your own mother, tell the children, tell our friends, sort out the house, throw away the memories in it, fabricate whatever grounds you fancy for divorce, it's your worry, you want it, I won't fight it, I won't cooperate with it, I won't sign anything, I won't demand anything, I won't accept anything, Happy Christmas.

Once the shock had worn off, the wondering where her mother had gone, and the sadness that the letter had only mentioned Jackie herself as one of the tasks her mother would no longer concern herself with, Jackie was able to smile nervously at the defiant words. They represented a victory of sorts. She hadn't realised her mother had been listening to her.

13

"Do they let you home for the holidays," said Mary, "from the Nut Cutlet Commune?"

"One more crack like that – " Jackie began, and stopped. At least Mary's tone was faintly jocular now that they were actually in the taxi on the way to King's Cross, at least she was helping with Jackie's and Dora's migration, passionately though she opposed it. Mary's help had never come free, one always had to listen to jokes, the chief motif of the current spate being that Jackie and Dora were bound for the strictest of boarding schools, or hospitals, or jails. Or convents.

"I seem to remember that when Audrey Hepburn gave her life to God, she first gave all her worldly possessions to her friends."

"I offered you my dresses."

"Only because you knew they wouldn't fit me. And to prove some crack-brained theory that you're never going to wear a dress again." Mary was wearing a full-length purple caftan and a fur coat from Petticoat Lane. She liked to shock her office with her clothes while at the same time insisting that a certain sympathy with some feminist ideas did not mean foreswearing all fabrics but denim.

The taxi pulled into the station rank. A traffic-jam up Grays Inn Road and along Euston Road meant that Jackie's last sight of her city would be of it at its noisy, irritable, tangled worst, slush in the gutters, poison in the air. She was glad of it; glad, too, that Mary had given up questioning her very sanity, even though Mary's ghost paced at Jackie's side while the real Mary paid the fare and capably sorted out tickets, suitcases, platforms, and Dora.

It's not just a figure of speech. I think you're mad. Post-natal depression, a bit delayed. You ought to see a shrink.

"I know," said Jackie calmly.

You know?

"I know you think that. You told me before."

But I'm right.

"Of course. People always think their own opinions are right By definition."

But you're going to drag that poor little mite off to this nut house . .

"If I'm mad, a nut house is where I belong." This was a new riposte, and Jackie wished they could have the conversation again.

You're going to walk out on the women's movement, which you got me into, I might add, not that I'm really in it, and go off and grow potatoes and eat nut cutlets and freeze to death.

"It's typical," said Jackie, "of women who live in London to think that anyone who so much as travels to the end of the Northern Line has walked out on the movement! You've got all the zeal of the new recruit, Mary, telling me what feminism is and what it isn't. Look. You can have your equal pay and your equal opportunities – "

Thank you. How?

"By fighting for them. At work. I don't go to work. I've got to find a new way to live. No, not a new way. The old way."

The ghost and the real Mary were coming together under the indicator board like twin images in binoculars. Mary wasn't even looking at Jackie, she was pointing out trains to Dora, who had been in a doll-like state of shock since she was taken from her cot this morning and dressed in layers and layers of wool till her hands and feet could hardly touch each other. But as Jackie approached, the *Nun's Story* was resumed.

"I seem to remember her father's last words before the iron bolts closed were that there was no disgrace in changing her mind and admitting she'd made a ghastly mistake."

Jackie's sudden fear that she might do just that was equalled only by an urge to administer a snub so devastating that it would end their friendship for ever. Fortunately, she couldn't find the words. She grabbed Dora and strode towards the train, knowing that Mary would follow with their cases and a kind farewell, but she told herself even that didn't matter any more. The train was a terrifying sleek beast, getting ready to roar and carry her off to new friends – the second letter from the commune had seemed to cost them a lot. It said that they still weren't sure they were all into kids, but one of their number was now pregnant, and they thought that if they were going to have to get into kids they might as well get into them properly and rescue Jackie and Dora from their difficult living situation. The very ungraciousness of the phrasing had seemed to prove to Jackie that the invitation was meant, but she had not shown it to Mary.

Jackie and Dora were in the train, Mary was outside, leaning on the window. Game to the last, she said, "Lift up your daughter, Jackie, and let me kiss her. Now, Dora, remember, I'm always at the end of a phone, and I can get you made a ward of court just like *that*."

"There's no phone at Auchendene," said Jackie, and the train started to move with Dora held between the two of them. *What if Mary grabs and I let go?* But Mary gave her back of course, mouthing something about "*Lunch?*"

"I forgot – "

"Ye gods – " And Mary ran along with the train, pressing pound notes into Jackie's hand, her face hopeless, laughing and near tears.

The journey took all day. Jackie had never been north before. At Watford she had to fight off memories of her father's jokes about barbarianism beginning at this point. She wasn't going to think about anything, least of all him. Every reason she had for seeing the final sundering of her parents' marriage as a triumph and a relief could be countered with one for seeing it as a tragedy.

She looked out of the windows as Dora blessedly slept. She saw great pottery kilns out of school geography books, smoky, slummy cities, radar installations in the middle of plains. People were standing in the corridors of the train, looking at empty seats with reserved signs. A young couple shared out pages of the *Guardian* as Dora woke up to play her latest game, which consisted of her standing on Jackie's lap, hugging her fiercely, then grabbing her nose and twisting it with blood-curdling little growls. The young couple weren't young at all, they were thirty at least, it was funny how having a child made you feel older than anyone who hadn't. She tried to interest Dora in the grey stone villages, the station inns, the long climb up through the Pennines, "the Backbone of England", she supposed she would one day teach her. How old must a child be to appreciate such a metaphor? Four, seven, thirteen? It was impossible to imagine. Dora's daily growing could not be ignored, but Jackie had no sense of a real future for either of them.

Muddy drifts of February snow clung to the sides of hills. "A noble time of year to come," the commune had written, "with nothing to eat but perpetual spinach."

A steward swung nimbly through the swaying carriage, handing out plastic tickets for what he called luncheon. The price was breathtaking but Jackie took one. Her last meal.

"Sit here, madam, please."

"I'll need two seats, I've got my little girl."

"Seats for diners only," the steward sang out, adding apologetically, "if only we weren't so busy . . ."

Jackie's cheeks burned as she brought some cheese sandwiches and made her way back, empty, to her seat. She wanted to lean low into the faces of businessmen swilling bright red soup and say, *May it give you ulcers.* She felt a grim satisfaction that even on her journey of escape she was being proved right.

A chill evening was falling as the train pulled into Edinburgh, an awesome sight, towering and chiselled in rock. Dora cooed and grizzled and pulled Jackie's nose with increasing frenzy. They should have travelled up overnight, to arrive with the sunrise. Smears of sleet fell on the windows; the icy air as they got off the train shocked Dora into silence. At the barrier an old lady stood, craning her neck to peer into the advancing crowd, her face pleased and anxious. Unhampered by babies or luggage, a young girl rushed into her arms. It was too sudden; Jackie had no chance to shut off her grandmother's voice saying, *Of course you must go, dear,* as she sat in a row of old women in a lounge that was comfortable enough but slightly too warm and slightly too fragrant with aerosol air-freshener.

Jackie took Dora to the Ladies and changed her nappy on a

bench. Dora's bottom was all red from the wet, disposable nappy that Jackie had lacked the bravado to change in the crowded train. "Proper ones from now on," she crooned, "and lots of nice aunties to wash them. Much more ecological. And uncles."

She found her second train, a small one, nearly empty, shedding its few passengers and picking up none as it made its way for over an hour along its single track into darkness. It reminded her of the branch line to Leehaven and ended just as abruptly. The station was a windswept halt in the middle of nowhere – what a place to put a station, there was a town but it seemed very far away. The sound of the sea and the smell of raw salt hung in the cold air. Dora howled. There was nobody there, not even to collect tickets; the train shook itself huffily as if it had expected to be thanked, and reversed, and took itself back with its lights and its seats and its warmth towards Edinburgh. The end of the railway was no satisfying full stop as at Leehaven; it was more like an amputation, the stony track ran on without rails into the wilderness, towards the sea.

"It's all right, Dora," said Jackie, "they're coming to meet us." She left the station and peered along the empty road.

It felt like an hour before she heard the tramp of feet on stones and saw two figures loom up out of the dead railway track: a woman who walked as if she was pregnant but did not bulge, and a huge, shaggy older man in a sheepskin.

"Jackie?" said the man, "and Dora?" Jackie warmed to him at once because he acknowledged Dora. Some people treated Dora as if she didn't exist just because she couldn't talk. "Sorry we're late, the van wouldn't start." His voice was soft and musical, almost womanly, with a faint trace of Scottish accent emphasised by the woman's upper-class English tones. "I'm Lucy, this is Dugan." Dugan and Lucy. She tried to remember. Lucy was the the one who was going to have a baby. Dugan's? No, Lucy's husband was called Tom. Dugan scooped up Dora, who made no objection, and sat her on his big shoulders. Jackie half-protested, she looked so precarious, but Dora gurgled with delight as her tall mount carried her off into the darkness.

Soon they were out on the dunes and the sea was in sight, single lights winking from boats and buoys.

"Is it far?"

"Not this way. It's five miles by road, but the railway track goes past our door. It's a lovely walk in daylight, especially in the summer." Dugan sounded like a big bird calling through the night, just loud enough to be heard. "They closed the railway but nobody told the flowers."

But it must be far, Jackie thought. I can't even see any buildings. Maybe they're so hardy, their idea of far is different from mine. It's like a dream, or a Sunday-school story: keep right on to the end of the road. Lead, kindly light. They can see in the dark. So can Dora, what's she laughing at? And what about the man – Dugan – who's acting like her father already? Is it really going to work out? Now it's like one of those TV commercials when you come in all cold and wet and your mother meets you with a bowl of soup.

Whose mother? Not Jackie's mother. Jackie's mother had a career now, a living-in job at a children's home. Jackie had gone to see her to say goodbye and to pass on her father's message that he thought the best thing, now that he wanted to buy a flat with his latest girlfriend, was to sell the house (Kate could go and stay with one of her brothers till she left school and went to France) and share the proceeds amicably; but he couldn't do it without his wife's signature, her parents having put the house in their joint names. Jackie had found her mother flushed and busy in an overall, with children clustered round her and a younger woman in another overall telling her what to do. She had shrugged to hear of her husband's plans and repeated what she wrote in her letter: "I'm not going to do *anything*, Jackie. He started it, let him finish it. And remember your promise not to tell him where I am. He can start by playing Find the Wife."

They climbed up the last ridge of dunes and there was a cosily lit house. Jackie nearly fell over log-chopping equipment as she went through the garden gate. A tangle of dogs bounded out to greet them, and Dora clutched Dugan's hair in terror. He squatted down, perched her on his lap, and performed introductions until she was calm. Jackie was surprised by the size of the house, she had been expecting a cramped cottage, she had been listening to Mary too much. The sitting-room was warm, light, slightly smoky from the fire and very untidy. There was stuffing leaking from the big old sofa and chairs, piles of books everywhere, a packet of Dried Blood on the mantelpiece and a very young-looking girl kneeling on the floor pondering over a large piece of complex and oily metal set down on several sheets of newspaper. She was small and intense-looking, with hair cut militarily short around her ears and a dress-length grey sweater over jeans and multicoloured socks. She nodded to Jackie and said she couldn't shake hands because she was mending the van. The far end of the room was occupied with a large loom, a spinning wheel and several boxes of grey wool.

Another woman, called Sue, came in. She was comfortable and plump, in a muddy patchwork skirt. She gave Jackie some soup with what appeared to be stinging nettles floating in it. The sixth commune member, Tom, was asleep in a chair with his mouth open.

The soup tasted better than it looked.

"Nettle soup," said Sue proudly.

"Where's Dora?" Jackie asked the room.

"Who?" said Bernie, the one who was mending the van.

"My daughter. I want you to meet her."

"I've got her," Dugan sang out from somewhere. "Just showing her her new domain."

"Oh, you'll never get her back from Dugan," said Bernie, wiping her hands on a cloth, "he's really – "

"– into kids?" Jackie supplied.

"Right. It's thanks to him you're here. I won't have any, you see." So Dugan was Bernie's man.

Lucy said, "It's not just thanks to him, Bernie, for heaven's sake." She patted her own stomach. "You're not making Jackie feel very welcome. We all wanted you, Jackie."

"Of course we did," Bernie agreed. "We've had a lot of struggle over the kids thing, Jackie. But it's all right. I know I can't be with women if I won't be with kids." Jackie wasn't sure what to make of this, but they *had* invited her. She would save it to ponder later.

The bedrooms upstairs were big and bare and cold. The fireplaces showed no sign of recent use. But there were plenty of blankets, and Bernie showed Jackie how to pile newspapers under her mattress to stop the cold seeping up from the bare floor. "We'll be making rugs this year," she said. "Do you know how to weave?"

"No."

"I'll teach you."

Everyone had their own room, except Dora, of course, and Jackie was glad to have her cuddled in her arms for warmth. She wondered who else was sleeping with whom, if they changed partners or even stayed monastically alone. Dora woke once in the night and sobbed a bit; Jackie soothed her to sleep, then couldn't sleep herself. She sat by the window with a blanket round her shoulders and watched the moonlit sea break on the beach. She started to write to her grandmother, but fell asleep before she had managed more than the bare details of the journey.

14

First there was the blue-black dome of sky, perfect as paint. Beneath it was a strip of paler blue. Then purple intruded, and pink, and red, and then the sea began, reflecting the stripes of the dawn sky which faded into white as foam broke on the shadowy beach. The beach was flat and sandy this far out, dotted with rocks and seaweed.

Somewhere out there was a horizon, indistinguishable by Jackie's eyes from the colour play of morning.

Sounds were not the same, a delicious, tantalising jumble. The sea inhaled itself, and exhaled like her own breath. Seagulls made their mournful riot, taunting the domesticated poultry back at the house. Released from their night shelter, breakfasting on potato-peel before another day of rich foraging, the hens squawked back at their cousins of the cold sky.

Jackie was supposed to be gathering driftwood with Dugan, but she couldn't stop walking. She felt the wet sand give and suck. She balanced on one leg, then the other, to pull of her boots and socks. Soon her feet were naked, and she felt a sharp shell bite into her left heel. She walked towards the sea, the sky hardly changing, her feet feeling the same whether still or moving. It was like being suspended in time and space. At last she reached the water's edge, and threads of cold tightened in her feet like metal wires. She turned and saw the inland hills becoming green, the house waking up, and the carefully prepared soil of the vegetable patch waiting for spring planting. Between there and here was the tide line, with Dugan loading bits of wood into a handcart while Dora watched, putting sticks into a bag.

Jackie walked back. "Found much?"

"Enough." He straightened up. The wind blew his soft brown hair into a halo. Dugan seemed to move in a permanent cloud of wool and hair. He smiled kindly at Jackie as he enquired, "And you?"

Dora said, "Wood."

"Did you hear that, Dugan? She said wood."

"Hm. Sounded like a burp to me."

"You said wood, didn't you darling?" Jackie picked her up and hugged her passionately. Dugan had cut down an old oilskin for Dora, and with that and her uncut red hair she looked like a Pict warrior pretending to be a fisherman in an advertisement for sardines. She struggled to be free and went back to her bag of sticks.

"You've done better than your mother," said Dugan solemnly.

"I have, haven't I?" said Jackie, stretching and surveying the landscape of her new life.

"I was speaking," said Dugan, "to Dora." And he nodded at the sticks.

"Sorry. I haven't been very helpful, have I? But I love the way you can walk and walk out on that beach and never seem to get anywhere. I'll push the cart back."

"It's heavy, now."

It was also rather inexpertly made. Grinding through rocks and shingle, up the dunes and across the flinty railway track, each of its wheels seemed to have a mind of its own.

"Let me take it, Jackie."

"No!"

The handles opened blisters on her hands as she pushed. A necessary pain, scraping away her soft, town-bred skin. It would harden. After two months she felt proud of her strengthening body, her growing knowledge of what must have been second nature to her ancestors, ancestresses. Crop rotation, milking, planting. She delighted in the circles she perceived, work producing food to nourish the bodies that did the work. Hot water soothing bones aching from sawing up wood for fuel. Jars of last year's fruits, sacks of flour, bottles of eggs in water-glass, dwindling in the storerooms but holding out until this year's harvest. Her own recent tensions melting into well-being, the marks where she had once hit Dora long disappeared, turned into good new flesh.

She tipped the wood on to the grass near the sawing table. One soft, rotten chunk crumbled. She said, "That one looks like a Fru-Grain."

"A what?"

"A Fru-Grain. They were a kind of cereal my grandmother used to give me. I used to think they looked like wood."

"You never say much about your family, Jackie."

She laughed shortly. "Next time you've got a week with nothing to do, I'll make a start." Dugan's family was a source of much mirth. They were landowners, so rich that their idea of cutting off their dropout son without a penny was to give him this small farm. Perhaps it was because they were such public property that Dugan was curious about Jackie's background. But she enjoyed being a little mysterious. It served her purpose of not thinking, just moving with the cycles of the days.

"Is your grandmother still living?"

"Yes." Why had she made that idiot observation about Fru-Grains? "She's in a home. I do write to her." *And she doesn't reply.* "She's very old."

The kitchen walls were lined with rotas. There was a calendar of seasonal tasks, and lists of jobs that had to be done every day. A pink sheet of paper catalogued traditionally male jobs that the women must make a special effort to do, and a blue sheet did the reverse. Popular jobs were listed in brown ink on yellow paper, unpopular ones such as weeding and cleaning up in red on white. This colour scheme used to be the other way round, Jackie learned, but Sue had objected that it was racist.

Sue was always quick to notice things like that. She spent a lot of time consciousness-raising in the women's group at the university where she was in the final year of a modern languages degree, and insisted on doing more at home. She was a very diligent student. She rose before dawn on lecture mornings, did her jobs, then hitch-hiked (if she couldn't persuade anyone to drive her) the twenty-five miles to the university. She left books with markers in them all round the house and the out-buildings for casual study, she said she had no interest in paper qualifications, and only remained enrolled in the course in order to get her grant.

Shopping was top of the popular jobs list, along with milking, building and breadmaking. Jackie was surprised at how much they bought: canned food, tea, newspapers, occasional tobacco, and sweets from the village store, where a cryptic silence fell among the shopping women when they entered and conversation buzzed when they left; tools and seeds and building materials from nearby merchants. They discussed the implications of their purchases. Sue was worried about the conditions of tea pickers in the third world.

"So we drink herb tea which we all hate and put them out of work?"

"Do we actually *need* to eat sugar?"

"Possibly not, but Mrs Mac needs to sell it."

"Ah, the contradictions . . ."

"If I could change the subject," said Jackie, "it's still very cold in the evenings, and I'd like to light a fire in the bedroom for when I put Dora to bed. I don't mind getting the extra wood."

Bernie said sharply, "There's no extra wood, just wood, and all get it. No-one has fires in their bedrooms."

Dugan mediated. "You could undress her downstairs."

Needled and uneasy that she might be thought selfish, Jackie retorted that Dora was entitled to her privacy like anyone else, and at one and half did not understand about being cold for the revolution. Everyone at once took her side and Bernie spread her little red hands to indicate that she accepted the will of the majority.

At nineteen, Bernie was older than she looked, but still the youngest of the group. Jackie privately thought her and Dugan a very unlikely couple, almost father and child; he babied her and never rebuked her for her sharp tongue. Everyone else tried, in their group discussions, to be consistent and coherent, but Bernie felt entitled, when things got heavy, to say things like, "Oh, this is such crap," or walk out of the room. Since nothing could be decided behind anyone's back, that effectively ended the meeting.

But one day, when Jackie was getting ready to dislike her totally, Bernie took Jackie's side in a quite surprising way. Jackie had been worrying about money. She felt wretched to bring it up, but she had to. For the truth was she felt she wasn't contributing. Dugan owned the house. Sue had her grant. Tom worked on local people's cars on a freelance basis from time to time, and Lucy wrote stories and sent them off. Admittedly they always came back, chequeless, but there was a chance.

"Where's the nearest social security office?" Jackie asked timidly.

"Don't know – why?"

"I could claim. Unsupported mother. Unsupported in their terms, I mean," she added hastily, looking at the shocked faces.

Dugan's forehead folded into a gentle frown. "Jackie. We've got enough for the bills. Once you start getting money from them, they'll be round here, asking questions, checking up on us . . ."

"But we're not doing anything wrong . . ." She gave up. They were terribly hurt. Everyone wanted to know if they had said or done anything to make her feel unwelcome. Bernie said, "You are thick, you lot."

"No, they're not, Bernie, I'm sorry," said Jackie. Then she feared an immediate tirade against herself for assuming she was not included among the thick. Instead, Bernie demanded to know why Jackie claiming supplementary benefit would be different from Sue's grant. "Either we say fuck the state, or we screw it for all it's worth. Or both. Jackie's a fully-fledged one-parent family. I say she should claim."

But she didn't. She let the subject drop. There was nothing she needed, and the commune's money was there for her to take, like anyone else, if she did need something. Dugan was very quiet with her for several days, and she feared that she had somehow unfairly implied that he was pulling rank as landlord. And what about Bernie? Her forthright support had been as welcome as it was surprising, but what lay behind it? "A fully-fledged one-parent family." Bernie's behaviour with Dora could not be faulted, but she never went out of her way to play with her or take pleasure in her as the others did. Was this her way of establishing Jackie and Dora as separate . . . separate from Dugan in particular? Bernie didn't bring money in either, but her deft little hands could turn themselves to a bewildering array of crafts above and beyond the basic skills Jackie struggled clumsily to learn: Bernie had apprenticed herself to Tom to learn car mechanics, and after a session she would wipe her hands and bend her thin back over some impossible piece of darning or some frivolous, incongruous thing like a tapestry tray cloth. Often she gave these away, but anyone could see they were saleable if the need arose.

Bernie would willingly teach her skills to anyone who asked, but she had none of the encouraging small talk of a good teacher.

"Like this," she would say, her needle rapidly dipping in and out of her fabric. "That's wrong," she would say. "Unpick it." "Not bad," was high praise . . . and as such, welcome as a bouquet when Jackie presented her with a ball of wool, gathered from hedgerows and spun and dyed under her instructions. Jackie ventured a joke.

"These, er, instinctive female skills aren't quite as instinctive as I thought."

"Eh?"

"Historically, women always knew how to spin. That's where *spinster* comes from."

"Really?" said Bernie politely. They were alone. Jackie looked at her wool, which Bernie was testing for strength and burst out, "Oh, Bernie, why don't you like me?"

"Like you?" The hard little face looked very distressed. "Of course I like you. Why do you think I don't like you?"

"You're so . . ."

"Tough? I'm tough with everyone. I'm practising. Women have to be tough. One day I'm going to have a whole chain of craft shops." Touchingly, she took Jackie's hand. "I just say what I think. I'm no worse to you than I am to anyone else, am I?" Jackie considered, admitted that she was not, and apologised. Bernie decided that she shouldn't apologise so much. Sue always said that when giving way in an argument you should give the other person an opportunity to give way on something too, to keep things equal; and with this in mind, Jackie considered apologising for apologising so much, but suggesting that since Bernie was aware of her own sharpness she should try sometimes to curb it. Instead she said, "It's Dora, isn't it? You don't like Dora."

"I think Dora's a darling. As kids go."

"But you're not into kids."

"*No.* Not in this society. I hate to see women getting lumbered."

"But aren't we trying to make a different society?"

"Oh, I suppose so. I'll tell you one thing, though. I think Lucy's round the bend to say she's going to have the birth here. She ought to go into hospital. What if the baby gets stuck and there's a snowstorm?"

Jackie felt suddenly maternal, almost powerful. "Do you really expect snowstorms in July? You need to come to terms with your fear of childbirth, as Sue would say."

"There aren't any terms! I'd feel the same if we started pulling each other's teeth out." Jackie started a lecture about childbirth not being an illness, but Bernie interrupted to ask whether Jackie had given birth in a mud hut or a modern hospital; and Jackie had to admit that not only was it the latter, but also she didn't remember much about it, and Lucy's confidence that she would be as good as any midwife might therefore be misplaced.

"Anyway, I shall go away for the birth," said Bernie. "I'd only be a liability."

"I don't think anyone would want you to think that." Jackie was surprised and pleased by the turn the conversation was taking . . . not because Bernie was upset but because she herself felt able to help. "I think Lucy will want you there." She was quite unprepared for what came next.

"Why did you decide to have Dora?" Bernie seemed very much the child as she asked this.

"We-ell. You don't always decide these things."

"But you could have got rid of it."

"You see . . . I felt . . . my mother had just had an abortion, and I . . ."

Bernie laughed fiendishly. "And you didn't want to be like your mother? I know all about that trip. I ran away from mine when I was seventeen."

"With Dugan?"

"He was a teacher at my school."

Jackie hadn't known that Dugan had been a teacher.

Summer started, the wheat came up and the vegetable patch was covered with hopeful green foliage. Lucy was tired and huge and ecstatic. Everyone read books on childbirth. Dora took to staying awake all night, squatting by the window, imitating the calls of night-birds.

"She keeps me up," Jackie told the meeting, "and then I have to do the same work as everybody, even though I'm tired."

Bernie pointed out, "You're the only one who hears her." She checked herself. "Perhaps Dora could sleep in a different person's room each night."

Dora let off a wail from under the table. Jackie knew it was because she had crawled in to explore and was now panicking in the forest of legs, but the wail was taken as fair comment on that suggestion.

Dugan said, "I wouldn't mind staying in Jackie's room from time to time."

Jackie stared into his eyes which seemed to say, *Have I said something wrong?*

"Yes, we all could," said Bernie quickly, "take in our sleeping bags and see to Dora if she wakes up."

"There's a tension between Bernie and Jackie," Sue sang out.

"No there isn't," said Bernie and Jackie together, and everybody laughed. Bernie added, "It's just a bit funny to hear you say you want to sleep with someone else, Dugan."

Jackie waited for Dugan to deny that he had meant that. But he said, "You've said yourself we don't own each other, Bernie."

Jackie fought with her face. She had been having fantasies about Dugan. They were not sexual, exactly: more about his bigness and gentleness and power, holding her as she held Dora, all night.

But she said to Bernie later, "There's nothing between Dugan and me."

"You heard what the man said. No-one owns anyone."

Was this a wry admission that the ideological chickens had come home to roost? Or was it permission? Was Dugan even interested? He was nice to Jackie, but he was nice to everybody. And he worshipped Dora. Maybe that was it. She was seeing him as a father for Dora, she was oppressing him! She must control her dreaming. Not hurting Bernie was more important.

But the child-care thing must be sorted out before the birth of the new baby put it really to the test. They would take turns to have a day and night of total responsibility for Dora, and anyone who had been up in the night could rest the next day. Dora was delighted. She was mopping up words like blotting-paper and rapidly learned what could be got away with with whom. With Dugan it was midnight walks on the beach.

Jackie woke one night to find Dora back in bed with her, sleeping cradled in the hands of Dugan, who was kneeling by the bed in his jeans and T-shirt, watching the two of them as if it was the most natural thing in the world.

"Don't wake up," he whispered. "You look lovely asleep."

"Don't you want to sleep?"

He nodded at Dora. "Don't want to move her."

She hesitated. She couldn't tell if that was all he meant. She didn't know what to do or say. What she felt was unlike the defiant hunger of being with Calvin, when love and pleasure were nothing compared with the exciting outrageousness of what he did, what he made her do. Dora shifted, smiling like a tousled angel, and Dugan released his hands. "Dreaming," he said.

"Dugan" – Jackie swallowed – "is it true that you . . . took Bernie away from school?"

He frowned puzzled. "That's a funny way of putting it. She wanted to leave."

"But you were her teacher?"

"Teachers have feelings too, Jackie. I didn't force her, I assure you. On the contrary, I tried to dissuade her, but she knew her own mind. She still does," he added darkly.

Of course, thought Jackie, relieved. And what business was it of hers anyway? Who was she to approve or disapprove? Something else was her business.

"Is it true that you both . . . have other people?"

"Bernie has had . . . we've exchanged no vows. I don't want to tie her down, and she doesn't want to be tied." How did he know to say all the things she needed to hear? "She's always been enough for me. Until recently."

Jackie said slowly, "Why don't you come in with us?"

"Would Dora mind?"

"You're fond of her, aren't you?"

"I love babies."

All babies? Not Dora especially? And she won't be a baby for ever; will you still love her then? She made a space for him. She was naked and embarrassed. He took off his own clothes with the air of that king in history who saw an uncultured guest drink from his finger bowl, and promptly drank from his own to put the guest at ease.

It was a hot night. His body was very cool in the sticky bed. For a while he did nothing, waiting for her. Calvin always used to announce what he was going to do, then do it. Dugan started to stroke her, long cool strokes with his big hand, from her shoulders to her knees, making her feel tiny, touching but never lingering. She wished he would linger.

"You're not on the pill or anything, Jackie?"

"No, but I'm sure it'll be all right."

He smiled and moved away. "Silly girl." He was instantly apologetic. "Unless you mean you want another baby?"

"The others would love that, wouldn't they?"

"I wouldn't mind. You make a lovely mother, Jackie."

She started to cry. She didn't feel sad, exactly, but there was a delicious luxury in letting tears flow on to his bare shoulder. "I'm not, I'm not. I had her for all the wrong reasons, and I –" should she tell him? "– I hit her once."

His voice was still kind, but she could feel him tense. "I don't suppose you meant to, Jackie. But if you were having difficulties, you should have mentioned it at the meeting."

"No, it was before . . ."

"Before you came here?"

"Yes, and there was so much, I – "

"But she must have been tiny!"

"Yes, I'm sorry, I – "

"Was it just the once?"

"Oh *yes*. It was part of the reason why I knew I had to get away."

That seemed to satisfy him, but she wished she hadn't told him.

"If you'd like to make love, I could fetch some things."

Things! She smiled at his delicacy. Calvin once said they were like eating candy with the wrapper on. Where would he fetch them from? Bernie's room? And why did he have them anyway, wasn't Bernie on the pill? She said no. But she wanted him to stay.

"It's all right," he said.

His fingers played deliciously. Calvin used to do this, but for educational purposes or as a grudging preliminary. For Dugan it seemed to be pleasure enough. "You're like a flower down here, luscious with honey. Mothers have sweet cunts." *Cunt!* She hated the word, it sounded like a thud of meat. *But it means what it means, and there's no other. One thing about having a child: you learn to make sounds quietly, even these sounds.*

Bernie was skinning a rabbit. It was one of the compromises they had made on vegetarianism. They would not buy meat or slaughter their own stock. But if one of the dogs brought in a rabbit, they would eat it.

The rabbit hung by its hind legs, still warm. Bernie cut up the insides of its thighs with sharp shears.

Jackie went and squatted beside her. Bernie said quickly, "It's quite all right."

The rabbit still smelled of life. "How do you do that?"

"You *cut*."

"It was just – "

490

"I'm not asking."

"We didn't actually – "

Bernie smiled tightly. "Wasn't his night, then, was it?"

"What do you mean?"

"I told him I'd gone off the pill."

Jackie felt sick. "You want to get pregnant?"

"I do not. But it just hit me. Here we are, crippling ourselves to produce healthy food, and there was I popping pills to stop my body behaving as it should."

"But you'll use something else?"

"Nothing else is safe. Not a hundred per cent."

"You truly don't want him?"

"I didn't say that. I don't want the consequences. Could you pass me that bit of wire?"

"What's it for?"

"To dry the skin."

"Bernie. It's important. Are we still friends?"

"Of course we are." The skin came off the pink shining carcase. It was all in one piece, like a tube. Bernie turned it inside out. "Of course we are, we live together."

15

Sue said, "Look, there's something I've been meaning to raise."

They were all sitting on the grass in the sun. Lucy had her head in Tom's lap and Dugan was garlanding Dora with daisy-chains. Bernie, with some sewing on her lap, was staring out to sea. Jackie felt much too lazy for heavy discussion; and she guessed the others felt the same, the way they rushed in with their own ideas of what Sue meant.

"I don't think anyone'll mind if you want to work less and study more, Sue," said Dugan, "till after your exams."

"Could we plant a bit less lettuce and a bit more something else next year?" said Jackie, "I'm turning into a rabbit."

"And we all know what Bernie does to rabbits," said Tom slyly. He added quickly, "Talking of next year, pigs are very efficient animals."

"I am *absolutely against pigs*," said Bernie, not turning round. "Raising animals for slaughter is a wasteful use of the earth's resources."

"I didn't mean any of that, as you all know," said Sue calmly, "I think we ought to talk about . . . well Dugan and Bernie and Jackie."

"Why?" said Bernie.

"There's, well, a strain . . ."

"Oh? Who's under strain?"

"You are," said Sue, going to sit beside her, "and I think it would help if we talked about it."

"What is there to talk about? Jackie and Dugan are together. It's no-one else's business."

Jackie knew she ought to intervene, but she didn't know what to say. She felt gratitude to Bernie for not minding, and worry that it might all be pretence; and exhilaration too, that it was all possible, that one woman could grow tired of her lover and he could go to another woman and all three of them could stay together in a community. Now that Dugan slept with her and made love to her night after night, Jackie let herself love him totally. The sunshine, the blooming of the garden and their love all seemed to be one.

"All right, not now," Sue sighed, "but I'd like to put it on the agenda for next week."

"Put it on your fucking agenda. I won't be here."

"Bernie!" Jackie was appalled.

"It's not *you*. Lucy's as big as a balloon. I said I wasn't going to stay for that. I'm going to go to London for a month or so. I've never been to London, and I hear there's a lot going on."

There was no arguing with her. They voted her the money for her fares and Jackie gave her Mary's address and a note asking the women's group to look after her. Bernie loaded a rucksack with little things she'd been making, socks, mats, purses, gloves, woollen hats that she would sell. She looked younger than ever as they saw her off at the station. "See you in September," she sang. "Have a nice birth, earth mothers."

Lucy's baby was lazy. It didn't want to be born. It just wanted to sleep and grow in the darkness, unimpressed by all the flowering and ripening outside. Lucy's date came and went and she pored with Jackie over calendars, checking that they had worked it out right. They had; they had given themselves a generous margin for error, and even that had been overstepped. "It's like an omen,"

Jackie said. "Doesn't anyone want to live with us any more?"
Sue's results came: first-class honours. Everyone exulted while
she turned up her nose. Her professor asked her if she wanted to
do a Ph.D. "Might as well say yes," she said. "We still need a
bit of money."

Tom's nerve was the first to crack. He had been enthusiastic
about the home birth; it appealed to his mechanical mind to think
that they could manage. He had also been at the forefront of
dismissive discussions about biological parenthood, declaring that
his child, like Dora, would have six co-equal parents. Now he
was frightened, possessive. Without consulting anyone he went to
the village and telephoned the hospital. Then he bundled Lucy
into the van and drove her away, the noise of their argument
drowning the roar of the engine.

It was the right decision. The baby had to be born by Caesarian.
He was a hefty boy with wrestler's shoulders and a wrinkled face
that looked oddly like a dog. "He looks like a St Bernard," Lucy
declared. "We're going to call him Bernard."

"You can't," said Jackie. "We'll get him confused with Bernie
when she comes back." But more and more they were talking
about Bernie in the past tense. Apart from a note to say that she
had arrived safely and was staying at Mary's, they had not heard
from her. Even their telegram, REJOICE A SON IS BORN YOU CAN
COME BACK NOW, had brought no response.

"We'll call him what we want," said Lucy sharply. She was
pale and irritable and smelled of illness.

"I think it's up to them, Jackie," said Dugan.

"And that's another thing, what about his surname?" said Sue.

"He should have Lucy's name, after all she's been through,"
said Jackie.

"It's not his fault. I'm not claiming him as some sort of reward,"
said Lucy.

"Anyway, a woman's surname is only her father's name," said
Dugan, "after all."

"Maybe he should make up his own mind when he's older,"
said Sue.

Tom and Lucy looked at each other, relieved and ashamed.
Lucy started to speak, but Tom restrained her with a squeeze of
her hand. "In the meantime we've registered him in my name.

"Why?" Jackie asked.

"Because that was what the hospital kept calling both of them, and Lucy's been in no state for a lot of hassle! I would have thought you of all people would realise that, Jackie!"

It was a difficult autumn. With Bernie still away, Lucy not fully recovered, and Tom working full-time at a garage to get the extra things he insisted his wife and son needed, too much harvesting and preserving and wooding fell to the others. And Bernard was not an easy baby. He seemed determined to make up for his late arrival. He howled night and day, a furious, piercing sound that hit the edge of everyone's nerves. He was prey to dramatic ailments which always cleared up en route to the clinic. His nappies had a foul, penetrating smell. Lucy and Tom denied hotly that this was different from other babies' nappies' smell, and it became the subject for furtive jokes. Dora didn't like the baby at all. She sulked at the way she perceived Dugan giving him more attention than he gave her; and she was grudging in her acceptance of the bed Dugan built her, partly as a consolation, partly so that he and Jackie could have free run of the mattress.

Dugan kept up everyone's morale, and Jackie loved him for it. He listened to complaints, mediated, allowed himself to be snapped at so that they should not snap at each other. He was like a sort of Christ-figure, she thought, taking the sins of the world on his shoulders. Or a lightning conductor.

"Either that dog goes, or we go!" Lucy shouted one day when the dog snapped at Bernard.

"You shouldn't make threats like that; we discuss things here," Sue retorted.

"Lucy's anxiety is understandable, Sue," said Dugan.

"Oh, trust the father of the world to take the side of the mothers!" Sue clapped her hand over her mouth and apologised at once, and everyone resolved to keep a special eye on the dog.

"I don't think we should worry too much about all this," Dugan said later, soothing Jackie's tension. "We can't expect it to be easy all the time, and we're a real family now."

Jackie lay in his arms, listening to the wind blowing up the beginnings of winter outside.

"Do you think Bernie will come back, Dugan?"

"I don't know."

"Do you want her to?"

"I want," said Dugan, "whatever will make her happiest."

"I don't think she'd be very happy here now."

"It's no place for someone who isn't into kids."

She yawned. "Bernard'll get better. First babies are always a problem, especially boys."

"Listen to you!"

No-one was surprised when Bernie's letter came, saying she was staying in London. But they were upset by its tone.

"I don't see why she had to be so self-righteous about it!" said Lucy. "All right, she's going to live in a women's squat and campaign for a sex discrimination law. We can't all do everything."

"She obviously thinks it's more *relevant*," said Dugan, with a rare touch of acid in his voice. "This friend of yours is obviously very persuasive, Jackie."

Jackie said nothing, and Dugan went on. "All right, so now we've got a spare room. Maybe they'll be able to take a little time off from legislative reform to find us another single mother who needs a home. If they think it's relevant enough."

Everyone agreed that this would be a good idea, but Jackie felt suddenly unnerved by the vision of the new arrival, frail and shy, with a clinging baby, walking along the railway track. Was it her imagination that Dugan had taken so strongly to Bernard, that he had less interest in Dora the growing child than he had had in Dora the baby? Of course, of course. Bernard was the one who needed all the care. How could she doubt her luck in having found a man who not only mouthed feminist theories but put them into practice . . . and loved her into the bargain?

"I think we ought to devote a whole meeting to this," said Sue faintly, "only not now, because the prof's had a manuscript sent specially from Paris for me, and I ought to go through the motions of reading it."

Sue was writing a thesis. Bernie had left, as she had every right to do. Tom had a job. Lucy had threatened to leave if she didn't get her way over the dog. It had been an entirely understandable threat, Dugan had defused the situation with his usual tact, it had not been repeated, but its words and its significance still hung in the air.

"I'm feeling insecure here," Jackie whispered to Dugan when they were alone.

"Are you?" He looked at her in surprise. "I'm sorry to hear that. I won't say what I was going to say, then."

Then, of course, she had to make him say it. She insisted that she was not feeling insecure at all. He said that he had been thinking – just thinking – how nice it would be if she had another baby. His.

The idea was rather romantic. She couldn't understand why she reacted so savagely. "You mean nail the lid down even more firmly? So that you can't get out?"

Calmly, devastatingly, he said, "That's a rather ugly way of putting it, Jackie. But I suppose, yes, if I'm to have the responsibilities of fatherhood and it would be nice to have its reality too."

"Dugan, of course, I'm sorry, I – "

"But only if you want to, and when you want to. I didn't mean now this minute! And you know I'd be willing and happy to marry you, if you thought the security was worth the, er, compromises. I love you very much, Jackie."

"I love you too," she said. She had said it dozens of times before, but this time it sounded like an ending.

Ruby and Jackie
1972 . . .

Ruby woke up. The early morning autumn sky in the square skylight was an indeterminate purple-blue that told her nothing of the time. It might be later than she thought.

She pressed the button of her bedside light, taking care not to touch the emergency call switch instead. Dingy light filled the white-painted single bedroom and the skylight turned black.

There was a bible on the bedside table. Every room had its Bible. Under Ruby's were her cigarettes and her matches. She had seven cigarettes left, but only one match. She put a cigarette between her lips, determinedly steadying her hands. She was still lying on her back, quite still, not wanting to test out her bones yet. She must be very careful with this match. There would be no ringing for another one if it failed.

The prospect of an unlit cigarette and no matches was worse than the memory of her accident. She chuckled appreciatively at this realisation.

"Smoking is not allowed," they would say, "in residents' bedrooms."

"It is a requirement," they would continue, "of our insurers."

"It is in the interests of all residents."

"Hah!" said Ruby, and scraped the match on the side of the box too hard. The phosphorus tip split and a drop of fire fell on the sheet. She brushed it aside and the flame stayed on the match. She waved her chin around, struggling to marry the flame with the cigarette. At last.

She smoked it down to the tip, knocking the ash on to a sheet of foil from a chocolate bar that she also kept hidden under the bible.

Usually she wrapped the ash in the foil and threw it out of the window, fanning the room with the curtains. This morning she might not have to. Was it this morning? She would know as soon as she tried to move. What a sly, cunning blessing this rheumatism was, now afflicting her like knives in her bones, now letting her be. She didn't have it as badly as most of them. Mrs Nutt's fingers were twisted like pipe-cleaners. Mrs-speechless-dribbling-Nutt, whom they always sat next to Ruby, Mrs Nutt and Mrs Orange, Fruit & Nut, *that's a good one!* They meant well. Probably. Possibly. They did not.

They were too stupid to mean anything. The laugh would be on them. Just because everyone else's rheumatism got better in summer and worse in winter, they never guessed that Ruby was approaching her most agile time of the year.

"You're not a prisoner, Granny Orange!" they said whenever she announced she was going to the pub. She remembered a saying about somebody protesting too much. They didn't like having their petty routines upset by a troublemaker who was not content to watch television all day – puppets, professors, whatever was on.

Not a prisoner! See what happened when she escaped!

She shifted her leg, wincing in advance, for it had still been stiff yesterday morning. It moved with the ease of a baby's hip. Today, then.

She put on four pairs of knickers and a clean pad. She had perfect bladder control, however much they might like to blame her for other women's accidents, but it was going to be a long journey. And lavatories on trains to Scotland were not always as clean as they might be, she was sure. Not these days.

They were clean enough on the Indian trains.

India! Journeys! All her life it had been journeys, she thought, as she slowly put on three vests, her white blouse, her blue blouse, her tweed skirt, her cardigan and the lime-green dress that Jackie liked. The important thing was not to be seen carrying a suitcase, even if she did look a bit funny. Her coat would cover it all.

Journeys? All her life? Less than a third, if she worked it out, had been spent travelling to India, travelling from India, travelling around India, with Walter, with the children, without the children, without Walter . . .

Most of her life she had stayed put. She had only married Walter to get away.

She opened her bedroom door. It squeaked faintly. Her joints felt as if they had been oiled. She felt she could take the stairs two at a time. She smelt porridge cooking. That was why it was always served up cold at breakfast. They started cooking it in the middle of the night.

Married Walter to get *away*? No, no, she had not even been that courageous. She married him because . . . there was no *because*. What on earth was she asking?

What a welcome they would give her at Jackie's farm, with all the history she could tell them and all the farming advice she could remember from her days as a land-girl.

She had married him so that she could have a story. It might have been a better story with that young poet, but what happened to him? Walter gave her a story for a while, then ended it by dying. He left the children, of course. Weren't your children supposed to give you a story? Would Emma have, if she hadn't been killed? Would she have been killed if Ruby had taken her side against that officer who was so shocked about the black market meat? She should have. She should have taken her side.

And Randolph? Spoiled young lord. Well, of course she had spoiled him. Her son. And this place, with the bills paid and monthly visits, was how he thanked her.

But that was men.

She was starting to sound like Mary!

Now there was a girl who was going to have a story, though heaven knew where it would end. Ruby had met her once or twice at Jackie's and never taken much notice; but she had very kindly come to visit Ruby the day Jackie went off to Scotland because she was missing Jackie and guessed that Ruby was too. Ruby remembered the conversation.

"Jackie has her own life to lead, dear."

"Oh, I *know*. But why can't she lead it here?" Ruby was touched. She couldn't remember having a friend who was so fond of her. Mary looked quite bereft in spite of her brightly coloured clothes and her row of defiant badges. "I've known her all my life, practically, and I won't have anyone to tease. I'm always getting into hot water with the others, they take me too seriously."

"Never mind, dear."

Mary cheered up and said, "What *about* her mother, then?"

"What about her?"

"Total non-co-operation. I love it! Serves him right too, Jackie's father's always been a . . . your son." Her face fell. "You see? I'm doing it again."

"I know he isn't perfect, dear. Would you like some tea?"

"If there is any."

Ruby summoned a maid. "They haven't got anything else to

do." The maid heard and winked at Mary as she gave her tea. Mary looked perplexed. "It's a shame about the house, though," she began again, "standing empty while they argue. We could use it if only Jackie would live there. My bedsit isn't big enough for me, never mind a duplicator and assorted waifs and strays. We need a big headquarters for a campaign for a sex discrimination law, and a refuge for women who want to leave their husbands."

"What sort of law, dear?"

Mary grinned. "A law that says any man who won't give a woman a job because of her sex should be hanged."

"Good gracious!" It was a joke. Mary talked some more about her own job as a personal secretary. Her liveliness was starting to depress Ruby. "I don't suppose the house will be empty for long."

"Oh . . . then we'll squat a block of flats or something."

Wanting to contribute something of her own, Ruby spoke of her own secretarial days and the Misses Parley. Mary urged her on, laughing till Ruby thought she would make herself ill.

"I might send a few anonymous letters myself," Mary wiped her eyes. "Actually, Mrs Orange, I knew that story."

"You knew it?"

"Jackie told it to us once. In class."

There was a frozen silence. Ruby was aware of Mary's youth and immobile age all around her. There was a dim buzz of grumbling about the noise they were making.

"Then why did you make me repeat it?"

"Oh, I wanted to hear it from you!"

"I am not a music-hall act."

She would not accept Mary's apology. Mary went away. If Jackie wrote, she would not reply. Better not to get upset.

Young people thought themselves so clever, but sometimes they were too clever by half. Take that Scottish maid, for instance, who came in on Tuesdays and Thursdays.

"How do you get to Scotland?" Ruby had asked her.

The maid had laughed. "Are you thinking of taking yourself off there to give us a bit of peace?"

"My husband is there."

"Did you hear that, girls? Granny Orange has got married again and she's off on her honeymoon."

"Don't do anything I wouldn't do, Granny Orange."

"That'll give you plenty of scope, Granny Orange."

What did they know.

It didn't matter anyway. She had Jackie's first letter, describing the journey. King's Cross was the station to go from.

It was just as well Mary hadn't kept up her visits. Ruby would never have resisted the temptation to tell her her plans, just to hear her say, *Go it, Granny Ruby!* (the cheek of it!) *and bring her back.*

With Jackie or without her, Ruby had no intention of coming back. There weren't many trains to Edinburgh. She had to wait two hours, after buying her ticket. She should have thought of this. It was a long way, and she was frightened of arriving in the dark.

She got some funny looks as she sat on the bench. As if they expected her to take out a bottle of methylated spirit.

On the Indian trains they brought gin and lime to your seat, ice disappearing before your eyes, and your husband paid.

The cost of the ticket was a shock, and she was penniless.

When she finally boarded a train that seemed to be bound for Edinburgh, she winked at businessmen to see if they would take her to the bar. They would have, once!

The train wasn't very full. She had a whole compartment to herself.

"You sure you know where you're going, love?"

"Is my ticket not in order?"

"Yes – "

"Then attend to your business, and I shall attend to mine."

She supposed she must look rather odd in all her clothes. It had been silly to think she must bring so many. They made all their own clothes at Jackie's. Jackie would make her a coat out of fox's fur, to pay Ruby back for all the things she used to buy her in Leehaven.

It was like the middle of the night when the train reached Edinburgh. And still another train to catch, she hoped they were still running. Her leg was starting to hurt and she was cold. She should have taken some of her things off on the journey, in order to feel the benefit of them now.

She hobbled towards the indicator board. Doors were slamming, a whistle blew.

"You wanting this one, hen?"

"Yes . . . yes."

He bundled her aboard. Too late now, of course, but she might as well check Jackie's letter. She did, and she was right, it was the right train! She could remember Jackie's station on the list of destinations. It was fortunate . . . she had no idea where she was. The train was emptying at each stop. There was no-one to ask now, even if she wanted to. Were nights ever this dark at home? At home? Where? Stalcross. She drowsed for hours or was it seconds? She was going to work for the Misses Parley. She must be sure and tell Jackie and her friends about the Misses Parley. Or had she already done so? She wished she had brought a note-book in which to write down what she had told them and what she had not. Old people could be such bores, repeating everything.

The train stopped. The station had no name, no lights. A guard thumped the door. "This is as far as we go, now." He eyed Ruby. "You know where you are, hen?"

"Naturally. My granddaughter is meeting me. In the . . ." She searched around for the name of a car. ". . . Renault." That shook up his ideas. He had no respect. Pain shot in a direct line from her hip to her toes and her head. She seemed suspended in blackness. The train carried off its light and warmth. It was the end of the earth, death. Then she saw the abandoned railway track, remembered, consulted Jackie's letter again. This was the short cut to the farm.

She had better wait before setting out, in case Jackie was coming.

Perhaps she should have written . . . but what if Jackie had said it wasn't convenient?

Convenient! Would Jackie dare say such a thing? It hadn't always been *convenient* to have her at Leehaven.

Yes it had. There was nothing else for a Leehaven widow to do but have her grandchildren to stay.

She set out.

Wind whipped a thin rain of sand into her face. The track was uneven with sharp stones. Out there, beyond the darkness was the sea, not the seaside sea of Leehaven, but wild, endless sea. Nobody was coming to meet her. But Jackie had said that if you walked along the railway track and up over the dunes, you couldn't miss . . .

Could she do it? Of course Always great travellers on our side of the family.

2

Where was she? There was a faint smell of wood smoke and something rotting, but she was quite comfortable. She was lying on a mattress covered with blankets on the floor of a room piled high with clutter. She could hear a dog barking.

She remembered everything. She had got lost on the dunes, had fallen and been unable to get up. She didn't know how long she had been lying there when a dog licked her face.

That had been bad enough. But the dog's owner! She had doubted whether he was a man at all, more like the abominable snowman looming up like that! But he was kinder than he looked, he had brought her here. And where was here? Her journey's end, Jackie's farm, and here was Jackie staring down at her, looking more or less the same as before, although shocked, of course, and anxious, poor girl. Ruby couldn't blame her. Jackie's jeans looked as if half an hour with a needle wouldn't come amiss.

"Hello, dear."

"Thank goodness! I thought you were dead."

"Very much alive. Aren't you surprised?" She waited for the words of welcome that didn't come. Jackie was still in shock. Ruby would make conversation and put her at ease. "Have I been asleep for long?"

"No . . . it's still tonight. Now just keep still, Dugan's gone for a doctor."

Dugan? The hairy man? Something about the way Jackie said his name made her uneasy. "I don't need a doctor."

Jackie sat down heavily on the mattress. Ruby saw her very clearly. "What do you need, Granny Ruby? I mean . . . what are you *doing* here?" Jackie's dark, curly hair, the hair that ran in the family, cast shadows on her white face. *What do you need, Granny Ruby?* Where was the invitation, the welcome? Had she made this outrageous journey only to be politely doctored and asked what else she needed, like when she went into the newsagent's to buy her *Telegraph*?

She said the only thing that came into her head, which was, "I can't go back to that absurd home."

"So you've come to . . . stay with us?"

Ruby looked away. The room needed redecorating, the smell of smoke suggested the chimney should be swept. She had thought that she would stay . . . but it was not what she had expected.

Jackie recovered herself a little, though she was still deathly pale, her eyes dreamy. "I blame myself. I should have thought of it." She hugged Ruby. "Oh, it's *lovely* to see you. But you see, I couldn't . . . can't just invite you. It's not just my home. We discuss everything together at our meetings. We'll discuss it in the morning." Her voice faded out. "Now just get well."

"I," said Ruby, "am not ill." When the doctor came, he seemed to agree. He said she was just cold and confused and he seemed quite annoyed at having been called from his bed. Not a bit like Dr Cameron on the television, except perhaps in the way he seemed to take the view that one crazy person more or less in this household was neither here nor there. "Plenty of rest," he said, "and, er, good food. Build her up," he added to Jackie.

Ruby hardly heard him. All her attention was on the man Dugan who kept his arm round Jackie's shoulders while they listened to the doctor, detaching himself only when the doctor ordered Jackie to bring food. He went himself, returning a while later with a bowl. Ruby had never seen such food in her life, but on the other hand it seemed perfectly in keeping with what had gone before that she should be offered a bowl of hot water with leaves floating in it. That wasn't what unnerved her about him. It wasn't even the way everything he wore seemed to be unravelling before her eyes.

"Granny Ruby's going to stay with us for a while, Dugan," said Jackie when the doctor had gone.

"I'm delighted," he said slowly, courteously. There was nothing about him to dislike. Just something to be afraid of, for Jackie's sake. *For a while*. He put his hand in Jackie's. He seemed unable to speak to her without touching her, and Jackie in turn edged closer and closer to him, surreptitiously, as if she had already read Ruby's mind.

"Do you think you could sleep now, Granny Ruby?" Jackie asked.

"I don't feel as if I'll ever sleep again!" she replied wildly.

"Then I'll sit with you for a bit. You go to bed, Dugan."

"You won't be long?"

"No."

"Goodnight, then, er, Granny Ruby."

"Goodnight, then, er, Dugan."

Before he could leave, the door opened and a mop-headed child in a nightgown looked in, grizzling and rubbing her eyes. Little Dora, how she had grown!

"Dora, here's your great-granny come to see you."

"Tell her to give me a kiss, Jackie."

But Dora refused, raising her arms to Dugan, who lifted her.

"Ah well, I suppose I'm not a very pretty sight," Ruby laughed.

"We must have woken her. She'll be all right in the morning."

In the morning! Everything would be all right in the morning. Dugan took the child away and Ruby was alone with Jackie, who wouldn't meet her eyes.

Jackie. Dora. She could remember Jackie when she was Dora's age, two, half the age of her own earliest memory of herself, perched on Aunt Sarah's knee as the century changed.

"Teach that child to type," Ruby said. The words had not been through her head, they had come straight to her lips.

Jackie looked relieved, as at a good joke in a difficult moment. "Who? Dora?"

"I'm dreaming, dear. It's what my aunt used to say. About me."

"The suffragette one?"

"Yes."

"Oh well. You see, it was different in those days. The typewriter was a symbol of women's independence. Now it's a symbol of servitude. Excuse me, I want to be a microbiologist. Yes, but can you type?"

It was a relief to Ruby to feel her blur of emotions come together into sharp, simple anger. "*Do* tell me about *those days*, dear."

"Sorry."

"Are you going to be a micro . . . what you said? Aunt Sarah would have approved."

Jackie ignored this. She ignored everything and sought an escape. "Do you really not think you can sleep now? I can't believe that journey you made . . ."

"Your young man wants you. Or should I say your husband?"

"My young man has a name! It's Dugan!" How well Ruby recognised the feeling of being in the wrong and then having the other person say the wrong thing too. Now Jackie would want to push the advantage home. "You've taken an instant dislike to him, haven't you?"

"On the contrary, dear, he reminds me of your grandfather.

He's very polite. Are you married?" She winked. "Have I guessed right?"

"As a matter of fact, no. But he has asked me and I am thinking about it. We want another baby." Jackie seemed shocked by her own words. She retreated to safer ground. "Oh, Granny Ruby, I wish you'd written first . . . everything's so uncertain at the moment. We just don't know what's going to happen. We've got a baby here, you see, and he's got some intestinal trouble, you might be able to smell – "

"No," said Ruby.

" – and his parents are thinking of moving somewhere nearer the hospital, just until he's better. And Sue – you'll meet her tomorrow – has to go to France next month to look at some manuscripts for her thesis."

"But you and Dugan are staying here."

"Oh, *yes*. It's just a question of who with. We have to discuss it. Of course I want you. But I'm only one person."

"Does this *Sue* have a room?"

"Yes."

"I could have that, then. While she goes to France."

"But Sue can do heavy work, and you . . ." Jackie seemed near tears now. "Don't make it more difficult for me! I said we'd discuss it."

Ruby sighed. That was enough. "All right, dear. Thank you."

"Perhaps we'll get a typewriter and you can teach . . ." Jackie's words faded. Ruby fought the resurgence of her anger. Did Jackie really think she was senile? Then she had to say what she meant to say if only for her self-respect.

"Your friend Mary has a good job. Typing is the first rung up the ladder." The mention of Mary seemed to upset Jackie more than anything else. She got up from the mattress and started pacing about.

"She's blocked by sexism at every stage. And maybe I don't want to climb that ladder. There are other things – "

"What things? Oh, you've got a lot of things, Jackie. You've got a good brain and a lovely daughter and a good friend in London working away to make things easier for people like you – "

"People like me?"

"Silly girls who have everything and don't know what to do with it!"

"Learn to type, you mean!"

"Learn to do *anything*, dear." Jackie was crying properly now. "There's plenty of time for having babies and marrying nice men. Life is very long."

"I know . . ."

Ruby wished Jackie would argue. She had said more than she meant and felt dully exhausted. Who was she to urge rebellion on Jackie, when she herself had had so many opportunities, so many instincts, to rebel, and had shied away from all of them? Was it any of her business? Turning up here and making Jackie cry? Had she ever allowed an older generation to advise her?

"Oh, marry him, dear, I can see you're fond of each other." She added, "That's the trouble," but only under her breath.

3

Jackie thought she wouldn't mind the sleeping compartment being so small if only there were more air. But the ventilator wasn't working, it was too cold to open a window, and Granny Ruby was smoking a cigarette on the lower bunk.

Dora made it clear that she had no intention of sleeping. She alternately shrieked with glee at the novelty of the night train, the moving beds, the top bunk, and banged the pillow wailing, "Dugan, Dugan, Dugan!"

Jackie made no attempt to quieten her. She was wailing for the two of them. Jackie felt no pain yet. She wondered when it would start. She could see his face quite easily, stunned by her plans. "Jackie, you can't mean it! What have I done?"

She had said she couldn't explain. She would write to him.

Let it hurt. She could come back. She could deliver Granny Ruby to her home, get on the train and come straight back. This time tomorrow she could be on her way.

But she knew she wouldn't be.

The knowledge that she wouldn't was as sharp and sure as a knife to her throat. "Dugan, Dugan, Dugan," she whispered.

She looked over the edge of the bunk at her grandmother. If there was triumph in her face she might kill her. But the blue glow of the night-light showed no expression at all.

"I'm sure you're not supposed to smoke in these sleepers."

"Then why is there an ash-tray?"

Impossible old woman! What was she thinking? "Did you come all this way to bring me back?"

"Nothing was further from my thoughts, dear."

The train swept throught the night. Jackie raised the blind and watched the gleam of sleeping cities as they hurried by. Just two days ago she had been so content, her world quite still. Now what was happening to her?

It was the wrong question. Nothing was happening to her. *She* was doing something. What was she doing?

Running away? No, for what would she be running from? Life with a man she loved, as his wife or his lover, whichever she preferred; a man who would look after her but not impose on her, and who would let her do the same for him. What was there in that to be afraid of?

The things he had said at the meeting had been very reasonable. The essence of reasonableness. "Is this a suitable place for an old woman? She'll be bored and uncomfortable once the novelty wears off." A perfectly fair comment, one to which Jackie had no answer. "What if she gets ill? We haven't coped as well as we might with Bernard – we need time to get used to these problems." What indeed? "She'll be a mouth to feed who can't do much work. Can we afford that?" Probably not.

No, it wasn't that. A voice like Dugan's was needed to prevent sentimental gestures that could not be lived up to and would cause more pain in the long run than if they had never been made.

It was something else. Granny Ruby's astonishing appearance, and then her words, had woken Jackie from a dream. Her grandmother was old but looked like her. With or without Jackie, the future was going to happen. Jackie remembered her uneasy adolescence; the excitement, fury and hope of her discovery that women felt the same discontent in the past. How had that turned into a belief that she must live in the past? Was this ignoring of the future that she was practising in the name of liberation so different from the way she had shied away from making serious plans for adulthood in her teens, because she didn't know any adult women she wanted to be like?

"Did you love your husband, Granny Ruby?"

"He was a *very nice* man indeed," the old woman replied solemnly.

That wasn't what I asked.

"And did you get married because you couldn't think of anything else to do?"

There was no reply. It was too cruel a question. And less important than the question of why Jackie had come so near to doing the same thing herself.

She had the vote. She had an equal pay act. If Mary had her way, she would soon be able to claim any job she could do. She had had as good an education as she could have wished for. She could have had an abortion, unthinkable though that now was with Dora grinning back at her. Why had that not been enough?

Was it some failing in her, or was it something else? How could she know?

She would explain to Dugan that she had to find out these things.

"I shall go to college and become a teacher and teach girls women's history and make them realise there's a future."

"Yes, dear."

"And none of my girls will ever start to see there's something wrong with her life and think, 'no-one's ever felt this before. I'm on my own. What's wrong with me?'"

"No, dear."

"And we'll have the Women's Centre at the house – and you can live with us, Granny Ruby – I don't know what himself will say, but as long as Helen goes on dragging her feet . . ." She would call her mother by name from now on.

"Which I think she might," said Granny Ruby, "and anyway, by the time all *that's* sorted out, Mary will have her block of flats."

Jackie leaned down towards her. "Granny Ruby, you had all this planned with Mary. You came to get me."

"On the contrary, dear. My motives were purely selfish."

"Our history teacher always said we should get a bit of experience of life before going on to higher education." She looked at Dora. "I'm not sure that you were what she had in mind, though." Perhaps when she was qualified . . . perhaps when she felt more independent of Dugan . . .

But would he wait that long?

Would she ever find such a man again?

She had to give him up. She only wished she could hate him for his commune and his kindness and his love of children, and of her, and his love-making, and all the other things that had prevented her from seeing that withdrawing from the world was one thing when you had the confidence and the qualifications and the money to go back to it whenever you chose; and quite another when you were twenty-two and scared, and had A-levels in English, Latin, and history, and a baby, and nowhere to feel at home.

Granny Ruby had fallen asleep with her cigarette burning. Jackie reached down and stubbed it out.

It was a shock to find that the train had stopped, for she had thought she wouldn't sleep. It was dark outside but she could see signs that said this was King's Cross. The sitting passengers were being turfed off into 5 A.M. North London, but the sleepers could linger for an hour or two. Jackie listened to her daughter and her grandmother snoring in quiet unison. Outside, the station was waking up with soft sounds.

She edged out of the bunk and dressed herself. Dora did not stir. Jackie considered moving her to the bottom bunk, but that would wake both her and Granny Ruby. She pushed her instead as far from the edge as possible and put pillows round her for further protection. *I have to do this alone. You won't wake up, will you? And if you do, you won't fall? I'll only be five minutes. And I have to be on my own to do this.*

The station was big and bare and intimate. There were more bits of litter blowing about than people moving. She looked at the immobile trains which later today would be going back to Scotland.

She proceeded a few paces along the platform, sighed, went back to the carriage and scooped Dora out of the top bunk. She carried her, sleeping and wrapped in her British Railways blanket, towards the public telephones.

She dialled with her free hand. Dora grew heavier and heavier as the phone rang in Mary's bedsitter and Jackie wondered what to say. It was absurd to feel shy in front of Dora. She was asleep.

Mary's voice said, "Yes?"

"Is that the Women's Centre?" Jackie croaked.

"No it *isn't*, it's my home, or trying to be – " Dora was slipping and waking up. Jackie tried to squat down to hold her on her lap but the phone wire wasn't long enough. Mary's voice softened a little. "I mean, sorry, yes, this is the Centre's number." She sounded tired.

Jackie said, "I'm sorry to trouble you at this hour. But I was given your number. I've had to leave home. I've got an old woman with me and a toddler and no money. And I don't know what to do." She heard her own voice crack. Just as quickly she wanted to laugh. Mary said, "Where are you?"

"King's Cross."

"Wait there. Get yourselves some breakfast and I'll pay when I arrive. I'm not sure if there are any tubes yet, but I'm coming, okay?" Dora opened her eyes and, taking in her new environment, howled like a small wolf. Jackie put down the phone and hugged her into silence. She had no idea whether Mary had recognised her voice and was playing along (*playing along with what? Everything I said was true*) or thought she was helping a stranger. Either way, Jackie felt entitled to be proud of both of them.